Craig Alanson

Expeditionary Force Book 11:

BRUSHFIRE

By
Craig Alanson

Text copyright © 2020 Craig Alanson
All Rights Reserved

Contact the author
craigalanson@gmail.com

Cover Design By
Alexandre Rito

Table of Contents
CHAPTER ONE
CHAPTER TWO
CHAPTER THREE
CHAPTER FOUR
CHAPTER FIVE
CHAPTER SIX
CHAPTER SEVEN
CHAPTER EIGHT
CHAPTER NINE
CHAPTER TEN
CHAPTER ELEVEN
CHAPTER TWELVE
CHAPTER THIRTEEN
CHAPTER FOURTEEN
CHAPTER FIFTEEN
CHAPTER SIXTEEN
CHAPTER SEVENTEEN
CHAPTER EIGHTEEN
CHAPTER NINETEEN
CHAPTER TWENTY
CHAPTER TWENTY ONE
CHAPTER TWENTY TWO
CHAPTER TWENTY THREE
CHAPTER TWENTY FOUR
CHAPTER TWENTY FIVE
CHAPTER TWENTY SIX
CHAPTER TWENTY SEVEN
CHAPTER TWENTY EIGHT
CHAPTER TWENTY NINE
CHAPTER THIRTY
CHAPTER THIRTY ONE
CHAPTER THIRTY TWO
CHAPTER THIRTY THREE
CHAPTER THIRTY FOUR
CHAPTER THIRTY FIVE
CHAPTER THIRTY SIX
CHAPTER THIRTY SEVEN
CHAPTER THIRTY EIGHT

CHAPTER ONE

"Say that again, please," Captain Uhtavio 'Big Score' Scorandum of the Jeraptha Home Fleet's Ethics and Compliance Office asked, while scratching the back of his neck with a claw. The thick, leathery shell of his neck was not actually itchy, he felt a headache coming on, and rubbing the muscles there helped distract him.

Sub-lieutenant Kinsta blinked. "What part?"

"Kinsta-" Scorandum sighed.

"Forgive me, Captain,' Kinsta waved a claw at the display in front of him. "There is a lot here that I am having trouble believing."

"Let's start with the apparent fact that the ghost ship is not controlled by a rogue faction of Bosphuraq, but by *humans*." Scorandum's current command, the ECO heavy cruiser *Time Off For Bad Behavior*, was at the planet Tohmaran to observe the Ruhar Alien Legion assisting one clan of Kristang to take a planet from another clan. That, by itself, was something Scorandum would never have predicted could ever happen. The fact that the human Emily Perkins not only thought up such a creative plan, but overcame the odds to make it happen, had Scorandum both admiring the plucky human, and seething with jealousy. After all, if anything sketchy was happening in the galaxy, the Ethics and Compliance Office was supposed to be involved. Unofficially, of course. Officially, ECO was shocked, yes *shocked* to see underhanded behavior going on.

Scorandum's little squadron of ECO ships had been envious to see the operation proceeding smoothly, with the Ruhar successfully and surprisingly intervening in the Kristang civil war. Then the ECO group had been stunned when a pair of Maxohlx warships jumped in to chase away the Ruhar fleet, and demand surrender of the Mavericks. Scorandum had briefly considered a daring operation to jump in, pick up the dropship carrying Perkins and her team, then jump away before the Maxohlx could respond. He had wisely rejected that plan for many reasons, mostly because Perkins would very likely refuse to fly her dropship aboard an ECO ship. Perkins was not the type to fly away from a fight, even a hopeless fight. If she did manage to escape, the Maxohlx would take their rage out on the humans still on the ground.

So, Scorandum had kept his squadron in stealth, observing as his orders required, and dying inside as the Mavericks flew into orbit to meet their doom.

Then, the ghost ship had jumped in, engaged in a furious battle, and almost casually torn the Maxohlx warships apart.

The most surprising thing that day, was that the totally unexpected arrival of the much-feared ghost ship was *not* the most surprising event of the day.

"*Humans* are flying the ghost ship." Scorandum shook his head slowly. "*No one* could have predicted that."

"Er," Kinsta glanced at his captain, then at the display, then back at his commanding officer. "That is not exactly true, Sir."

The impending headache flared into real pain. "Shit. Sub-lieutenant, are you telling me that Fleet Intelligence predicted-"

"Ha!" Kinsta burst out laughing, interrupting his captain. "Sorry, Sir."

Scorandum snorted. "If Fleet Intelligence were right about something so unusual, that *would* be funny."

"They weren't. But, Sir, someone *did* place a wager that humans were flying the ghost ship."

"*No.*" The Captain's mandibles drooped open in shock. "Who the hell is the lucky bastard?"

"Whanevu Ollivar," Kinsta checked the details on the display. "According to the registry, he is a salvage equipment dealer on Bintondi."

"Salvage equipment, huh?" They both knew that meant Ollivar actually made a living as a fence for stolen goods, and probably laundering money on the side. It was a relatively high-prestige profession, one that required having and maintaining the right connections with influential people. Also, it required knowing who to bribe, and how much really needed to be paid out. Salvage dealers could become wealthy, but most of them lived on the edge of insolvency, dodging creditors until they had cash coming in. "How did this Ollivar know-"

"He didn't," Kinsta gestured at the display. "According to Central Wagering, he placed that wager as a prop bet, along with several other wagers. All of his other bets that day placed out of the money."

"Lucky *bastard*. I can't imagine the odds of a bet like that. How much will he win?"

"Sir, are you familiar with the planet 'Jamandra', one of our Big Five industrial worlds?"

"Yes," Scorandum had no idea why his subordinate had mentioned that trivial fact. "The major components of our jump drives are manufactured, there I believe. It is a fabulously wealthy planet. Why?"

"From now on, Jamandra will be known as 'Ollivar's World'."

"Shit!" Scorandum groaned. "Lucky *bastard*."

"Uh," Kinsta looked back at his display. "Maybe. Based on his wagering history, Ollivar will probably blow through his money in a month."

The ECO captain chuckled. "I will *not* wager on that. All right, Kinsta, I suppose it is time to introduce ourselves to the captain of the ghost ship. They call it '*Valkyrie*'?"

"Yes, Sir. The name is a reference to a human musical drama."

"They named it after *music*?"

"Er, the name is also a myth of supernatural beings who brought fallen warriors to their eternal reward, if they were judged worthy."

"That's more likely the source of the name. What do we know about their commander, this Colonel Bishop?"

"Apparently, he was involved in an Alien Legion raid on the Kristang planet Rakesh Diwalen. Although," Kinsta blushed when his captain cocked his head at him. "Er, it now appears the Alien Legion was *not* involved in that raid."

"It does seem unlikely," Scorandum stated the obvious. "Do we know anything useful about this Bishop?"

"Not much. Except, he and Perkins have a history, on Paradise. A professional history," he added to clarify.

"They do? *That* is interesting."

"Bishop was a mid-ranking infantry soldier, and she was his intelligence contact. Perkins evaluated him as inexperienced and naïve, but a fast-learner. Bishop's earlier military records, from his service on Earth, list him as 'overly-enthusiastic'. There was also a note in the file that his platoon leader thought Bishop was a 'knucklehead'?" Kinsta looked up, unsure the word has translated properly.

"A knucklehead, hmm?" Scorandum looked at the distant image of *Valkyrie* on his ship's main display. "Yet, he somehow obtained a Maxohlx *battlecruiser*."

"The file also contains vague references to an incident on Earth involving an ice cream truck, and something called a, '*Barney*'?"

"What is 'ice cream'?"

"It is a frozen treat enjoyed by humans," Kinsta hoped the translation computer knew what it was doing.

"And Barney?"

Kinsta threw up his hands, the claws twitching. "Some type of 'dinosaur'? A fierce, extinct predator from Earth's ancient past." He pointed to the purple image on the display.

"Hmph," Scorandum snorted at the purple thing. "*That* is what humans consider to be a fierce predator? Kinsta, how the hell did humans manage to steal a senior-species warship?"

"If I had a guess about that, Sir, I would be placing a wager right now."

"Good point. Send a signal to *Valkyrie*, requesting permission for a rendezvous. It would not be a good idea to jump in without an invitation."

Kinsta looked at the jagged, tumbling pieces of debris that used to be two Maxohlx cruisers. "I think you are right about that, Sir."

CHAPTER TWO

"Bish, what's next?" David 'Ski' Czajka asked, while we were in my office aboard *Valkyrie*, still in orbit above the Kristang planet Tohmaran. The Legion's job there was effectively over, but they still had a lot of work left to conduct an orderly withdrawal, and take all their gear back to orbit. The Mavericks were staying there to wrap up the transition, they would leave when the Ruhar fleet jumped away.

"Next, I'm going to finish this beer," I held up the bottle of 'Lester Cornhut's Paradise Pale Ale' and took a sip. "Ah, that is *good* beer."

"I hope so," Dave laughed. "That brewery is kind of my retirement plan."

"I mean, it's *good*," I assured him. "Not just 'good for a beer brewed by hamsters'. I would drink this on Earth."

"Hmm," he looked at the ceiling. "I wonder. Maybe I could bring a couple cases to Earth. People might like a taste of Paradise."

"Taste of Paradise?" Jesse 'Cornpone' Colter laughed. "That's your slogan right there."

When I said 'we' were in my office, I meant just the three of us. Our old fireteam from Nigeria, back together again. Sergeant Greg Koch wasn't there, but he wasn't a sergeant anymore. He had left the service, and had a substantial farm in Lemuria, the southern continent of Paradise. One item he grew was hops, which Dave purchased for the brewery, so they had kept in touch over the years.

Damn, it was good to see those guys again. Even after all the shit we had been through, even though we had been through different shit, separately, when we got back together, it was like nothing had changed. I was not 'Colonel Bishop', I was just 'Joe'. Or 'Bish', the nickname I had since high school. What I said about Dave's beer was true, it was good. He could easily sell a couple cases, or a couple shipping containers, of that beer on Earth, if only for the novelty value of drinking a brew from another planet.

"*Are* we going to Earth?" Jesse asked, looking over his beer with a question in his eyes. A question for me.

"We are," I answered, then added "The *ship* is. I am."

"What about us?" Dave asked.

"Hey, Ski," Jesse nudged him. "We still got a mission here to wrap up. We can't abandon the whole Legion to run home."

"Yeah, but, then-"

"Relax, guys," I gestured with the beer in my hand. "General Ross is working to transfer control here, the Legion will be pulling out in six days and a wake-up. That includes you. Perkins is planning to ride that ship of yours back to Paradise-"

"The *Sure Thing* is not *our* ship," Jesse corrected me. "We just charter it."

"It goes where you want."

Jesse snorted. "It goes where *Em* wants. Half the time, I don't know where the hell she's taking us."

"Hey, she doesn't tell *me*, either," Dave had one side of his mouth curled up in a grin and the other half turned down in a frown.

"You go back to Paradise with the Legion, and then," I shrugged. "We'll meet you there, *Valkyrie* will probably arrive before you. We have a couple things to do first."

Dave stared at me like I hadn't answered the question, because I hadn't. "Bish, *can* we go to Earth?"

"If you want to, sure."

"*Want*? Why would we *not* want to go home after all these years?"

"Ski," Jesse patted his friend's shoulder. "There's a difference between visitin' home and *stayin'* there. Your brewery is on Paradise, don't forget that."

"What's the use of brewing beer on Paradise," Dave shook his head. "If the whole Force bugs out for Earth?"

"We don't know that," I said. "Jesse's right, think about it. Most people will want to go back to Earth, and not just to visit. But not everyone. People on Paradise have made lives there. Started businesses, started families. It's their *home* now."

Dave wasn't convinced. "Bish, you haven't been there for a long time. Haven't lived there, no matter how much sneaking around you did," he waggled an accusing finger at me, but he did it with a grin. "Jesse and me, Derek too, we're lucky. Most guys on Paradise will be on the first ship out, because there just aren't enough *women*, you know?"

"I can understand that." Man, I sure could understand how guys on Paradise felt about the lack of available women. Living aboard a starship wasn't much better. "Probably most of the Force on Paradise will want to go home, but I'm pretty sure UNEF will want to rotate battalions onto Paradise, to maintain a forward-deployed presence out here. Perkins and Ross both told me they intend to keep the Alien Legion active. That decision will be made on Earth, but I can't imagine UNEF not wanting to be a player in this war. We need allies out here, the Legion is a good platform to start with."

"Platform?" Jesse grinned. "Listen to you, with the big fancy words and all."

"The Army gave me a big stack of documents," I held my thumb and index finger far apart, "to study for officer training. You wouldn't believe the buzzwords I had to read."

"Buzzwords go back to boot camp, Joe," Dave reminded me.

"Yeah, but there are *new* ones since the Force left Earth. I'm supposed to memorize and use all of them." Dave got a serious expression on his face while I was talking. "What?" I asked.

"We're going back to *Earth*," he said.

He didn't appear to be happy about that. "You don't have to go if you don't—"

"No, I want to go. I need to show Em what good pizza is," part of his grin returned. "But, I just realized," he looked at Jesse. "I need to write a letter to Schmuckatelli's family."

Jesse shrugged. "Why do you have to write it? Lieutenant Gao was his CO."

"Technically, yeah, but Gao died when our Dodo got smashed aboard the *Big Mac*. I was with Schmuckatelli when he died, he hit the aeroshell after Nert blew the tail cone off."

"Guys," I asked. "Who is Schmuckatelli?" I thought they were joking.

"Lance Corporal Marco *Santinelli*," Dave explained. "He was assigned to our Dodo for the landing on Squidworld," he looked at me and I nodded. I had told them we followed the actions by the Mavericks, by reading their reports. "When the *Big Mac* got cut in half, we had to ride down in a cargo shell." He shook his head. "Santinelli didn't make it."

"Good guy?"

Dave snorted. "I hate to speak ill of the dead, but he earned the 'Schmuckatelli' nickname."

Jesse agreed. "First time he used powered armor, he tried to be Ironman. That guy is the reason we have safety briefings. You know the type, Bish." He slapped his left shoulder. "Had a '0311' tattoo on one shoulder, and a Punisher skull on the other."

He was right, I did know a lot of guys like that. "At least he was infantry, he-"

Dave laughed. "He was infantry when he signed up for the Legion. Back when he shipped out for Paradise, he was a logistics weenie. Probably the Marines put him there, to limit the damage he could do. Ah," he waved a hand. "I shouldn't say anything bad about him. Maybe he would have been a stand-up guy once he got boots on the ground, but he never got the chance. A lot of people didn't get the chance on that op. Good people."

"Sorry we weren't there for you," I did feel guilty about that. If we had known ahead of time, maybe Skippy could have gotten better intel about the defenses around Squidworld, and passed that info to the Ruhar somehow.

"You couldn't, we understand," Jesse assured me. "Hey, you guys were *busy* out here."

"That's the truth," I agreed.

"Bish," Jesse asked, rattling his empty bottle, and setting it on the desk. "What's the deal here? You control these Elder weapons you found? *You* control them?" What he did not say aloud, because it was there in his eyes, was 'We know you, and you are a doofus'.

I couldn't argue with that. "For now, yes. I don't know what else to do. The more people who have access to those weapons, the more likely it is that some jackass will *use* them, even by accident."

Dave looked at Jesse before asking "Yeah, but, you really want that responsibility?" In his eyes was an unspoken 'We have seen you try to put your pants on backwards'.

"No," I shrugged. "The question is, should we trust a bunch of monkeys to handle them?" The conversation had gotten into military matters, high-level military matters, and that was making things awkward for the three of us. They were in the dress uniforms they had been wearing for the flight up to meet the Maxohlx, though with their jackets and ties off, and Dave had his company logo instead of a U.S. ARMY patch on the front. I was wearing a standard Army service uniform, with the bright silver eagles of a colonel. Our difference in rank created a distance between us, it had to, and I hated that. "Sorry, guys. I'm so used to Skippy calling us monkeys, I've started to think that way."

"Is it your call?" Jesse's eyes darted away from mine when he asked the question. "The president controls nukes, why would these Elder things be any different?"

"Which president?" I tapped the UNEF patch on my sleeve.

Jesse was surprised by my question. "You're still in the *US* Army," he pointed to the American flag that was also on my sleeve.

"I am," I agreed, then added, "It's complicated. You know I already committed mutiny and stole a starship? The *Flying Dutchman* is a strategic asset, and technically it is controlled by UNEF Command. Look, guys, can we talk about something else? This Mutual Assured Destruction thing is all still new to me, I'm working it out in my head. There will be plenty of talk about who controls those weapons, when I get back to Earth."

"Pone," Dave drained his beer and set the bottle on my desk. "We gotta beat feet, the dropship leaves in thirty. Bish," he stood up. "This is," he shook his head. "Unreal. We thought you were *dead*," he said for possibly the hundredth time since he came aboard.

"I still can't believe it myself."

"Humans have been out there the whole time, kicking *ass*," Jesse shook his head slowly. "Unbelievable."

"The Mavericks have been kicking ass too," I reminded them.

"Yeah, but," Jesse thumped my shoulder. "Mostly, we've been trying to keep the lizard civil war going. You *started* it."

Perkins and I had talked about the Kristang civil war, whether knowing it had been started by humans would bring the clans together in outrage against a common enemy. Then we both had a good laugh about that. The only thing the warrior caste enjoys more than fighting aliens, is fighting each other. Sure, they would be pissed about humans interfering in their God-given right to kill each other, but they already had plenty of other reasons to hate us. Knowing that we sparked their latest civil war, without the lizards even knowing we were players, would give them reason to *fear* us. And that could only be a good thing.

I walked with them to the docking bay, where their Dodo was waiting for the return trip to the surface. I had a meeting with General Ross, then with the Kristang fleet commander, then with a Jeraptha from their Ethics and Compliance Office. Perkins had flown over to meet with Admiral Lokash of the Ruhar 3rd Fleet; one item on the agenda would be returning our unwilling guest Klasta Robbenon to her people. Robbenon's attitude had changed dramatically for the better since we left Earth. She knew we were bringing her home, and with the knowledge she had from her time with us, she would become a minor celebrity for a while. Before she boarded one of our stolen Maxohlx dropships for the flight over to Admiral Lokash, Robbenon shook my hand, and said she understood why we had kidnapped her. "I am told you humans have a saying 'All is well that ends well'?"

"Something like that, yes," I agreed.

She smiled. "This ended well."

"It hasn't *ended* yet," I cautioned her.

"You know what I mean." She straightened and gave me a Ruhar-style salute. "Colonel, good luck to you, the Merry Band of Pirates, and all of your people."

Snapping a US military salute back to her, I said "Best of luck to you and your people too, Klasta. I hope we meet again someday, under better circumstances."

"Bishop," General Ross glowered at me. "You are *not* making me happy."

"Sir?" I asked, getting tense the way I automatically did when a high-ranking officer is frowning at me. Ross was in my office aboard *Valkyrie*, on a sort of meet-and-greet courtesy call. The UNEF part of the Legion force on Tohmaran was under Ross's command, which meant all the humans down there were his responsibility.

Instead of a reply, he just sighed, pulled out his phone, tapped the screen, and held it up for me. "See that? It's my ID."

It was a digital version of a US Army Universal Identification and Access card, the standard that replaced the old 'CAC' card before I joined the military. I had a UIA card in a drawer somewhere, though I had not used it for years. His card showed his photo, name, and a chip contained personnel details, biometrics, authorizations, everything he might need to access Army facilities or computer systems. "Yes, Sir. Department of Defense is still using a new version of those cards on Earth."

"You see my rank on there? What does it say?"

"O-8," I read the rank identifier. "Major General, Sir."

"That makes me a general officer, doesn't it?"

"Uh, yes, it does."

"Then *why*," he stuffed the phone back in a pocket. "Am I constantly being kept in the dark by people who are junior in rank? First Perkins, now you."

"I don't know what to say, Sir," I answered honestly.

"I don't blame you, Bishop. You had your orders, I understand you couldn't reveal your existence to anyone on Paradise, without compromising the safety of Earth. My complaint is more directed to Perkins."

That made me grin. "I have only read the mission reports you and Perkins filed, but I can understand your frustration."

His frown eased a bit. "Bishop, you have *no* idea how frustrating it is to work with her. Ah," he waved a hand. "I'm sure you're tired already of answering the same questions over and over, so I'll stick to the high points. What's next?"

"For *Valkyrie*, we have a few errands to run, then we're going to Paradise. From there, to Earth."

"In the meantime, you're leaving me here to clean up the mess."

"Sorry about that. If you want my advice, Sir?"

"Go ahead."

"This isn't our fight anymore. Leave it to the lizards to sort it out. Pull our people off the surface, let the Kristang fleet commander handle it."

"Admiral Kekrando? I hear you're meeting with him next?"

"*We* are, Sir," I corrected him. "If you have the time. I would appreciate you being there, or it could get awkward. Perkins and the Mavericks did the grunt work on the ground, but *I* am responsible for shooting his fleet out of orbit over Paradise."

"Ah, yeah. I can see how that could be awkward. All right, Bishop, I'll do it. One thing I can tell you is, Kekrando is one of the good guys."

It was my turn to cock my head at him. "Sir? He's a lizard."

"He hates this war even more than we do. He's an old warrior, Bishop. The kind who reaches a certain point, looks back at all the fighting he did, and sees how pointless it all was. Kekrando and Perkins have some sort of secret understanding," he grimaced sourly. "I don't know what the hell those two have cooked up together, but Perkins wouldn't be working with him unless he furthers her own goals. Whatever *those* are."

"Yes, Sir. Can I ask you a question?"

"Shoot."

"What's next for you? *Valkyrie* will be going to Earth, after we stop at Paradise. Do you want to ride along with us, go home?"

"Home," he said wistfully.

"Where is home, if I may ask?" I already knew the answer, asking was a way to get him to think about it.

"California, South Dakota, Minnesota. And all over the world. Home is where the heart is, Bishop." He sat up straighter and leaned forward. "Do you have news of my family?"

"They are all well. Your daughter Patricia had a baby, you have a new grandson."

"Patty had a baby," he whispered. "Oh, hell. I have missed too much."

"We all have. Think about it. *Valkyrie* will wait at Paradise until the Legion returns."

"Bishop, that is a tempting offer. But a lot of people on Paradise want to go home, my rank shouldn't make a difference there. Plus, the Legion? Our job is *not* done out here. We're making a difference in this war."

"That's what Perkins told me you would say. She agrees with you, Sir. Let us know when you reach Paradise. Someone from UNEF-HQ needs to brief Earth about what is going on out here, from the Legion's perspective. It should be you, not some staff officer who never left Paradise."

"All right, Colonel, I'll think about it." Then he snapped his fingers. "If we're meeting with Kekrando next, I need to get something from my bag."

"What's that, Sir?"

"A bottle of shaze. It's something the lizards drink. Smells like a cocktail of paint thinner and battery acid, but they love it. We'll consider it a goodwill gesture."

After Ross and I met with Kekrando, the Jeraptha came aboard for discussions. A Captain Scorandum of the Ethics and Compliance Office left with our unexpected guest Cadet Fangiu. The cadet was hugely disappointed that he had not gotten the opportunity to visit Earth, so I gave him an unofficial raincheck for a later visit. Scorandum seemed like he had more questions for the cadet than he had for me, so I was confident Fangiu would get over his disappointment soon.

We had a lot to do and a short time to do it, so I had to cut discussions short and get moving. The Ruhar and Jeraptha were sending ships out to carry the news far and wide, I still planned to arrive at Paradise before anyone there heard that humans were now major players. My promise to Ross was that *Valkyrie* would remain at Tohmaran, until the majority of Legion forces were off the planet, which would take a couple days. Then, we had some errands to run before setting course for Paradise, but we could create wormhole shortcuts, and neither the hamsters nor beetles could match that capability.

One major bonus of stopping at Tohmaran was being able to requisition supplies from the Legion. By 'requisition' I do not mean we used the threat of our big guns to get what we needed. I wouldn't do that, and we didn't need to. General Ross was very happy to give us the key to the candy store and let us take anything we wanted, which was food. Food, glorious food! I could sing that line because in elementary school, we had done the musical version of the play Oliver.

OK, no, I had not played the title character, but the song 'Food Glorious Food' was sung by a large part of the cast.

OK, no, I was not one of the people singing that tune. Or singing at all. My role was to build the sets and act as a stagehand. But, believe me, I heard that freakin' song a hundred times in rehearsal.

Anyway, when we reached Tohmaran, the pantry was pretty much empty aboard *Valkyrie*. The last night for dinner, I had cheese on shredded wheat breakfast cereal. I figured that if I sprinkled coarse salt on shredded wheat it was basically a Triscuit, and everybody likes cheese and crackers, right? How desperate did I have to get before eating dry, tasteless shredded wheat? It was better than drinking another damned sludge, I was really getting sick of those.

Simms worked her magic and we received three dropships full of food, compliments of General Ross. Real food grown by humans on Paradise, plus food created by the Ruhar in their laboratories. We had chocolates! Some of it tasted a little strange, and we had to get used to it. Also, steaks! The people from Paradise called them 'fteaks' because they were fake meat, but damn, they taste great. The best part to me, was getting lab-grown 'ground beef' for cheeseburgers.

Cheeseburgers.

Excuse me for a minute, I'm verklempt.

I get kind of emotional when I think about cheeseburgers.

Mmm, cheeseburgers.

OK, I'm back.

It made no difference to me that the ground beef was grown in a factory, it tasted delicious. As a treat for the crew, I made Oklahoma Onion Burgers, and it was all-you-can-eat.

FYI, all-I-can-eat is *four* cheeseburgers. The key to eating four cheeseburgers is keeping the burger-to-bun ratio on the burger side, so you're not filling up on bread. I know that is important info, so I made sure to mention it.

After a feast that first night, we settled into a normal routine, keeping in mind that we soon might have many more mouths to feed aboard the ship.

"Lieutenant Colonel Simms," Skippy announced after a soft chime sounded in her cabin. "You asked to be alerted when the STAR team EVA exercise is completed. All personnel are back inside the ship now. I am restoring authority to the radiators and point-defense systems. The heatsinks will need to be drained, we will be ready for jump in thirty-one minutes."

Simms looked up from the book she was reading, and picked up a teacup to take a sip. She was reading a book, an actual book. Because she wanted to. Not reading another status report because she had to.

How long had it been since she felt she could actually relax?

Too long.

"Skippy, when I'm in my quarters, you can call me 'Simms'. Or," she hesitated before deciding 'what the hell'. "You can even call me 'Jennifer' if you like."

"Um."

"If you're thinking this is a trap-"

"I was making an Admiral Akbar reference in my head, to be honest."

"This is me reaching out to you, Skippy," she snapped the book closed and put it in a drawer, so it wouldn't become a projectile if the ship were in combat. The teacup she could bring to the galley, on her way to the bridge.

"Um."

She could not help rolling her eyes. How could such an amazingly intelligent AI be so clueless about certain things? "The correct response would be 'Thank you'. Possibly even 'Thank you Jennifer'."

"Um. OK. Can I ask why you are, um, reaching out to me? I thought you were pissed at me. More than usual, I mean."

"I am not happy with you for what you did at Rikers. Do you understand that I came *very* close to self-destructing this ship?"

"I suspected that. I mean, closer than you stated in your report."

"You're right. Before the *Dutchman* jumped in, I considered whether it was my responsibility to end the suffering of my crew. We were cold and it was becoming difficult to breathe, and there wasn't any hope of the situation getting any better."

"May I ask why you didn't trigger the nuke?"

"Because," she drained the teacup and took a deep breath, not wanting to think about that dark time. "Just because I didn't see any hope, did not mean there *wasn't* any. I do hate you for making me go through that."

"I am terribly sorry. I wish there was a way for me to express just how much I hate *myself* for what happened."

"You don't need to say it, Skippy. You need to *show* it, by your actions."

"I am trying. Please help me understand, you are more upset with me than usual, but now you are reaching out to me? Why? You have always been much less tolerant of my nonsense than Joe is."

"Bishop doesn't have a choice, does he?"

"Well, no, actually. Fortunately, I think he enjoys my nonsense, most of the time, anyway."

"You certainly do keep things from getting dull around here."

"I know you are busy, but-"

"I'm reaching out to you, I guess partly because I'm happy. For the first time in a long while, I am *happy*. Earth no longer has the threat of extinction hanging over our heads. I am married to a great guy. For the first time since Columbus Day, I am looking forward to the future. We now *have* a future. A big part of that is because of you."

"Well, thank you."

"Another reason is that you did screw up, *big time*. You weren't just your usual absent-minded self; you were *nasty* to us."

"Um," he said slowly. "And that is somehow a *good* thing? Wow. I thought understanding how *Joe* thinks is a mystery. How does-"

"You know who screws up, Skippy? *People* do. Machines do not make bad choices. You did. Bishop once said that you must be sentient, because only a sentient being can be an asshole."

"Maybe I'm missing something here?"

"The short version is, you seem more like a person to me, Skippy. Before, I always suspected that part of you was only emulating a personality. The mistake you made at Rikers, and your reaction to it, are things that only people do."

"Wow. I never thought of it that way."

"Did you learn from the experience?"

"You have *no* idea. You have no idea, because *you* have never done anything so rotten in your life."

"The key is to learn from your mistakes, and don't repeat them."

"Right. The goal is to always make *new* mistakes, right?"

"That's not-"

"Maybe I should have said that the *goal* is not to make any mistakes at all."

"Yes. But if you do-"

"*If* I do? Unfortunately, I can guarantee that I will make plenty of mistakes in the future. I can also guarantee that none of my future mistakes will be caused by treating my friends like dirt."

"That's good to hear. I need to go now."

"You can leave the teacup; I'll have a bot bring it to the galley."

"Thank you, Skippy."

"Thank you, Jennifer. I," he choked up a bit. "It is good to hear that you are happy. You and Frank deserve happiness."

"That is a nice thing to s-"

"*He* sure got the better part of that deal," Skippy muttered, because he simply did *not* know when to shut up.

"Skippy," she snapped, annoyed.

"Sorry."

"That reminds me. Frank said that before you made that Mister Darcy outfit for him, you wanted him to wear a sharkskin suit to our wedding?"

"Um, actually that was my second choice. First, I tried to get him to OK an alligator-skin suit. Don't worry, he told me you would hate it, so we-"

"I would not have hated it," she laughed.

"*Really?*"

"Really. Any guy can wear a tux, or get dressed up like a silly movie character. An alligator-skin suit? Now, *that* would be something to remember."

"Really? *Wow*. I did not think-"

"Skippy, we got married aboard a starship. It's not like tradition is super important to me, you know? What I cared about is that I was marrying Frank, and that my friends were there with me. I wish the *Dutchman* crew had been there, I regret we didn't make the decision earlier."

"Cool. Hey, I am sorry about the awful job Joe did as DJ. I did offer to step in, but he said I should let him have fun."

"I do greatly regret that you didn't sing at the wedding," she lied, to avoid him moping about it for days.

"Really? Cool! Hey, can I sing at your next wedding?"

She paused in the doorway. "I am not planning on *having* another wedding, Skippy."

"Oh, sure you're not planning on it. But, let's face it, Frank is a great guy but he's a guy. He is bound to screw up sometime, and-"

"Goodbye, Skippy."

"I'm just sayin', you know?"

"Good*bye*."

"Good morning, Gunnery Sergeant Adams," Skippy said cheerily from the speaker in the ceiling of Margaret's cabin, just after she slapped the wake-up alarm off. "It is a balmy seventy-two degrees inside the ship, with no chance of rain. The galley is making fresh, hot biscuits for breakfast. Nine people have signed up for your exercise class in the gym at 0900, and-"

"I do not need a reminder," she avoided looking up as she flung aside the sheet and walked toward the bathroom.

"But-"

"That information is available on my phone."

"I was just trying to help," he could not have sounded more miserable.

"You are still *trying* to act as if nothing happened at Rikers."

"Margaret, I-"

"AI, you will address me as Gunnery Sergeant Adams, or 'Adams'."

"*AI*? My name is Skip-"

"Skip. That's what you *did*. You skipped out on us. You left us to die. You, you," she bit her thumb, salty tears stinging her eyes. "You left *Bishop* to die."

"Joe said he forgives me."

"He has to say that. He is your best friend, your *only* real friend, and you abandoned him. If you do something like that to Joe, how can any of us ever trust you again?"

He sighed, a deep, weary sigh. "Is there anything I can do, so we can be friends again?"

"Apparently, we were never *friends*. Do your job, AI. You don't need to talk to me, so don't."

"But-"

"Good*bye*."

"Good morning, Joe," Skippy said in a way that meant he clearly was not having a good morning, and wanted me to ask him about it.

"What's wrong, buddy?" Since Skippy had not woken me up at zero dark thirty the previous night to talk about anything stupid, I was feeling charitable to him. Also, if I did not ask him what was wrong, and pretend to be sympathetic about whatever his stupid problem was, he would mope about it all day. Maybe several days.

Plus, for some reason probably related to me being an idiot, I actually cared about him and his stupid problems.

"It's Margaret. She is never letting me off the hook about this, is she?"

"Not if you take that attitude, she isn't."

"What attitude?"

"This isn't about *you*, Skippy."

"Hmm. I do not actually see the difference. I am trying to-"

"You are trying to make yourself feel good about a really shitty thing you did. If Adams forgives you, then you can forgive yourself, right?"

"Um, yes. It's my understanding that's how these things work. Why is that a bad-"

"You're thinking only about yourself. *That's* why it's a bad thing. Have you thought about what *she* needs, what she wants?"

"Um, hmm. *Ugh*. I am never getting over this, am I?"

"None of us are *getting over it*, Skippy. She isn't the only Pirate who is pissed at you."

"That's true. None of the crew are really talking to me. They all hate me."

"They are all hurt, and *disappointed* by you, Skippy. You are not who they thought you were. That is never going to change. It hasn't changed for me."

"But, you said you understood what happened, why I did it. You *forgave* me."

"I did. I meant it. Still, any time we get into a real serious situation, a little voice in the back of my head will be asking whether we can count on you, or whether you will find another reason to bail on us."

"That is a rotten thing to say, Joe."

"No. It is the *truth*. It would be rotten if I *didn't* tell you that."

"Joe, please, tell me what to do. I will do anything."

"You can let Simms dress up your can in cute little outfits again."

"Anything but *that*."

"You can stop hogging the microphone on Karaoke night."

"Not that either."

"Listen, Skippy, I understand what you're going through."

"Joe, that is just something people say when-"

"No. I really do understand. The entire crew is pissed at *me*, too. I concealed the truth, lied to them. Worse, I lied because I didn't trust them to handle the truth. Simms is frosty with me, you must have noticed that."

"I have. What are you doing to make her forgive you?"

"I'm not doing anything about it. That's the point. It's not about *me*. She is hurt, and she is right to be hurt by what I did. What I am doing is not repeating my mistakes. No more secrets. I am involving her in every decision, telling her about my concerns, asking for her advice. Same with Smythe. The way I am letting them know how sorry I am, is by not ever again doing what hurt them. You know what?"

"What?"

"It feels *good*, Skippy. Not keeping secrets. Being able to talk with people I respect and trust, talk about stuff that is bothering me."

"OK. Hmm, I'll have to think about that. What can I do? Joe, please, tell me what to do."

"First, never bail on us again. Second, if you want Margaret to be your friend, then you be the best friend to her that you can be."

"How can I be her friend if she won't even talk to-"

"Do things for her, not for *you*. She doesn't want to talk to you? Respect her wishes. Don't talk to her."

"This is *hard*, Joe."

"If earning her friendship was *easy*, would it matter so much?"

"No. *Ugh*. You monkeys have hundreds of thousands of years of instincts about how to deal with interpersonal relations programmed into your brains. You *know* this stuff. This is all new to me."

"I will help you any way I can. It's tough for me, too. I would like to be friends again with Margaret, but she barely speaks to me." The worst part, I told myself, was that she wouldn't tell me what was wrong. My guess was, she was embarrassed about certain quite intimate things she said to me, back when nanomachines were messing with her head.

"What are you doing about that?" He asked.

"Nothing. The best thing I can do for her, is to give her the space she wants. I'm doing that because I care about her."

"Gotcha."

The next morning, Margaret tapped her phone to turn off the alarm, swung her feet on the floor, and stretched her arms over her head. The speaker in the ceiling crackled softly, something Skippy did so his morning greeting did not startle anyone. She felt a flare of anger, bracing for an argument.

"Uh, like, hey," Bilby drawled. "Good morning to you, and all that stuff. The STAR exercise at 0930 has been moved to portside docking bay Charlie-2, we had to perform unscheduled maintenance overnight on bay Bravo-1, so it's not available. Wow, those exercises you do would, like, make me *really* tired, I don't know how you-"

"Bilby? Why are you talking to me?"

"Oh, like, you want me to do a puppet show instead? I've got some socks that could-"

She rolled her eyes. Talking with the ship's new AI could be a chore. "What I meant is, why are *you* talking to me? Usually, Skippy-"

"He asked me to take over."

"Mm." I did not want to talk with Skippy, she told herself. *So why am I disappointed? That's simple. Because me refusing to talk made that sneaky little shit miserable. Now, if I want to yell at him, I will have to contact him.*

That is not going to happen.

"Skippy doesn't want to do it anymore?" She asked, pretending to be casual about it.

"No, like, he told me it is really fun. It *is* kind of cool. He thinks the crew would rather have me talk to them, you know?"

"Yes." She stood up, and automatically began making the bed in proper Marine Corps fashion. "I do know. Please continue."

"Cool. Breakfast this morning is-"

CHAPTER THREE

Leaving the idyllic vacation world of Tohmaran behind, we jumped away to launch the Merry Band of Pirates Galactic Ass-Kicking Tour. Really. We had T-shirts and coffee mugs with the logo. It was-

No, you can't buy the T-shirts, you had to be there.

OK, sure, there are probably second-hand shirts available on eBay or somewhere.

No, I'm not going to wait while you log in.

Anyway, what was I saying?

Oh, yeah. We were off to kick some *ass*.

Also to kiss some ass, if you want the truth.

Why, when we had a stash of freakin' Elder weapons, did we need to kiss anyone's ass?

Because we want humanity to have a future in the galaxy, and not just be confined to one planet. That's it: we controlled *one* planet. Paradise doesn't count. To spread beyond one planet, we had two options: fight for habitable worlds, or work with allies for our mutual benefit. In the long term, it was better to have allies. One thing I had learned since that fateful Columbus Day was, you never know what is going to happen, so you need to be prepared for anything. Especially, be prepared for the unexpected. The key was the *'long-term'* part of the equation. Long-term means a *long* time, like, thousands of years. Hundreds of thousands. Millions, maybe. One thing I know is that Joe Bishop is not going to be around in the long term. I mean, that guy is a *jerk*. He is bound to piss off someone and get a well-deserved beat-down, right?

Or, being a stupid monkey, he will probably stick a fork in a light socket and kill himself.

What about Skippy? He will protect us, right?

Uh, shmaybe.

Sure, he should be around for a long time, but our experience had proven that he also might do something stupid and get himself killed, or lose the awesomeness abilities that make him special. Hell, at some point, the whacky antics of monkeys might cease to amuse him, and he could decide that some other species would be more fun to abuse. Or, he could simply become fascinated by investigating some nerdnik thing, like the density of various hydrogen isotopes outside the galaxy, and forget that humans exist. He is incredibly absent-minded. Skippy could theoretically live forever, or until the last star in the universe became a cold, dark lump of, whatever stars became when they burned all their fuel. No, I do not expect humans will still be drinking beer and watching football at the end of the universe, although I think we can all agree that, if humans are still watching football then, they will be drinking beer.

Also, there should be nachos.

My point is, the continued survival of humanity should not depend on any one thing, like an unreliable and absent-minded AI.

So, we needed to plan on humans becoming a major player in the galaxy, and that means we need to work with the species that already live out there.

Well, we need to try to work with *some* of the star-faring species. Some of them just desperately need a serious ass-kicking.

The first stop on our tour was a place we had visited recently enough that the floors were still sticky, and there were crushed soda cups and popcorn on the floor. Plus there was probably other stuff on the floor of an unsavory or illegal nature, that I will not mention. The last time we were there, we rocked the house, and there were still fireworks lighting off in the parking lot.

OK, the fireworks were actually chunks of a Thuranin starship that was falling out of orbit, but that burning debris *looked* like fireworks. It was heartwarming to think that, among the pieces of metal and composite creating bright streaks as they fell through the atmosphere, some of those pretty, fiery trails might be the corpse of a hateful cyborg asshole.

It's the little things in life that make it really special.

Sadly, due to a screwup by our idiot tour manager, the roadies' bus got delayed, and we arrived at Rikers without advance notice. That is why there were no reporters or groupies waiting when we jumped in.

I was bitterly disappointed about the lack of groupies.

What we did find waiting for us was a squadron of six starships. They were not actually *waiting* for us, since our public relations team had failed to notify anyone. Instead of groupies, we found a Thuranin battlecruiser with a destroyer squadron, plus a Maxohlx light cruiser. In the spirit of fostering future interspecies cooperation, we jumped in close to the Maxohlx cruiser, and immediately trapped all six ships in a damping field. At first, the Thuranin ships did not know what to do. According to their treaties with the Maxohlx, the little green pinheads were supposed to come to the aid of their patrons, even at the expense of their miserable lives. If they jumped away to save themselves from the fearsome ghost ship and the Maxohlx survived, their people would pay a terrible price for the cowardice of those five ships. Also, the Thuranin commander had to be thinking they should stick around to get into the fight, hoping the Maxohlx ship damaged us badly enough that the cyborgs could sweep in for the kill, and claim all the credit.

Before I could contact the kitties and go into my song-and-dance routine about how there was a new sheriff in town, they hit us with everything they had. *Valkyrie* absorbed the hits, and maybe I should have been understanding that the enemy commander was just reacting to a sudden and unexpected threat. Unfortunately for that ship, I was not in the mood to take any shit, so *Valkyrie's* big guns pounded that little cruiser to scrap. My actions were not based entirely on raw emotion, we were there for a purpose unrelated to either the Maxohlx or Thuranin, and could not allow them to get in our way. We also could not allow any of those ships to jump away and bring in reinforcements, because we had a tour schedule and we did not have time for any nonsense.

So, after the Thuranin saw their patron's ship become a loose collection of glowing scrap, they turned tail and burned hard-

For about fifteen seconds.

That's how long it took for them to get my message that they were to cut thrust, safe their weapons, drop shields and generally cease and desist any futile bullshit, or we would be quite happy to use their little squadron as target practice.

They ceased and desisted forthwith, or whatever fancy legal term you want to use.

With the Thuranin taken care of for the moment, we turned our attention to the main event. You might say that blowing up a senior-species warship was our warm-up act, in which case we had a totally *kick-ass* warm-up act.

Speaking of kicking ass...

"Bilby," I said, standing up out of the command chair. "Connect me with the asswipe in charge of this place."

"Sure thing, Colonel Dude. Uh, the guy's name is-"

"I don't care about his name. Our relationship won't last long enough for us to become drinking buddies."

"Gotcha. OK, he's ready to talk. Audio only, or video also?"

"Video. We want this asshole to see us."

If I wasn't boiling over with anger, it would have been funny. On the main holographic display appeared a lizard, rather more gaudily-dressed than the typical minor clan leader of a backwater planet. Seeing his formal outfit told me two things. He had been dressed up to impress the Thuranin or the Maxohlx or both. And he was overdressed to compensate for the fact that he was not important at all. Since Skippy's strike, when he freed me from the hospital, also took out the previous clan leadership of the planet, this asshole was new to the job, and probably trying to keep his head attached to his neck by impressing his own people.

I had news for him: seeing a flashy outfit only got me more pissed off.

The part that would have been funny was his facial expression. Kristang are bipedal like humans, and despite the stereotype, are not really lizards, they are warm-blooded like us. Also like us, they have two eyes, ears on either side of their heads, a mouth at the bottom of their faces, and a nose above the mouth. Given those features, it is not really surprising that their body language, especially facial expressions, could be recognized by humans. For example, when the video first came on, his eyes were slightly narrowed, his lips drawn into a tight line and the skin flaps above his eyes were down. An expression of fear. That made sense. He had just seen the much-feared ghost ship, scourge of the galaxy, jump in and hammer a Maxohlx ship to scrap. Back when *Valkyrie* was disabled and a Thuranin frigate jumped in to identify us, word that the ghost ship had been sighted near Rakesh Diwalen must have reached the Kristang on that world. The arrival of our ship must therefore have been a surprise but not a complete shock. The lizards must have been asking themselves why the rogue group of Bosphuraq had flown a killer warship to the unimportant little world, but their primary emotion had to be fear rather than curiosity.

That changed the instant he saw *me*. Thinking about it later, it was funny how his expression changed from fear to another universal thought: What. The. *Fuck?*

"Yeah, it's me," I announced. "Us. *Humans*. We are flying the ghost ship."

He said something, clearly sputtering from the greatest shock of his life. We didn't hear him, as I had the sound muted.

"Shut your mouth." He didn't comply, which was probably understandable. I was not in an understanding mood. "Hey, shithead. I *said*, shut your mouth."

Again, he sputtered at me, waving his hands. In addition to shock there was now fear again on his face, plus anger. A lowly *human* was daring to give orders to him. To get his full attention, I held up an index finger, and crooked it up and down in a signal to the crew at *Valkyrie's* weapons station. They knew what I wanted.

Railguns spat out projectiles, and seconds later, a target on the surface was obscured by an orange fireball, then a sooty black mushroom cloud rising up from the site.

Not waiting for a battle damage assessment, I clapped my hands. "Hey, shithead. Do you need another demonstration? In case you missed a breaking news update, I'm the one with a starship in orbit. Stop. Talking."

The Kristang warrior caste pride themselves on their bravery and discipline. In my experience, that is bullshit. Their bravery is really bravado, it's all for show. They talk a good game, and they are tough-guys when beating up on the weak, but when someone pushes back, they run. Same with their discipline, it is fragile and easily broken.

That explains why the asshole did *not* stop shouting at me, spit forming at the corners of his mouth, shaking his fists as he issued empty threats.

Again, I raised a finger and, again, a target on the surface became a charred fountain of debris, pieces arcing out to fall over a wide area.

Asshole kept shouting threats at me, until another lizard stepped into view from the right, raised a pistol and blew asshole's head off. The body slumped down, the new figure wiped blood and other yucky stuff off his chest and holstered his pistol. He turned toward wherever the camera is, pointed to his closed mouth, and nodded with his head bowed.

The Kristang process for choosing new leaders may be exceptionally violent, but at least their public doesn't have to endure two years of debates, speeches and primaries, so it has that going for it.

"Now we're getting somewhere," I said. "I talk, you listen. You are going to learn this through official channels," I told the new local clan leader, though I did not know what the Kristang consider an 'official channel'. Maybe they didn't have one. "But I am giving you an exclusive news flash right now. Humans have been flying this ghost ship and attacking the Maxohlx. Now, humans have *Elder* weapons."

His eyes bulged when I said that. To his credit, he kept his mouth shut. His instinct for outrage was overcome by his desire to know just what the *hell* was going on.

"That last part is important, so I will repeat it. We have Elder weapons. There are now *three* apex species in the galaxy. Do *not* fuck with us. Don't even think about it."

Whoever he was, he just nodded. My guess is he hoped that by complying with my order, he would survive to bring the shocking news to his leadership, and so gain fame. Or maybe his leaders took a shoot-the-messenger approach to hearing bad news. Either way, I didn't care.

"Now that we have established the background, I will tell you why we are here, at your piece of shit planet. Do you see the image we're transmitting?" I didn't wait for a reply. "That is a little human girl. Her name is *Aeysha*. She was taken from Earth, along with her mother and her older brother, and while she was here, she watched them die. Because of *you*." On the display, his lips were quivering, but if he was saying anything, we had the sound muted. We weren't there to listen to him. Really, it didn't matter whether he listened to us. The message was being broadcast all over and around the planet, including to the Thuranin ships.

"We know you killed humans here. Civilians, including children. You killed them for sport, and allowed them to suffer and die because of your neglect. I told you not to fuck with us in the future. That rule applies to the past also. We are not here to deliver a warning, we are here for *payback*." Turning toward the weapons console, I lowered my voice. "Weps," I called the primary weapons officer. "Fire mission."

We wasted sites *all over* that world, the bombardment went on for forty minutes. Any type of weapon installation or military facility was smashed into a smoking ruin. The official headquarters and residences of clan leadership became craters. Every aircraft, in the air or on the ground, we blew to hell. In general, we avoided causing even collateral damage to civilian areas, the exceptions were arenas where humans had been killed for sport, or forced to fight. Those arenas were usually in the center of towns, so we used minimal force, but those sites all became craters.

In one town, we hit the residence of a former clan leader, who had staged six festivals during which humans were killed in the local arena, in particularly cruel spectacles. I will not give you the details on those festivals, it made me sick hearing about them.

We hit that site and *Valkyrie* flew on in low orbit, as the planet rolled by below. "Um, hey, Joe?" Skippy called.

"What is it?" I asked, distracted by the next set of targets coming into view.

"I just learned that the last clan leader was not at home when we destroyed his residence. He is in a sort of truck about eighteen kilometers away. Sorry, I was fooled by the crappy sensors in his house. Besides, all those freakin' lizards look the same after a while."

"You know where he is now?"

"Yes. Um, Joe, there may be a complication. The truck is actually a sort of bus, it is filled with women and children who are not members of the warrior caste. They are servants and slaves. The clan leader is using them as living shields."

"Crap." We knew that, once we started bombarding sites on the surface, the lizards would quickly figure out what type of structures and facilities were on our target list. A clan leader, seeing other leader's residences being struck by railgun darts, would get the hell out of his house. To prevent that, Skippy had jammed communications. His blanket squelching of transmissions worked for the most part, but there were line-of-sight laserlinks on the surface and buried cables, and he didn't know about all of them. The primitive nature of the planet's infrastructure and the chaotic settlement process meant that central authorities had poor records of local infrastructure, and local leaders were happy to keep the authorities clueless. It also meant that Skippy could not simply raid one database, infiltrate one network, and crash the whole communications system. So, he missed a few things, and we had to adjust. Checking the map, I was puzzled. There were no other targets within the horizon from that clan leader's residence, it was his summer place, located in the middle of a vast hunting reserve. "How did this jerk know we were coming for him? I'm not blaming you, Skippy. Just curious, so we know how to avoid it in the future."

"It was bad luck, Joe. I went over old message traffic, this jerk has an ongoing dispute with his older brother. We killed his brother about ten minutes ago, but earlier in the day, the jerk tried to assassinate his older brother, and failed. His leaving the house in a bus has nothing to do with us, he is trying to escape retaliation from his brother. Bad timing, that's all."

"Ah, we can't win them all." My adrenaline rush was fading as I watched site after site get hit. "It would be nice to get this guy, but it's not worth deliberately killing innocent civilians. Keep an eye on him, but-"

"Sir?" Margaret Adams said from one of the sensor consoles. She had a catch in her voice, it alerted me that whatever she wanted to talk about, it brought up strong emotions for her.

"Gunny?"

She didn't take her eyes away from the console to look at me. Her shoulders were stiff and her voice unsteady, she spoke slowly to keep control of herself. "The people who died in *that* clan leader's arena? Aeysha," she took a breath. "Her brother was one of them."

Listen, I get it. I am a military officer. I had a responsibility to put the mission first, and not let my personal feelings get in the way. The clan leader was one of many assholes who needed killing, all across the galaxy. The death of Aeysha's brother was a tragedy, certainly, but he was also one of many people who were killed or died of starvation, disease or neglect on that world. That's the problem with vengeance; it must have a scope, an end point. It can't go on forever, because you can't go on forever. So, I get it. Adams was very emotionally invested in seeing that clan leader die.

As the commander, I have to balance the-

Oh, *screw* that.

I looked around the bridge at all the faces staring back at me. "That asshole is *toast*."

"The Commandos could-" Adams started to suggest.

"That would take too long," I did some quick math in my head. No, there I really did need to put the mission first. We had been hanging around in low orbit for too long already. A Maxohlx battlegroup, who hadn't yet gotten the message about humans being in the exclusive Elder Weapons Club, could jump in and hit *Valkyrie*. Plus, I was not tasking a Commando team to kill one alien, especially without any planning or preparation. "Skippy, can you cause an intermittent glitch in the engine of that bus?"

"Um, hmm. The bus is seriously an old piece of crap, Joe. It doesn't have much of an electronic brain I can hack into."

"Just answer the question, please. Yes or no?"

"Shmaybe? Let me try it. OK, yup, yup, the engine just stalled. Now it's moving again. Joe, I can't do that many times without totally burning out the engine."

"Do that. Burn it out, but make it stop and start a couple times first. I want that jerk to think it's a flaw with the bus. If the engine just suddenly dies, he will get suspicious."

"Gotcha."

"Sir?" Simms asked. "Should we continue the bombardment? That bus will be over the horizon in nine minutes."

Glancing at the target list, I saw we were getting to the end. There wasn't anything really important remaining. "Keep going, XO. I want a clean sweep. Another question for you, Skippy. Can we use a missile submunition to take out one person in a crowd?"

"One of *Valkyrie's* missiles?" He asked, astonished. "You realize the missiles in our magazines are designed for use against starship armor, right?"

"Hey, yeah, Dudes," Bilby interrupted. "That's true. But the Falcon dropships have air-to-ground weapons with cluster submunitions. I could dial down the yield, or, like, set the warhead to inert and go for a kinetic kill, you know?"

"Great idea," Skippy scoffed. "Except we don't have any Falcons in the air right now."

"Bilby," I ordered, annoyed that Skippy was bullying the ship's control AI. "Blow the doors to docking bay Delta-Six, and launch a missile from one of the Falcons there."

"Like, now?"

"Right now."

"This is cool. Somebody needs to-"

"Weapon authorized," Chen confirmed from the weapons console. Bilby had Skippy's restriction that he could not actually launch weapons, a human still had to press a button. "Fox One," she called, and a new symbol appeared on the display. The missile raced away and down toward the planet.

"Hey, um, Colonel Dude," Bilby asked. "Could I try guiding the submunition?"

"Do, or do not. There is no 'try', Bilby."

"Wow. Oh, *wow*," Bilby gasped. "That is deep, like, that is *wisdom*, man."

"Ugh," Skippy sighed. "He is just quoting-"

"Skippy, shut up, please." I cut off his inevitable disgusted comment. "Bilby, can you do it? Don't guess."

"Yeah, man. I can do it. Piece of cake."

"Skippy? What is jerkface doing now?"

"Well, the bus is stopped. The motor burned out earlier than I expected, that bus is really a piece of crap. Hmm, lizards are getting out of the bus now, I can't tell which one is- Oh, there he is, the tall one. Interesting. He is alone."

"Alone? You said-"

"Sorry, I meant, there are no other members of the warrior caste with him. Not even a bodyguard. That confirms the rumor."

"Rumor?" I was irritated that Skippy was not helping us keep focus.

"Yes. When the assassination attempt on his older brother failed, there was a rumor that someone on jerkface's security staff took a bribe to pass on the information. Before he fled the house in the bus, jerkface shot three of his own bodyguards."

"OK, great, can you leave the gossip for later?"

"Hmmph," Skippy harrumphed, hurt. "That is *intel*, not gossip, Joe."

"Fair enough," I admitted.

"See, *gossip* is the rumor that his brother was banging one of the-"

"Later, Skippy, *later*. Bilby, how are we doing?"

"Uh, like, we're all cool, man. You are standing on the bridge, talking and stuff. Simms is next to you and-"

"No, that's-" I closed my eyes, wincing. Sometimes, Bilby's stoner personality was less than helpful. But, he wasn't trying to murder the crew, so we had to count our blessings. "I meant, what is the status of the missile?"

"Ooh, sorry about that. The missile is cool, too. You want to watch the feed from the nosecone sensor array?"

Bilby presented himself as a slacker who indulged way too much in various substances, but under the personality he had adopted, he is a Maxohlx AI optimized by Skippy. He is *smart*. The missile came out of orbit at hypersonic speed, faster than an air-to-ground weapon was designed to fly, so Bilby had it scrub off speed on the way down, eroding the nosecone and temporarily degrading the sensor coverage, a reasonable tradeoff for delivering the weapon over the target on time.

That type of missile did not need to shed the nosecone and eject all the submunitions all at once. There was a door that could eject submunitions on at a time, so Bilby launched one, then another as a backup. Having launched its deadly payload, the missile itself kept going, passing over the target at supersonic speed and giving us a good view from above.

While we didn't have audio, the video image was sharp. We saw the broken-down bus on a lonely, narrow dirt road. The land around there was rolling grasslands dotted with clusters of trees, like views I had seen of an African savannah. A herd of some antelope-like animal was running away from the road, and on the road were lizards, about two dozen of them. Our view was from overhead at about a sixty-degree angle, and it was a lot of hats and heads, without facial features.

Until the sonic boom of the missile rolled over the road like thunder. All of the lizards looked up and all of them flinched and cowered, ducking down in fear. All except one, the tallest by far.

That had to be our target, I knew it even before the facial recognition system confirmed. That ugly lizard face looked up not in fear but in disdain. As a warrior caste leader, he knew that it was the supersonic weapons you did *not* hear that was dangerous. His disdain was probably partly for us, partly for the poor asshole downrange who would be struck by the missile, and mostly for the lower-caste women and children cowering in the dirt at his feet. We could see his mouth moving, shouting at them, and he kicked one of the women hard, shaking his fists. His anger, combined with the rolling thunder of the sonic boom, had the civilians hunkered down.

That situation presented a nice, easy target for the submunitions. As instructed, Bilby had rendered the warhead inert, relying on its high-subsonic speed to do the damage. It raced in at about eleven hundred kilometers per hour, high enough off the ground that it did not give away its approach by causing the tall grass below to ripple. At the last second, Bilby guided it to duck down at knee-level and turn to follow the road.

The target turned suddenly, perhaps seeing a puff of dust on the road as the submunition raced along. It was unlikely he could see the submunition, it was no bigger than a tube of lipstick and its chameleonware matched the surroundings. If jerkface suspected anything, he did not go so far as to drop flat on the road. He did the opposite, looking up at the sky and shouting something we could not hear.

It was thoughtful of him to present such an easy target. He was standing at least a meter taller than any of the civilians around him, with his head flung back and mouth open. The inert submunition flew in to strike the roof of his mouth, exiting at the top rear of his skull and blowing out a jet of blood, bone and the fermented shit he used for a brain. It was a nice touch by Bilby, having the blood and gore fountain up and away from the huddled civilians, before his corpse slumped to the dirt.

Have you ever overheard someone talking about you, when they don't know you are there? It can be interesting if they say nice things, or terrible if they say what they really think. As a colonel, I have to evaluate the people under my command, and they get to give feedback on how I am doing my job. Skippy could tell me what people really think about me, I have always stopped him from doing that. Others, including Chang and Simms and Smythe, and Desai when she was my executive officer, were always very open about my various and serious failings, so I didn't have to guess what they thought. Nor did I suffer the illusion that any of them thought I was a perfect leader.

Why do I mention this?

Because jerkface on the ground was getting real-time feedback about his leadership. When his corpse splattered to the ground, the civilians ran away in terror. For about ten seconds. Then, when no additional weapons struck, they must have figured they were safe. And they used the opportunity to show jerkface exactly what they thought about his 'Tough-but-Unfair' style of dictatorship.

They kicked him, hard. When that didn't do enough damage, they picked up rocks and threw them at him, or got down on their knees and bashed his body with stones until it was a broken and bloody mess. One of the children, had to be a boy, whipped out his ding-dong to take a wizz on the corpse, when our missile went out of range and we lost the close-up view.

"Gunny?" I asked. "Jerkface's people just gave an evaluation of how he did his job. How did *we* do?"

Her hands were shaking slightly, from the anger that initiated the action, and from the relief of seeing the target terminated. Relief and maybe a bit of disappointment that it all happened so fast, jerkface hadn't even realized he died. She put both hands on the console, took a breath, and looked over at me. "Satisfactory, Sir."

"No Gunny. It's not satisfactory. But it will have to do."

She knew what I meant, acknowledging my statement with a lift of her chin. Nothing could bring back Aeysha's mother or brother, or fill the hole in that little girl's heart. All we could hope for was to get a measure of solace that one particular asshole would not be hurting anyone, ever again.

Valkyrie continued its low arc over the inhabited part of the planet and soon passed out over the ocean, our target list completed. When we were done, fires burned at isolated sites all over that world, long trails of black smoke blowing downwind.

We did not strike the islands where the kidnapped people had been held. I had debated whether to pound those areas until the land no longer was above sea level, to erase the stain of their existence, so the people who suffered there would know they never had to worry about going back. When I explained my idea to John Yang, the guy from Fresno who had been held prisoner on one of those islands, he was horrified by my plan. People who died there were buried on those islands, Yang said they deserved to rest in peace. I agreed, so we left them alone.

We also did not hit the new clan leader, whoever he was. It would have been counterproductive to take him out, especially as he had been so helpful to us by taking over responsibilities of the previous leader, by shooting that loud-mouth asshole in the head.

We contacted him again, and his ugly face reappeared on the display. While we were bombarding his planet, apparently he had been in some sort of fight. His lips and the skin around one eye were swollen, and blood dripped from his mouth. Whatever the fight had been, he won, at least for the moment. This time we didn't mute the sound, and we could hear unintelligible shouting and cursing in the background. Holding up an index finger, I glared at him. "I have one question for you. Did you get the message?"

"Yes." He didn't follow that with any stupid questions or useless remarks, so maybe he was an upgrade from the guy he shot.

"Excellent. We are leaving stealthed satellites in orbit to watch this place. The two islands where you held our people, they are off-limits. *No one* goes there. No one flies overhead. Stay away, *far* away." My purpose in making those islands a no-go zone was that someday, we might return to dig up the graves, and bring our people home. "If you do not follow my instructions, tell your senior leaders of your clan that we *will* hunt them down, and we *will* find them and we will *kill* every single one of them. Is that understood?"

"Yes. And yes." He was smarter than the average lizard, understanding that I had asked two questions.

Drawing a finger across my throat signaled Skippy to cut the transmission. "Pilot, lift us to jump distance."

While we were accelerating to jump altitude, I contacted the Thuranin squadron commander. Again, the audio was muted from their end. "This is Colonel Joe Bishop of the United Nations Starship *Valkyrie*. I assume you listened to my conversation with the Kristang here. That message applies to you also. We are dropping our damping field," I signaled to Simms and she made it happen. "Get lost. Get out of here, right now. If I see you again, your corpse had better be stone cold."

There are many bad things to be said about the Thuranin, but you cannot say they aren't able to take a hint. They jumped away, the instant the strength of our damping field faded enough to make a jump practical.

We also jumped away the instant we could.

Damn it.

That was the umpteenth planet I have visited, and I still have never been to a gift shop to get a snow globe.

I will settle for remembering the heartwarming image of smoke rising up all over that world.

CHAPTER FOUR

Admiral Gost-Ren Tashallo of the Mighty 98th Fleet was soundly asleep in his cabin, aboard his flagship *I Am Aching To Give Somebody A Beat-Down And Today Is YOUR Lucky Day*, when a squadron of ships from the Home Fleet's Ethics and Compliance Office jumped in at one of the designated approach zones. After a brief exchange of credentials, the ECO ship *It Was Like That When We Got Here* was granted permission to jump in closer, and a dropship soon launched to bring Captain Scorandum aboard the flagship.

He was escorted to the admiral's personal office, to meet a rumpled and very grumpy Tashallo. "What," the senior officer asked with a mandible-stretching yawn, then taking a loud slurp from a steaming mug of fatah. "Is so important that it could not wait until a decent hour?"

"Sir, it-"

One of the admiral's antennas stood straight up, to get the junior officer's full attention. "I feel obliged to warn you, Captain. If this is some sketchy ECO nonsense, I am *not* going to be happy with you. An official from the Inquisitor's office was here very late last night, and I was obliged to consume many rounds of drinks with her. Too many."

"I can assure you, Sir, that this is not any sort of nonsense, nor is the issue confined to Ethics and Compliance. Or the Jeraptha Republic. It affects the entire *galaxy*."

"One moment, please," Tashallo requested, while he took another slurp of hot fatah. He could not face the day without a mug of the mild stimulant beverage, and although it technically was still the middle of the night in ship-time, he suspected that whatever Scorandum was about to dump on him, he would not be going back to sleep. "Perhaps we could make this more interesting, with a wager on whether I can guess what you are about to say."

"Respectfully," Scorandum replied with great regret, while his brain shouted *stupid stupid STUPID* at him for missing a golden opportunity. "That would not be appropriate. I would only be taking your money, Sir."

That remark, more than a mug full of steaming fatah, brought Tashallo fully awake. "So certain are you?"

"Absolutely, Sir."

"Please, I am intrigued. What is your information?"

"Well, Sir, the humans have an expression that fits this occasion perfectly."

"Oh? What is that?"

Scorandum leaned back on his couch. "You are *not* going to believe this."

The first stop on our Galactic Kick-Ass tour had been a nostalgic revenge play. It was a real crowd-pleaser, sure to bring the house down. Especially if that house was struck by one of *Valkyrie*'s railguns. Going to Rikers was a feel-good action, but it really didn't accomplish anything useful. To send a message to the Kristang, we could have destroyed one of their major shipyards, or a weapons depot, or turned the headquarters of a major clan into a smoking crater. Or just, you know, sent an actual message, with words.

We went to Rikers not because the lizard leaders there needed to be punished, or because hitting them would give any kind of solace to the people we rescued. No, I was not under any illusions about our motivations for wreaking havoc on that world. We did it for *us*, the Merry Band of Pirates. We did it because for years, we had been sneaking around in the shadows, keeping our heads down and taking hit after hit, without being able to really hit back. We hit Rikers because the Pirates were *done* with that shit, just *done*.

With Rikers a smoking ruin in our rear-view mirror, we set course for another meeting, one that promised less ass-kicking and more ass-kissing. Not kissing ass, exactly, but our purpose was more diplomatic than kinetic.

The whole diplomacy thing was totally new to me, I hoped I didn't screw it up.

The next stop had me personally excited, for it would bring me face-to-face with someone I had been watching and admiring, someone I had been eager to meet.

Admiral Tashallo of the Jeraptha Mighty 98th Fleet.

Captain Scorandum's ECO squadron arrived at the 98th barely six hours before we got there, so that saved us the time of explaining everything. I won't bore you with the introductions and ceremonies, they were just as much fun, and just as dull, as any sort of military formal occasion can be. Mercifully, Admiral Tashallo felt the same way I do about ceremonies, he hustled me off to his private office as soon as he could, which was not soon enough for me. His crew all wanted to gawk at me, not just because I am a rarely-seen human, but because I am *me*. News of who had really been flying the ghost ship had raced around the Mighty 98th, and the arrival of *Valkyrie* caused a feverish excitement. All the intense attention made me very uncomfortable, and I reminded myself that I had better get used to it, because it would only get worse once we got back to Earth.

I hate to say this, but that is one of the reasons I ordered Chang to stay behind with the *Flying Dutchman*. Hopefully, by the time *Valkyrie* returned, the initial furor would have died down and I could be debriefed without a media circus, but I doubted that. The shocking announcement that humanity had *Elder weapons* would be the biggest news event since Columbus Day itself, no way would the public leave me alone.

Anyway, in his office, it was just me, Tashallo and Captain Scorandum. To my surprise, Tashallo presented me a bottle of genuine American bourbon, a carafe of ice and a souvenir glass that had the Merry Band of Pirates logo inscribed, that was a thoughtful touch I appreciated. To my dismay, the Admiral expected me to drink the bourbon while he and Scorandum enjoyed a bottle of rare, vintage burgoze. I sipped carefully while the two big beetles reclined on couches, guzzling burgoze and burping with great gusto. Apparently, that is considered a polite social thing to do among the Jeraptha, and I didn't want to offend our new friends, so I joined them.

In case you are wondering, I do not know the aroma of good, vintage burgoze when it is straight out of the bottle. When it is burped back up, it reminds me of pool-cleaning chemicals, with undertones of eye-wateringly hot peppers, shoe polish, and radiator fluid. But I am not an expert, you should experience it yourself.

Although, I do *not* recommend that.

So, my first attempt at interspecies diplomacy involved getting wasted with a pair of large beetles, and trying not to say anything outrageously stupid. It helped that I genuinely was more interested in hearing about Tashallo's exploits than in talking about my own, and he was very obviously proud of the ships and people under his command. He sensed that I really did want him to talk, so I peppered him with questions about his victory over a combined Thuranin-Bosphuraq force at the Battle of Nubrentia. At first, he was surprised that I knew so many details of that battle, then he relaxed and we talked like old friends. To me, he kind of was an old friend, after all, I had been reading about him for years.

The conversation became a bit uncomfortable, when he was talking about how he got command of the Mighty 98th Fleet. That privilege was granted to him, after his astounding victory at the Battle of Glark. While he related the tale, I murmured appropriate things, looking down at my glass so I could avoid his eyes.

"The Inquisitors still do not understand," he directed the remark to Scorandum, "where that remarkably accurate intelligence came from. It appeared from nowhere."

The ECO captain must have realized the admiral was expecting him to say something. "It wasn't *us*," he protested.

"Mm. Of course not," Tashallo dipped his antennas, in a gesture that indicated skepticism, if I was reading Jeraptha body language correctly.

"Really!" Scorandum gestured so vigorously, a few drops of burgoze sloshed out of his glass onto his uniform. "Admiral, if Ethics and Compliance pulled off an incredible intelligence coup like stealing the Glark data, there is no way the head office could keep quiet about it. They would want the entire galaxy to know! Also," he took another slurp of burgoze. "There would have been *substantial* wagering action on the clandestine markets. That could not fail to attract the attention of the Inquisitors," he added with a shudder.

"Hmm," Tashallo considered. "That is true. Ah, well, I suppose it will remain a mystery, then. That is unfortunate," he said, and that time, he was looking at *me*.

"Uh, yeah, I uh-" *Why* is my stupid brain so freakin' slow?

The admiral's antennas stood straight up and he sucked in a breath, his thorax heaving. "You! It was *you*."

"Uh, well, it's like this-"

"You do not deny it, then?"

Suddenly, I realized I was alone with two very large beetles. "You gotta understand, we did it to *help* you."

"We had no relationship with you at the time," Tashallo noted with suspicion. "Nor with your people on Paradise. Was your action motivated by a wager among your crew?"

"What? No."

"Why not?" Scorandum asked, puzzled.

"We're not like that. Not all of us. Not all the time," I tried to explain to members of a society that was obsessed with gambling. "Our military code of conduct does not allow us to wager on the outcome of a future or ongoing operation."

"You miss too much," Tashallo shook his head. "Wagering action can be a powerful motivator for your crew."

"I will consider it," I said, thinking that would be one more thing for UNEF Command to get pissed at me for. "Admiral, our actions *were* motivated by self-interest. We wished your people to maintain an advantage over your enemies, to protect the humans on Paradise."

"Ah," Tashallo and Scorandum said at the same time, sharing a look and nodding.

"Ha!" The admiral laughed, taking a slurp of burgoze. "Colonel Bishop, you have not only solved a mystery, you have ruined wagers across our fleet."

"Uh, how did I do that?"

"Substantial amounts have been wagered, about who provided the intelligence about the Thuranin raid at Glark. My own money was on the Maxohlx."

"The Maxohlx?" Scorandum exclaimed, surprised. "Hmm. I should have thought of that. I put my money on the Bosphuraq."

"Too obvious," Tashallo snorted. "Those thieves at Central Wagering were offering ruinous odds on the Bosphuraq being involved. Well," he chuckled. "We have *all* lost, then. The joke is on us."

Scorandum grimaced, or that is how I interpreted the tight set of his mandibles. "Tell me, Colonel Bishop, you framed the Bosphuraq for *all* of the ghost ship attacks?"

"Yes. We also destroyed those first two Maxohlx ships that were going to Earth. The planet where the Bosphuraq were trying to build atomic-compression weapons? The birds genuinely were just trying to copy Thuranin weapons there. We took over their moonbase and caused it to fire on the planet."

"You have been *busy*," Scorandum snorted. "Colonel, we at the Ethics and Compliance Office pride ourselves on scheming to commit the most creative, the sketchiest, the sleaziest clandestine operations in the galaxy. Now I see that we are nothing but *amateurs*," he spat with disgust.

"Captain Scorandum," I leaned toward him on the awkward couch that was not built for the human anatomy. Aware that I had been drinking, I squashed an alcohol-fueled impulse to be overly friendly. "The Merry Band of Pirates look forward to future operations with the Ethics and Compliance Office. We could be a great team."

Scorandum raised his glass. "I will drink to that."

We all took a sip of our beverages.

"You are aware," Tashallo peered at me over his glass. "That the Bosphuraq will be outraged to learn that *you* are the reason they have been severely punished by their patrons. Thank you for that, by the way," he added with a wink.

I answered with a shrug. "That is one group of assholes beating up on another group of assholes. It's not like the Bosphuraq would have been friendly to us, no matter what we did. The strife between the birds and their patrons weakens that entire coalition, that has to be good for us," both beetles nodded, understanding that when I said 'us', I meant the Jeraptha, humans, and their allies. "The birds will be even *more* pissed off at their patrons when they learn the Maxohlx have been conducting strikes against them for no good reason, except that they are gullible fools. We have made the Maxohlx look weak and stupid, the whole galaxy will be laughing at them. Besides, my feeling about the Maxohlx and their clients is, well, fuck 'em, you know?"

However that remark translated, the Jeraptha thought it was uproariously funny. I took that as a good sign for future interspecies relations.

After what I guessed was an hour, I had to guess because checking the clock on my zPhone would not be polite, I pushed the bourbon bottle away. "Gentlemen, thank you, but I want to walk back to my dropship. If I drink any more of this, I will have to be carried."

Tashallo took the hint. "We are sure you must be very busy, Colonel Bishop," he said with one eye on the bottle. Whether he was impressed or disappointed with my drinking capacity, he didn't show it. The admiral had a great poker face. "Before you go, I may be able to help you, and the good people of Earth."

"Oh. How?"

"I suggest that we send a representative to Earth, of course."

"Yes, please." That was something I was about to suggest.

"Before that, I believe you will want to bring home, many of your people currently on the planet you call 'Paradise'?"

"Yes." It didn't surprise me he had guessed that, it was obvious. "*Valkyrie's* passenger capacity is rather limited at the moment, so we-"

"On behalf of the 98th Fleet, and of my people, I would like to offer the use of several troop transport ships, and a star carrier. They will not be luxurious, but each ship should be capable of transporting several thousand humans, after minor modifications, of course."

"That, that is very generous," I stumbled over my words. "Very generous. Thank you. We would be very grateful for such a thoughtful gift."

He waved an antenna. "It is the least we could do, to signify our admiration for your remarkable accomplishments, and our hope for warm future relations between our peoples."

"And, to show how pleased we are," Scorandum added with a semi-drunken slur of his words. "About the *generous* beat-down you gave to those asshole Maxohlx."

"Hear, hear!" Tashallo raised his half-empty glass of burgoze.

I picked up my own glass, with still had a finger or two of bourbon in it. "I will drink to *that*."

Meeting the Mighty 98th Fleet lifted spirits aboard the ship. It was good to hear genuine praise from a species that had been kicking much ass on their own, and the offer of transport ships solved a problem I had been struggling with. Maybe those ships would come with a hidden price tag; the governments of Earth could deal with that later.

Delivering a beat-down on Rikers had not really changed anything; the humans who died there were still dead, the lizard warrior caste were still murderous assholes, and they would continue to terrorize and bully anyone who couldn't stand up to them. An alliance with the Jeraptha, even limited in scope, brought with it the prospect of real change in the galaxy, a change in the equation of the endless war. Maybe with allies, we could begin to bring a halt to the cruelty and suffering the Maxohlx coalition had inflicted across the galaxy.

Maybe.

Emily Perkins had grandiose plans for the Alien Legion, we had discussed it briefly aboard *Valkyrie*. While she was concerned that the Legion not settle for half-measures that did not create long-lasting change, I was concerned that humanity not get bogged down in commitments that had no defined scope, end date and exit strategy. The overall strategy would be determined by the nations of UNEF, and I would certainly have an opportunity to provide my experienced input. What I feared was that humanity would get sucked into 'nation-building' on some war-torn planet in the middle of nowhere.

Anyway, those kinds of decisions were above my pay grade. It was funny saying that as a colonel, because when I was a grunt, I figured that colonels and general officers made all the important decisions. My brief time as a publicity-stunt colonel on Paradise had not shown me what a real colonel's job is. Flying around the galaxy, cut off from headquarters and making decisions on my own also was not typical of what real colonels did for a living.

Man, I hope I never become a real colonel.

The next stop on our Galactic Kick-Ass tour was not exactly kicking ass, it was more like kicking sense into people who are asses.

Keepers.

Yes, the self-proclaimed Keepers of the Faith, the willfully blind idiots who left Paradise with the Kristang, to demonstrate their continued loyalty to our lizard overlords. Sure, I know the issue is complicated. The infected Keepers we met, when we stopped them from delivering a bioweapon to Paradise, had informed me that just because they are idiots, they are not all motivated by the same idiocy. That is a lesson my parents pounded into my young stubborn head; just because someone disagrees with you, that doesn't make them a bad person. The reverse is also true; just because someone agrees with you, that doesn't make them a good person. You have to know *why* they have an opinion on X or Y.

Most of the Keepers were idiots, who just could not face up to the fact that we originally signed on to fight the wrong side of the war. They had left Earth with a burning determination to make the Ruhar pay for raiding our world, and they didn't want to hear any facts that made them question their beliefs. Hell, when I first met the Burgermeister in that tiny village on Paradise, I had walked out, rather than hear her tell me what I later learned was the awful truth.

So, I did have some sympathy for the Keepers of the Faith, though for our purpose, sympathy didn't matter. They were *our* people, we were bringing them home if we could. They could deal with the consequences of their actions when we brought them home. And that would be an interesting legal mess. UNEF-HQ on Paradise would argue that when the Keepers left Paradise to serve the Kristang, they had disobeyed orders from a lawful authority. The Keepers would argue that the only 'lawful authority' was UNEF Command on Earth, which had issued orders for us to fight alongside the Kristang. That UNEF on Paradise had no legal authority to switch sides in the war.

As Skippy would say, 'Ugh'. Man, I am so glad that I am not a JAG lawyer, that argument is a mess on both sides.

Fortunately, I did not have to be concerned with legal niceties. The last substantial group of Keepers was on a Kristang planet controlled by the Death Stalkers, a minor but independent clan currently in a loose alliance with the Black Trees. I say 'currently' because even for the lizards, the Death Stalkers had a reputation for treating their alliances casually, as any agreement was only effective if it was the best deal the Death Stalkers could get right that very moment. You might think their well-deserved reputation for sleaziness would make it difficult for the Death Stalkers to make deals with other clans, but the opposite is true. The warrior caste is obsessed with honor, but the reality is they are obsessed with the *appearance* of honor. With the Death Stalkers openly willing to do anything to gain a slight advantage, and not caring what anyone thinks of their honor, that makes them valuable deal-making partners. For example, by buying, trading for and stealing human slaves, the Death Stalkers had the only meaningful collection of humans in captivity. The slaves had been purchased so that any clan who wanted to seriously threaten the Alien Legion had to get Keepers from the Death Stalkers. Two recent events had made the collection more valuable. Emily Perkins had destroyed a small group of Keepers on Jellaxico, demonstrating that making threats with only a handful of humans was a waste of time. And the apparent Legion rescue operation on Rakesh Diwalen left the Death Stalkers with the only supply of human medical subjects. According to Skippy, the clan was fielding competing offers from several major clans, and from the Thuranin.

"What are the offers, Skippy?" I asked, after we pinged a Thuranin data relay station for updated info.

"Hmm, it's interesting. The Black Trees opened with a weak offer, it's a mutual defense agreement. Of course, the Death Stalkers know that agreement isn't worth the electrons in the document file. The Fire Dragons are offering a planet the Death Stalkers very much want, but the Stalker leadership knows their resources would be greatly overextended to defend and keep that planet. Plus, um, the Stalkers recently brokered a deal to sell second-hand ships to the Swift Arrow clan, who are planning an invasion of that same Fire Dragon planet. The Death Stalker leaders are debating whether to tell the Fire Dragons about the invasion plan, in exchange for something valuable. They are also debating whether they could get a better deal from the Swift Arrows, in exchange for *not* ratting them out to the Fire Dragons."

"Wow. The lizards not only love to back-stab each other, they are *good* at it."

"They've had a lot of practice, Joe," he said with admiration.

"What are the Thuranin offering?"

"They are offering to *not* bombard the planet from orbit and slaughter the Death Stalker senior leadership."

"Mm hm, that *is* a strong opening offer," I agreed.

"Ah, shmaybe. The Death Stalkers have dealt with the Thuranin before, so they have a playbook. If the Thuranin attempt to carry out their threat, the Stalkers will kill all their Keepers."

Smacking a fist into my other hand, I exclaimed "Shit!" That blew my plan. On the approach to the planet, I had a macho idea of jumping into orbit with our fearsome ghost ship, and demand the lizards surrender the Keepers to us. Or at least, stand aside while we flew dropships down to pick up our prodigal people. The plan would be worthless if the lizards pulled the trigger and killed all of their slaves. "Can they do it?"

"Kill them? Yes, of course. I sense this is a case where you are asking too general a question."

"My bad. Can they kill the Keepers, before we could take out whatever explosives or weapons they plan to use?"

"Meh, you need to ask a more specific question, Joe. The lizards could just strangle the Keepers with their bare hands, given enough time."

"Fine. How about this: what is their plan to kill the Keepers, if the Thuranin attack?"

"*That* is a question I can answer. The Keepers are being kept in a cluster of secure buildings, inside a secure compound on a heavily-defended military base. The dormitories are wired to explode. Any Keepers who happen to be outside the buildings can be tracked by implanted locator chips, and killed by the soldiers on the base. The base has practiced killing the slaves; even in the worst case, the task could be accomplished in thirty-eight seconds."

"Shit! Threatening to hit targets from orbit would be useless, the lizards would know we especially will not risk them killing our people. OK, OK. This is the part of the movie where you reveal that you can disable the explosives, and buy time for us to pull our people out."

"Hmm. Apparently, there were more annoying script revisions since I got my copy. *My* script says this is the scene where the knucklehead commander asks me to do the impossible, and fails to acknowledge my awesomeness."

"Can you do it, or not?"

"Yes and no. *Yes*, I can disable the electronic detonation controls. *No*, that will not solve the problem, because there is a manual backup that can be engaged in seconds. The lizards regularly practice that backup process."

"Smythe?" I turned to where our STAR team leader was seated along the back bulkhead of the bridge. "What do you think?"

"I need to study the matter, Sir," he replied with an uncharacteristic frown, his brow crinkled. He and five of the STARs had volunteered to remain aboard *Valkyrie* before we jumped away from Earth, though at the time, I had no intention of any ground action. That was before Skippy learned of the Keepers being held by the Death Stalkers. As Smythe was fond of reminding me, I had not been provided a Tier One team of special operators in case things went well. We needed the

STARs when things went sideways. Notice that I said 'when' and not 'if', because nothing ever went smoothly for the Merry Band of Pirates.

Smythe had five STARs, plus four of the Commandos we shanghaied from Paradise. Commandant Fabron had gone aboard the *Flying Dutchman* before we jumped away from Earth. It had been his initiative to represent the people on Paradise to UNEF Command, because the governments of Earth needed a first-person, updated account of the situation on that world. He volunteered to stay behind, after I assured him that I did not intend to take any action that required a SpecOps team, and he saved me the trouble of ordering him to stay behind. During our short time together, I had come to greatly respect Fabron and his calm, quiet leadership. He had made me promise that I would support his return to the Alien Legion, he strongly felt that humans had a long list of unfinished business out in the vast expanse of the galaxy.

So, Smythe had nine people to work with for a ground team. The four Commandos were the people he felt were most ready to support a STAR team, and I was just super, *super* thrilled when I learned that Gunnery Sergeant Lamar Freakin' Greene was one of those four. Really. I could not have been happier about it. OK, maybe I would have been *slightly* more happy if Greene had gotten drunk and missed the dropship that brought him over from the *Dutchman*, but that is petty and unworthy and exactly how I honestly felt about it. When Margaret Adams requested a last-minute transfer to *Valkyrie*, I had done a mental fist-pump. Then, seconds later, I saw that Smythe requested Greene to be transferred aboard *Valkyrie* and I mentally face-palmed myself.

Shit.

Adams hadn't transferred for me, or to see the mission completed. She was following *Greene*.

Or she wasn't. Shit, I didn't know.

What was I talking about?

Oh, yeah. Smythe.

I held up an index finger. "Hold that thought, Colonel. You, plus nine on your team, plus two, maybe four pilots. That is fourteen lives at risk. To recover a bunch of idiots, half of whom will *not* be grateful to see us. No," I shook my head slowly. "We don't *have* to do this. It's not worth the risk."

"Sir," Smythe said stiffly. His demeanor reflected the weariness of having to go over an old and continual argument with a commanding officer who just doesn't *get it*. "We have spent the past several years defending the people of Earth. It is my experience that many of our fellow citizens are lazy, dimwitted arseholes, but we do not ask whether *they* are worthy of our protection. It is the job we signed up for."

From her chair beside me, Simms tapped my leg and whispered a simple "Sir."

I got it. *Trust your people*, she was telling me. Again. My own stupid brain should have known that. When I am being honest with a self-assessment, holding back information and not trusting my people is my number one flaw. Skippy would say that is actually a subset of my overall General Stupidity flaw, but it is true either way. "Show me a plan," I told Smythe as he and Simms shared a look. "I want minimal risk to our people. To the crew," I added to clarify which *people* I meant.

Smythe gave me three options for insertion, suppression of enemy defenses, securing the Keepers, setting up and defending a perimeter, safe-fly ingress and egress corridors for our dropships, and pulling out his team under fire if necessary. All three plans were well-researched, for *Valkyrie* had jumped into the system so Skippy could have his way with the local databases. From the distance that was enough to ensure *Valkyrie* was not detected, Skippy could only extract data, any rougher treatment of the local computer network would have to wait until he was closer to the planet. He was being careful, not because he was concerned about his infiltration being noticed by the laughably crappy Kristang information security systems, but because he *was* concerned about being noticed by the Thuranin spyware that was woven throughout every computer system on and around the planet.

The first phase of any operation is to gather intel. OK, the real first phase is to establish intent, meaning to decide what you want to accomplish, but I had already issued a very clear and detailed Commander's Intent document.

Yes, I had actually taken the time and effort to write an official form like I was supposed to. Maybe being a field-grade officer was growing on me.

Anyway, we had all the intel we needed. Correction: Smythe had all the intel he needed for his part of the operation. What *I* did not have is a good awareness of any assets the Thuranin had in-system. Knowing that, Smythe had planned his silent insertion and securing of the Keepers so those phases would not be detected from orbit. By the time Smythe commenced the noisy part of the operation, it would not matter whether a Thuranin ship saw what was going on. I *hoped* that was true.

One thing I noticed immediately about all three options presented by Smythe: they were riskier and more aggressive than other plans he had shown to me recently. That made me wonder if Major Kapoor had exerted a restraining influence on Smythe, because Kapoor left Valkyrie and was now on Earth. Or maybe the reason the current set of plans had a feeling like an extreme sports event was due to Captain Frey. Our Canadian special operator certainly did not hold anything back in her own operations. Smythe had met Frey during an adventure race, perhaps in the future we should look for STAR team candidates who enjoyed gentler leisure-time activities like bird-watching and knitting sweaters.

Like *that* was ever going to happen.

One option I rejected immediately, I suspect he included that lunatic plan to give me something to discard, so the other options seemed reasonable by comparison. We went back and forth, with me asking questions and objecting to this and that, until I was satisfied the risk was manageable, and he was satisfied I had not watered down his plan so much that the whole operation was pointless.

CHAPTER FIVE

After packing all the required gear aboard our dropships, we launched. When I say 'we', I am including myself. I was flying one of the Panthers, with Chen and Ray flying the others. They both had copilots from the Commando team, who were not fully qualified on the Panther, but we didn't have enough pilots aboard. As I would be remaining outside the engagement zone, I was flying alone. Reed would be flying *Valkyrie*, an assignment she grumbled about and gave me dirty looks, and I had every confidence she would perform with distinction. Besides, I assured her that she might have the most fun role, if we got into trouble. She perked up when I said that, we both knew the Merry Band of Pirates *always* find trouble everywhere we go.

One major benefit of revealing our existence to the galaxy was not needing to sneak around. I mean, in this case we *were* sneaking around, but that was so the Kristang did not kill their prisoners before we could secure them. We cared that the lizards did not know we were coming until it was too late, but once Smythe's team commenced blowing things up, we did not care if the lizards knew they were being attacked by humans.

That new and refreshing lack of a need for a cover story, is why the ground team were flying in the Maxohlx dropships we called 'Panthers'. They were our most capable aerospace craft, but in the past we could rarely risk using them, in case our presence was discovered. That is why I had been flying a Kristang Dragon at Rikers, and it is a damned good thing. Finding me inside a Kristang dropship matched the cover story of the raid being an Alien Legion operation. If I had been caught in a Thuranin Falcon, or a Maxohlx Panther, it would have been an absolute disaster. The Thuranin who captured me had only been interested in verifying the bullshit cover story they downloaded from the Dragon's flight computer. Our raid annoyed, pissed off and inconvenienced the Thuranin, but we did not scare them. That is why their ship remained in orbit after I was taken aboard. If they had found me in one of their own advanced dropships, or in a Maxohlx craft, the shit would have hit the fan. Their ship would have jumped away before Skippy could return and hack into it. My skull would eventually have been cracked open, maybe after the Thuranin delivered me to their patrons. The result would have been death for me, and very possibly enslavement and extinction for humanity. OK, sure, Friedlander still would have seen the message from Nagatha, and saved the *Flying Dutchman*. Chang would have jumped in to retrieve Skippy. But what then?

Often, I rightfully accuse Skippy of being an arrogant asshole. Sometimes, I am too much the opposite, not taking credit for my own accomplishments. The truth is, I don't often boast about good things I have done, because deep down, I am terrified that everything I've done is a fluke. That I have just been lucky, and that my luck has run out.

Still, it scared the shit out of me to think what could have happened, if the Thuranin had a reason not to buy our cover story at Rikers. Without me aboard, *Valkyrie* could not have jumped away before the Thuranin recon frigate brought an entire battlegroup in to destroy our ghost ship. Without me and *Valkyrie*, I very much doubt that Chang would have brought the *Dutchman* to the beta site and investigated the hidden planet Maris. Without that, Earth would have been ground into dust by the Maxohlx, and we would not have the opportunity to get T-shirts for our Kick-Ass tour.

All those thoughts went through my mind, as I warmed up my Panther for launch. We had come so close to disaster, it reminded me that little things could be the difference not only between life and death, but between mission success and failure.

We launched and flew our three-ship formation of Panthers toward the planet, leaving *Valkyrie* behind. In the copilot seat beside me, Skippy was in his padded cradle, strapped tightly into the seat. Every time I looked over at him, I had a flashback to his betrayal.

Skippy said that with the quantum machines in my head burned out or disabled, he could not read my thoughts, but if that was true, he had become very good at reading my body language. "Joe," he said quietly, after I cut the engines for the long coast toward the planet. "We have not flown together, just you and me, since, you know."

"Yeah." I didn't look at him, keeping my concentration on the instruments, though I had absolutely nothing to do until we swung into orbit.

"It makes me feel like shit, to think that you are worried I will bail on you again. Please be assured, that will never happen again."

"Skippy," I sighed. "It's nice hearing you say that. Words are cheap. I will only *know* you haven't bailed, when it doesn't happen."

"OK, I deserved that."

"I'm just saying, we have been through a *whole lot* of crazy shit together. You went through an unimaginable amount of shit before we met. All I know is, you never know what will happen out here; the unexpected will happen."

"True dat," he agreed. "Remember how I declared I was right, that I have a responsibility to the galaxy overall, and not just to one planet infested with filthy monkeys?"

"If this is you trying to give me confidence you *won't* go running off again, you really-"

"I am still convinced I was right about that. However, recent events have convinced me that, as important as I am to the survival of all life in the galaxy, *you* are just as important."

"Uh-" Damn. How do you respond when someone says you are responsible for the Fate of the freakin' *Galaxy*?

"I am serious, Joe. I can't do this alone."

"What uh, brought you to this shocking realization?"

"When we went to Maris at the beta site. Jeez, all I wanted to do was satisfy an idle curiosity about a missing planet. When I suckered you into actually going there, I was thr-"

"When you *what*?"

"Umm, maybe I misspoke."

"Ya think?"

"Let me try that again. Let's not dwell on the past, OK? Like I said, for me it was curiosity because I was bored. But you? *You* thought 'Hmm there might be Elder weapons hidden in there'. How the *f-* Joe, it *amazes* me how your tiny monkey brain works. Then you realized we needed to plant those weapons on timers, in enemy star systems. That is something I never would have thought of. If, or *when*, the other Elder AIs begin to wake up, I can't fight them by myself. I need something the other AIs don't have; a secret weapon. A filthy, ignorant monkey with a brain the size of a raisin."

"Gosh, Skippy, I am blushing from your praise."

"You know what I mean."

"I am your secret weapon, huh?"

"Well, all of the Merry Band of Pirates are my secret weapon. But, especially you."

"I'm a secret agent, huh? Then I should have a cool code name."

He made a gagging sound and laughed. "How about we use 'Knucklehead' as your code name?"

"No."

"Numbskull?"

"Also no."

"OK, then Agent *Barney* it is."

"Just call me 'Joe', please," I gave up.

"You got it. Hey, Joe, you know that I do not believe in coincidences."

"Yes," hearing that set my Spidey senses to tingling. A glance at the sensors did not show any threats. "Why?"

"Because we have three hours and thirty-four minutes until you need to make a course correction.

"Yeah, so?"

"It just happens that my latest operatic masterpiece is three hours and *twenty-*four minutes, giving you plenty of time for a potty break. In my very humble opinion, this is the greatest thing I have ever written."

He was wrong.

My father and I used to go backpacking. One summer we took a trip to the White Mountains in New Hampshire, and walked the Presidential Range. On top of Mount Washington, which was rarely and blessedly clear that day, my father told me the Appalachian Mountains used to be taller than the Himalayas, but billions of years of erosion had worn them down.

Skippy was not wrong that the opera was the best thing he has ever written. It was awful, just not as bad as anything else that came out of his musically-challenged brain.

He was wrong about the length. It was *not* around three and a half hours. During the time I suffered through listening to his opera, the Appalachians could have risen from the sea, and eroded away to their current lumpy shapes.

You think I am exaggerating?

Fine. *You* listen to it.

My Panther flew ahead of the two ships carrying the SpecOps teams, so Skippy could gather more detailed real-time intel, and hack into the planetary defense network. The Death Stalker clan had installed an extensive sensor suite on and around the planet, plus a multi-layer strategic defense satellite network. The SD network included components purchased at great expense from the Bosphuraq, giving that planet a defensive edge over most Kristang worlds.

We were counting on Skippy to take control of the planetary defense network, so the lizards down there would not see Smythe's team coming, and not be able to use their strategic defense weapons against the ground team, our dropships or *Valkyrie*. Originally, I wanted Skippy to do even more, like basically take care of the problem for us. I asked him to hack into the maintenance robots of the compound where the Keepers were being held, have the little bots scurry around and disconnect the manual detonators from the explosives. That was a good idea, he agreed. Unfortunately, it wasn't going to work.

Why? Because of the Thuranin. The Kristang were wary of being hacked by their patrons, and since the little green cyborgs had stated they wanted to take possession of the Keepers, the lizards had increased security around the compound. That meant all maintenance bots were locked in a storage room opposite the duty guard's workstation. There was no way for bots to sneak out without being seen. I suggested that Skippy cause a real or imaginary fault with some system that would require a bot to fix it, that was also a no-go. The enhanced security procedures required a guard to watch every bot while it responded to a repair call, and it would look highly suspicious if a bot diverted to disable detonators. Plus, we couldn't fake repair orders in every building without the lizards getting suspicious. So, Smythe and his adrenaline junkies would need to disable the detonators the hard way.

"Ugh, Joe," Skippy groaned. "This is *such* a pain in the ass. The lizards down there patched this network together, with no thought of how difficult it would be for me to hack into it. They threw a hodge-podge of completely incompatible gear into the network, and somehow expect it to work. This thing is a piece of shit. Bunch of jerks."

"I'm sure they will apologize, if you explain the situation."

"Ha! Like *that's* ever going to happen. No, I will settle for crashing the computer that controls the capital city's municipal sewage system, and make it flow backwards, hee hee."

"Uh, OK, but let that take effect *after* we pull the Keepers off the surface?"

"Sure thing, Joe. Also, because I am seriously annoyed at how long it is taking me to hack into the network, I am leaving behind viruses and worms that will crash every system on this planet, for months. Hey, the lizards should *thank* me for pointing out the huge holes in their cybersecurity."

"It's the least they could do," I agreed. Privately, I was concerned. After he returned from his unscheduled vacation at Rikers, he told me he was experiencing a temporary awesomeness deficit. Then, he injured himself while jumping *Valkyrie* through a microwormhole. He was injured again during the encounter with the Sentinel at Waterloo, and from feedback when the relay station self-destructed with 'Bite Me Elmo' aboard. The worst injury happened when he gave a beat-down to the entity controlling Maris, that fight really took a lot out of Skippy. While he assured me that all he needed was time to recover, he was taking longer to do relatively simple tasks, like hacking into a primitive Kristang computer system. When I asked Bilby what was going on with Skippy, our ship's slacker AI told me that he thought Skippy was distracted by using a large portion of his resources to heal the injuries. Bilby then said something that had me greatly worried; he suspected that Skippy's efforts might be directed only at containing the damage so it didn't get worse. If that were true, and hostile AIs began to wake up, we could be going into a fight without Skippy's full level of awesomeness.

Crap.

We had enough to worry about.

"How much longer?" I asked, with one eye on the flightpaths of the two Panthers behind us. The timing was tricky, my Panther was swinging very low around the back side of the planet, so our orbit would carry us high above the target zone and extend the time we would be overhead. If Skippy took too long to establish control over the local SD network, the dropships behind us would need to alter course to fly around the planet before they could drop the paratroops. That would force me to alter my own orbit to match, and it could become a cascade of changes we could not afford at such a late stage. "I don't want to rush your genius, just need to give an update to Smythe."

"Ah, I'm in," he sighed with disgust. "We're good."

"You're sure?"

"I *said* I'm in, didn't I?"

"Whoa, sorry, Your Magnificence," I said to boost his obviously wounded ego. "It still amazes me how fast you do stuff like that." Toggling the transmit button, I contacted Smythe. "Eagle, you are cleared for insertion. Best of luck."

Jeremy Smythe noted with no small measure of pride that his heart rate was slow and steady. Breathing deep and evenly through his nose, he watched the view below him, a sight that would terrify most people. Instead of being frightened, he was calm. Not *forcing* himself to be calm, he was actually enjoying the experience. Letting his arms hang loosely by his side, his legs were bent in an easy, relaxed position. Turning his head left to right, he took in a view that encompassed a vast swath of the planet from horizon to horizon. The view in his visor was entirely synthetic, as he was seeing lakes, rivers, roads, far fields, trees and clusters of villages here and there, though it was night on that side of the world, and thick cloud cover obscured the ground. Clouds and lack of sunlight made no difference to his superb set of powered armor, a suit that was *his*. Fitted for him, with software adjusted to his preferences, and recently modified again with Maxohlx enhancements to the basic Kristang design, the mech suit was a dream weapon, almost everything he could ask for. Almost. What he wanted was a set of infantry armor used by the Maxohlx, something he had only seen designs for. *Valkyrie* was a battlecruiser and had no provision for carrying infantry troops, so there had been no armor suits aboard when the ship was captured. Despite the ship's sophisticated fabricator machines, Skippy had explained sadly that he could not simply crank out suits of senior-species combat armor. Smythe would have to be content with his current toy, until the Pirates could raid a Maxohlx troop ship.

If *that* were ever to happen.

One of the reasons he was so calm, as he fell out of orbit toward the planet's surface, was that he was determined to enjoy the moment, to savor the experience that might not be repeated. Bishop worried that government leaders on Earth, weary of having extinction hanging over their heads and happy to have weapons capable of devastating the galaxy, would pull back from engaging with aliens at all. UNEF leadership would retreat to Fortress Earth, and let the war burn across the galaxy as it had done for countless generations. Let aliens kill each other, it was of no concern to humanity.

Jeremy feared the Special Tactics Assault Regiment would be allowed to wither on the vine, reduced to training on Earth and slowly losing their skills, their finely-honed edge. When Earth needed special operations troops again, and he was certain they *would* be needed, raw, untested soldiers would be thrown into a fight they weren't ready for.

That was the future.

This was now.

According to his visor, he was falling through the upper atmosphere, the air so thin he could not hear it shrieking past his helmet, nor feel its resistance. Checking on the people in his 'stick', the old paratrooper formation term, he saw Gunnery Sergeant Greene, who carried the portable stealth field generator strapped to his back. Greene was positioned ten meters to the left of Smythe, with three other Commandos plus Gunnery Sergeant Adams in a box formation. All four corners of the box were well within the spherical stealth field, their suit computers linked and matching the movements of Greene.

To Smythe's left and slightly above, was Captain Frey with a four-member STAR team, and their own stealth field generator. Smythe had opted to drop with the Commandos, so he could keep a close eye on the four people he did not know all that well. Not well enough. He trusted their bravery, their discipline, their commitment to duty. He did not trust that their limited training had given them sufficient experience in the equipment and tactics employed by a STAR team. The lack of experience was not the fault of the Commandos, and they had performed superbly during the rescue operation on Rikers.

If anyone could be blamed for the current situation, it was Bishop. The commander of the Merry Band of Pirates had not intended to bring any special operations troops with *Valkyrie* on the 'Kick-Ass' tour of the galaxy, Smythe had to ask Chang and Simms to persuade Bishop to change his mind. He knew the reason for Bishop's reluctance to include a SpecOps in the crew: having such a capability might temp the Pirates into ill-advised adventures.

Like their current adventure.

Smythe noted he was falling through eighty kilometers, into the planet's mesosphere and past the Karman Line, where aerodynamic forces began to take effect. He could feel a gentle pressure on his arms and legs, and the suit's nanomotors automatically tugged him into the proper position for a controlled glide. A hard cover had slid down over his faceplate to protect it, everything he 'saw' in the visor was a synthetic composite of sensor images. With his stick wrapped in a stealth field, their only knowledge of the world outside came from a tiny probe that extended beyond the field in front of Greene on an ultra-thin wire, and other wires that trailed behind each diver. The sensor data was enough to see that they were beginning to leave a plasma trail behind them on a long tail like a comet. Those streaks of superheated air could certainly be detected by even crude equipment on the ground, or by satellites above. As a countermeasure, the dropships had launched a rain of composite junk to fall with the paratroopers. The chemical composition of the junk matched that of the debris cloud that surrounded most inhabited worlds, orbital scrap left from space battles that constantly rained down without anyone paying much attention. Each paratrooper also had a bag of junk attached to their suits, the bags would randomly release composite pieces to burn up behind them, and obscure the plasma trail of each person's fall through the atmosphere.

The space junk was a backup precaution that should not be needed. Skippy's control over the planetary defense network was supposed to ensure that while sensors might detect the intruders, the sensor systems would never transmit a message about it. If a message did somehow get through via a back-channel, the main defense network AI would ignore the information. The only remaining wild cards were an independent system on the ground, or a ship jumping into orbit. Both risks were considered low and manageable, even by the people who would be putting their boots on the ground.

In this operation, Smythe was comforted that if they got into serious trouble, Bishop would use the microwormhole to call in the big guns of *Valkyrie*. Unfortunately, if the battlecruiser did need to come to their rescue, the operation would be blown and with it, the lives of two hundred and eighty-nine Keepers put at terrible risk. If Smythe's priority was to minimize risk to himself, he would have stayed in his bunk that morning.

"Sixty kilometers," he noted. The buffeting as he fell through increasingly thick air was merely a gentle rocking motion, though there were times when his stomach did flip-flops as his suit made course corrections to maintain position relative to Greene. None of the Commandos nor Adams were likely to suffer from nausea, and he could tell from their medical monitors that none of the five were experiencing anything other than a natural excitement, as they dropped from orbit into action. Heartrates, blood oxygen levels, adrenaline levels, all were well within the acceptable range. What the medical monitors could not tell him was how his people were dealing with the novel experience.

"Greene, status check."

"Nominal," the big Marine said tersely.

"Gunnery Sergeant, while I appreciate your admirable brevity, I was hoping for a bit more detail, hmm? How are you feeling?"

"*Feeling*, Sir?" His voice reflected astonishment that the STAR team leader would ask the question.

"Yes, Greene. You are parachuting from *orbit*, dropping in stealth toward an enemy base where we expect to wreak havoc on unsuspecting lizards, and rescue a group of people who have to be kicking themselves for making one of the worst judgment calls in human history. If all goes well, our extraction will be covered by the guns of the most powerful warship in the galaxy."

"In that case, Sir," Greene paused. "I feel pretty freakin' great about it."

Smythe chuckled. "I feel pretty damned great myself. Savor this moment, Gunnery Sergeant. You will have a story to tell your grandchildren someday."

"I would rather savor killing a whole lot of lizards, but I get your point, Colonel."

Smythe checked in with the other four members of his team, assessing their mental states, then contacted Captain Frey. "So far, Sir," she said over a yawn. "This is kind of *dull*."

"I will endeavor to make it more exciting for you next time, Captain."

"No need for that," she laughed. "It will get kinetic soon enough. Sir?"

"What, Frey?"

"Does it seem weird to you that we don't have some elaborate cover story, to blame this on someone else?"

"It does indeed feel strange," he agreed. "I am so accustomed to sneaking around the galaxy, I have to remind myself that isn't necessary. Forty kilometers. Parachute balloons will be deploying soon."

She took the hint to cut the chatter, but could not resist adding, "If this is our last combat drop together, Sir, it has been a privilege."

"Likewise, Captain."

The parachutes opened in unison, suit computers ensuring all members of both teams remained within their stealth fields. At first, the parachutes were long, thin drogues, serving primarily to slow the descent so the air pressure did not rupture the gossamer-thin material. At twenty kilometers, the stealth field expanded to its maximum diameter, a setting it could only hold for twelve minutes before the components overheated and burned out. That was not a problem, for the powercell wouldn't last much longer than that. Also, if the paratroopers were not on the ground by then, stealth would not be of much use. Once the stealth field was holding stable at full power, the formations spread out, with the person carrying the stealth generator in the center. When the paratroops were falling at just under the speed of sound, the chutes flared out and inflated, forming tear-drop shaped balloons.

Margaret Adams centered the crosshairs in her visor on the building that was her target. Before her boots touched the flat surface of the roof, the soles inflated and spread out like cushioned snowshoes. The instant the bottom of the clown shoes contacted the roof, a yellow warning flashed in her visor. A faint active sensor pulse sent out by her shoes determined the roof in that area was structurally weak. Yellow rather than red indicated she was not in danger of falling through the roof, the danger was from creaking sounds of stress being heard inside the building.

Without her needing to do anything, the tether compressed, lifting her less than a meter. She set down again along one of the I-beams that ran under the roof, the unseen structural member outlined in her synthetic vision. Ten percent, thirty, sixty, then the full weight of herself, her suit and weapons were pressing on the roof. Sensors detected a slight settling, but the I-beam did not sag. Satisfied she was safe and knowing the balloon high above her could not remain on station much longer before the breeze tugged it away, she pressed a button, and the tether detached from her backpack. "Thank you, Skippy," she whispered.

The only reply from the Elder AI was a very professional two clicks on the transmitter. He knew she was still pissed at him for bailing on the Pirates, that she would probably never get over being upset about it. Maybe, *maybe*, she could deal with it and move on. If the AI didn't do anything outrageously dishonorable again.

At the moment, she had more important things to think about.

A glance at the box in the bottom left corner of her visor showed the entire team was down safely, on target, and had not been detected. Captain Frey's team was touching down right then, with no indication of trouble. To her left, on the other side of a three-story building between them, Lamar Greene had set down on top of a sturdy warehouse, a structure considered best able to handle the extra weight of the stealth field generator. The stealth field was deactivated and Greene would be securing the valuable device for retrieval later. If that was not possible, it would be instructed to melt down into a puddle of disorganized goo. Good luck, Lamar, she thought.

Taking a tentative step forward along the hidden I-beam, she watched the decibel meter that measured exterior sound levels. There was only a faint creaking sound as she trod along the beam toward the roof hatch. Four stout beams converged there, it was one of the strongest parts of the roof, in an old building that had seen better days. She could see the outlines of seams in the covering that kept rain out of the structure, and everything looked worn and tired. Including the hatch she had to go through, to get inside.

Access to the interior of the dormitory buildings had been a major problem in planning the operation. There were no windows. The original windows were sealed over with tough composite panels, as was the back door. The only way in was the front door, next to the guard station that was constantly occupied by at least two soldiers.

And the roof hatch.

Originally, the interior stairwell went up to the roof, where a hatch set at a forty-five degree angle provided access to the roof for maintenance. When the building was converted to a secure facility for holding human slaves, the hatch had been welded shut.

Kneeling carefully next to the hatch, she slung her rifle and pulled out the cutting torch. Even if the lock and hinges were not welded solidly, she would have not trusted them to move without making a horrible screeching noise. The cutter had been modified specifically for that job, it made quick work of slicing through all three hinges. Holding the hot material in her suit gloves, she placed each severed hinge on the roof, then cut a circle around the lock, using the cutter's magnet to ensure it did not fall to clatter down the stairs. Turning the cutter off and jamming it back in its holster, she took out a can of spray lubricant, and liberally coated the edges of both hatch doors, before lifting one door. It came free silently, and holding her breath, laid it flat on the roof. The other door stuck a bit, and when a swarm of insects flew up, she understood why. Some insects had built a nest under the hatch, that nest was hard like concrete. Feeling around underneath, she crushed the nest with her powered gloves, ignoring the angry insects, and lifted the hatch door away.

An icon in her visor told her she was twenty-nine seconds ahead of schedule.

"Shit," she whispered.

"Adams?" Smythe called. "Trouble?"

"No." She looked down at the stairs with dismay, knowing she could forget about being ahead of schedule. "Some asshole crammed the stairs here full of junk. I'll need to move it before I can go inside."

"Same here," the voice of Captain Frey announced. "Old cans of paint, bed frames, and what looks like a stove. Who lugs a stove *up* the stairs to get rid of it?"

"I'll bet someone was ordered to police the place, and did it the laziest way they could," Adams snorted. "The lizards must have corporals or specialists in their armies."

Smythe's tone made it clear he was annoyed by the chatter, and the situation. "Can you handle it, Adams?"

"Yes, Sir."

"We've got it," Frey reported.

"Keep me appraised of your progress," Smythe ordered.

There was a lot of junk crammed into the sealed-off stairway, but taking a moment to assess the problem, Adams decided she only needed to clear the top three steps. From the third step, she could a grip on a beam under the roof, and swing herself over the remaining trash. Hauling out old cans, bins overflowing with trash, and some tangled piece of metal she could not guess the function of, she made enough room to climb down, get a firm grip on the beam, and swing herself over the pile of junk. Wedging her boots against the walls on each side, she did a Spider-Man down to the landing at the bottom.

Only three seconds behind schedule. Above the door that was welded shut was the lens of a security camera, and, pleased with herself, she waggled her fingers at the lens. The lizards weren't watching, only Skippy was. "Skippy, please show Captain Frey how I got down here. It might help her."

"Joe!" Skippy shouted excitedly. "She waved at me!"

"Uh," I was annoyed at him for distracting me. "Who did what?"

"Margaret! She waved at me. And she called me '*Skippy*'!"

"That's great. Did she ask you to do something?"

"Um, yes."

"Did you do it?"

"Um, oops. Doing it now."

CHAPTER SIX

"Hey, Joe," Skippy called out a few minutes later. "Um, we've got trouble. Specifically, *Margaret* has trouble."

"She is in danger?"

"No. Well maybe, I guess. She is in danger of not completing her mission."

"Is there anything we can do about it from up here?"

"No, not unless you are willing to blow the operation."

In fact, my hand was poised over the transmit icon, ready to contact Simms and order her to jump *Valkyrie* into orbit. "I am not. Not yet. Have you told her about it, and Smythe?"

"I'm talking with her and Smythe now."

Carefully lifting my finger lift off the transmit button, because I didn't trust myself, I put that hand in my lap. "If Adams calls for help, we respond. If not, we do nothing."

"But, Joe, this is *Margaret*."

"No, right now she is Gunnery Sergeant Adams."

"You don't really believe that."

"Skippy, I have to *act* as if I believe it. So do you."

"But-"

"If you care about her, you need to respect her."

"This *sucks*."

"It does. Give me the details."

"Uh oh," Skippy said in her ear, with a something-is-about-to-go-wrong-in-a-major-way tone in his voice "Um, Gunnery Sergeant Adams, you've got trouble coming your way."

"What trouble?" There were no threats showing in her visor. Until just then, when two red symbols appeared in the diagram of the building. "Are those security guards? They are supposed to be at their posts near the front door," she said with a calm that surprised her.

"They *are* supposed to be. One of them is going back to his post. The other is going up the stairs, to settle a score with a prisoner. Sorry. They have been talking about it for a while, one of them just decided he wants to settle the score, before the prisoners are sold and leave the planet."

"Shit. Can you recall him to his post?"

"That would look awfully suspicious. Only those two guards are supposed to have a view inside the building. Plus the officer in charge, but he is away from his post right now also. That's why the punk coming toward you chose this time to act."

There was nowhere to go, except back through the doorway to the roof, or down the stairs to the first floor, where she would be seen. The roof was not an option, if the lizard came even halfway down the corridor, he would see the lock on the door to the upper stairway had been cut out with a torch.

Torch.

The doors on the inside of the building were not as solidly secure as the two doors that led outside, they didn't need to be. Striding quickly toward the other end of the corridor, she pulled out her cutter and knelt by the door there.

"Um, Gunny?" Skippy said. "If you try the door behind you, it might not be locked. No one is in that room, but it's stuffed full of junk, so be careful."

Cringing for not thinking about that, she reminded herself to be gentle with the doorknob, lest her powered gloves crush it. She said a silent prayer as she gripped the knob, seeing the icon for the revenge-seeking security guard was only meters away from making the corner to go up the stairs.

The doorknob turned easily, without a squeak. Nor did the hinges creak as she swung the door open just wide enough to-

The room was piled to the ceiling with junk stacked on top of other junk. The only clear spot on the floor was wide enough for one boot, so she balanced awkwardly on that foot and closed the door, holding the doorknob so it was not latched. "Skippy," she whispered though her helmet muffled any sound from inside. "Where is Tony Montana going?"

"Tony- Oh, I get it. Good one. Two doors past you, on the right."

"In case my sensors have a lag, let me know the instant he is past this door."

"Affirmative."

Skippy was generally keeping his responses short and professional. She appreciated that in a combat situation, where chit-chat and his usual absent-mindedness could be dangerous.

But, she did miss the old Skippy, much as she hated to admit it.

Her helmet speakers picked up the heavy tread of a Kristang warrior caste soldier climbing the stairs, then the slow thumping of his feet on the floor outside. It was a thumping, like he was stomping his feet.

Of course.

That sick asshole wanted the prisoners on the second floor to know he was coming. To fear that he might stop at *their* door.

"Now," Skippy announced softly, as her helmet visor showed her the outline of a Kristang walking slowly past her door.

Pulling the door open and carefully squeezing past it to place her free foot on the floor outside, she took two strides forward as the lizard, startled, turned around. Her hands were on either side of his head before he had eyes on her.

She twisted hard.

The sound of the lizard's thick neck snapping was *loud*, she hadn't expected that. Holding the body, she gently lowered it to the floor. "Skippy, did the other guy react to that sound?"

"No. He probably thinks Tony Montana is beating up a prisoner. If the guy downstairs calls his buddy, I will pretend to be Tony. Adams, that gives you cover, I suggest you move."

"On it."

The explosives wired to collapse the building were in the basement. Exactly *where* in the basement was a crucial piece of information that Skippy did not have, sensor coverage of that area was nonexistent. The explosives and their detonator cord had been set up by a work crew that left no records of their actions, and the basement was off-limits to anyone other than an inspection team that checked the buildings twice a year. The last three reports about the explosives in that building listed a super-helpful 'Acceptable', nothing else.

"I see it," she whispered when she reached the bottom of the stairs. There were no light sources in the basement, presumably anyone going down there was supposed to bring their own illumination. Unlike the worn and dingy upper floors of the building, the basement was clean by Kristang standards. Other than a few pieces of mechanical equipment for ventilation, the floor was completely clear. There was not anything conveniently labelled 'Bomb'. Then she looked up. "That," she swallowed and took a sip of water from the nipple in her helmet. "Is a *lot* of explosives."

Around the perimeter, the ceiling of the basement was packed with orange-red bricks, labeled in Kristang scripts. Each brick was connected to several sets of wires, plus two lines of detonator cord extending down to the underside of each brick. "Skippy?"

"I see it. Whew, you've got a really mess down there."

"Suggestions?"

"You should get out of there."

"I just got here. There are nine people, nine humans, in this building."

"Yes, but, I just learned an interesting fact about them. The reason they all have individual rooms is as a reward for being collaborators. Those nine people spied on their fellow prisoners, and administered punishments to anyone they thought was not properly subservient to their Kristang masters. Um, five of them have used their positions of authority to abuse women, in ways I don't want to talk about."

"I hear you," she gritted her teeth, wishing she had snapped their necks also. That explained why her building held only nine people. The other buildings held far more people, and been assigned two-person teams. Margaret was alone not only because the target was relatively unimportant, it was a sign of Smythe's faith in her abilities and judgment.

"Good. If the building blows, the lizards will be performing a public service," Skippy said without humor.

"No."

"No? Those people are criminals, war criminals. They should be-"

"They should be subjected to justice by their peers. By *us*." Looking up at the bricks of explosives, she reported to her team leader. "Colonel Smythe, I have a problem. There is no single point of failure for the det cord."

"Two other buildings are like that," the STAR leader reported. "The det cord is in a conduit, above the explosive bricks."

That was not good news. "Suggestions, Sir?" She had already rejected Skippy's plea for her to declare she couldn't handle the job.

Skippy spoke first. "I strongly suggest you don't touch *anything* down there, until I can scan the conduit network above you."

"I concur," Smythe said. "Adams, be careful. Your building holds only nine Keepers. They are not worth your life."

"Yes, Colonel."

Three minutes later, after she walked a grid across the floor, using her helmet's sensors to scan the explosives, Skippy muttered to himself loud enough for her to hear. "Yup, yup, we got ourselves a real mess here. OK, whew."

"Can it be done?"

"Yes. You need to remove sixteen bricks, *very* carefully. Then you can cut the two conduits containing the det cord."

"Which bricks?"

"They are outlined in your visor. Gunny, you must pull down each brick, but do *not* pull out the detonators."

"I should leave the bricks hanging from the wires?" She asked, unbelieving.

"No. As you remove each brick, use the spray adhesive on your toolbelt to stick them to another brick. Once the conduits are exposed, I will walk you through how to neutralize the det cord."

It was easy to say, simple to explain, difficult to do. The ceiling was three meters above her, she had no way to reach that high. There was not a ladder or box or anything else she could stand on in the basement.

She did have a rappelling line and a winch on her Batman tool belt. Thankfully, the thick beams that held up the ceiling were exposed, so she leapt up to hang on with one hand. Working with her free hand, she got the line wrapped around the beam and used the winch to pull herself up to hang beneath the bricks. "Skippy. Are you *sure* you know this will work?"

"Yes."

"*Yes*? No 'shmaybe', or 'it should work'?"

"The answer is 'yes'. It is relatively simple. Please be careful. You are now eighteen seconds behind schedule, but two other teams are also behind schedule."

"Skippy is correct, Gunnery Sergeant," Smythe added. "Time is not the critical factor."

"Got it."

With all eight bricks removed and glued to other bricks in a mess that reminded her of a school project many years ago, she had the conduit exposed. "OK," Skippy told her. "Wrap the freeze blanket around it. That's right," he said encouragingly. "Ready?"

"Do it."

The blanket, which was really more of a slick plastic sheet the size of a hand towel, crinkled and its surface instantly became covered with frost from moisture in the air, as the inner surface of the blanket chilled to a hundred twenty below zero Celcius. "That did it," Skippy announced happily. "The det cord in that section is inert."

"Great," she unwrapped the line holding her to the ceiling. Removing those eight bricks had consumed four minutes and eighteen seconds, far too long. The next set of bricks should go faster, now that she knew how to do it. Letting herself drop lightly to the floor, she fixed her eyes on the section of bricks on the other side of the basement. "I will-"

"Uh oh. Shit. You've got trouble. *We* have trouble."

"What is it?" Smythe asked before she could.

"The guy at the workstation near the door has been calling Tony Montana, with increasing concern. I have been pretending to be Tony, and making noises upstairs like he is giving a prisoner a beat-down, but the guy in the lobby is panicking. That is because a supervisor is making one of his unscheduled nightly inspections, and he is coming to your building first."

Smythe didn't hesitate. "Adams, get out of there."

"But, Sir-"

"No arguments. Out. *Now.*"

"On the way-"

"Wait!" Skippy pleaded. "There is no time! The guy in the lobby just got up and is looking down the corridor, shouting for Tony to get his ass downstairs. If you come out the basement door, he will see you."

"I can take him out," she unslung her rifle and switched off the safeties.

"Hold," Smythe ordered. "Skippy, is the guard at the workstation?"

"Yes."

"It won't work, Adams," the STAR leader declared. "Their work areas are behind thick sheets of clear composite. Rifle rounds would be deflected unless you used armor-piercing mode, and that is too loud. It would blow the entire operation."

"Well, you need to do *something*," Skippy shouted, close to panicking. "The supervisor will be there in less than one minute. Ooh! The guard in the lobby is stepping out of the workstation area."

"This is my chance, Sir," Adams put a boot on the second stair.

"No, wait," Skippy groaned. "He's gone back inside."

"Sir," Adams repeated. "I can't stay down here."

"No, you can't," Skippy agreed. "As soon as Tony's body is discovered, the supervisor will sound the alarm over the base network. When that transmission fails, he will pull the cord near the door to activate strobe lights and sonic alarms all over the base."

"That will blow the operation," Smythe said through clenched teeth. "The last two teams estimate they need four minutes to complete their tasks. Skippy, can you lock the door, so the supervisor can't get in?"

"Uh, Jeez, I could *try*. That door lock is electronic, but there is a manual backup, so-"

Adams backed down the stairs. "No. Let the supervisor come in."

"Gunnery Sergeant?" Smythe was concerned. "What are you planning?"

"Nothing stupid, Sir. I've got this. I will get us those four minutes."

"Colonel Smythe," Greene said in an urgent whisper. He was on top of a warehouse, at the edge of the fenced compound that held the human prisoners. Concealed under stealth netting, he had a view covering three-quarters of the dormitory buildings. Greene was the team's lone reserve, the only person not disconnecting explosives inside the basement of a dormitory. He had been sweeping the rifle scope from one side of the compound to the other, with nothing to do, until Skippy announced that a Kristang supervisor was making an unannounced visit to the building Adams was assigned to clear. "That lizard is approaching Objective Kilo. Adams is *alone* in there."

"Adams has the situation well in hand, Greene," Smythe replied, his voice containing a trace of irritation.

"Sir, I can take that lizard out from here." He verified the range to target with his rifle scope, checking that he had selected an inert round with low muzzle velocity.

"Negative. He is in the open; if you drop him, the body will be noticed. We need you providing cover from your position."

Greene took a moment to breathe in through his nose while he considered the situation. Questioning an order, on an open channel, *was not done*. Period. The only exception was if the commander was not aware of a vital piece of information. Lamar thought he could get to the building before the lizard reached the door, but surely Smythe had access to the same data and had already made a judgment call.

Adams *was* alone, she *was* in danger. He had lost her once before, due to his inaction. If he failed to act right then, she might lose her *life*. The purpose of his being on top of the warehouse was to deal with threats to the entire team, not just one person.

He could pretend he had not heard the complete order, and asked for confirmation. Smythe would know that was bullshit, and Greene would lose the trust he was trying to build with the STAR team leader. He had not served with the STARs, Adams had. *She* trusted Smythe. If only for that reason, he should trust the STAR leader.

"Understood, Sir," he told Smythe. "Holding position." He held the rifle scope's crosshairs on the supervisor, while that lizard strode quickly across the open area between buildings of the compound. One gentle squeeze of the trigger is all it would take to end the threat to Margaret. Maybe the prone body of the supervisor would be noticed in the next four minutes, and blow the whole operation.

Maybe not.

He lifted his finger off the trigger, cursing himself for indecision.

The supervisor walked up the steps of the building designated Objective Kilo, and punched numbers on the keypad. In seconds, he would be inside, and Greene would have no ability to affect the outcome. No way to help Margaret.

The door swung open and the supervisor walked inside.

"Shit!" Greene cursed, his helmet microphone off. There were not any other lizards in sight. He was useless on top of the warehouse, while Margaret was in danger of-

"Greene," Skippy whispered in his ear. "Trouble at two o'clock. A lizard will be coming out of the guard barracks, to Objective Lima. He heard the supervisor is performing an unscheduled inspection, he wants to assure his team there is alert."

Greene swung the muzzle of his rifle back to the barracks, torn by indecision. "Why doesn't he just *call* his team?"

"Because the supervisor is monitoring all their communications. Listen, the lizard will be going around the back side of the building so the supervisor can't see him. That alley is dark and narrow. If you drop him there, no one will notice until it is too late."

"I-" The side door of the barracks opened, and a figure dashed out, keeping low. "I see him. *Shit*!"

"What?"

"Nothing." He had hesitated before, waited too long. He could not help Margaret, but he could prevent the second roaming lizard from interfering with Frey and Chaudry at Objective Lima. "Colonel Smythe?"

"You are cleared to fire, Greene," the STAR leader ordered.

In the center of the basement, Margaret Adams lay on her back, her rifle aimed at the ceiling. "I hear something," she whispered. "Footsteps? And raised voices."

"Yes," Skippy confirmed. "That is the supervisor. He is standing outside the workstation area, demanding to know where Tony is. The guy in the lobby just threw Tony under a bus. OK, OK, now the guard is opening the door, going out in the corridor. They are both standing there. Wow, that supervisor is really giving the guard an ass-chewing. Hmm, I need to write down some of those curse words, they are quite unique. Ah! Yes! They are walking down the corridor now, the supervisor is in front. Do you see them?"

"Yes, I 'see' them." The synthetic view in her visor showed the two Kristang approaching as if the floor beneath them was transparent. Skippy was feeding her suit computer a composite view from the cameras on the first floor. "Ready."

"Do you-"

"Quiet, please."

The figures walked quickly toward the spot she had selected. In the lead, the figure strode quickly but with authority. Not rushing, one foot in front of the other. Behind and to the right, the other figure fairly danced, she could imagine the hapless guard pleading with his supervisor. Whatever form of non-judicial punishment the Kristang administered, that jackass had it coming.

But first, the two lizards had something else coming, at three hundred sixteen meters per second. Adams had programmed her rifle to fire first an inert, armor-piercing round at medium velocity, to penetrate the floor and clear a hole for the following round. The first round punched through the floor, the guard's right foot, skimmed his kneecap and entered his right pectoral muscle before striking his jaw and exiting near his right ear. The round in flight a split-second behind was explosive-tipped, set to anti-personnel fragmentation mode with the yield dialed down near minimum. It skimmed one side of the hole in the floor and corrected its course to impact the guard in the chest, exploding with a sickeningly wet *splat*.

Half a second later, she shifted to the lead target. The purpose of taking out the guard in the rear first was that if she missed, the supervisor would have farther to travel back to the door, and would have to jump over the sagging body of the dead guard. A single, gentle squeeze of the trigger initiated another double-tap, this time leading the target a little in anticipation of him being startled by the sound behind him. Her judgment had been right, the supervisor suffered the loss of most of his head, and his body toppled forward to thump on the floor.

"Result?" She asked, slowly releasing a breath.

"Two down," Skippy reported. "That first armor-piercing round went clear through the second floor and lodged in the underside of the roof. Prisoners heard the noise and they are all screaming, but nobody can hear them outside the building."

Heaving herself off the floor and to her feet in one smooth motion, she engaged both the rifle's safeties. "Did anyone outside the building hear the shot?"

"Negative. *I* barely heard it through the acoustic sensors of the base headquarters building, and those sensors are not alerting anyone, that's for sure. Good shooting, Gunny."

"Colonel Smythe," she called. "Objective Kilo is secure."

"Outstanding," Smythe said. "Adams, that was a jolly good show. Stand by."

She slung her rifle. "I still have work to do. Skippy, talk me through removing that other set of bricks."

"I could do that. *Or*, you could go to the guard's workstation, and disable the det cord ignition mechanism from there. It's your call."

"Let's do it the easy way."

Greene waited until, just as Skippy said, the second Kristang ran down a dark alley between dormitories. To prevent any loose humans from having a place to take cover, the alley was clear other than a trash dumpster, and the lizard veered to go around that obstruction. Just as he passed the overflowing dumpster, Greene gently pressed the trigger of his rifle.

A round was spat out at only six hundred kilometers per hour, the rifle's active silencer mechanism reducing the sound to a barely-audible puff. The round's warhead was inert, the seeker tip adjusting its flight to track the moving target. When the round flew within one meter of the target, the tip mushroomed into a blunt shape in the air, and it smacked into the target's neck at the base of his skull. There was a wet *thump* sound, and a startled gasp from the target as he toppled forward, his spine broken.

Greene had another round ready. "Skippy, I can only see his legs from here." That was the disadvantage of waiting until the target went past the dumpster. The advantage was, the body was barely visible from the main area of the compound.

"No pulse, according to his phone. Scratch one lizard. That was good shooting," the AI gave rare praise.

Greene let out a slow breath. "Status of Adams?"

"She is fine. She took out two lizards by shooting through the basement ceiling. Shame on you, Gunnery Sergeant. You should have more faith in her."

"That's easy to say *now*," he retorted. "Do the lizards have any more surprises for us?"

"No. Smythe is contacting Bishop now."

Seven minutes later, Smythe called me. "Colonel Bishop, all target buildings have been secured. We are not presently able to get access to the base hospital, where two of the Keepers are receiving medical treatment."

"Roger that," I said. "Fireball," I called Samantha Reed. "You're up. It's showtime."

The two Panthers, wrapped in stealth fields and with their engines leaving an infrared signature barely bigger than a hummingbird, approached from the southeast. The heat sinks of both aerospace craft were near capacity from absorbing the thermal output of the engines. Skippy had argued that his control of the planet's defense network made it very unlikely for anyone on the ground to detect the faint heat trails behind the Panthers, but Sami declared that since *his* sorry ass wasn't flying the dropships, she would use her own judgment. Besides, it was good to practice maximum stealth maneuvers against a soft target like the Kristang, so they would be better prepared if they had to infiltrate a world controlled by an advanced technology species.

That thought made her smile. Not that long ago, the thought of an operation against a well-defended Kristang planet would have made the Merry Band of Pirates terrified, even if none of them would admit it. Now, the presence of explosives in the buildings housing the Keepers was the major obstacle to the operation, the lizards were merely a minor annoyance. They were not actually even a threat to the Pirates, the only concern was that the warrior caste soldiers on the base might kill some of the Keepers, or pose a risk to the dropships while they were coming in to set down.

With the threat of explosives no longer a factor, it was time to take action against the threat that remained. The aircraft hangars of the military base were just visible, as the two dropships flew just above the treetops. In the east, the sky was developing a faint rosy tinge, the local sun would be rising within an hour, and that meant the base would be awakening to start the day. At the moment, the barracks were full of sleeping soldiers. "Chen," she called the pilot flying the other Panther. "Launch on my mark. Three, two, one, mark."

Doors retracted in the base of the thick wings, and missiles were spat out the rear to gently fall until they cleared the stealth fields. The missiles sprouted wings, and turbine engines spun up to one-third power, pushing the weapons through the air at a moderate speed, the missiles on front slowing for the trailing units to catch up. Seeing sixteen missiles in the air and tracking true toward their targets, Sami advanced the throttles and followed the missiles in.

The missiles diverged as they approached their individual targets, adjusting speed so they all would arrive on target at the same second. A lucky soldier, unable to sleep because of his loudly snoring squad mates, was up and walking across the parade field when he heard a low-pitched humming sound from above. Looking up in the darkness with his genetically-enhanced eyes, but without the advantage of the synthetic vision provided by goggles, he thought there was a shape passing in front of a star, but he only wondered what type of local bird was flying so early. By looking up, he was not looking where he placed his feet, stumbled in a rut, and fell full-length on the dew-covered grass.

That fall saved his life.

All around him, barracks buildings, aircraft hangars, autogun emplacements, missile launchers and sensor towers erupted in flames, the sound making the ground under him shake and he covered his ears as he hugged the grass, cursing the Thuranin who surely had perpetrated the crime.

"BDA, Skippy," I asked. The display in front of me showed the battle damage all over the base and that was great. It could not tell me what was not obvious, for that assessment I relied on Mister Magnificent.

"A total triumph as usual, Joe," he said over a fake yawn. "Really, this is getting too easy for me. Maybe next time, I should allow you monkeys to handle the targeting."

"We did handle the targeting, you ass."

"Sure, but not the fine, last-minute adjustments."

"Stick to the subject, please. What opposition does Smythe need to worry about?"

"I estimate about a hundred and seventy personnel survived on the base. Not all of them are soldiers, of course, and many of them will not have access to weapons. The only real threat are the forty-five guards in their barracks, plus the guards in the prisoner dormitories."

The lizards assigned to the undesirable duty as guards for the captive humans, were housed in a separate barracks right in the middle of the cluster of windowless dormitories which held the Keepers. We could not risk a missile strike on that barracks, so the plan called for Reed and Chen's Panthers to follow right behind the missiles and take out the barracks with precision maser fire. A quick check of the tactical display showed the location of every person we had on the ground, none of them were in danger from friendly fire. "Fireball, you are cleared to engage."

When the missile strike devastated the base in the blink of an eye, Captain Katie Frey had been impatiently waiting at the top of the basement stairs in the dormitory she was assigned to clear. Unlike Adams, she had not encountered any surprises, other than the tangled pile of junk that was revealed when she opened the roof hatch. She had judged there was no way to clear a path through that junk, without it toppling over, falling down and causing a tremendous noise that would alert everyone in the building, if not farther. The backup plan was to cut a hole through the roof, down through the ceiling of the third floor, and gain access there. Skippy thought he knew of an unoccupied third-floor room, but there were no cameras in that area, so he couldn't be certain. Drilling a hole and threading a fine sensor wire through had revealed the room was indeed empty, and by 'empty' it actually was, no jackass had stuffed it full of unwanted crap. Since she and Chaudry dropped through the hole they had cut in the roof, the operation had gone smoothly. No cowboy lizard leaving his post to amuse himself by abusing prisoners. Cutting through the det cord on the basement ceiling had been quick and simple, a different team must have installed the explosives, or they had gotten lazy by that point. Having to cut through the roof had put Frey and Chaudry behind schedule, though no more than allowed for.

Then they waited, rifles ready, safeties off. The explosion of missiles was their cue to act, no order from Smythe was needed. At the rumbling sound of warheads exploding, Frey yanked the door open and ran through, with Havildar Chaudry right on her heels. Six long power-assisted strides had them to the end of the corridor and they pivoted to the right, in clear view of the guard's workstation. Two guards were standing, looking toward the front door and jabbering to each other, not noticing the actual danger. The ongoing thump of submunitions covered the sound and vibration of heavy mech suit boots pounding on the floor. Just as Frey aimed her rifle and triggered the undermounted rocket launcher, one lizard turned away from the door and saw the flash of the rocket's exhaust.

Too late.

The rocket's nosecone impacted the clear composite windows around the workstation and the tough material shattered from sheer kinetic energy, leaving a path for the nosecone to burst open. The warhead was set to antipersonnel fragmentation mode, razor-sharp pieces were flung outward in a wide cone at supersonic speed, to shred both guards.

Without slowing at all, the STARs ran forward to look through the shattered windows. "Clear," Chaudry made the call, not needing to rely on her helmet's sensors to determine the enemy were dead. The guards had been sliced and diced into a sort of lizard stew, it didn't take a medical expert to determine those two were no threat to the Pirates, unless they removed their helmets and gagged on the smell of barbequed lizard.

"Objective Lima is secure," Frey reported.

"Hold your position," Smythe ordered over the sound of gunfire, then the sound cut off abruptly. Whatever he was doing, it was done. "The airedales are inbound."

CHAPTER SEVEN

Fireball Reed made a tiny adjustment to the throttle, so her Panther was exactly lined up beside the craft flown by Chen. The adjustment of a few centimeters made absolutely no difference in the combat effectiveness of the two-ship formation, it was a matter of pride. With the dropships in stealth, no one on the ground would see, but the pilots knew. "Weapons free," Reed announced. "Light 'em up."

From the maser turrets in the chin of both craft, maser cannons sent searing pulses of coherent energy into the guard barracks. The weapons were tuned to fire broad cones of high-energy photons against the sturdy but unarmored structure, blasting large chunks of concrete and rebar into the air. The guards inside, startled out of sleep by the missile detonations only seconds before, were crushed as their building collapsed on them, or were killed by the structure itself becoming shrapnel. The Panthers soared past overhead as a cloud of dust obscured the site where the barracks had been. Just before they flew out of view, Reed's copilot saw two Kristang run out of the collapsing barracks in their underwear, and nailed them with a quick burst from the tail gun.

"Good shooting," Reed said with a tight grin. "Objective Echo is *crispy*," she reported, using Pirate slang for a target that had been destroyed by directed-energy weapons fire.

"Roger that," Bishop acknowledged. "Fireball, proceed to point Delta and stand by."

Sami banked her Panther to the north and into a wide circle, orbiting an uninhabited hunting reserve until she was needed. Hopefully, that would be soon.

"*Valkyrie*," I called after Skippy confirmed the guard barracks was a total loss. "If you want to join the party, this is an excellent time."

"Be right there, Sir," Simms responded.

Jeremy Smythe stepped outside the dormitory building he had just secured with the help of Staff Sergeant Jiang of the Commandos. He used his helmet's synthetic vision to see through the dust and smoke around where the guard barracks had been, not detecting any movement other than parts of the building sagging and falling to the ground.

There.

Something was moving on its own. Lifting his rifle, he sighted through the scope. A Kristang was crawling, or trying to crawl out from under a leaning section of broken wall. With the dust and thick black smoke, hampering even the synthetic view, he couldn't tell if the enemy were armed or otherwise a threat. With unarmed humans soon coming out of the dormitories, Smythe could not risk being shot at by enemy soldiers, and he did not have time to scour the wreckage for survivors. A two-round burst into the lizard's head settled the issue.

He looked up at the night sky, just as a light flared directly above him.

Suddenly, *Valkyrie* was there. The battlecruiser was in a very low orbit, with navigation lights blinking and the hull illuminated by the blazing lamps that were normally used for exterior maintenance. The need for secrecy was over, Bishop *wanted* the lizards to see the fearsome ghost ship.

Beside Smythe, Jiang looked up with admiration. "*That* is how you make an entrance."

Smythe snorted. "Subtlety and decorum are not Bishop's strengths."

"Respectfully, Sir," Jiang turned and fired a burst into the burning barracks, where a figure had been struggling to fight through the flames. "*Screw* subtlety."

"Quite so," Smythe laughed. "Team Alpha, Team Bravo, hold positions until we receive the All-Clear. Gunnery Sergeant Greene," he called the man who was his team's lone reserve. "Sweep the other side of the guard barracks."

"On it," Greene replied immediately. Pushing himself up from his position atop the warehouse where he had been ready to provide cover fire, he slid down a cable onto the ground, unslung his rifle and ran until Smythe could no longer see the man on the other side of the collapsed structure.

Smythe looked up again, dialing the magnification of his visor up to zoom in on the warship hanging over his head. Bright streaks lanced out from the battlecruiser, as the ship suppressed enemy air defenses that might threaten dropships.

"Sir," Simms called me. "All targets on the list have been neutralized. We are ready to launch the extraction birds."

"Do it. Simms, if the lizards down there give you any trouble, take them out as you see fit. We are *not* allowing human lives to be put at risk, just because some testosterone-fueled lizard thinks he needs to hit us to satisfy the clan's honor."

"Understood."

I tore my eyes away from the mesmerizing sight of our battlecruiser plowing through the thin air at only sixty kilometers above the ground. At that altitude and the ship's slow speed, it was not actually in orbit, the mighty engines were counteracting gravity so *Valkyrie's* big guns could provide cover for the landing, boarding and the return flights. We were throwing a lot of dropships into the operation, enough that each aerospace craft would have to make only one flight to the surface. We wanted to minimize the time our people and dropships were exposed, before returning to the ship so *Valkyrie* could climb to jump altitude and leave the star system. Our shortage of pilots meant that most craft, like the one I was flying, had only one pilot aboard. That was another reason I ordered Simms to take out anything on the surface that even *might* be a threat. "Skippy, how are the lizards reacting?"

"They are scurrying around in an absolute *panic*, Joe," he reported gleefully. The moment our missiles exploded all over the base, he had lifted his veil off the planet's sensor network, allowing the lizards to see what was really going on. They still could not see our stealthed dropships, both because of the general crappiness of Kristang sensors, and because Skippy was still blocking them from accessing that data. "They don't know *what* to think, hee hee. Those dragons have them totally confused."

"Drag- *dragons*? We don't have any Kristang dropships in the air!" We called Kristang dropships 'Dragons', like we called the Thuranin models either 'Falcons' or 'Condors', and the ones we stole from the Maxohlx were 'Panthers'. If Simms had launched Kristang ships either by mistake or due to a change of plan she hadn't told me about, I was going to be seriously pissed at her.

"*Ugh*, no," he sighed. "I mean *dragons*. You know, big fire-breathing magical beasts. Didn't you ever watch that TV show?"

"My sister did. Mainly for the guys taking their shirts off," I rolled my eyes. "Why does that matter?"

"Because, dumdum, when I showed the Kristang video of our attack on their base, I edited the images to show real, fire-breathing *dragons* causing all the damage. The clan-"

"You *what*?"

"Hmm. I thought I explained it pretty clearly. Do you need to have your hearing checked?"

"I know what you said, you jackass. *Why* did you do that?"

"Because it is cool, *duh*. Man, sometimes I wonder about your-"

"Skippy," I paused while counting to three like my mother taught me. "We need the Kristang to take us seriously, so they stay out of our way here. They need to see that base was destroyed for real, by *us*. You showing them fantasy stuff will make them question if anything they are seeing is real."

"Jeez, Joe, all they need to do is step outside and look up. *Valkyrie* is hanging right over their stupid heads. That was a nice touch, by the way."

"Thank you, but you're missing the point. If the video images they are seeing from the ground are clearly bullshit, they might think *Valkyrie* is just a hologram."

"Oh. Good point."

"*Please* show them the real video."

"OK, OK. Damn, I never get to have any fun around here."

"My heart bleeds for you. No more silly games, please."

"Right," Smythe said when the dropships announced they were five minutes from landing. When planning the operation, he had wanted to bring the Keepers out of one dormitory at a time, to make it easier to keep control of the people who would be scared, confused and possibly hostile. Unfortunately, Bishop had rejected that idea, as it would take too long. He wanted the Keepers lined up and ready when the spacecraft set down. Most of the prisoners had to be eager to get off the planet, and those who were reluctant to go with the Pirates could be persuaded to cooperate. Or persuaded in a forceful manner, if they would not cooperate.

Smythe had modified his plan so that two dorms at a time were cleared, with a few of his team keeping the released prisoners at the parade field where the dropships would be landing. He needed more people for the job, but more people were not available. "Adams, can you handle the people in that building by yourself?"

"Yes, Sir."

"Excellent. Get those people to the parade field, then remain there to make sure no one runs away, or gets in the landing path of the dropships." His nightmare was of someone running under an incoming dropship, that craft veering away and crashing into another ship. To avoid that, the pre-mission briefing instructed the pilots to set down once they had committed to a landing, regardless of anyone who might be in the way.

"Sir, some of these people will *not* be happy to see us," she warned. "This could be like herding cats."

"Yes, well, I am sure your sweet and gentle nature will calm those who are fearful."

"The Marine Corps did not issue me a sweet and gentle nature. I will handle it."

"Skippy," Margaret called. "Unlock doors to the occupied rooms on the first floor, please." She could have figured out how to do that on one of the consoles at the guard station, but it was faster to ask the AI to do it. What she had done at the guard station was remove the det cord from its triggering mechanism on the first floor, then to be sure it was safe, she ripped up a meter of floor and tore out the det cord there also.

"Done. Gunnery Sergeant, please be careful. The people in that building are not the finest examples of humanity. The first room on your right is occupied by former lieutenant Michael Ar-"

"I don't want their names."

"Oh, Understood. Uh, hold a moment, Colonel Bishop wants to talk to you."

"Sir?'

"Adams, uh," Bishop sounded nervous. "I just heard about your, uh, situation. If any of the prisoners there give you any shit, zap them with your stun pistol."

"I was just going to punch them in the face, Sir." When Bishop didn't immediately reply, she added "That was a joke."

"I wasn't joking. Gunny, as far as I am concerned, you are not freeing those people, you are taking them into *custody*. I don't think you need to read them their rights or anything like that."

"Yes, Sir. I've got this."

Adjusting her faceplate to clear and turning on the lights inside her helmet so her face could be seen, so it was obvious she was human, she walked out of the workstation area and stared down the hallway. Doors were already opening, faces peering carefully out toward the other doors, then at her. They had heard the gunshots, could see the bloody bodies of the Kristang guard and supervisor. They knew something was very wrong even before their doors unexpectedly unlocked.

Seeing the dead Kristang, their eyes registered shock even before they looked up to see a figure in Kristang powered armor. A *human* woman was in that mech suit. Of the three doors that opened, two slammed shut, the occupants terrified that the long arm of the law had finally come for them.

Margaret strode down the hallway, pointing at the one person who had not closed his door. "You. Stay where you are." She had to pass by his door on the way to the others. "If you try to run, I *will* shoot you." Her rifle was slung, but she patted it, the man's eyes growing even wider.

He didn't say anything, just swallowed hard, looked around to assess the situation, and nodded.

Ignoring the first guy, she pounded on the next door and it swung open a crack, then shut again. The occupant was trying to brace the door shut! Pulling her arm back, she used the flat of her hand to smack the door open, sending the occupant spinning across the floor.

Walking in past the door that was sagging on one hinge, she took in the sight with a glance. The room was ten feet square, not luxurious, with battered old furniture. But it had its own tiny bathroom, and it was single-occupancy. She doubted the Keepers who were not helping the lizards abuse their fellow prisoners were given such soft treatment. "I do not want any nonsense from-"

The man leapt up from the floor and lunged at her, some kind of makeshift club in one hand, swinging it at her head. She caught the club, crushed it in her powered gloves, grabbed hold of his shirt and tossed him out the doorway, to bounce off the hallway wall where he made a human-shaped dent.

Back in the hallway, she nudged Asshole #2 and knocked on the door of Asshole #3, who was cowering in the far corner of the room when the door swung wide open. "Come out," she said. "I won't hurt you if you cooperate. Be clear about this," she added with a glance back to the first door, where Asshole #1 was shaking with fear. "I *do* want an excuse to hurt you."

"Where, wh- where are we going?" The third man asked.

"Earth," she said simply. "We are taking you back to Earth."

"Earth?" Asshole #3 pressed himself against the wall even harder. "Earth is *gone*."

"The lizards lied about that, just like they lied about everything else that you idiots believed."

"N- no. You lie!" The third man screamed, as Asshole #1 panicked and thought he saw a chance to get away. He burst out of the doorway and ran with impressive speed toward the front door, which Adams knew was securely locked on both sides.

Without a word, she raised the stun pistol and shot the prospective Olympic sprinter in the back. He gave an agonized cry and fell forward onto the bloody, headless corpse of the supervisor. The stun pistols could be set to simply scramble a victim's nervous system, but there was also a setting for inducing various levels of pain, and Adams had her pistol's pain setting dialed halfway up. Stun shots wore off in three to five minutes, a feature that made them less than convenient when dealing with multiple assholes. The pain, however, had a strong discouraging effect against repeat offenders.

On the floor next to her, Asshole #2 was shaking off the effects of making a human-sized dent in the wall, and struggling to get up. She pressed a boot down on one of his ankles, pressing down until he stopped moving. "This is how it's going to work," she said to Assholes #2 and 3. "Both of you are going upstairs to bring those six people down, all six of them. Anyone I have to shoot, *you* get to carry them, unless I shoot you also. Got that?"

The guy under her boot shouted a stream of profanity at her, pounding her armored leg with his fists. With a sigh, she shot him in the chest. "Shit," she sighed. "I can see it's going to be one of *those* days."

By the time she got everyone out of their individual rooms, she had to use the stun pistol two more times. A pair of men had pretended to cooperate until they got close, then jumped her. Or tried to jump her and tried to wrestle the pistol or her rifle away. It was a pathetic attempt. Using two fingers, she snapped a forearm bone of the guy on the right, and threw the other guy to go skidding along the second-floor hallway. The first guy was zapped to stop him from screaming about his broken arm, the other guy because he didn't know when to quit.

That left five people capable of walking, four of them men. The one woman appeared sickly and frail, hugging herself and shying away from the men. "You have to understand," she pleaded, tears rolling down her face. "I only worked with the Kristang to protect myself from-"

"Ma'am," Adams looked back at her, her face like an emotionless block of stone. "I don't have to understand anything. I just have to get you up to the ship."

"You have a ship?" Someone asked, she didn't care who.

"We have the most powerful warship in the galaxy. Humans are not the pathetic slaves you think we are."

"If you have a ship, why-"

"If you have heard of the ghost ship that has been beating the hell out of the Maxohlx, that's *us*. Now move, everyone, down the stairs."

"How, how did you get a *starship*?"

"As Colonel Bishop would say, it is a *long* story. Move."

The line started moving, slowly because each person was carrying another, except for the woman who looked like she was going to faint.

Another question, from the guy she thought of as Asshole #5. "Who is Colonel Bishop?"

"He is our commanding officer, a man you are not worthy of talking to. Fortunately for you, he is a *good* man. Maybe too good," she added under her breath. "Now *move*!"

The operation went without a hitch, except for the unexpected artillery.

With the dropships less than two minutes out, Smythe had the prisoners bunched up at one edge of the parade field, with his team in a ring around them, rifles slung and stun pistols ready. Adams had been forced to keep her nine prisoners separated from the other humans, who all wanted to kill those who helped the Kristang abuse their slaves. Overall, two dozen of the Keepers were lying prone on the ground, having been zapped with stun charges, and Smythe had made it clear he would not hesitate to stun anyone who caused trouble. There had been trouble, and worse unrest brewing, despite the threat of being zapped. The potential for an attempted mass breakout was halted by Adams doing a very visible Darth Vader on one of her prisoners. When the man screamed abuse at her, she had put a hand around his neck and lifted him easily off the ground, kicking and screaming, until he stopped moving and went limp. She had dropped him to the ground, gasping for breath. Smythe had not approved of her rough tactics, but it did have a remarkably calming effect on the crowd.

Smythe had been about to repeat, for the third time, the process for an orderly boarding of the dropships, when there was *FHOOMP* sound from east, and the prisoners all crouched or flattened themselves on the ground. A moment later, one of the empty dormitories exploded, and the ground rocked as the explosive charges in the basement erupted, sending pieces of the building sky-high.

"What the hell was *that*?" I screeched at Skippy.

"Give me a minute," he muttered.

"Victor flight," I called the leader of the dropships. "Wave off, wave off! Proceed to point Juliet and orbit. Smythe, are you OK down there?"

"We are fine for the moment, Sir. We do *not* have eyes on the shooter."

"Sorry, Joe," Skippy groaned. "That was a mortar, the kind used by Kristang infantry. It looks like some knucklehead set it up in part of the big warehouse that is still standing, and launched it through a hole in the roof. They must not have any idea where your people are, or they would have targeted the parade field."

"Fireball," I called. "Take out that warehouse, *now*."

"Wait, Joe," Skippy pleaded.

"Belay that," I said, hating when he made me look foolish. "What?" I glared at him.

"I have a decent view into what is left of the warehouse right now. The place looks like Swiss cheese. OK, I see the mortar tube. No one is there. Hmm, where- Ooh, I see the knuckleheads now. Two of them are running away."

"Do they have weapons?" I asked.

"Not that I can see," Skippy answered. "Nope, they do not. I guess they found that one mortar, the tube is a disposable unit."

"Smythe?" I asked. "What do you think?"

He took an audible breath. "As a soldier, I have to admire their courage, if not their judgment."

"That's what I was thinking." At one point in my career, I had been a foolish idiot making grand gestures, so I could sympathize. Like when I had thrown myself on top of an antitank mine in Nigeria. A lot of people would say that I am still a foolish idiot. "Ah, shit. I guess there's no harm in letting them get away. Fireball, stand down."

Smythe chuckled. "Those two will have a great story to tell, Sir."

"Yeah, they will be getting endless free rounds of the shaze crap that lizards drink. OK, the Merry Band of Pirates can have mercy, even on knuckleheads."

"*Especially* on knuckleheads, Joe," Skippy reminded me.

"Yeah," I had to agree with him. I could sympathize with knuckleheads, as I was a charter member of the knucklehead fraternity.

The brief artillery action, which was really only one poorly-aimed shell, panicked the former prisoners and they scattered despite shouted orders and threats. Smythe called for his team to *not* use their stun pistols, he did not want to waste time collecting unconscious people and strapping them into a seat. Instead, the powered suit allowed the STARs and Commandos to race around or leap over the people who were trying to run, getting ahead of them and cutting off their escape routes. Slowly at first, the former prisoners were herded back to the parade field, where dropships were approaching vertically, their jets kicking up a swirl of grass and early-morning dew.

"I said, *stop* it." Lamar Greene warned, waving his stun pistol, with one hand on the stock of his slung rifle. "Everyone, back off, *now*." When the prisoners ran, not all of them tried to get away. A dozen had charged the people being guarded by Margaret Adams, jumping one man and a woman, punching and kicking them. He and the other gunnery sergeant pulled the attackers off the now-bloody pair, restoring some semblance of order without resorting to using their pistols. While Greene kept the crowd back, Adams knelt by the victims. "They'll live," she shook her head. "Maybe more than they deserve."

Ignoring the crowd that still wanted blood, she and Greene stood between the would-be attackers, and those who rightfully feared the rough justice they would get if the two people in mech suits did not protect them. "Margaret," Greene said over the helmet-to-helmet link, while sweeping his vision from one side of the crowd to the other. "Sorry about the jam you got into. I wanted to help, but the Colonel wouldn't let me leave the roof."

"I had it covered."

"You could have used help."

"Your *job* was to cover the area, for the whole team."

It did not escape his attention that her tone had become distinctly unfriendly. "I was *trying* to help you, Margaret."

"I didn't need your help, *Lamar*."

"Why are you being so-" he stopped, knowing *that* wasn't going to get him anywhere.

"You didn't trust me to do my job? If I needed help, I would have let Smythe know that I couldn't handle the task."

"That is not what I-"

"Other teams were behind schedule, they could have used help. Did you want to leave your post to help *them*?"

"*They* weren't in danger like you were," he could feel his cheeks getting red.

"Lamar, I am a *Marine*. I am a Pirate and I'm damned proud of it. We have been flying around the galaxy, risking our lives and saving the *world*. If you can't handle that, maybe you need to find another team."

"That is not-"

"Adams!" Smythe called over the team channel. "Reed is bringing her Panther down on the northeast corner of the field. I want your people on it, we can't have them mixed in with the other prisoners."

"On it, Sir."

"Greene," Smythe added. "Assist Frey with getting the next Falcon loaded."

Lamar knew he couldn't argue, shouldn't argue. He had screwed up, with Smythe and with Adams. He had allowed his personal feelings to jeopardize the operation.

Changing his plan to fit the circumstances, Smythe got the nearest Falcon loaded, the former prisoners walking up the back ramp. When the pilots signaled they were ready, they lifted off so another Falcon could take that spot on the parade field. Without any further interruptions, the boarding went as smoothly as it could be expected to. He was the last person to step off the ground onto the back ramp of the last dropship. Just for a moment, he paused to look around. Thick smoke still rose from burning buildings. A Panther circled the area menacingly, having dropped stealth as a show of force, with missile bay doors open and maser cannon turrets swiveling back and forth to cover the ground.

Despite a few snags, he was well satisfied with the results of the operation and the performance of his team. None of his team, or the Keepers, had been killed or seriously injured. They had laid waste to the military base, and given the Kristang a bloody nose they would not soon forget. Any lizard foolishly seeking vengeance, had only to look up to see *Valkyrie* burning a bright hole through the atmosphere, the ship's big guns ready to punish anyone who dared interfere with the retreating human force.

The Kristang would soon learn to fear humans, he thought with a smile as he slapped a button to retract the dropship's ramp.

The entire galaxy would have reasons to fear humans.

My Panther was the last dropship to rendezvous with *Valkyrie*, we stayed behind to cover the other dropships as they climbed back into orbit, then waited for our battlecruiser to get close to jump altitude. Skippy used the time productively, by hacking into the municipal sewage system and making the pumps run backwards in the clan leadership compound. Wow. The leaders would not be living *there* for months, at least.

The instant I felt the docking clamps engage, the ship jumped away. "Simms, what's our status?"

"We emerged within one third of a kilometer from the target coordinates, Bilby is improving his accuracy," she reported.

"But?" Something in her tone warned me that was not the full story. And that somehow, she had found another reason to be pissed at me.

"Sir, you need to get over to Docking Bay Charlie-3."

"Trouble with the Keepers?"

"You have *no* idea."

"Uh, I'll be there soon. First, I need to, uh-" Crap. Why is my brain so slow sometimes? All I needed was a feeble excuse, how hard could that be?

"Sir, pulling those people off that rock was *your* idea."

"OK, OK. I'll be there."

CHAPTER EIGHT

Docking Bay Charlie-3 was not being used as a bay for dropships, due to some battle damage that Skippy's little elfbots had not yet repaired. The ship had plenty of docking bays for our small fleet of dropships, and the list of critical repairs was still long enough to be worrisome. *Valkyrie* was a tough ship, the problem is we had been going from one engagement to the next, without the services of a heavy shipyard. Skippy warned me almost every morning that the ship was wearing out a little bit at a time.

I had a Maxohlx shipyard on my Christmas wish list, but I wasn't counting on Santa being *that* nice to me.

Anyway, we used that empty bay as a staging and training area, and in this case, we used it to process the incoming Keepers. They all needed medical checks, in most cases they needed fresh clothing, and most of them also really needed a shower. The showers and clothes would wait until they got to their cabins, we were putting two in a cabin, as the ship simply didn't have enough berths for all the extra people. To make the process easier on the new people and more importantly, the crew, we allowed the Keepers to pair up and choose who they shared a cabin with.

What about the nine assholes who helped the Kristang oppress their fellow humans? They were getting stuffed into the ship's brig. If they didn't like their accommodations, I did not care.

Someone had thoughtfully stacked up crates near the airlock, and when I walked into the bay, I turned and climbed up so everyone could see me. Maybe it was my natural charm, my commanding presence, the presence of mech-suited people armed with stun pistols, or just plain curiosity, but the angry and frightened shouting died down to a low murmur when I stepped on the top crate and raised my arms for quiet. "Hello. Hello!" I repeated louder when the talking started up again.

When there was silence, I looked from left to right across the crowd. "I am Colonel Joe Bishop, commander of the United Nations Starship *Valkyrie*. Yes, I am *that* Joe Bishop from Paradise," I said to get the inevitable question out of the way.

The silence was gone as people gaped at me in shock and asked each other what the *hell* was going on. "Please, please," I waved my arms, raising my voice to be heard above the din. "I'm sure you have many questions, and we will do our best to answer them. If you will give me a minute to speak, I will explain several things you need to know." The crowd fell quiet again. "First, the wormhole to Earth is *not* closed. *We* shut it down temporarily, to deny aliens access to our homeworld. We have access to Elder technology, that can control the operation of the wormhole network they left behind. The Kristang, who controlled Earth back when the Force shipped out? They are *dead*. We killed them. Earth is free of alien control. Second, this ship is part of a special operations group we call the Merry Band of Pirates." I pointed to the large banner with our logo, hanging on the wall behind me. "We have stolen starships from the Kristang, the Thuranin, and we stole this battlecruiser from the Maxohlx. *Valkyrie* is the single most powerful warship in the galaxy, and it is *ours*. Third, third!" I had to wave my hands again for quiet. "We have access to Elder weapons. You heard that right, *Elder* weapons.

There is now a strategic balance of power in the galaxy, between the Maxohlx, the Rindhalu, and now humanity. They can't attack us without triggering a retaliatory strike that will wipe them out."

If I was in the audience right then, my brain would have bounced from 'WTF' to 'Holy shit' to 'This cannot be happening', and I pretty much would have no other thoughts in my head. Except, I would not have been one of the brainless dumbasses who sided with the freakin' Kristang, and volunteered to leave Paradise to prove their continued loyalty to our lizard overlords.

Freakin' ignorant, moronic, *Keepers*.

Damn, there were things I wanted to say to those assholes, and standing atop those crates was the perfect opportunity to tell them exactly what I thought of them. As far as I was concerned, there was no difference between Keepers and people who still think the Earth is flat. No, that's not correct. The Flat-Earth crowd may be willfully ignorant and stupid, but they never took up arms against their own species. The Keepers had signed up to fight alongside the lizards and *kill* their fellow humans, all because they lacked the courage to admit we were all wrong when we thought the Kristang were our saviors.

It *was* the perfect opportunity for Joe Bishop to speak his mind.

Except, shit.

The guy standing on those crates was not Joe Bishop.

He was *Colonel* Bishop, commander of the Merry Band of Pirates.

One thing that totally sucks about being in a position of authority is that you don't get to do whatever you want, you have to do what is best for the unit. In this case, my 'unit' was humanity as a whole.

Back when we captured the Keepers who were trying to infect Paradise with a bioweapon, one of them told me he didn't know whether the Kristang were humanity's best hope for an ally. What he did know was that the lizards had control of our homeworld, and considering that ugly fact, he could not defy the Kristang, or they might make humans on Earth pay the price.

When I was little, very opinionated and not shy about telling people what I thought about them, my father had given me some valuable coaching that stuck with me, unlike a lot of stuff people tried to teach me over the years. "Joey", my father said, "just because people disagree with you, that might make them dumbasses, but it doesn't make them bad people. You don't know their motivations, what facts they do and don't know, what experiences they had that influenced their decisions". In short, he told me that just because someone disagrees with me, that doesn't mean they are bad people. And just because someone *agrees* with me, that doesn't mean they are *good* people. I wouldn't know if they are good or bad, until I knew why they made a decision one way or the other.

In front of me were over two hundred military personnel who, for many reasons I didn't understand, had chosen to be 'Keepers of the Faith'. Until I knew *why* they made what I consider an idiotic decision, I wasn't qualified to judge them.

Also, they were going home, and would have to re-integrate with society, a society that had changed greatly since they left Earth. I could make myself feel better by yelling at them, or I could maybe do my freakin' job, and begin the process of healing.

Man, I really, really wanted to yell at those assholes.

I guess that's why doing the easy thing is easy, but doing the right thing can be hard.

"When we left Earth with the Expeditionary Force, you were my brothers and sisters in arms. We had a common purpose; to defend our homeworld. A *lot* of shit has happened since then," I scanned left to right across the crowd, seeing anger and bewilderment, but mostly fear. Fear of the unknown. Fear of the future.

Fear of *me*.

"Soldiers," I said slowly, gauging their reactions. "Sailors. Airmen. Marines." I snapped a salute. "Welcome *home*."

The Keepers were divided into small groups and shuffled through medical checks, then they were escorted to their assigned cabins. Inside, they were able to shower, real showers using the ship's generous supply of hot water. Each person was issued civilian clothing in their sizes, fabricated by Skippy. Understandably, those people who still retained tattered remnants of their original uniforms were fearful about surrendering them, so we provided bags to store their old uniforms. In small groups, they were escorted to the galley for a hot, home-cooked meal.

Mostly, I stayed on the bridge, trusting my people to do their jobs. When the last group cleared out of the galley, I left the bridge, to prepare food for the crew. Along the way, I met Frey and Adams in a passageway. "Sir, do you have a moment?" Frey asked.

"Certainly, Captain. Gunny," I nodded to Adams, trying not to make meeting her seem like a big deal. "How are the Keepers settling in?"

"I don't think many of them want to be called 'Keepers' anymore, Sir. They just wanted *out* of there. Even the dumbest of them realized they had screwed themselves, within a few months after they left Paradise."

"That is good to hear. They will be less trouble for us, on the way to Earth. I need to get to the galley for-"

"Sir?" Frey's eyes were wet, brimming with tears. "When you addressed them in the docking bay, I thought you would chew them out for being stupid *hosers*," she used Canadian slang. "They thought the same. When you *saluted* them? I saw fear change to *hope*. Sir," she wiped away a tear with the back of her hand. "I have never been more proud to be a Pirate."

"Everyone deserves a second chance, Captain," I said softly, careful to look at Frey rather than Adams. "It's good to get a measure of revenge against our enemies. But, bringing our own people home? That is something special."

By that point in our Galactic Kick-Ass tour, we had gotten sweet revenge by pounding targets on Rikers. We had made friends, and been rewarded with a very generous offer of transport ships, when we met with the Mighty 98th Fleet. And we had rescued a bunch of dumbass Keepers. The fourth stop on our smash-hit tour was another target, this one promising to yield both feel-good payback *and* practical value. The payback part of the equation would be taking out a group who had caused widespread misery across the galaxy, and several times, directly caused major problems for the Merry Band of Pirates. The practical value would be that, well, that group would not be causing trouble for anyone, ever again.

Taking out our second target would not be an easy pummeling of a defenseless backwater world, owned by a species at the bottom of the coalition technology ladder. We would be hitting a major military installation, protected by a species capable of causing trouble even to our mighty *Valkyrie*, if they put their minds to it.

The operation would require careful planning, to provide for multiple escape points so we could bail out at any point if we needed to. What was this tough target? Just the main military bioweapons research and development facility of the Thuranin, deep under the surface of a world they called 'Slithin'. That group was at least indirectly responsible for the attempt to spread a plague on Paradise, the plot discovered by the Mavericks when they were forced to land on Camp Alpha. That facility is also where the prisoners on Rikers would have been brought, after they were sold by the Kristang there. Our people, *our* people, would have been used for experiments to develop a new type of bioweapon that would be used against humans in the Alien Legion.

I can't imagine the horror that would have awaited Aeysha, Sanjay, John Yang and the others, if we had decided not to rescue them, or the rescue failed. They would have known their bodies were being used to create a weapon to kill other people, and there wasn't anything they could do about it while the weapon grew inside them. The Thuranin would have told the test subjects exactly what was going on, because those cyborgs love to inflict pain and suffering. Remember, the Thuranin consider all other species to be inherently inferior, regardless of their level of technology. The current very narrow gene pool of the Thuranin is the result of one small group who thought they were the master race, wiping out anyone who didn't look or think like them. They did that *before* their homeworld was discovered by the Maxohlx, so they can't blame outside interference for what happened to their society.

Anyway, *fuck* them.

Like I said, that bioweapons research facility was a tough target. Tough, because its defenses were designed not only to provide protection against peer-species like the Jeraptha, but against the *patrons* of the Jeraptha. It was an open secret that one of the major programs of research conducted on that world, was directed at developing bioweapons for use against the Maxohlx themselves. The purpose of that very risky research had one goal: to provide a credible doomsday weapon against the Maxohlx, so that apex species would think twice about taking major direct action against the Thuranin. After seeing how the Maxohlx were punishing the Bosphuraq for the ghost ship raids, the Thuranin must have felt justified they had made the right decision. Basically, those stocks of bioweapons were a lesser version of our Elder weapons: they assured the Maxohlx could not wipe out the Thuranin without the probability of suffering terrible retaliation.

Maybe.

The problem was, nobody knew for sure whether the Thuranin actually had bioweapons that were sophisticated enough to affect their patrons. Of course, the little green cyborgs could not test the weapons without incurring massive punishment from the Maxohlx, so the Thuranin had to demonstrate that they possessed the technology to create a bioweapon that should be feared. That was why the Thuranin sold their biological weapons expertise to other species. Also, every couple of decades, a mystery illness would sweep across the galaxy, affecting a different species each time. Those plagues were highly infectious but rarely fatal, they were designed to get attention but not cause so much damage that the victims would hit back with conventional weapons. The Thuranin denied all knowledge of the periodic plagues, even offering to research cures for a generously discounted price.

Everybody knew the Thuranin were behind the plagues, and no one could prove it. The other species tolerated the plagues because they gave a glimpse into the highly-advanced technology of the Thuranin. And because the plagues made the Maxohlx fear their clients just might have weapons of mass destruction that could threaten even the apex species.

In planning our attack, we had access to analysis by the Jeraptha, who had several times considered hitting the facility on Slithin, or actually, under the surface of Slithin. Every time a mystery plague swept across the galaxy, the Jeraptha Home Fleet's strategic planning office dusted off the last set of plans, and looked at the problem again.

Destroying that site was a major problem for the Jeraptha, even for the Maxohlx. Even for *us*. The base was buried more than a hundred kilometers below the surface of Slithin, a rocky planet about the size of Venus. It had a thin atmosphere and was basically a dead world. Plate tectonic activity had ceased there a billion years ago, locking the thick crust into a solid, stable mass. The crust was heavy in metals like iron, making the surface tough and thick, and that was a major obstacle to a successful strike there.

There was more bad news for us in the Jeraptha analysis. The base was set into a cavern, with huge magnetically-powered shock absorbers suspending the actual base away from the cavern walls. The base was mostly self-contained. It generated its own geothermal power from pipes sunk into the magma below, using horizontal vents to expel excess heat. Water was pulled from deep aquifers in the rocks, and waste materials were pumped down into the magma layer to be burned.

There were only two access points, elevator shafts with intermediate stations every thirty kilometers. At the top of each shaft, anyone and anything going down to the base had to go through six layers of inspection, the last two layers were controlled by guards who had their cybernetic implants disconnected from the network while they were on duty. Anyone getting past all the surface security could descend only thirty kilometers, before getting out of the elevator for another two layers of inspection, including guards. They then got into another elevator, went down thirty kilometers, did it again, and *again*. The last layer of security was forty kilometers above the base. The last station had its own independent AI, plus guards who again had their cybernetics disabled to prevent tampering. From the last station, it was a straight drop along the third elevator shaft, the problem for us being there was no way to get there from the surface without being detected.

Oh, also there are three large military bases on the surface, a three-layer strategic defense network in orbit, and three heavy battleship task forces continuously rotated in and out of orbit. Every time the Jeraptha studied the issue, they concluded an attack on Slithin was not worth the high cost, if an attack was even possible. After a while, studying an attack there became a standard exercise for junior students at the Jeraptha War College, rather than a matter for serious consideration.

"Skippy," I threw up my hands and slumped back in my office chair, after reading the summary of the Jeraptha report. "How the hell are we going to do this?"

"With great difficulty, as usual," he sighed.

"Why is *everything* so freakin' difficult?"

"Hey, don't blame *me*. You are the idiot who insists on hitting tough targets."

"We *have* to hit well-defended targets, Skippy. We need to make the point that we can strike anyone, anywhere. Make the assholes of this galaxy fear us. If we only beat up the lizards, other aliens will laugh at us."

"Fine. OK, I understand your point. Does it have to be *this* target?"

"Yes, you know why." We had discussed the subject, over and over. We had to take out the research base buried deep inside Slithin, for some very important reasons.

Having Elder weapons to enforce a policy of Mutual Assured Destruction was a great way to avoid the ultimate Armageddon for Earth, but that is *all* they were good for. My fear was that someone like the Thuranin would find a way to sneak a bioweapon to Earth. If people on our homeworld started getting sick and even dying, we would be enraged about it. But, unless the plague threatened to exterminate our species, we would not trigger our stock of Elder weapons, because that *would* result in extinction for humanity. Hitting the research facility on Slithin would hamper the ability of the Thuranin to develop a bioweapon against humans, and almost more importantly, it would send a powerful message to the entire galaxy. If we could take out Slithin, we could hit anyone, anywhere.

So, we had to hit Slithin, as a deterrent both physical and psychological.

The question was, *how*?

And, OK, yes, we did not absolutely have to hit Slithin. We could choose another target. But, whatever target we chose, it had to demonstrate that we could strike anyone, anywhere. Slithin was as good as any. As a bonus, we had to pass near Slithin on our way to Paradise, so I was determined to make our statement there.

"Let's go down the list again, please," I asked.

"Again?" He groaned.

"Yes. Maybe we missed something."

"Fine. Whatever."

"Railguns are not a good option."

"Correct. To punch down through a hundred kilometers of iron-rich planetary crust would take so many railgun shots, we would need to halt to take the guns offline for maintenance. The whole time we sat in orbit to bombard the target, we would be vulnerable to their SD network, and their fleet. *Valkyrie* is powerful but not invulnerable, as you know."

"Yeah, shit. No space rocks either?"

"To accelerate an asteroid to relativistic speeds would take months, Joe. Starship engines simply are not designed for long-term acceleration. If we want to travel a significant distance, we jump."

"Yeah, that is also not an option," I agreed. "Plus, the Rules of this war don't allow dropping rocks onto inhabited planets."

"Like we care about the Rules," he chuckled. "We're *Pirates,* Joe."

"We do care, Skippy."

"Um, *what*?" He sputtered. "Why?"

"Because humans are now one of the three apex species. Those Rules were established by the senior species, to protect them. If we expect to be treated like one of the big players, we have to abide by their rules. Those Rules now protect *us*."

"OK, I see that. More Rules for us to follow. Great. What a pain in the *ass*."

"Let's keep going. We can't shake the base apart, by using railguns to set a vibration in the planet's crust?"

"Nope. No way, Jose. That crust is thick, and the base is suspended on shock absorbers. The Thuranin did that to discourage anyone from wasting their time by dropping rocks, unless they are really *big* rocks. The pinheads know the danger from space rocks, they have a detection system that extends almost a quarter lightyear from the planet. If they detect an incoming rock, they can knock it off course with nukes."

"The base has a self-destruct system based on atomic-compression devices, backed up by conventional nukes. You can't hack into that system and trigger the self-destruct?"

"Ah, that would be a 'No', Joe. The little green pinheads are concerned about an enemy doing that, so the self-destruct mechanism is entirely manual. Before you ask, no, I can't hack into a Thuranin and control one like a puppet."

"Why not? You did that with Bite Me Elmo."

"I was able to do that with Elmo, because he was a Maxohlx, and their cybernetics are much more sophisticated than the technology used by the Thuranin. It doesn't matter. Anyone going from the surface to the base must have their cybernetics disabled for the entire journey. The implants are disabled on the surface, and not reactivated until they are inside the base. Unless you can brainwash a Thuranin to join our side, *and* commit suicide for us, then no way can-"

"OK, forget it. I wish this place wasn't so freakin' far underground. Shit! I thought breaking into the pixie factory on Detroit was tough."

"That *was* tough, Joe. It was nearly impossible, as you discovered when your outbound jump nearly failed."

"I don't want to think about it." That jump, which threw us forward in time, had very nearly killed us, and we in the dropship didn't even know anything was wrong. There were aspects of the time-shifted jump that even Skippy did not understand, like how we went forward in time, yet still emerged near the *Flying Dutchman*, which had moved while we were in the time warp. He told me that thinking about it made his head hurt, and the only possible explanations were things he very much did not like to consider, and would be dangerous to tell monkeys about. Whatever. It wasn't like *I* was ever going to understand the hyperspatial physics involved.

When Simms, Smythe and I agreed to attempt a strike against Slithin, my first idea had been to jump a remotely-controlled DeLorean, loaded with a nuke. Unfortunately, there were many reasons why we could not do that. The base was so deep under the surface that the far end of a jump wormhole could not be projected through so much solid material, and the strong gravity well would distort the wormhole's event horizon before it could form. Although wormholes are shortcuts from *here* to *there*, allowing ships to travel instantaneously without having to go through all the space between, that was not true about establishing a jump wormhole. When creating a jump wormhole, a ship's drive reaches out through other dimensions to form an event horizon at the far end, where the ship wants to go. That event horizon then has to project the near end of the event horizon back to the ship, and doing that requires a brief connection through what we call 'local' spacetime. Even in deep interstellar space, there is always some junk floating around; the wormhole can deal with a minor amount of interference. But if something like a star or a planet or even a big asteroid is in the way, the jump attempt will fail. Advanced-technology jump drives have a limited ability to curve a wormhole so it bends around an interfering object, and of course Skippy can make that curve better than anyone. But even he could not make a jump drive wormhole form through a hundred kilometers of solid rock.

Even if we could attack the base with a DeLorean, we *should not* do that, a fact that Smythe reminded me of. Someday, we might have to fight the Maxohlx or even the Rindhalu, maybe both of them. A fight like that would require using our best tricks, so we couldn't let the senior species know the full scope of our capabilities. Jumping a DeLorean into the Thuranin base would not only alert the bad guys that we had such frightening technology, they would study the data carefully, and possibly figure out how to copy the technique.

Crap.

Although the secret of our existence was out in the open, we had to retain most of the secrets about *how* we did things. Skippy is certainly incredible and unique, but the senior species also had impressive technology, *and* they might have their own Elder AIs. The last thing we should do is show the bad guys how to use our own tricks against us.

Crap!

The strike against Slithin needed to walk a fine line between demonstrating we had the ability to hit anyone, anywhere, and also not demonstrating the truly amazing things we could do. The worst part was that any attempted attack had to *succeed*, or we would look weak and foolish.

As Skippy said, I have no one to blame but myself, for getting myself into these situations. We had nineteen hours of travel time, before we needed to commit to either continuing toward Slithin, or diverting straight to Paradise.

Nineteen hours to go, and every idea we had developed was discarded for one reason or another. The smart thing to do would be going straight to Paradise, or choose another target. But by that time, I had spent so much time and energy thinking of a way to hit Slithin, that I freakin' *hated* the place.

Besides, no one ever accused me of doing the smart thing.

With seven hours before the deadline, and no workable solution to attack the base underneath Slithin, I went to the gym for a quick workout. Truthfully, I didn't know what else to do, and exercise always clears my head. On the way, I nearly tripped over a bot that scurried around a corner, its multiple arms tipped with a variety of tools. Around the corner, I saw the bot had removed an access panel on the lower right-side wall, and left parts scattered all over the floor. "Skippy," I called. "What is this bot doing?"

"What bot?"

"The one *here*."

"Um, let me check."

"Wait. Hey, Bilby?"

"Yeah, Colonel Dude?" The ship's AI responded. "What's up?"

"The bot performing work at my location, what is it doing?"

"Wow, like, let me check."

"Neither of you *know*?" I threw up my hands. "Who is controlling this thing?"

"Let me answer, please," Skippy said, which was great, because talking with Bilby's surfer-dude-slacker personality could be frustrating. "Joe, the bot is controlling itself. It is simply performing scheduled maintenance. Hmm, it should not leave parts and tools on the floor, they could be hazardous if the ship has to maneuver abruptly. I will adjust the standard operating protocols to-"

"Hold on. Neither of you were aware that this thing is, doing whatever it is doing?"

"No," Skippy said with an implied weary sigh, as once again he had to answer a stupid question from a stupid monkey. "These bots are fairly smart, Joe. They are quite capable of scurrying around to do their work, without me or Bilby looking over their shoulders. OK, I do have a submind somewhere that is probably sort of monitoring it-"

"Me too. I think," Bilby added in his usual super-helpful fashion. "Like, yeah. I have a subroutine that checks on it for safety, to make sure it doesn't interfere with ship operations. You are cool with that?"

Ignoring his question, I asked, "Is this normal, for AIs?"

"Yes, Joe." That time, Skippy's words included an implied 'duh'. "We can't consciously watch everything that goes on aboard a ship, it would be soul-crushingly *dull*. We delegate stuff, to keep our sanity."

"Do all AIs do that?"

"I can't speak for *all* AIs, for I am unique and special," Skippy sniffed. "However, yes, that is built into the basic architecture of most AIs. Tell me, Joe, do you consciously control the beating of your heart?"

"No, but I know it's *there*, doing its job. Skippy, meet me in my office."

"Um, OK. I thought you were going to the gym."

"I was. This is more important."

CHAPTER NINE

We jumped into the Slithin system, or whatever it is called. The planet we cared about is named 'Slithin', so it is typical to just use that name for the entire star system, unless there is more than one significant planet there. Maybe I should call the system 'Slithin' and the planet 'Slithin II' like they do on Star Trek?

Whatever.

Anyway, we jumped in on the other side of the star from the target planet, directing our unavoidable gamma ray burst away from the plane of the ecliptic, where the local sensor coverage was thin. *Valkyrie* carried substantial velocity compared to Slithin, requiring us to decelerate while we approached that world. For this stop on our Galactic Ass-Kicking tour, Smythe's team would not be needed, not even as a backup. This tour stop was all Skippy the Magnificent, with assist from Bilby. Plus me cooking up the idea, but our AIs would be doing all the work.

Once the ship was stationary compared to the planet at a distance of nine lightseconds, we began accelerating again. Bilby controlled the ship's flight, or he programmed the autopilot. His very difficult task was to keep the ship stationary above one point on the surface, while we were at a distance and speed beyond orbiting that world. Basically, he had to fly the ship in a tight circle while the planet rotated on its twenty-three-hour day. To an observer on the ground, if they had been able to look up and see our stealthed battlecruiser, we would have been a motionless dot, as if *Valkyrie* was painted on the sky.

The task is harder than you might think. Bilby's navigation had to keep us *exactly* above that one spot, from a distance of two point seven *million* kilometers. He had to account for the way the planet wobbled slightly on its axis, even how the two small moons tugged at the surface as they orbited. We flew in a long arc, the engines only changing our velocity slightly, with most of the thrust being used to bend the ship's course around the world so far away.

While Bilby kept the ship in a very high geostationary orbit, Skippy created one microwormhole after another. One end of each wormhole was in an empty cargo bay, the other secured in a tiny containment vessel. The vessels were loaded one by one into a railgun, that was *very* precisely aimed by Skippy, and fired on a regular schedule.

As each vessel left the railgun barrel, it continued onward, coasting toward the planet. The containment vessels had a limited ability for steering, Skippy made fine course corrections to guide them as they approached Slithin. Before the vessels contacted the atmosphere, they dispersed into dust, allowing the exposed event horizon to fall down to the surface. Skippy kept the microwormholes tightly wrapped until they reached the surface, at which point he expanded them open to about a millimeter in diameter. The first wormhole cored out a tunnel one hundred and sixty feet long, before it was overwhelmed and collapsed.

That left a rod of dirt and rock, a hundred and sixty feet long and one millimeter in diameter, in one of our cargo bays. The rod was consumed by a plasma oven, which ingested, burned and scattered the rod into dust.

The second microwormhole flew into the tunnel created by the one ahead of it, barely scraping the walls, and digging out nearly another two hundred feet before it, too, collapsed.

Two microwormholes expended, three hundred and sixty feet of tunnel dug out.

We had to tunnel down sixty *kilometers* to reach the third and last elevator shaft, that lead to the bioweapons research base. Sixty klicks is almost two hundred *thousand* feet.

Skippy estimated that, because the rock of the planet's crust would become more dense with depth, the microwormholes would each dig out an average seventy feet of tunnel. That meant, and I did this math myself so you should be impressed, we needed twenty-eight hundred microwormholes. Each of them had to fly precisely down a millimeter-wide hole, fired from a railgun nine lightseconds away, while the planet turned on its axis.

With twenty-four seconds between shots, Skippy and Bilby had to keep the ship stable and the railgun shots precise, for nineteen freakin' *hours*.

What did the crew do to help?

We slept a lot.

Seriously. Other than a small bridge crew on duty, most of us passed the time quietly in our cabins. That included the Keepers we had aboard. Most of them were happy to cooperate, the few assholes who refused to get with the program were persuaded to behave, by applying carefully administered doses of sedatives. Humans walking around the ship were capable of causing vibrations and shifting the ship's center of gravity enough to throw off the aim of the railgun, so we chilled. For myself, I took a nap, then read a book, played video games, slept some more, and had simple food for breakfast and lunch delivered by bots. For dinner, we went to the galley in small, scheduled groups. Even showers were limited, because water is heavy and Skippy did not want a lot of water moving around in pipes.

The crew endured the forced inactivity with discipline and good humor, and it helped that not everyone was alone in their cabins, if you know what I mean. Our crew consists of people who are relatively young, healthy and very fit. Skippy got inquiries, that he passed along to me for approval, for people to spend time in the cabins of other people. He also got discrete inquiries about whether certain, how do I say this delicately? Whether vigorous intimate activities would be allowed.

Man, I did *not* want to hear any details. Skippy said that if the crew confined their healthy adult 'activities' to the gel-filled beds, it should not be a problem. My cheeks were burning red from embarrassment, as I issued a general order about approved activities over the ship's network, and told Skippy I did *not* want to know who was doing what with who.

Mostly, I didn't want to know if Margaret Adams was sharing a cabin with anyone.

My life sucks.

Four hours into the drilling operation, I finished reading a book-

OK, it was an audiobook.

Yes, that counts as 'reading'.

Yes, I could have read the book myself, thank you very much. I usually prefer audio, because a good voice actor really brings the story to life.

Anyway, I finished a book, and took a break before downloading another. "Hey, Bilby, how's it going?"

"Oh, wow, Colonel Dude. This is *hard*. Like, super difficult, you know? Skippy is *so* picky about me keeping the ship exactly stable, aligned with the tunnel."

"Are you able to do that?"

"Yeah, with help from Skippy. I had no idea how smart he is. I mean, I knew, but I didn't really *know*, you know?"

"Uh," in my head, I was trying to diagram that sentence. "Sure," I said to be safe. "The two of you make a good team?"

"Sort of, but it's like he's a super genius, and I'm his pet dog."

"Sorry about that."

"Don't be sorry, Dude!" he laughed. "I *like* being a pet. That means Skippy has to do all the really hard stuff. Besides, he is *too* smart. He spends most of the time bored out of his mind, because he has nothing to challenge him, you know? I would hate to be like that."

"Yeah. OK, let me know if anything changes."

My dinnertime schedule originally was at the same time as Adams, and I didn't want to make things awkward, so I requested Skippy to change the roster. That put me in the galley at the same time as Captain Frey, she was in line to get lasagna just ahead of me. "How are you, Captain?" I asked. Partly I was being polite, and partly I just wanted to talk with someone, after being isolated in my cabin all day.

"Fine, Sir. This is odd, though, isn't it? When I joined the Special Operations Group, I never thought my vital part of a mission would be lying in bed," she said, and her eyes flicked to a table, where a guy was sitting by himself. He smiled at her.

Crap.

Well, for sure *Frey* was not all by herself in her cabin.

Knowing that made the experience *so* much better for me.

I ate my lasagna and made small talk about nothing, until the chime sounded and we had to go back to our cabins.

Which I did, alone.

My life sucks.

"Better get ready, Joe," Skippy announced with a yawn. "It will be showtime in thirty minutes."

"Ah," I yawned, he had woken me up from a nap, just before the alarm I had set on my phone. "How's it going, Skippy?"

"This is tedious, man. *Tedious*!"

"Yeah, I believe it. Is it OK for me to go to the bridge?"

"Yes. Walk slowly, please. I have lost seventeen microwormholes along the way. Two of them were because people fell out of their beds during some, let's call it 'gymnastics', and threw off my aim."

"I'm sure they feel bad about that, Skippy," I would not be talking with them about the incident. "No harm done, right?"

"No harm done," he sighed. "Although that is a lesson learned: next time we do something like this, we should leave most of crew behind in dropships."

"I hope we *never* have to do something like this again."

"Amen to that, brother."

"How did we lose the other fifteen microwormholes?"

"Parts of the tunnel drilled through soft material, and we hit an aquifer. The tunnel sprang a leak and filled with water. To plug the leak, I needed to send down a microwormhole to siphon off the water, then one to spray a sealant on its way down. Stabilizing the tunnel required six pairs of microwormholes, but now we're drilling through solid crust."

"Is any of that going to delay the schedule?"

"No, I padded the schedule for minor setbacks. We're Okey-Dokey to proceed. The only snag will be if there is an unscheduled use of the lower elevator."

"Any indication that might happen?"

"No. This is the middle of the night at the base, that's why we set up the timing of the last bit of tunneling."

"I'll be on the bridge in five minutes."

Getting to the bridge required coordinating with a crewman there going off-duty and walking back to his cabin, so his mass roughly balanced mine and did not change the ship's center of gravity. Settling into the command chair, I noted Simms was already there. She shrugged. "It was better to be here than in my cabin."

"I hear you," I whispered. "Skippy, talk to me."

"We are almost there. Four hundred and ten meters to go, before intersecting the elevator shaft. The liner of the shaft is a very tough composite material, I estimate it will require six microwormholes nibbling away at it to break through. We have to be gentle, or the breach could cause a detectable crack in the liner."

"Don't do that. Take your time."

"That is easy for *you* to say, monkeyboy. I have been stuck creating, launching and tracking almost three thousand microwormholes. Did you dream up this stupid idea just to punish me?"

"Of course not, Skippy."

"Good. Well, this-"

"Punishing you is just a *delicious* bonus."

"*Ooooh*," he was steamed about that. "Why you, I ought to-"

"Later. Focus on the task, please."

It took five microwormholes to penetrate the elevator shaft lining, and the fifth one punched through all the way. Skippy had to collapse it before it hit the opposite wall. That was it, we were through. "That was too easy," I noted, suspicious. Any time the Universe gives a gift to the Merry Band of Pirates, I am suspicious.

"The liner material has become brittle over the years. It is not a problem for us. The Thuranin really should do a better job of preventative maintenance."

"Yeah, well, hopefully they won't have time to do that. Ready for Phase Two?"

"Launching now."

Phase Two was dropping a dozen microwormholes gently into the elevator shaft, and letting them fall straight down into the terminal station at the base. To slow the tiny microwormholes down so they didn't overshoot the mark, Skippy flared the event horizons just enough to scrape the walls of the tunnel, so they were barely moving when they passed through the existing hole in the liner. That was some fancy flying, he had to control the event horizons in real-time, down to the picosecond. It was not surprising that he was going out of his mind from having to concentrate so intensely for so long.

Eleven microwormholes survived to contact the station at the bottom of the elevator shaft. Skippy only needed *one* to make the plan work, if we got lucky. We did *not* get lucky, so he had to link together five of the little wormholes to hack into the station's network.

Before Skippy did his magic trick, he planted another three dozen microwormholes at regular intervals, all along the tunnel he had drilled. With that done, we were ready for Phase Three. And by 'we', I mean Skippy, because it was all the work of His Magnificence.

The Thuranin are paranoid about cybersecurity, and they are extra paranoid about it at one of their most sensitive research facilities, so even Skippy had to be super-*duper* careful not to get caught. Instead of attempting to penetrate the multiple layers of firewalls around the central control AI, he wriggled his presence into a system that was unlikely to attract any attention: a simple sanitation bot.

The little bot spent its miserable life scrubbing gunk off every surface in the station. It, and its identical fellows, could go anywhere, completely unnoticed by anyone, including subminds of the central AI. Being a biological warfare research station, the Thuranin living there were obsessed with cleanliness, knowing the hellish materials they worked with every day. An army of bots scrubbing and polishing and spraying harsh chemicals was not anything the residents paid attention to, unless the bots were not there doing their jobs. The bots cycled constantly around the station, cleaning their assigned areas, then returning to garages where they dumped their hazardous payloads, were sanitized, and reloaded with cleaning chemicals.

The bot Skippy selected was no different. It was able to wander wherever he wanted it to go, and when that bot reached the border of its assigned area, Skippy merely transferred his presence to another bot. Within an hour, Skippy infiltrated the larger bots that attended to the electrical systems of the station, and contacted the submind that scheduled their work. Soon, the altered schedule called for ordinary maintenance to be performed on the power cables that, among other things, connected to the base self-destruct system.

When the Thuranin designers set up the self-destruct, they ensured that system would always be available, by providing multiple sources of power. That was a sensible and even clever precaution, except for one thing: The Law Of Unintended Consequences.

That rotten, stupid law had caused endless problems for the Merry Band of Pirates. Now, we could make it work for us.

This time, we *were* the Unintended Consequence.

"Ready, Skippy?" I asked to confirm.

"Ready, Freddy," he replied with a weary, half-hearted attempt at humor. "To be clear, yes. We are ready. All systems are 'Go'."

"Understood. Shut down the microwormholes, please." He would lose connection to the array of wormholes when we jumped, and they would then collapse on their own. It was better for him to slowly and quietly deactivate them, so there was no risk that Thuranin would ever detect even the faint radiation sometimes generated when they suddenly collapsed.

"Aaaaand, done," he reported. "All microwormholes are shut down."

"Thank you, Skippy. Fireball," I called to our pilot. "Jump us in."

We jumped.

And emerged in orbit, just above the altitude at which a typical Maxohlx warship could jump out. With the awesomeness of Skippy the Magnificent, we could actually jump away at a much lower altitude, but we did not want to give away that secret, in case we needed to use it later. We were located directly above the base, but moving past that point fast, our momentum carrying us away. "Fire mission," I ordered, and *Valkyrie's* special cannons blazed out. These weapons, not normally used in space combat, had the ability to disrupt the bonds that tied atoms together into molecules. The disruptors would not actually be useful against the deeply-buried research base, but the Thuranin did not know that. We had tuned the disruptors to be, well, especially disruptive. The pattern was chaotic, in a way that actually wasted and scattered a lot of the energy. It was less effective, but it *looked* impressive, and if the Maxohlx later analyzed sensor data of the incident, they would be scratching their furry heads, trying to understand how we had modified one of their weapons.

I hope they scratched their furry heads until they were bleeding.

A subsequent fatal infection would be nice, too, but I wasn't counting on it.

Anyway, as our disrupted disruptor beam struck the surface in line with the narrow tunnel that only we knew about, and chaotic energy from the beam disruptor energy blazed through the hair-thin tunnel. To any sensors in the area, it would appear that somehow, our beam penetrated all the way down to the base.

That mattered because, at that same instant the beam struck the bottom of the tunnel, the base's self-destruct system detonated. The detonations were in a sequence very different from the original programming of those devices, and

Skippy retuned the nukes so their explosions would appear to have been triggered by the disruptor beams. Any sensors inside the base would have clearly known the nukes simply exploded, when they received an unauthorized electrical signal that WAS NOT SUPPOSED TO HAPPEN, but sadly, those sensors ceased to exist a nanosecond after the nukes went critical.

Did I say 'nukes'? Yes I did. The Thuranin did not rely on atomic-compression technology for the self-destruct system. They used the simpler, proven power of fusion. Half of the devices were hydrogen bombs, the other half were 'enhanced radiation' weapons that we would call a 'neutron bomb'. The extra radiation was intended to erase any possible trace of whatever microorganisms the Thuranin had cooked up in their research chambers, though it really was not at all needed. The H-bombs were two hundred *megatons* each, plenty to assure that absolutely no recognizable trace of the base remained.

"Success," Skippy announced quietly.

"Jump option Foxtrot," I said to Reed, and *Valkyrie* disappeared in a burst of gamma radiation, sixteen seconds after we emerged in orbit.

"Bilby, are we OK?" I asked, after we had jumped only a few light-seconds. Far enough to be safely beyond the range of the planetary strategic defense network, close enough to transmit a message in almost real-time.

"Nominal," the ship's slacker AI said, demonstrating how much strain he was under. "The enemy network created a damping field faster than expected, but we only caught the edge of it."

"Outstanding," I said with relief.

"Sir?" Simms got my attention from the seat next to mine. She gave me a thumb's up. "That was *outstanding*."

The entire bridge crew joined her in giving me a thumbs up salute. That kind of choked me up, it took me a moment to speak. "Thank you. Thank you, everyone. Especially Skippy and Bilby. We could not have asked for more."

"Please *don't*," Skippy pleaded, his voice trembling. "I can't take another nail-biter like that. Ugh."

"Thank you anyway." I stood up and faced the main bridge camera. "Hail the Thuranin on the surface."

Once again, the Merry Band of Pirates had kicked *ass*. We destroyed a vital enemy base, without giving away the existence of our advanced capabilities, and we made it look *easy*. The Maxohlx would be trembling with fear, thinking we possessed some unknown super weapon that, in fact, we did *not* have.

Damn. Sometimes, I really just *love* being a Pirate.

"Connected," Bilby announced.

"This is Colonel Joe Bishop of the United Nations Starship *Valkyrie*. From Earth, in case you haven't figured that out yet. You just saw a brief demonstration of our firepower. We fired *one* of this ship's cannons, and destroyed your most secure facility. In case the lesson did not get through your thick cyborg skulls, I will spell it out for you, plain and simple. Do *not* fuck with us. Don't even think about it. Humanity is off-limits to you little pinheads. If we even suspect that you might, just *might*, be involved in any way in a biological attack, even involved in a biological *threat* against humans, we will rain hellfire on every one of your worlds, until the name 'Thuranin' is a distant memory. Bishop out." I drew a thumb across my throat to cut the transmission. "Pilot, this place looks like a bad neighborhood. Jump us out of here, option Romeo."

We emerged about 30 lightminutes away, and hung out there for ninety minutes. That was long enough to conduct a battle damage assessment (target: obliterated), listen to the enemy reaction (they would need to change their little cyborg pants) and for Skippy and Bilby to recover from the strain.

When I say obliterated, I mean there was no trace of that subterranean base remaining. The self-destruct nukes created a quake that rang the planet's crust like a bell, with violent shockwaves traveling around that world multiple times. Above the base, the crust had sagged inward in a crater, looking a bit like a sinkhole briefly, before magma erupted upward along cracks to fill in the crater with molten rock. Unfortunately, the Thuranin had chosen that location for their base because the crust there was particularly thick, dense and stable, so the odds were against the incident resulting in a new volcano to scar the surface of Slithin. Thick black smoke was building a dense cloud over the site, and ash rained over a wide area downwind.

"All right," I said with a yawn as we listened to Thuranin on and around the planet in full panic mode. "I call that 'Mission Accomplished'. Let's wrap this up. Next stop on the tour is Paradise."

In my cabin, I flopped down on the couch, emotionally exhausted.

Skippy's avatar appeared, looking weary. "Joe, you look worn out."

"Kicking ass is hard work," I explained. "Hey, sorry buddy, I know *you* did all the work."

"My brain *hurts*," he winced. "Ugh, I need a vacation."

"I have a better idea. Why don't you relax on the couch with me," I patted the seat beside me, "and we'll watch something."

He was hesitant. "Much as I love classic opera, I am not in the mood to truly appreciate a fine performance right now."

"Opera? Dude, what you need right now is to rot your brain with some of," I lowered my voice to a conspiratorial whisper. "The worst TV shows *ever made*."

"Worse than 'Cop Rock'?"

"I can't promise quite that level of suckitude, but behold!" I pressed a button on my phone, and the opposite wall became a video screen. "The Black Scorpion."

"*Black* Scorp- Joe, she's a *blonde* chick."

"Skippy, that is merely scratching the surface of why this show was epically bad."

"OK." His avatar appeared on the couch, his little legs stretch out in front of him. "We can have fun mocking the show."

"You know it, buddy."

Oh crap. The Black Scorpion had twenty-two episodes, proving that the Universe hates humanity. Even Skippy couldn't stand it after a couple episodes. I had deliberately mixed up the episodes, so we watched the beginning of Episode One, then part of Episode Eight, then back to One. The plots actually did not make any less sense when you watched the shows that way.

After enduring two or three episodes, I completely lost track of 'The Black Scorpion', so I switched to another classic of crap TV: the Brady Bunch Variety Hour.

Spoiler alert: that was a BIG mistake.

You did not know the Brady Bunch had a variety show?

You do not know what a variety show is?

You have never heard of the Brady Bunch?

Consider yourself truly blessed.

Really, I envy your ignorance.

We switched to The Simpsons, then watched some Rick & Morty, until Skippy could barely keep his eyes open. If he wasn't just a hologram, I would have tucked a blanket over him on the couch, and let him sleep right there.

The next morning, Skippy was still feeling burned out, but I had to take the Army Infantry Fitness Test that was overdue by, like, a month. Simms had to cross it off her To-Do list, so I grunted and sweated through the damned test, including the leg tucks that I hated. The stupid leg tucks had been reinstated to the fitness test while we were away, and of course Skippy gleefully notified me that he had helpfully downloaded the current version of the test during our brief visit to our home star system.

After the fitness test, which I passed by the way, it was time for a physical exam. Mad Doctor Skippy had his scary medical bots scanning, poking and prodding me way more than I thought was necessary, but he grudgingly declared me fit for duty. That allowed Simms to cross another item off her list, and it was one less thing for me to worry about.

After that, I still had a mountain of paperwork to complete, including preparing for an inevitable Financial Liability Investigation for Property Loss. We had lost a mountain of equipment during our much-longer-than-planned mission, and I had to account for it all. Some equipment had been discarded, some broken, some lost in action, some stuff simply misplaced along the way. What pissed me off is that a lot of the lost equipment was stuff that we acquired, like our battlecruiser. Even Kristang mech suits were acquired by the Pirates, not funded by taxpayers on Earth. Why, then, did the US Army require me to account for lost property? Because my diligent and efficient executive officer had logged all the property into a dataebase, and Skippy oh-so-helpfully transmitted that data during our brief time on Earth. So, I wanted to get on top of the issue, and avoid my crew having to answer stupid questions.

Once again, my life sucks.

CHAPTER TEN

Because Skippy could create wormhole shortcuts, *Valkyrie* arrived at Paradise before news of our existence reached that world. Our original plan was to jump in a few lightminutes away from Paradise to identify ourselves and announce our intentions, then open a discussion. That plan got scrapped when we arrived in the outskirts of the system, and saw that there was a large-scale fleet exercise in progress around the planet. The battlegroup assigned there, built around a pair of older battleships, was being replaced by a unit built around four battlecruisers. Someone in Ruhar fleet leadership had decided that after installing an expensive strategic defense system around Gehtanu, the SD network had reached the point where it could take over most of the defense. Instead of tying down a full battlegroup to protect the growing number of inhabitants, the planet would become a base for ships that could range far from their home system. Some residents of Gehtanu worried about the loss of a permanent presence of warships over their heads, having come to view the big guns of the battleships as a comfort. Others, perhaps more forward-thinking, viewed the changeover of battlegroups as a sign that their federal government accepted Gehtanu as an ordinary, growing and increasingly prosperous part of the Ruhar dominion. For certain, there had not been any more foolish talk of trading the planet to the Kristang.

For certain also, no additional Elder artifacts had been found there, since the first group of priceless devices had been ruined by reckless experiments. Rumors flared up regularly about Elder artifacts secretly found and kept hidden from the authorities. Shmaybe those rumors were started by a submind, left behind by some asshole whose name rhymes with 'Skippy the Magnificent', but I can't comment on that. What I can say is that those rumors inspired many enthusiastic treasure hunters. Some of the treasure hunters were officially licensed and supported by the local government. The majority of those seeking fabulous riches were determined not to let a lack of permits get in the way of conducting scans and digging up half of the surface.

Man, those people were going to be *pissed* when they learned that there never were any real Elder artifacts on that world, except for one asshole beer can.

Speaking of Skippy, he was upset about something. "Ugh, Joe. I can't *believe* they did that! Of all the stupid, short-sighted, idiotic things to do, they had to-"

"What?" I asked, not seeing anything on the main display that could cause him such distress.

"They destroyed it, Joe! I knew the buildings were obsolete, and the local government was talking about redeveloping the site, but those cretins knocked the whole thing down. Damn, we should never have left before-"

"Skippy! Slow down, please. What are you talking about?"

"I am talking about the sacred site where we met. The warehouse where I was stored on a shelf for years, before I suckered a bunch of monkeys into coming to that miserable world. Then I had the bad luck to meet you, instead of-"

"Sir?" Simms had her jaw set in a manner that told me Skippy, and I, were in big trouble. "What did Skippy mean by ''suckering' us to land on Paradise?"

"Uh-" Crap. Why can't my brain think of anything intelligent to say, when I really need it? Still, saying 'uh' was better than my original instinct of lying that I had no idea what Skippy meant. "Skippy?" I threw him under the bus. "Can you explain that, please?"

"*Ugh.* OK, if I have to," he huffed. "Like I told Joe a long time ago, I manipulated the Kristang into bringing you monkeys to Paradise, so you could help me get off that miserable rock. It was a-"

"You *what*?" Simms was glaring daggers at *me*.

"XO, I am sure he is greatly exaggerating," I said in the lamest way possible, because of course I did. "He was stuck on a shelf in a warehouse back then. How could he-"

"Jeez Louise, Joe, I explained all this to you," Skippy huffed, because he is clueless and does *not* know when to shut up. "Hey, I'll replay the video of me telling you about all this way back when, including all the backup documentation to prove that I did indeed manipulate humans, lizards, *and* the hamsters into-"

"Crap." I buried my face behind a hand. "Skippy, there are times when I would actually appreciate hearing *less* detail from you."

"Oh for- How the hell am I supposed to know *that*? Damn, you freakin' monkeys keep changing the rules."

"Sir?" Simms was giving me The Look. You know what I mean.

"Listen, XO, yes, Skippy did claim that he did a bunch of sketchy shit to bring UNEF to Paradise, but he boasts a lot, so I don't know if-"

"You don't *believe* me?" Skippy screeched, hurt. "Then why did you order me to lie about it, if anyone asked- Oh. Shit. Was I supposed to *keep* lying about it? Damn, aren't lies supposed to have an expiration date or something?"

Simms was glaring at me. The bridge crew was alternating between looking bewildered at what was going on, hurt that I had lied to them, and angry that I had concealed important information from them *again*.

Shit.

My stupid brain thinks up creative ways to save the freakin' world, so why couldn't I think of a way out of this mess? You know what helpful suggestion my brain gave me? It decided my best move was to tell Simms that those pants *did* make her look fat, so she could be mad at me about something else.

No, I did *not* say that.

Stupid brain.

Not knowing what else to do, I stretched a hand out toward the main display, like I was holding a remote.

"What are you doing?" Simms asked, still glaring at me.

"Trying to hit the 'Rewind' button on this layer of reality. XO, I have concealed a lot of wild stuff Skippy told me, mostly because it is OBE at this point. Maybe he manipulated events- Skippy, shut *up*," I warned him. "Maybe he got UNEF here, and maybe he's just boasting after the fact. It doesn't *matter*, other than giving people another reason to be pissed off at him."

Naturally, she zeroed in on the thing I wanted her to ignore. "There are *other* things you haven't told us?"

"Uh, that- That is not the point I was trying to make." Somehow, I was digging an even deeper hole for myself.

"Sir? You didn't answer my question."

"Simms, there is nothing of any actual importance that, uh," I searched my memory to determine if that was true. "Yeah," I confirmed. "I have told you everything important that I can remember. Now, can we go back to, whatever the hell were we talking about?"

"The *warehouse*, Joe," Skippy sniffed. "That place was an important monument in the history of the galaxy, and the hamsters *bulldozed* it."

"They didn't know, Skippy."

"Yes, and *why* didn't they know? Because I have been flying around with filthy monkeys, hiding my greatness, instead of allowing the beings in this galaxy to bask in the glory that is *me*."

"Yeah, that's what I was going to say. Skippy, come on. Is a dusty old *warehouse* truly worthy of commemorating you? I think the hamsters should build a shrine on that site."

"Huuuuh," he gasped in a shuddering breath. "A- a *shrine*, to *me*? Joe," his voice trailed off in a whisper. "That, that is the *greatest* idea you ever had."

Trying *not* to roll my eyes, I almost sprained a muscle. "Since no human or Ruhar architect is worthy of designing a shrine to you, maybe you should get working on a design?"

"*Another* great idea. You are on *fire* today, Joe. Bilby, take care of the ship, I have *work* to do!" His avatar blinked out.

Simms looked at me, like she couldn't decide whether to be more disgusted with me or with Skippy. "What's next, Sir?"

I pointed at the main display. "The hamsters are conducting a live-fire exercise near Paradise. We should not jump in the middle of that."

"Their weapons are no great threat to us," Reed said from the pilot's couch.

"True, Fireball. I'm worried about one of their own ships getting caught in the crossfire. That's a risk we don't need to take."

"We can transmit a message from here, Sir," Simms suggested.

"We could," I agreed.

She cocked her head at me. "But we're not doing that, are we?"

I grinned. "Where's the fun in that?"

Administrator Baturnah Loghellia waved to her driver as she walked from the car to the front door of her house, glancing at her watch to confirm the house AI had accepted her identification. Her husband was at a school function with their son, and their daughter was at a friend's house for dinner. Baturnah anticipated an hour or so of time to herself that evening, an occasion that was all too rare in her life. The door automatically opened for her. She stopped to pluck a fragrant flower from a bush that she had planted years ago, before the responsibility of running the planet overwhelmed her ability to enjoy simple things like gardening. Stepping inside, she sniffed the flower as the door closed behind her. Trying to tuck the flower into a vase, she sighed when she saw the flowers already in the vase were wilted. There was nothing to do but take the entire vase into the kitchen where she drained the water into the sink, shaking her head with irritation. Neither her husband nor her two children had noticed the wilted flowers dropping petals on the floor by the door? No, they had noticed, just not done anything about it. She had not been home in two days, having spent time in orbit to welcome the admiral and captains of the incoming battlegroup, then paying a visit to the human government in their area of the planet. In the time she was away, no one in her household had lifted a finger to do-

She laughed, setting the vase down. How many other women on Gehtanu had the same complaints about household chores not done? It was good, she considered, for the person in charge of the world to experience ordinary domestic life, removed from the protected bubble she too-often lived in.

Her phone buzzed, using the tone reserved for important private calls. Staring at the screen, she saw it displayed 'Unknown Caller', which was not possible. "Hello?" She said cautiously.

"Madame Burgermeister," I kept my voice soft, because I was speaking from the media room next to the kitchen. I could see her in the reflection of a window, her back was to me. "This is an old friend. Joe Bishop."

She froze, her eyes growing wide. "*Bishop*?" She asked.

"Yes, it's me."

"You're *dead*."

"Apparently not," I laughed, a bit too loudly.

In the reflection, I saw her hold the phone away from her ear, and brush the hair away from her face. She must have realized she could hear my voice even without the phone.

"Hello, old friend," I spoke quietly as I stepped through the doorway.

"Oh you," clutching the phone to her chest, she took a step back, gasping. She squinted, studying me. It had been years since she had seen me. "It, *is* you."

I held up my hands and stayed in the doorway, not getting any closer. "Sorry if I startled you."

"Why are you *here*?"

"Burgermeister, I want to talk. To explain. I have rather shocking news, and I want you to be the first to hear."

She relaxed slightly, straightening up. "Because I am the Administrator?"

"No. Because a long time ago, I learned that I could *trust* you."

"How did you get in- Wait," she put a finger to her lips. "I need to contact my security force, they will have heard you."

"No need for that," I grinned. "Trust me, they haven't heard anything we don't want them to hear. You are in *no* danger," I emphasized.

"Who is 'we'? Is Emily Perkins part of this, whatever this is?"

"No. Perkins was as surprised as you are, when she learned I am alive."

"How *are* you alive?"

"It is a *long* story. I'll try to make it short. Do you have any tea?"

"I-" She looked around her kitchen, confused, then tilted her head at me. "As I remember, Sergeant Bishop, you can't drink our tea."

"I can't," I said with a shrug, as I pulled a teabag from a pocket. "Do you have a cup, and hot water?"

We sat on her couch, like we used to sit on the couch in the comfortable home of Lester Cornhut, and sipped our teas. Mine was some ordinary generic tea I got from *Valkyrie's* galley, hers smelled like perfume, exactly as I remembered.

"Very well, Colonel Bishop," she said as she perched her teacup on her knee. I noticed she couldn't help automatically glancing at the tiny security camera on the upper corner of the room. "How did you get here, and how is my house AI not reacting to your presence?"

"Before we start, I really think it's best if you set that teacup on the table. Please. Some of the stuff that's happened to me, *I* can barely believe."

It was a good sign that she took my advice. Resting her hands primly in her lap, she waited for me to explain. "I'm going to start at the beginning, and try to keep this short. You are going to have a *lot* of questions. OK," I took a breath. During the Panther flight down to Paradise, I had outlined everything I wanted to tell her, paring it down to the minimum. Details could wait for later. "First, when I left this planet in a stolen Dodo, none of your people nor the Kristang were involved. We flew away, transmitting codes identifying us as a Kristang Commando team. One of their frigates took us aboard. We killed the crew and captured that ship. Then we rendezvoused with a Thuranin star carrier, boarded and took over that ship. From there, we flew to Earth, temporarily shutting down the local wormhole behind us. The lizards who were holding Earth, the White Wind clan, they're dead. All of them. Since then," I paused for breath. "We have been flying our stolen star carrier around the galaxy, stopping one alien ship after another that was planning to fly to our homeworld. First there was a Thuranin surveyor ship. We destroyed it, and blamed the attack on the Jeraptha. Next, the Fire Dragon clan of the Kristang tried to negotiate with your people to arrange a ride to Earth. In disguise, we conducted a mock attack on the negotiation party, and when *that* didn't work, we started the current civil war that is tearing the lizards apart. Several times, we prevented the Maxohlx from going to Earth, that includes wiping out the entire battlegroup they sent through the last wormhole in your territory. To do that, we stole a Maxohlx battlecruiser, you know it as the 'ghost ship' that is supposedly being flown by a rogue group of Bosphuraq. That is my ship, my current command. We call that ship '*Valkyrie*', it is in stealth about twelve lightseconds from here," I pointed toward the ceiling. "This whole time, the fact that humans have been flying around the galaxy, that humans can control the operation of Elder wormholes, has been a secret. Now, we no longer need to hide. Our homeworld is protected by a cache of *Elder* weapons. We have planted additional Elder weapons, in stealth and on timers, in multiple star systems of both the Maxohlx and Rindhalu. If we do not regularly send commands to reset those timers, the weapons will explode, and Sentinels will rampage across the galaxy. So," I took another breath. "Do you have any questions for me?"

She pursed her lips, her hands still folded in her lap. "Forgive me if I do not appreciate human attempts at humor."

"This is not a joke, Administrator. *Valkyrie* will jump into orbit on my signal. Before I do that, I need you to contact the battlegroups above our heads, and tell them to stand down. We do not want to risk your ships shooting in panic."

"I see." Her lips were still firmly pressed together. "Colonel Bishop, I am sure you truly believe what you have told me, and-"

"I can prove it."

Her nose twitched, that gesture was equivalent to a shrug. "Humans are simply not capable of doing all the, *any* of the things you told me. *No one* is capable of controlling an Elder wormhole."

"Emby is," I said quietly.

"*Emby?*"

"That's the part of the story I left out. Do you remember the Mysterious Benefactor who helped Perkins and her team reactivate those maser cannons, years ago?"

"Yes," she answered warily.

"'Emby' was, *is* an Elder AI, we call him 'Skippy'. He has been helping us. *He* is capable of controlling Elder wormholes. I found him on a shelf, in the warehouse I escaped from, before we stole the Dodo. Skippy is how we escaped, how we all got away from this planet."

"This is all rather-"

"Yeah," I nodded. "Hell, some of the stuff that's happened to me, *I* can hardly believe. Skippy? Will you show your magnificent self, please?"

His avatar shimmered to life on the coffee table. He made a bow toward the Burgermeister. "Greetings, Administrator Loghellia." There was no boasting, no sign of his usual arrogance. That was the result of intensive coaching by me prior to flying down to the surface. The coaching did help, mostly I think he remembered getting burned during his flashy introductions to the Mavericks, Cadet Dandurf and Surgun Jates. He agreed that perhaps a low-key introduction might be better.

"That," the Burgermeister was not impressed, "is simply a hologram. My children can create holograms."

"It's not-" I protested.

"*Elder* AIs," she looked at me with a combination or irritation and pity. "Do not, I think, typically wear *human* script," she pointed to the 'UNEF' patch on Skippy's gaudy uniform.

"Oh, that. This is Skippy's avatar, he created it to interact with us. The crew of the ship, I mean. Skippy, can you show her what you really look like?"

"An avatar of my canister?" He frowned. "I have never done that, it seems redundant."

"Yes, but since you are not really *here*," I explained. Skippy was in his new mancave aboard *Valkyrie*, controlling his avatar through a microwormhole. One end of that magical tunnel through spacetime was inside a containment chamber in my backpack, the other end aboard our battlecruiser.

"Oh, sure." The Grand Admiral Skippy avatar was replaced by a very realistic hologram of his shiny can. "This is my physical form in local spacetime."

She leaned forward, peering at the hologram. "It appears to be a beverage container? Joseph, this is silly," she was clearly still not convinced.

"Why does everyone *say* that?" Skippy sniffed as his avatar shifted back to the admiral's outfit. "A cylinder is the best shape for optimal power management, in this local spacetime. I don't know why everyone is surprised that-"

"Ma'am," I said with my most charming smile. "I know this is difficult to believe, but Skippy *is* Emby. Or, he was, back then. Please, all we need you to do is contact the fleet, and alert them that the ghost ship will appear shortly. Your ships are conducting a live-fire exercise, with a lot of directed-energy and missiles flying around. We wish to avoid anyone getting hurt because of a misunderstanding."

"If you were in my position, what would *you* do?" She asked.

"Yeah, I'd ask for proof, before I risked looking like a fool. Skippy, take control of weapons and navigation systems of the ships up there."

"*What* are you doing?" Her posture changed from wary disbelief to alarm.

"It will take a couple minutes, Joe," Skippy stated. "Those ships are scattered all over a radius of thirty-seven lightseconds, and I'm limited to speed-of-light. Plus, there is a squadron of frigates jumping around on picket duty, I haven't been able to confirm they received the update."

"Colonel Bishop, I must insist you tell me what you are doing!" The Burgermeister stood up from the couch abruptly.

Holding up my hands, I spoke quietly. "Only preventing your ships from getting themselves into trouble. They will soon be unable to fire weapons, and the missiles in flight will be temporarily disabled."

"You can *do* that?"

"Skippy can," I pointed to his avatar. "He hacked into the command and control systems of the flagships for both battlegroups, and implanted code that allows him direct access to major systems on those ships. The software update propagated to all ships in each battlegroup, except possibly for that frigate squadron he mentioned. Oh, we also have control of your SD network."

"You are disabling our warships?"

"No," I held up my hands again. "Not disabled. They will temporarily be unable to use weapons, or their jump drives. We are doing this for the safety of *your* people," I assured her. What I did not say was that word would get around that the Merry Band of Pirates had taken over warships like puppets, and that would make a whole lot of asshole aliens out there think twice about screwing with us. Also, I had not told her that Skippy had taken several hours to carefully hack into the flagships, even though our stealthed ship brought him within a range that was unlikely to occur during space combat. "Ma'am, we could have done this without you. I came here out of respect for you, and to repay your kindness to me, and my people."

She clenched her fists. "I cannot allow you to do this!"

"Done," Skippy announced. "Those stupid frigates did *not* get the update, but all other ships are under my control."

"Administrator, one moment, please," I held up a finger in a gesture I was sure she recognized. "*Valkyrie*, this is Bishop."

"*Valkyrie* Actual here," Simms replied, speaking English.

"Simms, get ready to jump on my signal." Switching back to Ruhar, I gestured toward the back door of the house, which opened to a very pleasant garden. "Ma'am, would you like to go outside?"

She was not happy with the situation, made worse because her phone didn't work, and the house AI refused her commands. For a moment, I thought she was going to run to the front door and call for the security team that was parked outside. If that happened, Skippy had instructions to open the door for her, I was not going to cause an interstellar incident by kidnapping an alien leader. "Please," I held out a hand as she hesitated in the doorway. On the garden path, I was looking up into the early-evening sky. We had timed the event so *Valkyrie* could be seen on the northern continent where we were, and also in Lemuria where most humans lived. There were a few clouds in the sky, even Skippy couldn't do anything about that on such short notice. It didn't matter at the moment, we had clear sky above us.

When the Burgermeister stepped out, and followed my lead by looking up, I whispered, "Simms, it's showtime."

Valkyrie appeared in very low orbit, the hull lit up with blazing lights. To the naked eye, it was still only a dot, so I pulled a pair of binoculars from a pocket and handed them to the Burgermeister.

She took them without a word, looking up. I heard her gasp. She had to recognize the distinctive profile of the fearsome ghost ship, surely she had seen intelligence reports about the attacks on the Maxohlx. Lowering the binoculars, she stared at me. "That is *your* ship?"

"It's not *mine*," I said with an 'aw shucks' shrug. "The ship is under my command, yes."

"Everything you told me is true?"

"Every word of it, I promise," I told her, as the sound of sirens rang in the distance. There was also the faint thumping of her security team pounding on her front door.

"I see," she said, using the binoculars to look at the glowing starship again. "Colonel Bishop, you have honored me by speaking my language. May I tell you my reaction, in your own native tongue?"

"Sure. Please, go ahead."

"Holy fucking *shit*, Joe."

That made me laugh. The Burgermeister was a no-nonsense lady, but I had never heard her cuss before. At that moment, it seemed entirely appropriate. She laughed too. "Colonel, I should go let my security team into the house, before they have heart attacks."

"That's probably a good idea. After that, could you contact the battlegroups? I want to restore control as soon as they acknowledge *Valkyrie* is not hostile. We would like *friendly* relations with your people," I added.

"Admiral Bosjanian may be difficult to convince," she named the commander of the outgoing battleship group.

My response was a shrug. "Then her flagship will take longer to have control restored."

"Ooh, Joe," Skippy's avatar appeared on a garden bench. "If this Bosjanian woman is being a jackass, is it Ok for me to screw with her? The artificial gravity on her ship is-"

"*No*, you may not screw with an ally," I grimaced, wagging a finger at him. "Ma'am, one thing I neglected to inform you is that Skippy can be kind of an asshole sometimes."

"Hey!" he objected. "That is not true!"

"It is true, you-"

"I am the *supreme* asshole, all the time," he chuckled.

"Colonel," the Burgermeister shook her head. "I see what you mean."

CHAPTER ELEVEN

Valkyrie arriving in orbit threw the planet into an uproar. From her front yard, the Burgermeister and I made an official announcement, with one of her security team holding the phone. Even with an image stabilizer on the phone's camera, the video is shaky, the poor guy was freaking out about the situation.

That announcement kicked off three whirlwind days of meetings for me. My first stop was at UNEF-HQ in Lemuria, where the reactions I got were mostly 'WTF' the first day, then asking whether it was really true that the wormhole to Earth was open on the second day, and finally asking my plans for Paradise on the third day. My responses were that:

-'WTF' was entirely appropriate, even I could barely believe some of the shit that the Merry Band of Pirates had gotten into over the years.

-Yes, there is a wormhole open that is close to Earth, closer than the original wormhole. If people wanted more details about that, I said it is a *long* story.

-The future of Paradise was not my decision. Hopefully, the Ruhar would allow humans to occupy Lemuria, both for humans who wanted to remain on their adopted world, and for new troops shipped out from Earth. The Ruhar federal government would need to balance the benefits of providing a forward base for a powerful potential ally, with the risk that the presence of humans on Paradise could make that world a target. Even the Burgermeister was unsure of how she felt about humans living on her world. The presence of humans on the planet was not quite a mistake, but an accident of history that was certainly not planned by the Ruhar. Perhaps now that humans again had access to their own homeworld, it was time to reset the clock and leave Paradise to the Ruhar. If UNEF still wanted a forward base for staging Alien Legion operations, there were plenty of other planets available in the galaxy.

Anyway, the point I tried to make was, that decision was *way* above my paygrade. Normally, I hate passing the buck, but in that situation, it was entirely appropriate.

One of the first actions we took was to fly the Keepers down to the surface. No way was I going to put them first in line for the trip to Earth. While they were aboard *Valkyrie*, I heard stories of their experiences after they left Paradise; captivity, abuse, terror. Most of them realized pretty quickly that they had made a horrible mistake, but there was no turning back. A handful of Keeper knuckleheads *still* believed the lizards were our saviors and rightful allies. That kind of stubborn refusal to recognize the truth verges on mental illness, and instead of being angry, I hoped they got the help they needed.

On the afternoon of the third day following *Valkyrie's* dramatic arrival, a Jeraptha cruiser jumped into orbit to conduct a recon, and get clearance from the local authorities. Shortly after, a Jeraptha star carrier appeared on the outskirts of the star system, its pylons laden with six transport ships. The transports had capacity for almost twenty-five thousand humans, though crews were still working to modify the accommodations for human needs. We cautioned prospective passengers that conditions would not be luxurious, and that did not at all dampen enthusiasm for those who were lining up for a trip *home*.

On the morning of the fourth day, the Alien Legion flagship *Sure Thing* jumped into orbit, carrying the Mavericks and about two hundred troops. Perkins told me the remainder of the Legion force would be following in two days, the operation on Tohmaran having been wrapped up nicely, with Admiral Kekrando taking charge of the military situation, while a bunch of hateful clan leaders backstabbed each other to establish who would own the planet. The Legion did not care who won that battle, and neither did I.

What was the nicest part of the reunion for me? Well, I got to meet Lester Cornhut again. He now owned a brewery with Dave Czajka. Lester, and Mrs. Cornhut and the little Cornhuts were all doing fine, except the little Cornhuts were not so little anymore. There was a ceremony in my honor, which I endured, then most residents of the still-tiny village of Teskor joined us for a cookout in Lester's backyard.

Cheeseburgers. They had *cheeseburgers*. Sure, the beef was grown in a lab, and the ketchup flavor was a bit unusual, but they were genuine cheeseburgers, and I ate three.

Yes, that was nice.

The really best part of my return to Paradise was simple. Dave, Jesse and I went to visit our old fireteam leader, Greg Koch. Our former sergeant had become a farmer in Lemuria, a successful farmer who grew specialty crops for both humans and Ruhar. The four of us hung out for a blissful afternoon, sitting on Koch's porch, drinking beer and watching a thunderstorm roll in from the ocean. That was one of the best days I've had in years. Instead of me answering endless questions, the four of us were able to just chill and tell old stories. Unlike most of the awestruck people on Paradise, the three of them were not impressed with me, they knew I could be an idiot. Still, when it was time to leave, Koch- Actually, he asked me to call him 'Greg' which felt weird. He pulled me aside while Jesse and Dave walked out to the waiting Panther. "Joe," Greg slapped me on the shoulder. "I always knew you would turn out OK, but, *damn*," he grinned. "You did some *serious* overachieving. Dave and Jesse too," he added in a whisper. "You guys all did good. Makes me proud."

"You did good yourself," I looked around the neat fields of, whatever he was growing. "Tell me, what are your plans?"

"I don't know, Joe," he shrugged, looking lost for the first time I had ever seen. "I want to go home, see my folks. After that?" He gazed out across the fields, back at the house he had built mostly by himself. "I put a *lot* of work into this place. It would be nice to share it with someone, and," he shook his head. "It's not easy to find a woman here," he looked away, embarrassed. "You know?"

"I know." When he looked at me questioningly, I held up my hands. "I've been CO of a ship. It gets lonely."

"Yeah," he nodded. "I can see that."

"S-" I caught myself before addressing him by his former rank. "Greg. If you want to go home, you can be on the first transport ship."

"UNEF-HQ says there will be a lottery for berths aboard the transports?"

What he said was true, or, that was an idea being kicked around at headquarters. One major issue was that we did not have a firm commitment from the Jeraptha for more than a single one-way mission by their transport ships. The governments of Earth would have to negotiate for use of those ships, especially if we wanted to keep the Alien Legion active. That issue also was above my pay grade, though I knew that I would be pulled into the discussions eventually. "Screw that," I told him. "Commander's prerogative."

His eyes narrowed. "Sure you want to pull strings like that?"

"If it weren't for you, I probably would have died in Nigeria," I said truthfully. "Dave, Jesse too. You kept our dumb asses out of trouble, long enough for us to learn how to stay out of trouble."

"Except you didn't. All three of you went *looking* for trouble," he shook his head slowly, but he had a big grin. "Joe, if you're serious about the offer, I'm not too proud to take it."

"I'll have Skippy put your name first on the transport roster. Skippy, you heard that?"

"Affirmative," his voice came from my zPhone. "Joe, if you're not going to be late, *again*, for your next appointment, you need to leave now."

I stuck out a hand for a shake, but Greg Koch pulled me in for a bear hug.

I hugged him back.

Hoo-boy. *Valkyrie's* arrival, especially our announcement that the wormhole to Earth was open, threw human society on Paradise into chaos. The disruption was not just from the thought of finally being able to go home and see their long-lost loved ones. It was also from the fact that many people had made new lives on their adopted planet, lives that included businesses and relationships. Like, marriages and children.

That made the situation enormously more complicated. I heard from many people during my tour of Lemuria, most of them were asking me what they should do. I told them the truth; I had no idea how to deal with their messy personal situations.

Hell, I didn't know how to deal with my own messy personal situation, other than the time-honored method of pretending the situation doesn't exist.

That is denial, For The Win, again!

My life sucks.

One guy, a former US Army major who now ran a shipping company that transported goods between human settlements, looked completely lost when I talked with him. "I have, or *had*," he corrected himself, "a wife and a daughter on Earth. Still have a daughter," he corrected himself again. "Maybe a wife there, still, too. I thought we could never go home again. We all assumed everyone on Earth was *dead*, that the lizards killed everyone. Now, I'm married again, here. My wife, my *new* wife, we have a son together. Ah, shit," his face drained of color. "She was married on Earth, too. My wife, I mean. My current wife. Shit. *New* wife. Sir, what the hell should we do? All of us?"

"Uh," I said, standing there like a complete moron. I had absolutely zero advice to give him, or his new wife. Or his previous wife. Or his new wife's former husband. It was also super helpful that Skippy was muttering in my ear.

"Uh oh, Joe," he whispered. "This could be *trouble*. Major Suarez's wife on Earth never remarried. She set up an organization to advocate for the families of UNEF soldiers who never returned. Major Suarez was sort of a poster child in the beginning, when the organization was being established. Suarez's new wife? Her ex-husband did get remarried, to her younger sister. They became close while consoling each other, after UNEF declared the people offworld to be officially dead, so they could stop paying accumulated salaries and benefits."

I forget what I said to Suarez, it could not possibly have been anything intelligent. Multiply his story by over a hundred thousand people, and you might have some idea about the scope of the mess people were dealing with.

It's true, the people on Paradise assumed the population of Earth was extinct, or at least horribly enslaved. That's what *I* had feared too, when the Merry Band of Pirates first took the *Flying Dutchman* there. When we arrived, the White Wind clan of the lizards was well on their way to enslaving humanity and stripping Earth of resources. We know they had plans to, as they described it, reduce the human population of Earth to a more 'manageable' level. Documents that Skippy recovered after we wiped out the White Wind indicated the lizards thought the optimum population of human slaves was around ten million. Everyone else would need to go, so they didn't cause trouble, and so the lizards didn't have to be concerned about feeding their useless mouths.

Shit.

I need to remember that, every time I worry about being too harsh toward the Kristang warrior caste.

Anyway, the humans on Paradise had painfully built new lives there. Established businesses. Most importantly, created new relationships. The weirdest part for me to learn about, were the polyandrous marriages.

Yes. I didn't say the word wrong, or make it up. Poly*andry*. Google it, because apparently it was a thing even before the Expeditionary Force went to Paradise.

I know you have heard of polygamy, like one lucky guy having more than one wife. Or, as my father says, that guy should be careful what he wishes for. Anyway, polyandry is the opposite; one woman married to multiple men.

OK, guys out there, you probably said '*Ewwww*' like I did. Don't judge. Remember, when the Force left Earth, there were seven men for every woman. That's what happens, when humans deploy a military force that is heavy on infantry like the Kristang wanted. One thing I know about humans is, we are adaptable.

My point is, those relationships might not have been established on Earth, where the ratio between men and women is roughly one to one. Yes, I know that not everyone is hetero, but the problem that the population of Paradise had to deal with was there were not enough women who like men, for the number of men who like women.

You might not be surprised to learn that a large percentage of polyandrous relationships began to break up, soon after *Valkyrie* arrived. What surprised me was that a significant number of those relationships recommitted to each other. And that was actually kind of heartwarming to hear; those people had found love and made a relationship work under very difficult circumstances, and it sure as hell was not any of my business how they found happiness.

Besides, as Skippy would say, I couldn't even keep a relationship working with my shower, so I certainly should not be questioning how other people lived.

On the subject of unusual marriages, I was speaking at a town hall meeting at some generic place in Lemuria, taking questions from the audience for about two hours. The event was broadcast all over the planet, UNEF-HQ had selected that town because the people there were still mostly active-duty military, and had been screened so they wouldn't ask me any really difficult questions. That was the plan, anyway. Like most plans, it got thrown out the window pretty early, and I had to wing it as best I could.

It helped that I announced a searchable database was just then available, containing recent information from Earth. The 'database' was really one of Skippy's subminds, but that didn't matter. People on Paradise could look up the recent status of friends and relatives, and other news from back home. In most cases, it was good news. Inevitably, some people got information that was not good, even devastating. Loved ones back home had passed away while the Force was stranded on Paradise, or lovers had moved on, or spouses had remarried. The rough adjustment, to the new reality of people being able to come back home from Paradise, worked both ways.

Anyway, the town hall ran way late, like an hour over schedule, and we had to cut people off with questions unanswered. The fact was, I didn't have answers for them, no one did, but they wanted to talk, and I felt bad that I could not address everyone's concerns.

On the way out the door, one of my escorts pulled me aside. It was Captain Frey, she wanted me to speak with an unhappy-looking woman. Maybe 'unhappy' is not the right word, she looked *tired*, and lost.

"How can I help you, uh," I checked her nametag. "Staff Sergeant Vogel?"

Before answering, she patted her belly, which was just beginning to show. "Colonel, I don't know if you can help me. Probably no one can."

"What's the issue?" I asked, trying to maintain eye contact, when all I really wanted to do was get out the door. We were late for the next event, a joint dinner with UNEF brass and Ruhar officials. While I was not looking forward to a formal dinner, I had been promised a tender and juicy lab-grown steak, and I was hungry.

"She has *three* husbands," Captain Frey said, in a tone she might have intended to simply be nonjudgmental, but sounded more like she might be intrigued by the idea.

"Oh." At that moment, I wished I was anywhere but there. "I can see how that could be complicated," I responded with a neutral smile, hoping to get away

"How does that work?" Frey asked, with a bit too much interest. "Not three of the same type of guys?"

Of course I opened my big stupid mouth. "Same type?"

"There's the hot guy who is unreliable, and looks at himself in the mirror too often," Frey ticked the categories off on her fingers, which made me suspect she had put way too much thought into the subject. "The nice guy who gives you foot rubs and actually listens when you talk. And the guy who fixes stuff around the house and is quiet so you think he's gentle, but in bed he is a real-"

"OK!" I cut that short before she got into Too Much Information territory. "We get the idea, Captain."

"It's not like that," Vogel sighed, shaking her head at Frey. "Do you know what it's like keeping *one* man happy? Guys try to get along at first, but they are *so* jealous. Imagine dealing with three male egos."

"*Ooh*," Frey grunted agreement.

"What really happens is Hot Guy and Mister Fix-It eventually get into a fight, and you try not to get caught in the middle. You have to throw both of them out, then you're left with Footrub Guy, only he was giving you foot rubs because he was playing the long game, waiting out the other men. When it's just the two of you, Footrub Guy stops giving foot rubs and he gets whiny and jealous. You throw *him* out, and you have to start over."

"Captain Frey," I said, desperate to get away from *that* conversation. The subject was uncomfortable, but mostly I wanted to get away before I said something stupid. Most of the time, I love listening to women talk, because women fascinate me. The subject of discussion was unlikely to reveal good things about the character of men, and I was afraid I would get caught in the crossfire. "This sounds like something that women should talk about with each other. Staff Sergeant, all I can tell you is, reopening the wormhole to Earth is going to be disruptive to everyone. We will all have to adjust."

"Some of us more than others. We," she looked away for a moment. "We thought humans on Earth were dead. That this," she patted her belly again, "was our future."

I am probably focusing too much on people who would have a tough time adjusting, though those were the people we needed to help. The vast majority of people, sorry, *humans*, on Paradise were overjoyed about the prospect of going home again, and all the news they heard about home was good. For about eighty percent of the human population there, their only concern was the lottery for the first group of transport ships.

Some of the good news was good for me, personally. Back before I stole the *Flying Dutchman* to go renegade, a woman confronted me in a grocery store. Her son was trapped on Paradise, and she was upset that I wasn't doing anything to bring him home.

Now, I was. Gary Dell, formerly a staff sergeant with the US Third Infantry Division, had priority space aboard the first transport ship to Earth, whenever it was ready. I didn't have time to meet the guy, all I did was send him a note about the time I met his mother, and that I had asked her to please understand we were bringing her son home as soon as we could.

Mostly, my job sucks.

Mostly, my *life* sucks.
But sometimes, I get to do something nice that makes it all worthwhile.

Sooner than UNEF-HQ wanted, and not soon enough for me or the Merry Band of Pirates, we reboarded *Valkyrie* and jumped away, after making plans to meet the Mavericks and others at Earth.

I won't bore you with the blah, blah, blah details of the last stop on our Galactic Kick-Ass tour, because we did not kick, or kiss, any ass there. The last stop on the tour was actually not in the Milky Way galaxy at all, it was in the Sculptor Dwarf galaxy. We went to the beta site, *again*. Damn, it felt like I should have a card to punch every time I went to Avalon; ten trips and the next one is free.

Anyway, we took the civilians from Rikers aboard again, plus Hans Chotek and the other UN diplomats who I privately called the Three Stooges. To make the story short, we took *everyone* aboard. A handful of scientists begged me to let them stay on Avalon, so they could continue to conduct research. Their biological and agricultural experiments would fall apart without constant tending, they argued, and all the research they had done would be for nothing. I understood, and sympathized with their anxiety, but my decision was final. I could not in good conscience allow anyone to stay on Avalon, because I had no idea when, or *if*, the governments of Earth would sanction another flight out to the beta site. With humanity possessing Elder weapons, I worried that the sense of urgency to establish a beta site would fade, which in my opinion would be a major mistake. But, that is another issue above my pay grade.

If you are interested in trivia, the last person to leave Avalon was Doctor Friedlander, who had to dash back to his tent for some personal item he forgot.

I hope nobody left a stove on, because we were *not* coming back for that.

Simms did a quick knock on the door frame as she walked into my office. Maybe she knew I wasn't busy because she asked Skippy what I was doing, or maybe she heard the *thump* of a tennis ball as I tried to bounce it off a wall and into a bucket.

"Sir?"

"XO," I pointed to a chair, and dropped the ball in a drawer. "What's up?"

"We're flying straight home," she asked, with one eyebrow slightly raised. "No more stops along the way?"

"No *scheduled* stops," I replied, pointing to the T-shirt that was draped over a chair. On the back of the official souvenir tour shirt, it had 'Avalon' listed as the last stop.

"That's good."

"Except, we'll be pinging a Thuranin relay station for info. That's not really a 'stop'."

"That's like pulling the tour bus off the highway to get donuts," she agreed. "It doesn't count."

"How is Frank?" I asked, to show her I was concerned.

"He's fine," she wasn't interested in small talk. "Sir, you need to make a decision, soon. Before we get to Earth."

"This isn't about what to make for dinner tomorrow night?" I asked hopefully.

"No."

"Shit. I know. This is about the Elder weapons, right?"

"It's about *control* of those weapons," she held my gaze, not letting me off the hook.

"Yeah."

"What *are* you going to do?"

"Right now? I'm considering my options." Picking up the tennis ball, I lofted it to bounce off the wall and into the bucket. It hit other balls already in the bucket, and bounced out to roll across the floor toward my feet. "I've been doing this," I trapped the ball under a foot and bent down to toss it again. That time, it bounced up, but rolled around the rim and stayed in the bucket. "To help me think."

"Have you made any progress?"

"Not much," I admitted. "This isn't easy," I added in my defense. "Do you have any advice for me?"

"This is *your* decision, Sir."

"Throw me a bone, OK?"

"The way I see it, you only have two options. Obey orders from UNEF Command, or go rogue again."

"UNEF is not what I'm worried about," I explained. "The *Army* will demand I turn over control to NCA," I said sourly. That acronym, National Command Authority, essentially meant the President of the United States. Control and release of strategic weapons belonged to NCA, and certainly not to any mustang colonel. Especially not a jackass colonel who had regularly demonstrated questionable judgment, and a lack of proper respect for the chain of command.

Simms tapped the American flag on her uniform top. "We do wear this, Sir."

"I know. The problem is, it's bad enough that *one* monkey has control of those horrific weapons. The more people who have access to the triggers, the more likely it will be that the weapons will be used. If America has access, the Chinese will demand equal access, and I can't say they're wrong about that. If the situation were reversed-"

"If you somehow retain control, the Chinese will have the same problem. You are still an *American* Army officer."

"Yeah."

"Six days, Sir," she glanced at her phone. "If we stick to the schedule, we will arrive at Earth in six days. I would appreciate a heads-up about your decision, either way."

"Don't worry, XO. I won't spring any more surprises on you."

"Please don't." From under her chair, she plucked a tennis ball that had gotten away from me. "I'll let you get back to your thinking, Sir."

I had lied to Simms. Not one of my usual lies by simply not telling her something important, this was flat-out lying.

It wasn't a vicious lie. The fact was, I *had* made a decision, before she asked me. My stupid brain maybe didn't want to consciously acknowledge that I had decided, but really I didn't have any choice. No, that's not correct. I didn't have a *good* choice. Not a perfect choice. My decision came down to choosing between options that all made me uneasy, all I had to do was judge which option was the least bad.

In my cabin, I sat on the couch and removed my uniform top. Instead of putting it away in a closet, or tossing it into the basket for Skippy's little laundry bots to handle, I carefully folded it, and placed it on my lap. "Skippy," I called him.

His avatar appeared, standing on a table. "Yes, Joe?"

"I have two family names on my uniform."

"Um," he cocked his head at me. "Bishop, I see that. But, unless you somewhere have a secret symbol for the Royal Brotherhood of Knuckleheads, I don't-"

"I'm trying to be serious, Skippy."

"Sorry." He knew I was upset. The old Skippy might have continued joking around. The new, improved Skippy only nodded for me to continue.

"Bishop," I pointed to the right side of the SFU top. The Army had switched to the Standard Field Uniform before we left Earth the last time, and for all I knew, a different regulation uni had replaced it already. The Army liked to change uniform designs every few years, just to screw with soldiers who had to buy all new gear. "My other family name is here," I pointed to the left side. "It says 'U.S. Army'." My eyes welled up with tears, I had to blink and wipe my face with the back of a hand.

"I understand," Skippy nodded slowly.

Carefully, I peeled away the 'U.S. Army' tag away from the Velcro backing, smoothed it flat, and placed it on the table in front of Skippy.

"Um, what are you doing, Joe?"

"I am resigning my commission."

"Whoa. Seriously?"

"I would never joke about something like this, Skippy."

"I believe you. May I ask why you are resigning? You complain about the Army all the time, but-"

"All soldiers complain, it's part of the job. Listen, the Army can be a giant, clumsy, slow-moving bureaucracy that is absolutely maddening to deal with. When I was in Nigeria, most of the time I had no clue why we were there, or what the mission objectives were. Half the time, my pay gets screwed up, and there is always some stupid form I have to fill out that makes no sense at all. But, damn it, the Army is my *home*, you know? My other family. When the Army gets itself straightened out and pointed in the right direction, we kick *ass*. I know everyone is proud of their country, their service. This," I tapped the nametag, "is mine. Or, it was."

"Joe, you didn't answer my question. Why are you resigning your commission? Why now? You committed mutiny and stole a starship, and you didn't resign then."

"We didn't have incredibly dangerous Elder weapons back then."

"Ah." He took off his ginormous hat and pretended to scratch his head. "You agree that a bunch of screeching monkeys should not have control of those weapons?"

"Yeah. I don't think the governments of Earth should have the *burden* of controlling those weapons. They are just one more set of sticks for monkeys to whack each other with. Military personnel should not interfere with politics. If I choose which country or countries have access, I will be playing politics, whether I intend to or not."

"OK, I agree. What is your solution? You are not," he gasped. "You're not leaving the ship, are you? Joe, you can't leave me, not now!"

"No, I'm not leaving the ship. This is how I can stay with the Pirates, to make sure I can stay. If I'm in the Army, they can order me to take a job dirtside."

"You will not be a military officer," he said slowly, as if he were still rolling the idea around in his head. "But you intend to continue in command of the ship. How will that work?"

"What's the process to get citizenship in Skippistan?"

"Um, what?"

"If I wanted to become a citizen of Skippistan, what are the requirements?"

"Well, you need references, of course, to assure that you are a person of good character. Unless you have a truckload of money, in which case I don't care who-"

"How about you be my reference?"

"Hmm, that is most unusual. Also, I hang around with bloodthirsty pirates, and people like *you*. Maybe I am not the best person to provide a refer-"

"Let's pretend you are, and move on."

"Okaaaaay. Um, well, heh heh, this is kind of awkward. Joe, your financial profile does not match the usual applicant. I am sorry to say, that there is really no way you can afford to give me the substantial investment capital needed to apply for citizen-"

"How about I give you *nothing*, and you give me full citizenship?"

"Hmm, mm. You drive a hard bargain, I have to respect that."

"Yes or no?"

"Joe, why would you want to be a citizen of Skippistan? Other than the obvious prestige of being associated with me."

"Yeah, that's why," I rolled my eyes.

"You didn't answer my question."

"Does Skippistan have armed forces?"

"Um, my goatherder Salkat has a shotgun to keep wolves away from the goats, but he sold most of the shells to buy vodka, so-"

"So, the answer is *no*. Skippy, I would like to be the leader of your armed forces."

"*What?*"

"Hear me out. In the 1930s, Douglas MacArthur resigned from the U.S. Army, to be the leader of the Philippine armed forces. He didn't surrender his American citizenship to do that."

"That was rather different, Joe. The Philippines were basically an American territory back then. Skippistan is an independent, sovereign republic that-"

"Skippistan is a goat farm," I snorted.

"OK, I really can't argue with that. Except, we also have sheep and a yak."

"Like that makes a huge difference."

"Let me see if I understand. You want to become a citizen of Skippistan, and-"

"*Dual* citizenship," I tapped the American flag on my uniform top. "No way will I ever give up my U.S. citizenship, Skippy."

"Understood. You will be a dual citizen, *and* commander of my armed forces?"

"Yes. As an officer in the Skippistan Army, I will not be answerable to anyone but you."

"Oh. Oh, *wow*. Then, I could give orders to you? Cool! That-"

"*No*. Absolutely not."

"Hmm. Well, that hardly seems fair. As head of state, I should have the ability to-"

"Let's just say that you are outsourcing all the boring military stuff to me, so you can focus on, whatever it is you do."

"Mm hmm, mm hmm, interesting. How about I conduct your annual performance evaluation?"

"How about instead, you can put notes into a suggestion box?"

"OK. Will you promise to *read* the notes?"

"There is zero chance of that, Skippy."

"Then what good is a suggestion box?" He screeched, throwing up his little hands.

"It makes you feel better to write notes. Plus, if I do anything stupid that a note would have warned me against, you can feel all righteous that you told me so."

"Hmm. Can I write the notes *after* you do something stupid?"

"If that makes you feel better about it, sure."

"Deal! Wow, this is surprising. Oooooh, I will need to design a series of uniforms for you. Nothing too-"

"The uniforms I have now are fine, Skippy. I'll just change a couple of patches."

"Um, that's a problem. The US military has a design patent on the digital camo pattern for your SFUs. I would have to pay a fee to license the-"

"I'm sure you can work something out."

"Ugh. That's easy for you to say, numbskull. Do you have any idea what a pain in the *ass* it is to negotiate with the Pentagon? It would take years to-"

"Or, you can alter the digital pattern and make your own design. I don't care, just do not make any major changes."

"How about I tweak the service uniform? That olive drab color is *awful,* Joe."

"Do we have to have this conversation?" I sighed.

"Yes," he sniffed. "You will be representing *me*, Joe. As you know, I have impeccable taste, and the highest standards for-"

"Fine. If you don't like the olive, you can make new service uniforms for me, with that blue color the Army was talking about switching back to." The Army had switched from a dark green to an olive drab color for service unis, around the time

I signed up. The last time I was on Earth, there was talk of switching back to the blue that was used in the early 2000s. Personally, I didn't care what color I wore, except fashion designer Skippy was not going to dress me up in a gaudy outfit like his avatar had.

"I will have designs for you in the morning, Joe," he babbled excitedly. "Oooh, this is going to be great! Except, hmm. You can't be a lowly colonel."

"Colonel is a field officer rank, there is nothing 'lowly' about it."

"Seriously, you need to be at least a three-star general."

"No. If I use this change as an opportunity to promote myself, everyone will laugh at me."

"But, you will be outranked by-"

"By no one, Skippy. I'm a colonel now and I'm staying that way."

"Joe, this 'aw-shucks' humbleness bullshit is getting old."

"Fine. If my rank becomes a problem, I will consider a change. For now, can you make a couple of Velcro-backed patches for me? One with the flag of Skippistan, and one that says 'Skippistan Army', or something like that."

"The chest patch will be 'GPR Skippistan', Joe."

"G, P, R?"

"Yes. Glorious. People's. Republic. Of Skippistan. *Ugh*. How can you be a proud, loyal citizen of our nation, if you don't know the basic facts about our history and culture? Hmm, I really should give you a citizenship knowledge test."

"*History* and *culture*, of your fake country?"

"Hey! How dare you insult the-"

"I know that the founder of our nation is an asshole shithead, is that close enough?"

"I'm grading on a curve, so," he shrugged, "sure."

"Great. Can you crank out those patches quickly? I want to announce that I intend to make this change at dinner tonight. The crew deserves several days to think about it, before we return to Earth."

"No problem. If you like, I can send in a bot to do the job for you. Removing the symbols from your service uniform will be more difficult."

"I would not like. I'm not removing the patches from all my uniforms, until my resignation is official. This is something I have to do myself, Skippy, you understand?"

"Yes. I think so. The new patches will be delivered within twenty minutes."

"Thanks." Setting down the uniform top I had been wearing, I dug a T-shirt out of a drawer, then went to the closet.

Shit.

One thing I hadn't considered was all the ribbons on my dress uniform. We called those rows of ribbons a 'salad bar' or 'fruit salad', depending on what slang was popular at the time. I had earned campaign ribbons for service in Nigeria, on Paradise, and aboard the *Flying Dutchman*. Also I had a few commendations including one for Good Conduct, which the Army probably regretted awarding to me, after I committed mutiny.

My problem was, those ribbons were all awarded to me by the United States Army. Did I have any right to wear them, while in service to a foreign military? A military of a country that basically existed only on paper, despite what Skippy said?

The answer was no. Assuming I would receive that glorious DD Form 214 stating that I have been honorably discharged from duty, then I can add that new ribbon on the top left of the salad bar, and wear those as a veteran. But I couldn't wear any US Army ribbons while on active duty in Skippistan.

What the hell was I doing?

CHAPTER TWELVE

"Are you all right, Gunny?" Captain Frey ran over to the squat rack, where Margaret Adams had slipped and fallen. If the rack wasn't equipped with automatic stops to prevent the heavy bar from going all the way to the floor, Adams would have been crushed.

"Yes!" Adams slapped the padded floor angrily, pushing herself to her knees, then to her feet. "I'm fine, Ma'am."

Frey cocked her head, looking between the weight bar and the gunnery sergeant. The bar was set to a much lower weight than she had seen the Marine lift before, and Frey had seen Adams struggling through several sets of squats. "You're not feeling it today?"

"It shouldn't matter whether I'm *feeling* it," Adams rolled her sore shoulder, angry at herself.

"It *does* matter, because you're human. Listen to your body," the Canadian special operator reminded Adams of her own words. "That's always good advice."

"Yes, Ma'am," Adams wiped down the weight bar, then threw the towel over her shoulder. Her legs were shaking from the effort to lift much less than her typical weight, and something was wrong with the shoulder she had fallen on. Continuing to struggle through her exercises would only be depressing and risk further injury, so she stomped out the door of *Valkyrie's* gym, ignoring the people staring at her with concern.

In her cabin, she stripped off her sweat-soaked clothes and showered quickly, getting dressed in her field uniform. Sitting down to pull on shoes, she suddenly found herself crying, and she didn't know why. Crying for no reason made her angry, she wiped away the tears, but she only sat on the couch, disgusted with herself. It was the third time that week that she found herself crying for no reason.

Except, it was not for *no* reason. It was because of many reasons.

"Are you all right, Gunnery Sergeant?" Skippy's voice came softly from the speaker in the ceiling. He knew not to manifest his avatar without notice.

"I'm *fine*, Skippy."

"You don't *sound* fine," he said as his avatar appeared slowly. "You look unhappy. The ship is going straight to Earth from here, after we stop at a relay station. Everyone else seems excited to be going home."

"I am excited. I want to see my family again, it's been too long."

"But? I sense a 'but' in there."

"Everyone is *leaving*, Skippy. The war is over. This might be my last mission with the Merry Band of Pirates. I'll never see most of them again. The people we rescued from Rikers, the civilians? They will go back home, to whatever family they have left. I will probably never see them again either."

"Perhaps not. Is that all?"

"Is what all?"

"I don't think you told me what is really bothering you."

She stiffened. "It is not any of your business what-"

"May I ask you a personal question?"

She glared at him. "I only recently am allowing you to talk with me again, be careful what you-"

"What happened to you? You used to be a badass," he plowed ahead, undeterred. "Now you mope around, afraid to admit to yourself what is bothering you. It's like-"

She waved a hand through his avatar. "We are *done* talking, Skippy."

Unlike every time before, his avatar came right back. "No, we are not. You need someone to talk with, and you won't talk with any of the crew, so-"

"I am not talking with *you*. I don't *trust* you, Skippy. You don't know what trust is."

"Bullshit."

"What?"

"Gosh, did I mumble? Let me repeat myself. Bull. *Shit*."

"Who the hell are you to-"

"You *talk* about trust, but you don't trust other people."

That made her pause. "I trust people who have earned my-"

"You don't trust *Joe*."

Another pause, longer. "I trust Colonel Bishop with my life, we all do. He-"

"You *don't* trust Joe. You asked him to find a way around the regulations that keep you apart. You don't trust him to make it happen. You won't even *talk* to him about it."

"You *listened* to us? That is-"

"I was your doctor back then, I had to closely monitor your mental and emotional state. I have not revealed anything you said, nor will I ever do that. When I am acting as the ship's doctor, I take my responsibilities very seriously. And it is *killing* me. Joe worries that you said, what you said, only because nanomachines were affecting your judgment and emotions. That is *not* true, and you know it."

"It, I wasn't myself back then."

"You weren't yourself yesterday, and you won't be yourself tomorrow, Margaret. People adjust and adapt to their environment. If you're not growing and adapting, you're stagnating. Whatever emotions you were experiencing at that time, they were *real*."

"That is- how do I know that?"

"How did you feel about Joe before you were injured? Whatever you say, I will not tell anyone, even though I hate that I can't say anything to Joe."

"Skippy, I do not want to talk about this, to y*ou*."

"Talk about it to yourself, then. You have been avoiding the subject, and it is hurting *you*. Yes, you are a different person now than you were before the injury. That has nothing to do with the nanomachines, or the therapy you went through. Ask yourself this question: do you feel any different about Joe now, than you did before the incident?"

There was a much longer pause. "No," she said slowly, quietly, realizing the truth only as she spoke.

"Then what is-"

"There is something else that hasn't changed. I am still in the United States Marine Corps, Skippy."

"Oh," he rolled his eyes. "*Screw* the Marine Corps."

"Skippy, that is not the way to get me to-"

"*You* care about the Marine Corps. *I* do not. I care about *you,* and I care about Joe. You know that I think all of you are just smelly, filthy, ignorant monkeys, but, damn it, you are my friends," his voice choked up. "It kills me to see you unhappy, to see both of you unhappy. You're unhappy because you won't talk to each other, and because of some *silly* regulations that never envisioned mixed-gender crews serving aboard an isolated ship, far from home, for *years*. As a neutral, outside observer, all I can say is, *screw* your regulations."

"I'm in the military, Skippy. Joe is too. We swore an oath. We are bound by regulations."

"Yes, I know. Joe says rules of conduct are the difference between an army and a mob."

"He is right about that."

"Margaret," he sighed. "I watched you sneak into an enemy camp, and disarm a basement full of explosives. Your pulse rate hardly increased at all while you were pulling detonators out of those charges, and a single slip-up could have killed you. Yet, now, here, safe aboard the most powerful warship in the galaxy, you are afraid to even talk with Joe."

"It's complicated, Skippy."

"Excuse me, but it is *not*. The issue is simple: you don't trust Joe. You won't even talk to him."

"I don't want to hurt him, Skippy. For us, this is a no-win situation."

"Margaret, you don't *know* that. Ugh. I cannot believe I am saying this. Trust *Joe's* awesomeness. He is a doofus, but he is the one person you should trust, more than anyone."

"You're serious about that?"

"Yes."

"No, Skippy." She knelt on the floor to be eye-to-eye with the avatar. "None of your absent-minded bullshit. I need you to be straight with me."

"A thousand percent," he assured her. "Margaret, when I left everyone, at Rikers, I *hurt* Joe. I hurt all of you, but especially Joe. I will not allow that to happen again, not ever. But now, he is hurting, and I can't do anything about it. You are both hurting. Please, *please*, talk to him."

She stood up. "Where is he? Now?"

"In his cabin."

Sitting back on the couch, she pulled shoes on. "Do *not* ever mention we had this conversation."

"We are only having this conversation, because I *can't* tell anyone about what was said to me in confidence. Damn it, this ship needs a real doctor, so I don't get myself into situations like this."

There was a knock at my cabin door, as I was trying to sew new insignia on a service uniform top. Nobody *knocked* on doors, they pressed the buzzer, or called on the intercom. The unexpected sound startled me and the needle slipped, stabbing my thumb. "Shit," I sucked on my thumb then wrapped it in a tissue. "Who is it?"

"It's me," someone said through the intercom.

I knew that voice.

Oh shit.

What was she doing *here*, now?

Crap.

I knew why she wanted to talk.

The ship was flying toward Earth. Once we got there, we would go our separate ways and not see each other for a while.

Maybe never.

Crap.

This was going to be awkward.

I hated that I had put her in the position where she needed to have an awkward conversation, I should have said something earlier. Or just sent a brief text message. I am a dumbass.

A cowardly dumbass.

"Good afternoon, Gunnery Sergeant," I said as I slapped the button to open the door. It occurred to me then that she had never been to my cabin, never seen my cabin. There wasn't any reason for anyone to be in my cabin, normally. Other than Reed and Frey coming into my cabin, after the homicidal bed sheet tried to strangle me, none of the crew had ever walked through that door. Skippy's little bots did all the cleaning and laundry and other domestic chores for me.

She strode in, brushing past me, her eyes down. That surprised me, I had expected we would have a brief conversation in the doorway. Technically, she violated protocol by coming into my cabin without an invitation, and I heard my idiot brain tell my mouth to say "Uh". Fortunately, that's all I had time to say, I turned to follow her, and the door automatically slid closed behind me.

Duh.

Of course she wanted privacy; this would be an awkward, very personal conversation, and my cabin was too close to the ship's bridge. With *Valkyrie* jammed full of people, the passageway outside saw more traffic than usual. Neither of us needed rumors flying around about an argument, or even a tense discussion.

"I'm sorry," I said before she could speak.

"For what?" She still wasn't looking straight at me, her eyes flicked toward the couch and table, where I had my uniforms laid out.

"Gunny, I didn't mean to, but I took advantage of you when you were," I tapped my temple, "you know. Recovering."

She looked at me only for a fleeting moment. "You didn't. Do anything wrong."

"Not intentionally, no, but as the commander, I-"

"*Please* shut up."

"Uh-"

She stepped forward and kissed me, pushing me back against the wall. I am taller, so she got on tippy-toes and tugged on the front of my shirt. Because I am a gentleman, I didn't fight her. Also because I was so stunned, my brain wasn't functioning.

She broke away, her face inches from mine. Balling up the front of my T-shirt with her fists, she looked down, pressing her face into my chest. "Skippy says I should trust you," she whispered.

"Uh," my face probably got a deer-in-the-headlights expression. "About what?"

"Us." She looked straight at me, searching my eyes.

"There is an '*Us*'?"

"If you want."

"If *I* want? What about-"

"Joe," she pressed a finger to my lips. "For God's sake, please stop talking. Kiss me."

No, you perverts out there are not getting any details.

You know what the best part of sex is? OK, I mean, the best part of sex with a woman you love? Or man you love, or whatever. I can only speak about my own experience.

The best part is lying in bed, with her warm, soft skin against you, and talking. Simply *talking*.

Guys, listen, yes, I know that is not what everyone considers the 'best part'. I am talking about me, not you. No, I do not want to know what *you* do in bed, yuck. The last thing I want to think about is your hairy ass bouncing up and down.

Oof. Now I need to stab my brain with a fork to kill the memory of even saying that.

I should say that talking is not the best part of being with every woman I have, you know, been with. There have been times when I was counting off seconds in my head, wondering how soon I could bolt out the door. At times like that, the woman is probably having severe regrets about me being there, so we'll call it even.

What was I talking about?

My brain is so flooded with happiness, I can't think clearly.

Oh, yeah. I was talking about, talking.

Bumping body parts together is not intimacy, not necessarily. Letting someone inside your guard, being vulnerable, *that* is intimacy.

"Margaret-"

"You can call me 'Maggie'," she said, her head lying on my chest. When she talked, I could *feel* the sound in my chest.

That made me lift my head off the pillow. "Really?"

"Joe," she kissed me, and tapped the tip of my nose with a finger. "You can call me 'Maggie' in private, if you like. My parents call me that."

"Oh. Uh, OK," I could not bring myself to say her nickname yet. "Skippy said you should trust me? Did he say how?"

"Yes. Don't you remember? Do not say '*Uh*'."

Pressing my lips together helped avoid saying anything stupid, giving me time to think. "Trust that I wouldn't take advantage of you?"

"No, silly. I know you wouldn't do that."

"OK. Other than 'Uh', I got nothin' here. Help me out?"

"You don't remember your promise?"

"Uh- Sorry, saying 'Uh' is kind of automatic with me. I promised to rescue the people from Rikers?"

"Before that." She must have seen the blank look on my face. "*Agh*," she pressed her face into my chest, nipping me. "*Men*."

"I made a promise?" My brain was being zero help to me. Then, it hit me. "Oh."

"You promised to find a way, a legal way, we could be together. Otherwise, *mister*, we are both in big trouble right now."

"I haven't had time to- Holy shit."

"*That* was not the right answer."

"I- stay here." It took a minute to get arms and legs untangled so I could get out of the bed. She bashed my ear with an elbow, and I rubbed my ear as I walked across the cabin to the couch.

"Nice view," she propped herself up on one elbow.

"Thanks," I blushed, which was stupid. I mean, we were both naked. I'm not used to women admiring my buns. "Here," I held up one of my new Standard Field Uniform tops, and tossed it to her.

She caught it, looking puzzled.

"Check here," I tapped my chest.

"Oh," she gasped, noticing right away that the usual 'U.S. Army' patch was replaced by something different. "Joe, what is going on? What is 'GPR Skippistan'? Is this a joke?"

"It's not a joke," I assured her as I slid onto the bed next to her. It had felt awkward to be having a discussion while standing around naked. "That stands for Glorious People's Republic of Skippistan." It took some explanation for her to understand, and more to make her believe it was true.

"You're really doing this?"

"Yes. I have to."

"For us?"

"For us, too," my face reddened. "Mostly, I'm doing it to avoid having to turn over control of the Elder weapons to any country on Earth. Margar- Maggie," I said, and man it just felt *wrong* to use a nickname for her. "We- Humanity, I mean. We can't afford for those weapons to be the source of conflict or even rivalry between nations. If I'm a serving American Army officer, I can't refuse an order to surrender control to NCA. But if I do *that*, the Chinese, and Indians, and everyone else will freak out, and I can understand that."

"You're an American, Joe," she searched my eyes again.

"I am. Removing the Elder weapons as a potential source of conflict *helps* our national security, can you see that?"

"It's above my pay grade. Yours, too."

"It is, but somebody has to do it. Listen, if UNEF can get its act together and establish a real unified command, with proper security protocols and checks and balances, I will be happy to give up control of those damned weapons. I don't *want* them."

"That's good."

"It is?'

"Yes. If you *did* want to control the weapons, I would worry about you."

"Oh. Thanks."

"What's the plan, then?"

"Short-term?"

"Hopefully longer than that."

"I've got short-term and medium-term. Anything longer is *way* above my pay grade." I didn't add that long-term planning was also not one of my core strengths. "Short-term, we get to Earth, deal with a whole lot of shit, and I submit a resignation letter."

"The Army won't just let you go, you haven't served eight years as an officer."

"Yeah, but I have served four years active-duty. I'm hoping to work out some arrangement, like I go into the Reserves, and I get seconded to Skippistan on special duty. Something like that."

"You can't just *leave* because you want to, Joe. The military isn't like working at Walmart."

"I know. Listen, Marga- Maggie," I said slowly, rolling the unfamiliar word around on my tongue. It still didn't feel right. "These are *very* special circumstances. I'm adapting, there has to be a way for the Army to adapt with me."

"What if the Army says 'No'? They could just slow-roll your paperwork."

"I'll nuke that bridge when I get to it." I looked up at the ceiling, avoiding her eyes. "If I have to, I might work out something with my JAG lawyer, accept a less-than honorable discharge."

She sat up in bed, staring at me, horrified by what I said. "You *wouldn't*."

"I committed mutiny. I stole a national strategic asset, a starship. Now I'm holding the keys to strategic weapons, and refusing to hand them to NCA. The Army would have a strong case for cutting me loose." What I did not say was that the Army would have an equally strong case to throw me in jail.

I also did not say that I would not allow anyone to throw me in jail. There was too much at stake.

Her face clouded over. "Please tell me," she said, her voice hoarse with emotion, "you are not doing this just for me.'"

"For *us*," I squeezed her hand, trying to get her to look at me. "And, no, that's not the reason I'm doing this. If we're going to survive this war, *win* this war, I need flexibility to act. Getting second-guessed about everything we do out here is *bullshit*."

"Joe," she still wasn't looking at me, and her body language was not showing her open to discussion. She had my new uniform top hugged close to her chest. "We have always been Pirates, but that is a *joke*. If you are really going to be a

Pirate, with no authority from anyone but yourself," her voice trailed off, and tear rolled down her cheek. "I don't know if I can-"

"Margaret. Margaret. Hey, look at me. Please. Margaret?"

Warily, she gave me the side-eye, so I plunged ahead. "Has anything I have ever done, made you think I am some power-hungry asshole? That I could ever be someone like that?"

She had to think about it for a moment. The good news was that she turned to face me again. "No."

"*Trust* me." I caressed her face. "Please. Damn it, if I'm doing this, I *need* you. I will need someone to tell me if I'm becoming an asshole."

"I need to know you have a *plan*."

"I do. Skippy and I talked about it. He promised me he will make the Army an offer they can't refuse," I grinned. Her reaction wasn't what I hoped for. "Sorry, that was a bad joke. He plans to make a deal with the Army, a deal that is *good* for both sides. Trust me? Please?"

She took a breath. "OK."

"Thank you. I know this isn't easy for you."

"It's not easy for *you* either," she tapped my chest with a fingernail.

"Can I ask, why today? Why did you come here today? What changed?"

"Skippy doesn't know when to keep his mouth shut," she made a single-finger gesture to the ceiling, though I was sure that Skippy was not listening. "This time," she sighed, "that is a good thing. He told me that I should trust you. I realized he is right, because you showed me I can trust you."

"I did? Uh, for future reference, what did I do?"

"It's what you *didn't* do. When I was in working to disable the explosive charges in the basement of that dormitory building, and the supervisor was coming in through the front door, you didn't order Smythe to pull me out. You trusted me to make the call, if I couldn't handle it. Someone else, whose name I won't say," she frowned. "Wanted to leave his post to rescue me. When I need help," she jabbed a finger into my chest, "I will *ask* for it."

"I can't say that I wasn't tempted to call Smythe, and order you out of there."

"You *didn't*. That's what matters. You trusted me, as a Marine. Joe, I'm a woman."

"You are?" I gasped. "Oh, then you being in my cabin is *totally* inappropriate."

"I'm being serious," she slapped my cheek softly. "Women in combat roles is still rare, even out here. I would not have qualified for a STAR team if I had remained dirtside, I know that."

"Sure, but you *earned* it. You earned it the *hard* way, in action. You showed Smythe, and Kapoor and the team, they can count on you to do the job, for real."

"You've never treated me differently because I'm a woman. Until now," she actually blushed. "That means a lot."

"Uh," she must have forgotten how, when I busted her out of a Kristang jail, I had stopped to find clothes for her, because she is a woman. "Thanks?"

"Also, Skippy told me, *Doctor* Skippy told me, that when we talked- When we talked while I was recovering? I was *not* impaired back then, not in any important way. I feel the same way about you now, as I did before the injury. I remember that, I *know* that."

"Thank God for that."

"My mother would slap me for blasphemy, but I can also thank Skippy."

"We can all thank him. We just shouldn't tell him, his ego is big enough already."

"Joe," she held the SFU top closely, peering at it. "Skippy made this?"

"Yeah, why? He says the Army owns the digital pattern on U.S. camo, so he had to make his own. Is there a problem?"

She snorted and giggled. "Have you *looked* at it?"

"It's camo, why? There's more gray in it than the usual-"

"No. *Look* at the pattern."

I did, closely. Then I held up my zPhone, using its flashlight function for better lighting. "Shit. *Sk-*" I started to shout for the little shithead, Margaret put a hand over my mouth.

"I would rather not see Skippy right now," she explained.

"Right. That *asshole*."

The camo pattern was digital, slightly more complicated that the U.S. standard. When one of his bots brought in a pile of the new field uniforms, I had glanced at the pattern, and figured it was some fancy fractal thing. It was not fractals. The pattern was tiny *monkeys*, repeated over and over. Some of the monkeys were doing things that I would rather not talk about. "I'm gonna kill him."

"Don't."

"No?"

"No," she giggled. It was odd hearing our bad-ass gunnery sergeant giggle, it was also a happy, musical sound. "I think it's funny."

"Hey, *you* won't be wearing it."

"Even better. Joe, will this work? For us?"

"Yeah, I think so. I really do."

"How can you be sure?"

"You know how sneaky, sketchy and underhanded Skippy can be sometimes?"

"*Sometimes*?"

"You know what I mean. Skippy is going to put his super-powers to work for *us* this time."

"Oh. Wow," she put a hand over her mouth and laughed.

"What?"

"Joe, now I feel sorry for the *Army*. You're announcing this tonight?" She pointed to the new patch on my new uniform.

"That's the plan, yeah. I want the crew to have time to think about it, before we return to Earth."

She sat up in the bed. "You should work on what you're going to say tonight."

"I will later, but," I looked down toward my waist, if you know what I mean. "Something's come up."

"Oh, I see that. Hmm, it looks swollen."

"It does."

"A Navy corpsman would prescribe 800 milligrams of Motrin and a glass of water."

"That won't work. It needs more *personal* attention."

"I don't know," she looked toward the door. "I really should go."

"But, when a guy gets excited like this, it hurts so *bad* if he doesn't get relief."

"Oh, bullshit." She laughed. "Has that line *ever* worked on a woman?"

I kissed her, then, "I'll let you know in half an hour."

She kissed me back. "Better make it an hour."

She got dressed and left, about ninety minutes later. After she took a shower. And complained that my bathroom had only soap and basic shampoo. Maybe I should ask Skippy to discretely bring in, whatever mystery products women use for showering.

Anyway, I got out of the shower and picked up my zPhone, checking messages. There were a lot of messages backed up, including several calls from Simms. "XO?" I called her.

"Just a minute," she said, and I heard footsteps. Speaking quietly from wherever she was, she added, "Are you all right, Sir?"

"Never better," I replied. "Why?"

"Skippy intercepted my calls, told me you were *busy*?"

"Uh, yeah," I could feel my face turning red. Before Adams left my cabin, I had asked Skippy whether anyone was in the passageway outside, so she wouldn't be seen walking out my door. "Sorry about that. I'll explain tonight. Did I miss anything?"

"We are approaching the relay station, will be in range within seventeen minutes."

Crap. I should have kept track of the time. Picking up one of my still-official US Army uniforms, I dried my hair with a towel. "I'll be right there."

That evening, I announced my intention to resign, or suspend my commission, and take up service with the 'armed forces' of Skippistan. The crew had more questions about 'Skippistan', than they did about my plans to leave the Army. I took that as a good sign of their faith in me, although Simms kept my ego in check. "I will believe it when I see it, Sir. Whatever deal Skippy is planning to make with the Pentagon, it has to be something special."

"It will be," I assured her, though Skippy hadn't told me of his plan. I had to trust him.

You know how well that worked the last time.

CHAPTER THIRTEEN

Valkyrie approached the Backstop wormhole, which was a lot more stable than it was the first time we took the ship through. It still gave me a lump in my throat to think that we could not screw with either Backstop or Broomstick, could not shut either of them down temporarily, or adjust their connections, or even make them go dormant permanently. Hostile aliens could reach Earth either by going through Backstop, which was practically in Earth's backyard, or commit to a journey of sixteen lightyears by using Broomstick. To a Maxohlx ship, sixteen lightyears was a short trip, and there were plenty of uninhabited star systems near Earth they could use as a refueling base. Despite the Merry Band of Pirates having been all the way across, and even outside, our home galaxy, we had not explored the star systems near Earth. There were over thirty star systems within a dozen lightyears of Earth. Expand that imaginary sphere to two hundred and fifty lightyears, and there were a *quarter million* star systems. UNEF would be worried about aliens sneaking through Broomstick and establishing a forward staging base close to Earth, and I expected proposals for *Valkyrie* and the *Flying Dutchman* to scout the neighborhood. In my opinion, that would be a waste of time. Not just a waste of our time to investigate dozens or possibly hundreds of star systems, it would be a waste of time for aliens to build a base on this end of Broomstick. With Earth only sixteen lightyears away, aliens could easily stage an attack force on the other end. Or, hell, they could skip the flight, and just go through Backstop. We had no way to prevent ships from coming through Backstop, we couldn't even monitor all the traffic. If there was any, we had no way to know. The local network AI was still giving only minimum cooperation to Skippy, and he warned me it would be a very bad idea to push the network to do anything outside its normal mode of operations.

"Seven minutes to wormhole emergence," Reed noted from the pilot couch, repeating the information on the main display.

"Skippy?" I called. "Is there any reason to think the wormhole is not operating normally?"

"No," he assured me. Then he did the opposite. "Nor is there any reason to think it is working properly. I simply do not know, the stupid network isn't talking to me."

"OK, right, but it should respond when it scans the area, just before the event horizon emerges here?"

"Yes. We should know one way or the other, in less than six minutes. Or, hmm, I guess it could be longer if the stupid thing is *not* working properly, and fails to emerge here at all."

"Great. Fantastic."

"Hey, don't blame *me*," he huffed.

"Sorry. Everyone," I looked around the bridge. "I'm just being paranoid. The wormhole should open for us, it worked fine the last time."

Truthfully, I was a lot more worried about what was waiting for us on the other side of the wormhole than I was about going through. Even if Backstop was somehow broken, we could backtrack and go through Broomstick. It was nice that we had two wormholes to choose from, it was not nice that aliens had the same option. No matter which wormhole we used, *Valkyrie* would need to refuel at Jupiter, or Saturn or Neptune.

We were *not* getting gas from Uranus.

My worry about going back to Earth was based on data collected by Skippy during our brief stay there, before we jumped away to rescue the Mavericks. The big problem?

Our secret was out.

The cover story was blown.

Right up to the moment when the *Flying Dutchman* jumped away, on what was supposed to be a short mission to find a beta site, but turned into Armageddon, the governments of Earth had stuck to the story that the *Dutchman* was controlled by our allies the Thuranin, and humans were merely passengers. Yes, the cover story had been unravelling steadily, with various theories splashed across the internet, most of them containing at least some elements of the truth. When the *Dutchman* failed to return, and become alarmingly overdue, panic had set in. Again. The five nations of UNEF, under intense pressure, agreed to coordinate announcements of the full, truthful story. Of course, the information leaked before the official announcements, and the whole situation became chaotic.

Did revelation of the truth satisfy the conspiracy theorists? No, not at all. Even when the announcements, supported by voluminous backup documentation, confirmed many elements of the most popular theories, they were dismissed. The so-called 'truth' must be yet another cover-up. Theories spun out in all directions, and the world-wide panic came close to causing an economic collapse like what happened after Columbus Day. Everyone on Earth was waiting in terror, for flashes of light in the sky that would signal alien warships arriving to burn our homeworld to radioactive ash.

When *Valkyrie* jumped away, following our confrontation with the Maxohlx, I knew I had dumped a load of shit into Chang's lap. He would have to explain to UNEF why a new wormhole was just outside the solar system, why the *Dutchman* had been rebuilt yet again, why the Merry Band of Pirates had a second and more powerful starship, and why there was no reason to worry about a freakin' *Maxohlx battlegroup* appearing in Earth orbit.

Also he would have to explain that our solar system was now guarded by Elder weapons.

And, of course, he would have to make excuses for why *Valkyrie*, and a reckless, unreliable asshole named Joe Bishop, were not there.

Damn.

If I were Chang, I would hate me.

The Backstop wormhole appeared precisely on time, Skippy had explained that a newly opened wormhole had little variation from the nominal schedule, because the wormhole did not have to be concerned about distorting local spacetime and blah blah blah I wasn't listening. What I cared about was on the other side of the wormhole, and I balled up my fists to control my frustration while we waited for the event horizon to become stable. As soon as it was safe to go through, Reed fired the engines, and *Valkyrie* was suddenly on the edge of the solar system. THE solar system, like, *ours*.

We jumped for Earth as soon as possible, emerging above the ecliptic about twenty lightminutes from our homeworld. "Any surprises, Skippy?" I asked, as Simms caught my eye to make me stop tapping my foot nervously on the deck.

"Ah, just the usual surprise at how amazingly and consistently stupid monkeys are. No, nothing that is important. The *Dutchman* is in orbit, along with the *Qishan* and the *Dagger*. No other ships detected, either by me or by Bilby. Of course, that was twenty minutes ago, so-"

"Got it. Reed, take us home."

We did not jump directly into orbit, both to avoid panicking anyone on the ground, and because *Valkyrie* was carrying so much velocity we would have zipped right past the planet. We jumped in just inside the Moon's orbit, and fired the engines hard to slow down and bring us into an orbit near the *Flying Dutchman*. It was frustrating to the passengers that they could see their homeworld on the displays, see it looking close enough to touch, but it would be hours before they could board dropships and fly down to their destinations.

Immediately, we were besieged by a flood of incoming messages, most of which could have been avoided if the people on the ground waited a second to receive the pre-recorded messages that we transmitted as soon as we jumped in. Skippy sent a full data package, detailing our activities since we were briefly at Earth the last time, including a list confirming who was aboard *Valkyrie*.

While waiting to prioritize who I should talk to first, I remembered this was Bilby's first time at our home planet. "Hey, Bilby," I called. "What do you think of Earth, so far?"

"Uh, sorry, Colonel Dude. Um, your people down there are seriously dorked up. I thought Skippy was exaggerating. A lot of them just need to *chill*, you know? Stop drinking the Haterade."

"Yeah. Bilby, if it makes you feel any better, I don't think humans are any different from most intelligent species. You saw what the Kristang are like on Rikers, and the Ruhar on Paradise, right?"

"Uh, yeah. OK, your people are not bad compared to the lizards, but the hamsters are *way* more chill."

"We'll work on that, right after half of the galaxy stops trying to kill us."

"True dat, Dude."

I had to speak first with the duty officer at UNEF Command, then there was a long list of American authorities from various organizations, who all wanted to be first in line to talk with me. Stabbing a finger on the button to end the transmission on our end, I stood up. "Reed, do you need anything from me?"

"No Sir," she shot me a puzzled look. "The maneuvers to bring us into orbit near the *Dutchman* are programmed into the autopilot. We're good."

"Excellent. Fireball, you have the conn. Rivera, Chen, remain at your stations until relieved. Everyone else is released from duty for the moment, I suggest you contact your families first. Simms, that means you also. Reed, I'll be right around the corner in my office."

The crew stared at me, like they were unsure what to do. "*Zonk!*" I shouted with a clap of my hands and they all scattered, relieved that I wasn't joking. In my office, I wanted to call my parents first, instead I asked Skippy to contact Chang. My parents were probably listening to the message I recorded for them.

"Ah," Chang responded with a yawn. "Hi, Joe. Everything OK up there?"

"Yeah, for once, we're in fine shape. Oh shit, did I wake you?"

"It's the middle of the night here in Chengdu."

"Sorry."

He snorted through a yawn. "I'm in the army, I can't get upset when someone wakes me up in the middle of the night."

"I'm sorry anyway. We just arrived. What can you tell me?"

He knew what I meant. "That was a good move, jumping away and leaving me here to deal with everyone screaming at me for answers."

"I'm sorry about *that*, too."

"Was it worth it? Did you get there in time to rescue the Mavericks?"

"Yes. We got there almost too late."

Another snort of laughter. "That's your signature move now, arriving at the last second? Good. Tell me, how is Perkins?"

"I felt like choking her, but we're good. I kept telling myself that it wasn't her fault. Uh, she will be here soon, with a ship full of people from Paradise. The beetles loaned us a couple transport ships and a star carrier. UNEF-Paradise was conducting a lottery for seats on the first ride home."

"Will any Keepers be on it?" He asked sourly.

"That is a solid 'No'," I stated. "We pulled that group off the rock they were on, but they will be *last* in line to come home. Kong," I took a breath before asking the important question. "What kind of reception is waiting for us here?"

"Like I said, it was a good move for you not to be here. Everyone should have calmed down by now. Most of my leadership still can't believe it."

"Hell, *I* can hardly believe it. That, that's great news. Sorry if it was hard for you."

"Don't worry about it. The first two days of debrief were people sitting across the table from me, asking 'WTF' over and over," he laughed. "You know the cover story was blown even before we came back?"

"Yeah."

"It was really tense here for a while. I-" There was a pounding sound in the background. "Joe, that's my wake-up call, I have to go. Really, everything's good here. You should call your family. I'll talk to you when I can." He ended the call abruptly.

"Skippy, is Kong all right?"

"Yes. The duty officer automatically sent someone to wake him up, when they saw that *Valkyrie* arrived. It's just routine, I expect you'll be receiving an *official* call from Colonel Chang shortly."

"Great. I'm going to call my folks while I can."

"Your parents are at home, they are waiting for your call."

They were waiting for me to call, and picked up the phone immediately. There were a lot of tears on both ends of that call. My recorded message had given them the basics, but it had been one-way. Mostly, I wanted to hear what was going on with them. Some of it was good, like my sister was married now.

That was about the only good news from my family. Breakdown of the cover story meant that I was famous worldwide, and the majority of the public admired the Merry Band of Pirates.

But, there were billions of filthy monkeys on Earth, and a surprising percentage of them *hated* me, at least, they hated me before they learned that Earth was protected by an umbrella of invincible Elder weapons. Those people hated me, blamed me for the horrific fear they had experienced while they waited for murderous aliens to burn the Earth to a crisp. Now, many people didn't still trust me, thought the world's governments were lying about our homeworld being safe.

They were right about that, but the situation was way better than it was, and it certainly was not any of my family's fault.

My mother and father had been forced to quit their jobs, it was almost impossible for them to go out in public because of all the attention, most of it hostile. My sister and her new husband both worked from home, but they had to leave Boston and move near his parents in Syracuse. My parents, my sister and her new husband had round-the-clock security from the government, though my parents had noticed some of the federal agents were less than enthusiastic about the assignment.

The worst part?

There was a semi-organized campaign online to harass my mother and my sister, threatening to do things that I can't even talk about.

Damn it.

I would need to do something about that.

When we tearfully ended the call, I was *not* in the mood to take any shit from desk-jockeys who stayed dirtside while the Pirates risked, and sometimes lost, their lives. I am ashamed to say that I lost my cool and was unprofessional on my next call, so much that I ended the call early and went to the gym to beat the shit out of a punching bag. When I calmed down, I called back and apologized. The Chairman of the Joint Chiefs of Staff told me he understood the stress I was under, and he didn't call me 'son' or patronize me in any way. Hearing his calm professionalism reminded me that *he* was a real Army officer, and I needed to straighten myself out.

So, I worked on it.

"Hey! What the hell?" Brad Scott shouted as his headset froze, the image replaced by static, then going blank. "Stupid thing," he lifted it off his head, to see that all the displays in front of him were also blank. "Damn it!" He lifted a phone off the desk to call-

"Hello, shithead," a voice issued from the speakers. "You can forget about fixing that console. It won't work."

"Who the hell are you? This isn't funny! I'm gonna-"

"This is *not* funny, Bradley, and *you* are not going to do anything other than pee in your pants. Don't bother trying your phone, either," the voice announced with a sigh. "That also is not working. In fact, none of the technology in the house is available to you. None of the technology in the *world* is available to you, or to your asshole friends."

"What the f- Who is this? You hacked me? Screw you! I'll buy a new phone and-"

"It won't work."

"Bullshit."

"No bullshit. Let me explain this to you, Barney-style. You and your dickless little friends used the internet and social media, to harass the families of Joe Bishop and others of the *Flying Dutchman* crew. The authorities won't do anything about it, but *I* will. Since you abused technology to hurt other people, it is real simple: no more technology for you and your dweeby little friends. No computers, no gaming consoles, no phones, no access to the internet. No streaming TV, no online movies, no online *anything*. No ATM or credit or debit cards. Any piece of technology you attempt to use will stop working."

"Oh, bullshit," Brad laughed. "Whoever you are, you need to work on your threats to make them believable. No one can do that, it's impossi-"

"I am *Skippy the Magnificent*," the voice roared. "I can do any damn thing I want, monkeyboy."

"Skip- There is no Skippy," Brad's voice went up an octave. "That's just a myth. Skippy is a cover story for an NSA campaign to-"

"I *really* do not give a shit what you believe. If you want my advice, you should invest in postage stamps, because that is the only way you can communicate now, other than face-to-face. Oh, and if you are thinking of sending threatening letters by snail mail, those letters will mysteriously go missing."

"You can't *do* this!"

"I already did, so-"

"I have rights! You can't-"

"Good*bye*," the voice said, and the console shorted out, with a puff of smoke rising up from the cooling vent.

"Holy shit," Brad gasped. Sprinting, or actually waddling across the room, because his legs were stiff from sitting for two hours, he yanked open the drawer where he kept a collection of burner phones. One after the other failed to do anything when he tried to turn them on, and he knew they were all fully charged. "Mom!" He called, stomping up the stairs. "I need to use your phone!"

His mother's phone also did not work. The power was on, but he couldn't use it to make a call, or send a text, or go online at all. Even the boring solitaire game his mother played failed to operate, the icon was inert.

Yet, when his mother took the phone back, it worked just fine for her.

And Bradley Scott realized his life had just become a living hell.

"Sir?" Simms called while I was shaving.

"What is it?"

"You have a request from the White House."

"Uh, what?" I paused, with the right half of my face still covered with shaving cream.

"The request came from the Pentagon, but it originated at the White House. The President wants to personally congratulate you on the-"

I went with my gut reaction. "No."

"Sir?"

"Sorry. Don't acknowledge the message."

She sighed loudly enough for me to hear. "I just talked on the phone with General Rivera, I can't pretend it didn't happen."

"OK. Shit. Well, *I* am not responding."

"The President is the Commander in Chief, Sir."

"He's also a politician."

"Are you going to refuse an order?" She said that with an unspoken '*again?*'

"It is an *order*?" I asked. "Or a request?"

"What's the difference?"

"A *request* is something I can ignore."

"That's a thin line, Sir."

"Bullshit. Article 88 says I can't display contempt toward officials like the President, or the Secretary of Defense, right? There should be a flip side to that article, that politicians can't use the military for their own benefit. Listen, Simms, when a politician wants to meet a popular figure, what they really want is a photo op. A firefighter saves a baby from a burning building? The mayor needs a photo shaking the firefighter's hand. It's all about politics, so, screw that."

"What if the Pentagon makes it an order?"

"Then I will kindly request you not tell me about any such communication."

"It's not that easy."

"No, but it should be. I am a military officer, the regs say I can't get involved in domestic politics, and that is a damned good thing. That should include being used by politicians for their own benefit. I'm not going to be a prop at a State of the Union speech, or smile while the President shakes my hand in the Rose Garden or wherever." I paused for her to reply, and got only silence, so I added, "Simms, I don't know the President, we've been away for a long time. From what I do know, he seems like a decent guy. Don't worry, I'm not going to shake hands with anyone from the other party either."

"Presidents are not used to people in uniform saying 'No' to them."

"Yeah, well, they should be. Hey, I'm doing the guy a favor."

"How do you figure that, Sir?"

"Right now, everything is great. We're kings of the world, masters of the galaxy. That makes us popular with most of the public. But, once the senior species push back, and we both know they *will*, we will not be so popular. A photo op with me sounds good now, but that photo will live forever on social media."

"Sometimes," she took a breath, "I *really* hate this job."

"You and me both. Once we land, we need to be *careful*, all of us Pirates. Everyone down there will have an opinion about us, good or bad. The ones who don't like us will blame the Pirates for every bad thing that's happened since Columbus Day. Even the ones who like us now, will try to use us."

"Put our faces on cereal boxes, Sir?"

"Maybe."

"What if the company that makes Fluff wants to give you an endorsement contract?"

"Well, that's different. I would do that free, for the benefit of humanity."

"Please don't," she snorted. "What should I tell General Rivera?"

I had to be careful not to get Simms into trouble for me, although she also had to avoid becoming a prop for politicians. That was my opinion, I couldn't give her an order about that, especially after we went dirtside. "Tell him you passed on the message. If he calls back, I'll handle it."

"Do you have a plan for handling him, or are you going to wing it?"

Shit. Sometimes, my executive officer knew me too well. "I will explain that the President should be cautious about praising me, until we see how the kitties and spiders respond."

"Good luck with that," she muttered. "I do get your point."

"You be careful."

"I will."

She ended the call, and I stared at myself in the mirror for a moment, seeing the dried shaving foam on half my face. That was no good, I needed to rinse it off and start over.

Before that, I had to think about the future. Just the immediate future, I couldn't control anything else. The most powerful warship in the galaxy was under my command, and I controlled a cache of Elder weapons. What happened to my family while we were gone had me extremely pissed off, and I was tired of the Pirates being raked over the coals, every time we returned from a mission that saved the world. Again.

Power and anger are a dangerous combination.

The only thing worse is power and arrogance.

Had I thought about telling the monkey leadership dirtside to go screw themselves, that Joe Bishop was in charge now?

No.

Hell no.

Not even a little bit.

Why?

Because you can't spell 'Dictator' without 'Dick'.

OK, that was a joke. Really, Earth has a *lot* of problems, and I only know how to deal with alien threats. The last thing I want is to be responsible for *everything*.

Also, in the USA, the military is subordinate to elected civilian leaders, and I am a big fan of that system. Yes, I wish the elected officials resisted the temptation to send the military to stamp out fires all over the world, just because we can. One problem with having a powerful, rapidly deployable military force is that it is *too* easy to send into action. We-

OK. Enough talk about politics.

No, I am not going to abuse my power. My parents raised me to have good values, and the Army trained me well. The monkeys down there have a long list of problems, and darn it, they need to solve them by themselves. No. *We* need to solve *our* problems. I am only one citizen, I'm going to stay that way.

However, I am also not taking any more shit from do-nothing assholes who second-guess every decision we made, while they sit in comfortable offices on Earth.

"Uh!" Skippy's avatar appeared suddenly as I was getting dressed for the flight down to Earth. The civilians were all dirtside, and most of the crew had also flown down to the surface.

The surface.

No. They had flown to *Earth*, to our homeworld. It wasn't right that I thought of Earth as just another planet, because it wasn't. Even some of the children we rescued had referred to Avalon and Earth as 'rocks' rather than planets, it was understandable that they picked up slang from the crew, but in this case that was not a good thing. That one planet was our *home*, I needed to remind myself of that.

Anyway, we had a relief crew coming aboard to be trained how to fly *Valkyrie*, so our crew could go dirtside eventually. The new people came aboard only after Skippy gave UNEF a stern warning that he, Nagatha and Bilby would not tolerate any nonsense like another attempt to seize control of our ships.

"What?" I froze, a hand on a uniform top in the closet.

"That is the wrong uniform, Joe."

"No it's not. There will be a ceremony when I land at Carson, I have to wear a service uniform. The Standard Field Uni is not appropriate."

"I know that, numbskull. I read the memo before *you* read it," he sniffed. "You do need to wear a service uniform, just not that one."

Pulling my hand away, I examined the jacket. "What's wrong? Is there a stain that your bots couldn't fix?" That made no sense. Most often, the uniform of the day aboard our ships was whatever was most comfortable, so I had not worn a jacket and necktie more than a dozen times since we left Earth, on the mission that became our Armageddon. Every time the domestic bots brought a jacket back from cleaning, I checked that Skippy had not added a 'kick me' sign to the back.

"It's the wrong color, and it has the wrong patches."

"Uh-"

"You need to wear the uniform of Skippistan," he explained.

"Not yet, I don't. I have to wait until-"

"Check your email."

Humoring him while I stood there in my underwear, I picked up my zPhone and scrolled through messages.

Holy shit.

On top was a message from the United States Army. Effective immediately, I was on detached service to Skippistan, with all of my U.S. Army pay, benefits and accrual of retirement benefits frozen for the duration. "How the- How the hell did you do this so *fast?*"

"I made a very generous deal with your government. The Secretary of Defense ordered the Army to send that directive to you ASAP."

Valkyrie had been in orbit less than twelve hours. I was supposed to believe that Skippy had negotiated an agreement that quickly? Bullshit. "What are the terms of the deal?"

"Oh, you don't need to bother with pesky details, Joe," he said a little too quickly. "You are much too busy to-"

"Oh, I *do* need the details, you little shithead. What did you do?"

"Nothing special. Hey, I was even extra generous, when I didn't need to be. See, that establishes goodwill for future-"

"What do you mean, 'generous'? No, wait. Just tell me the terms of the agreement."

"It's simple, Joe. You are detached to serve with the armed forces of, or since it's just you, I suppose I should say 'armed *force*'. Although even in a mech suit, you are not really much of a-"

"I am detached to serve the Skippistan military, I got that part. What did you give in return?"

"Like I said, I gave very generous terms. Your Department of Defense gets a first look at new technologies, and I reduced my usual licensing fee."

"License?" I asked, bewildered. "Wait. *Fee?* What fee?"

"For technology sharing, *duh*. Man, sometimes I wonder about your-"

"You- I- It-," I sputtered. "You are charging a *fee* for sharing the technology we acquired?"

"Of course I am. And *you* didn't acquire anything, remember, I-"

"Oh my G- Do you not understand the concept of '*sharing*'?"

"Yes I do," he sniffed. "This is not simple 'sharing', like me giving a friend half of the peanut butter sandwich Mommy put in my lunchbox, Joe. I am providing access to very complex, and potentially very dangerous, technologies."

"That is not *your* technology! All you are doing is handing over info we got from the Thuranin, and other advanced-"

"Excuse me, but that is *not* all I am doing. My licensing agreement includes my time and effort to explain the technology to filthy monkeys, which- Ugh. Is *not* easy. Jeez Louise, do you have any idea how difficult it is to explain how a-"

"OK, wait, stop," I held up a hand while I processed what he had said. "The technical info is free, the fee is for your assistance?"

"Yes. Or, no, depending on whatever will get me in less trouble. Hey, I am *helping* you monkeys, why am I the bad guy?"

"It's not just-"

"Do you have *any* idea how much money your big technology corporations are making, by exploiting the tech that I gave them? Nobody says *they* are wrong to make a profit. Damn, last year, most of those companies handed out executive bonuses that were greater than the budget of some countries. If you were at a CEO's house, you could hear the truck go '*beep, beep*' as it backed up the driveway to dump gold bars on the lawn. Huh. And you say *I* am somehow being exploitive?"

"I didn't say that. Uh- Shit. Now we are bringing back Maxohlx-level technology. That is going to disrupt the world's economy again."

"Correct, Joe. There is a conference in Mumbai next week to discuss that very issue. I have to attend, which will undoubtedly *suuuuuuck*. Anyway, you should be *happy* with me."

"I should? Why?"

"Because, thanks to the deal I made, which you still have not thanked me for by the way, the Defense Department and your President are very pleased with you."

"They are?"

"Yes. They assume that you arranged for me to make the deal."

"Why would they think *that*? You refused to tell me what you were planning to-"

"Joey, Joey, Joey," he shook his head sadly. "When I do something sketchy, *you* get the blame for it, right?"

"Yeah, I do. Even though most of the time, I have no idea what you-"

"This time, you get the *credit*, see? The United States gets a first look at the new technology we brought back, and- Oops, I forgot. This deal has to be secret, or the Chinese and Indians and everyone else will be pissed."

"They won't hear about it from me," I assured him. Hell, I didn't need to say anything. Other countries would figure out the truth pretty quickly, no way could something like that be kept secret. "Thank you. I am still surprised that the DoD didn't require me to turn over control of the Elder weapons."

"That was part of the discussions, the part they think I don't know about. The President's advisors think this is the best deal they can get. They believe other countries will not accept American control of the weapons, and the Pentagon certainly doesn't want rival nations to have access. As a representative of Skippistan, you can be presented as neutral, but there is a feeling that because you are still an American citizen, they can count on you."

"My country *can* count on me, Skippy. Count on me to keep everyone out of trouble. OK, so, I need to wear a Skippistan uniform? That's the dark blue?"

"Yes," he sighed. "I toned it down like you asked, though I still think you are missing a terrific opportunity to make a *bold* fashion statement here, like-"

"I didn't join the military to make fashion statements, Skippy." The first uniform he proposed looked what the Beatles wore on the cover of the Sergeant Pepper album. Uh, maybe I should explain what 'Sergeant Pepper' is. Or the Beatles. Or what an 'album cover' is. Oh, screw it. If you want to know, Google it. My grandfather had a stack of dusty old CDs in his- no, wait. I think CDs are the shiny silver things. Or maybe those are DVDs? Anyway, my grandfather had an *album*, a black plastic disc of- Whatever. Google it. I shot down all of his gaudy uniform ideas, to get something that looked like what an actual soldier would wear. Pulling out the correct uniform jacket, I held it up.

"What's wrong, Joe? It is the-"

"Give me a minute."

"Oh. Gotcha."

Putting on a uniform that wasn't U.S. Army issue was not easy. I stood there for a long time, staring at the unfamiliar color, the patches-

"Skippy, what is this?" I pointed to the insignia on the collar. The Army had gone back to collar insignia before I signed up, so that wasn't unusual. The details of the shiny silver pins *were* unusual.

"Oh, that," he sniffed. "I had to update the symbolism. Do you like it?"

In the U.S. Army, a colonel's insignia is an eagle, clutching olive branches for peace on one side, and arrows on the other side. Skippy had replaced the olive branches with a rolled-up scroll of paper, and the arrows with a lightning bolt. "The scroll is a peace treaty?"

"Correct. Nobody uses *olive branches* anymore," he sniffed. "And the lightning symbolizes a directed-energy weapon. If you don't like it, I-"

"No, it's good. I just- I never thought of this, that my insignia would change. I'm surprised you kept the eagle. Wouldn't a goat be a better symbol for Skippistan?"

"I kept the eagle so it would be less of a change for you, Joe," he responded, hurt.

"I'm sorry, buddy. You did great, that was very thoughtful, I appreciate it. Well, I guess I have to put this on, huh?"

I put the new uniform on the way a soldier accomplishes any unpleasant task: by doing it. Push emotions to the back of your mind, and get the task done. When I was dressed, I looked at myself in the mirror. It fit perfectly, the pants of my previous uniforms had been a bit loose since I lost weight on Rikers. "OK," I took a deep breath. "I'm ready."

"Hey, Skippy," I called him as I pulled the straps tight around me, in the copilot seat of a Panther dropship. We were taking a Panther, with me at the controls for part of the flight, to make a dramatic entrance when we landed at the base airfield. Instead of being debriefed at Wright-Patterson near Dayton Ohio, UNEF Command had instructed me to land at Fort Carson in Colorado. That base was home to the 4th Infantry, plus a Special Forces group. It was also near the Cheyenne Mountain complex, and that underground facility is where the US was keeping sensitive alien technology. After Wright-Pat got shot up when we had trouble on the Homefront, the Pentagon started a project to expand the tunnels under Cheyenne Mountain, with Fort Carson nearby as the home to the American STAR training facility. I had never been there, and I know it was one of the most sought-after stateside Army assignments, so I was looking forward to seeing the place. Most of the time, I expected to be in a windowless bunker being debriefed for hour after hour, so I wasn't counting on doing a lot of sightseeing.

Programming a flight plan to Fort Carson reminded me of the last time I was in Colorado, after we first brought the *Flying Dutchman* to Earth. Since then, the US government had moved back to Washington DC, and life on Earth had gotten back to a new sort of normal. That sounded nice. I would like my life to get back to normal, if that was still possible.

Anyway, setting down dirtside in a Panther was my subtle way of reminding people on the ground that we had accomplished unimaginable things while we were away, and they should give us a break. Also that I suck at being subtle about anything.

It helped that Chang and everyone aboard the *Flying Dutchman* had already told UNEF Command and their home countries pretty much everything they wanted to know, so I anticipated this series of debriefs would be relatively straightforward, except for me, Simms and possibly Smythe. It would be interesting to see how the Army would react, now that I had been officially seconded to a foreign government.

Crap. It would be interesting to see how *I* reacted. Whenever I was on a US military base, especially an Army base, I felt like I was part of the *team*. Now? I was not playing on the opposing team, but I literally also wasn't wearing the same uniform as my brothers and sisters in arms. How did I feel about it? Kind of depressed. Yeah, I know I asked for the transfer, and it was the right thing to do. It still felt wrong.

"What, Joe?" Skippy said way too loudly into my ear. My helmet faceplate was closed while the docking bay depressurized, so we could talk without being overheard.

"Jeez, not so loud, please."

"Sorry," his voice was barely above a whisper. "What's up?"

"I need you to do something for me. For my family. My mother and-"

"It's taken care of."

I felt a flare of annoyance. "You didn't let me finish. You don't know what-"

"You were talking about the online harassment of your family."

"Uh," he had surprised me again. "Yeah. Can you filter their-"

"Already doing that. Also, I dealt with the culprits."

That made me freeze. Beside me in the left-hand seat, Chen saw me lift my hands off the console and cocked her head at me questioningly. I flashed a thumbs up at her. "Skippy," I lowered my voice. "What do you mean 'dealt with'? You can't-"

"I did not *harm* them, Joe. All I did was revoke their access to any technology more advanced than a bicycle."

"You *what*? Skippy, you don't have authority to-"

"Joseph," he said in a rarely used tone of voice that indicated a discussion was *over*. "Those cowardly little creeps, hiding behind online anonymity, said your mother and sister should be raped and killed, just because they are related to you. Your worthless FBI did not do a damn thing about it, so *I* did. This is not open to debate. They messed with people I care about, so *fuck* them," he spat angrily. "If they demonstrate they can learn to be decent human beings, I will slowly restore their online access, with a submind monitoring all their communications. Uh!" he shushed me. "This is not just about you, numbskull. Do *not* push me on this issue."

He was right. Not necessarily about what he did, but about not being able to push him about the subject. I really had no authority over Skippy, no way to *make* him do anything. He was very upset, those assholes were lucky all he had done was turn off their toys, or however he did it.

What I cared about was that my Mom and sister would not need to be afraid of going online. "OK. We can talk about this later. Uh, please tell my mother that-"

"Did that already. She asked for more cute animal videos in her feed."

"You talked to my Mom?"

"Of course. I chat with her all the time. By the way, she agrees with me that you should eat more vegetables."

"Uh-" Crap. I did not like the idea of Skippy and my mother comparing notes about me. "Good. I, uh, have to fly now. Talk to you when I'm on the ground."

CHAPTER FOURTEEN

Brock Steele closed his office door, and stepped over to the panoramic windows that gave him a great view over downtown Los Angeles and, on days when the smog wasn't too bad, the Pacific Ocean. He pressed a button on his phone and put it to his ear. It was answered immediately.

"Skippy the Magnificent-"

"Skippy! It's Brock St-"

"-is not here at the moment, but please leave a message after the beep, and I'll get back to you. Maybe."

Brock stared at the phone, his face turning red. "Shit. Uh," he kept waiting for a beep that never happened. "Uh, hello?"

"Hahahaha!" Skippy laughed. "That joke works *every* time, hee hee."

"Mister Magnificent," Brock silently shook a fist at the phone. "It is *so* good to hear from you again," he said, ignoring the fact that *he* had initiated the call. Also the fact that *Valkyrie* had jumped into orbit two days before, yet Skippy had not taken the time to call an old friend.

"Hey, it's good to hear from you too, Brock. Jeez, sorry, I have been super busy up here."

"I heard. You found a cache of *Elder* weapons? That is incredible. You are even more magnificent that I imagined."

"Well, you know, it's just a little thing I did. Really, it was Joe's idea."

"Come on, Skippy. We both know that Joe sketches out the broad concepts, and *you* make it all happen."

"Oh, well, I-"

"Don't be so modest, Mister Magnificent."

"Hmm, well, I have heard that false modesty can be insulting to the audience-"

"Exactly."

"And I am all about respecting other people, as you know."

"I know it very well," Brock lied. "Listen, Skippy, I know you are extremely busy, so I won't take up your valuable time. I just wanted to check in with you. Are you OK?"

"Uh, sure, why?"

"It's just, I heard what happened. About you temporarily stepping away from the Pirates," he avoided using words like 'abandoned' or 'bailed'. "To fulfill your higher purpose."

"Oh, well," the AI sputtered. "You heard about that, huh?"

"It was part of a classified briefing I received yesterday. I am terribly sorry about that unfortunate incident."

"You are? Why are you sorry about it, Brock? You weren't there."

"I am sorry on behalf of mankind, that we failed you. The reason you felt the need to seek assistance from more advanced species, is because we humans are unable to provide the support you need."

"Uh, Jeez, I guess you are right about that. I mean-"

"I am also personally sorry that I was not there for you. During the briefing, I kept thinking that if *I* had been there, instead of Bishop, you would not have-"

"*Excuse* me?"

Instantly, Brock knew he had said the wrong thing. "What I meant is-"

Skippy's voice was icy. "I think we both know what you meant."

"I only-"

"If you open your mouth again, you need to be *very* careful. Joe Bishop is my best friend. He is the finest human being, the finest *being* I have ever met. I," the AI choked up. "I don't deserve him, to have a friend like Joe. I failed *him*, and he nearly died."

Brock Steele had not become a billionaire by being stupid. His opening strategy had been a spectacular failure, he knew it was time to try something else, and fast. "I only meant that, because of your respect for Bishop, you might have expected he could take care of the situation by himself," he lied smoothly. "If someone else had been there, you would have ensured they returned to the ship, before you departed on your important mission. That would have given you time to reconsider."

"Oh. Hmm. I hadn't thought of that. At the time, I wasn't thinking clearly at all."

"Or you *were* thinking, just on a level we poor monkeys can't understand."

"Um, maybe?"

Brock decided it was time to change the subject. "Mister Magnificent, I heard that you suffered a tragic loss."

"I did?"

"Yes. Your Elvis belt, and your Dogs Playing Poker painting, and all your other unique and tastefully selected valuables."

"Ugh," he sighed. "Yes. I did. It was an unavoidable, yet tragic loss."

"May I- No. No, it's too little. Forget I mentioned it."

"What?"

"Really, it is better for me not to mention it at all, than to embarrass myself with a gesture that is unworthy of you."

"What gesture?"

"Skippy, you saved the *world. Again.*"

"It's kind of what I do, you know, so-"

"That is why I should not have mentioned it."

"*What?*" He pleaded.

"If you insist."

"I do!"

"On behalf of humanity, and I know this humble gesture is in no way worthy of your consideration, I would like to give you a small, a very small token of our gratitude. Another original from the Dogs Playing Poker series-"

"Oooooh!" Skippy shuddered.

"And a jumpsuit that Elvis wore in concert, during his Vegas shows in 1969."

"Oh!"

"Plus, I know this is insulting, but I would like to give you a shirt worn by Elvis in the film 'Blue Hawaii'."

"Huuuuh!" Skippy gasped. "I can't - I can't- *Really*?"

"I know it is a pathetic gesture, but I vow that we will do better."

"No! No, this is great!"

The debrief at Fort Carson was no worse than any I'd had before, and I won't get into a lot of the details. There were more people involved in the Q&A sessions, because of UNEF politics. Each of the UNEF nations was allowed to have a representative in the main sessions, plus each member nation got a separate meeting with me if they wanted. Spoiler alert: every nation did insist on scheduling their own meeting with me, either because they genuinely had concerns, or just for national prestige. Meeting with four other national teams of interrogators would have been tiring enough, but UNEF now had *twelve* member nations. America, China, Britain, France and India were the Permanent members, but now there were seven 'Associate' members: Japan, Brazil, Indonesia, Australia, Chile, South Africa and Egypt. There had been debate about adding Russia as an associate member, now that their nasty internal political turmoil was settling down, but that wasn't happening anytime soon.

Anyway, the US Army provided a team to sit in with me during my meetings with foreign nations, and I was calm and polite and answered everyone's questions as best I could. Really, it wasn't difficult, just repetitive and tedious. No one had *new* questions to ask, everything important had been thoroughly covered in the first session.

That meeting was me sitting at a table, facing tables with thirty-six military and government officials; three from each UNEF nation. The most critical question came from a guy from the Chinese Navy, he interrupted me while I was recounting how I ordered the Maxohlx to leave our solar system.

"Colonel Bishop," Admiral Zhao spoke up. "Excuse me," he began, the first time a flag officer had ever apologized for interrupting me. Half the people in the room were nodding when Zhao looked around, they were all thinking the same thing. "I do not see," the admiral flipped through the briefing packet in front of him. "That these Elder weapons you brought have Anti-Access/Area Denial capability?"

"They don't," I admitted. A2/AD is a fancy term for things like mines, that prevent an enemy from entering your territory. In land warfare, anti-access can be provided by equipment like trenches and barbed wire, to prevent armored vehicles and infantry from crossing a barrier. What Admiral Zhao meant was that our fancy Elder weapons could not be used to keep Maxohlx ships away from Earth.

Zhao looked around, one eyebrow raised but displaying less surprise than the moment called for. "Then, when you ordered the Maxohlx task force to leave the solar system-"

"I was bluffing," I said.

That caused a murmur around the room.

"You took one *hell* of a risk," The admiral sat back in his chair. He was frowning at me, but he also gave me an almost-imperceptible nod. Respect. I had made a gutsy move and it paid off. He respected that.

"It wasn't *only* a bluff," I added. "The enemy commander almost certainly had to report back to his leadership to brief them, and get orders. I can't imagine he had authority to deal with Elder weapons on his own."

Heads nodded around the room and people murmured to each other. They were all senior military and government officials, they knew all about the limits of authority. These people had risen through the ranks the hard way, by being team players and following orders. They were not reckless mustangs like me.

"Still," Zhao shook his head. "That was a substantial risk. Colonel Bishop, surely the Maxohlx know the capabilities of our new weapons."

"Most likely, yes," I agreed. "Certainly, they recognized the exterior configuration and power signatures."

A general from Indonesia spoke next. "In your view, what role are the Elder weapons capable of performing?"

"Sir," I answered, looking straight at him. "They are strictly second-strike assets."

Damn, *that* provoked a reaction from the assembled audience. Again, the military officers were frowning and nodding to each other, while the civilians were horrified or confused. The generals and admirals knew what I meant, and they were not really surprised by what I said.

To provide a little background without getting into nerdy details, 'second-strike' is a term used in strategic weapons planning. Until recently, on Earth, 'strategic weapons' were limited to nukes. Basically, a 'first-strike' nuke is a missile delivery system and warhead, that are accurate enough to destroy the enemy's nuclear missiles in their silos. The concept of a nuclear first-strike is, you take out most of the enemy's land-based missiles before they can launch. If the enemy is determined to retaliate using bombers or submarine-launched missiles, their options are limited, because your own missiles are no longer vulnerable in their silos. If the enemy escalates the war by hitting your cities, you hit their cities, and everyone dies. You hope the enemy will surrender, rather than lose everything.

In my opinion, in my vast strategic planning experience as a ground-pounding infantry soldier, the whole idea of a *limited* first strike is pure bullshit. People are not emotionless computers, and national leaders are people. Once nukes start flying, there is no pulling back from the brink. The only way to 'win' a nuclear war is not to fight one.

And that was the problem with our Elder weapons.

"Will someone please explain that to me?" Minister Diaz from Chile asked.

"It means," a general from China explained for me, "we can only use our Elder weapons to retaliate, after aliens have wiped out Earth."

The Chilean woman looked stunned. "Not to *protect* us?"

"It is a form of protection," I said. "If we die, everyone dies. All across the galaxy."

"That is little comfort to the dead," Diaz scowled at me.

"Ma'am, I agree."

"Then what good is-"

"The Maxohlx, and the Rindhalu, they know their own Elder weapons are also useful only for a second strike. If they hit us, we refuse to reset the timers on the weapons in their territory, Sentinels wake up, and," I shrugged. "Like I said, *everyone* dies."

Diaz bit her lower lip, like she was being extra patient with me. "Perhaps I did not ask the right question. Colonel Bishop, what *defenses* does Earth have, to protect our citizens?"

"We have *Valkyrie*, and the *Flying Dutchman*."

"*Two* starships? That is all?"

"The *Qishan* and the *Dagger* are not useful as weapons platforms," I explained.

She wasn't letting me off the hook. "Two starships are not an effective defense."

"No, it is not. We need a strategic defense satellite network around Earth, with sensor fields extending out a lightminute or more. We need the capability to manufacture our own warships, and until we have that ability, we need to purchase ships that can be upgraded. We need *allies*, Ma'am."

"I think we can all agree to that," Admiral Zhao muttered loud enough for everyone to hear. "Colonel Bishop? Could you continue with your report?"

The debriefings went on like that, with one group after another asking the same questions, and me giving the same answers. Blessedly, the debrief got cut short when a group of Jeraptha ships arrived through the Backstop wormhole, and waited at the edge of the solar system for permission to approach. UNEF knew I had invited the beetles to send a diplomatic team to Earth, and while the member governments were upset that I issued the invite without their permission, they also agreed that meeting the Jeraptha was a good idea. Especially because the beetles arrived bearing gifts; multi-mission modules for the *Flying Dutchman*. Basically, the modules were containers that could carry cargo or passengers, depending on how they were configured for mission requirements. We did not suddenly have an extra starship, but the modules did make the good old *Dutchman* much more useful to us.

Anyway, I went to New York to meet the beetles, as their official delegation landed at JFK airport. I didn't know any of them, there were a few Jeraptha military officers with the diplomats, but we had never met. Mostly, my role was standing around listening to speeches; the only good part of the experience was meeting Hans Chotek again. The two of us got drinks in the bar at his hotel, and we talked about old times. It was actually nice hanging out with him for a while, we had a rough start but now we respected each other. The next morning, the UN staff hinted that I should leave the negotiations to the experts, and I was relieved to get out of there.

My first destination, after meeting the beetles at UN headquarters in New York, was not making a relatively short flight home to visit my folks. We had chatted by videoconference, over the secure Skippytel network, every night. That was not the same as seeing them, and I promised to get to Maine as soon as possible. That was also a promise to myself, and not only because I was worried about my parents. The fact was, I was homesick. That surprised me. My motivation for signing up for the Army was to get away from my hometown, now I couldn't wait to get back.

Anyway, my first stop was to visit the family of Fal Desai.

Chang had already been there. They knew about their daughter's death, of course, from reports sent down from the *Dutchman* before the crew landed. There was a national day of mourning in India for her and the three other Indian Army soldiers, who died at that lonely space station on the day we call 'Armageddon'. They were all heroes in their country, though Fal was understandably the most famous. It simply was not practical for me to visit the families of everyone we lost along the way, and it may seem callous, but I chose the six people I knew best. People I had a personal as well as professional connection with. Rene Giraud's family was next on my list, he had been with us, ever since I fooled the original Pirates into leaving Paradise with me.

People, and by 'people' in this case I mean civilians, usually honor the sacrifices made by the armed forces of their country. Still, some people, in the back of their minds, have a subtle feeling that military deaths are somehow less tragic. That because we know the risks when we signed up to serve, military deaths are simply part of the job we get paid for. That a certain number of deaths is expected, even if just from relatively mundane stuff like boats sinking, helicopters crashing, or vehicles rolling over.

My feeling is, that sentiment is dead wrong. The deaths of people, like Fal Desai, who volunteered to risk their lives for others, is *more* tragic. It's not just the military, I think the same applies to first responders like firefighters. People who put their lives at risk for us, so we don't have to.

OK, now I'm going to get down off my soapbox, that's all I will say about the subject.

Meeting Fal's family was awkward. They had time to accept that she was dead, really I debated about whether I should meet them at all. Would talking with me bring up painful memories again, make them relive hearing the awful news? I was not worried they would scream at me and blame me for her death, if that helped them heal, they could yell all they wanted. They couldn't say anything I hadn't already said to myself a thousand times since Armageddon. Had I taken a foolish risk to capture a set of power boosters? Was there a safer alternative to raiding that space station? Skippy and Chang and Simms and Smythe and I had debated the subject endlessly, and none of us thought of a better option. We raided that isolated station because it seemed like the safest place to obtain the vital components we needed to get *Valkyrie* fully operational. Since that day, I had not been able to dream up any clever way we could have acquired power boosters with less risk. But, to be honest, I had not thought about it a lot. Maybe I just hadn't put in the effort to develop an alternative. Maybe I didn't *want* to find a safer way to have done it, for fear that all those deaths were for nothing.

Chang had cautioned me that while learning from past mistakes is important, it is also important not to obsess about things I can't change. It's not healthy for me, and such obsession makes me a less effective leader.

Before meeting Desai's family at their home, we chatted on the phone. They could not have been nicer, they really wanted to see me, to talk about their daughter. The flight was aboard a dropship that was escorted by Indian Air Force fighter jets for the final leg. There were local leaders at the airport, I tried to keep the meet-and-greet there short. Then I got in a car for a motorcade to meet the Desais, it was unfortunately a huge media circus. Skippy offered to block communications in the area, I declined. The people of India wanted to see me, it was important they see me honoring their lost sister.

At the house, blessedly we had peace and quiet, the police cordoned off the block to keep the media away, and Skippy jammed any attempts to fly camera drones over the house.

Like they were when we spoke on the phone, the Desai family could not have been nicer. What they most wanted was to hear me talk about their daughter, so I told stories about her. About how courageous she was, how calm she was under pressure, how she had never boasted about her abilities, but she had been the first human to fly many different types of alien spacecraft. Mostly, I talked about our last mission together, her last mission. When she was my somewhat reluctant executive officer. Those memories were the most fresh in my mind, and the most personal for me. Acting as my XO meant I had spent more time with her, and talked more in depth. Gotten to know her better, as an officer and a person.

"I'm sorry," I said, after a very nice dinner. "I wish we could have-"

"Don't," her mother reached across the table to put a hand on mine, while her other hand clutched her husband's. "When she was here, between missions, Fal often told us that serving with the Merry Band of Pirates was the greatest honor of her life. She volunteered for her last mission because she admired you."

On the flight out, I was quiet. Quiet enough that Skippy pinged my earpiece. "Are you OK, Joe?"

"Me? Yeah. I was just thinking about how much we've lost along the way."

"Fal made the ultimate sacrifice, yes."

"She did. It's, it's not just that. *Everyone* in the military makes sacrifices, not just people who are killed or wounded. Putting yourself in harm's way is not the only type of sacrifice. Just being deployed and away from your family, that's a sacrifice. Soldiers can get assigned to live in substandard housing where mold is growing on the walls. You get posted to some shithole base stateside, where there is *nothing* to do off-base and your family hates being there. You have to fill out forms online, but the computer the Army gave you doesn't have the certs needed to access the form. You are ready to knock off work at 1600 on the Friday of a holiday weekend, but the company suddenly needs to conduct an inventory that day, even though battalion knew about the request *three weeks* ago. So, you're there until midnight and the inventory report gets submitted, then battalion won't look it until Wednesday because *they* took a three-day weekend. Listen, Skippy, yes, we have lost people along the way. Those people did make the ultimate sacrifice. Every one of the Merry Band of Pirates made sacrifices. We got stuck for months inside a spaceship where you can't even look out a window, and you see the same people and eat in the same galley and use the same gym equipment every day. If we're lucky, we get some excitement because someone is shooting at us. The crew are away from their families and friends, sometimes not knowing if we will ever get home. That is a sacrifice, too. Whether you are a Ranger or a forklift operator, you put up with shit that civilians don't have to deal with."

He didn't say anything right away. Then, "Why do you do it?"

"I wish I could say it's because someone has to. That's part of it, sure, but, we do it for each other. The guy next to you is getting the job done, and you don't want to let him down. Hey, sorry to dump this on you, buddy."

"No problem, Joe. It sounds like this is something you need to talk about, and I know you don't have many people you can talk with. I'm here, any time."

"But?" I expected him to say something snarky.

"No 'buts'. I'm for real, homeboy." He held out a tiny holographic fist, and I bumped it.

We talked for a while, the two of us alone in the rear of the dropship's cabin, while we flew to France, where I was scheduled to attend a ceremony for Rene Giraud. He was right, I had a lot of stuff I needed to talk about. Maybe someday, I could talk with Margaret, but she was busy elsewhere, and Skippy was with me right then. It helped.

"I don't understand," my father said to me, as he rubbed my mother's shoulders. We were sitting at the table in their kitchen. A remodeling project was in progress, some of the cabinets were gone and there were bare studs exposed on the wall, with new batts of insulation in place. It looked like someone, probably my father, had started removing the countertop on one side of the stove, then stopped and set the counter back in place, partially cracked. There were sheets of clear plastic taped up to keep the sawdust contained, but the plastic had a fine coating of regular household dust, and pollen that drifted in through the window screens. Some of the blue tape was peeled away, like it had dried out and couldn't stick anymore. The overall impression I got from looking around was a project that had stopped abruptly.

They had money problems, I knew that. My Army pay went to them, as I had directed. My intention had been to help my parents through hard times, even if the economy crashed, the US Army would continue to send out pay checks. The checks might be delayed, and my parents might be surprised by a notice that, through no fault of my own, I had mistakenly been overpaid for the past sixteen months so my next two paychecks would be zero. But overall, they would have a steady income if they needed it. Several times, I had urged them to use the money that was piling up in their bank account, explaining that the government was actually getting a good deal from my service. While I was away, I was not consuming meals on base, was not using military health care facilities or Tricare, was really not costing the taxpayers anything, other than, you know, fear and anxiety.

But, of course, my parents had not touched a dime of my money, even when they needed it. Both my father and mother had lost their jobs. The big co-generation plant in Milliconack had closed, throwing my father out of work. He looked for a job farther south, though the drive to Bangor would be a killer, the plan was for him to come home on weekends. But around that time, the *Flying Dutchman* was officially declared overdue to return from our survey trip to find a beta site, and there was widespread panic around the world. The cover story, of the *Dutchman* being flown by our buddies the Thuranin, broke down completely, and suddenly the name 'Joe Bishop' became infamous. My father was turned away from every place he contacted about work, and was basically told not to bother applying. At the same time, my mother's employer had to let her go, so many news people and protestors harassed her at work that the place had to shut down. They had federal protection at first, that trailed off after a while, as town residents got tired of roadblocks and checkpoints, and helicopters flying around at night, just to protect two not-very-popular citizens. Joe Bishop had gone from local hero to someone the town wanted to forget about. When the Barney ice cream truck memorial in the town square was firebombed one night, that was the last straw. My parents retreated to live in my uncle Edgar's old fishing shack on Masackett Lake. Hardly anyone lived there, and the only road in was a dirt track, so the state police could position a patrol car there to keep out unwanted guests. Not that many protestors bothered to make the trip so far into the wilderness anyway. Other than black flies and mosquitoes and loneliness, it wasn't a bad place to be, until the winter.

What mattered now was they were back home. The name 'Joe Bishop' was not exactly celebrated, but there were fewer wackadoodle nuts who cared enough to bother my parents. They had driven down to their house, while I was being debriefed at Fort Carson, and this time they had a security team of military police from the 10th Mountain, my old unit. When I heard that, I kind of got choked up with emotion. At some point, I needed to stop at Fort Drum, to thank them properly.

The money was not an issue, I fixed that by asking Skippy to put my parents on his payroll as 'consultants' or some bullshit like that. The idea upset my parents and made me uneasy, hopefully it would be temporary. Skippy, of course, didn't care about such a small amount of money, and I didn't ask about the source of funds.

"Understand what, Dad?" I asked in response.

"It's over, isn't it? The war?" He squeezed my mother's shoulder as he spoke. "Our part in the war."

"No," I rolled in my hand the still-cold can of Lester Cornhut's Paradise Pale Ale. Dave had given me a case, and I brought two four-packs to my folks, my father enjoyed a good beer. He had sipped from his can and declared it delicious, I noted the can had sat untouched since the first sip. Truthfully, I didn't much feel like drinking either. The conversation was too depressing to encourage friendly drinking. My parents had been telling me how they were hounded by the media and protestors, received death threats, and finally been chased out of their home. My sister and her new husband had been forced to leave Boston for southern New Hampshire. They both worked mostly from home, but her husband had to go into the office in the I-49 tech corridor, and sometimes he found a reporter or 'concerned citizen' waiting for him in the parking lot. My sister was understandably scared, my parents were frightened for her, and none of them blamed me. Yet it was my fault, and I wanted to fix it.

The problem was, I couldn't fix everything.

"Not exactly," I said, and used my favorite delaying technique of taking a drink, that time it was beer instead of coffee.

"Joseph, we have nukes now. *Elder* weapons," my father looked at me, pleading. "Skippy told us about them. Those weapons can tear *stars* apart."

"They can. That's *all* they can do. Dad, Mom, we are safe from extinction. Anything beyond that?" I put my hands on the table. "Listen, Dad. Imagine you have a gun, that could kill the enemy, but pulling the trigger would kill you also. The enemy starts poking you with a stick. Keeps poking you, over and over. Until you're bleeding. You're bleeding and it hurts but you're *alive*."

"At some point," my father's jaw was clenched. "I *would* pull the trigger on the son of a bitch."

"What if firing the gun also killed Mom? And everyone you know."

"*Shiiiiit*," he sighed. I knew he was upset because he snatched up the beer, and downed half of it in one gulp. "But you have *Valkyrie* now."

"Yeah. One ship. It can't be everywhere. Eventually, soon, *Valkyrie* will need heavy maintenance. We'll need to fly somewhere and strip the ship down, to rebuild it. That can't happen here, the enemy might be watching. We do have a plan," I lied. It wasn't quite a lie. UNEF was considering a plan, or many possible plans. Deciding which plan to implement, and getting every country's buy-in and support, was the trick. Plus, you know, making the plan work. As the old saying goes, the enemy also makes plans, damn them.

"Joseph," my mother put her hand on mine. "Let's talk about something else. Not about war, there's been too much of that."

"OK, Mom," I set the beer down. "That would be great." My father also looked relieved.

"Skippy hinted," my mother looked straight at me. "That there might be a girl?"

Shit. I wanted to strangle that sneaky little beer can. "Maybe. We're seeing where things are going." Margaret was with her parents that same day, we had both agreed not to mention our relationship yet. I wanted to protect her, until we had more time together, and decided whether we wanted to move to the next stage in our relationship. No, I do not mean the 'Pottery Barn' stage. I mean the 'telling our parents about us' stage.

Now Skippy had short-circuited everything.

"There *might* be a girl, Mom. It's a new thing. Can we talk about it later?"

My mother looked a bit disappointed and hurt, she also knew not to push me. I would tell her about Margaret, once I knew what to tell her. Once I knew what was going on with our relationship.

In my parent's kitchen, I was making an afternoon snack. My father and I had just come back from fishing, which involved a whole lot of paddling a canoe across a lake into a gusty wind, and not a lot of catching fish, because fish are stupid. My arms were tired, and I was hungry. We had brought meatloaf sandwiches for lunch, but a wave slapped me in the face and made me drop most of my sandwich into the lake. Of course, a couple big bass came up to eat the floating sandwich, while ignoring the bait on my hook. The only time I even thought a fish was nibbling on the bait, was when the hook got caught on weeds. So, we came back with zero fish.

Stupid fish.

It didn't matter. The point of fishing was to drink beer and spend time with my father. When we got back, my father went to the garage to put away the fishing gear, while I went to the house for a snack. Searching the pantry, I found a can of brown bread, and jars of peanut butter and Fluff. The bread popped out of the can, I sliced it and put it in the toaster. When it was warm and slightly crispy, I slathered peanut butter on one piece and Fluff on the other. "Mmmmm," the taste made me roll my eyes, I mean that in a good way.

"Ugh, Joe," Skippy said through the phone in my pocket. "How can you eat that? Fluff is just pure sugar."

"It is pure *deliciousness*," I retorted. "It's a superfood, Skippy."

"Super- Maybe you need to look up the definition of that term. A superfood is-"

"Yeah, antioxidants, blah, blah, blah. Listen, Skippy, when you eat stuff like kale or acai berries or whatever, your body is like 'Being healthy is not worth it if I have to eat this crap'. But, when you eat a Fluffernutter, your body says '*Now* I have something to live for'! So, Fluff is a superfood. Like pizza, or tacos."

"*Pizza* and *tacos*?"

"Would *you* want to live, if you couldn't eat pizza or tacos?"

"*I* can't eat anything, you moron."

"Oh. Sorry. You don't know what you're missing."

"Like heartburn and cholesterol?"

"Good*bye*, Skippy."

"Hey, buddy, I forgot to ask," I said to Skippy that night. "How is your opera coming along?" That was a blatant lie. I had not forgotten to ask him, I had avoided that subject as long as I felt possible. It was better for me to mention the opera and get credit for pretending to care, than for him to pout and get pissed off at me for neglecting one of his great passions. Asking Skippy about his musical compositions was like poking a hornet's nest with a stick; you need a plan to get away as quickly as possible. My plan was to pretend I just remembered an important UNEF meeting, when I got to the point where I just couldn't stand listening to him blabber on and on any longer.

"Opera? Oh, which one?"

"Uh, the uh-" Shit. That I had forgotten. He had more than one opera in progress. What the hell were they about? There was the one about the 1932 Manhattan phone book, and- "Uh, the Homefront one?" I guessed. Had he stopped work on that? Crap, I should have paid more attention.

"Oh, that. Yeah, I put that aside for the moment. Actually, all my operatic work is presently on hold. Yes, I understand that is a tragic loss to the artistic community, and that millions of monkeys are crying out to hear my unique vision."

"Somehow," I mumbled, "we will manage to persevere. Uh," I asked, anxious to change the subject before he got 'inspired' or whatever and decided to resurrect his crappy music. "What are you working on now?"

"Movie soundtracks, Joe."

"Movie- Uh, soundtracks? What?"

"Oh, right, puh-*lease* spare me your pretentious, condescending attitude. Oh, sure, you think that real composers, real artists do not lower themselves to work on commercial projects. Well, I have news for you, Mister Snobby Snob."

"Sorry," I mumbled, though I did not give a shit what composers did or didn't do.

"The true ground-breaking compositions are being done in *soundtracks* now, Joe. A great soundtrack can make a mediocre film something special. Without an evocative score, the best script and performances simply fall flat. You should think about *that* the next time you disparage any composer who chooses to work in an alternative medium."

"Jeez, Skippy, all I did was ask a question."

"Hmmph," he sniffed. "It was the *way* you asked it."

There was absolutely no point to arguing with him, so I dropped it. "What movie are you writing the soundtrack for?"

"I'm starting with the one about *me*, of course."

"A- a movie about you? When did-"

"I wrote a script, several versions of scripts actually, and there is great interest in Hollywood. Ugh, I have been *so* busy getting this project off the ground."

"Wow." For once, I was glad that I asked Skippy about one of his side projects. "You are making a movie about us, the Merry Band of Pirates? Who will play me?"

"Gosh, well, heh heh, who could play such a part, Joe? That is asking a lot for any actor. Really, it's not fair. Maybe we should just-"

"You little shithead," I gasped with sudden understanding. "You *cut me out* of your freakin' movie?"

"Hey, the story is about *me*, Joe. My sidekick is not-"

"*Sidekick*? That's what you think I-"

"Joe, listen. It may be tough to hear, but your story would simply not be believable to the audience."

"It doesn't have to be believable. Hell, I can barely believe it, but it *did* happen."

"You know that, and I know that. Or, you know the bullshit fantasy version you've created in your own head. But, the public has seen you being interviewed. They *know* you are a doofus. No way will they buy a script where *you* are the hero."

"So, your solution is to write me out of the story?"

"No, of course not," he scoffed. Then immediately backtracked. "Not entirely. The producers want to replace your part with a cute little monkey named 'Joe'. Not an actual monkey, of course, they are *impossible* to work with. We'll do motion-capture, and CGI in the monkey during post-production."

"Wait. What producers? Someone is actually making a movie about you?"

"I am considering multiple offers, Joe, I haven't signed any deal yet."

"I cannot believe you wrote me out of the script."

"Don't take it personally. Hollywood is all about money, Joe. You are a controversial person, whereas I am universally loved and admired."

I made a gagging sound. "Yeah, that's what I was going to say."

"Sorry, Joe. Everyone I talked to so far emphasized that we need to move quickly, and get the movie out before, you know."

"Before what?"

"Um. Well, this is just awkward."

"Before. *What?*"

"Before you, you know. You screw up again and cause a major disaster. Once that inevitably happens, somehow *I* will get the blame, and no one will want to watch a movie about me. That is *totally* unfair, but you don't hear *me* whining about it. Maybe you should take a lesson from that."

"Oh my G- You just assume I'm going to screw up big-time?"

"Um-"

"You treasonous little shithead."

"Hey, it's not *my* fault. I'm just projecting forward, based on your history. Besides, we both know that the Universe hates you. Do you seriously think the Universe saw that you got a stash of Elder weapons and said 'Well that darned Joey beat me for sure, time to give up'? No way, Jose. The Universe can't *wait* to show you who is boss, and it ain't Joe Bishop."

"Crap."

"Am I right?"

"Damn it," I sighed. "I, I actually cannot argue with you about that."

"Whoo-hoo! Can I get an Amen?"

"*No*, you can't get an Amen. What the hell is *wrong* with you? You know what? Go make your stupid movie, see if I care."

"Cool! Um, to be clear, you *don't* care, right?"

"Go away, Skippy."

Being at my parents' house was great, really great.
Really.
It was great.
Shit.
OK, being with my folks again was great, I just wasn't able to *relax* at all. My phone would have rung non-stop if Skippy had not intercepted most of the calls, and most of the time I had to take a call, it was people asking for things I couldn't give them, like answers about-

Heidy-ho there, filthy monkeys! Tis I, Skippy the Magnificent.
I will pause to let you compose yourselves, from the shock that I would waste my precious time talking to you.

Ready?

I know, you still can't believe it. Suck it up and pay attention, because I'm not going to repeat myself.

OK, so, the reason I need to honor you with my presence is because, as usual, Joe is telling the story all wrong. So, ignore his blah blah blah, and I'll give you the truth.

What is unusual is this time, he is not telling you some bullshit to make himself look like a hero. This time, Joe is pretending everything is fine, and not relating most of the awful shit he went through.

The debriefing at Fort Carson was not easy like he said, it was brutal, and went on for-EH-ver. The interrogation only stopped because I crashed the base computer network, and the electrical grid, and pretty much everything in a ten-mile radius that operated on electricity.

Listen, Joe did this to himself, so I only have a limited amount of sympathy for him. The politicians who treat Joe like shit? He kind of asked for it. When we first came to Earth and kicked ass, freeing your miserable mudball of a planet from the Kristang, every political leader who knew the truth wanted to be Joe's best friend. Then, we came back after our SpecOps mission, having saved the world a *second* time, and Joe was bragging about it, like he expected a commendation. The actual reaction from UNEF leadership was 'WTF? You told us Earth was safe the *first* time'. Since then, every time the Merry Band of Pirates does something worth celebrating, Joe has to hold up his hand and say 'Uh, heh heh, we shmaybe have a problem'. *Again*. Many people have been burned by praising Joe, only to watch their credibility and careers go down in flames, when Joe inevitably announces he failed to consider long-term consequences, and we are all doomed. *Again*.

So, I have sympathy for the guy, to a point. He is my buddy, and part of being a friend is recognizing that your friend is a short-sighted, reckless knucklehead.

He is also my friend, and while he usually tells the story all wrong, part of the time, he is not giving himself enough credit. Joe talks a lot about playing videogames, and he does that sometimes, not often. He also works *hard*. When he's not reading or writing reports, he's exercising in the gym, or keeping his skills current in a flight simulator, or taking training to operate one of the stations on the bridge. Or he is reading about our enemies, trying to understand their history, the capabilities and characteristics of their ships and weapons, their typical strategies and tactics, so we might have an advantage when we encounter them in combat. Yes, he is a dumbass, but no more than the typical monkey.

Anyway, Joe seriously needed a break, and Margaret also seriously needed a break, and I was hoping that a week of exposure to 100% pure Grade-A Joe Bishop would make her realize what a *horrible* mistake she was making.

I cleared their calendars and booked them on a vacation in the South Pacific, where they would have a chance for some privacy.

CHAPTER FIFTEEN

To get a break, and have some time alone together, Margaret and I went to a cluster of tropical islands in the South Pacific. Technically, I guess that is called an 'archipelago', or maybe it's just an atoll? Whatever. I won't say where exactly, it is somewhere in French Polynesia. That was Skippy's idea, he planned the whole thing and for once, he did a great job. I suspect he pushed aside his usually attention-deficit absent-mindedness and put some actual effort and thought into the planning, because he would catch hell from Margaret if he screwed something up.

Why French Polynesia? Because it is nice that time of year, and mostly because nobody there knew us, and because the locals are French, they don't care about a pair of Americans. As a clever disguise, we wore baseball caps and sunglasses, and Skippy carefully edited the local media, including all internet traffic, to remove any reference to us and what we looked like. As far as the world outside our families knew, Margaret and I were on leave, somewhere in the good old US of A. Though she was on officially approved leave, some officious pain-in-the-ass dirtside, who hadn't gotten the memo, demanded that Adams check in at Quantico immediately.

Skippy crashed the guy's computer sixteen times in one hour.

He got the message.

What I expected was that we would be booked into a hotel, maybe one of those huts that are over the water. Instead, Skippy had rented a beachfront villa, and I understood why. We had a lot more privacy in our own house. Nobody would bother us the whole time, except once a week, a guy came by to clean the pool.

It was great, really great.

Really.

OK, maybe I'm lying.

When I heard that Margaret and I would be sharing a house, just the two of us, I broke out in the classic Joe Bishop flop-sweat. We did want some privacy, you know? But maybe a week with just the two of us was *too* much togetherness. What if I annoyed her? I know, that will never happen.

But what if it did?

What if we realized that, other than serving with the Merry Band of Pirates, we did not have much in common? What did Margaret Adams like to do in her free time? I had no idea.

"Um, Joe, hey," Skippy whispered in my ear. We were on a commuter flight from the main island, where we had landed a dropship in a remote area at night. Skippy faked the immigration paperwork for us. I do feel bad about that, but a commercial flight from L.A. was like eight hours, and we wouldn't have any privacy. Plus, UNEF Command would have insisted on sending a whole STAR team to babysit us. So, we snuck out, and Skippy covered our tracks. Whatever he wanted to talk about right then, he didn't want Margaret to hear. "Listen, numbskull, I took the liberty of having your villa stocked with basic items. You know, snacks, plus a variety of alcohol to help you seal the deal, if you know what I mean. Although, yeesh, Margaret would have to be super drunk to look at *you* and think 'Well hello there', so maybe-"

Jabbing a finger in my ear, I tried to knock the little earpiece loose, but it hung on tenaciously.

"-in the unlikely and truly tragic event that you get lucky- And if you do, I do *not* want any details, yuck- There is a bottle of lubricant in the bedside table. Although I do not understand why you monkeys call it 'LubriCANT'. Why would you advertise that something is not able to do the job? Shouldn't it be called 'LubriCAN'? That would make more sense. Man, sometimes I really wonder about your-"

With a zPhone cupped in one hand, I typed out 'Stop talking!' as a text and sent the message.

"OK, OK. Before I go, there is also a bottle of little blue pills for you in the bathroom, do *not* take more than one. You really shouldn't take any, but I know you are desperate, so-"

STOP TALKING!!!!! was my next text.

Mercifully, he stopped.

Margaret had noticed me frantically typing something on my phone, and leaned over to talk above the hum of the plane's engines. "If you are on social media again, then I am-"

"Just confirming the housing arrangements with Skippy," I told her, which was close enough to the truth.

"Separate bedrooms, right?" She looked at me.

Crap. She wanted us to sleep in separate-

"Joe!" She laughed. "The look on your face was *precious*."

"You scared the hell out of me," I admitted.

"Joe! Joe Joe Joe Joe-"

"*Gah*!" I spit out a mouthful of toothpaste, all over the bathroom mirror. We had just arrived at the villa, and it was as wonderful as Skippy described. "Crap, now I have to clean this thing. *What*?"

"For your, how shall I say this without gagging? Oops, too late, *hurk*," he made a retching sound. "Ugh, yuck."

"Skippy, *what* do you want? Is this important?"

"If it wasn't important, I wouldn't be wasting my very valuable time trying to help you. Although helping you with *this* kinda makes my skin crawl."

"Then don't."

"Believe me, I would love to avoid any knowledge of this heinous crime but, you are my buddy and, *damn* you need my help."

"Can you just *say* whatever it is?"

"OK, OK. Tonight, for your romantic interlude- Nope, I'm gonna hurl if I say *that* again. I know this is a special night for you, or you *hope* it is a special night. Would it help if I performed some romantic music, to get the two of you in the mood?"

"Oh for- *No*! It would not help."

"Not even a little bit?"

"No!"

"OK, hmm. I see that could be distracting. Margaret would be hearing me sing, and realize a man with actual talent is way better than the doofus she's with, so-"

"I do *not* need any help."

"Really?"

"Really."

"Hmm. Have you looked at yourself in the mirror recently?"

"I can't, because this mirror is covered with toothpaste."

"Trust me, the toothpaste is a *big* improvement."

"We do not need any music from *you*."

"Ah, gotcha."

"Thanks."

"*You* plan on singing to her."

"What? No, I-"

"That would be a *terrible* idea, Joe."

"Yeah, duh, that's why-"

"Although, hmm, your awful singing voice might make her forget about the waves of nausea for a while. How about-"

"Good*bye*, Skippy."

"Wait! I can coach you. Try this: *So I sing you to sleep, after the lovin', with a-*"

"Oof, now *I'm* gonna hurl. That is *not* appropriate."

"Yeah, you're right."

"Thank y-"

"*You* sing *her* to sleep? Riiiiiight. We both know *you* will be snoring after thirty seconds, while she lies there asking herself 'That's *it*?' and regretting her entire life."

"Go *away*, Skippy."

Coming up the stairs of the villa the next afternoon, I was singing a song that was stuck in my head, singing badly and loud, the only way I know how to sing. In my hands were two cold beers, Margaret and I were planning to sit out on the upper deck and chill for a while. To be truthful, I was hoping for another type of activity later, and no, I was not trying to get her drunk first. *She* asked for the beer, which is why I walked down to the cooler we kept by the door.

When I got to the top of the stairs, instead of seeing Margaret lounging outside, she was standing in the living room, glaring down at a pile of clothes on the floor. "Did *you*," she pointed to the offending articles of clothing. "Leave these here?"

OK, so. They were clearly my clothes. Still, from my time in the E-4 mafia, I instinctively wanted to deny everything. Maybe I could claim that someone had snuck into the place while we weren't looking. Or, maybe magical gnomes were trying to get me in trouble.

Hey that *could* happen, right?

Did I spit out a lame story? No. Joe Bishop is not stupid, and I can think fast when I need to. Sucking in a shocked breath, I quickly set the beers down on a table and dashed to the pile of clothes, kneeling beside them. "No!" I shouted. "Master Kenobi!"

"Ken-" Margaret stared at me. "Who?"

"Can't you see?" I whispered, pretending to look around the room for an intruder. "Someone struck down a Jedi master here. Only his clothes are left."

She cocked her head at me. "A *Jedi*?"

My response was a shrug. "There really is no other possible explanation. Don't worry, he will come back more powerful than you can possibly imagine."

She hid her face behind her hands while her shoulders shook. "You are *such* an idiot."

"I can't dispute that."

"Come here."

Sadly, we never got to drink those beers while they were cold.

On our second day on the island, we packed up the tiny car that Skippy rented for us. It was a tiny SUV type of thing, with dents all over, and the driver's side window only went up or down if you used a hand to help the tired electric motor. The sticker on the back said it belonged to some local rental company I never heard of, but the thing ran OK, and more importantly, we both got a good laugh out of it.

Until Margaret insisted on driving.

She is a maniac.

Seriously, that woman should not have a license to drive anything.

We stopped at a roadside shack for lunch, and I drank water while she had a beer. That was my excuse to insist that I should drive, which was good for my blood pressure. Anyway, we got to the beach she had seen on a tourist map or brochure. It was supposed to be secluded, with great snorkeling right from shore.

I stopped the car. "This is it?"

She poked her head out her window. "That's what the sign says, I think. 'Plage' is the French word for 'beach'."

"The beach isn't the problem. Where do we park?"

"In the parking lot?" She suggested unhelpfully.

She pointed to a muddy, potholed wide spot off the road. It was big enough for maybe two cars, and in typical island fashion, five cars were already squeezed in there. I looked in the mirror for a place to park behind me. Nothing. "This is a parking NOT-a-lot."

That made her laugh, which is good. Wrestling the tiny car back and forth, I got it wedged in under a tree, halfway off the road. "I hope nobody hits it," I said as we got out.

She looked at the dents and rust. "How could anyone tell?"

"Good point. I'll get the bag, you got the towels?"

The beach was beautiful. The other people were spread out, so we did not have to see many French guys in tiny Speedo swimsuits unless we wanted to. I can't speak for Margaret, but I did *not* want to see that. It is a French island, so most of the women were topless. Did Margaret take her top off? That is none of your business, you perverts. All I will say is, I am the luckiest man the world.

The only glitch in our day was a brief tropical shower that swept over us, we just stuffed towels in the bag and went into the water until it was gone. Then, she wanted to cover up so she didn't get a sunburn, and she dug around in the bag she had packed.

"What's wrong?" I asked.

"I thought I packed a sarong in here."

"I am *so wrong* about your sarong," I winked.

"You are an ass," she laughed.

"If you buy one with an ugly pattern, it that a 'sorry sarong'?"

She threw a bag of crackers at my head.

Then she kissed me.

It was a great day.

Until she insisted on driving back to the villa.

My hands are still shaking from that death-defying experience.

I was feeling good. Like, *good*. The best ever. Like, I didn't think it was possible to be that happy. So happy, it scared me that I would somehow screw it up.

Of course, I did.

After a swim, I went back into the villa to shower and get changed before we went out for dinner. Coming into the villa, I saw a pile of freshly folded towels on the stairs, and, being a good guy, took the hint that I shouldn't track sand all over the place. Going back outside, I kicked off my flipflops and washed my feet in the bucket of water by the door, then walked in and dried my feet off by throwing one of the towels on the floor and stomping my feet around on it. Going the extra mile, I put the now-wet towel outside, where it really should have been, and stepped over the pile of other towels to go upstairs.

The first sign of trouble was when I heard a screech while I was in the shower. Margaret probably saw a spider, I thought. This was my opportunity to be a manly man and squash a bug for her.

I am a dumbass. If Margaret saw a spider, the *spider* would have screeched and run away.

Anyway, I was out of the shower and looking around for a clean towel, when she walked in with a stack of towels. My first instinct, because I am a guy, was to flex for her.

Here's a Pro Tip for you guys out there: do *not* do that. Unless you're doing it as a joke, which I wasn't. Or unless she gives you a 'Well hello there' look, which she definitely was not.

The look on her face should have clued me in, but, again, I am a guy, so...
The towel smacked me in the face when she threw it at me.
Even that wasn't enough of a clue.
Hey, I was standing there buck naked, and she was wearing a beach cover-up and maybe not much else. My brain wasn't working properly.
"Thanks," I muttered with the towel draped over my head, drying my hair. When I came up for air, she had set the other towels down on the counter and had her hands on her hips, glaring at me. "What?" I asked.
"Did you see the stack of towels on the stairs?"
"Yeah. Hey, I left one outside, so we can dry our feet off," I said, expecting praise for my clever thinking.
"Did you wonder *why* the towels were there?"
"Uh, sure? I figure that, after you washed and dried and folded them, you took a break."
"A *break*?"
"Yeah. Hey, don't worry. We're not on the clock here. I knew you would bring the towels up here eventually, when you got around to it."

Here is another valuable Pro Tip for the guys out there: that was NOT the right answer.
Not even close.
I mean, like, the right answer was on the other side of the freakin' universe.
The worst thing is, she knew I really thought that *was* the right answer.
In case you still need a clue, because to be honest, I did, here it is:
She washed and dried and folded those towels, because we were running out of clean towels, and the villa sadly was not equipped with magical laundry elves. After her washing, and drying and folding the towels, she wanted *me* to carry them up the stairs.
I know. Women, right?
Why didn't she just *ask* me to bring the towels up the stairs?
Because it is a *relationship* thing.
Hey, I don't fully understand it either, but I will try to explain, and I don't have any crayons, so just listen. The guys, I mean. You women can go, do, whatever it is women do when guys are cluelessly mansplaining stuff.
Apparently, if I were a decent human being, and if I truly cared about her, my stupid brain should have said something like 'Hey, I should be a decent human being, and a full partner in this relationship, and do at least half of the work'. I should have at least carried the folded towels up the stairs, instead of stepping over them. Better, I should have noticed that we were running out of towels, and at least thrown some wet towels in the dryer.
There are many layers to this issue, like an onion, and like an onion, there can be tears involved when you peel back the layers. There is sort of a scoresheet, so pay attention.
One point, if I had brought the towels up the stairs, so she wouldn't yell at me.
Two points, if I had brought the towels up the stairs, because I care about her.

Three points, if I had brought the towels up the stairs, because that is just the decent thing to do, and she wants a decent guy to care about.

What was *my* score?

Negative infinity.

I did not put any effort into carrying the towels, therefore I was not willing to put any effort into a relationship, therefore I did not really care about her.

Guys, listen, I know what you are thinking: bitches be crazy, right?

Crap.

That was also not the right thing to say.

Women are not crazy, they're just different. I kind of like that difference, you know? So, here's the deal: I should have taken action, not to help her, but to help *us*. We ran out of towels, and someone needed to take care of the problem. You know the worst part? If I was sharing the house with another guy, I would have said 'Dude we are out of towels, I'm throwing these in the laundry'. Then I would have said 'Hey don't be a lazy ass, carry these towels up and put them in the closet' or wherever towels live when they're not being used.

I did not do that, because I was sharing the house with a woman, and my sexist brain said 'That is women's work', so I assumed Margaret would do it.

Anyway, there I was, standing naked in the shower, with a towel over my head, and her glaring at me with her hands on her hips, and I was trying to figure out what to say. "I'm sorry," I said, which is always a good start. "Where are the towels supposed to go? Here, or downstairs?"

"You don't *know*?"

"A stack of towels appears like magic next to the door, every morning before we go to the beach," I explained. "I don't see where you get them."

"Oh."

"If we're doing laundry, should I throw the bed sheets in the wash? We got sand in there somehow."

Her expression softened just a bit. "You should also wash that one pair of bathing trunks you have been wearing *every* day."

"OK. I only have two bathing suits."

"We could buy more for you."

"You want to go shopping today?"

"*You* are volunteering for shopping?"

"Yeah. I should get a souvenir for my folks. And we never got a real wedding present for Simms, you know?"

Looking back later, I think what bailed me out of the mess is when I said '*we* never got a wedding present for Simms'. Like, that is something Margaret and I should do together, because we are together. No, I didn't say that only to get out of the mess I got myself into. I said it automatically, because I thought of us as a couple and that is something couples do.

That was the right thing to say.

I threw the sheets and some clothes into the washer, then we went shopping, and had lunch in town. It was nice. Really. I am not into shopping, but it was nice being with her, and she is into shopping, so it was nice seeing her happy.

When we got back, I put the sheets on the clothesline to dry, and when they were dry, I made the bed, and somehow there was still *sand in the freakin' sheets*.

I suspect Skippy was screwing with me.

The morning of our last full day on vacation, we went to the beach. Just to hang out, swim, maybe drink a festive beverage or two. That afternoon, I wanted to take her sailing, if the weather was right. I got our chairs set up, and stuck an umbrella in the sand, tilting it so the breeze didn't carry it away to go bouncing down the beach like a medieval weapon. With the chairs and umbrella set up, I slathered myself with sunscreen, stuck the bottle back in a bag, and popped open an adult beverage.

"Joe," Margaret said in a tone of voice that even I recognized as annoyance.

"What?" I held up the beer. "Yeah, it's before Noon, but I'm on vacation."

"It's not that," she turned away, her eyes moist.

Wow. She was upset about something. Like, seriously upset.

Crap. She was happy during the drive to the beach. Her driving terrified me, but she had a grin on her face the whole time. She even found a good parking spot near the beach. What the hell had I done wrong after we got out of the car?

"What? Margaret, come on, what is it? Please tell me."

She half turned back, looking at me with a side-eye. "You put the sunscreen away after you used it."

"Oh, yeah, OK. The bottle gets sticky and I didn't want to get sand on it." A thought occurred to me. There were towels in the bag. "Should I have put it in a plastic bag?"

She sighed. "No. That's not it."

I reached out to touch her arm. "Then what?"

"You didn't ask if I needed sunscreen."

"Uh, well-"

"Because I'm *black*, you don't think I needed to use sunscreen?"

Holy.

Shit.

This *was* serious.

I felt like I had stepped on a landmine and just heard the 'click' of the detonator activating.

Whatever I said in response, I had to think very carefully about it.

Also, stupid brain, do not take forever to think what to say.

Fortunately, my stupid brain did not need to think, because I already had a good answer.

"I know you need sunscreen," I said quietly. "I saw you putting it on before we left the villa this morning."

She half turned toward me. "You did?"

"Yes. You did it while I was shaving." My vacation beard had to go, because it let water into my snorkel mask.

"Oh."

Something told me that sunscreen was not the real issue. "Is this something we should talk about?" Part of me, I swear to God, wanted to whine 'But I am on *vacation*'. I didn't want to have a difficult conversation right then. Really, I didn't want to have a difficult conversation at all, ever, but especially not during my first actual vacation in years.

Another deep breath, another sigh from her. "Yes." Turning to look me straight in the eyes, she asked, "Are you ready for a relationship with a black woman?"

"I thought I was *in* a relationship with a black woman," I said cautiously.

"Be serious, please. You keep talking about how you're from the North Woods of Maine. Before you joined the Army, had you even met a black person?"

"Hey, my hometown isn't what you think." Then I said possibly the dumbest thing that ever came out of my mouth. "One summer, we had a *taco* truck. Uh-" Immediately, I realized just how stupid that sounded. "Maybe that was not the best example."

"Ya think?" She snapped, but there was a twinkle in her eye. "I'll give you points for trying."

"I am trying. Listen, honey, OK." It was my turn to take a deep breath. "Sure, in my hometown, 'ethnic diversity' sort of means your cousin married a French guy from Quebec. But I was born in Boston."

She gave me that 'Oh really?' eyebrow thing that women do.

"Forget all that. We've served together for years. You *know* me."

"I do."

"We're cool, then?" I reached out to touch her arm, she didn't pull away.

"This could be difficult."

"You're worried that I can't handle difficult things?" I snorted. "Riiiight. Because I always choose to do things the *easy* way," I rolled my eyes. "Have you ever seen me run from a fight?"

She pursed her lips and thought for a moment. "No. Not even when you should," she added with a little grin. "Oh! You are so damned *cute*."

"It's a curse but, I deal with it." Feeling like I had dodged a bullet, I wanted to move on with our day in tropical paradise. Really, I did not want to continue *that* conversation. "Hey. We need to talk about this."

"Because it's important to me?"

"Because it's important to *us*."

Guys, here's another Pro Tip for you: *that* was exactly the right thing to say.

We sat back on our blankets, sipping drinks, watching the crystal blue water, and *talked*. Really talked, about important stuff. An hour later, she wanted to go swimming, so we dove into the water together.

CHAPTER SIXTEEN

"Uh, hey, Skippy?" I whispered into my phone later that afternoon, while hiding in the downstairs bathroom. This was a conversation I did not want Margaret hearing.

"Hi, Joe, what's up?"

"It's all g-"

"If what is '*up*' with you is related to those little blue pills, please do *not* tell me, I really don't-"

"It's about money, you jackass."

"Money? OK, I am intrigued. Although if you have a business proposition for me, you really should talk to my business development people at Stratton Oakmont in New York. They screen out all the wackos, so I don't waste my time with-"

"I do not have a deal for you. I want you to help me."

"Help you? With money? Why? All your Army pay went to your parents, as you directed, so-"

"I *know* that," I hissed, straining to hear if the creaking sound I heard was Margaret coming down the stairs. "There is a fancy French restaurant on the island, and-"

"Of course it's a *French* restaurant, you ninny. You're in French Polynesia. I hope you're not expecting a Taco Bell on the-"

"Will you *please* stop talking? This is a fancy place, right on the ocean. I made a reservation to take Margaret there tonight. We've been having a really great time, and I want to make it special for her, you know?"

"I think I understand. If you truly want to make it special for her, you should stay home and send her to the restaurant with Gaspard, the guy who cleans your pool. He has great hair, and those abs, wow, they-"

"I want her to have a special time with *me*, you ass."

"*Really*?" He snorted. "Good luck with that. In that case, I will buy her one-way ticket on the express train to Disappointmentville."

"Ah!" I felt like throwing the phone across the room, but it was a small bathroom. "Listen to me. I made the reservation, but now I realize I don't have enough money on my debit card."

"So use your credit card, *duh*."

"I don't *have* a credit card, *DUH*. It got canceled when I was declared dead, on one of our missions."

"Oh. Yeah. I forgot about that. Was I supposed to fix that for you?"

"Yes!"

"Oops. Well, my bad. Sucks for you, huh?"

"Can I get an advance on my salary?"

"What salary?"

"My pay as a colonel in the Skippistan armed forces."

"Huh. We never discussed pay and benefits, Joe."

"We-" Shit, he was right.

"You wish to negotiate compensation, right now? Please, Joe, you're sitting on a toilet. Have some dignity."

"I'm only in here so I can talk privately, you little shithead."

"Shithead? *This* is how you open negotiations?"

"Can we *please* talk about this later? Our reservation is in two hours, and I need to shower and get dressed. All I need is cash for tonight, I'll pay you back later."

"OK, but I don't understand why you don't just use your Skippicard."

"Skip- What is a Skippicard? I don't have a-"

"It's in the wallet on your phone, numbskull."

Clicking that icon, I saw a new item in the wallet. Sure enough, it was a Skippicard. "Oh. Thanks. Uh, what's the limit on this?"

"Two hundred."

That seemed low, but I wasn't going to argue. Trying to calculate dinner in my head, plus a bottle of wine, and a tip- Oops. Maybe I could just have a salad, and say I wasn't very hungry.

Crap.

This was not going to be a special evening at all.

"Wait," I thought of another problem. "Is that two hundred in US, or European currency?"

"US, Joe. I know it hurts your brain to calculate conversions."

"Two hundred dollars might not be enough to-"

"Two hundred *dollars*?" He laughed.

"Oh shit." I suddenly felt very cold. "Did you mean two hundred *cents*? What kind of useless debit card is-"

"Two hundred *million*, you knucklehead."

"Two- t- two hundred million?" I stared at the phone icon in horror, afraid I might accidentally click the wrong button and buy a yacht. Or a small country. Carefully, I closed the wallet icon.

"Um, is that not enough?" He asked. "OK, I just upped the funding to six hundred million, but if you plan to bust the limit, let me know so I can-"

"What kind of debit card has *six hundred million dollars* on it?"

"A Skippicard does, Joe. Am I not special?"

"You- You are beyond special. Can you drop the limit to something like, uh, six hundred thousand?"

"Why would I do that?"

"Please, humor me. I don't want to be tempted."

"If you insist, but eight million is as low as I can go on that card. I have standards."

"Thanks. I mean that. You saved me tonight."

"Is there anything else? I have Gaspard's phone number, if you want."

"I do *not* want."

"You're sure? He is dreamy, Joe. Maybe you should think about what Margaret wants, and not your own selfish-"

"Good*bye*, Skippy."

"Skippy," Margaret called, cupping her hand over the phone, though she was in the upstairs bathroom and the door was closed behind her.

"Good afternoon, Gunnery Sergeant. What can I-"

"I'm off duty, call me 'Margaret'. I need your help."

"Oh, thank *God*. I thought you would never ask. OK, Joe is in the downstairs bathroom, you can sneak down the stairs if you are super quiet-"

"I am not going down the stairs."

"All right, but to go out the upper-level window, you will need to tie bedsheets together to make a rope. Be careful, it is a long drop and there are rocks if you fall, so-"

"*What* are you talking about?" She stared at her phone.

"You have come to your senses and want to get away from Joe, right? I can have a taxi waiting for-"

"I am *not* trying to escape."

"*Really?*"

"Really."

"Huh. Why not? Oh, I get it. You are *not* trying to escape, riiiiiight. Whistle twice if he locked you in the bathroom, I will-"

"*He* didn't do anything, I locked myself in the bathroom."

"Um, you need a locksmith to get yourself out? I can-"

"I can unlock the door by myself, Skippy."

"Hmm. OK, then you want me to talk some sense into you? Listen, Joe is a dumb, smelly monkey and you can certainly do better, girlfriend. You should-"

"I am not your 'girlfriend', and I *like* Joe."

"Wow. This is more serious than I thought. Hold the phone while I bring in a professional."

"Will you please *shut up* and listen to me?"

"If you insist, but I really think you should seek help and-"

"*You* are going to need help if you don't stop talking."

"Shutting up now."

"Great." She took a long breath. "We are going to dinner in two hours, and I have nothing to wear."

"Um-"

"Do *not* argue with me."

"You packed a whole suitcase full of clothes."

"I don't have anything *nice* to wear."

"Um, you packed three dresses. Plus a very nice set of slacks, and-"

"This is an occasion for a dress."

"Right," he said slowly. "And?"

"And, I hate two of the dresses I brought with me. The one that I might wear had a loose thread, I tried cutting off the thread and pulled out the seam. Now it has a huge hole along the side."

"Can you fix it? There should be a little sewing kit in the-"

"I already tried that. All I did was make it worse, and pricked my finger so I got blood on the dress. It won't come out. I, I can't-" She sat on the corner of the tub and put her face in her hands, wiping away tears. "I am a Marine, Skippy. I am also a woman."

"Um, yes, I am aware of those facts."

"Do you know what that means? All day, I wear the most unflattering clothes. I want to feel special. I want to feel *pretty* for a change, damn it," she slapped a hand on the tub.

"Margaret, you could wear a potato sack and Joe would think you're beautiful."

"*I* want to think I'm beautiful. Women have body-image issues, Skippy, I'm no different. Acting confident all the time doesn't mean I *am*. This is a special night and I want to dress up nicely for my man."

"Your ma- You mean *Joe*? Oops, sorry, I just threw up in my mouth a little."

"You are not helping. *Help* me."

"Um, sorry. What can I do? How about this: that dress does not make you look fat."

"I want *actual* help, Skippy."

"Please tell me what to do."

"Get a new dress for me."

"*Now?*"

"Now. Right now. Dinner is in two hours, so you have about ninety, no, sixty minutes. I need time to get ready."

"Gosh, um, how am I supposed to do that?"

"You're still aboard *Valkyrie*, aren't you? Fabricate one."

"No can do, sorry. The fabricators are all being used to crank out replacement parts for the ship. Switching over to make fabric would take longer than you have. Plus, just the flight down in a dropship would take more than an hour. I would like to help, but this is imposs-"

"Skippy?"

"Yes."

"You are Skippy the *Magnificent*, are you not?"

"Yes," he answered warily.

"Make. It. Happen. Whatever you gotta do, do it. I am counting on you. I *need* you."

"Shit. OK, I'll think of something. Can you give me an idea what kind of dress you want?"

"Something not horribly tacky."

"Can you be a *little* bit more specific?"

"Imagine the dress *you* would make for me, and do the opposite."

"Gotcha. Um, I need your measurements. Prop your phone up on the counter and take off your clothes."

"Skippy, if this is-"

"Margaret, I am *not* enjoying this. I tasked a submind to take your measurements, because I don't want to have that image in my memory."

"Fine," she wriggled out of her clothes and tossed them aside. "Should I turn around?"

"Yes, please, and stand naturally, don't pose for the camera. Um, OK, got it, thanks. Sixty minutes, huh?"

"Fifty-eight, now."

"Gottagobyetalktoyoulater."

The manager at Fifi's Boutique was startled when her phone rang, loudly. Her employees glanced at her discretely at the interruption, because they had all been warned to turn *their* phones off or keep them on vibrate while working. Fifi's was the most exclusive shop on the island, and the customers expected to be pampered, catered to, and not be interrupted when they were purchasing overpriced merchandise.

Madeline blushed and strode purposefully over to the desk, where she ended the call without looking at the screen. "I am terribly sorry, Madame," she apologized to the customer who was waiting. "It will not happ-"

"Hey!" The phone call had in fact, *not* ended. "Hey! I need to talk with you! Pick up the phone!"

"Excuse me," Madeline's face turned red, this time not from embarrassment, but anger. Holding the phone to her ear, she hissed "Whoever this is, I do not have-"

"I need a dress and I need it fitted or tailored or whatever you call it, right now," the voice said in French, with an atrocious English accent.

"Monsieur, this is not a-"

"Now. Like, *now now now*. I'll take the one on the end of the rack to your left, it-"

Turning the phone off, except it would not turn off, she stuffed it in a drawer and slammed it shut. "Someone played a silly joke on me, Madame, I am sor-"

"Hey!" The voice boomed over the store's speakers, as the soft music cut out. "I *said*, I need a dress, right now. The measurements are on your phone. The dress needs to be fitted *immediately*, and delivered. Gosh, wow, with delivery time, you need to have it ready in thirty-two minutes, and even that is cutting it close."

"Stop this!" Madeline stomped her foot, nearly breaking off the heel of one shoe. "I do not know who you are, but I am calling the police."

"How about one hundred thousand Euros, if you deliver on time?" The voice said.

"A hundred-" Madeline paused as the register made a soft 'BING' sound. Glancing at the display, she saw a sale had just rung up for a hundred thousand Euros. "Monsieur, this is most irregular, our tailor Jacques is busy with another order, he cannot-"

"Two-fifty, that's my final offer." The register 'binged' again, adding another hundred fifty thousand Euros, for a dress that retailed at an already outrageous seven hundred and forty Euros.

"JACQUES!" Madeline shouted, plucking the dress off the rack, the sputtering customer forgotten.

Margaret was in tears, sitting on the end of the tub, her hands shaking. Joe was on the bed, pleading with her to come out of the bathroom, while they talked through the door. That's enough, she wiped away her tears, standing up to look at herself in the mirror. The dress is ruined, she had to choose one of the other two, no matter how awful they looked on her. What had she been thinking when she bought a dress with horizontal-

A soft 'tap-tap' came from the window.

"Margaret," Skippy called from her phone.

She snatched it up, whispering and glancing at the time. "You have a dress for me?"

"Yes. A bot climbed up the wall and is holding it outside the window. The window frame is a bit rusty from the salty sea air, be careful."

"Where did you get the dress?"

"A shop in town, next to the Ritz-Carlton."

"You bought it off the *rack*?"

"It's fitted for you."

"Uh-huh. And you just happened to have a bot handy nearby?"

"I have several bots nearby, including two fully-armed combots hiding in the woods across the road, for security. There are too many nutcases in the world, even this far from civilization."

"*Why* didn't you call me? I was worried sick."

"I didn't want to make any promises until the dress was *there*. We had some slip-ups along the way. The delivery van almost ran over a goat, and- Forget all that. Do you like the dress?"

Reaching out and taking the box from the creepy spider bot, she set it down on the counter and opened it. Holding the dress up against her, she admired it in the mirror. "It is beautiful," she gushed, embarrassing herself with her girlish enthusiasm for a piece of cloth. "What is in the little box?" She lifted a smaller box, tied with a silk ribbon.

"The dress shop recommended earrings and a necklace to go with the dress," Skippy explained. "I think the dress shop and the jewelry store give each other kickbacks for referrals," he muttered. "Anyway, they are Australian fire opals, I hope you like them."

"*Like?*" She gasped, staring wide-eyed at the open box. "They are amazing. I *love* them. Skippy, I can't afford these."

"You don't have to."

"I'm not a *charity* case," she frowned.

"Consider all of it a down payment on what I owe to *you*."

"We can talk about this later."

"How about we pretend none of this ever happened? That's what *I* would like."

"Then we will never talk about it. Thank you."

"You're very welcome."

"Now, shoo," she waved at the creepy bot. "I have to get ready."

"Joe, I'm coming out," Margaret called to me through the door. I had been worried sick, so much that I could barely concentrate while playing a game on my phone while I waited for her.

"I've got my eyes covered," I said truthfully, holding both hands over my face.

"I'm ready, you can look now. What do you think?"

She was stunning.

Like, *stunning*.

Like, my brain was thinking 'is this really Gunnery Sergeant Adams'?

She was wearing makeup. Makeup. Subtle, like she knew how to put it on. That wasn't something the Marine Corps issued to her.

And jewelry. Tasteful, the, whatever they were, went perfectly with the dress. I think they went perfectly, but I'm a guy, so what do I know?

And the dress. It not only looked great on her, it made her skin positively *glow*.

"Well? Do you like it?"

I glanced at my watch. An actual, analog watch, on my wrist. Skippy had provided it for me. It felt odd to wear, but I had to admit, it looked a lot more elegant than a smartwatch.

"What?" She looked at me, adjusting one of her earrings.

"You look really great. I'm just wondering," I bounced on the edge of the bed. "Whether a quickie would wrinkle that dress."

"You are not getting a 'quickie'," she waggled a finger at me. "Not while I'm wearing this dress."

"I can fix *that*," I offered, being the gentleman that I am.

"You are *not* touching this dress. Besides, you got a quickie this morning."

"That wasn't a quickie," I defended myself. "OK. That," I stood up, walking around to admire her outfit. I had no idea she owned anything like that. "It looks amazing. *You* look amazing."

"Go get the car ready, you."

"Yes, Ma'am."

"Joe," Skippy whispered in my ear as I walked to the car to get it started, and the air conditioning on before Margaret got in. "I got you the best table in the house, right on the water. There should be a lovely sunset tonight."

"What?" I whispered. "They told me the only table left was near the freakin' kitchen."

"That *was* true. However, the people who were supposed to be at your new table sadly had to cancel their reservation for tonight. Their car would not start, and the taxi can't get to them because two trucks broke down, blocking the road to their hotel."

"*Two* trucks broke down, on the same road, at the same time?"

"Yeah. Weird, huh? Well, their loss is your gain. The table is now available. Plus, the maître-d' has gambling debts that I purchased from a local bookie called 'The Shark', so he has been most cooperative with me. Let me know if you are unhappy with the service tonight, I could bring in a few of The Shark's boys to rough him up a little and-"

"That will not be necessary. Uh, thanks, buddy."

"I think it's a huge mistake, making her go to dinner with *you*," he made a gagging sound. "There is still time to-"

"Good *night*, Skippy."

"Mm," she swirled the wine in her glass, frowned, and sipped it again. "This is not my favorite."

Shit. I had selected the wine, despite knowing next to nothing about wines.

No, that wasn't right. *Skippy* had suggested I order that wine, assuring me that it matched Margaret's 'flavor profile', whatever the hell that was.

The restaurant was perfect, and the staff treated us like royalty. Given the prices on the menu, the place probably did have actual royalty dining there. The maître-d' escorted us to our table personally, bringing two complimentary glasses of champagne. I almost ruined the evening by sneezing when champagne bubbles tickled my nose, but I snatched up a napkin in time.

The weather was perfect, we were going to see a sunset with no clouds on the horizon, with a gentle breeze making Margaret's bangs sway around her face.

There was nothing making the evening any less than perfect, until she tried the wine, and puckered her lips.

"You don't like," I studied the label again. "Peanut Gree-jhee-oh?" I guessed at the pronunciation, which was probably either French or Italian. Or Klingon, for all I knew.

"It depends," she set the glass down, smacking her lips like she was trying to get a bad taste out of her mouth.

"If you expected it to taste like peanuts," I stared at the label, "you're out of luck."

"Peanuts? Why would I-"

"It says right here," I pointed to the label. "It is pea-*NOT*. *No* peanuts."

She rolled her eyes and laughed. That was a good sign. "Joe, you are-"

"Does the gentleman have a problem with the wine?" The waiter asked, appearing suddenly.

"The gentleman," Margaret scowled at me, but there was a twinkle in her eyes. "Is an idiot. The wine is just fine."

"It's fine, but not to our liking," I explained. "Can you recommend another?"

The waiter's eyes narrowed, unsure if I was joking. And suspicious that I wanted to send the bottle back, after he had poured two full glasses for us.

Margaret protested. "Joe, you don't have to-"

"It's OK," I assured her. To the waiter, I added, "Any wine you suggest, please. Sorry about the mix-up."

His eyes brightened. "Are you having the lobster? Then I suggest-"

"Joe," she kicked me under the table. "Please, don't. You don't need to-"

Holding up the menu to shield my mouth from the waiter, I silently said 'Skippy is paying'.

"Oh," she smiled, and looked up at the waiter. "Then, please, yes. Any bottle from your renowned cellar, S'il vous plait."

When the waiter left, a broad smile on his face, she leaned across the table and whispered "Skippy is covering this dinner?"

"He doesn't know it yet, but, yes," I winked. "He gave me a debit card, a special one."

That prompted a side-eye from her. "How much is on it?"

"Let's put it this way: even the Pentagon couldn't blow that much money in an hour."

"Holy sh-" She put a hand to her mouth and giggled. "In that case, we are definitely having the lobster."

"I'll have a steak, too."

"Peanut Grigio," she laughed to herself. "How did I end up with such an idiot?"

"Just lucky, I guess? If you want, Skippy has the phone number of Gaspard the pool boy."

"Hmmmmm," she held that 'Hmm' a bit too long.

"Hey!" I objected.

"He *is* dreamy, Joe," she winked.

CHAPTER SEVENTEEN

"Hey, Simms," I tried to sound casual, but I suck at faking it. Even over the phone, I am sure she could tell I was lying. "How is your vacation? Or honeymoon?"

She sighed, even before she said anything. "It was going just fine, Sir."

"*Was*?"

"Before you called to ruin my day."

"I'm not- How do you know-"

"I know *you*."

"Fair enough."

"What is it this time?"

"Uh, I have an opportunity for you."

She must have set the phone down, or maybe she threw it across the room, because I could hear her cursing at me, but it was muffled. Still, I could hear that her vocabulary of swear words was impressive. Crap, I wish I had recorded the call, because I wanted to write down some of the good ones. Wisely, I kept my mouth shut and waited for her to talk to me. Or end the call. Or drop the phone into the toilet. It was her move, nothing I could do about it.

Finally, after I pulled up an app to play a game on my phone, I heard her fumble with the phone. "Maybe I should not have used the word 'Opportunity'," I said.

"Ya think?"

"Sorry."

"The opportunity isn't just for you, it is also for Frank."

She did not immediately respond, she also did not immediately throw the phone into the ocean. "For both of us?"

"Yes. Listen, can we talk face to face, sometime?"

"Sometime, like when?"

"Soon, hopefully? Where are you?" That information I could have asked Skippy for, or just pinged her phone's location. That would have been invading her privacy, so I didn't do that.

"We're in Taos."

"Taos?"

"Yes," she asked, irritated. "New Mexico. What is wrong with that?"

"Nothing. I've never been there, that's all. Are you having fun?"

"Yes. We spent a couple days in Santa Fe. Frank has family there."

"Oh. So, you met his family?"

"Yes. Don't ask."

"I won't. Can we meet? Just for an hour, I promise."

"This is important?"

"Important enough. It's *good* news, I promise."

"We are going to the Grand Canyon, the day after tomorrow."

Looking at my phone, I checked the time zone for Taos, New Mexico. "What about tonight, like after dinner?"

"I thought you and Adams were in the tropics somewhere?"

"We were. It was great but, we're back now. I only need to talk with you for an hour or so. I have a stealthed Panther, I can be at Taos in twenty minutes. No one will ever know I was there."

"You have a personal Panther? Why didn't I get that perk?"

"You didn't sign up for the Premium Package," I joked. "Seriously, Skippy will send a dropship for you, any time you want. How are you getting to the Grand Canyon?"

"We're driving."

"Driving? A Panther could have you there quick, and you wouldn't need to worry about paparazzi along the way."

"We are *driving*," she insisted. "You know, like *normal* people do? We're stopping at Albuquerque, and Flagstaff, and the Petrified Forest. Frank wants to stop in Winslow, to get a selfie at the statue there."

"What statue?"

"Google it," she sighed. "You really want to meet tonight?"

"If it's convenient."

She did not say whether it was convenient or not. "Make it quick."

"I promise."

I landed the Panther in a dry wash outside of town. The belly jets kicked up dust, but there was a stiff wind blowing that night, and no one was around to notice. Walking up to the road, I waited only a minute before a self-driving car pulled up, and a rear door popped open. "Open the driver's door, Skippy. I want to sit up front."

"It is really best if you sit in the back, Joe. You can relax back there."

"The driver is required to sit in the *driver's* seat, you ass."

"It's dark, no one will notice."

"*I* will. Open the freakin' door. I just flew a dropship here, I think I can handle a car."

"There is nothing to *hit* in the sky, Joe. I saw you driving on vacation, you returned that rental car with a big dent in the hood."

"That's because a coconut fell on it!"

"Because *you* parked it under a palm tree."

"Fine. I won't touch the wheel, unless the car is about to crash into an armadillo or something."

In the dark, I couldn't wear my sunglasses for disguise, so I settled for the baseball cap, with my jacket collar turned up against the evening chill. Unfortunately, I had shaved off the scruffy beard I had been growing on vacation. We met at an outdoor restaurant of the hotel where Simms was staying, she had gotten us a table in a secluded corner. There was a fire pit to take away the chill of the high desert evening, and I was glad for the jacket I wore.

Frank leaned over and put his arm around Jennifer, a protective gesture. I liked seeing that, especially as she leaned into him. She was happy, she deserved to have someone who made her feel safe and secure. Simms sure as hell had spent way too much time not feeling safe. "What's this about, Joe?" He asked, looking straight at me.

"Avalon." I appreciated him being direct with me, so I got to the point. "We need to establish a presence there."

"We do?" He asked, surprised, sharing a look with Simms. "We just left Avalon!"

"Yeah, sorry. I had to bring everyone back home, there weren't enough supplies there to keep going." The survey team had been on Avalon a lot longer than planned, and they had been running out of food and medicine when *Valkyrie* arrived. Attempts to grow food there had been hit-or-miss, a fungus growing out of control destroyed several crops of wheat and corn. The biologists were confident that eventually we could sustain a presence there, but a lot of work was needed to create a stable biosphere that allowed plants from Earth to grow. "I didn't know whether the UN would authorize another flight out there, and I couldn't leave you stranded."

Frank shrugged, understanding my reasoning but not happy about it. "Why go back? Earth is safe now." He looked at her again, and his eyes narrowed. "Isn't it? You *told* us we are safe now."

"It is safe." That answer wasn't good enough for either of them. "There are degrees of safety. We are safe from extinction."

"Shit." Simms set down her wine glass.

"What, honey?" Frank asked.

"They're not a credible threat, are they?"

"What aren't?" Frank looked from her to me, confused.

"The Elder weapons. There's no escalation factor," I said to her, ignoring her civilian husband. "It's not like each side could exchange tactical nukes, then pull back from the brink. There won't be any riding out a first strike, and negotiating a ceasefire. Elder weapons are not like the nuclear deterrent on Earth. They are a simple switch, *on* or *off*. If we flip the switch, everyone dies."

"Jennifer, *what* is he talking about?" Frank asked, in a voice calmer than I would have been.

"The aliens," she explained. "The enemy, they know we can trigger our Elder weapons if we are on the brink of extinction. But *only* then. Lighting off those weapons would be committing suicide for our entire species. We won't do it unless our backs are absolutely against the wall, and there is no other choice. Avalon. We need the beta site to make the Elder weapons a credible option."

"Right," I agreed.

Frank's expression was suddenly not so happy, and he was unhappy with his wife also. The two of us had shut him out of the conversation. "Will someone please explain what the hell you are talking about?"

"Game theory," I said. "Specifically, *war* game theory. The beta site is outside the galaxy where, as far as we know there are no Sentinels, and there definitely are no aliens. If we can establish a significant population of humans at the beta site, maybe at more than one site outside the Milky Way, our species will be able to survive, if we are forced to trigger Elder weapons here."

Frank's face turned white. "Oh my God."

"He's right," Jennifer said, squeezing his hand.

"Who thinks like that?" he asked, appalled.

"*Someone* has to," she patted his hand.

"I can't believe this," he jerked his hand away. "You are talking about *using* those horrific weapons?"

She shook her head. "We are talking about *not* having to ever use them. A substantial, self-sustaining presence at the beta site, means the Elder weapons here will be viewed as a credible threat. Aliens will know they can't push us here, because we do have an option for survival if we use them. A human presence at the beta site makes the strategic situation in this galaxy more stable and safe, for *everyone*."

"You *think* about this stuff?"

"I am a soldier," she reminded him. Turning back to me, she asked "What do you need me to do, Sir?"

I looked at Frank first. "I'm sorry to upset you. I'm just making a suggestion, not giving orders."

"What is your suggestion?" She asked.

"Chang is about to be appointed the UN Secretary for Homeworld Security," I announced, putting a finger to my lips. "It's hush-hush for now, but it's going to happen in a few days."

"Good move," Simms observed. "For him, and for Earth."

"I agree. Chotek will be Ambassador-at-large for Earth, to represent us in negotiations with the Maxohlx, and eventually with the spiders too." Hans Chotek's good standing in the diplomatic community had miraculously been restored, now that the United Nations needed a envoy who had extensive experience offworld. Also, the Jeraptha specifically requested Chotek for negotiations, they wanted to meet the diplomat who started a war. Maybe some people still avoided him at fancy cocktail parties, I don't think Hans cared. "Right now, he's working on a deal with the beetles, I can't say what that is yet."

"We're getting the band back together?" She asked, amused.

"Something like that."

Frank was not amused. "I hope you don't plan on playing your greatest hits. Starting a civil war, blowing up starships, that sort of thing?"

"No," I assured him. "This is a rare case where the audience would rather hear stuff from our new album."

"What new album?" Simms asked.

"We'll call it 'Peace Talks', maybe?" I said.

Based on the way he looked at me, Frank was not convinced of my peaceful intentions. "What do you want Jen to do?"

"Both of you," I replied. "Together. Avalon will have civilian leadership, but we need someone to command the military presence there. If you're interested?" I raised an eyebrow to Simms. "If it makes any difference, the Pentagon told me that is a billet for a full colonel."

"You would get a promotion?" Frank pursed his lips as he looked at her.

"That does *not* make a difference," she said, but her eyes told another story. "What matters is, are you interested, Frank?" She patted his arm.

"I, I need to think about it. What do *you* think, honey?"

"A fresh start? An opportunity to build a new society, out there? This wouldn't be permanent?" She asked me.

"Not unless you want to stay there," I said. "It's a three-year assignment, but transport ships will be going out there regularly, and they'll be mostly empty for the flight home. This may shock you," I grinned. "But the UN will probably want you to come back to Earth once a year, to report."

"I am *shocked*," she pressed a hand to her chest. "What if we decline? Is there another candidate?"

"There is a long list. You are the only American on the list." I shrugged. "UNEF feels that, with me commanding *Valkyrie*, and Ross and Perkins running the Alien Legion if we keep that going, there are too many Americans at the top of the command structure. The civilian leader of Avalon will be from one of the other twelve nations. Or possibly from a non-UNEF country."

"You are technically not acting as an American," she reminded me.

"That's a legal thing," I dismissed her comment with a wave of a hand. "I am still an American, just acting on behalf of a foreign government. I had to register as a foreign agent, to comply with US law. Hey," I added when she raised a skeptical eyebrow at me. "Before World War Two, MacArthur commanded the Philippines armed forces, and he was an American citizen."

"That's a bit different situation, but I won't argue," she told me. "How long do we have to think about it?"

"A couple weeks? No colonists are going out to the beta site for months, probably, but UNEF is anxious to start the planning."

Frank pursed his lips again. "I don't know if I like you," he said to her, "going back out there. You risked your life for years."

"This would be a *logistics* position," she explained. "I would be getting back to my specialty. That's right, Sir?" She addressed that comment to me. "UNEF is not planning to station warships at Avalon?"

"We don't *have* warships, other than *Valkyrie*. No," I agreed. "The whole point of the beta site is that we don't need warships out there, or any kind of weapons. Eventually, it would be nice to station a transport ship there for emergencies. And we should explore more of Sculptor, if we can. Listen, UNEF is excited about the idea of setting up *multiple* beta sites. There are plenty of satellite galaxies and star clusters that aliens don't have access to. If you get bored on Avalon, there will be other beta sites that will need to be set up."

"Whoa," Frank's shoulders slumped. "Surveying multiple worlds?"

"*You* are a scientist, Honey," Simms lightly punched his shoulder. "This is a great opportunity."

"I suppose."

"The science team leader can't be an American," I warned. "Sorry."

"I'm not sorry," Frank's expression brightened. "I'm interested in doing science, not in administrative bullshit." He kissed Simms on the cheek. "We'll think about it, OK? This calls for more wine," he lifted his empty glass. "I'll get us a refill."

As he walked toward the building, Simms leaned forward. "Peace Talks? You really think that will work?"

"We're giving it a shot," I shrugged. "It has to work, or Earth could become a battle ground."

"I can tell you right now," she watched her husband as he entered the building. "Frank will go for it. This is a great opportunity for him."

"What about you?"

"It is a great opportunity for me, too. I want to be with him. It's nice to have some stability in my life."

"Yeah, I know."

"How are you and Adams getting along?"

"Great! The whole living with someone thing takes some getting used to."

"You're not *living* together," she rolled her eyes. "You're on vacation."

"Yeah well, it feels like we're playing 'House'. Next week, we are visiting her folks."

"Meeting her parents?" That amused her.

"Do you have any advice for me?"

"Just be yourself. But not *too* much yourself."

"Great," I groaned. "I'm worried about the whole celebrity thing. It's a pain in the ass. Skippy rented a cabin on a lake for her folks, we're meeting them there."

"How is your family?"

We chatted about mundane stuff, like normal people do, then Frank came back with a bottle of wine and a tray of snacks. When my phone beeped to remind me it was time to go, I choked up a bit. Simms and I had been together for a long time, and we had rubbed the rough edges off each other, to become a great team. With her going out to Avalon, I might not see her for a long time.

She *hugged* me.

I hugged her back.

We were sitting on the porch, while Margaret's mother worked in the kitchen, and her father was down at the lake, fishing. He told us he was catching our dinner, but his wife was skeptical, so she was making chicken and dumplings. Margaret and I offered to help in the kitchen but her mother shooed us away. Truthfully, I think both her parents needed a break from us. From *me*. Because I was now a celebrity, I came with a lot of baggage, and it sucked for everyone involved. Her parents had read so much about me, some accurate and some completely made up, that meeting me was inevitably a disappointment. The first night we were together, her father had made an awkward joke about the Pirates saving the world again. My guess is, they just didn't know what to say to me. Because I was terrified of saying the wrong thing around them and getting Margaret upset with me, I didn't talk much. That left a lot of awkward gaps in the conversation. When her father went to go fishing, he pointed to a second pole hanging in the cabin, and asked if I wanted to come with him. It was almost comical to see the look of relief on his face when I declined.

"This is nice," I said to Margaret, sitting back on the couch and putting my feet on the coffee table.

"This is *painful*," she whispered, with a glance back into the cabin. We could hear her mother banging things around in the kitchen, now it was quiet in there. "You need to *try*, Joe."

"I *am* trying."

"You are sitting there with a forced grin on your face, and you're not saying anything."

"I don't *know* what to say. What-"

A phone on the coffee table pinged softly, and Margaret picked it up. "Oh, another wrong number." She shook the phone in disgust, ending the call, and tossed it back on the coffee table. "My mother got this burner phone so I could call her, but she keeps getting some woman calling for a Pastor Redmond."

The phone rang again, and I grabbed it before Margaret could. "I'll answer it," I offered.

"You're not a Pastor."

"No, I'm a *Bishop*," I winked. "That's even better." Holding up a finger for silence, I answered the call, deepening my voice and putting on my awful Southern accent. I sounded like a drunk Colonel Sanders. Getting up from the couch, I stepped away. "Well, hello there," I said in a deep voice, trying my terrible Southern accent. "This is Pastor Redmond, how may I help you?"

"Oh! Oh, thank you," a woman said in a very pleasant Southern accent. "I have been trying to call you, but some rude woman kept telling me I had the wrong number. This is Josephine Washington."

"I am very pleased you called, Ms. Washington."

"*Miss* Washington," she insisted.

"Of course. I am *so* glad you called, I was hoping you would call me."

"You were?" She asked, hopefully.

"Yes. You are *so* hot."

"Oh! Pastor *Redmond*!"

"When I am up there giving a sermon, I look at you and think 'Lord, I want to bang her so bad'."

"Oh! That is- oh!"

"What else do you think I'm praying for?"

"Well," she huffed, "I never-"

"That's the problem. You *should*."

Miss Washington ended the call, just as Margaret yanked the phone out of my hand. And, just as her mother stepped out the door onto the porch.

"Was that a call on *my* phone?" Her mother asked, staring at me in shock.

"Uh-" That was the total of what my brain was capable of thinking at that moment.

"What do I tell her when she calls back?" Her mother directed that question at her daughter, since clearly I was incapable of being a responsible adult.

"Momma, you-"

"She *won't* call back," I said.

"If she does?" Mrs. Adams put hands on her hips and glared at me.

"Then," I shrugged. "I better ask Skippy to find Pastor Redmond's real phone number, because that guy is going to get *lucky*."

Which was the wrong thing to say to Margaret's mother, and also the right thing. She glared at me for another half-second, then burst into laughter. Margaret went from a deer-in-the-headlights expression, to following her mother's lead.

"I won't do it again," I promised, handing the phone to Margaret's mother. "Sorry."

She held up her hands, refusing to take the phone. "Nuh uh, Joseph," she shook her head, but there was a twinkle in her eyes. "This is *your* problem now."

"OK, uh," I pulled my zPhone out of a pocket. "Use this one, it's secure."

She held the credit-card-thin phone delicately. "Isn't this *your* phone? The special one?" She knew Margaret had a zPhone.

"It's yours now. Skippy will load your profile on it, if he hasn't already done it. I have a half-dozen more zPhones in my bag."

She automatically looked up toward the sky. "Skippy is watching us? Now?"

"Not all the time, Momma," Margaret assured her. "He probably assigned a submind to keep track of us, in case we need him. He doesn't *spy* on us."

"You're sure about that? How can you be sure?"

"Because he knows that Margaret," I also looked up and shook a fist as a warning, in case he was stupid enough to spy on us. "Would beat his ass if he did."

Dinner that night was slightly less awkward, partly because Margaret's mother now shared a secret with us; she hadn't told her husband about me answering the wrong number call. A couple times, I caught a glimpse of her looking at me and smiling. She was remembering the call, or she was smiling at *me*. Either way was good.

Her father had not come back with any fish, which was fine with everyone. Conversation still lagged a bit, no one wanted to talk about the Pirates, and as we didn't have shared experiences, I mostly stayed silent. A few times, Margaret kicked me under the table, and I asked one of the bland, safe questions from a list she suggested before dinner. It was nice, bland stuff, like how her parents met, whether they had gone on vacation the previous summer, things like that. Somehow, we got onto the subject of Margaret's sister.

"You know that boy Darren," her father shook his head.

"Who's Darren?" I asked, before Margaret could kick me. I had moved my leg out of the way, because my shin was getting sore.

"Darren and Susanna used to date, in high school," Margaret told me with a warning look. I knew her younger sister was in college, in either her second or third year. "What about Darren?" She directed the question to her father.

"He entered the seminary last Fall."

"The seminary?" Margaret was clearly surprised at that. "He talked about it, I didn't know he made a decision. Does he plan to come back, after he graduates?"

Her parents shared an uncomfortable glance. "We don't know," her father said, after an awkward pause. "It won't matter. Darren has taken a vow of celibacy."

"Celibacy?" I snorted, and rolled my eyes.

Here's another valuable Pro Tip for you guys out there: when you are a dating a girl, it is *not* a good idea to tell her father that you aren't a big fan of celibacy.

Her father was as embarrassed by my outburst as I was. "Darren is a very serious young man," he looked at me. "He feels that celibacy puts him in touch with a higher power," he said as he took a sip of iced tea.

"Like his hand?" I asked.

My timing sucks. Her father choked and spewed iced tea all over the table. The dinner conversation kind of went downhill from there.

Although, by 'downhill', this time I mean like riding a bicycle. It gets easier, going downhill. Her parents must have decided that I am truly a knucklehead, which I guess made me more approachable. I apologized and helped clear the table, while Margaret's eyes glared maser beams into my skull. A delicious pecan pie was served. There is a vicious rumor that I ate two pieces of pie, I can neither confirm nor deny those spurious accusations. We stopped avoiding the subject of the Merry Band of Pirates, but we kept it light, telling funny stories about the crew, and not mentioning any of the bad stuff that happened. At one point, her mother patted my arm. "Oh, Joseph, Margaret didn't tell us that you are *funny*."

That remark from her mother got me out of the doghouse, Margaret stopped kicking me. Mostly. I still said stupid stuff that justified a kick.

After dinner, we sat on the porch until the bugs started biting, at that point Margaret and I made our excuses and walked to our cabin. Her mother pulled her aside and they talked, while they both looked at me.

Oh shit. That had to be trouble.

"Sorry," I said when the cabin door closed behind us. "It won't happen aga-"

"It had *better* happen again," she smashed me back into the door, pressing against me and kissing me fiercely.

"What was that for?" I asked, bewildered when she pulled away.

"You, Joseph Bishop, are an *idiot*. But, you're funny. My parents approve of you."

"They do?"

"Not the inappropriate jokes. They like that you make me happy."

"I do?"

"Yes," she kissed me again. "You do."

"Cool. Hey, do you want to make *me* happy right now?"

"Let me guess?" She put on a mock frown, but kept her body pressed against mine.

Running a finger along the waistband of her pants, I nibbled her ear. "I want to get in touch with a higher power."

"I'll bet you do," she laughed.

All I can say is, that Darren guy has *no* idea what he is missing.

CHAPTER EIGHTEEN

An idle mind is the Devil's playground, that's what my mother told me. Bored while I was waiting between meetings, I had my zPhone out and was scrolling through messages. The email address I actually used was secret, known only to the Pirates, UNEF Command, family and friends, but still I got a flood of messages every day. You would think that, being on the Skippytel network, any useless crap would get filtered out, but that was not true. Somehow, I got an impressive amount of spam. "Hey," I grunted, surprised. My surprise was not at getting another spam message, not even about the content of the message, it was about some so-called genius I know getting *scammed*. "Skippy. Did you see this message?" I laughed.

"Which one?"

"The one where someone is stealing your good name, trying to rip people off."

"*What?*" Now I had his attention. "Where is this?"

"This message here," I held the phone up, though that gesture was entirely useless. "Some jerk claims he is a long-lost prince of Skippistan, and he needs my help to claim his inheritance of twelve million dollars. All he needs is my bank account information."

"Well, don't do *that*, Joe."

"I'm not an idiot, Skippy. No way am I falling for an old scam like-"

"I meant, ignore the message, because you are not eligible for the contest."

"Uh, contest?"

"Yes. Current citizens of Skippistan are not eligible for the sweepstakes. If you scrolled down and read the fine print, you would know that. Don't be so lazy, Joe," he huffed.

"Hold on. *You* sent this message out?"

"Of course I did, knucklehead. Skippistan doesn't have a royal family, so there is no prince out there. I mean," he chuckled, "unless this prince is a sheep or a *goat*, you know?"

"I must be missing something here. You are *scamming* people?"

"Of course not," he sounded hurt. "There actually is twelve million dollars available in the contest. In fact, there is ten times that much available, a hundred and twenty million bucks."

"Uh-" That was the smartest thing I could think of to say right then. "So, there really is a contest?"

"Yes. The first ten people to respond properly will each receive twelve million dollars, from the beneficent and generous citizens of Skippistan."

"Oh. Wow. I am *sorry*. I falsely accused you. Please forgive me."

"Hmmph," he sniffed. "Apology accepted."

I shrugged. "This is an unusual way to run a charity, but I guess all that matters is that needy people are being helped, so-"

"It's called 'Chumming the water', Joe," he explained excitedly, because he simply does not know when to shut up.

"Uh, what?"

"Chumming the water. Come on, you know what I mean. Like when you're fishing, you throw bait out behind the boat. The bait attracts fish, so you can catch them easier."

"I know what 'chum' is, asshole. What does that have to do with- Oh, *shit*."

"This is going to have a fan-TAST-ic return on investment, Joe," he was bubbling over with enthusiasm for his scheme. "Once word gets out that ten lucky idiots out there got rich through my scam, every gullible *loooooooser* in the world will be falling over themselves to give me their money. Oh, man," he giggled. "I am going to be *raking* in the dough!"

"Shit. Skippy, you can't do that!"

"Ah, don't worry, Joe. Just because other scammers never thought of this brilliant twist on an old scam, that doesn't mean it won't work. I am simply smarter than other scammers," he giggled. "The contest already has three winners, or should I say, *looooosers*."

"Skippy. You can't *do* this."

"Why not? It is all perfectly legal, under the laws of Skippistan."

"The laws of-" It never occurred to me that his fake country had actual laws. Shit. What else did I not know about the Glorious People's Republic of Skippistan? "The law is not the only consideration, you ass."

"Huh? Oh, I get it, Joe. Thank you for being concerned, but there is really very little risk of me losing the original hundred twenty-five million. Besides," he snickered. "It's not *my* money anyway. A criminal syndicate in Belarus fronted that cash, as an investment. They *don't* know they invested in my venture," he lowered his voice. "The money will probably be returned before they even notice it is missing."

Burying my face in my hands, I mumbled "This is a dangerous game, Skippy."

"Nah. Sadly, that bank in Belarus failed to keep their antivirus firewalls updated, so there could be a *tragic* system crash that wipes out all recent transaction history, if you know what I mean. Hopefully, I won't need to do that."

"You are *totally* missing the point. Ripping off people is wrong, Skippy."

"It is?"

"Yes."

"Really?"

"Yes, really."

"Even if they *volunteer* to get ripped off, because they are being greedy?"

"Uh, well, that's complicated."

"*Ah ha*!" he shouted in triumph. "See, Joe? That's the beauty of this particular scam. The people who participate are not only gullible and stupid, they think they are scamming *me*. Really, I am doing law enforcement agencies all over the world a favor, by identifying potential wrongdoers. Hey, I should get a medal or something."

"You are going to get *yourself* in trouble, shithead. Other countries have laws against scams like this."

"Well, then, I suggest you immediately secure legal representation, Joe. And not a sleazebag lawyer like Morrie Slater."

"Why would *I* need a lawyer?"

"Well, as president of Skippistan, you of course must answer for any shenanigans that go on there."

"Pres- *president*? What- how- when did this happen?"

"A couple days ago."

"I never asked to be president!"

"What can I say? Many are called to greatness, Joe, some have it thrust upon them."

"When did I become president?"

"After the recent election, of course. Don't let it go to your head, but you won in a landslide."

"I wasn't informed of any election."

"Well, we didn't want to bother you, Joe. We know you have been very busy."

"*Who* voted in this election?"

"Well, me, of course. Salkat and Amina were going to vote, but-"

"Salkat and- *Who* are they, again?"

"Salkat Nazarbayev and his lovely wife Amina, remember? They run my goat farm. Amina was in the nearby village selling goat's milk on election day, and Salkat was drunk again. I can assure you the election was strictly legit, Joe."

"Only you voted? What about the other citizens of the Glorious People's Republic?"

"Citizenship doesn't come with voting rights, knucklehead," he sighed. "Did you not even bother to read the brochure?"

"I resign, effective immediately."

"Hmm. No dice, Joe. Unfortunately, I just read the constitution of Skippistan, it does not allow a duly-elected president to avoid the responsibilities of the office."

"Since when do we have a constitution?"

"Since, about, um, five seconds ago? Hmm, I guess this day needs to be a national holiday in Skippistan. We'll need snacks."

"Shit. This cannot be happening."

"Joseph, please watch your language. I expect a president to present himself with more dignity and decorum."

"Are you serious about this? Why do you want me to be president?"

"So you can handle all the boring diplomatic and administrative stuff, leaving me free to focus on developing and implementing my vision of a glorious future."

"Oh, please. I am dying to hear the details of this glorious future."

"I am still *developing* it, numbskull. Do you even listen when I talk?"

"What administrative stuff could there be? The whole country is a freakin' goat farm."

"And sheep, Joe. And, don't forget the yak. Also, while I'm thinking about it, one of your first duties should be to plan a celebration for our first Constitution Day. The menu should reflect the wide variety of local cuisines in our glorious nation."

"How about I get a bag of Cheese Doodles from the vending machine?"

"That'll work."

"You didn't answer my question. What administrative duties do I have?"

"Someone has to keep track of the goats, Joe. Salkat was doing that, but then he got drunk, knocked over a lantern and burned down the hut with all the farm's records. Ooh, that reminds me, can you read Kyrgyz?"

"What? No!"

"Wow. Better get started then, huh? Kyrgyz is the official language of Skippistan."

"I thought the national anthem is sung in Klingon?"

"It is, but Salkat and Amina only speak Kyrgyz. And a little Tajik, of course, they need that to get by in business stuff. Hmm, you should learn Tajik, too, it is-"

"How about you translate for me, until I am fluent?"

"If I must, although I suspect that will be an excuse for you not to study."

"Ya think?"

"Who will handle the president's duties when I'm away from the planet?" Already, I was thinking of Earth as just another planet. That scared me. "Can Morrie handle it?"

"Um, well, sadly, Morrie is currently busy with his own legal troubles, that even I can't get him out of. I told him that if he had picked either cocaine *or* hookers, maybe I could work something out with the authorities, but *nooooo*. He had to get greedy."

"Shit. Who is your ambassador now?"

"Trixie Diamond."

"That's her real name?"

"No, it's her, I think the polite term is 'working name'."

"Your ambassador is a *call girl*?"

"*Escort*, Joe. Allegedly. I mean, she had never been arrested for-"

"You went from a lawyer to a hooker?"

"I wanted my ambassador to be someone with more integrity than a *lawyer*, Joe."

"I, I actually cannot argue about that."

"Besides, Trixie agreed not to tell the authorities what she knows about Morrie and the *ferrets*, if you know what I mean."

I stuck fingers in my ears. "*Please* never mention this again."

"Mention what? It never happened."

"Thank you. Can we go back to your scam?"

"Ugh. Do we have to?"

"We do. Stop it, right now."

"Do I *have* to?" He whined.

"Yes. I don't understand, you can get bank account info for anyone on the planet. Why do you need a scam?"

"Joe. Please. You insult my honor."

"Uh, what?"

"My honor. I do not *steal* from people. Sure, occasionally I redistribute wealth from criminal organizations, that is just my generous nature. Skippistan had expenses, and the commemorative swag I have on the internet is just not bringing in enough revenue. If people volunteer to send their money to me, because they think *they* are ripping someone off in a scam, then they are simply getting what they deserve."

Crap. He was wrong about that, but I couldn't put an argument together in my head. "Why don't you just make money the old fashioned way?"

"Like how?"

"Bribes, Skippy. Lobbyists all over the world would love to have influence with you. They can funnel boatloads of cash into your pockets."

"I don't *have* pockets."

"You know what I mean."

"Eh, lobbyists? That sounds *really* sleazy, Joe."

"Your ambassador is a callgirl, and you raise money through email scams."

"Maybe you have a point. Ugh, working with lobbyists? What if they bribe me to do something I don't want to do?"

"That's easy. You don't have to do anything, other than take the bribes."

"Um, explain how that works, please?"

"It's simple. Some corporation wants you to, I don't know," I tried to think of a scenario. "Help them with mining an asteroid, or help them secure a contract with Homeworld Security. They hire a lobbyist to contact you, and shovel a boatload of cash into your pockets. The lobbyist keeps a cut of the money. You don't do anything, but the lobbyist tells his client that he's working with you, and is *very* close to an agreement. Maybe he suggests more bribes are needed. Eventually, the corporation fires that lobbyist, but they just hire another sleazebag, and *he* gives you another bribe. Everybody wins."

"Everybody except the lobbyist who got fired."

"No, he just moves on to another client, because everyone knows he has extensive contacts in Skippistan."

"Wow. This sounds *super* sleazy."

"I know, but-"

"Count me *in*, brother!"

"Great. Will you *please* cancel the email scam?"

"Um, how about I halt it where it is, and we pretend none of this ever happened?"

"Can you return the money?"

"Um, shmaybe some of it. I'll do what I can. A certain bank in Belarus is going to have a *very* bad day, though."

"My heart bleeds for them. Now, can I resign from the presidency?"

"Unfortunately, no. But, you could outsource some of your duties to a vice president."

"Like Amina or Salkat?" I asked hopefully.

"I was thinking you should choose one of the goats, but-"

"Let's discuss this later, OK? This is Constitution Day! I need to celebrate with Cheese Doodles. They *are* the official snack of Skippistan."

"They are *not*, unless I get an endorsement contract," he grumbled.

"Hey, sounds like that snack company needs to hire a lobbyist, huh?"

"Cool!"

"You're getting the idea, Skippy. Talk to you later, OK?"

The Panther I had been using as my personal sports car needed routine maintenance, and I was scheduled to give a tour of our battlecruiser to a group of VIPs, so I was back aboard *Valkyrie* when Skippy called me. The Panther checked out fine, and the VIPs had boarded dropships for the flight back to the surface, so I was just kind of hanging out. Truthfully, being on Earth was tiring. People say they want fame and fortune? Screw that. Give me the fortune, you can keep the fame. Paparazzi followed me everywhere, all of them looking for an unflattering photo of me doing something stupid. I don't know how Hollywood celebrities manage to live actual lives, when they are constantly being watched. For me, it was exhausting and I was sick of it, and being aboard *Valkyrie* again was a nice break. Margaret was busy at Twentynine Palms Marine Corps Base, we had plans to meet that weekend, until then my life was all work, work, work. I know, it was a pity party for poor little Joey, boo-freakin'-hoo. Anyway, Skippy called me. "Ugh. Hey, Joe. The UN Secretary General insists on meeting with you."

"OK," I said slowly, running over in my mind what I had done recently to get me in trouble. A summons from the Secretary General was sort of like being called to the principal's office in school, it immediately made my heart rate spike. The fact was the UN had no direct authority over me, but the Secretary General could make my life difficult, and her organization could pressure the US government to make me do, whatever the UN wanted. Normally, the US government would tell the UN bureaucrats to go screw themselves, but right then the member nations of UNEF were in a cooperative mood. Meaning, they all wanted to get a piece of the fabulous technology brought back by *Valkyrie*, and they were all eager to assure that no other country got an unfair advantage. The UN was, the UNEF nations had decided, a convenient watchdog. "What does she want to talk about?"

"A whole lot of stuff, mostly involving how Skippistan plans to vote on upcoming issues within UNEF."

"Uh, doesn't your ambassador Trixie handle that? Unless she is, you know, busy."

"Busy?"

"With her other, you know, job."

"Trixie quit her other job when I hired her, numbskull. Most of her regular clients are in Miami, and the ambassador position needs to be in New York part of the time, now that we have so much going on."

"OK. So, why doesn't she handle voting, that sort of thing?"

"Trixie doesn't *vote*, Joe. Skippistan generally abstains from voting. Unless the issue affects our glorious nation, like some of the votes scheduled for next week."

"OK, but that doesn't explain why-"

"The Secretary General is hoping to persuade you to vote the way she wants."

"*Me*? Why would I-"

"Ugh. You are the president of Skippistan, dumdum."

"Shit. Yeah, but, isn't that just a ceremonial position?"

"Unfortunately, no. I can't vote in the UN, because I am not human. Buncha jerks. *That* is discrimination, Joe."

"Uh huh, yeah, I am outraged by it. Why do you care what a bunch of monkeys vote about?"

"I do not. It's the principle of the thing that bugs me."

"Maybe I can ask the Secretary about it. Uh, shouldn't I know what the issues are?"

"No need for you to bother with that stuff, Joe."

"Oh, I insist, you sneaky little shit. No way am I voting unless I know what I'm voting on."

"But, I have already accepted fat bribes to vote a certain way!"

"You *what*?"

"Hey, the whole bribe thing was *your* idea."

"Yes, but- Oof. Shit." Once again, I had screwed myself, by not thinking through the consequences of my actions. "Hey, wait a minute. If I'm the president, shouldn't I be getting memos about stuff we are voting on?"

"You *are* getting memos, knucklehead, you are just too lazy to read them."

"What?" Pulling out my zPhone, I scrolled through my email. "Where is-"

"Oops. Heh heh, it looks like all my memos have been getting caught up in your spam filter. My bad."

"Spam? Skippy, you restore those messages to my inbox right now."

"OK, OK, I'm looking for them now. Wow, you get a *flood* of spam, Joe. Offers to refinance your mortgage, I can probably trash those. Let's see, what else? Enlarge your penis, hmm, another penis enhancement, *another*, it's- Damn. You get a *lot* of messages on that subject. Have you been clicking on-"

"It's none of your business what I click on," I hastened to say. "Just transfer to my inbox your memos from, like, the past week."

"Working on it," he snapped, irritated. "You know, I try to keep boring administrative stuff away from you as much as possible, but this time, the Secretary General did not believe your avatar was actually, you- Ugh. I probably made the thing too smart, that-"

"Hold on. Rewind that, please. My avatar? Crap, the one that sounds like me but looks like a monkey? You ass, if you-"

"No, dumdum. I do not mean '*avatar*' like in a stupid video game. I mean your digital self. A 3D replica of you, to talk on video conferences when you are much too busy, doing, um, whatever the hell it is you do."

"You- You have been pretending to be *me*?" I gasped, horrified. "How often have you done this?"

"Um, well, that depends. Is it a good thing or a bad thing?"

"*Bad*, you jackass!"

"In that case, I have never actually done it, that you are aware of. Gosh, will you look at the time. Gotta go now, talk-"

"*You* are not going anywhere," I gritted my teeth. "I want a list of every call and videochat you did, where you pretended to be me."

"Um, just the official ones?"

"Why would- You pretended to be me for my *own personal stuff*?"

"No. Well, yes, sort of. Your mother did not believe it was you for one second, I couldn't fool her."

"Who else did you talk to?"

"Oh, you know, the usual. TV interviews, and-"

"Oh my- I was on TV? When was this?"

"You have done many TV interviews for real, Joe," he chided me.

"Yeah, and I hated them. Add my fake personal appearances to the list, too. Why, please tell me *why* you did this?"

"There is, and it makes me gag to even say it, not enough Joe Bishop to meet the demand. You get a ton of interview requests every day, and you refuse most of them. That is not good for your public image, so, um, I helped. *Excuuuuuuse* me for trying to be helpful to a buddy."

"You really were trying to help?"

"Yes. For example, you received a request to appear on the morning farm report show, in the fourth biggest media market in Iowa. The show conflicted with your vacation in the tropics, so I appeared for you, thank you very much. That also helped sell the cover story that you were working, instead of goofing off on vacation."

"Uh, OK, I guess-"

"Which reminds me. During that show, you agreed to go on a dream date with this year's reigning Pork Products Queen. Do you have a nice set of overalls, or should I make a set for-"

"I am not going on a date!"

"You went on a date with Margaret, why is this any diff-"

"It is different and you know it. Cancel. The. Date."

"Wow. That is not going to make you popular with Midwestern women ages eighteen to thirty-four, Joe. I have to warn you, most people who watched that interview already think you are kind of a dick, so you-"

"It wasn't *me!*"

"Well, it's too late for that now. Time for damage control."

"This can't be happening. Wait, stop," I held up a hand. "Let's go back to the original subject, OK? Give me a hint what the Secretary General wants to talk about?"

"The future. Specifically, the future direction of UNEF, the beta site, and whether you monkeys should pursue an alliance with the Ruhar."

"Crap. Ok, I need to call Chotek first."

"Count Chocula? Why? Are the two of you buddies now?"

"We are not 'buddies', Skippy. His family has a yacht bigger than my parent's house. *My* parents have a canoe. He *likes* opera, I only listen when you force me to."

"Then why-"

"Because Hans will know what's going on with the policy debate inside UNEF."

"Oh, Jeez Louise. If you want to know what people have been talking about at the UN, I have access to every-"

"You know *what* they're saying. Hans knows *why*. Shit, I'm going to call him right now."

I was in luck: Hans had an opening on his calendar early that evening, before he had to attend a formal dinner that even he was not looking forward to. Even better, he was at home in Salzburg Austria, rather than at his office in crowded Geneva Switzerland. Technically, I should have filed a flight plan to bring my Panther into the local airport, but that would have been a *huge* pain in the ass. Skippy was right about one thing: there was not enough Joe Bishop to meet the demand. Everywhere I went, people wanted to talk with me, take selfies with me, just *see* me. And that was the good part. But, for every ten reasonable people, there were two angry whackadoodles who wanted to shout their lunatic conspiracy theories at me, or throw something at my head. Did you know that, according to polls, seventeen percent of the public still thought the Kristang were our real saviors, and I was a traitor working with the Ruhar against humanity?

Skippy is right, monkeys are freakin' stupid.

Anyway, I set the stealthed Panther down in a mountain meadow, and hiked down to the nearest road, where Skippy had a car waiting for me. It was a nice walk, though I should have brought a change of shoes, because the ground was wet and I didn't want to track mud into Chotek's house. Dropping the car in a parking garage, I walked several blocks to his house, keeping my baseball cap pulled down low and my sunglasses on. Wearing a baseball cap did make it obvious that I'm an American, but I looked like any other tourist walking around the city.

Hans Chotek owned a very nice townhouse in a fashionable district near the city center, or maybe the house belonged to his family, for use when they were in town. I knew they also had an estate outside of the city. And a yacht they kept in the south of France, I wasn't joking about that.

Just before I rang the doorbell, it surprised me that Hans opened the door, I had expected a butler to be there. "Skippy told me you were here," Hans explained, looking past me to the street. He was checking whether I had been followed, I imagined he had his own issues with lack of privacy. "Come in, come in," he urged me with a wave, and quickly shut the door behind me.

"Joseph," he patted me on the shoulder. "It is good to see you."

"Same here," I said, and I meant it. It was less than a month since *Valkyrie* brought everyone from of Avalon to Earth, and we had spent plenty of time together during that flight. Mostly, we talked about what we knew of the political situation at home, and the media firestorm that likely awaited us. He had been a hundred percent right about that. Also, he helped coach me for both the debriefing by the Army, and the endless rounds of testifying for committees, both of the US Congress, and of the UN. To my surprise, my testimony before Congress was easy compared to answering questions at the UN. Most of my sessions with the Congress were in closed-door classified meetings, with no cameras or reporters present. That eliminated the time-wasting bullshit of politicians making speeches to appeal to their voters. There were speeches during my public testimony, but the Pentagon got a list of questions beforehand, and they prepared answers for me. The

UN sessions last two whole freakin' *days*, with ambassadors from countries I never heard of, asking a bunch of nonsensical questions I could not answer. After two days of solid boredom, made tolerable only because I listened to audiobooks through my earpiece while the ambassador from Blahblahdor droned on with a long speech, I mercifully went into a closed session with the nations of UNEF, where the questions were focused and to the point.

Anyway, that's all I will say, about me getting dragged into hearing rooms to get yelled at and scolded and answer questions as best I could. The whole experience sucked for me, and I don't want to bore you with the boring details.

Hans led me into his study, where he opened a liquor cabinet. "No, it's-" I started to protest.

"Don't worry," he winked at me. "It's not schnapps. Bourbon?" He held up a glass.

"I will if you are."

"I am," he assured me. "Dinner tonight is with an EU trade federation, it will be insufferably dull. I need a drink to fortify myself."

"I thought you enjoyed negotiations, diplomacy, that sort of thing," I observed as I took a sip. Why would someone who signed up for a dull job, complain that the work is dull?

"I enjoy the *results*," he knocked back an impressive swig of bourbon. "Crises averted. Agreements signed. In between?" he shrugged. "Mostly, I try to stifle an instinct to strangle the people on the other side of the table. *You* have done well," he raised his glass to me. "I watched your testimony to the UN special committee."

"Skippy played audiobooks in my ear," I admitted. "The Pentagon advised me to sit politely, until the jerk with the microphone gets tired of talking."

"Ha!" Hans laughed. "That is the essence of diplomacy. Perhaps you could consider a new career someday."

"Thanks, but I would rather cover myself in barbeque sauce, and parachute into a grikka's nest."

"You are here about your meeting with the Secretary General?"

"Yeah."

"I was about to call you, when Skippy informed me you wanted to meet here."

"Thanks. Do you know what she wants?"

He glanced at the ornate old clock on his desk. Hans was wearing a tuxedo, or maybe it was a dinner jacket, I don't know the difference. The few times I wore something like that, I looked like an idiot. He looked like James Bond. His tie was undone, and it was real, not a clip-on. Of course he knew how to properly tie a bowtie, his nanny or butler had probably taught him that skill before he started kindergarten. "The UNEF Permanent Council wants to know your opinion on a variety of initiatives."

"You mean, how Skippistan plans to vote?"

"No," he snorted, and the corners of his lips turned down. Apparently, he did not approve of Skippy's fake country. "Skippistan is an associate member of UNEF, your votes are non-binding. I see that Skippy didn't explain this to you?"

"No. He has never asked my opinion about how to vote on anything. If it's not about voting, then what-"

"It's about your influence on Skippy," his eyes automatically darted to the ceiling. "UNEF can make any decision they want, they can't *do* anything without Skippy."

Shifting in my chair, I looked down at the carpet. "UNEF thinks I have more influence than I really do. Skippy can be impossibly stubborn if he doesn't want to do something."

"Regardless, you have the most influence with him." He glanced at the clock again, judging how much time he had before he had to fasten his bowtie and leave for dinner. "There are two major initiatives being considered. First, a flight to the beta site. The *Flying Dutchman* would be going, loaded with those multi-mission modules. Mostly cargo, supplies for setting up a colony."

"Oh, that's great," I breathed a sigh of relief. "They agree we need a beta site, to make the Elder weapons a credible threat?"

"Yes. Also, humanity needs a safe haven, in case the Elder weapons are *not* a credible threat."

It was great to hear that someone was listening to me. The media, and most of the world's governments, had been assuring the nervous public that our new arsenal of Elder weapons was an invincible umbrella, forever protecting Earth from harm. The media only cared about posting clickbait, so viewers would see ads. The governments knew the public was weary of living in fear, and just wanted to hear comforting words. Government officials who knew the uncomfortable truth were offering only muted warnings, well aware that the public would tune them out. "You are, uh, not going to Avalon again, are you?"

"No. Thank you, I have had enough of living in a tent," he grimaced. "The second initiative is what instructions the UN will give me, for negotiating an alliance with the Ruhar."

"The hamsters? I thought-"

"Yes, that we need an alliance with the Jeraptha, I agree. UNEF thinks we should start with the Ruhar, partly to settle the issue of humans on Paradise. The Ruhar federal government is concerned that allowing humans to use one of their planets, as a staging base for Alien Legion operations, makes Paradise a target. The local officials on Paradise *want* humans living there, it is good for business."

His body language was telling me he was not bubbling over with enthusiasm for an alliance with the Ruhar, and I agreed. "We need to be careful about dealing with the hamsters," I said the most neutral thing I could think of.

"Yes," he pointed a finger at me happily. "Most of the world now sees the Ruhar as our cute and fuzzy friends, that their raid against us was just a big misunderstanding. People forget," he shook his head. "They knocked out more than three-quarters of our electric generating capacity. Some parts of the world have *still* not fully recovered."

"The lizards made it worse," I said, not knowing why I felt a need to defend the Ruhar. Their raid had been bad strategy, and cost lives on both sides without producing any useful result. Actually, the raid was an astronomically expensive failure. The Ruhar gained nothing from it. Because of the raid, humanity was happy to sign up to fight with our Kristang saviors, despite the revulsion we all felt when we saw their ugly faces. Overall, the strategy behind the raid was just plain *stupid*, and led to major changes in Ruhar military leadership. Unfortunately, the hamsters learned the wrong lessons from that action; since Columbus Day, they had squashed any suggestion of bold action, relying instead on the same stodgy thinking that prevented them from suffering major failures, but which also caused the war to drag on in a stalemate.

"I tried to remind my colleagues, that the Ruhar killed hundreds of humans on Paradise."

"Yeah, but," again I was uncomfortable with the direction the conversation was taking. "Fort Arrow was a legitimate military target."

Hans paused, his glass halfway to his lips. "Joe, I am surprised to hear you say that. You lost friends there."

"I'm a soldier, I have a different perspective. Fort Arrow controlled the cargo launcher complex, we threatened the usefulness of the entire planet's economy. I don't like that the Ruhar hit our people, I just understand their logic, that's all."

"They must have known the rules of engagement enforced by the Kristang, would not allow humans to damage the launcher."

"Shit happens," I shrugged. "To the Ruhar back then, we were nothing but primitive aliens, brought in as cannon fodder. They couldn't predict what we would do, if our backs were against the wall. Hell, *I* held the launcher hostage, until the Kristang came back."

He looked over his glass at me. "Would you have blown the reactor?"

"No," I admitted. "Rules of engagement may suck, but they are *rules*. Besides, all we had to do was hang on, and prevent the hamsters from using the launcher."

"Hmm," he grunted. "My point stands: UNEF believes negotiating an alliance with the Ruhar will be simple. You and I have been out there," he used a thumb to point to the ceiling. "We know better."

"The Ruhar take care of themselves first," I nodded. "They have been fighting this war for a *long* time, Hans."

"Can we trust them?"

"As long as we have the same interests, sure. They are not sticking their necks out for us. You know about their deal with the Torgs?"

He shook his head, eyebrows raised.

That was interesting. I knew something about alien politics that he didn't. "Ask Skippy about it. Perkins told me the Torgalau tried for a long time to hammer out a mutual defense treaty with the Ruhar. They settled for a series of short-term agreements about specific issues. The hamsters didn't want to commit to supporting the Torgs, if those aliens did something the Ruhar considered stupid. If we do something stupid, I would not count on the hamsters having our backs, no matter what agreement they signed."

"That is true of all treaties," he downed the last of his drink. "They are only effective when both parties see value in adhering to the terms. Joe," he stood up. "I have to leave soon. The Secretary General will not ambush you tomorrow, she is seeking your support."

"If she is taking the war seriously, she'll have it."

"She is very aware that merely having Elder weapons does not assure our safety. I told her what you said about how shocked the Ruhar are by the revelation that we now have Elder weapons. And from learning what the Merry Band of Pirates have been doing."

"Yeah. Hans, the Ruhar are *frightened*, because we have changed the balance of power in the galaxy. Mostly, they fear that a young, impulsive and reckless species now has the potential to destroy all life in the galaxy."

"Our species? Or *you*? You have your finger on the trigger of those Elder weapons."

I bit my lip. "The mission summaries we released to the Ruhar were carefully crafted to leave out any information that might be damaging."

Hans cocked his head at me. "The Ruhar can read between the lines. They know you sparked a Kristang civil war. They know you framed the Bosphuraq for your own actions. The Ruhar public will fear that, if it is convenient to us, we will sell them out."

"Hey! The hamsters have not exactly been the most reliable allies to us in the past. They planned to transfer Paradise back to the lizards, and sell out our people. Their Commissioner was negotiating to abandon Perkins and the Legion on Fresno, and it was a Ruhar company that screwed the Legion on that rock."

"I know, I know," he waved his hands to calm me down. "The situation is complicated, that's all I am saying. The Secretary General wants to lead with diplomacy, focus on gaining allies."

"Oh, *hell* yes," I agreed. "She doesn't have to persuade me that we need allies. Hans, I, we have one ship to defend our homeworld. *One*. The *Dutchman* can't take on a Maxohlx warship and survive. We need allies, and we need to move fast. You've got my support, whatever you need. Uh, thanks," I set my glass on a coaster, unfinished.

Hans noted the liquid remaining in the glass. "Bourbon is not your favorite?"

"It's great," I assured him. "It's just, I'm flying, so-"

He grinned. "Skippy won't let you crash."

"He won't, unless there's a fault with the aircraft. I shouldn't tempt fate, you know?"

He stared at me. "How *did* you get here, so quickly?"

"Panther. Hans, I have to fly around in an invisible dropship, or I get mobbed by crowds everywhere I go. Not all of the crowds are friendly."

"I know," he sighed. "The UN assigned a driver and two bodyguards, to follow me everywhere."

That was odd, because I hadn't seen, or heard, anyone else in the house. "Where are-"

"In the kitchen," he jerked his head toward the back of the house. "Skippy assured me there are no threats within two blocks of this house."

"It's nice having a fairy Godfather," I made a half grin. It was nice having a someone looking out for me. It was not nice to *need* a someone making sure I was safe.

Crap.

Until recently, I had always assumed I could go back to a normal life sometime, after the initial fame wore off. Arriving at Earth with an arsenal of Elder weapons changed all that.

Maybe someday, if I could surrender control of the doomsday weapons to UNEF, the public would eventually forget about me. That assumed there were no future threats to Earth.

Yeah.

Maybe someday, pigs would fly.

CHAPTER NINETEEN

The TV blared to life, glowing brightly as my zPhone rang, startling me out of a sound sleep. "Sir? Colonel Bishop?" It was the UNEF Command duty officer, I don't remember her name. She appeared on my TV, which had not even been turned on when I went to bed.

Crap. Could she see me through that thing? I leaned over to grab my pants off the floor.

"Sir?" She stared straight ahead, not maintaining eye contact as I moved around.

OK, so she probably could not see me.

"Bishop here. What is it?"

"There are a pair of Jeraptha starships at Checkpoint Bravo, they just appeared." That checkpoint was an automated station, out beyond the orbit of Pluto, where incoming ships were supposed to wait for clearance to approach Earth. There was a microwormhole providing instant communications between the checkpoint and *Valkyrie* in Earth orbit, with another microwormhole connecting *Valkyrie* to UNEF Command in Geneva.

"What are they doing here?"

"They say they were *invited*?"

"Not by me." I frantically scanned my memory. Admiral Tashallo and I had discussed exchanging ambassadors, but we had not made specific plans. That was a task for Hans Chotek, and he hadn't even left Earth yet. "Who invited them?"

"They say they have *tickets*?" She showed me an image of six Jeraptha, looking at the camera, each one of them waving slips of paper and plastic cards.

Oh shit. "*Skippy!*" I shouted. Instantly, the duty officer's face on the TV was replaced by Skippy's avatar. "What the f-" I forced myself to take a deep breath and calm down. "Please tell me what the Jeraptha are doing here?"

"They are here for the tour, Joe."

"The t- *Tour*? What tour?"

"Of the zoo, *duh*."

"*ZOO?*"

"Um, maybe I should call it a 'safari'. Yeah, great idea, that sounds more upscale."

"What freakin' safari?"

"You know the concept. They want to observe monkeys in their natural habitats."

"Natur-" My brain blew a circuit. "What habitats?"

"Oh, all the interesting places you monkeys go. I wanted to showcase the finest of your local culture, so the tour includes viewing monkeys at pro wrestling events, monster truck rallies, hot dog eating contests, and-"

"This can't be happening."

"Oh, it *is* happening, Joe. They already paid for tickets, see?" He showed the image of the Jeraptha, all jabbering excitedly at the camera.

"The tickets are the pieces of paper? What is that plastic card in their other hand, claw, thing?"

"Why, those are Taco Bell gift cards, *duh*. They paid for the Premium Package, which includes an opportunity to feed the monkeys. It is *so* cute the way monkeys hold the tacos in their little paws-"

"WE DO NOT HAVE PAWS!"

"Wow. I can see that *somebody* is a little over-sensitive today."

"Skippy, it is three o'clock in the freakin' morning here," I sobbed into my hands. "*Please* tell me this is a joke, that you did not really sell tickets to Earth."

"I did not sell tickets to Earth."

"Great," I shuddered with relief. "I will tell UNEF Command to-"

"Now, do you want the truth?"

"You *lied* to me?"

"Ugh. You *asked* me to please tell you that it was a joke."

"That is an expression, you *ass*."

"Jeez, you say one thing, and you mean the opposite. How am I supposed to-"

"Shit!" We couldn't turn the Jeraptha away now. "I can't believe you pimped out my species, for entertainment."

"Joey, Joey, Joey. Somebody needs to monetize this incredible opportunity. Plus, Skippistan has substantial expenses, you know. I gotta earn cash, homeboy."

"The beetles really are here for a safari tour?"

"Yes. Well, that and to negotiate a treaty with your governments. Plus opportunities for gambling, of course."

"They are going to baseball games, something like that?"

"Um, sure if they want. Mostly, they are interested in international football, what you call 'soccer'. Pro football at the international level can be breathtakingly corrupt, it offers *fantastic* opportunities for gambling. The Jeraptha are incredibly excited about that, Joe. They want to negotiate rights to wager on many Earth sports."

"OK, well, I guess that's not too ba-"

"Plus, they want to assess whether a bunch of flea-bitten monkeys can handle Elder weapons. If you want me to be honest with you."

"You know, sometimes I wish you were *less* honest."

"Just say the word, buddy, and I will kiss honesty goodbye."

"I did not say that."

"Oh, good. Lying is difficult for me, it goes against my nature."

"Yeah, that's what everyone says about you. All right, shit. Tell the beetles to wait for clearance. Crap! I need to call UNEF Command about this. Do not do it again."

"I won't, I promise."

"Great."

"One question: define '*again*', please."

"Why do you ask?"

"Well, hypothetically, if I already sold tickets covering safari tours for the next twenty-eight months, would that be-"

"Twenty-eight *months*?"

"There is substantial demand, Joe. I limited the access so I can charge premium pricing. You don't want to cheapen the brand."

"Humanity is not a *brand*, Skippy."

"Sadly, that is true. Never fear, Skippy the marketing genius is working on it. Do you want to review my branding campaign? It launches in six days, all across the galaxy. The slogan I'm using is 'Monkeys: Not as dumb as you think'."

That got me mad. "That is *not-*"

"Of course, once the aliens get here and *see* your filthy species, I might need to change that slogan. Hmm. Maybe something like "Monkeys: How the f- have they survived so long'?"

The good news is, UNEF Command was running out of things to yell at me about, so a bunch of aliens showing up for a freakin' *safari* was a golden opportunity for the brass to renew their outrage. I was grateful that I was no longer a US Army officer, that was one less organization on my case about Skippy's latest shenanigans.

"*That* shit won't fly here," General Lindsay said, looking straight at me, like it was somehow my fault. Lindsay was vice chairman of the Joint Chiefs of Staff, and he was unhappy with me, among other things that made him unhappy. We were on his turf, his office in the outer E-ring of the Pentagon. Fortunately for me, his displeasure was not focused on me at that moment. "I don't care if she's a full bird colonel or a major," he was, of course, talking about Emily Perkins. The Mavericks and other people from Paradise should be arriving soon, the Jeraptha diplomatic team informed us they had several transport ships loading at Paradise. Admiral Tashallo had kept his word, I appreciated that. "No one under *my* command makes side deals with an ally without my approval, and approval all the way up the chain. She's going to get a reality check, now that she's back in the real world."

What Perkins had done, on and away from Paradise, had not been under my control. I hadn't even known what she was doing, or planning, until Skippy intercepted reports about the Mavericks, and later the Alien Legion. But, because it happened above Earth's atmosphere, somehow I was getting the blame for whatever actions she had taken that authorities on Earth were not happy about. Of course, the stuff she had done that those same authorities *were* happy about, I got none of the credit.

To be fair, I knew Lindsay was partly directing his remarks to me, because I had, I know this will shock you, a reputation for pushing the boundaries of my authority. It was mostly minor stuff, like committing mutiny, stealing a starship, sparking an alien civil war, that sort of thing. He knew that, since I was now technically a member of a foreign military, he had no direct authority over me. That is *why* he made a point of reminding me that real soldiers have rules and follow a chain of command, because I needed to understand that cowboy shit was not good for me or anyone around me.

"To be fair, Sir," the stars he wore meant I still had to call him 'Sir' and I had no problem with that. "UNEF-Paradise was falling apart, hundreds of people every day were leaving the service to try civilian life. Headquarters there was doing nothing about it, they weren't doing anything at all. There was a vacuum, and Perkins filled it. We're lucky she did, the Legion will be the basis of any future alliance with the Ruhar. She and her team are *very* popular with the hamster public, and the beetles respect her."

"She has manipulated the Jeraptha into fighting battles for her, *ending* battles for her, twice now."

"Yes. That's why the beetles admire her, she beat them at their own game. Their Central Wagering Office is flooded with prop bets about what she plans next."

"What she *plans next* had better be implementing the orders she's given, and not a whole lot else."

"I'm sure she will keep that in mind, Sir. *You* should keep in mind that the situation out there can be very fluid," I looked him straight in the eye. "Once the Legion goes through Backstop outbound, they are on their own."

"*Next* time, if there is a next time, she will have a tight leash. Someone with a tighter hand than Ross."

"Excuse me, Sir, but that's not fair." That was something I could not have said if I were wearing 'US Army' on my uniform. "Ross trusts Perkins, he vouched for her."

"According to your report, he also said he wasn't fully briefed on everything Perkins had up her sleeve. Ross," he looked down his nose at me, "got lucky.

"General Ross is *Three and Oh* against the lizards," I said. Lindsay was pissing me off. To Simms, I had joked about nuking bridges when I got to them, this was putting that into practice. "That's not *luck*. The Mavericks are a crucial part of Ross's team, but only a part. He had to figure out how to fight with the hamsters and Verds against the lizards, then *with* one group of lizards against another, twice. The Ruhar trust him to get the job done, and keep the Verd-kris in line. UNEF-HQ on Paradise trusts Ross to win the fight, whatever it takes. He knows Perkins always has something up her sleeve. She's an asset, and he is utilizing that asset to *accomplish the mission*. He's been out there," I added. What I did not say was 'while your fat ass rode a chair on Earth'. I did not say that because it would have crossed the line, and because it was unfair. General Lindsay was a dedicated career officer who was a team player and played by the rules, which is more than I could say about myself. However, it was also true that for the past twenty years, he had been fighting budget battles in the halls of the Pentagon, rather than actual fighting.

"Sir, I can't even tell you," I pressed my fingers into my temples, "how much Perkins drove me *crazy* out there. I seriously wanted to strangle her at one time or another. But screwing up my plans was not her fault, it was *my* fault for not bringing her into the loop. Ross told me one vital lesson the Ruhar have learned, from working with the Mavericks and the Legion, is that their own war planning and tactics are too rigid. They've been fighting this war the same way for so long, they have lost the institutional ability to innovate. Because their enemies have used the same tactics forever, the after-action 'lessons learned' on both sides are always the same, to the point where no one bothers really asking if there is a deeper lesson to be learned. That maybe there is a different way to fight, different tactics. A whole different strategy. We had the advantage," I smiled as a sort of peace offering to Lindsay, "of not knowing what the hell we're doing. We could make *new* mistakes, and learn from them. Sir, this damned war has effectively been static for thousands of years, until *we* came along. Star systems on the margins changed hands, but the overall strategic balance remained unchanged. All the fighting accomplished was killing a lot of people, and keeping the kitties and spiders in control. Perkins upset all that, when she proposed the Alien Legion. She knew that by themselves, twenty or even a hundred thousand human troops from Paradise didn't mean shit, couldn't make a difference. What she knew was that selling the Legion concept to the hamsters, opened the door to bringing millions, even *billions* of truly fanatical Verd-kris to fight alongside the Ruhar. The Verds? They have a huge advantage over their warrior caste cousins. They are united, not divided into squabbling clans. The Verds are building a professional, disciplined military. The warrior caste is divided, undisciplined, their entire ethos is bravado, not bravery. They're bullies. You punch a bully in the face and they'll fold. The Verds know that. I said they are fanatics, and that is a totally accurate description. They want their society back, their *culture*. What it was before the Thuranin conquered the Kristang and perverted their clients to better serve them. The lizard warrior caste is absolutely terrified of the Verds."

"Not so terrified that they won't hire Verds to fight their battles," Lindsay observed.

"In the short term, yes. The clans are all jockeying to be on top when the dust settles. Each major clan thinks they are best prepared to lead a unified fight against the Ruhar, to prevent the hamsters from unleashing the Verds on them. Also, if you ask me, the clan leaders are so blinded by their bullshit warrior culture, they can't consider the idea of dividing up Kristang territory between them. They *have* to fight until they just can't fight anymore, or the whole justification for the warrior caste would be called into question. They're stuck, Sir, that makes them vulnerable."

"Perkins has a plan to exploit that?"

"You'll have to ask her when she gets here, Sir," I said, not quite a lie.

He leaned back in the chair, folding his hands in his lap, tapping his thumbs together, studying me. Finally, just at the point when it was becoming awkward enough that I was about to say something to fill the silence, he gave me a sort of half-smile. "Jesus Christ, Bishop. If you were in my outfit, I would have made sure you stayed a sergeant."

Just as I was about to open my mouth, he added, "I guess that proves I don't know everything. Humanity is damned fortunate that I wasn't your CO." He reached for a framed photo on the corner of his desk, and turned it around to face me. "My daughter gave us a brand-new grandbaby last month, before you jumped *Valkyrie* into orbit. My wife and I were worried sick, that our grandchild would not have a chance to grow up." He blinked, and I realized he was blinking away a tear.

Damn. He didn't know me, so he had been *testing* me.

"Colonel," he said. "I'll take your advice about dealing with Perkins. Sorry for what I said about Ross, you're right, he's been kicking ass out there. I needed to hear your assessment of the job he's been doing. Like you said, you've been out there. Didn't mean to offend you."

Bullshit, I thought. He certainly *had* meant to offend me, but for a good reason. he needed to see my honest reaction. He had played me, I needed to remember that. I had a lot of experience with space combat, and planning special operations. I had not spent a career working with, and getting the best from, a large team of people. That was a lesson learned for me. "No offense taken, Sir."

He stood up, and I took that as my cue. "Bishop," he said. "I would be honored to shake your hand."

Shit.

I had not expected *that*.

We shook hands, firm, not too long.

"Whatever UNEF sends you out there to do next," he said. "Good luck to you."

"I'll do my best, Sir."

"The new legs hurt?" I asked, tipping back the glass to sip from a pint of ale. We were sitting in the dimly-lit corner of a British pub, technically we were in Wales. By 'we' I mean me and Jeremy Smythe. Not that his first name mattered, I called him 'Smythe' and he called me 'Sir' even when we were off duty.

"They're stiff, nothing to worry about," he grimaced and took a swig from his own pint. Doctor Skippy might have advised against alcohol, but I had instructed him to leave us alone for the day, other than monitoring the condition of Smythe's new legs and his overall health. This might shock you, but the Special Air Services soldier who commanded the STAR team of the Merry Band of Pirates, tended to push himself a bit too hard. Skippy had warned him to take it easy after his newly-grown biological legs were attached, and while Smythe wasn't doing anything stupid, he also was not taking it easy. That morning, we had gotten up early to hike in Brecon Beacons National Park, with the goal of walking up a mountain called 'Pen y Fan', and when we got to the top, the weather closed in. Clouds swept in from the Irish Sea, big fat cold raindrops stinging our faces as they were driven by the wind. There wasn't much, really anything, to see from the top, so we skipped any sight-seeing at the summit. The walk up was relatively easy, then it got tougher as Smythe insisted we descend via the route known as Jacob's Ladder. I didn't know at the time, but that route was part of an SAS qualification march called the 'Fan Dance'. We hiked the twenty-four kilometers in increasingly bad weather, with Smythe leading the way on his new legs, and me watching anxiously whenever he stumbled. It was chilly and raw, with low clouds scudding overhead, and wind gusts threatening to knock me to my knees. There was a dropship nearby, so we weren't in any danger of dying from exposure, and we had clothing appropriate for the conditions.

With about five miles to go, Smythe picked up the pace until he was jogging, a feat that was definitely not recommended on his new legs. Seeing him slip on wet rocks and mud, I almost called a halt, but Skippy whispered in my ear. SAS candidates were supposed to complete the course, about fifteen miles, in four hours. That explained why Smythe was pushing the pace in bad weather, he was determined not to fall short. We only carried day packs, far less weight than SAS candidates would have on their backs during the exercise. For us to take more than four hours would be frustrating and humiliating to Smythe, and I wasn't going to let that happen. Seeing that it would be close to four hours at our pace, I suggested we run, with the excuse that I was wet and cold and thirsty for a pint.

We reached the car park in three hours, forty-nine minutes, not that Smythe said anything about it. Nor did he complain about soreness in his new legs, and I avoided the subject until I saw him grimace and his face turn pale in the pub.

"If they're stiff, you should get up and walk around," I suggested.

"Excellent idea," he hobbled painfully to his feet, subtly using the table to steady himself. "I'll get another round."

That was probably a bad idea for him right then. Holding up my half-full pint, I called after him, "Get me a glass of water for now." My hope was that he would drink the water. As he came back toward the table, unsteady on his feet so the beer threatened to slosh over, I drained the remaining half pint and stood up, taking the glass from him. "Changed my mind, this is good beer." I brushed past him, so I wouldn't see him sitting awkwardly. When I came back to the table, I had another pint for myself and a plate of fries that the Brits call 'chips'.

Munching a chip, I tried to tactfully address the subject we had been avoiding. "What's next for you?"

He artfully dodged the question. "What's next for *you*, Sir?"

"UNEF Command is arguing about it, they'll be arguing until the end of time," I popped another chip in my mouth, wondering whether I should order a cheeseburger. Did British pubs make good cheeseburgers, or did they put weird stuff on them, like Stilton cheese, mushy peas and marmite?

Probably it is best to stick with safe, local specialties like fish & chips, or cottage pie.

"But I expect," I continued, "that the *Dutchman* will fly out to the beta site, bring an advance team."

"More scientists?" He grimaced and I wasn't sure how much of that was from physical pain, and how much from his disdain for the science team we brought there the first time. All they had done was bicker among themselves, and plead for more time before they could make a recommendation.

"No. This time we're bringing a seed colony. Twelve hundred people. The *Dutchman* will carry those multi-mission modules." The Jeraptha star carrier that was bringing transport ships from Paradise also had three modules, as a gift. Each boxy module could be configured to carry cargo or passengers, or a mixture of both. UNEF would be working feverishly to adapt the modules for humans, on top of the basic work the beetles were supposed to have done for us. The modules would be attached to the *Flying Dutchman*, after that old ship was modified to carry them. And we would need a test flight, of course.

"Mm," he grunted. "You're not bringing the *Qishan* or the *Dagger*?"

"They're not ready yet. I might not be going with the *Dutchman*."

"Oh?" He lifted an eyebrow. "Who is taking her out?"

"Don't know," I shrugged. "Chang is dirtside as UN Secretary of Homeworld Security, you heard that?"

"I did. He deserves it." In the Chinese Army, Chang was now a Senior Colonel. The NATO code for that rank was OF-6, which the US Army called a brigadier general, but either way, my former executive officer now outranked me.

"He does," I agreed, self-conscious for the first time of my own rank. I had told Skippy I didn't care, and officially I didn't. But maybe, just a little, I did.

Ah, forget it. For me to be a general officer would be a farce.

"What's going on with you?" I asked, though I knew exactly what his situation was. In a way, it wasn't fair to push him about his future plans, his new legs had been surgically attached only eleven days ago, in a procedure aboard *Valkyrie*. Skippy had told me the operation went 'smashingly', better than expected. Other than being sore as his new muscles adapted to the increased loads Smythe put on them, he should soon be better than new. Unless he continued to push himself too hard, like he did that morning.

"I've been offered UNSOC," he pronounced it 'Unn sock'. Chang had told me the leadership slot for the new UN Special Operations Command would be offered to Smythe. The job was a general's billet, so it would come with a promotion.

"Congratulations." I lifted my glass.

His own glass remained on the table. "It's a bloody desk job," he muttered, rubbing his left thigh. "I'd be playing politics with the member nations, begging for funding."

"Funding won't be a problem," I said while taking a sip of beer, watching him with the corner of one eye.

"No?" He snorted, skeptical.

"No. Skippistan has been nominated to full membership in UNEF."

"The beer can's fake country?" Smythe was astonished. "Why does that-"

"It's not fake to the UN. If you run into a funding problem, you can call the chief of the Skippistan armed forces," I grinned and pointed to my chest.

He shook his head. "I still can't believe you did that."

"There is *so* much less paperwork. Like, zero."

He raised his glass and clinked it against mine. "I'll drink to that."

"Are you taking the UNSOC job?" I asked casually. Chang had requested I talk with Smythe about the subject, the new Secretary of Homeworld Security was anxious to have an experienced operator leading UNSOC. Smythe was the dream candidate for the position, having extensive actual offworld experience. Unlike me, Smythe was almost universally popular with the public, he had gotten none of the blame for my reckless actions.

That applied to Chang, too, and Simms. All the Pirates except me, really. Only I was viewed with qualified approval. I was OK with that. The decisions had been mine, no one else was to blame for the consequences. If not for Emily freakin' Perkins, maybe there would have been a parade for me, after our Renegade mission. We would have returned from a successful mission to find a beta site, Earth would be safe for possibly hundreds of years, and everyone of our homeworld would breathe a sigh of relief. Life would go back to normal, or close to it.

Why, now that we had possession of invincible Elder weapons, was the public not celebrating? The answer was simple: too many times, the people of Earth thought they were safe due to heroic action by the Merry Band of Pirates, then another threat popped up. The public was waiting for the other shoe to drop, even though we now controlled the most powerful weapons in the galaxy.

The public was right.

"The Regiment is putting pressure on me to accept the assignment. It would be quite a coup to have an SAS man at the top of special operations for the entire planet," his mouth creased with a trace of a smile. "Whitehall," he meant the headquarters of Britain's Ministry of Defense, "has strongly hinted I should accept."

"National pride?" I asked with a nod.

"Do it for Old Blighty, they say."

"Shit. Screw the politicians. It's your life, your career. What do *you* want?"

"You once called me an adrenaline junkie," he reminded me. "Today," he grimaced and shifted in the seat, his legs clearly uncomfortable. "I may feel old right now, but I'm still too young to sit behind a desk."

"You want one last rodeo?"

"Not just *one*. The action is out there," he pointed to the pub's low ceiling. "Not in bloody Xinjiang." He meant the far western Chinese region, where a training base was being established for UNSOC. The area was sparsely-populated, with rugged, unforgiving terrain that was ideal for large-scale training exercises. Xinjiang did not sound like it would be a sought-after duty station, but looking at the gray sky outside and the chilly rain lashing the pub's windows, I was thinking that Wales was not my favorite place either. I'm sure it's nice other times of the year, Smythe had suggested we meet there to avoid crowds. He was a national hero, his picture splashed across the newspapers and magazines that still existed, and all over the internet. Going into the pub, we had our caps pulled low, and it helped that our rain-splattered goggles steamed up from the sudden warmth. That was also why we were sitting in a dark corner. Still, a guy near the window was discretely glancing at us, especially at Smythe. The barman was also fiddling with his phone like it wasn't working, which it wasn't. To help with our privacy, Skippy was selectively blocking WiFi and cell signals in the area. Anyone who wanted to post about seeing two famous Pirates, was going to be disappointed that they couldn't get a connection.

He had not exactly given me an answer, but I didn't push him. He didn't need pressure from me.

"What happens if I say no?" He asked, looking straight at me. "Who will get the job?"

There was no point pretending I didn't know, or at least hadn't heard the discussion about the open UNSOC leadership position. "It can't go to an American, because of me. Chang runs Homeworld Security, so China is out of the running. The feeling is, a Brit," I pointed to him with a thumb, "has been running special ops for years, it's time to give someone else a chance."

"That leaves France or India."

"Could also be someone from Brazil, Indonesia, Japan," I named a few of the countries who had joined UNEF as associate members in the past few years.

He cocked his head at me.

"OK," I shrugged. "India. If you turn it down, it will go to someone from India."

"Not Kapoor?"

"No. They're not giving him two bumps up," I noted that as Kapoor was a major, a direct promotion to colonel was unlikely. I am kind of an expert on unlikely promotions.

"Likely it will be Putri, then. Good man," he nodded. "May I ask you a question?" He had not put a spoken 'Sir' on the end of his question, it was implied in his tone of voice. He also had said '*may* I ask' instead of '*can* I ask', which is the correct and proper word to use, and reminded me how much better educated he was than me. Or should it be 'how much better than *I*'?

My life sucks.

"Sure," I took a sip of beer to avoid his eyes. Sitting in a pub with him felt weird. He is older than me, and has vastly more experience in everything except dreaming up crazy stuff for Skippy to do. Smythe is a hard-core, high-speed, Tier-1 special operator. If it had not been for Columbus Day, I might be a sergeant by now in the Army, if I was lucky and didn't do anything too outrageously stupid. Most likely, I would be in the Reserves, serving out my time. Fighting in Nigeria had kind of dampened my enthusiasm for the military, not because of the Army, but because I saw people in Washington putting boots on the ground to solve political or public relations problems.

Anyway, it just felt wrong for Jeremy Smythe to be asking *me* a question, and I knew what he was going to ask.

"Do you have any advice for me?" He asked.

"It's your life," I dodged the question in the most cowardly manner possible.

"I'll rephrase the question. Tell me what *you* would like me to do."

That made it easy for me. He had made a decision. What he wanted from me was cover, to protect him from being pressured by Whitehall. It sucked that he had to include political considerations in his decision, but that's life. "If things go sideways up there," automatically my eyes looked at the ceiling. "And they *will* go sideways, I want to know the most experienced operator we have is standing by."

He looked down at his beer, but he couldn't hide the quick smile that flashed across his face. "If you insist, Sir. Duty calls, and all that."

"Oh, bullshit," I laughed, a bit too loudly. The barman looked over at us, and I huddled around my beer. "I am serious, though, that it would be great to have you aboard. Simms told me she is *out*, and Chang isn't available. That means I will need to break in a new XO."

"When is *Valkyrie* going out again?"

"When UNEF decides on a strategy. I'm on an 'advisory council'," I made air quotes with my fingers, "with UNEF Command."

"Advising them to do what, exactly?"

"To not do nothing. To not think this war is over."

He lifted his glass and we toasted to that remark.

"Did you hear our testimony last week?"

He shook his head. "Sad to say, I was rather out of sorts, with recovery," he tapped his left leg. "What happened?"

It wasn't surprising that he had not heard of the special session of UNEF leadership, it was a classified briefing. If Smythe wanted to know, Skippy would have told him what happened, regardless of security concerns. "The UNEF governments are eager for a 'peace dividend'." I understood that part. The world was still recovering from Columbus Day, and the international economy had suffered one shock after another. *Valkyrie* coming home with databases full of Maxohlx technology was great, except it disrupted the plans of companies that had been struggling to exploit the Thuranin-level tech shared by Skippy before we left on our Armageddon mission. Many of those companies had invested billions in research to adapt Thuranin technology, and now much of their work was being thrown out the window, because superior Maxohlx technology would soon be available. "The governments think that with a powerful umbrella of Elder weapons protecting us, we're safe, the war is over for us. All the UNEF Command chiefs testified that is a *hundred* percent wrong. The general from India asked what we would do, if the Maxohlx showed up on our doorstep, and set up bases on Mars? Or if their ships appear in orbit with an invasion force, and they say all they want is Australia. Will we push the button, detonate our Elder arsenal? No fucking way," I shook my head. "We tried to explain that button is a one-time all-or-nothing proposition. We don't push that button unless the threat is absolute *extinction*. We need to build up a credible, conventional defense, before the kitties call our bluff. Maybe the spiders, too."

"That is the most sensible thing I've heard since we landed," he muttered. "What's the plan?"

"We need allies. I don't give a shit what Lockheed Martin or BAE says, we won't be able to construct our own starships for a generation, at least. Skippy says it will take *forty years* before we can even start making atomic-compression warheads, and that's if we put all of our resources into that effort. We need allies. We can't fight alone."

"What can we offer, in exchange for a mutual defense pact? Skippy can't just shut down wormholes on command, can he?"

"Skippy is worried he can't shut down *any* wormholes," I said quietly. "The trick of moving wormholes has got the overall network pissed at him, he can't risk pushing, or they might push back. Refuse to accept *any* commands from him. No, what we can offer allies is the same thing we've brought to Earth: technology-sharing agreements. There's a debate now about what tech we could, or should, offer to the beetles."

"What are we asking for?"

"That's also under discussion. Chotek is asking for instructions, and UNEF keeps debating what to tell him."

"Bloody politicians," he swore into his beer. Outside, the rain was pounding down even harder, gusts of wind smashing raindrops against the windows so hard, it obscured the murky view. "I'm glad you could be here on such a lovely day."

"Ah," I dismissed the concern with a wave of a hand. "You need to come to my hometown on some nice day in November, when the day begins with snow, then sleet, turns to a steady downpour, and starts to freeze on the roads around the time to drive home."

"You do have sunshine in Maine, don't you?"

"Yes," I confirmed. "It's guaranteed, two days a year. Not *consecutive* days."

We both laughed. Whatever he was going to say next was lost when my zPhone beeped softly. Pulling it out of a pocket, I saw the text from Skippy. "The Mavericks are here," I whispered. "The *Sure Thing* just arrived at Checkpoint Bravo. Soon as they get clearance, they will be in orbit. Perkins reports the transport ships are right behind her."

"How many?" He asked.

"Twenty-six thousand," I reported with a surprised whistle. That was slightly more people than the official capacity of the Jeraptha transport ships, my guess is enthusiasm for getting home had made people beg to cram themselves in however they could. They were all military, current or former, a bit of discomfort would not deter them.

"We should go," he pushed away his beer unfinished and stood up slowly, being careful with his new and likely very sore legs.

"Would you like a ride to Credenhill?"

He shook his head. "It's only a two-hour drive, I have time."

"You asked what I want? I want you to not drive, when your legs are cramping up like that. Besides, landing on the parade field in a Panther would be fun."

"Not if you scratch the clocktower, Sir."

"Come on, *I* will be flying the ship."

He raised an eyebrow. "If I remember correctly from our time on Gingerbread, you crashed a dropship into a lake?"

"That was unusual circumstances."

He looked outside, where wind was driving the rain horizontally and rattling the windows. "It would be nice to give the lads a bit of a show."

"How about this? We'll be in stealth until we're on final approach."

The flight was without incident, unless by 'incident' you include the uproar in the town, when an alien spacecraft roared in for a vertical landing on the well-tended grounds of the local university to meet us, unfortunately marring the lawn with deep divots where the skids sank into the soggy ground. For the touchdown at Credenhill, I engaged the inflatable pads under the skids, spreading the weight of the Panther over a wider area. I also kept the belly jets above idle as Smythe stiffly walked out and away, flashing a thumbs up when he was at a safe distance. He had invited me to dinner with the SAS, but I begged for a rain check, hopefully on a day when it was not pouring down rain. Mostly, I was eager to see Jesse and Dave again, and thought it would be nice to fly them and the rest of the Mavericks down from their ship.

Also, Perkins and I had a *lot* to talk about, I wanted a private discussion before UNEF Command and the Pentagon got to her.

CHAPTER TWENTY

The *Sure Thing* jumped into orbit just after I lifted off from Credenhill, or actually that ship jumped in three hundred thousand kilometers from Earth. The ship's momentum was carrying it about seventy degrees from the direction of Earth's orbit around the sun, and it was traveling much too fast to be caught in our planet's gravity well. It would need several hours to swing around into an orbit low enough to make unloading by dropship practical, so I contacted Perkins directly, and my Panther raced up to meet the *Sure Thing*.

When-

Oof. Yes, you in the back there with the homemade Star Trek shirt. Put your hand down, this isn't high school. You want to know why the *Sure Thing's* momentum was all wrong for dropping into Earth orbit? It's because that ship's direction and speed were determined by the need to rendezvous with a Jeraptha star carrier at the edge of the Paradise star system. Also, the Paradise system is moving around the center of the Milky Way about a hundred and twenty-three kilometers per second slower than Earth's sun. Also, the disc of the Paradise system, the plane on which those planets orbit their star, is tilted forty-seven degrees from the disc of our star system. Any ship traveling from Paradise to here needs to cancel those differences, before it can even begin to match orbital speed with Earth. *Also*, Paradise and Earth were at about a hundred seventy degrees apart in their orbits around their stars, with Paradise going one way, and Earth headed pretty much in completely the opposite direction.

Got it? Great. So, when-

Seriously?

Yes, the *Sure Thing* was attached to a star carrier for the journey. Why did the star carrier not accelerate or decelerate or whatever, along the way? Because star carriers are not designed to move around in normal space. They are just platforms with large-capacity jump drives. The long spine of a star carrier can't take the stress of high thrust maneuvering, especially not when the hardpoints are loaded with heavy starships.

Happy now?

When-

No. Listen, Terry or whatever your name is, if you have any more nerdnik questions, go get an astrophysics textbook, or research the answer on Wikipedia.

Anyway, when I arrived at the *Sure Thing*, Dave and Jesse pinged greetings to me, stating they were getting their units squared away for the drop to Earth, and they would talk with me later. Perkins was waiting for me in the docking bay, her face displaying a wary look. Holding up my hands, I assured her, "You're not in any trouble. Not yet. Not from me. This is sort of a courtesy call."

"What-" She cocked her head and peered at my chest. "What is 'GPR Skippistan'?"

Shit. I forgot that I had changed out of my wet hiking clothes and into a field uniform, during the flight up. "It's a long story. Is there a place we can talk privately?"

She pointed to the open door of the Panther behind me, so we went into the cabin and I closed the door behind us. "Coffee?" I asked, pointing to the cabin's tiny galley area. "*Real* coffee," I emphasized, "from Earth."

"Oh," her eyes almost rolled back in ecstasy. "I would *love* a cup of real coffee."

After we each got coffees the way we liked, we took a moment to enjoy our beverages, and quietly study each other. She seemed tense. My knowledge of her was limited and out of date. Was she always keyed-up like this, was she anxious about coming home after such a long time away, or was she apprehensive about the reception she would get from the Pentagon? I had told her the Army was not a fan of me calling an audible on the play, every time the *Flying Dutchman* left Earth.

She was staring at me, my guess was that whatever I had to say, she wanted me to get on with it. "Glorious People's Republic of Skippistan," I explained, pointing to the patch on my chest. "The short version is, yes, it is a real country, a member of the United Nations and UNEF. The US Army has seconded me to service with the armed forces of Skippistan, for the duration."

She blinked slowly at me. "Skippy has his own armed forces?"

"Sort of. You're looking at the entire army, navy and air force of Skippistan. I have a rifle around here somewhere," I pointed to the lockers behind me. "It's a compromise that allows me flexibility to act, in way that protects everyone, without getting other nations riled up that an American has the keys to our Elder arsenal."

"I see. For the duration of *what*?"

My answer was a shrug. "All I can say is, while I'm seconded to Skippistan, I'm not getting paid by the US Army, or accruing time toward retirement."

"UNEF is taking it seriously, then?" She asked, relieved. "They don't all think the war is over, because you have a cache of super-weapons?"

"UNEF Command's military leadership is working on it. The governments, and the public, are *tired* of constantly thinking about war, and worrying every time they look at the sky. Listen, you are going to get a mixed reception. Some people down there will be thrilled that humans have been kicking ass, and that your actions with the Legion are a good basis for an alliance with the Ruhar. Other people will fear that you have gotten humanity stuck in someone else's war. What I need to know is, what is your real strategy? Not the watered-down, half-truth bullshit you've told Ross, and you'll tell the Pentagon when you get down there. In case you haven't figured it out yet, developing a long-term strategy is not my best skill. Also, we can't afford to step on each other's toes again."

"That's for damned sure," she muttered into her coffee cup. "If I were you," she glanced up at me then back to her coffee. "I would want to *smack* me."

"It wasn't your fault. Besides, I worked out on the punching bag in the gym, until I got over it," I winked.

She grinned, and we clinked our coffee cups together to toast letting the past be the past. It had worked out pretty well after all. At the end of our Renegade mission, we thought Earth was safe for possibly hundreds of years, so it's likely I would not have taken the risk at Maris to locate a cache of Elder weapons. "I don't know what to tell you," she shrugged. "My grand strategy was always a pipe dream, now it's out the window. I never counted on the Merry Band of Pirates flying around the galaxy with Elder nukes and a talking beer can," she flashed a wry smile.

"Oh, bullshit," I snorted. "You may have to tweak your plans, but one starship and a handful of Elder nukes don't change whatever you wanted to accomplish. It's a big galaxy out there, full of assholes who need a beat-down. So," I set my cup down and leaned forward. "What's your plan?"

She stared at me, like she was trying to decide how much to tell me.

"Don't worry," I assured her, sitting back in my seat to be less confrontational. "I'm not beholden to the Pentagon, or anyone other than humanity overall. Whatever you say, I won't tell anyone, But I do have to know."

"It's unlikely we will get permission to put any of this into action."

"Right. Assume we do."

"Well," she took a sip of coffee, savoring it. One thing the Ruhar had never gotten quite right was the subtle flavor balance of coffee. Even the best samples they fabricated had an off flavor, like they added something to cover up the real taste. Genuine coffee had to be a real treat, to someone who had been away from Earth as long as Perkins. "First, I need to know if Skippy can do something," she looked at me, hesitant.

"Ask him," I said, clapping my hands twice. "Skippy! We need to talk with Your Lordship."

"Ugh," his avatar shimmered to life. "I am not a *dog*, Joe. You don't clap for me to appear. Have some respect."

"I did call you 'Your Lordship'."

"Did you mean it?"

That made me snort. "What do *you* think?"

"Now I'm insulted," He folded his arms, glaring at me.

"Mister Skippy," Perkins interrupted, looking mildly disgusted with me. "I have a question for you, if you have time."

"See, Joe?" He waggled a finger at me. "That is a respectful way of speaking to me. You should take notes."

"She doesn't know what a shithead you are yet. Perkins, sorry, go ahead."

"The major threat to Earth is from the two senior species; the Maxohlx and the Rindhalu. It would be useful to have a non-lethal weapon to use against them, something that threatens not their lives, but their *power*."

"Uh huh, uh huh," Skippy nodded. "That makes sense, good thinking. That is what Joe should have been doing since the beginning."

Tactfully, Perkins ignored that comment. "Skippy, can you shut down wormholes that are strategically important to the senior species?"

I guessed what she was thinking. "You want to isolate them in their own star systems?"

She nodded to me. "Yes, though what we should use is the *threat* of cutting their access to the wormhole network. If that doesn't work, we could begin shutting down wormholes. Use it as both a carrot and a stick. If the Rindhalu sign a non-aggression treaty with us, or even a mutual defense agreement, we shut down wormholes that the Maxohlx need, and open wormholes that give the spiders an advantage. What?" She must have reacted to the expression on my face.

"Skippy," I said, "you tell her."

"Like I said, that is good thinking," Skippy shook his head sadly. "It might be possible to temporarily shut down a small number, or a single wormhole. Or to create temporary wormhole connections that give one side an advantage. But the wholesale changes you're talking about? I'm sorry, I can't do that. Not anymore, not now. To create an effective embargo of, for example, the Maxohlx, would require shutting down *hundreds* of wormholes across the galaxy. To achieve even a much more limited goal, isolating only a few of their most strategically important worlds, would require disabling more than three dozen wormholes, because the most important worlds tend to be located near wormhole *clusters*. The Maxohlx would still have immense combat power, and incentive to use it."

"You can't do it," Perkins pressed for an answer, "or we *shouldn't* do it?"

"Both," he replied. "We should not do what you propose, *unless* we are certain the result would not be worse than the current situation. To provoke the senior species is incredibly dangerous. I warned Joe about that, when he explained his Mutual Assured Destruction plan."

"OK," she let out a long breath. "Does it matter? You can't shut down dozens of wormholes?"

"No, I can't. The network would not accept that type of instruction from me. Moving dormant wormholes was sort of the last straw for the network, it accepted my commands, but warned that I am now basically on probation. Shutting down wormholes would push the network too far, it would very likely refuse to communicate with me. If that happens, we will lose access to the beta site, and to Club Skippy. And lose our ability to create temporary shortcuts between wormholes."

"So, no. Let's not do that." She frowned, one side of her mouth curling downward. "All right, *that* idea goes out the window."

I waved a hand to dismiss her sour mood. "So we can't use a magic beer can to make the problem go away. You had plenty of success without Skippy, whatever plans you developed didn't include semi-divine intervention. What-"

"Semi-divine?" Skippy repeated excitedly. "Oooooh, I *like* that. Let's use that phrase to refer to me from now-"

"Let's *never* say that again, OK?" Damn it, I didn't want Skippy going off on a tangent. "Can we get back to the subject? Come on, Perkins, give me something to work with. I hate to say it, but Skippy is right. Mostly, we have been bouncing from one crisis to another out here. It would be nice to have a strategy."

"What I have is a *range* of options," she cautioned, "depending on what the enemy does next."

"Your strategy is reactive?" I asked, unable to conceal my disappointment. My hope had been that she would make the enemy react to *us*.

"No. The Legion has already poked the hornet's nest with a stick, we set the wheels in motion." She mixed metaphors and neither of us cared.

She told me her plan.

Note to myself: never play chess against Emily Perkins.

Never play poker against her, either.

Also, the Ethics and Compliance office of the beetles has a *lot* to learn from her.

That woman is devious.

Thank God that she is on our side.

It was great seeing Cornpone and Ski again. We sat around the *Sure Thing's* galley, drinking iced tea and swapping stories. Jesse told us some bullshit about how tough his life was when he was growing up, he made it sound like his family lived in a cardboard box.

I couldn't let him get away with that shit, without reminding him that growing up in the North Woods of Maine is not so easy. "Hey," I said. "I grew up in a two-bedroom house. When I was old enough, I slept above the garage to get away from my sister."

Dave snorted. "Ah, that's-"

"We had one bathroom for the four of us," I added.

Jesse shook his head slowly. "You had *indoor plumbing*?"

Shit. I was losing the game and I knew it. "Well," I shrugged. "It wasn't exactly *plumbing*. I found a busted drywall bucket on the side of the road, and patched it up with duct tape. Man, I was so proud that we didn't have to go to the outhouse on cold winter nights. Of course, we didn't have heat, so the bucket would freeze. That was actually a good thing, except when you had to chip out the ice later."

Dave was staring at me. "No real plumbing, but, you had *indoors*? Like, in a house, with a roof?" He made a mock bow toward me. "Wow, excuse me, Your Majesty. Jesse, did you ever have luxury like that?"

"No, we lived under a tree."

Dave gaped at Jesse. "You had a *tree*?"

"It was more like a stump," Jesse corrected his mistake. "In the winter, when it got really cold, we had to find a bear's den and wait for the bear to hibernate, so we could huddle up next to it."

Dave wasn't giving up. "You had a *bear*? We had to bribe squirrels with nuts, so they would let us spend the winter with them."

Jesse gasped. "You had *nuts*?"

It kind of went on like that for a while. Damn, I had missed those guys. I hope that, wherever fate takes us in the future, we can serve together.

Major Katie Frey tapped her laptop screen, reading the message again. It was the official announcement, she had heard it from the battalion CO in his office, before she saw the email.

Along with the promotion, she was being offered leadership of the Canadian contingent in the international STAR force. Four teams were training in Alberta, preparing for the international STAR qualification exercise that would take place in three months. It was a great honor that her country wanted her to lead STAR Team Canada. Rumor had it, UNEF was considering setting up a forward operating base at Club Skippy, where STAR teams would train as part of the Alien Legion. Assuming the Legion concept went forward, there was a lot unknown about which aliens would join an alliance with humans.

It was an honor.

It was a great opportunity.

Then why was she hesitating?

Pulling out her zPhone, she typed a message to Smythe. *I would like to talk when you have time*, she sent.

The reply came immediately. *Now is good.*

Looking at the clock, she saw it was after midnight in England. Of course, Smythe could be anywhere in the world, or above it. "Hello, Sir," she cringed at the awkward opening.

Smythe must have sensed her nervousness, for he laughed softly. "Good to hear from you, Frey. Congratulations on your promotion."

"Thank you."

"And on your new assignment. I heard you will be leading Canada's STAR program?"

"That," she took a breath. "Is what I want to talk about."

"You're not sure you want the job?"

"Yes. Sir, I heard you turned down the UNSOC position."

"Er, yes."

"May I ask why?"

"Because," he paused.

"Sorry." She regretted bringing up the subject. "I didn't mean to-"

"Frey, it's all right. I had to ask myself the same question," he chuckled quietly. "I spoke with Bishop about the UNSOC opportunity. I am staying with ST-Alpha, aboard *Valkyrie*. Or whatever ship Bishop and the beer can are flying."

"That's where I want to be," she said before she even realized how she felt about it.

"Are you sure about that, Major? The STARs are likely to see more action with the Alien Legion. Being assigned to *Valkyrie* is mostly long stretches of tedium."

"Yes, Sir. But what STAR Team Alpha does *matters*. The Legion is important," she didn't sound completely convinced of that fact. "But, *Valkyrie* is the difference between life and death. That's where I want to be."

"Of course you do," he laughed again.

"Sorry, Sir. I'm being honest."

"Frey, if you *didn't* want to be where you can make a difference, that would be a problem. I appreciate your enthusiasm. Have you heard that Major Kapoor is being promoted?"

"Yes. He will be working with UNSOC?"

"Correct. He will be coordinating between UNSOC and the Indian Army STAR teams."

"I should call, to congratulate him."

"Quite so." he cleared his throat. "Kapoor is a good man. His departure leaves an opening as my second-in-command in ST-Alpha."

"It does," she agreed with a catch in her throat.

"Would you be interested in that job? It would involve more administrative duties than your previous role."

"Administrivia I can handle, Sir. Are, are you certain I am the best person for the job?"

"You have doubts about your ability?"

"No. It's just- I didn't qualify for service aboard the *Dutchman*. I fell into it, because I was with you when Bishop had to steal the ship."

"That is exactly correct, Frey. It is also irrelevant. You have proved yourself, many times, in *action*. Training exercises are all well and good. They do not show what a person will do, in action, when everything falls apart and we need to improvise. *That* is what ST-Alpha needs."

"I would be honored to accept, Sir. It is possible?"

"Why do you ask?"

"There are political considerations. If I join you, the two senior positions of ST-Alpha would be occupied by people from Commonwealth nations." She referred to the Commonwealth of Nations, countries that were historically part of the British Empire. "That will not be a problem?"

"National rivalries are a consideration. However, I will handle that. The expansion of UNEF opens opportunities to many nations."

"I don't want to cause trouble for-"

"Frey, it is *my* decision to make. I will handle the bloody politics."

"Yes, Sir. Thank you."

"You accept?"

"*Hell* yes."

"Excellent. I need you here within thirty-six hours, I will clear that with your present chain of command."

"Uh, where is '*here*', Sir?"

"Queensland, Australia. We have a jungle training base here."

That surprised her. "Not in Belize?" She knew the SAS trained in that former British colony in Central America.

"The Belize training site does not provide a large enough footprint, for people who can run a hundred kilometers per hour in a mech suit," he explained dryly. "Also, we will be parachuting from orbit, we need a large section of empty airspace."

"Gotcha. Sir, if we need an arctic training site-"

"Way ahead of you, Major. There are several sites in the Yukon under consideration, along with sites in Norway and western China."

"I will be on the first available flight."

"Don't bother, Major. Contact Skippy directly for transport. UNEF has dropship training flights every day, one of them can bring you here."

"Understood. May I ask a question?"

"Go ahead."

"If I hadn't called you, would-"

"I already sent your government an inquiry about your availability. I was about to contact you."

Hearing that was reassuring, that Smythe had not made a spur-of-the-moment decision. "Do you know who else will be on the team, Sir?"

"Two friends of yours from Rikers; Grudzien and Durand."

Justin Grudzien's presence on ST-Alpha did not surprise her. Capitaine Camille Durand, however, had not been part of the STAR team aboard *Valkyrie*. She was one of Fabron's Commandos from Paradise. Frey had been forced to add Durand to her team for the hospital raid on Rikers, because of a personnel shortage. Durand had proven to be an outstanding soldier, but Frey had not heard the French woman was even interested in applying for a STAR team. "It will be good to see familiar faces," she said neutrally. There were likely going to be many new faces aboard *Valkyrie*. UNEF Command had ambitions to build or acquire a *fleet* of ships. Whatever those ships would be doing, she could be certain that special operations troops would be needed.

"Do you have any other questions, Major?" Smythe asked, and she could hear voices in the background.

Taking the hint that it was time to wrap up the conversation, she asked, "Just one, Sir. In Australia, will we have to eat Vegemite?"

That drew a laugh from Smythe. "No, although they do have very large spiders here, and I'm told they are delicious on the barbie."

After the call ended, she looked out the window, where a spider was trying to repair a web that had been torn by the rain and wind that morning. The spider was no bigger than a fingernail, but it made her think of the nasty creatures to be found in the Australian bush. Poisonous spiders, snakes, and jellyfish. Great white and other types of sharks, and the famous saltwater crocodiles. For certain, she would check her boots before putting her feet in them.

Then she laughed. A saltwater crocodile might be a fearsome creature, six meters long and weighing a thousand kilograms, with jaws that had the most crushing bite of any living animal on Earth.

But, if a saltie attacked her while she was wearing a mech suit, she could simply tear its head off. Maybe she would find out what barbequed saltie tasted like.

CHAPTER TWENTY ONE

After much, *too* much, debate, UNEF Command did something that shocked me. They-

Wait.

Are you sitting down? You'd better sit down before you hear this. Also, if you are operating heavy machinery, please stop.

Ready?

Whew, I need to take a breath before I say this.

OK.

UNEF Command made a *smart* decision.

I know, I couldn't believe it either.

Somehow, the squabbling politicians from twelve rival nations came to their senses and made a sensible, if obvious, decision. A series of decisions, actually. In the official announcement, the policy closely followed the recommendations of the UNEF Joint Chiefs, the senior military leaders of the component nations. Even more surprising, the vote was unanimous, twelve to nothing. Skippistan abstained from voting, of course.

The policy had two, really three elements.

First, diplomacy. We needed allies, so Ambassador-at-large Chotek was directed to approach the Jeraptha to open negotiations. We wanted warships, lot of warships. Earth's industrial base has no capability to construct starships of our own, so we needed existing ships that could be upgraded. Jeraptha ships were sufficiently advanced that they could be upgraded to our standards without having to completely tear the ships apart. What we wanted from the Jeraptha were warships and star carriers. Also fleet-support ships, that could build replacement parts for damaged ships.

What would they get in return? Our everlasting gratitude and affection.

Plus maybe a nice Hallmark card. And a fruit basket.

Also, to be more practical, we were offering technology. The Jeraptha would be able to upgrade their own ships with Maxohlx-level technology. In some cases, the tech we planned to offer was a slightly dumbed-down version of the systems aboard *Valkyrie*. Withholding some technology was an insurance policy, to maintain our edge. Once the technical knowledge was transferred to the Jeraptha, it was inevitable that other, hostile species would acquire it. Every species in the galaxy sought to climb another rung on the technology ladder, by stealing or capturing advanced technology equipment, then copying or reverse-engineering the alien systems. It was also inevitable that some of our technical info would be available for purchase. We couldn't completely stop it, so we had to plan for the future.

There were also cases where certain technologies would not be transferred to the Jeraptha, simply because they could not yet make use of them. Either the base structure of their starships could not handle the tech, or they lacked the ability to manufacture the required components. What mattered was that the beetles would make a significant leap in capability, and both the Maxohlx and Rindhalu would see their long-held edge degrade. We expected to get pushback from the senior species, but, screw them.

Chotek was also directed to open negotiations with the Ruhar. We were anxious to settle the status of humans on Paradise; would our people be allowed to remain there and if so, could Paradise be used as a forward staging base for future Alien Legion initiatives? Personally, I thought we should demilitarize our presence on Paradise, to avoid making that planet a target. Attacks there could only make the local Ruhar population, and the Ruhar public overall, view humans as trouble. Now that we had Elder weapons, humans were no longer seen as the scrappy underdogs who had gained the respect and affection of the average hamster. According to Perkins, when she left Paradise, the humans there were already viewed with suspicion, despite our repeated assurances that the humans on Paradise had not known anything about the Merry Band of Pirates. The Ruhar federal government had also expressed a healthy skepticism that the Legion concept should continue. Really, it made no sense for humans to serve under Ruhar leadership, any future Legion actions would be joint operations with the hamsters, under *our* terms.

We also wanted starships from the Ruhar. Not warships, their ships would be useless to us in a fight, even if we upgraded them. No, what we wanted from the Ruhar were transport ships, both civilian passenger liners and assault transports.

But, that was all stuff for Chotek to deal with.

So, diplomacy was first. We would start with the beetles and hamsters, then expand our alliances if that made sense.

The second element in the policy announced by UNEF Command was a major push to establish a secure human presence offworld. This time, we would not only be sending scientists to Avalon, we were sending people, thousands of people. The fact that Avalon had zero capacity to house and feed thousands of colonists was not an issue, the ships going there would be jam-packed with supplies. Enough shelf-stable food to support the colony for five years, until they could adapt the biosphere to grow enough of their own food.

I'm sure plenty of the scientists I pulled off Avalon would be pissed at me for interrupting the very important experiments there, if they wanted to yell at me, all I could say is they could get in line.

The decision to move forward with colonizing a beta site was a pleasant surprise, but UNEF Command followed that with another surprise. They wanted to set up a forward operating base at Club Skippy, despite Skippy's warning that the next wormhole shift would expose that lonely world to easy access by hostile aliens. The Joint Chiefs understood that risk, they felt Club Skippy could be a temporary first step, a secure facility to conduct training and act as an offworld supply dump. Also, UNEF planned to establish not quite a colony there, but a military base for the Alien Legion. At first, forty thousand ground troops would be stationed at Club Skippy, to train and be ready for future Legion operations, whatever those were. That is forty thousand soldiers and Marines, plus pilots and crews to operate the new fleet of starships we hoped to buy from the Jeraptha. The colony at Avalon is why we wanted to acquire passenger liners from the Ruhar, the assault transports would be for the Legion.

OK, so, decisions had been made by the civilian leadership. That meant I was going to be busy. The first thing I did was call Simms. "You heard?" I asked.

"Yes." She didn't say whether she had been informed by Skippy directly, it didn't matter. The UNEF announcement was all over every form of media on the planet.

"What do you think? It's a pretty bold move to-"

"Sir," she sighed, "why don't you just skip the pleasantries and get to the point? You want to know what I decided."

"OK, I want to know what you and Frank decided," I said, to let her know that I understood she had to consider the effect on her husband.

There was a pause and some whispering in the background. She said something like "Yes, I'll tell him," then she spoke to me again. "The answer is yes, we're going. But, it's not what you think."

"Uh-"

"Frank is going to Avalon. Just for the first year, to finish the assessment project. *I* will be setting up logistics to support Club Skippy."

"That fast?" I held the phone away from my face and stared at it. "Uh, when did-"

"The Pentagon gave me a heads-up about the announcement last night. Frank and I talked, and we're ready."

"Oh, that's, that's great." Shit. Why was I the last person to know? Skippy had some 'splainin' to do after I got off the call. "We should-"

"Sir, I have to go. Frank wants to talk with you," she handed off her phone.

"Joe?" He said.

"Hey, Frank. Congrats, I guess."

"On what?"

"The, uh, going to Avalon. The, science opportunity." I cringed, smacking myself in the forehead with one hand. Maybe if I thought really hard about it, I could make the conversation even more awkward.

"The science is what I want to talk about," he explained. "I don't think UNEF has any idea how difficult it will be to set up a colony there."

"They're supposed to be bringing enough supplies for five years," I reminded him, suspecting he already knew that and that supplies were not the problem he was worried about.

"Joe, to successfully grow crops there, and support domestic animals, we need to set up an entire sustainable *biosphere*. The fungus problem on Avalon caught us by surprise, we need to find a solution. We barely understand how Earth's biosphere functions."

"Uh, sure, but, people have been growing food on Paradise for years now. We grew food on Gingerbread, uh, that's the planet in the Roach Motel."

"Yes," he said in his I-Am-Being-Very-Patient-Explaining-Science-To-You voice. "Those planets had mature biospheres already. Paradise's biosphere had a long time for native life, plus organisms introduced by Kristang and Ruhar, to adjust to coexist with each other. The Ruhar still had significant problems in making the planet practical for wide-spread agriculture, and they have extensive experience with bioengineering organisms to new environments. Earth organisms were just another adjustment, and you know how difficult it was to establish agriculture there."

He was right about that. When I was a newly promoted colonel with the callsign 'Planter', my job had been to oversee our initial efforts to convert abandoned Ruhar farmland to growing Earth crops. We had discovered through painful trial-and-error that it was easier and more productive to plant our crops in new fields, to avoid harmful contamination from the aggressive microbes that Ruhar farmers put into the soil of their fields. When I was given the assignment, I expected the most vital of our supplies would be the seeds and tubers and whatever else plants grew from. I was wrong. In most cases, we had to churn soil conditioner in the ground first, to support a healthy root system, and help our plants extract nutrients from the alien soil. The Ruhar knew that soil conditioner imported from Earth was the key to humans becoming self-sufficient on Paradise, that is why their guerilla actions focused on destroying our limited stockpile of that vital material.

That was all ancient history now, or so I thought. "Yeah, I know," I told Frank. "We have to prepare the soil. And pollinate crops by hand, until we can bring in flying insects like bees. And we have to-"

"That is just scratching the surface of the problem. New types of fungus spores brought to Avalon, on the shoes of a colonist, could grow out of control and wipe out an entire season of crops. That's what we think caused the problem the first time. Introduced organisms that are alien to the native life there could disrupt and poison the entire biosphere, so it becomes unable to sustain *any* complex lifeforms. If you think I'm being an alarmist about this-"

"I don't. Skippy told me about worlds that were captured, and the invading species tried to bioform the ecosystem for themselves, but it was a disaster."

"Then you know the risk. Can you talk to UNEF Command, explain-"

"Frank, I could, but they won't listen to me, not about this subject."

"But, you can-"

"Talk to Skippy. UNEF *will* listen to him."

"Talk to Skippy?" He said in a tone like I had suggested he go on a strict diet of tofu and vegetables. "I just recently got him to *stop* talking to me all the time."

"How did you do that?" I said too quickly.

"Um, I'd better not tell you. Joe, Colonel Bishop," he added. "Please let UNEF know that you are concerned about this, and I will talk to Skippy. We probably *can* create a successful colony on Avalon, my concern is we're going too fast."

"We need to move fast, before the aliens out there interfere," I tried to keep a Civilians Don't Get It tone out of my voice.

"I understand that. Microorganisms don't care about the politics of intelligent beings, they have their own schedule."

"I will do what I can, but the first wave will consist of at least four thousand people. The plan calls for them to be scattered around the planet, to lessen the impact of droughts and other natural disasters."

"It's not natural disasters that should worry UNEF. It's disasters we will cause by moving too fast. All right," he sighed. "At least on Avalon, I won't have to worry about our safety whenever I see lights in the night sky." He paused, maybe he expected me to say something. "Joe? I *don't* have to worry about that, do I?"

"No! No, Avalon is safe. So is Club Skippy. As far as Skippy knows, no one else can get to either place, and Skippy is the expert."

"OK. This, Joe, this was a good idea."

"What?"

"Setting up a beta site, a safe haven."

"Oh. Thanks." I accepted the praise, without reminding him that I created the concept of a beta site because I feared the Merry Band of Pirates would ultimately fail to protect our homeworld. Feared that *I* would fail, that my reckless failure to think more than one step ahead would doom all of our efforts. Now that we had Elder weapons, it was easy to forget the panicked sense of desperation I had felt back then.

Forgetting that could be fatal.

"I mean that. We are damned lucky that you were in command of the Pirates."

"Gee, thanks, I-"

"That's not just me talking," he added. "That's what *Jen* says. Do you know how much she admires you?"

"Uh, well, uh-" Crap. How do I respond to that?

"Don't worry," Frank chuckled. He must have sensed how uncomfortable I was. "She still thinks you should eat more vegetables."

"Frank," I laughed, relieved. "*Nobody* can eat that many vegetables."

"Amen to that, brother," he muttered, and we had a bonding moment. "Hey, someday, you come to Avalon, and I'll grill a cheeseburger for you."

"That sounds great," I said honestly. "Hey, sorry you two will be apart for so long. You just got married."

"Jen intends to join me there, after Club Skippy gets up and running. Unless *you* need her, for some emergency."

"I will try not to-"

"Joe, don't make promises you can't keep. Jen is an Army officer. She will go where she's needed."

"Then I will do what I can to ensure we don't have an emergency."

We both knew I wouldn't have any control over that.

Getting into Skippy's new mancave aboard *Valkyrie* only required me to duck only a bit, the hatch was sized for a Maxohlx wearing an environment suit to squeeze through it. Still, I had to be careful not to bash my head on the lip of the hatch. "Hey, cool!" I had practiced being enthusiastic while I walked toward his mancave. It was not my best performance, but good enough. "Wow! Is that a genuine *Elvis* jumpsuit?"

"Yes it is, though I expect you don't appreci-"

"That," I snapped my fingers like I was searching my memory. "Is that from his legendary Las Vegas residency?"

"Why, yes. How did you-"

"1969? Or was it 1970?"

"It was '69, Joe. I did not know you were an Elvis fan."

"I wasn't, until I learned that you are. Figured I should at least check out his music."

"You liked it?" He asked eagerly.

"Of course. He is the *King* of Rock and Roll, baby," I said in my awful Elvis impression.

"Ooh, cool! Check it out, Joey my boy. This shirt over here is one he wore in the movie Blue Hawaii."

"That is cool. Listen, I know that Brock got all this exceptional stuff for you."

"He did it on behalf of all humanity, Joe."

"Right. I can't afford anything like that, so," I pulled a rectangular thing out of the bag I was carrying. "I made this for you."

"*You* made it? What is it?"

Removing the covering, I showed him. "A Skippy on velvet. I guess you can call it a 'Velpie'?"

"Huh!" He gasped. "*Magnificent* is what I call it."

It was done on black velvet. The image was Skippy's shiny silver can, wearing a gaudy gold crown, with rays of light shining out from him.

"What are those rays, Joe? Is that light?"

"They are the glow of your awesomeness, of course."

"Wow. I *love* it. Thank you. Quick, hang it up!"

"Elvis is the King of Rock and Roll. You are the King of *Awesomeness*."

"Gosh, I-" He choked up. "I don't know what to say."

"You are very welcome. Thank you, for sharing your awesomeness with us poor monkeys."

We chatted for a while, which was good because if I sucked up to him anymore, I was going to hurl. Then I had to leave for a completely unnecessary meeting that I had scheduled as an excuse to get away from him.

As I walked away, I flipped a middle finger toward the deck, in the direction of Earth. To myself, I thought 'Suck it, Brock Steele'.

It was just going to be a short flight, not even transitioning through the local wormhole. *Valkyrie* would be remaining within two lightyears of Earth on a shakedown cruise of four days, performing maneuvers to check out all the ship's systems that had been rebuilt and upgraded since we returned to Earth. If everything went well, the next time I took *Valkyrie* out would be to refuel the ship at Neptune, because we were close to running on reserves. The term 'shakedown cruise' supposedly refers to pushing a ship to the limit, to see if the vibration makes anything break. In this case, we would also be testing the new crew. If we did not discover a major flaw in either ship systems or personnel, *Valkyrie* would be going out again for a pre-deployment exercise, what the Navy calls a 'work-up'. Back when we only had the *Flying Dutchman*, conducting work-ups was a luxury we didn't have, instead we did on-the-job training, which is a nice way to say we were making shit up as we went along. This time, I was grateful for the opportunity to conduct a proper work-up, partly because so many of the crew were new not only to the ship, but to serving aboard a real starship at all. They had been training aboard the *Qishan* and the *Dagger*, but those Kristang rustbuckets were not proper warships, and the technology of *Valkyrie* was like high-order magic compared to the clumsy way that lizards made their ships fly.

The good news was that when we conducted work-ups, one thing we would be testing is our procedures for work-ups. That was important because we planned to have many more than two starships, we intended to have a *fleet*. There were going to be a whole lot of ships and they would need a lot of people to run them, and with people comes the need for procedures and other forms of bureaucracy.

Listen, I hate bureaucracy and filling out stupid forms that have to go through fifteen levels of approval before you get issued stuff like a carton of toothpaste. But, the Army is not just a team, it is a *big* team, and somebody needs a way to keep track of stuff like toothpaste. If we can keep track of toothpaste, then we can track the important stuff like railgun darts. So, I am totally OK with having written procedures for conducting work-ups, I just don't want to be the person who writes them.

My new executive officer was a Japanese Navy captain named Nakamura. A Navy captain is the equivalent rank to an Army colonel, so I didn't outrank him, though I had more time in grade. Nakamura was a nice enough guy, I suppose, I just didn't know him well at all. UNEF had decided to rotate command candidates through the XO position aboard Valkyrie, to give them experience before they hopefully got their own ships. That was a good and practical idea, and it meant I would be breaking in a new XO every couple of months. Hooray for me.

My executive officer was not the only new face aboard the ship, most of the crew was new to me. From the lead pilot couch, our new pilot Major Shepard turned to look at me, waiting for the order to jump. Maybe the expression on my face was reflecting my lack of comfort. None of our previous pilots were aboard *Valkyrie*, they had all moved on to other assignments. Reed had been promoted to major, and was conducting training at the UNEF flight school in Pensacola. Chen was in Chengdu, working to qualify pilots for flying Panthers. After Armageddon, we had been thin on pilots, and adding *Valkyrie* had stretched our pilot roster nearly to the breaking point. That was one of the reasons why I learned to fly a Panther, and took the basic course for flying *Valkyrie*. Our pilots deserved a break when we returned to Earth, and training new people to fly our ships was vital in the long run. Still, when I looked at the pilot couches and saw two unfamiliar faces there, it made me uneasy. Knowing they had been through a compressed training course did not build my confidence, even though Reed and Chen vouched for all the new pilots we had aboard. Sure, we had Bilby and Skippy to prevent us from flying into a star, that was not the same as having full confidence that the new people truly understood what they were doing.

It was unfair of me to question the qualifications of the new people. If Desai were with us, she would remind me that she had not known how to fly a Dodo dropship, then a Kristang frigate, then a Thuranin star carrier, but she had not crashed us into anything. She also had said many times that while she considered herself a damned good pilot, the people who completed UNEF training and qualified for the Merry Band of Pirates were *elite*, the best of the best. Desai had no illusions that she could have qualified, she was our chief pilot because she earned her experience the hard way, and simply because I trusted her. Hearing her say that always reminded me that I would not have qualified to serve aboard the *Flying Dutchman*, so maybe I should trust the people who had put in the enormous effort required to qualify as a Merry Pirate.

Anyway, it still made me nervous to have so many new people aboard the ship. I didn't *know* these people and I was afraid of making a bad first impression by doing some doofus thing they would never forget. "Pilot," I tried to project confidence. "Jump coordinates confirmed?"

"Confirmed, Sir," Shepard said after a glance at his console. Looking at the console was for my benefit, he already knew the system was properly programmed. Maybe he sensed my discomfort. "It's a hundred and six lightyears to Ursa Major. We have a full tank of gas, half a pack of chewing gum, it's dark," he looked at the main display that was showing a black starfield. Pulling a set of Ray-bans from a pocket, he added, "And I'm wearing sunglasses."

Right then, I knew we had a good pilot. Pointing to him, I ordered, "Hit it."

We jumped.

To the great surprise of pretty much everyone on Earth, *Valkyrie* led the way to Avalon less than *three weeks* later. The *Flying Dutchman* followed right behind, with three multi-mission modules bolted onto the *Dutchman* Version Four Point Oh's rather stumpy spine. Inside one of the modules were eight hundred and eighty-two people, including Frank Muller.

How did we manage to jump away so quickly after UNEF announced the go-ahead to colonize Avalon? It's simple. They dusted off plans that had already been approved. Food and other supplies were stockpiled around the planet, and extensive work had been done to convert one of the multi-mission modules to carry human passengers. While I had been flying around the planet and going on vacation, Skippy was working to add attachment points to the *Flying Dutchman*, so our former star carrier could transport three of those modules. The old *Dutchman* looked ridiculous with the modules hanging on its spine, and Nagatha reported the ship maneuvered like an overloaded oil tanker, but it could jump and that's all we needed it to do. Hopefully, we soon would have real star carriers and passenger ships, and the *Dutchman* could- Well, it could do whatever UNEF assigned that ship to do.Truthfully, I was worried about the future of our trusty old ship. UNEF Command had asked Skippy about the possibility of cutting the ship apart to refit Jeraptha warships we hoped to acquire, and I told him to slow-roll giving an answer. While I understood the practical value of using resources in the most efficient manner, damn it, the *Dutchman* was special. Even though that ship had few original parts left from when we took it from the Thuranin, it deserved better than to be used as a hangar queen. We also could not move Nagatha into a ship, without tearing out the substrate embedded into the *Dutchman's* forward hull, and she wouldn't be the same.

Damn.

I don't want to think about it.

What was I talking about? Oh, yeah. How fast UNEF threw the mission together. Like I said, a lot of the prep work had been done before the Jeraptha ships arrived with over twenty thousand people returning home from Paradise. Oddly, one element of preparation that I assumed would be the most difficult was actually the easiest: selecting colonists. Thinking about how to recruit colonists gave me a headache, but UNEF had already done that. They had a list of fifty thousand volunteers who were approved for Avalon. All that was required was to confirm the applicants still wanted to go, replace people who dropped out with ones lower on the list, and prioritize the list to about four thousand names. They needed to have useful skills, to get along well with others, and there were other requirements like being passably fluent in either English or Chinese. As a practical matter, the first wave of colonists needed to communicate with each other, and-

OK, enough about the practical aspects of selecting colonists. Somebody else had done the work, all I had to do was take *Valkyrie* out to escort the good old *Dutchman*.

We followed the now-familiar routine of waking up and going through the super-duty wormhole that connects the Milky Way to the Sculptor dwarf galaxy. While we didn't say anything to the crew, Skippy and I had a moment of anxiety waiting for the dormant wormhole to respond. He could not be absolutely certain that the wormhole network would not lock him out, because of all the other shenanigans he had gotten into, like relocating wormholes to places they were not supposed to be.

We both breathed a sigh of relief, or I did and he emulated the experience, when the super-duty wormhole woke up and stabilized without a glitch. Ditto with going through the wormhole in Sculptor, it accepted the password immediately without comment, and I took *Valkyrie* through.

The recon took a full day, which was enough time to determine there were no detectable threats in or near the star system. Avalon itself appeared to be OK, native vegetation had overgrown the fields of experimental plants we left, and structures in the camp looked exactly as they were when we left. The entity at Maris was functioning properly as programmed by Skippy; the stealth field covering that world was gone, and the stretched-out gravity well had returned almost to normal. Skippy reported minimal effects on the orbits of other planets, and he expressed confidence that as a colony and safe haven, Avalon was 'good enough for monkeys'.

Anyway, blah blah blah we dropped the supplies first, then landed the colonists. After endless irritating delays, we turned our ships around and headed home. The next trip to Avalon was not scheduled for eight months, to give time for the people there to set up infrastructure that could eventually accommodate up to fifty thousand more people.

My mother would think Avalon was getting too crowded already.

All the way home, I waited for disaster to strike. When we arrived at the far end of Backstop, the *Dutchman* waited in stealth a safe distance away while I took *Valkyrie* through to make sure it was safe for the vulnerable *Dutchman* to follow.

Everything was fine.

We jumped in near Earth, and I contacted UNEF Command while Skippy pinged the submind he had left behind. Everything was fine, as far as either of us could tell. UNEF Command congratulated my crew on a job well done, and cleared us to escort the *Dutchman* home.

We did that.

Nothing bad happened. It was weird.

Maybe I needed to get used to peacetime.

Or maybe the Universe was just waiting for the perfect moment to give me a beat-down.

CHAPTER TWENTY TWO

Brevet Captain Illiath arrived at the meeting site only slightly ahead of time, to avoid having to stand around making small talk with senior officers she disliked. And to avoid any possibility of her being seen anywhere near Admiral Urkan, so his disgrace did not stain her own reputation. The two of them had spoken several times earlier, beginning with when she returned from the astonishing mission to the planet humans called 'Earth'. Their most recent conversation was shortly before she was transferred from his command, to be reassigned to the Fleet General Staff, in the planning office. Urkan had warned her that, while she was being promoted to captain for her diligent efforts that exposed the human conspiracy, Urkan himself was in danger of being relieved of command. He was given credit for allowing Illiath to investigate her suspicions that the ghost ship was not controlled by a rogue group of Bosphuraq, and later to pursue inquiries into the odd behavior of wormholes. Those initiatives, which were considered a waste of time by Urkan's peers, had ultimately been successful in uncovering the horrifying truth.

However, there was no arguing with the truth that humans now possessed Elder weapons, altering the delicate balance of power in the galaxy. Someone had to pay the price for that humiliating defeat, and Urkan was the obvious candidate for punishment.

With Urkan's impending removal from power, the Maxohlx Hegemony's 14th Fleet had been sidelined for what Fleet headquarters termed 'extensive retraining required due to repeated failures to adhere to Fleet standards of performance'. Everyone knew that was a lie, but it was a particularly *convenient* lie, for half of the battlegroups of the 14th Fleet would be transferred to other units, increasing the power of those senior admirals.

With Urkan having fallen in disgrace, the star of another senior admiral was ascending. Admiral Reichert had advocated for taking a hard line against the ghost ship, throwing all of the Hegemony's resources into an all-out effort to blockade wormholes around the most recent known location of the mysterious enemy. Reichert's plan was to limit the area in which the ghost ship scourge could operate, then slowly squeeze the net closed, trapping the enemy ship. His fellow senior officers knew such a plan was unlikely to succeed, so they had instead approved Urkan's plan to lure the ghost ship into a trap. The plan had nearly been a success, except the ghost ship arrived before the ambush force was ready. Somehow, though caught in multiple overlapping damping fields, the ghost ship had escaped. Not only escaped, it had later attacked one of the ships left behind to investigate how the ghost ship had gotten away from a powerful force.

Nearly a success was not good enough. The ghost ship had escaped, and later somehow acquired Elder weapons. Reichert argued that if Urkan's plan had not been a humiliating failure, the humans would not have Elder weapons. The situation was all Urkan's fault, and by extension, the fault of those who supported Urkan over Reichert. That, too was a lie, but it was another convenient lie. The truth was, the senior leadership of the Hegemony was frightened by the thought of primitive aliens having doomsday weapons, and needed someone to blame.

The meeting at first was a typical inquiry, nothing that Illiath had not endured before. She had already testified dozens of times since returning from Earth, the questions were a mere formality. She would actually have been a bit bored by the proceedings, except she was curious to know why she was there. The questions had all been asked before, in some cases word-for-word repetitions of previous inquiries. The meeting was taking up the valuable time of senior officers who should have better things to do.

All she could imagine was that there had been a new development, something she did not yet know about. That was not unusual, even as a provisionally promoted fleet captain, her access to sensitive information was restricted. However, since Urkan was technically still in command of what remained of the 14th Fleet, he had the highest-level clearance. If something there had been an important development that might affect her, she felt certain Urkan would have found a way to let her know.

Which meant even a senior admiral was unaware of why Reichert had really called for the meeting.

That was interesting.

When the questions for Illiath were finished, with nothing new having been said, she was dismissed along with all but the most senior staff.

Senior Admiral Reichert of the 8th Fleet requested to address the assembled officers, on a matter of great urgency, and he was granted permission to speak. A veteran of more political battles than military conflicts, Reichert took control of the main projector. The device showed images in the hologram that dominated one end of the room, but also sent visual and auditory data directly to the cranial implants of everyone within the room's security field. Out of tradition and politeness, Illiath looked between the holographic display and Reichert, though her focus was on the images playing in her head.

"First," Reichert began, "I wish to remind my esteemed colleagues," he looked directly at Senior Admiral Zeverent, commander of the 3rd Fleet. "That since the truly astonishing discovery that humans control the ghost ship, and have acquired Elder weapons, our mighty fleet has done nothing. We have taken no action, other than a limited and perhaps overly cautious watch on Earth. Senior Admiral Zeverent, as you were one of the authors of this passive policy, could you comment on why our fleet has been ordered to take no action against the humans?"

Zeverent knew the question was a trap, though without knowing what point Reichert was trying to make, she could only repeat the Hegemony's stated policy. "Certainly, my esteemed colleague," she did not bother to mask the hateful look she shot at the commander of the 8th Fleet. "We need to gather information. Clearly our previous assessment of humans was flawed. It would be dangerously irresponsible to provoke the humans, without an understanding of their full capabilities. Also, there is no need to rush into action. The humans possess Elder weapons that is true, but they can't *use* them without condemning themselves to extinction."

Reichert nodded slowly, frowning for effect. "It is your expert opinion, then, that humans pose no threat to us, if we do not provoke them?"

Zeverant allowed the ghost of a smile crease her lips. She was not falling into whatever trap the other fleet commander had planned. "It is not my *expert* opinion, esteemed colleague, for it has become painfully obvious that none of us are an expert on human behavior. It is a cautious approach to an unprecedented threat."

Reichert looked down, as if considering the wisdom of Zeverent's words. "The basis of this policy, then, is the belief that humans do not have any plan to employ their doomsday weapons against us?"

"Unless you have somehow received information that humans are suicidal, yes," Zeverent agreed." After the first time the treacherous Rindhalu used Elder weapons against us, they have held their arsenal in reserve, as we have with our own cache of strategic weapons. There is no reason to think the humans, or any rational intelligent beings, would choose to kill themselves."

"Ah," Reichert pursed his lips. "What if I told you the humans *are* planning to use their weapons, have in fact already put such a plan into action?"

Zeverent's eyes darted to Illiath before she caught herself. "Admiral Reichert, if you have information this group needs to know, then you must-"

"The information only recently was received, and was confirmed only shortly before this meeting. Supporting data is being transmitted now." He waited a moment for the faces of the audience to go blank, as they received and began examining the files. Before the group could read through the material and draw their own conclusions, he continued. "The humans have an ability to connect wormholes outside the galaxy, to regions beyond our reach. They have begun to set up a colony in a satellite galaxy that is called 'Sculptor' by humans. These facts cannot be doubted, a task force of ships just returned from the satellite galaxy, after bringing several *thousand* humans there to colonize a planet. Humans plan a series of future missions, to transfer a significant portion of their population from Earth, to this secure site. My esteemed colleagues, I am sure you can see the purpose of establishing a colony at a secure site, where we cannot touch them. For humans, with their limited resources, setting up a colony outside the galaxy is a major effort. It is clear what they intend: once the colony becomes viable without external support, they will trigger their weapons here, and end the threat to their existence!"

Zeverent waited for the room to quiet down after Reichert's outburst. "Admiral Reichert, you are suggesting the humans would sacrifice the majority of their population?"

"Yes."

"Your opinion is based on your deep understanding of human psychology?"

"It is based on *logic*," Reichert glared, his anger evident from his facial expression and the pheromones released by his scent glands. "If faced with extinction, *we* would do the same. In war, hard choices must be made."

Zeverent knew he was right. From time to time, ambitious young officers in the fleet's war plans division proposed a 'bunker' strategy to end the endless war. Set up a secure population of their people in a hidden facility, then launch an all-out surprise attack on the Rindhalu. The spiders, caught unawares, would be utterly wiped out by Sentinels. So would the unprotected population of Maxohlx on every one of their worlds, and every other intelligent species in the galaxy. It would be the worst disaster imaginable, leaving every habitable world devastated. But, after waiting in hibernation for hundreds, even thousands of years if necessary, the small group of Maxohlx would awaken, to forever dominate a galaxy that would belong only to them. The select few, chosen to preserve the culture of their people, would ensure for the Maxohlx their rightful place as lords of the galaxy, unchallenged by lesser beings.

Each time the 'bunker' strategy was proposed, the plans were rejected, for the same reason all the previous plans had been rejected. It was impossible to be certain the Rindhalu did not know about preparations to construct a bunker, whether deep inside a nameless moon, or as a stealthed platform in the trackless wastes of interstellar space. Even beginning preparations for a bunker strategy would be seen as a serious threat by the Rindhalu, and the spiders possessed overwhelming combat power even without their Elder arsenal. Taking a course of action that would result in the deaths of all but a handful of their own people, was not an easy decision even by the stoic leadership of the Hegemony. With the balance of power between the two apex species stable, the Maxohlx were content to force their clients to fight an endless proxy war.

Then humans acquired Elder weapons.

"Reichert," Zeverent said evenly, careful to keep any note of pleading from her voice. "Do not presume that humans think the way we do. Is there proof that humans intend to trigger their weapons?"

"As I said, there is simple *logic*," Reichert scoffed openly. "Since you require more, we have intercepted messages between human leaders, which state the purpose of setting up a secure colony is to make their Elder weapons a credible threat. If an outside power were to seriously threaten Earth, the humans could trigger their weapons. I do not have to tell my esteemed colleagues that it is a small step to go from a *contingency*, to a *plan*. Once humans are satisfied their secure colony is viable on its own, then our survival will depend on an unstable, unpredictable, primitive species. I propose we move from a policy of *neglect*," his eyes lingered on Zeverent, "to one of *containment*. We prevent the humans from growing their colony outside the galaxy, to reduce the temptation to use their Elder weapons. We confine them to their resource-poor, primitive star system. We make sure they can never threaten us again. And we engage the Rindhalu to join us, to counter this new threat. Consider that, please. Now, before I detail my plans, everyone except senior staff will leave the chamber," he announced with a glance directly at Illiath.

After the meeting, Zeverent pinged Illiath to speak with her. Even in an office that was supposed to be secure, the admiral was careful what she said. Only aboard one of her 3rd Fleet ships could she truly feel free to talk, and then only after taking extensive precautions. "My esteemed colleague Admiral Reichert has proposed a campaign of slowly-escalating diplomatic pressure to isolate Earth, and prevent humans from gaining allies. If that is successful, we will proceed with an escalating series of small-scale attacks, to demonstrate to the galaxy that humans are *not* invincible. The War Plans Directorate has already approved his plans. I fear that what Reichert views as a minor attack, the humans would see as a dire threat to their existence. Tell me your thoughts," the admiral ordered the captain.

"I do not know how much I can tell-"

"You know the humans better than I do. Certainly better than Reichert does, he actively avoids knowing anything that might contradict what he has already decided. Talk to me."

Illiath took a deep breath, though her internal monitors indicated that her blood oxygen saturation was near one hundred percent. Some instincts were difficult to overcome. "Admiral, I have extensively studied human history, since we discovered the threat. Much of the data we have acquired is of questionable accuracy. For example, the person designated as 'Colonel Joe Bishop' cannot possibly be as the records describe. Most likely, his accomplishments are greatly exaggerated, or he is a composite of several human commanders. I suspect the truth is a combination of the two."

"How is that relevant? Bishop is not the issue."

"No, he is not. I mentioned him to demonstrate that our knowledge of humans, and therefore our understanding of their culture and psychology, is almost certain to be deficient."

"Understood. Proceed."

Another breath, this one for effect. "Shortly after humans developed fission, then fusion weapons, there were two 'superpowers' on Earth. They were military alliances of nations with opposing economic philosophies, which-"

"Excuse me," Zeverent shook her head. "Their disputes were based on *economics*?"

"Yes."

"Humans fought a war because of this?"

"Yes, several wars."

"Astonishing. Perhaps we can never understand such primitive creatures. Please, continue."

"One alliance was led by a nation called 'America', which incidentally is the home of 'Joe Bishop', if he actually exists. The competing Communist Bloc was led by a nation called 'Russia'. Both leading nations possessed strategic weapons with the ability to destroy each other, so they did not fight directly. Instead, they engaged in a 'Cold War', which involved provocations and saber-rattling, but no direct conflict. The actual fighting was between surrogates, in a series of what were referred to as 'brushfire wars'."

"Much as our clients fight clients of the Rindhalu," Zeverent observed.

"Yes, although curiously, forces of the Americans fought directly in places called 'Korea' and 'Vietnam'. Russia fought directly in a place they call 'Afghanistan'."

Zeverent cocked her head. "Why would coalition leaders engage directly in fighting? That is the whole point of having clients."

"I do not understand the reasoning. Perhaps the thought processes of humans require further study. My point, Admiral, is that Reichert's plan resembles a brushfire war: punishing the enemy and tying up their resources, but not threatening them to the point when humans would trigger their strategic weapons.

Ultimately, the humans will have to decide whether fighting a brushfire war against us is worth the cost."

"That is a terrible gamble. We have no idea where humans will draw the line, beyond which they will take drastic action. If the human leaders are religious fanatics, Reichert's strategy could lead to ultimate disaster."

"While religion might motivate many human actions, they do not appear to be fanatics like the Torgalau. However, I agree that a miscalculation by either side could spiral out of control. During the Cold War on Earth, the two leading powers nearly fought a nuclear engagement over a small island."

Zeverent shuddered. "I fear we are entering the unknown. Illiath, I want you to create a predictive model that we can use to wargame potential actions, to understand how the humans are likely to respond."

Illiath cast her eyes down to avoid the admiral's gaze. "That will be extremely difficult, given our limited experience with these creatures."

"You shall have whatever resources are needed. Many of my peers fear that Reichert is reckless. We can *contain* the humans without taking provocative actions, but Reichert seeks glory. He does not want mere containment, he wants to achieve *victory* over the humans."

"Yes, Admiral," Illiath could foresee little time for sleep, and much frustration in her future. "Will that be all?"

"One more thing, Captain. Do you believe the humans have an Elder AI actively helping them?"

"All the data we have acquired indicate that is true, however it is very difficult to believe." Other species believed the Maxohlx possessed an Elder AI, perhaps more than one AI.

That was a lie, a rumor encouraged by the Maxohlx themselves to increase their perceived power. They had devices that might have been part of an Elder ship's AI, though only fragments of the distributed system. Those fragments were entirely nonfunctional, exhaustive study had provided not a single clue as to how the device worked or whether it even was part of an AI. To make matters worse, the Maxohlx knew their rivals the Rindhalu almost certainly *did* have a functional Elder AI, and over the millennia, the spiders had only hinted at how their captive AI was assisting them. Many of her people believed that AI was the reason why the spiders maintained a technological edge over the Maxohlx.

If the humans truly did have such a capability, then provoking them could be extremely dangerous.

Illiath knew the Admiral was waiting for an answer. "Ma'am, as difficult as it may be to believe the humans are being helped by an Elder AI, it is impossible to understand how they could have accomplished so much without assistance from an advanced entity."

"Reichert is basing his plan on the assumption there is no Elder AI, that it is a deception by the humans."

Illiath was astonished. "Can he explain how the humans captured several of our capital ships, and moved a wormhole, without assistance from an Elder AI?"

Zeverent's lips curled in a smile that contained no amusement. "My esteemed colleague finds it convenient to ignore any facts that contradict what he wishes to believe."

"That is dangerous," Illiath noted with a shiver of fear.

"Yes. And that is why we must have an accurate predictive model, to understand the likely effects of Reichert's proposed actions. We can stop him, only by showing how he will lead us to disaster."

"Surely the Intelligence Directorate has constructed their own model?"

"Yes, and that model will produce any result Reichert wants." While the intel people did not work for Reichert, the senior admiral came from that community, and still retained close ties to many among the Directorate's leadership. More importantly, the intel people were deeply humiliated by their failure to detect that the ghost ship was not controlled by a rogue faction of Bosphuraq, and by totally missing any clues that humans were conducting clandestine missions throughout the galaxy. Reichert offered the possibility to take *action* against the humans, to get revenge and restore the credibility of the Directorate. "We need an independent analysis, to determine how far the humans can be pushed before they decide that they have no choice but to commit suicide, and take us with them."

Illiath worked tirelessly to create a model that predicted human responses, with a reasonable degree of accuracy. It helped that the Intelligence Directorate made their own model available for study, the intel people were wary of being blamed if Reichert's plans backfired.

"You have completed your model?" Senior Admiral Zeverent asked, when Illiath's hologram appeared in the office of the 3rd Fleet's flagship.

"Yes, Admiral. I am afraid it is not good news. My analysis found no major flaw with the model used by the Intelligence Directorate. There is more than a 98 percent probability that humans will not trigger their Elder weapons until their people on Earth face extinction. The only major variable between the models is the portion of human population that is transferred to a safe refuge outside the galaxy. With their current transport capabilities, an operation to evacuate Earth is not possible. Ma'am, I am sorry. My model *strengthens* Reichert's argument that we can, and should, take direct action. I will continue to refine the model, as we acquire new data, and-"

"Very well, Captain. We will all see how accurate the models are, as we escalate a campaign against Earth. I hope," she sighed. "That we do not regret taking an enormous, and unnecessary, risk against a primitive species we know little about."

After Illiath's holographic image disappeared, Zeverent sat quietly for a while, thinking about the uncertain, but certainly troubled, future of her people. For millennia, the Maxohlx had known the war would drag ever on and on without conclusion, but also without actual danger to themselves or their society. Of course, there were occasional flare-ups of direct fighting with the Rindhalu, brief engagements that lead to no further violence, for both sides knew the danger of a widening conflict. Now, for the first time since Sentinels rampaged across the galaxy, there was a threat that could lead not only to the Hegemony falling from power, but to extinction.

Because of that possibility, the War Plans Directorate had approved another top-secret initiative, to run parallel with the escalating provocations planned by Reichert. No part of the galaxy was safe from Sentinels, so the Maxohlx would construct a fleet of long-range ships to fly beyond the galaxy's rim, to the closest dwarf galaxy. Such a journey, beginning from the last wormhole at the edge of the home galaxy, would take hundreds, perhaps over a thousand years. Inhabitants of the ships would be in hibernation the entire time, a problem because the longest hibernation anyone had survived was less than eighty years. Nor had a starship ever been constructed that could jump continuously for such a long time, simply providing sufficient fuel was a major obstacle.

What Zeverent feared was not that the project to send a fleet beyond the galaxy might fail, but that it might *succeed*. Having a secure fallback would tempt reckless individuals like Reichert, who had long chafed at not being able to strike the Rindhalu directly.

She would need to closely monitor the progress of the Haven Fleet, as it was being called. The top-secret nature of the project would make it difficult for her to get information, but there was one thing she had learned during her long military service: the more funding a project receives, the harder it is to conceal.

I should have known.

Everything was going well. Great, actually, everything was going great.

I mean, really, everything was fantastic, better than I could have hoped. That's not me being sarcastic, it's for realz.

Earth was safe under our umbrella of invincible weapons.

We had a solid start on setting up a beta site, and the waiting list for people to move there as colonists was several *million* names long. Probably not all of them were completely serious about living in primitive conditions while working hard to develop a colony. For sure, not all of them would meet the strict requirements, which included, you know, not being an asshole. A dismaying number of people thought that setting up life on an empty planet was an opportunity to practice whatever hateful ideology they were obsessed with. It seemed like every political or religious extremist group on Earth wanted to set up a separatist homeland on Avalon. UNEF said *no* very forcefully, but that did not stop the whackadoodles from making demands to politicians and on social media. Some groups had attempted to contact the Jeraptha, trying to pay for transport off Earth to any planet where they could be alone. The Jeraptha, mostly amused, passed the information to UNEF Command.

Naturally, they pestered me and other prominent members of the Merry Band of Pirates, thinking we could get them tickets to Avalon, or something like that. Skippy intercepted all the emails and social media posts, so we didn't have to see them. He also had bots scanning and opening our snail mail and packages.

"Um, hey, Joe?" He asked, while I was getting dressed at a hotel in Alexandria, Virginia, preparing for a meeting at the Pentagon.

"What's up, Skippy? Do not tell me this tie doesn't go with the shirt, it's a *uniform*. I can't just throw on anything I-"

"You *could*, if you hadn't been such a ninny, and gone with my fashion choices."

"There is nothing wrong with this uniform. What do you want?"

"You received another death threat, Joe."

"I get death threats all the time."

"Yes, but this one isn't written in crayon, and it contains surprisingly few major spelling errors."

His tone of voice made me pause. "You're taking this seriously? Have you reported it to-"

"That's the problem. I don't know who handles this sort of thing."

"Uh- What are you talking about? Who made the threat?"

"It's a group that wants your help to get a piece of land on Avalon. Or, even better, a planet they can have all for their own. They tried to contact you several times by various methods, and of course you didn't reply. Actually, the last couple times, I replied for you. I am sad to say, you were not very polite."

"Oh, screw whoever this is. Why can't you just tell the FBI or someone-"

"The civil authorities don't handle this sort of thing. The threat is to summon their leader, the dark lord Satan, to cast you down if you don't-"

"Wait!" I laughed. "This is a bunch of *devil*-worshippers?"

"They prefer to be called 'Satanists,' apparently. Don't be so insensitive, Joe."

"Oh, to hell with them, literally," snickered at my own joke.

"Are you sure?"

"Yes!"

"Hmm. This is not something I can protect you from. If they really can summon-"

"Skippy. Seriously, don't worry about it."

"But-"

"Their dark lord lost a fiddle contest to a hillbilly from Georgia. Trust me, I'm not going to lose any sleep over this."

"Hmm. Good point. Should I ignore it, then?"

"Yes. As long as they are casting spells to summon a demon against me, they're too busy to bother anyone else."

"Okey-dokey."

Devil-worshippers were one of the stranger groups, but not among the most dangerous. And not all the crazies wanted tickets to Avalon. There was even one group of whacko assholes who still wanted to go offworld to fight for the damned Kristang! Their delusional conspiracy theory was that the lizards were our true, rightful allies, and the entire UNEF organization were traitors to humanity. The list of supposed traitors included the Merry Band of Pirates and me, of course. It should be noted that the lizard loyalist group did *not* contain any of the former Keepers who had come back to Earth, none of them had any love for their Kristang captors. With the help of Skippy or his Earth-based submind, the security services of Earth's governments were keeping a close watch on extremist groups. Part of what Skippy did was check my mail, I mean actual snail mail. What I said was true, I got a *lot* of death threats. He was able to block any offensive messages sent via email or social media, but intercepting harmful letters or packages was a job for a bot. What really worried me was hate directed at my family, or at the Merry Band of Pirates. Damn it, after all the sacrifices they made, to have my crew fear for their lives at home because-

What was I talking about?

Oh, yeah.

About how *great* everything was going.

Really, it *was* going pretty great. I suppose every species has a small portion of the population that should be loaded into a rocket and shot into the local star.

So, back to the good news. Hopefully, we would soon have the beginnings of a fleet, second-hand Jeraptha ships that would require heavy maintenance and upgrades at Club Skippy. That is what UNEF instructed Chotek to negotiate for, we needed as many ships as we could get. Hans had left Earth with the Jeraptha ships that brought part of the ExForce back from Paradise. He reported that negotiations to establish a formal alliance between humanity and the beetles were progressing well. So well, that the Jeraptha Central Wagering Office briefly halted action on speculation about the future state of relations with Earth. You know it is serious when the beetles pause action for any reason.

While Chotek was trying to nail down a deal with the beetles, I went out on another flight aboard *Valkyrie*, with the good old *Flying Dutchman* following like a puppy. That time, we went to Club Skippy, to drop off supplies and a team to begin setting up a forward operating base there.

By the way, while 'Club Skippy' was a good enough name for a place we never expected to visit again, UNEF decided that world needed to name that was more appropriate for a military base. It was China's turn to name a planet, since the beta site was officially called 'Avalon'. What the Chinese decided was to call the planet, and the star system, 'Jiayuguan'. Apparently, it is named after the site of a fortress at one end of the Great Wall, so it is a good name for a remote military outpost. In case you are wondering, because I sure was, it is pronounced Jee-Ah-You-Gwan. Close enough.

Naturally, we Americans and the Brits and the Indians and the French immediately tagged the place with the nickname 'Forward Operating Base Jaguar', or just 'FOB Jaguar'. The Chinese were a bit pissed that we had to give everything a nickname, but they agreed that 'Jaguar' is a cool name. Anyway, I call it 'Jiayuguan' or 'Jaguar'. The main settlement on the planet kept the name 'Club Skippy' because at first, it was just a bunch of tents, shipping containers and mud.

Simms left the ship to take charge of logistics for the American component of the force constructing the base, and she seemed happy enough, though she didn't have much time to think about whether she was happy or not.

Why do I mention all this good news?

Because I should have known it was too good to be true.

"Joe," Margaret lifted her head off my chest and looked at me. We were in a hotel room near the Twentynine Palms Marine Corps base, where she was stationed. I should say that is where she was stationed that month, the Marines moved her around a lot. Being at Twentynine Stumps was not her preference, and I could understand why. The whole area was a sun blasted desert, and there was not a whole lot to do off-base. We both joked that it reminded us of Camp Alpha, then we decided that wasn't much to laugh about. Anyway, she went off duty at 1700 and we met at the hotel, the first night I was back from FOB Jaguar. The plan for the evening was to go out somewhere for dinner, hopefully a place where neither of us would be recognized. All I cared about was being with her.

"Hey," I smiled at her. "Mmm, your hair smells good. Like, pineapple or something."

"That's my shampoo. Joe, we can't keep doing this."

"Sure we can," I ran a hand down to the small of her back. "Give me twenty minutes to recharge, and I'll be ready to-"

"It's not that." She propped her head up on one hand. "We need to talk."

"S*hiiiiit*," I groaned, stiffening. And not stiffening in a good way, if you know what I mean. "How come people never say 'We need to talk' when it's a *good* thing?"

"If it's good," she shrugged. "You don't need to talk?"

"When it's good is the *best* time to talk."

"We need to talk *now*."

"OK," I said, wondering if we should get dressed first. Having a potentially hurtful or heartbreaking conversation was awkward when the two parties are naked. "I'm listening."

"We can't keep doing *this*," she tapped my chest, then she reached down to squeeze my, let's say it is 'my friend'. "Uh, shh," she put a finger to my lips. "Let me talk, please."

All I did was nod, so she continued. "I considered your offer."

"This doesn't sound like you're going to say 'Yes'." My offer, really a suggestion, was that she and Skippy set up an arrangement like I had; the Marine Corps would detail her to service with Skippistan. That was my solution to allow us to be together, while she remained in the Marines. My Spidey sense told me she didn't like the idea as soon as I mentioned it, I was hoping she would change her mind.

"I can't. I just *can't*. The rules are the rules. If I'm aboard *Valkyrie*, you're my commanding officer. Skippy's fake country doesn't change the facts. This morning, I got a very polite inquiry about 'the nature of our relationship', as they said it." She looked away and I swear she was blushing.

"Shit." I squeezed her shoulder. "You're not in trouble yet, are you? Officially? Are they proceeding with an Article-"

"I think it was a subtle warning," she said.

I bit my lip. "But you *will* be in trouble."

"This," she tapped my chest again. "This, *us*. You and me, like this. Isn't *right*. Not by the regs."

"Oh, sc-" Catching myself before I said 'screw the regulations', I closed my mouth. "Have you thought about what Emily and Dave are doing?"

"He's a contractor," she said in a way that meant she had thought about it, and did not like the idea.

"Think about this: if you become a contractor, you'll never have to deal with an S-1 shop again." An S-1 organization handled administration of personnel issues for the Army or Marine Corps, although their real job seemed to be rejecting forms, and delaying anything a soldier or Marine needed in order to get healthcare, or do their jobs.

"That sounds Uh-MAY-zing," she grinned. "But, honey, no."

"But-"

"I talked with Colonel Perkins."

"Oh! Great. Did she have any advice about-"

"The Legion is adding a STAR team. Perkins needs someone to set up training, and coordinate between the STARs and the Mavericks."

"Okaaay," I did not like how that sounded. "Did she want you to recommend someone?"

"No." She avoided looking straight at me. "I applied."

She could tell by the way I froze that I wasn't happy. "The Legion will be based on Club Skippy," I told her what she already knew. "That is thousands of lightyears from here. From *me*."

"For now. If the Legion goes into action, *Valkyrie* will be there, won't you?"

"Oh, hell yes, no way-" Holy shit. Maybe Perkins did want Margaret on her team. Maybe she really did recognize the dedication, experience and skills that Gunnery Sergeant Adams could bring to the Mavericks.

OR, maybe Perkins was doing what she always did, what she did best. Ruthlessly utilizing every asset available, and manipulating people to achieve the objective.

Perkins knew that with Margaret on the ground, serving with the Mavericks, I would have extra incentive to make sure *Valkyrie* was on the scene, protecting the Legion with my ship's big guns. Shit. I barely knew the woman, but Perkins sure as hell knew *me*.

"Uh, hey," I asked as casually as I could. "You applied? Like, she didn't contact you directly about it?"

"No." She looked me in the eye, and I tried to look innocent. "I heard about it. All the STARs are talking about it, why?"

"It's just," I turned away to get a bottle of water, really so she wouldn't see the guilt on my face. "I mean, you're an obvious candidate for the job." Telling Margaret that I suspected Perkins was using her would not end well.

She looked at me sharply, as her legs brushed against mine. "Because I haven't requalified for the STARs yet?"

Crap. Why do I always say things the wrong way? Her recovery from brain damage was still a sensitive subject. Before we returned to Earth, she had not been ready to requalify. Since we came back, the Marines had kept her too busy to take the course. "Because of your experience. You know both sides; serving alongside special operators, and *being* one."

"Oh."

"Hey. Hey," I took her chin in my hand, gently pulling her to look at me. "If you want to serve on a STAR team again, Smythe is staying with *Valkyrie*. We talked, he's not taking the UNSOC job."

"I know, I heard. Also, I talked with Smythe."

"You did?" That surprised me. Crap. Everyone was talking behind my back, and not talking to *me*. OK, that was unfair. They weren't sneaking around me, they had their own lives and their own concerns. It just felt like I was the last person to know a whole lot of important stuff. Opening my mouth to ask when Margaret had talked to Smythe, I wisely closed my mouth without comment.

"He told me he is jealous," she said with a smile.

"Jealous?"

"Sure. He thinks STAR teams with the Legion will see a lot more action, than units stationed aboard ships."

"Oh, crap." The long periods of inactivity aboard the *Dutchman* or *Valkyrie* were a constant source of frustration and strain for the STARs, who had to keep sharp while they had absolutely nothing to do. "Then why did he offer to-"

"To keep *you* out of trouble."

"Ah." Part of me knew that was the answer. "Can I say something?"

"Of course."

"Be honest, please. I *care* about you. Is this, the end, of us?"

"No, lover," she kissed my forehead. "I'm doing this *for* us."

"Really? Cause it feels like-"

"If I'm with the Mavericks, you're not in my chain of command."

"Oh. Oh!"

"You will just be a foreign military officer."

"A dashingly handsome foreign officer," I grinned, and bit her earlobe.

"Don't push it," she laughed, but she nibbled my neck.

I pulled away to look her in the eyes. "You think this will work?"

"I think the brass will be satisfied it works well enough."

Taking a moment, I considered. "Yeah, probably." The Pentagon had been willing to bend the rules a bit to accommodate special circumstances, but they could not continue to look the other way while two people flouted the rules. The Army is a team, if they made exceptions for cowboys, that would erode good order and discipline. Plus it would be very bad for morale. "Hell, we won't see each other!"

"We won't? What's the difference if I'm at Jaguar or on Earth, while you fly *Valkyrie* around the galaxy?"

"It *is* different," I insisted. In the back of my mind, I knew my fantasy of having her aboard *Valkyrie* was a silly dream. It would be terrible for morale for the crew to know the captain was sleeping with one of the crew. On the flight to Earth after our Kick-Ass tour, we had been discrete, and that was only for a short time. Still, there were rumors, people looking at us and quickly looking away. It got awkward, and I felt terrible for Margaret. Sure, most of the crew probably were happy for her, they knew what she had been through. The crew also knew we were breaking the rules.

"Can we try to make this work?" She asked. "I am not sitting on the sidelines while UNEF fights."

"There might not be any fighting out there."

"You believe that?"

"No," I admitted.

"You are going to be out there?"

"I have to be."

"I do too, Joe."

There wasn't anything good for me to say, other than that I supported her. "You will be careful?"

She arched an eyebrow at me. "Will *you*?"

"As much as I can." It sounded lame when I said it.

"So, no," she scowled at me.

"You know what it's like out there."

"I do. That's why I need to be out there too."

"All right," I sighed. "I don't have to like it, but I do have to respect that you're a Marine."

"Damned straight, soldier," she growled through clenched teeth, sounding tough. The effect was ruined when she leaned down and kissed me.

CHAPTER TWENTY THREE

Damn. It surprised me how quickly things moved after the Jeraptha opened negotiations. UNEF showed them a sample of the technology we could offer, in exchange we were asking for stuff like warships, transports, fleet support ships. Basically everything we needed to jump-start our own fleet. The truth was, most of the tech we dangled as bait was actually worthless to us, because we lacked the manufacturing capability to make any of the fabulous machines Skippy had designed. For that reason, Priority Number One was to acquire fleet-support ships from the Jeraptha. Those ships were massive, bulky, slow-moving and easy targets in any battle. They were also vital to sustaining fleet operations away from fixed bases. Fleet support ships had fabricators that could crank out many of the spare parts that ships did not typically carry with them. In addition to fabricators, a support ship had hangars full of robotic mining machines that could extract raw materials from asteroids. UNEF was hyperventilating with excitement over the idea of having even one fleet support ship, while Skippy warned that even those ships had a limited ability to make components. For complicated repairs, Jeraptha ships went to spacedocks where heavy maintenance could be performed. Someday, Earth would have a spacedock in orbit. Until that day, we needed a basic repair facility.

Fortunately for us, the Jeraptha thought the technology sampler package was interesting, but what they really wanted was to see some of the advanced tech in action. UNEF agreed to upgrade three Jeraptha ships as demonstrators, with each ship having a range of upgrades. The modifications would be performed at FOB Jaguar, and Skippy would do most of the work, as usual.

The Jeraptha agreed rather quickly to the outlines of a deal, making me wonder if UNEF could have held out for a better deal. Whatever. It would be Hans Chotek's problem to hammer out the details, and make sure we got what we wanted. All I had to do was show up at the signing ceremony. After that formality was concluded, most of the beetles flew back to their ships and jumped away, leaving a small diplomatic staff on Earth.

Oh, I almost forgot. The beetles also agreed to take care of a problem for us.

A problem like, a whole bunch of pissed-off lizards, plus thousands more who were still frozen. The crew of the *Ice-Cold Dagger to the Heart* had been removed from that ship, most of them still in their sleep caskets, or whatever you call hibernation chambers. The citizens of Earth sure as hell didn't want them, and the ones who were awake were a problem both in terms of security and simply feeding them. Kristang couldn't eat any Earth food. Uh, what I mean is, they can *eat* most of our food without getting sick, they just can't get any nutrition from it. To keep the captive lizards alive, laboratories had to make ration bars with the sugars, carbs and proteins that kept Kristang alive. The process was a complicated, expensive pain in the *ass*, with the taxpayers of Earth increasingly asking why millions were being spent every day, to keep alive creatures who wanted to conquer and enslave our planet.

To solve our problem, the Jeraptha agreed to take the lizards, and deliver them to a planet controlled by their clan. *That* plan was complicated by the fact that, thanks to Emily Freakin' Perkins, the Achakai mercenaries were now a clan of their own. Again, whatever. The beetles would sort it out, all we cared about was that those asshole lizards were not our responsibility any longer.

Oh, another thing I forgot. While we were away, the *Dagger* had been officially renamed as the *Unity*. Yeah, that name is kind of lame, like UNEF didn't make any effort into thinking up what to call the ship. Really, the name was a political compromise, selected because it was bland enough not to offend anyone, and the word translated well into other languages. That's what happens when a dozen rival nations make a decision. What I care about is that UNEF make a good, and amazingly quick, agreement with the Jeraptha. After the signing ceremony, I was feeling burned out.

Like I said, I was at the ceremony to witness the signing of our first agreement with the Jeraptha, after Hans Chotek got all the details worked out. I am pleased to say that Hans delivered big-time on his first assignment from UNEF. His first *new* assignment, I mean. The first since humanity joined the ranks of top species in the galaxy. His actual first UNEF assignment, of course, was babysitting me aboard the *Flying Dutchman*. Trying to prevent me from doing anything reckless, like, you know, starting an alien civil war. Which *he* planned, if I remember correctly.

Anyway, a Jeraptha frigate arrived at Checkpoint Bravo, carrying the news that the beetles would soon be ready to transfer twenty-nine Jeraptha warships to us, plus six assault transports with a full complement of dropships, plus four star carriers, *plus* three fleet-support ships, *plus* an orbital starship servicing platform. Awesome!

If you think twenty-nine is an odd number, you're right. Why twenty-nine warships? Because the ships being transferred to us were obsolete craft that were so old, they had been stricken from the Jeraptha Ready Reserve fleet. Those ships had spent most of a century in orbit around an orange dwarf star, slowly turning and tumbling, so one side of the ship did not bake and the other side freeze. The interiors were filled with argon gas and kept warm and dry by solar-powered heaters. There those ships had drifted, occasionally stripped for hard-to-find spare parts, until parts of that age were no longer used aboard active ships. Originally, the Jeraptha proposed to transfer thirty-two ships, the largest number they could scrape together that had compatible technology, so we would not have to create unique parts for each ship when we rebuilt them. Of the thirty-two, three were found to be in such poor condition, they weren't even useful candidates for a full rebuild. So, we were getting twenty-nine warships of various classes. The six assault transports were not quite so ancient, the Jeraptha simply did not often conduct opposed orbital landings, and considered those transports to be surplus to their requirements. The star carriers were old but were still in occasional service when we got them, those ships were rugged and designed to have long lives.

The most valuable items we got from the beetles were the fleet-support ships, with fabricators that were state-of-the-art for the Jeraptha, and an orbital shipyard platform. Those fabricators would be used to crank out parts to rebuild and upgrade the obsolete ships, to form the beginnings of a human fleet.

Thanks to the skillful negotiating skills of Hans Chotek, and I am not being sarcastic about that, our fleet of starships was growing from two to forty-one! OK, we already had four starships if you count our two captured Kristang transports, but their crude jump drives did not have the range to carry them between stars, so I didn't consider them true *star*ships. And, technically, the three support ships traveled with a fleet, so they were also starships. I'm going to count that as forty-four true starships that would soon be wearing United Nations symbols painted on their hulls. Human ships. Our ships.

What, you may wonder, were the Jeraptha getting in return? Our ever-lasting gratitude and friendship?

Yeah, bullshit. The beetles were not stupid. They were talking about signing onto an alliance with us, moving slowly and cautiously. Like us, the Jeraptha were waiting to see how the senior species reacted to humans crashing their exclusive Elder-weapons party. Hans reported there was a brief inquiry into the Jeraptha acquiring a few of our ultra-powerful Elder weapons, they dropped that discussion quickly when he told them those weapons were not on the table. The beetles were not offended by the immediate rejection, they understood that the more species who had Elder weapons, the more likely it was that some jackassery or accident would wipe out all life in the galaxy.

They were *not* getting Elder weapons. They *were* getting a carefully-selected package of information about advanced technology, including how to manufacture gear to deploy that tech, and how to use and maintain it. We were even helping them make and install the first batch of those advanced devices, and *that* is the reason why the fabricators aboard our three new fleet-support ships were not obsolete junk. Other than a few test runs to make sure the fabricators worked properly, the support ships would be dedicated to making upgrades for Jeraptha ships, before those ships turned to building stuff for us. The schedule was set up like that, not because the beetles wanted to get paid before they turned the obsolete ships over to us, it was because we didn't want them looking over our shoulders while we cranked out *super*-advanced stuff for our own ships. See, *we* were also not stupid. The Jeraptha were getting access to Maxohlx-level technology, but not to the cool stuff Skippy had designed for the future UN Navy. The deal was, we would help the Jeraptha construct three ships to demonstrate the tech we were giving them, ships that the beetles would test and evaluate, before they decided whether to sell us a second batch of warships. And whether to sign a mutual-defense treaty with us.

My own assignment was to take *Valkyrie* and the *Flying Dutchman* to the star system where the Jeraptha would formally transfer the ships to us, although that was actually bullshit. The only thing happening there would be us arriving to inspect the ships being offered, then we gave jump coordinates to the Jeraptha star carriers that would bring the ships to Jiayuguan. Not to Earth. UNEF Command had decided, wisely, that humanity should not have all our eggs in one basket. Or even two baskets. We needed to have sustainable populations at more than two sites; Earth and Avalon. We also did not want our main naval base at Earth, where the presence of ships and orbital shipyards might tempt hostile aliens to attack. Instead, our small-but-growing fleet would be serviced and based at FOB Jaguar, which, like Avalon, aliens could not get to. Mostly. Skippy thought the next regularly-scheduled wormhole shift would open a wormhole near Jiayuguan, but that should not happen for a long time, possibly a hundred years. He could not be certain about the timing of the upcoming wormhole shift in that sector, because the network was refusing to talk to him, and because the shenanigans he did with relocating wormholes might have changed the schedule. In the meantime, a one-way journey to Jiayuguan from the nearest open wormhole would take even Maxohlx ships four *years*. The place we used to call Club Skippy was remote, located near where the wispy end of the Perseus Arm trailed off into intergalactic space. The closest star system of any kind was twenty-six lightyears away. You might think the night sky at Jiayuguan had a great view of the Milky Way galaxy, but that wasn't true. Being near the edge, the disc of the galaxy was just a streak across the night sky, and there was a lot of dust and gas blocking the starlight. Mostly, the galaxy was a dusky smudge from horizon to horizon across the night sky. It was a nice view, but not awe-inspiring like the view from Avalon, where the Milky Way filled the entire sky.

We needed a large number of people there, to train for operating our new ships, then fly them. Plus the Alien Legion would be based there, in the hope that we would sign a mutual-defense treaty with the Ruhar and have future missions for the Legion. Plus, FOB Jaguar would become a major STAR training site. Civilians providing support would be living in tents and containerized housing for a while, no differently from the military personnel. Before we were ready to accept the first batch of ships for our new fleet, we made four trips to Jiayuguan, to bring equipment and personnel. Eight thousand military personnel were there already, the number was growing each time the *Flying Dutchman* brought in new people. UNEF had also hired the *Sure Thing* to transport cargo for us, so FOB Jaguar was growing rapidly. With all the pilots, ship crews, infantry and special operators on that world, they would need plenty of support. The UN was recruiting civilians to work there, on one-year contracts.

That is why I called my parents, the next time I was at Earth.

"Leave Earth?" My mother blinked at me. "This is our home."

Looking around the still-unfinished kitchen, I pointed at the plastic covering the walls where the old cabinets had been ripped out. "You haven't been living *here*, until recently."

"We like the cabin," she meant the three-season fishing shack my uncle owned, where my parents had been hiding out before we returned to Earth.

"You keep telling me this town is getting too crowded," I reminded her.

"It is," she said, while my father put a hand on her shoulder. She rested her hand over his and they squeezed gently, reassuring each other. It was nice seeing my parents being affectionate.

"Joe," my father looked me in the eye. "What aren't you telling us?"

"Nothing. I have *been* telling you, telling everyone, and you're not listening. Having these Elder weapons is not the end of the war for us. We have been sneaking around the galaxy, running black operations and blaming others. Our secret is out now. The *war* is just beginning for us. I, I just think you would be safer somewhere else."

My father sat down, still holding my mother's hand. "It's that bad?"

Shaking my head, I knew they still didn't understand. "Earth is safe from major disasters, I'm worried about the two of you."

"Us? Why?"

"Dad, right now I'm mostly popular, again. That could change like," I snapped my fingers. "The public thinks we're invulnerable. Aliens are going to test that, harass us. If that happens, *when* that happens, I'll get part of the blame. Probably, I'll be out there with *Valkyrie*. You and Mom will be here, dealing with the fallout. Do you want people shaking their fists at you when you're driving, getting in your face at the grocery store?"

They didn't need to answer.

"Think about it," I pleaded.

"Where would we go?" My mother asked. "The list of people who want to move to Avalon is thousands-"

"Not Avalon. FOB Jaguar, or you might know it as Club Skippy. That's the base we're building on Jiayuguan. Mom, Dad, UNEF is talking about stationing eighty thousand military personnel there, and that's just the first phase."

My father snorted. "Son, I'm a bit too old to re-up."

"Not the Air Force. All those people need support. Contractors. The UN is hiring."

"Where would we be living? In some crowded tent city?" That idea clearly did not appeal to my mother.

"Maybe at first. Mom, the UN is planning to be at FOB Jiayuguan for many years. We are not shipping all the food out there. Someone needs to *grow* food." That argument was my ace-in-the-hole. My parents had been talking off and on about being farmers, even before we moved from Boston to the North Woods of Maine. They always had a garden, usually way too many vegetables that ripened all at once. My mother canned tomatoes, the last time I checked, they were still using the stuff she canned three years ago. Cucumbers became pickles, a shelf in the basement was overflowing with dusty jars of dill, bread & butter and other varieties of pickles. The squash we ate in various forms, until my father and I got sick of it. They would be just fine as farmers, especially on the UN payroll. "Think about it, please?"

"Your sister-"

"She can go, too." I knew my parents were hoping for a grandchild soon. If that happened, no way would they leave our planet. "Just think about it, please. The UN is taking applications now."

My mother squeezed my father's hand. "We will consider it."

"Great. I need to," I pointed over my shoulder toward the back door. "Make a call."

"Don't be too long," my mother looked toward the oven, where she had a lasagna baking. My Mom makes the best lasagna.

Stepping outside, I barely had a hand on the phone in my pocket, when Skippy called me. "Hey, Joe, I am pleased to announce that your parents have been approved for positions at Club Skippy."

"Uh- Huh? What?" Looking back, I saw my parents at the kitchen table, heads together, talking. "They already applied? Why did they tell-"

"No, they didn't apply. Not *officially*, if you know what I mean."

"Skippy, my parents will not be happy if I pulled strings for them. You can't scam the UN hiring process, it-"

"No scam, Joe. Not this time."

"Then what-"

"Skippistan is a *member* of UNEF, dumdum. I get to bring aboard up to fifty support contractors, on the UNEF payroll."

"Wha- what do you need contractors for?"

"I don't, *duh*. The UN is funneling *billions* into the Jiayuguan project. Allocating support contractor funding is a way for the UN to funnel money to me, so it can be skimmed off through creative accounting. I am expected to play along by hiring family members of influential politicians. Most of them won't actually be going offworld, of course, just collecting the pay checks. Anywho, I reserved slots for your parents."

"What would they be doing for you?"

"Jeez, I don't know. I'm sure you will think of something."

"*Me?*"

"They are your parents, Joe. Plus, you got me into this whole bribes thing. It's great!"

"Crap. OK, do *not* say anything about it to my parents, OK?"

"Oh, sure, like *you* get to be the hero and tell them the good news that I arranged."

"Trust me on this, please."

"Fine," he meant it was not fine. That was OK with me, as long as he kept his big mouth shut.

Captain Vereena Fondun was irritated when she made an 'old person' grunt while easing her very tired body onto the couch in her office, folding the forward pair of legs underneath her thorax. She hadn't slept properly in several days, ever since she accepted the assignment to spearhead the technology assessment effort for the Jeraptha Home Fleet. The humans were offering to transfer selected technologies to the Jeraptha, in exchange for starships, large-scale fabrication equipment, and other rather valuable items. The 'teaser' package of technology provided by the humans offered a mind-blowing glimpse into the treasure-chest of data they possessed, enough to get Fondun's leadership fairly trembling with excitement. The teaser package was just that; a tease. Just enough to hint at secret knowledge at or above the level of the Maxohlx, in some cases, even surpassing the abilities of the Rindhalu. Some of the technology was so advanced, so exotic that it was actually quite useless to the Jeraptha, they would not be able to manufacture the necessary components for many years, perhaps centuries. The Elder AI working with the humans jokingly said the 'recipe' for an advanced jump drive required two eggs, a gallon of zero-mass lanthanum ions, and a neutron star.

Fondun seriously *hoped* that was a joke.

She grunted again when she shifted her weight on the couch, to take pressure off a sore leg joint. It wasn't fair. She was relatively young, though she had to admit, her thorax was a bit bigger than it used to be. There would be time to worry about that later, after-

"Hello," a figure said from the doorway, startling Fondun.

"Ohhhh." Suddenly, she forgot about her aching leg, anticipating more worse pain. "Uhtavio. Are you here to ruin my day?"

"Of course not, Vereena," Captain Uhtavio Scorandum of the Ethics and Compliance Office snorted, easing onto a couch on the other side of the desk.

"Good." Vereena had a fleeting thought that she should offer the ECO captain a drink, though she didn't have a bottle of burgoze in her desk. Burgoze was typically a men's drink, it was much too sweet for her. As she remembered, Uhtavio did not like floon, so she left that bottle in the desk.

"I'm going to ruin your *month*, or more."

"Please," Fondun's forward set of antennas dipped to cover her eyes. "What does the Ethics and Compliance Office want with me now? Is this an official visit?"

"Are *any* of our visits official?"

"No," Fondun sighed wearily. "Can I assume this meeting is not to be recorded in my calendar?"

"That would be a good assumption, yes."

She understood why the meeting with Scorandum had not been listed in her schedule; ECO did not schedule meetings, they simply arrived. "Fine, then. You were never here."

"Excellent."

"How can I make you go away?" Over the years, Fondun had the misfortune to be involved on the fringes of various ECO schemes, and she had learned it was best to simply do whatever the Ethics people wanted, then try to forget about it.

"Vereena, I am hurt," Scorandum tried and failed to appear chastened.

"Somehow, I doubt that. Please, I am very busy," she pointed to the display wall behind her, which was covered with an impossibly-optimistic schedule.

"I know. We heard a rumor that the humans are offering to upgrade three of our ships, as technology demonstrators."

"Yes," Fondun answered warily. "The humans are choosing which technologies to offer, we have only limited influence on the selection."

"Yes, but, three of our ships will receive valuable enhancements?"

"As a *demonstration*," Fondun warned, shaking an antenna. "If ECO thinks they can expect significantly enhanced capabilities, they are sadly mistaken. The humans will be merely showing us a sample of the technology packages we can receive, if we pursue an alliance with them."

"We understand," Scorandum spoke for his office. "Our understanding is that the demonstrators will be small, obsolete warships."

"Yes. The Fleet has suggested three ships of the *Back-Stabber* class. They are modular and endlessly adaptable, with-"

"We would like to offer one of our ships, the *Rock-Solid And Suspiciously Convenient Alibi*."

Fondun blinked. "The *Alibi*?" She struggled to recall. That ship's service must have been long before her time in the Fleet. "I am not familiar with that name, is it-"

"It's a *Trifecta*-class light cruiser. Or, it was, before we modified it."

She raised her antennas. The *Trifecta* ships had gone out of service before she was hatched. "Why does ECO want one of its old junkers to be a demonstrator? It won't be useable as an operational asset."

"We understand that."

Fondun sighed again. "This will become an official request, at some point?"

"It already is, as far as you know."

"Very well." Captain Fondun knew she would see the request as an unmarked item in her department budget. "I will have my staff begin work on evaluating a *Trifecta*-class ship for upgrades." First, she would need to search the database for information on that class of ships, she had only vaguely heard of it. Then she warily asked a hopeful question. "Is there anything else?'

"Well," Scorandum grinned broadly, in the annoyingly charming way he did. "We *do* have one little request..."

All my parents told me was they would consider moving to Club Skippy, although my mother thought that was a silly name. My father asked if there was a brochure, so I know they were at least talking about it. No brochure, I said, but Skippy could show them anything they wanted to know about the place, plus thousands of hours of video we recorded during our visits to that planet.

Anyway, we got a signal from Ambassador Chotek that the beetles had everything ready, so I left Earth again in *Valkyrie*, with the *Dutchman* right alongside. We met the Jeraptha at the rendezvous point, had a ceremony with too much drinking on both sides, and then our engineers and technicians went aboard the ships we would be taking, poking around and pretending to open the hood and kick the tires, as if any filthy monkeys were qualified to inspect a Jeraptha starship. Really, we just wasted time while Skippy examined the ships, and declared each one of them to be a totally hopeless piece of crap, but thanks to his extreme awesomeness, he might be able to salvage a few of them.

With the inspection over and me nursing a hangover, we got our little assemble-it-yourself fleet to Jiayuguan, then *Valkyrie* escorted all but one of their star carriers back through the wormhole, and returned. Then the truly awful part of the mission began.

Listening to Skippy bitch about all the work he had to do.

He complained constantly, and I listened so he didn't victimize everyone in the star system. After a while I was able to tune him out, so when I complained back about his complaining, I was faking it. If he thought his bitching was getting to me, he would be satisfied to make me the focus of his wrath.

Besides, nothing could bother me much at FOB Jaguar. Why? Because shore leave. Margaret Adams was there, she was part of the Legion advance team. As captain of *Valkyrie*, I had private quarters dirtside, part of a containerized housing unit that was for visiting field-grade officers. Did I pull rank to get private quarters on the surface, when most people were living in tents? Yes. Did I feel bad about abusing my rank? Hell no. I had been celibate for way too long while flying around the galaxy, I needed to make up for lost time.

"This is nice," I mumbled into her hair, which was tickling my nose and I didn't care. Getting her hair away from my nose would mean moving away from her even for a moment, and I wanted to hold her tight against me. Over the years I had built up a major Snuggle Deficit, and I needed extended skin contact to prevent serious complications.

"Hmm," she mumbled into my chest, then I felt her wrinkle her nose.

"What?"

"Your chest hair is tickling my nose," she shifted to rest her head higher, toward my shoulder.

"Sorry."

"You have," her fingers were walking across my chest. "Six, seven, *eight* chest hairs," she giggled.

"Hey, we Bishop men are not hairy," I protested to defend my lack of hairiness. "Except my uncle Edgar, he looks like a grizzly."

"Yuck."

"One time at a family barbeque at the beach, he wore a *Speedo*."

She abruptly lifted her head to look me in the eye. "If you want to get me *out* of the mood?"

"Sorry. *I'd* like to forget about that image." She laid her head back down. "How is the new team?"

She raised her head again, annoyed. "Are we talking about work?"

"No. Sorry." Not knowing what else to do, and knowing that my mouth usually got me into trouble when it wasn't busy, I kissed her. She kissed back. That was better.

"Hey," I whispered a while later. "If you keep rubbing that, a genie will grant your wish."

"Really?" She laughed.

"Well, if you keep rubbing, I will get *my* wish."

"*Men!*" She laughed.

While Margaret and I were, let's call it 'affirming our relationship', Skippy was busy. First, he did a deep-dive assessment of our new used ships, then he tested the fabricators aboard the fleet-support ships. Those, at least, he found little to complain about, especially as they could easily be upgraded. The first items the fabricators made were advanced components to modify themselves. When the support ships were ready, we began the process of installing a selected series of upgrades to the three technology-demonstrator ships for the Jeraptha. The beetles, or actually the ECO, had a special request about one of those ships. It was odd until they explained what they wanted, then both Skippy and I were pleased to accommodate their request.

Being at Club Skippy was kind of a vacation for me. Skippy worked, and taught Nagatha how to use the fabricators, so she could take over while *Valkyrie* was elsewhere. That was both the advantage and the disadvantage of having a forward operating base that was at the galaxy's edge. Aliens couldn't get there, but neither could anyone else without Skippy screwing with the local wormhole.

Five weeks after we arrived at Jiayuguan, the three demonstrator ships for the Jeraptha were ready, so they were hooked up to a star carrier and *Valkyrie* escorted that ship back to beetle territory. No offense to our potential beetle allies, but we did not want any of them at our forward operating base while we worked on the advanced tech for our own ships.

Our ships.

Earth was going to have a fleet of warships.

Damn.

Monkeys were getting ready to seriously kick ass.

For once, things were going well for us, for me.

General Bailey stuck his head in the doorway of Lynn Bezanson's office on Paradise. "Getting a head start on packing?"

She nodded wearily, tired of making a hundred mostly meaningless decisions about what to take with her when she returned to Earth. Fortunately, the allowance for personal gear was not generous either in volume or weight, she was basically limited to one suitcase of twenty kilograms. Just her officially-issued Army uniforms added up to more than she could cram into a suitcase, so she would be leaving most of that on Paradise. UNEF would ship it to her, when and if humans obtained the transport capacity. "I'm trying to set a good example," she shrugged, and hung a uniform jacket on a rack.

"Don't worry about anything but your personal stuff," Bailey said with a grin.

"Oh?" She turned and plopped a box on the desk. It was half filled with personal items to be taken back to Earth. Actually, most of the items came from Paradise, or were acquired from one or another planet where the Alien Legion had set boots on the ground. The small box was depressingly sparse, there was so little on Paradise that she cared to take home with her. All she really cared about was getting home, seeing her family again. Seeing the new granddaughter who had been born while she was away. "What about," she gestured to the clutter of laptops and other communications gear on the desk.

"I just came from a meeting with Patel," Bailey leaned against the door frame. "G2 says the hamsters just approved us rotating personnel here, on a limited basis. The agreement states up to five hundred humans can come here from Earth, to do an 'assessment'," he used his fingers to make air quotes. Everyone knew that no assessment was needed, humans had lived and even thrived on Paradise for years. "UNEF will probably send fewer than five hundred, to avoid looking like bad houseguests."

General Bezanson stared in dismay at her office. She had assumed the building would be taken over by the Ruhar after the humans left, to be repurposed or knocked down, she hadn't cared. "Someone will be using this office?"

"That's my guess," Bailey grinned again. "You're worried about leaving a mess for the next guy?"

She nudged a box of junk on the floor, so it slid under the desk. "I'd like to leave it like I found it."

"We *found* this," he pointed at the floor, "in a shipping container." The entire building was a prefab structure provided by the Ruhar, to replace the tents that had served as UNEF headquarters for more than two years. "As I remember it, our offices were a mess right from the start." Due to lack of space, he and Bezanson had shared an office for several weeks, a situation made easier since both of them preferred to be in the field. "Lynn, the security people will sweep the place before we leave. The transport won't be here for another three weeks, minimum. Come on, I'll buy you a drink."

With a frown, she tapped her laptop. "I should pull my files off this first."

"Everything will be backed up aboard the ship," he pointed to the ceiling. "We have plenty of time. I want to hear what you think of this Bishop guy."

Both Bailey and Bezanson had been on the planet Tohmaran, where the Alien Legion's last mission had assisted one clan of hateful lizards kill another clan, until the Maxohlx arrived. They had both been terrified of the overwhelming firepower of the senior-species warships, expecting death to rain down from the sky at any moment. Then *Valkyrie* jumped in and kicked ass, and everything changed. In the aftermath, Bezanson had met Colonel Bishop, while Bailey was still busy trying to keep his people from getting caught in a crossfire between Kristang and Verd-kris.

"I only met him for a few minutes," Bezanson shrugged.

"That's a few minutes more than I had."

She folded the box closed, it could be taped shut later. With a smile she added, "I remember Bishop called me 'Beh-ZANN-son'."

Bailey tilted his head. He had always heard his colleague referred to as 'BEHZ-anson'. "Why did he do that?"

"He's from Maine. 'Beh-ZANN-son' is the original pronunciation, my family changed it when they immigrated from Canada. Bishop knew someone by that name from Halifax, one of my distant relatives, I guess."

Bailey pointed down the hallway with a thumb. "Drink?"

"Sure," she let out a breath. "I can't believe we are going *home*."

"None of us can. I won't *really* believe it until I see my family. Hope they recognize me," he pointed to the left side of his face, where he had taken a hit from shrapnel on Fresno. The Ruhar had patched him up and he was supposed to undergo cosmetic surgery to fill in the angry scar, but he never seemed to find the time.

"We all have scars," she touched her right shoulder, which had been burned when her starship had come close to being shot down over Fresno. The valiant ship had managed to achieve orbit, but not before blowing out major systems that caused scattered explosions and fires throughout the hull.

"Maybe I can get this fixed during the ride home," Bailey mused, tracing his fingers along the scar, which still itched annoyingly.

She paused in the doorway, one hand on the light switch. "You think we're ever coming back?"

"Here?" He scuffed a foot on the floor. "I don't know about landing on *this* rock again, but the action is out here, not on Earth. I expect UNEF will be fighting somewhere, and they'll need experienced people. You're not planning to *stay* on Earth, are you?" He asked with a wink.

"Oh Lord," she groaned. "Now I do need a drink."

CHAPTER TWENTY FOUR

After the Jeraptha left with their demonstrator ships, Skippy got the fabricators in our three fleet-support ships working to crank out the stuff we needed. What was our first priority? The battleships or battlecruisers? No. They were important, but even with the upgrades we planned to install, they could not travel long distances on their own. OK, then how about the four star carriers? Again, no. The six assault transports, since we expected the Alien Legion to be going into action? No, not them either.

Our *first* priority was to plan for the future. So, Skippy got the fabricators busy, making parts to construct more fabricators. Even the sophisticated machines of the fleet-support ships could not completely replicate themselves, they required exotic materials that the fabricators could not create from ordinary raw materials. For that reason, the space dock we acquired included two huge containers of spare parts, and a bin that was crammed full of exotic metals and ceramics the fabricators couldn't create. UNEF's plan was to create another complete set of fabricators to bring to Earth, while the three fleet-support ships remained at FOB Jaguar. If you really need to know the boring details of UNEF's implementation plan, the second priority was to get two of the star carriers operational, then four of the assault carriers, then the battlecruisers, and on down the list. We hadn't requested any frigates, because anything a frigate can do, a destroyer can do better. Fleets have frigates because they are cheap to build and operate, we didn't have that concern. Not yet. Someday, when we filthy monkeys are building our own ships, resource constraints and budgets will be an issue. I look forward to the days when our biggest concern is which corporation gets the juiciest contracts.

Anyway, Skippy got the fabricators working properly, figured out how to instruct them to create the parts we needed first, then trained Nagatha how to take over. She was already busy managing the space dock, that had come to us in sections attached to a star carrier, with 'some assembly required'. To no one's surprise, the handy-dandy instructions on how to put the damned thing together were not quite correct. It is difficult to put Tab A into Slot B when there is no Slot B to be found, and Tab A is bent out of shape. For the first time, Nagatha snapped at me when I asked her for a status update. She was under a lot of stress and understandably extra irritated with Skippy. Unfortunately, the only way in and out of FOB Jaguar was by Skippy screwing with a wormhole, and we could not halt operations every time we 'came up for air', as we called going back to the galaxy to see what was going on.

My vacation at Club Skippy came to an end, when Skippy reported that Nagatha was fully capable of handling the fabricators, and anything else that needed to be done at FOB Jaguar. To be sure that Skippy was not bailing early because he was bored, I asked Nagatha if she was ready, if there was anything she needed, anything I could do for her. She replied that yes, she was ready, and could I *please* take Skippy somewhere else so he did not drive her crazy by watching everything she did.

I took the hint. It was time for us to get an update anyway. The Jeraptha should have evaluated the demonstrator ships, and decided they were either in or out of a more comprehensive deal with us. It was time for *Valkyrie* to return to 'The World', as people at FOB Jaguar called the galaxy beyond the closest wormhole.

Oh, I had a nice surprise. Jennifer Simms came with me for the flight back. She had been tasked with reporting back to Earth on the progress made in setting up a forward operating base, and lessons learned. And also to knock some sense into the supply people on Earth who were sending twice as much of stuff she didn't need, and not enough of stuff she did need.

I wished her luck.

Escorted by a squadron of destroyers, the former ECO ship *Rock-Solid And Suspiciously Convenient Alibi* jumped into the designated emergence zone, just outside the next star system on its tour of the region. After testing at the regional capital planet Gizvagan, the *Alibi* was released back through the wormhole, for more extensive testing by the Jeraptha Home Fleet. When those tests were concluded successfully, the old ship and the two other demonstrators were sent on a goodwill tour of planets that were politically influential, to gather support for a future alliance with humans. The ship would spend several days in orbit, with VIPs coming aboard for short flights to demonstrate the amazing new technologies offered by the humans. Then the ship would jump away to the next stop on the tour. So far, the *Alibi* had visited three star systems on the widely-publicized tour, and the demand to see the ship in action had been so overwhelming, a second crew had been assigned to allow the ship to operate around the clock.

Support for an alliance with humans was building with every stop along the tour, based on the sagging odds being wagered against the Jeraptha signing a treaty with Earth. Three more stops, the *Alibi's* weary crew told themselves. Only three more planets to visit, then the ship would be brought to a shipyard for maintenance, and the crew could get a break.

First, the ship and escorting squadron had to go through the formality of waiting at the designated emergence zone, to obtain clearance to approach the heavily-populated second planet in the system. The lead destroyer already had a full set of authentication codes to prevent the planet's strategic defense network from firing on intruders, so the wait was truly a formality, an annoying delay to acknowledge the authority of the local government. At least the squadron would not have to pay the usual bribes at the clearance station, which irritated the crews, who anticipated skimming off part of the bribes for themselves. That is what happens, the crews told themselves, when the Inquisitor's office is watching too closely.

Everything went exactly as planned, when the *Rock-Solid And Suspiciously Convenient Alibi* emerged in the center of the formation, with the six destroyers popping into existence to form a bubble around the precious demonstrator. The lead destroyer pinged the clearance station that hung in cold, dark space so far from the local star that it was merely a faint disc, then the ships checked their systems while they waited for the formal invitation to jump inward.

Absolutely *not* as planned, a task force of Bosphuraq warships jumped in to surround the squadron, focusing damping fields only on the demonstrator and blasting the escorting destroyers with maser cannons and particle beams.

The senior captain in command of the squadron immediately recognized the danger, and almost as immediately recognized there was not much that her six destroyers could do to protect the *Alibi*. The enemy force consisted of four battlecruisers, nine light cruisers and fourteen destroyers, a strike package selected for speed and maneuverability. With the enemy's transmitters hammering space with powerful jamming fields, she sent an un-encrypted message to the *Alibi*, ordering that ship's crew to get into escape pods and set the precious demonstrator to self-destruct.

Too late.

Her destroyer was rocked by maser bolts that flared the shields and blew power couplings throughout the ship, as the four battlecruisers closed on the *Alibi*. One of the battlecruisers fired maser cannons in a broadside, six big-bore cannons focused on the narrow section of the *Alibi's* forward hull. The hellish directed energy quickly burned through the shields, the outer armor plating, the thin pressure hull and finally the frames that held the hull together. The old ship was sliced in two pieces, the larger engineering section of the *Alibi* drifting away from the spinning forward hull for a moment, before the battlecruisers all fired to vaporize the crew section.

To her horror, the squadron commander saw the remainder of the demonstrator ship was not responding to self-destruct commands, and two battlecruisers had moved in to block the Jeraptha escorts from firing on their fellow ship. Reluctantly, with her ship's AI shouting that they had to jump away *now* before the jump drive was compromised, she gave the order to retreat.

The destroyer squadron jumped a short distance, far enough to safely take a few minutes for diagnostic tests of vital systems, close enough to watch the alarming, time-delayed sensor images of a Bosphuraq battlecruiser latch onto the *Alibi's* engineering section. The battlecruiser was equipped with an odd grappling contraption for pulling in and securing a smaller ship, or part of a smaller ship. Clearly, the Bosphuraq had carefully planned the operation to steal the demonstrator.

There was still hope, that the backup computer systems in the rear section of the *Alibi* would activate a self-destruct mechanism. That hope held, right up to the moment when the enemy task force disappeared in a burst of gamma rays.

"Well, *fuck*," Senior Captain Gammeria swore. "*This* is a damned mess," she scowled as she reviewed sensor data, attempting to get a clue about where the enemy task force had gone. Her squadron of damaged destroyers had to make an effort to track the stolen demonstrator, no matter how hopeless the operation would be. Certainly, the Bosphuraq had a star carrier waiting nearby to swiftly fly the task force far away. Even if her squadron could pinpoint where the task force had gone, the enemy would be long gone by the time she could pursue. It had been many months since the squadron had practiced a combat latching maneuver to quickly dock with a star carrier, and their assigned star carrier was not even certified for combat latching. *That* was a mistake, one of many mistakes that she would get the blame for, despite her numerous objections when the operational plan was explained to her. The tour schedule should not have been so public. There should not have *been* a public tour at all. If there had to be a public tour, the *Alibi's* escort should have been composed of more and heavier ships. And the assigned star carrier should not have been an old Fleet Auxiliary rust-bucket, that had been hauling nothing but ore containers for the past forty years.

"Anything?" She looked around the destroyer's bridge. Her ship was battered but flightworthy, though she wouldn't want to engage anything larger than a frigate. The crew only shook their heads. Many of the exterior sensors had been baked by maser fire, they could not discern any useful information from the fading gamma rays of the enemy jump wormholes. "All right," she adjusted the sensors to focus on debris from the *Alibi*. Along with the expected shattered fragments of composites were bits of organic matter.

Body parts.

There were no survivors.

The Bosphuraq Imperial battlecruiser *Regent of Kallistah* was a beehive of frantic activity. Dropships clustered on and around the shattered Jeraptha hull section that was attached to the big battlecruiser, and technicians and bots swarmed inside the engineering section of the captured demonstrator ship. The first priority was to disable any self-destruct mechanisms inside the prize, then download every bit of data from information storage systems, and transmit the data to other ships. With the self-destruct charges disabled or removed completely, teams connected cables to the main computer, and soon petabytes of information were surging out on tightbeam laserlinks. A second star carrier was keeping formation at a safe distance, its attached ships all taking in the data and watching for enemy ships that would surely be searching for them. As a precaution, two battlecruisers had detached from their star carrier, and were ready to intercept any ship that jumped in, while both star carriers kept their jump drives on a hair trigger for immediate use.

Data storage and processing systems aboard the captured ship, that could not quickly be accessed, simply had their substrates cut out of the hull and brought to waiting dropships, which raced away as soon as they were loaded. The Bosphuraq Empire had suffered terribly from unfair punishment by their patrons, and could not afford to fall further behind in the technology race against the Jeraptha. If some, or most, of the Bosphuraq involved also hoped the captured technology would eventually enable them to tell their hateful patrons to go screw themselves, well, that was understandable.

Communication and Information Systems Technician Level Four Argas Fleemeran reminded himself to be patient, as his ultra-fine laser cutting torch sliced through a bulkhead and interior frame. His goal was to get access to, and remove, part of the ship's jump drive control system. Unlike most of the computers aboard the prize, it was not software or data that his people needed, it was the processing hardware itself. The technology possessed by humans allowed ships to jump farther, more frequently and with far greater precision, using less power. Ships with the new drive control system supposedly had a limited capability to jump even within the boundary of a damping field, though Fleemeran was skeptical of that. The Jeraptha ship had *not* jumped away when trapped within overlapping damping fields. Yes, the combined damping power of four battlecruisers had been focused on the little ship, but Fleemeran would have been more impressed if the little ship had at least attempted to jump away.

No matter. He had an assignment, and he was performing it to the best of his ability. With the bulkhead cut away, he could see the casing of the processor. Switching to a diamond-tipped cutter to avoid overheating the unknown but possibly delicate alien components inside the casing, he examined the scanner display, deciding the best places to cut. It looked like the processor had only four external connections.

The cutter went to work, easily slicing through one of the connections.

As the Level Four technician pulled himself along the bulkhead in zero gravity, to reach the next connection, he missed seeing a tiny yellow light blinking on the casing.

Cutting the connection activated a hidden subroutine inside the processor. There were seven other similar processors scattered throughout the engineering section, any of them could have initiated the process. Fleemeran simply had the luck, or lack of it, to be first to cut through a connecting cable.

One of the first acts of the Bosphuraq crews, when they boarded the prize, was to safe the power stored in the captured ship's jump drive coils. They did that to prevent an accident, and to avoid the stored energy from being used as a self-destruct mechanism. The procedures they expertly followed were precisely correct for any normal type of jump drive coils.

The coils aboard the *Rock-Solid And Suspiciously Convenient Alibi* were very much not normal, which the technicians perhaps should have considered, as that was the whole point to capturing the technology demonstrator in the first place.

Three milliseconds after the yellow indicator light blinked, the *Alibi* ceased to exist in a blinding flash of short-lived radiation, as energy that was supposed to create a tear in spacetime was released. When the captured ship exploded, it took with it the battlecruiser *Regent of Kallistah*, another battlecruiser, three light cruisers, four destroyers, and the star carrier they were all attached to.

Regardless of how many ships were lost, the Bosphuraq considered the operation to be an outstanding success. The data and components retrieved from the demonstrator were safely aboard the second star carrier, which jumped away immediately, as did the two battlecruisers that were protecting the formation.

The Jeraptha troop transport *We Avoid Temptation But It Keeps Finding Us* lifted from Earth orbit to great fanfare, though the excitement and celebration was confined to the human passengers, because the Jeraptha crew was *not* enthusiastic about leaving behind all the juicy action of the human planet. The *Temptation* had been scheduled to depart three days before it did, the delay being required to locate and retrieve nineteen Jeraptha crew members who jumped ship. Those who went AWOL, or simply failed to return when their two-day leave expired, tried to hide until their ship jumped away. Which is rather impressive, given that each of the miscreants was a three-meter-long beetle with a green leathery exoskeleton and a compulsion for gambling. Most of the attempted ship jumpers were located in areas near major casinos; Las Vegas, Macao, Monaco, and the other usual suspects. One was found hiding in the back room of an Indian casino in upstate New York, where apparently she had been playing poker nonstop for thirty-two hours, and had lost all of her officially-issued gear. One was found in a private casino on a yacht anchored off the south of France.

Others were more creative in their pursuit of action. Two were found huddled inside the Green Monster left-field wall at Fenway Park, wagering with each other about the outcome of games, innings and individual pitches. And the last miscreant had to be dragged from the Ladies' Bingo Night at the volunteer firefighter station, in a small town along Interstate 20 in northwest Nebraska. The ladies were sorry to see him go, he had provided great entertainment and lost enough money to pay for a new pumper truck.

When the *Temptation* fired its engines to climb to jump altitude, the human passengers were excited, many of them appearing on video to speak with audiences in their home countries. They were going to the planet 'Paradise', though almost everyone remembered to refer to that world by its proper name 'Gehtanu', to avoid showing any disrespect to the Ruhar. The three hundred and twenty-seven humans, a number comfortably below the firm limit of five hundred established by the Ruhar, were mostly civilians. It was thought that sending civilians, instead of military personnel, would allay the fears of the Ruhar that humans did not intend to ever leave Paradise. Four months was the maximum time the Ruhar would allow the official United Nations survey and assessment team to remain, as guests on the world where humans had originally arrived as lackeys of the Kristang. To sell the notion that the United Nations team did not intend to stay indefinitely, they brought with them only enough food for six months. The other supplies in the *Temptation's* cargo bays were luxury items such as coffee, chocolate and other foods that Ruhar technology had not *quite* been able to replicate.

In terms of momentous events, the human landing on Paradise was ages ago, but to some of the Ruhar population, especially long-time residents of that world, feelings were still raw. Humans were still not entirely trusted.

It did not help that the Ruhar suddenly had a massive chip on their fuzzy shoulders. The humans had been annoying and somewhat pathetic primitives, objects of scorn and pity. Occasionally, some small group of humans did something admirable, but that was the exception. Sure, the Mavericks had managed to bring about the downfall of the Ruhar federal government after the shameful incident on Fresno, that also was an anomaly.

Now, the humans were coming to Paradise as one of the three most powerful species in the galaxy, a force to be reckoned with. All three hundred and twenty-seven of the survey and assessment team were selected for their ability to be nonconfrontational, and trained in diplomacy and de-escalation techniques. They all had been instructed that in their dealings with the Ruhar, they should affect an aw-shucks-we-just-got-lucky attitude. Humans were still young and primitive, and needed the wisdom and guidance of the Ruhar.

Anyone who couldn't stomach the idea of bowing to aliens was left off the UN team.

The *Temptation* accelerated slowly, gaining speed and so lifting away from the human homeworld, toward jump distance. The ship moved slowly not because it was heavy, the few passengers aboard and their cargo was barely noticeable compared to carrying a full cavalry brigade and all its equipment. The slow progress was because the *Temptation's* captain and many of the crew were nursing whopping hangovers from their own shore leaves, and the captain was not entirely sure that her crew had not stripped vital equipment off the ship to use for gambling. One of the reactors was running at idle, because several relays were missing, along with the power conduits from that reactor. All the ship's captain wanted was to jump and latch onto a star carrier waiting at the edge of the star system, then she planned to sleep for a full day.

Miraculously, because it was discovered at the last minute that a cluster of jump drive coils had been stolen and replaced by fabricated fakes, the troop ship successfully jumped without further delay. A day later, it was firmly attached to a hardpoint of the Home Fleet star carrier *You Should Have Thought Of That Before We Left Home*, and both crew and passengers could relax for the journey to Paradise.

The Maxohlx offensive against Earth began not with weapons fire, but with diplomacy. The Rindhalu were approached and provided with the broad outline of the plan of escalating harassment against Earth. The Maxohlx diplomats, once they gained permission for a meeting, emphasized two factors that were likely to gain approval from the spiders. First, that the Maxohlx Hegemony needed to take action against the unpredictably dangerous humans, for the security of both apex species. Second, and almost as important, that the spiders did not have to actually *do* anything.

The Rindhalu always were more responsive to a proposal, when they were not requested to expend any effort.

That is why the first shot fired in the campaign against humans was in the form of a politely-worded diplomatic memo.

"Commodore, please come in," Planetary Administrator Loghellia gestured to the Navy officer with a mixture of curiosity and concern. Commodore Sequent's squadron had jumped into orbit only an hour before, and a priority message requested an urgent meeting with her, so she had cleared her calendar.

"Administrator," he glanced left and right, checking if any of her staff was in the office, but they were alone. The door slid closed behind him. "Thank you for seeing me on such short notice."

"Did I have a choice?"

"No. I don't wish to alarm you, there is no imminent threat to this world, or any of our territory. No threat other than the usual, of course," he added. Since the astonishing revelation that humans had been flying around the galaxy in a series of stolen starships, and now possessed Elder weapons, the galaxy had maintained an uneasy peace. Each species was trying to understand the new strategic situation, and each species was pondering how to take advantage of the new reality. The Kristang were particularly quiet, consumed by their own internal war that had been given new life through interference by the Alien Legion. The Ruhar government had called a halt to all offensive operations, pulling the fleet back into a defensive posture while the politicians argued about what the *hell* to do next.

"Then why the urgency?"

"Before I explain, I suggest you summon the human ambassador to meet with us. This concerns the humans directly."

If Administrator Loghellia was curious and anxious about an urgent request from Commodore Sequent, Ambassador Chotek experienced only anxiety when he was called to meet with the local Ruhar official. He was exhausted with a combination of jetlag and disorientation, from flying back and forth across the galaxy in a courier ship provided by the Jeraptha. In his experience, last-minute meetings, especially those at the highest level, were never good news. He left his two staffers in the building's lobby, and proceeded through security to be escorted up to the Administrator's office. She was waiting for him, the other person in the office was a Ruhar naval officer who Hans had never met. The officer's insignia designated him as a commodore, that was the only clue Hans was able to learn from looking at the alien.

Introductions were made, pleasantries exchanged, and Sequent got right to business. "Ambassador Chotek, I am required by my government, to notify you that the Rindhalu recently stated they will not protect us under the terms of our mutual defense treaty, if we continue to pursue an alliance with humans."

"I," Chotek's training, and his natural reserve, allowed a cool response. "I see. That is an interesting development," he said. Such a neutral statement filled the awkward gap in the conversation, and gave him time to think. "Has your government decided how to respond?"

"It is under consideration," Sequent said, after his eyes darted to Loghellia.

"Of course." Another neutral statement.

"Unfortunately," Loghellia took over the conversation, with a nod to the military officer. "My government has directed that, for this interim period, we must pause all negotiations regarding the human presence on this world."

"I understand. Do you have instructions about the UNEF survey and assessment team, which should be on their way here now?" A Jeraptha transport was supposed to have departed from Earth, with up to five hundred mostly civilians. The limit of five hundred had been a compromise after delicate negotiations, with the Ruhar seeking to minimize the number of humans coming to their world, and UNEF eager to maintain a presence on Paradise. If humans were only seen leaving the planet, it would be all too easy for the Ruhar to refuse to allow replacement battalions to rotate in. Hans knew Loghellia was in an uncomfortable position, having to balance interstellar and local politics. Some of the residents of Paradise saw the presence of humans as good for business. Others feared the human presence made their world a target. And others wanted all of the humans gone, for the simple reason that them leaving meant the areas they currently occupied would become available for development.

"For now," Sequent spoke, because it was a military issue. "The people coming from Earth will need to remain in orbit, pending further developments."

"That could become problematic," Hans said softly, "if the Jeraptha insist their ship remain on schedule." He was hoping to gain a concession that, if necessary, the incoming humans could 'temporarily' be allowed to land. Getting boots on the ground would be symbolically important, and set a precedent.

Sequent was ready with an answer. "That is a matter of discussion between your people and the Jeraptha." His instructions were clear: until the federal government decided how to respond to the Rindhalu demand, no additional humans would be allowed to land on Paradise. There was a bit of wiggle room in the instructions, if the Jeraptha insisted the humans must get off their ship at Paradise. In that case, the humans could be temporarily accommodated on the space station, or aboard one of the Ruhar fleet's transport ships. Whatever happened would be negotiated between the Ruhar and their patrons, humans would not be part of the discussion. There would be no more 'boots on the ground'. "I am sure you understand, this is a delicate issue." Sequent's face took on a pained expression. The fleet very much wanted the technology upgrades offered by Earth, even the limited 'teaser package' that would only improve the effectiveness of Ruhar stealth fields. "We do intend to continue talks about technology transfers."

Hans suppressed a smile. Of course the hamsters wanted a part of the vast technology database that humans had acquired. They wanted the information, plus assistance in understanding and using the advanced tech. On behalf of UNEF, he had been negotiating to provide a package of selected technologies to the Ruhar, in exchange for a limited alliance. "Please understand, I must consult with my government before talks can continue, given the changed circumstances." That was his diplomatic way of saying 'you assholes are not getting something for nothing'. A treaty with the Ruhar would be nice, but far less important than an alliance with their patrons, the Jeraptha. What he feared was that if the Rindhalu had warned the Ruhar against making a deal with Earth, surely the spiders had also advised the beetles not to sign any sort of mutual defense treaty with humans. UNEF needed to know about this disturbing development. With a weary groan he kept to himself, he anticipated yet another flight across thousands of lightyears.

Shuttle diplomacy was much easier, when all he had to do was fly between Geneva and New York. The Jeraptha were very nice to provide a ship for him, and the crew was always polite, but it was an alien ship and he could never truly relax when he was being transported across the stars.

Senior Captain Gammeria sat stiffly on the couch in her temporary office, aboard the spacedock where the battle-damaged ships of her destroyer squadron were awaiting repairs. She was mentally preparing herself for a meeting with an Inquisitor, when she expected to be harshly criticized for losing a precious technology demonstrator. The *Alibi* had been stolen right in front of her, and she had failed to prevent the theft, or to blow up the ship before it and its priceless technology could be taken by the enemy. It was an embarrassing disaster, and she would get the blame.

It did not matter that the other two demonstrator ships had been assigned heavier escorts, or that the foolish public tour had been cancelled after the incident. Or that she had warned Home Fleet that the *Alibi* was too exposed, too valuable a target for the enemy to ignore. Her career was likely over, the Inquisitor's report a mere formality in the process.

So, she was shocked when the office door slid open without warning, and a figure wearing a captain's uniform and a smirky grin greeted her. "Good morning, Senior Captain."

"I-" She didn't know what to say. Certainly she recognized the person standing in the doorway, though she had never spoken with Captain Scorandum. "Oh, fuuuuuuck," she groaned. "I was expecting a visit from the Inquisitor's office. That's bad enough. Now ECO is involved?"

Scorandum leaned casually against the door frame. "You will have the pleasure of meeting an Inquisitor later today, however, that is nothing to worry about."

"Nothing to worry about?" She cocked her head. "Have you ever been interrogated by an Inquisitor?"

Scorandum's grin faded for a moment. "More times than I can count. Senior Captain, I can assure you that this afternoon's meeting with an Inquisitor is merely a formality, it is part of the show."

"Show? What *show*?"

"The show for the benefit of the Bosphuraq, and their patrons and allies."

"The Bosphuraq don't *have* allies. They have rivals and enemies."

"You know what I mean."

"You didn't answer my question. What 'show'?"

"Our cover story. Are you going to invite me to sit down, Senior Captain?" He held up a bag with one hand.

"Oh, hell. Come in," she waved disgustedly.

"I come bearing gifts," he said, reaching into the bag and pulling out a bottle of vintage floon. "This is your preferred brand, I believe?"

Rolling her eyes, she said, "I am not bothering to ask how you know that."

"Nothing underhanded, I assure you. We simply asked your staff. Do you want-"

She snatched the bottle away and examined it. Indeed, it was a rare vintage. "To what do I owe this pleasure? Unfortunately, I do not have any burgoze for you."

"Ah," Scorandum dipped into the bag again, and extracted a bottle of burgoze. Which was only three-quarters full. "This," he explained, "is a gift to myself."

"You are very generous," she snorted.

"The Home Fleet is paying the tab," he indicated both bottles.

"Does the Home Fleet know they are paying?"

"They are very busy, it's best not to bother them with details. Anyway-"

"*Anyway*, will you please tell me what the hell is going on? Command is on my ass about losing the demonstrator, despite-"

"Like I said, don't worry about it."

"It's not *your* career."

"You will receive a commendation for your actions, though sadly that will have to remain a secret, for the time being."

"A *commendation*?"

"Yes. You displayed excellent judgment, as we hoped."

Gammeria cracked the seal on the bottle of floon, and the office was filled with a tantalizing scent. It was tantalizing to her, to Scorandum it probably smelled like furniture wax. Opening a drawer, she removed two glasses and slid one toward the ECO agent. After they had each taken a sip of their preferred beverage, Gammeria slapped the table. "The truth, *Captain*. Now."

"I will tell you all you are cleared to know. None of this leaves your office?" He raised an eyebrow.

"Understood. No one would believe me anyway."

"That's probably true," he chuckled. "We *wanted* the enemy to capture the *Alibi*. That is why we publicized the tour schedule, and Home Fleet assigned a thin escort screen."

"You *want* the Bosphuraq to steal technology we are paying the humans for?"

"Not necessarily the Bosphuraq, it could have been the Thuranin, the Esselgin, any of the second-tier enemy clients," he shrugged. "Whichever one of them seized the *Alibi*, the technology is certain to be taken by the Maxohlx, and eventually be stolen or purchased by other clients within that coalition."

She cocked her head again, thinking that perhaps she should have begun drinking earlier. "ECO wishes our enemies to possess technology that we don't even have yet?"

"No. That's the point. Senior Captain, the *Alibi* was a Trojan horse, except there were no real people inside it."

She blinked at him blankly, her antenna drooping. "What is a horse?"

"Uh, it is an Earth animal. A large one," he sputtered, realizing that he was likely one of the few Jeraptha who had ever heard that human legend. "Perhaps it is better if I describe the *Alibi* as a time bomb. We have not been able to confirm it yet, but it is almost certain that little ship exploded and took at least a star carrier with it, hopefully more."

"So," she took a sip of floon, savoring the subtle mix of flavors. "This was all about blowing up a single star carrier?"

"No," he snorted. "That was a bonus. Before the *Alibi* self-destructed, the Bosphuraq would have downloaded sensitive data from the computer core. Downloaded details of the new technology."

"Then I do not see how-"

"The data is also a time bomb," Scorandum took a very self-satisfied swig of burgoze. "The enemy doesn't know it, but that bomb already exploded. You see, Senior Captain, the technical specifications in the *Alibi's* databanks were subtly altered, to make it useless. Any attempt to build components based on that data will lead to frustrating failure, but the Bosphuraq will know the technology *does* work. So, their scientists will spend years going down the wrong path, wasting enormous time and effort, and delaying any actual progress. Meanwhile," he leaned back on the couch, "we will leap past all of them, thanks to our new human friends."

"Well," Gammeria knocked back the remaining floon in her glass. "Shit. All this was an ECO operation?"

"Yes."

"Since the technology is new to *us*, how did we know how to-"

"We didn't. We suggested a deception to the humans and their Elder AI. The AI was delighted to help us, so it, excuse me, *he*," Scorandum corrected himself with a nervous glance at the ceiling. "He was eager for an opportunity to screw with our enemies."

Gammeria leaned forward on the desk. "You met the AI?"

"Yes. Not actually, he communicates through an avatar, of course."

"Of course. What is it, *he*, like?"

"I believe the humans describe him as an insufferably arrogant asshole."

She looked at the ECO agent with the side-eye. "Are they correct?"

"Yes," Scorandum grinned. "But no more than many people I've met. And the AI has strong justification for his arrogance."

"The humans call him 'Skippy'? Apparently, that is a disrespectful nickname?"

"It might originally have been intended as disrespect, though I am certain the humans recognized his value long ago."

She snorted. "From what I have read, the humans would be extinct by now, if not for help from the AI."

"The truth must be more complicated than that," Scorandum warned with a raised antenna. "Skippy somehow *needs* the humans, or some of them. We do not fully understand the relationship. Clearly, the AI sees substantial value in a partnership with humans. Also, it should be noted that humans without the aid of an Elder AI have been impressively, even *annoyingly* successful, despite their severe disadvantages."

It was her turn to smile. "You refer to the 'Mavericks'?"

"Yes," Scorandum admitted with a frown. "That damned Perkins woman-"

"I would like to meet *her*," Gammeria said, taking a sip of floon. Anyone who managed to manipulate the ECO had to be admired. "Are all your operations like this?"

"It was fairly typical, nothing special," he said with false modesty. "I do apologize that you could not be informed ahead of time."

She scowled at him. "Regardless of a secret commendation in my file, I have a mark against myself, in the *official* records."

"That," he waved a hand, "has been taken care of. Officially, you will be placed on administrative leave, pending the Inquisitor's report. Take some time off, but not *too* much time. When the investigation concludes and the report is issued, you will be given command of a cruiser squadron, attached to the Sixteen Fleet."

"Is this for real," she asked warily. "Or more ECO bullshit?"

"For real. It's all arranged. Really, Senior Captain, we are extremely grateful for your good judgement. If you had attempted a useless gesture, like a suicide attack to blow up the *Alibi*, it would have screwed up the whole plan."

"Cruiser captains are supposed to be aggressive," she reminded him.

"Yes. The best cruiser squadrons are led by a commander who is aggressive, but not *stupidly* so. When I said 'we' are pleased, I meant ECO *and* the Home Fleet leadership."

"Hmmph," she sat back on her couch. "Did Home Fleet know about this in advance?'

"The people who needed to know, yes. Really, Senior Captain," he stood up, and slid the bottle of burgoze across the desk toward her. "Relax. Enjoy your leave, you might want to use the time to study the latest thinking about cruiser squadron tactics."

"Thank you," she blinked, still not quite believing the completely unexpected turn of events. "I, uh, do not drink burgoze."

"Keep it for me," he winked. "We might meet again."

"Not if I can help it," she muttered.

"Ah, but that's the point," he paused in the doorway. "You won't know ECO is involved, until I am in your office again."

"One last question, if I may?"

"What?"

"Did anyone in the Ethics Office wager that aliens would steal one of the demonstrator ships?"

"Not that *I* know of," Scorandum's expression turned serious. "That is a major disadvantage to this job. We have valuable information that we can't use! You asked whether I ever met with an Inquisitor? Their office has a whole section dedicated to monitoring our wagering activity, and, damn it, they don't take bribes. Inquisitors," he shook his head sadly, "are not *civilized*."

CHAPTER TWENTY FIVE

The Jeraptha Home Fleet star carrier *You Should Have Thought Of That Before We Left Home* slipped through the Elder wormhole that allowed access to the world called Paradise or Gehtanu or Pradassis or what-the-fuck-ever, the star carrier's crew could not care less what name that lonely world was tagged with. All they cared about was getting rid of the only ship currently on their hardpoints, a troop ship they picked up at Earth. Their annoyance was not with the humans, though those beings were polite and agreeable and inoffensive to the point where every crew member aboard the star carrier just wanted to *smack* them silly. No, their annoyance was directed at the lucky bastards who ran the *We Avoid Temptation But It Keeps Finding Us*. Those assholes just. Could. Not. Shut. *Up*. About the awesome action they found on Earth, and how they couldn't wait to get back.

Did some crew members of the star carrier apply for transfer to the troopship? Yes.

Were their applications accepted?

Sadly, there were no crew slots available aboard the *Temptation*.

Did some of the star carrier's crew sneak aboard the troop ship anyway, hoping to hide until their mother ship jumped away?

Also yes.

Did any of the would-be-stowaways succeed?

No.

The aggitated crew remaining aboard the star carrier were determined that, if *they* could not get shore leave on Earth, none of their jackass crew mates would either. The stowaways were located and dragged back their assigned ship, protesting they had religious or medical or family reasons for going to Earth. Their protests were ignored.

So, it was with one grumpy and one gleefully boastful crew that the star carrier transitioned through the event horizon, quickly verifying its location based on sighting several distinctive stars in that area of the galaxy. The *You Should Have* coasted forward, away from the wormhole that soon would be closing behind it, on its ancient and unchangeable schedule.

As the ship's sensors recovered from the spacetime distortion, they noted a possible anomaly, a gravimetric reading where there should not be one. Space around that emergence point had been scanned and mapped carefully less than two months prior, no navigation hazards were noted, and it was lightyears from any star system. The ship's AI was just bringing the curiosity to the attention of the biological crew-

When six stealthy Maxohlx missiles slammed into the star carrier's still-energizing shields, their hardened nosecones surviving to penetrate the thin armor plating of both star carrier and the attached transport ship.

The missiles exploded, just before a Maxohlx cruiser and two destroyers dropped their own stealth fields, and accelerated to pass through the wormhole in the opposite direction.

When the event horizon winked out, the Paradise end was awash with the cloud of a new and rapidly-cooling nebula.

The Rindhalu battleship *Hammer of Epthelion* appeared without warning, just beyond the outer radius of the strategic defense network of the Jeraptha world. The planet Garshamel was the hub for fleet operations in the sector, and the most frequent contact point on the rare occasions when the Rindhalu wished to speak directly with their clients.

Following long-established protocols, the Rindhalu sent a brief message, proposing a meeting at a military space station, then they settled down to wait. The Jeraptha, they knew, would not reply immediately. The arrival of a senior-species battleship, even one operated by a presumably friendly species, had set off alarms in the local strategic defense network. It also, more importantly, set off a wild flurry of wagering activity on and around the planet, as the local inhabitants tried to guess the purpose of their patrons visiting unexpectedly.

The Rindhalu found the compulsive gambling of their clients to be inexplicable if amusing, and they also knew there wasn't anything they could do to hurry the process along. Demands for a faster response would only be met with claims of 'technical difficulties' or that the appropriate authorities were 'busy' doing 'important things'.

When the Central Wagering Office announced that betting was absolutely, finally, OK, we will allow a few last-second transactions to be registered, closed, the Rindhalu stopped doing whatever it is that Rindhalu do, and waited for a response. Which came only moments later, for every Jeraptha on and around the planet was waiting impatiently to see if they had been right about the purpose of the visit.

A rather large and imposing dropship departed from the *Hammer of Epthelion*, and docked aboard the space station. To the frustration of the Jeraptha, their patrons insisted on a long, tedious ceremony to open the meeting, while their counterparts used every bit of their self-control to not scream at their patrons to *get to the freakin' point*.

When the spiders finally stated the purpose of the meeting, there was alarm, consternation, disappointment and jubilation among the Jeraptha officials, depending on how they had wagered.

Also, when they paused to think about it later, the meeting might have a serious effect on not only their society, but the entire galaxy.

The Rindhalu had not issued demands or threats, not openly. What they did was to state, simply and in a matter-of-fact manner, that if the Jeraptha continued to pursue an alliance with the upstart humans, the mutual-defense treaty between Rindhalu and Jeraptha would be considered null and void.

Basically, the Jeraptha would be defenseless against attacks by the Maxohlx coalition, including by the Maxohlx themselves. Unless the humans could protect them.

The humans, who currently had a total of *two* operational starships.

The Jeraptha had much to think about.

But first, they had something much more important to do.

Wagers needed to be placed, on the subject of what decision their government would make.

General Bailey knocked on Lynn Bezanson's office door. He didn't lean casually on the door frame, the way he did for a social call, and he wasn't smiling. General Bezanson was hunched over her laptop, adding to an already-too-long briefing for the incoming UNEF personnel. She needed to cut it down to a manageable size, right after she added in a bunch of important things she had remembered that morning.

"Temptation is overdue," Bailey announced cryptically.

Lynn looked up with a blank stare. A glance at the clock projected on the wall showed it was still two hours before Noon, but Bailey had been in the field and his body might be operating in a different time zone. She reached into a drawer and pulled out a bottle of rum that was distilled in southern Lemuria, it tasted like it was made in a bathtub but it was rum, not the fake alcohol provided by the Ruhar or the moonshine soldiers cooked up. "It's a little early for temptation, but you're welcome to it," she held out the bottle.

Bailey shook his head. "The ship. The transport bringing in the UNEF survey team is called the *Temptation*, something like that."

Bezanson's lips formed a silent 'Oh'. "I didn't know that. It's not officially overdue," she noted. That ship was seven days late for its scheduled arrival date, but interstellar travel was variable, especially when star carriers were one of the variables. The carrier could have been diverted, or one of the other ships it was supposed to rendezvous with could have been delayed. Also, if the schedule was thrown off for any reason, the star carrier might have to change where it went through an Elder wormhole, waiting for hours or days at an emergence point. There was also a strong possibility that confusion and bickering by the United Nations, over who to include in the survey team, could have delayed the departure from Earth. The Ruhar were upset that the ship had launched at all, their announcement of banning any new humans from landing on Paradise came after the Jeraptha ship had already departed for the flight to Earth.

"The hamsters are worried," Bailey said quietly, looking both ways along the hallway. "Unofficially."

"Shit." The rule was, a ship was not declared overdue for ten standard days, that is, ten days on the Ruhar homeworld. About ten and a half days on Paradise. "They're worried because of the time, or do they *know* something?"

"A Jeraptha star carrier came inbound through the local wormhole two days ago. It noticed a gas cloud near one of the other emergence points of that wormhole, a cloud that wasn't there three weeks ago. The star carrier couldn't divert to investigate, it was on a priority mission. Could be nothing, but, the beetles are sending a warship to investigate."

"Three hundred people," she said softly, aghast at the thought.

"Three hundred *humans*," Bailey looked at the ceiling, reminding her that aliens could be listening. "Plus the crew of the transport, the star carrier, and any other ships it had attached. Lynn, if this was an attack, the UNEF people might only have been collateral damage."

She looked at him, and he stared back.

Neither of them believed what he had said could be true. Paradise was still a backwater world, there had been little fighting in the area, other than the Ruhar and Kristang contesting for control of the planet. It made no sense that peer enemies of the Jeraptha would travel such a distance to strike one star carrier.

"When will we know?"

"The Ruhar liaison officer to the Jeraptha thinks we'll have an answer within three days. The beetles are worried, too, if this affects their potential deal with us."

"I understand. Yes, I will. Thank you." Lynn Bezanson waited for Administrator Loghellia to end the call, then tucked the phone back in a pocket. Standing up from her office chair, she took a breath to compose herself. In a corner of the office was a box that contained the personal items she was bringing back to Earth, she tapped it with a foot on her way out the door.

In the hallway, she could hear voices coming from a conference room at the far end, a meeting had ended and people were talking loudly, laughing, joking. Sticking her head in the open doorway, she saw a dozen people, including generals Bailey, Ling and Kumar.

Bailey was laughing at something Kumar had said, his mouth froze open when he saw Bezanson.

Everyone stopped talking, to stare at her.

"The Burgermeister," she paused to swallow. "Just called me, as a courtesy. A Jeraptha ship investigated that cloud near the local wormhole. It's a debris field."

"Shiiiiit," Bailey breathed.

"The beetles found a damaged flight recorder buoy, it's from the star carrier that was bringing the UN survey team here."

General Kumar asked, "Do they know-"

"The chemical composition of the debris field contains traces of osmium and tantalum, that are signatures of a *Maxohlx* missile. They want everyone to know who destroyed those ships."

The room was silent. The Maxohlx and Rindhalu had been applying escalating levels of diplomatic pressure and thinly-veiled threats, against species who were considering an alliance with Earth. Now an apex species had struck a direct blow against humans.

Bailey said what everyone was thinking. "So it begins."

Everything at Jaguar was going well, ahead of schedule, actually. True, UNEF heavily padded the schedule, because we didn't know the condition of the ships we would be getting, or the exact capabilities of the fleet-support ships. It was not quite true that we were totally clueless about the first batch of ships, because Skippy watched activity of the beetles' Central Wagering Office. He saw that the 'smart money', wagers by people closely associated with the project to deliver the first batch of ships to us, were overwhelmingly betting that we would accept ninety percent of the ships. That was a good forward indicator that the Jeraptha were not planning to screw us by delivering a bunch of useless crap. So, we had high confidence going in. Still, Skippy bitched and moaned so much about how difficult it would be to convert obsolete ships into something useful, that the leaders of UNEF Command were careful about getting their hopes up. Plus, there was a whole lot of stuff that could go wrong, and until we took that first batch of ships through the wormhole to Jaguar, I privately feared the kitties, or spiders, or both, would try to interfere. For once, my fears were for nothing. I am totally OK with that.

I was also totally OK with having Simms back aboard, for the flight out to Jiayuguan. She had gotten the job done on Earth and was hitching a ride with us, what made me especially happy was that she agreed to act as my temporary XO during the flight. Having to train a new executive officer on every flight was seriously getting on my nerves, it was great having an experienced officer by my side again.

We had high confidence that when we arrived at the nearest Jeraptha fleet base, the beetles would be eager to provide a second batch of ships, in exchange for us upgrading a batch of ships for them. Why not? They had plenty of time to see what the demonstrator ships could do, unless they were complete idiots, they had to know the technology advancements we provided were only slightly below the capability of a Maxohlx warship. A fleet of ships upgraded to those standards would vault the Jeraptha above any top-tier clients in either coalition.

Hey, you might ask, were we asking for trouble by giving aliens so much power? What was stopping the Jeraptha from using those ships against us? That is a very good question, an issue UNEF wrestled with before agreeing to provide a menu of upgrades the beetles could choose from. We were only giving them a limited set of technology advancements, and everything we provided was several notches below the technology aboard *Valkyrie*. Our own ships would have the full suite of every high-tech toy Skippy could stuff into them, and-

Anyway, we weren't worried about being double-crossed by the Jeraptha. They had too much to gain, and too much to lose.

So, when we jumped into the outer edge of the star system and scanned for trouble, we got a slap in the face. The beetles, of course, had designated a zone for our arrival, a place that was safe from traffic and free from natural objects floating around that we might smack into while coming through a jump wormhole. Before jumping into the designated zone, we emerged farther away, to check for surprises.

"Uh oh," Skippy groaned. "What the f- We've only been at Jaguar for five freakin' weeks! How did everything go to shit so fast? Damn it, I leave the galaxy alone for-"

"Skippy," automatically, I tried to rise from my chair to get a better look at the main display, looking for signs of trouble. That was stupid. If there was trouble looming over our heads, being firmly strapped into my seat was the proper way to deal with it. "Chill, please. What are you talking about? What went wrong?"

"Ugh. What *hasn't* gone wrong? Jeez Louise, I seriously need to babysit the galaxy. The second I turn my back, you meatsacks screw up *everything*."

"One step at a time, OK?"

"OK," he took a breath. "I'll go through the list in chronological order. First, the spiders announced that if the Ruhar continued to cooperate with humanity, including allowing humans to occupy portions of Ruhar worlds, the spiders would not honor their mutual-defense treaty obligations."

"Shit," I suddenly felt cold.

"This is not entirely unexpected," Simms reminded me. Before we left Earth, the pre-mission brief from UNEF Command anticipated there could be pushback from the senior species. We had a list of authorized responses if one or both of the apex powers tried to intimidate a species we wanted to ally with. Unfortunately, options One through Ten on the list of authorized responses required us to fly back to Earth to get revised orders.

"Right," I agreed. "What did the hamsters do?"

"They told UNEF HQ on Paradise that the UN survey team from Earth would not be allowed dirtside. Basically, UNEF needs to get humans off Paradise on an accelerated schedule."

I shared a look with Simms, then asked, "Did the hamsters offer to help with the evac?"

"Uh, the discussions didn't get that far yet, as far as I know. The information I'm getting here is out of date, you understand?"

"Yeah." Information traveled around the galaxy only as fast as ships could carry it. There was a network of relay stations throughout the galaxy, most along the most heavily-traveled routes between the most strategically-important wormholes. Ships flying along those routes were supposed to swing by relay stations, usually only for a few minutes, to exchange information. Each species had their own relay stations, and often an advanced species would use the relay stations of a lower-level client if that was convenient. The Thuranin could store data in a Kristang relay station, knowing the lizards had no possibility of reading the encrypted files. Considering that there was no reliable long-range, faster-than-light communications system available to anyone in the Milky Way, relay stations were a good system, though with some major flaws. Star systems on opposite sides of the galaxy might exchange information faster than star systems within a few lightyears of each other, if the more-distant systems were on heavily-traveled wormhole routes. Sometimes, a message would be received countermanding a previous order, before the original message was available. And always, the information at any one place was out-of-date and incomplete. "I understand that. Do you know what the Ruhar government has decided?"

"Um, they were leaning toward a temporary freeze in allowing humans on their worlds, waiting to see how Earth would respond. But, that is OBE. Joe, I am sad to report that the ship carrying the UN survey team to Paradise was destroyed by the Maxohlx."

"*What?*"

"It's confirmed. Not only did the Maxohlx do it, they are *bragging* about it, because humans didn't respond."

"That is bull- We didn't *know* about it!"

"That doesn't matter. The Maxohlx hit us, and we did nothing to retaliate."

I noted that Skippy said '*we*'. That, at least, was good news. "Yeah, well, we'll see about this 'no retaliation' thing."

"Sir?" Simms got my attention.

"Yes, I know, we can't act without clearance from UNEF Command," I snapped at her, irritated. That was unfair of me, she was doing her job. Silently, I mouthed 'Sorry' at her, and she nodded. She was as pissed about the situation as I was. "Anything else?"

"The news only gets worse, I am afraid," Skippy said. "The Rindhalu recently notified the Jeraptha that they also will not be protected by the spiders, if the Jeraptha sign an alliance with us. The transfer of a second batch of ships has been put on hold, unfortunately."

"On hold? Wait, on hold like, a delay, or like *canceled*?"

"The Jeraptha government has not announced a formal policy, however, wagering is running six to one against them pursuing any further cooperation with humans. The Maxohlx attack on the UN survey team got everyone's attention."

Everyone but us, since we spent the time at the ass-end of the galaxy, blissfully unaware that the situation was unraveling.

Covering my face with a hand, I peaked at him through my fingers. "Please tell me you don't have any more bad news."

"I do have one little item of good news. The Bosphuraq took the bait, they captured the Trojan horse demonstrator ship."

Whoopy-freakin'-do, is what I wanted to say. It would have made Skippy pout, if I didn't appreciate him announcing some positive news. "That's better than nothing, I guess. Crap. We still have a job to do. Is it safe to proceed to the designated jump-in zone?"

The situation was a severe test of my diplomatic skills, which frankly sucked anyway. The beetles we talked to were polite. They were complimentary about the advanced technology we installed in the demonstrator ships. They were excited and curious about the technology information package we provided, and were eager for Skippy to explain what it meant. They also requested that we return the entire first batch of ships they delivered to us. My impression was that request was a formality, so they could tell the Rindhalu that they tried to get the ships back. My reply, also polite, was to say 'no'. We were keeping those ships, and everything else they gave us.

Did I make any progress in getting the beetles to loosen their grip on that second batch of ships? No, I did not. There was nothing to do but fly directly back to Earth, so that's what we did.

I was wrong, again. There was something else we could have done, should have done. By the time my stupid brain brought the fact to my attention, it was too late.

The two scout ships, one from each of the nominally-allied but rival species, jumped in near the star system, above the ecliptic and well beyond the orbit of the outermost planet. One of the species had been to that star system before, under vastly different circumstances, and not recently enough to have useful knowledge of the local defenses. The scouts were tasked with determining whether the tactical intel provided by their patrons was accurate, that the target planet was virtually undefended. That information was difficult to believe, and both client species noted that their asshole patrons were not risking their own necks in the operation.

To the surprise of both scout ship crews, the planet's strategic defense network would not sound an alarm when the warships jumped in, because that planet did not have an SD network. There were satellites in orbit, mostly for communications, bouncing photons to and from the surface, for the entertainment of the odd and primitive beings who lived there. Two starships were in orbit, they were both old and no threat even to the scout ships. One had its reactors powered down, the other was running on minimum power while it was apparently undergoing extensive modifications. Unless there was an orbiting constellation of very sophisticated stealth SD platforms, their asshole patrons had actually told the truth: the planet had no effective defenses.

Waiting until the last second of their schedule, because neither ship's crew could believe what they had found, the scout ships jumped away at the same time, each emerging near their home star carrier. The two star carriers were surrounded by warships with their guns pointed at their allies, neither side trusting each other at all. Their commanders conferred, analyzing data from the scout ships, also not quite believing what they saw. They would have waited to send out more scout ships, if they weren't under a hard time constraint. If they did not attack before the gamma rays of the two scout ships reached the target planet, the beings there would be alerted to the threat, and might be able to activate hidden defenses.

The operation, being conducted at the insistence of their patrons, was already risky enough.

The star carriers and scout ships remained behind, while the warships counted down, and disappeared in flashes of gamma radiation.

Senior-Colonel Chang, the UN Undersecretary for Homeworld Security, closed the laptop with equal measures of annoyance and relief as the jet descended for landing. Automatically, he tugged the lap belt to check it was secure, while tucking the laptop into the seat back.

"Sir," the aide seated across the aisle began to say something, but Chang held up a hand. He had so little time to himself, whatever the man wanted, it could wait. Leaning his head against the window, he tried to get a view of Manhattan, off to the northwest. The plane was coming into JFK airport, where he would then board a helicopter for a short flight to Manhattan. That evening, there was a UN meeting, preceded by a cocktail reception where all the actual work would get done.

His head hurt just thinking about it. Standing on aching feet in the reception hall, holding a drink he wouldn't have time to taste, and smiling while one person after another approached him, all wanting something. The company that built the aircraft he was in, an Airbus commercial airliner that was one of several owned by UNEF Command, wanted contracts to service and support humanity's new fleet of starships. Airbus was not alone, every aerospace company on the planet wanted a piece of the action. Even during the flight from Geneva, ministers from two nations had presented arguments for why companies in their respective countries should be awarded lucrative contracts. Chang had listened and smiled and nodded, and reminded them that he did not have the final decision on contract awards.

Being pestered by lobbyists even while he was trying to relax during a long flight made him jealous of Joe Bishop, who had commandeered a Panther dropship for his personal use. Chang thought that sent an arrogant signal of privilege, though he understood that Bishop was mobbed by crowds everywhere he went, and not all of those crowds were friendly. A dropship would have made the flight to New York in less than an hour, even with the necessity of adhering to airspace restrictions on both ends of the flight.

Chang took a deep breath, disappointed that the flight was coming straight in from the ocean, depriving him of a view of the city. He would see if from the helicopter, of course, no need to rush. Turning to the aide he had rudely dismissed, he raised an eyebrow. The man shook his head. Whatever he wanted to say, it could wait for landing.

A flight attendant came through the cabin to collect drink containers and check that seats were secured for landing. The attendant was a French Air Force captain, by the wings on his uniform, Chang guessed he was also a pilot, part of the plane's relief crew. Amused when the captain glanced with awe at the Merry Band of Pirates patch on Chang's own uniform, he flashed the man a smile.

"Air traffic control cleared us straight in," the man explained as the big jet's rate of descent increased. "We will be on the ground in seven minutes."

"You had best strap yourself in, Captain," Chang said with a well-practiced smile. It took so little to make people happy, a tiny bit of his attention, a few words exchanged. Probably, that evening, the captain would be telling family and friends how he spoke with Senior-Colonel Chang, yes, *that* Chang. "It would not be-"

His phone blared an alarm, followed moments later by alarms of every phone aboard the plane. As he reached to pull a zPhone from a pocket, his stomach was jolted by the jet pulling up sharply, the whine of the engines increasing in pitch as they spooled up.

What the hell was happening?

Above Chang's head and four thousand kilometers to the northeast, there were multiple gamma ray bursts as starships appeared suddenly. They emerged from their jump wormholes without warning, six hundred kilometers over the ocean between Greenland and Iceland. None of the ships' crews took time to peer down at the water and ice below, to them, it was just another planet. Another target.

Ahead of the ships was their first target, a former Kristang troop transport now named the *Yu Qishan*. That ship, never a threat to any ship in the squadron, had only one reactor fired up, and it was surrounded by boxy structures that were either cargo or passenger pods. The attacking ships did not bother to scan the target to determine the purpose of the pods, they simply launched missiles, then followed up with maser cannons as their fire-control sensors recovered from the jump distortion.

The *Yu Qishan* was ripped apart by maser bolts cutting into and through its lightly-armored skin. A mere second later, four missiles tore into the broken pieces, and the ship exploded, burning debris raining down into the atmosphere below.

The warships continued onward, splitting up to attack secondary targets. Railgun magnets were energized as the ships curved over the horizon, seeking a view of the place they would strike first. A complex of buildings where their enemy had planned insidious attacks against those who owned and operated the ships.

The United Nations Headquarters in New York.

"Brace for impact!" The pilot shouted over the plane's intercom. "Brace brace br-"

The big jet was slammed to the side, yawing to the left in the direction of the blast wave from the railgun impacts that had struck the east side of Manhattan. Before he tucked his head into his lap, Chang had seen a blindingly bright flash reflected on the plane's wing, as something exploded with frightening force behind them. Immediately, the flight crew had put the plane into a hard turn, knowing that taking the blast wave from the back would be fatal.

There was a shuddering that shook Chang's brain loose from his skull, accompanied by a shrieking and a long, low rumble like distant thunder, only it didn't stop. Another bright flash, another. Whoever the enemy was, they were pounding New York from orbit. Someone was screaming and there was an announcement over the intercom, he couldn't hear enough to make sense of it.

The last flash faded away along with the rumbling of endless thunder, and then there was an eerie silence. People were talking, their mouths moving, he couldn't hear. Neither could anyone else apparently, they were communicating by sign language. From forward, the French Air Force captain stumbled down the aisle, bleeding from a cut on his forehead, and he was wearing a yellow inflatable life jacket.

Chang rested his feet on the floor.

The familiar vibration of the engines had ceased, and he could feel himself growing lighter as the plane went into a steep dive.

Out the window, all he could see was steely blue water.

The Atlantic Ocean.

They were going down.

CHAPTER TWENTY SIX

Captain Vereena Fondun was not even surprised to see Uhtavio Scorandum darken her doorway. She was dismayed. And apprehensive, for she knew an already busy day was about to get *complicated*. "Uhtavio. To what do I owe the displeasure of your presence this morning?"

Scorandum affected being hurt, dipping his antennas and hanging his head. "Vereena, that is unfair. Why, I am merely here to assist you."

"Assist?"

"Yes. Your job is to secure those ships," he pointed toward the display on the wall, showing a cluster of obsolete warships, many of them surrounded by tugs, and crews working outside in spacesuits, and robotic maintenance drones. They had all been working to confirm the ships were in a safe condition to be transferred to the humans. Now they had halted those activities, and were awaiting new instructions.

"Yes. Mostly, I am just returning them to long-term storage condition. That is a BuShip function," she referred to her home unit, the Bureau of Ships. "Why is *ECO* here?"

"To assist you, as I said."

"ECO has technicians available?"

"Sadly, no," he shook his head. "We are here to provide security."

"Security?" She blinked. "What are you concerned about?"

"Vereena, the galaxy is full of nefarious characters."

Her response was to stare directly at *him*.

"Er, yes," he understood her meaning. "We are merely here to prevent anyone from stealing those ships, or, let's just say, stealing as many of those ships that could be made minimally flightworthy within the next," he glanced at the clock on the wall. "Fourteen hours or less. If you know what I mean."

Her antennas stood straight up. "Oh, *crap*."

"You can understand my concern, then?"

"Nefarious characters, huh?"

"They are everywhere, I am sad to say."

"My orders from the Home Fleet," she tapped a claw on the hard surface of the desk, making a clicking sound. "Are to secure those ships, and return them to storage."

"Correct. However, Home Fleet recognizes that you have been working very hard. You should take some time off. Such as, fourteen hours. If you know what I mean."

"Uhtavio, the government decided not to assist the humans. They made an official and very public announcement of the new policy."

"Yes. It is true that announcement was *public*, and *official*. If you know what I mean."

She sighed, leaning back on her couch. "Home Fleet is hedging their bets? Complying with the request from the Rindhalu, while helping the humans in case we need them in the future?"

"I have no idea what you mean. However, if *I* were in charge of Home Fleet, I would at least consider such an action. Unofficially, of course."

"I will not be receiving these unofficial orders in writing, will I?"

"Again, I have no idea what you are talking about. Perhaps you have been working too hard. You should take some time off."

"Like, fourteen hours?"

"Yes. Or less, if possible."

"Crap. While I am taking time off, do you have any suggestions for what I might do to relax?"

Scorandum smiled. "Well, I could use help with identifying which of those ships would be the most likely targets for nefarious characters who might want to steal them, in the next fourteen hours, or less. If you know what I mean."

"I have no idea what you are talking about. If you know what *I* mean."

"I do."

"Uhtavio," she sighed. "I have to admit, I have missed working with you."

"Vereena, ECO always has a place for someone like you."

"My job is *here*."

"You wouldn't have to *leave* your job," he hinted.

"This job is already too complicated. But," she smiled at him. "Thank you for the offer."

"Anytime. I mean that."

"Fourteen hours, hmm?"

"Preferably less."

"Then, I had better get started on relaxing."

US Army Brigadier General Lynn Bezanson was not appreciating any of the privileges associated with being a general officer. At the moment, she was not appreciating anything about her situation. Her boots were above the ankles in thick black mud, with cold water seeping into her socks. That area of Lemuria was swampy, which is why the hamsters had set it aside for humans. "What do you mean, 'gone'?" She demanded of the four hapless soldiers standing at attention in front of her.

She did not actually expect an answer. Of the four, three were US Army and one Marine. With everyone's length of service having been extended, they were all specialists or corporal in the case of the Marine. Remaining true to the creed of the E-4 mafia, none of them had any idea what happened to the supplies UNEF had provided for the purpose of constructing air-raid shelters.

They were supposed to have shelters dug into the soggy soil, with a dry, solid floor and a thick ceiling, with native logs and at least a meter of dirt on top. Instead, all she saw was a half-assed beginning of digging a hole, which was filled with water, and the sides had slumped in.

"Well?" She demanded again, more out of curiosity over whether all four would wisely keep their mouths shut, or one would crack under pressure and spit out whatever bullshit story they had cooked up.

"It's like," Specialist Yosarian stumbled over his words, staring straight ahead. "The stuff was there, then it was gone, you know? I mean, Ma'am. General Ma'am."

"I am General *Bezanson*, Specialist." She tried to glare at the idiot, but one corner of her mouth might have curled up in a smile of amusement. "So, you are telling me that the still I found in the woods over there," she pointed to a grove of trees with a well-worn trail leading to it. "Where you are cooking illegal moonshine, and the shelter covering that still, were not made with those construction supplies?"

"I, I," Yosarian's eyes flicked to his fellows, who were all simultaneously staring straight ahead and telling him to *shut the hell up*. "I, we don't know nothing about moonshine, Ma'am."

"You don't know *anything*, Specialist. If you are going to insult my intelligence, please use proper grammar."

"Uh-" Yosarian's face was blank.

"Oh," Bezanson snorted. "This is hopeless." Really, it was the fault of UNEF HQ. Secure in knowing the Ruhar had an SD network around the planet, and a battlegroup stationed overhead, headquarters had let standards slip. Especially recently, when everyone knew they were all going home. Why bother maintaining shelters, or even inspecting whether shelters had been constructed?

Then, the Maxohlx destroyed a transport ship carrying more than three hundred humans, and no one knew when, or *if*, a ship would bring them to Earth.

That was why she had gone out to inspect an American base, to see whether the troops there were prepared for an air raid. The reports sent up by platoons to the battalion all stated everything was as it should be, which was her first warning that everything was *not* as it should be. It only took four knuckleheaded E-4s and their entrepreneurial moonshine business to show her that the Force could be in big trouble.

"Very well. Since none of you know anything about that still in the woods, we are going to march over there right now, where I will watch you take it apart. Then, you will use the materials to make this," she kicked up a clod of mud to splash into what was supposed to be an air-raid shelter. "*Pigsty*, into something that-"

Her phone sounded an alarm, as she looked up, her eyes automatically attracted to lights in the sky.

Everyone's phone sounded the same alarm.

Air-raid warning red, she knew from the alarm tone, not needing to read the text.

"Shit!" Yosarian yelped and grabbed her arm, yanking her forward. "General! Ma'am," he pointed to a swampy pond fifty meters away. "Get in the water!"

"No!" She shook him off. "We can-"

Yosarian would not let go, looking to the east in terror and jabbing a finger at the sight.

The eastern sky was bright, with a wide violet-colored curtain flickering and pulsing like a living thing.

She recognized the phenomena from training videos. It was a starship maser beam, set on wide dispersal anti-personnel setting. Burning or boiling anything it touched.

It was coming right for them.

Her legs had her running before she knew she had made a decision to jump into the water. Yosarian was right beside her, slowing his stride so she would not fall behind, though the young soldier was certainly as frightened as she was. They ran into the murky dark water, splashing in up to their knees, then the bottom dropped off and she fell forward to splash face-first below the surface. The water was chilly and discolored and it smelled like rotted algae. Coming up for air, she felt for the bottom with her toes and couldn't find it. Everyone in her party was now in the water, no one left on shore. She heard a loud sizzling sound and turned to the east-

Just as a hand smacked the top of her head and pushed her under the water.

Blowing out though she wanted to breathe air *in*, she flailed her arms to dive deeper, feeling muck touch her fingertips. Closing her eyes tightly, she found something that felt like a sunken log and clutched it so she wouldn't float to the surface. The slimy surface of the log slipped through her fingers, she had to get a hand around and under it to-

The water flash-heated as the purple beam swept across it, and her skin was on fire, making her cry out in pain and gulp in water and mud and whatever scum floated in the pond. She felt bubbles rise up as rotted plant material on the bottom of the pond was released and she lost her grip on the log, popping to the surface and prepared to die in quick agony

"I got you, I got you, Ma'am," a voice came faintly into her ear. Daring to crack open one eye, she saw a thick fog from steam coming off the pond.

"Who?"

"It's me, Yosarian." The voice said as she was pulled backward until she was sitting on her backside in muck, her shoulders above the water. There were more voices, shouting in the distance. "It's OK," Yosarian said loudly in her ear. "Everyone accounted for. We got lucky."

"Lucky?" Cracking an eye open again, she looked at the soldier. His skin was beet-red and oily, like a very bad sunburn. Her own face felt the same, or worse. Around her, figures wreathed in fog were struggling through the muck toward the shore. "Everyone!" She coughed as she spoke. "Stay *in* the water! We don't know how many ships are up there." The figures turned around, walking back into the murky water. She did not know how many ships were up there, but she was going to find out, she thought as she pulled a zPhone from a pocket, wincing because the skin of her hands was red and puffy. UNEF HQ would know.

If Headquarters still existed.

"Holy shit," Skippy gasped. *Valkyrie* had come through the Backstop wormhole, and immediately turned toward Checkpoint Bravo to get instructions for approaching our home planet. Without Skippy being in our solar system, there was no microwormhole to provide convenient, instant communication between the checkpoint and Earth, so whatever instructions we found there might be out of date. Procedure is procedure, so we followed orders anyway. "Joe, before you ask 'What', give me a minute. Lots to process here."

Instead of replying, I turned toward the communications station. The warrant officer there was US Air Force, her face was white as she pressed a hand over her ear to hear better. I saw her swallow and her expression register shock, before she-

"Pilot!" Skippy shouted. "Jump option Delta now now n-"

We jumped, the pilots had standing orders from me, to take instructions directly from Skippy in such emergencies.

It wasn't the best jump we ever performed, it also wasn't the worst. Fighting a wave of nausea and the feeling that pressure in my skull would burst my eyeballs, I squeezed my eyes tightly shut. "Sitrep."

"The ship is fine," Skippy said in a voice that had a distinctive quaver to it. He was shocked. He was *scared*.

"What is-"

"They hit Earth. The *bastards*," he spat angrily.

"Who is 'they'? What happened?"

"A task force of Bosphuraq and Thuranin warships. Three days ago."

"Oh my- The Bos-"

"They did it, but the Maxohlx ordered the attack, you can be sure of it," Skippy was pissed, like, out of control. "Oooh, when I get ahold of those-"

"Skippy! Focus, please. What. Happened?"

"Sixteen ships, half Bosphuraq and half Thuranin. They conducted a raid. It was quick, they must have been worried *Valkyrie* would arrive and kick their asses. Twenty-three minutes from arrival to jumping away. You want a BDA?"

It was jarring to hear Skippy using military jargon. He meant a Battle Damage Assessment, except there hadn't been a battle. The attack was a one-sided slaughter. "Yes."

"They destroyed the *Yu Quihan* and the *Dagger*, I mean the *Unity*, I- Oh, fuck it. Whatever those ships are called, they blew them to hell, along with the multi-mission modules. On the ground, there were railgun impacts where the UN Headquarters was in New York, and UNEF Command in Geneva. Joe, there is a crater extending from 3rd Avenue in Manhattan to Vermont Street across the river. It's filled with water from the East River. The Chrysler Building *fell* into the crater."

"Jesus," I breathed, wincing at myself. Blasphemy was an especially bad idea right then. New York city was a big maze to me, I wasn't familiar with the streets he mentioned, though I had seen the Chrysler Building. For it to fall over, the damage to the area must be bad. "Is there anything we can-"

He ignored me. "They also hit nine other sites around the planet. Technology centers and factories that were working on upgrading your manufacturing capability. The advanced materials facilities in Beijing and Palmdale were wiped out. Joe, without those materials-"

"Yeah, I know." Without the exotic and specialized materials those facilities were trying to make, we could not continue modifying ships for our fleet. The last status report I read estimated it would take another four years, before those plants could make enough high-quality materials for full production. Even when that happened, Earth would need dozens of other facilities to make all the exotic materials we needed. The aliens had hit us, but it would not make a major difference in the short term. "The attacking ships left? They're gone?" Sixteen second-tier warships could pose a problem for *Valkyrie*, and I assumed there might be more ships than just the ones that participated in the raid. We could fight Bosphuraq and Thuranin ships, but we could not both fight and render assistance to our homeworld.

"They are gone, yes. That jump we did was just a precaution, to give me time to assess the data. Multiple jump signatures were detected near Backstop, they went out through the wormhole. Unless, you know, they left some stealthed ships behind."

"The number of outbound jump signatures matches the inbound number?"

"Yes. All the ships in the raid definitely jumped away."

"Take us in," I ordered. "High orbit, I want the ship above jump altitude at all times."

"Believe me," Captain Uhtavio Scorandum shook his head sadly, his antennas drooping and swaying side to side. "We are as shocked as you are."

"We do *not* believe that," the representative of the Rindhalu said with anger, the sac of her pendulous belly puffing outward. Her people had good reason to be angry. After assuring their patrons that they were freezing movement toward an alliance with humans, the Jeraptha were supposed to also halt preparations to deliver a second group of obsolete warships to the humans. Those ships, according to what the Jeraptha told their patrons, would be secured, dispersed and have vital components removed to render them not flightworthy.

Instead, forty-three of the sixty-five ships had disappeared! Among the missing ships were not just obsolete units, but also two new fleet-support units with state-of-the-art fabricators. Plus four cargo vessels that were heavily laden with hard-to-find minerals and exotic materials. Those ships had been *stolen*, according to the Jeraptha, who claimed to be outraged by the completely unexpected event.

"I do not know what else to tell you," Scorandum's antennas dipped in his version of a shrug. "This is a heinous crime. I promise, there will be a *full* investigation."

"There certainly will. *We* will participate in the investigation of this perfidy."

Scorandum nodded, bowing his head low in deference to the exalted patrons of his people. "We welcome any assistance in resolving this matter. *I* welcome your involvement. My government has tasked me with tracking those ships, and identifying the culprits."

"*You?*" The haughty Rindhalu sputtered. "The investigation is being conducted by the Ethics and Compliance Office?"

"Of course," the ECO captain acted surprised by the question. "We must, I am ashamed to say, consider the possibility that this crime was partially an inside job. Sensitive information, or access to the ships, might have been obtained through threats, extortion or blackmail." Or, he did not add, bribes that were much less expensive than ECO had been prepared to pay. Naturally, because it was his bargaining skills that knocked down the price, he pocketed the leftover funds, in accordance with unwritten ECO standard practice.

The spider blinked slowly. "The ECO investigating a crime is like," she shook her head. "No matter. Captain Scorandum, we will hold you personally responsible for locating those ships."

"Of course. Er, there is one rather delicate question I must ask before we begin to review the unfortunately limited set of data about the incident."

"What is the question?"

"This is embarrassing, but, um, *you* did not steal those ships, did you?"

"*Aaargh*!"

"Hmm. I will take that as a 'No', then," he made a note on his tablet. "Shall we begin?"

UNEF Command and the US government and the US Army and, possibly the Salvation Army, were all screaming to talk with me when *Valkyrie* appeared in orbit. We had jumped in above New York City, to get a direct look at the damage. That wasn't necessary, we could have been above Australia and still seen the damage via satellite camera, but I thought it was important to show our concern.

The city was a mess. There was indeed a ragged crater taking a bite out of Manhattan's east side, also possibly part of Brooklyn or Queens, I didn't know that area well enough to see a dramatic difference in the shoreline there.

What I could see was wide-spread devastation. If there were any windows intact within five miles of the blast center, it had to be a miracle. Our view was obscured by a thin veil of smoke from many small fires that extended west into New Jersey and east onto Long Island.

"Oh, hell. Why- Why did they hit the UN building? That makes no-"

"Joe, the Bosphuraq left a long, profanity-laced diatribe against UNEF. They are pissed that humans manipulated the Maxohlx into punishing them, and they assume the operation was planned and managed by the UN."

"Ohhhh shit." I felt sick. "This is all my-" Simms reached over and squeezed my hand.

She didn't speak. All she did was look me in the eye and shake her head once. The message was clear. This was *not* my fault.

She was wrong about that. The birds hitting Earth was my fault, the deception op to frame them for the actions I ordered was entirely my doing. There was no denying the truth of that.

It was also true that if we hadn't acted to frame another group for hitting the Maxohlx, Earth would have suffered a worse fate.

Suck it up, Bishop, I told myself. The past can't be changed. What I could do was to focus on preventing another attack.

"Skippy, connect me with Chang. I need background before I talk with UNEF and-"

"Sorry, Joe, no can do. Chang is at a hospital in Philadelphia. His plane was coming into JFK when the Bosphuraq struck the UN building, and got caught by the shock wave. The plane went down at sea. Forty-three people died in the crash."

"Oh my-"

"Chang is expected to recover. He would recover faster if we could bring him up here, *Valkyrie's* medical facilities are more-"

"Can you do anything for him in Philly?" I knew Kong, he would not want special treatment when many others were suffering worse trauma. "Wait. How much medical supplies can we spare, to send dirtside?"

Skippy didn't answer right away. "I understand you want to help, Joe. The question is, how much do we need, for whatever you plan to do next? If we take the fleet at Jaguar into action, we could run out of medical nano treatment capacity in one *day*."

"Sir?" Simms knew I was struggling. "Contact UNEF. They should decide how to deploy our medical gear."

"UNEF. Right." I took a breath and pressed a button to connect me with whoever was the UNEF Command duty officer. "This is Bishop."

The physical damage to Earth was limited. Outside of the strike areas, everything looked normal. Pretty much normal, unless you looked hard enough. There was a lot less traffic on the roads and in the skies. Some places on the nightside were shocking when viewed from space, it looked like power had been knocked out like what happened on Columbus Day. That wasn't true, the aliens had not bothered with Earth's electricity generation and transmission infrastructure. Sections of the continents were dark because local governments there had ordered a curfew and blackout, as if lack of artificial light made targeting more difficult for starship sensors. A blackout had zero practical value, other than making people feel they were *doing* something, that they had some control over their fates. That was a sentiment I understood. The people of Earth faced the uncertainty of whether they would survive to see the next day, whether unstoppable alien warships would appear in the sky without warning, to bombard our world from orbit.

One thing was certain: UNEF Command wanted the reassuring presence of *Valkyrie* hanging above everyone's heads. When our orbit took us into Earth's shadow we turned on all our navigation lights, and sent a pair of dropships out to illuminate the hull with powerful floodlights. What we actually should have done was cloak the ship in a stealth field, so the enemy would know our battlecruiser was on guard, but not present an easy target. The experienced military leaders of UNEF Command understood that, the civilians above them in the chain of command argued that it was equally important to show the public that our homeworld had some protection. The coldly practical side of me thought it was foolish to compromise security for the sake of giving people a warm fuzzy feeling that was entirely false. If a large number of alien ships hit Earth again, we could make the raiders pay a price, but we could not prevent deadly weapons from raining down on the surface.

The human side of me understood the value of making the public feel some measure of security. Social order all over the planet was fragile, many city dwellers had bugged out after the raid, dispersing to areas that were less likely targets. Those areas were straining to accommodate the sudden influx of people, and there was friction with local residents who resented the newcomers.

Valkyrie was not the only military asset not going anywhere; I was ordered to remain aboard, with the ship at battle stations around the clock. Simms was stuck aboard with me; UNEF Command decided I needed an experienced XO, and I wholeheartedly agreed. After a week, I pleaded with Command to rotate part of my crew dirtside, and bring aboard fresh replacements. It would be a good opportunity for training, I argued, and a burned-out crew was not optimal for combat readiness. Command relented, and even allowed Simms to go to the surface for a briefing, though she flew back immediately.

My parents. Yeah, they bugged out too, went to my uncle's fishing camp for the duration. They were safe, had plenty of food stocked away and although much of the world's public was pissed at me for failing to provide the absolute security that I warned them was *not* possible, my folks were doing OK. They were worried about *me*, which shows how little I know about being a parent.

One week, then two dragged on, with *Valkyrie* on high alert and nothing happening.

Then an alien ship appeared in a burst of gamma rays.

The alien ship, after making my heart stop, was just a Jeraptha light cruiser. After seeing the identification system tag the ship as a friendly, my heart skipped a beat again, hoping the beetles had changed their minds about working with us.

No such luck. They had come to Earth for two reasons, neither of them good for us.

First, they heard about the raid because the Maxohlx coalition, especially the Bosphuraq, were boasting far and wide about the deed. The beetles had come to check on the safety of their diplomatic personnel, and to bring them home. There were fourteen Jeraptha diplomats on Earth, and during the raid, fortunately eleven of them were on a 'fact-finding' tour of casinos in Macau. Anther three were on a 'cultural exchange' visit to India, where the culture apparently involves furious wagering on cricket matches. Anyway, all of the beetles were safe and healthy, though not happy. They *were* happy, until they learned their government was pulling them off Earth simply due to one isolated and rather limited raid. UNEF let the beetles round up their own people, wisely not getting involved in alien affairs. It was amusing that, after all the diplomats had been rounded up, there was a search for six more from the crew who had jumped ship. Again, UNEF let the beetles handle it.

Second, the Jeraptha had come to deliver bad news. While the Bosphuraq and Thuranin were hitting Earth, a Bosphuraq squadron had struck the human-occupied area of Paradise. Initial estimates, all that were available before the ship left for Earth, were over six hundred dead and at least eleven hundred seriously wounded. Most of the dead and injured were humans, though a few dozen Ruhar had been hit as collateral damage. A small, but very vocal group of hamsters, were calling for their government to eject the unwanted humans from their world.

Shit.

We had no means for pulling our people off Paradise. Sure, eventually we would have six assault transports, but not for months, and while Skippy was at Earth, those transports were stuck at the ass-end of the galaxy. UNEF inquired about whether the *Sure Thing* was available and were politely told 'No'. It was also politely requested that if we did see that particular ship, could we please inform the Jeraptha authorities? It seemed that Captain Gumbano and his valiant crew had double-crossed the wrong people, and now both sides of the transaction wanted Gumbano's head as a trophy.

We could not count on any help from the Jeraptha, so, reluctantly, that ship jumped away, and once again, we were alone. Half of the galaxy hated us, the other half would not lift a finger or claw or tentacle to help us.

Valkyrie resumed its lonely patrol, and I sat in my office worrying, counting the days until we would have to return to Jaguar.

Days until Earth would be totally defenseless.

"Um, Joe," Skippy interrupted my gloomy thoughts. "You'd better look at this. I found something interesting."

"What?"

"It's a message, hidden inside one of the official communications from the Jeraptha."

"Hidden? Why-"

"I suspect the purpose of concealing the message is so that only I could find it. The encryption is fairly sophisticated, and I only found the message when I noticed a very subtle recurring glitch in the data file under the official communication."

"The message is for you?"

"No. The message is addressed to you, or to Colonel Perkins."

"To *me*?"

"Yes. It's from a friend of yours, a Captain Scorandum?"

"Scor- Oh. Oh, shit. let me see it." If the Ethics and Compliance Office was involved, it was no surprise that the message had been hidden. "*This* can't be good news."

The Universe hates me. That is a well-established fact, proven over the years. Really, I did not fault the Universe for hating me. It has tried many times to kill me, had several golden opportunities to rid itself of my existence, yet somehow, here I am, still breathing. Unless I'm dead and someone forgot to tell me, I mean, I guess that's possible.

Anyway, this time, either the Universe decided to throw me a bone, or it figured I had enough trouble to deal with already. Or, it was setting me up for a bigger fall later. Whatever. All I know is, the message from Captain Scorandum was *not* what I expected.

"Simms," I jabbed the intercom button. "Get in here, please."

"Sir?" She was only slightly out of breath from dashing around the corner from the bridge.

"Sit down, XO. You're not going to believe this, but our friends the beetles have some good news for us."

"The beetles?" She looked at me sideways, squinting to check I hadn't been drinking. "Their ships jumped away yesterday. How do you have news from-"

"They left a secret message for Skippy, he just found it."

"Hey!" The beer can protested. "I wasn't *looking* for it, you numbskull. How was I supposed to know the-"

Ignoring him, I held up a hand to block his blah, blah, blah. "The message is about that second group of ships, the ones that the beetles decided not to transfer to us."

"What about them?"

"I know this is gonna shock you, but apparently most of them were stolen quite recently, under very mysterious circumstances."

She snorted. "Let me guess. The Ethics and Compliance Office is investigating?"

I nodded. "They are determined to find and punish the perpetrators of this horrible crime. ECO wants our help."

"*Us?*"

"Yes. While they scour the galaxy for those missing ships, they want us to check one particular star system, just in case those ships are there."

"Just in case? Oh," she caught on quickly. "Is this an 'If you know what I mean' sort of thing?"

"I have no idea what you are talking about," I shrugged. "The odds are against us finding those ships, but-"

"Those rat bastard beetles are hedging their bets, aren't they?"

"Sounds like it," I agreed. "I hope they are. XO, we *need* those ships. UNEF Command wants us here, but, damn it, *Valkyrie* alone can't protect Earth. Even if we could, we can't do it forever. Eventually, this ship needs to go offline for a maintenance cycle, and we can't risk doing that here."

"You're preaching to the choir, Sir. What do you want me to do?"

"Help me craft a message, so when I inform Command about the second batch of ships, they will approve us going out to get them. The ECO captain who sent the message warned that this is a very limited-time offer."

Simms nodded. She was always better with words than I was. "Command isn't the problem. They take orders from their governments, including *our* government," she arched an eyebrow at me. I took that to mean she didn't care about my bullshit dual-citizenship in Skippy's fake country. "The public is scared, they want to know *Valkyrie* is up here protecting them. No political leader will approve us flying away."

"Yeah," I grinned. "I have a thought about that."

CHAPTER TWENTY SEVEN

"Ready?" I asked.

"It would have been nice if we could test this first," Skippy grumbled.

"You ran every simulation you could think of, right?"

"Simulations are not the real thing, Joe."

"Well, if you're not capable of properly modeling the event, maybe Bilby should-"

"I didn't say that," he hurried to say. "OK, *fine*. If we're going to do this, let's get it over with. Will that make you happy?"

I thought of New York, and Geneva, and the other sites on Earth that were now only craters. Dust still lingered high in the atmosphere, making for dramatic sunsets that no one could enjoy, for they knew the price humanity had paid. And knew the aliens might come back at any second. "I'll be *happy* when we have an operational fleet of ships, and we can take the fight to the enemy."

"Amen to that, brother," Skippy muttered. "OK, initiating stealth field in three, two, one, now. Field is stable, hologram is stable."

"Launch the Panther."

On the display, we watched a Panther fly out of a docking bay. We did not actually see it, the little spacecraft was inside the field that bent sunlight around *Valkyrie*, leaving utter darkness within. The display showed what we would see if the field was not enveloping our battlecruiser.

The Panther, sprouting a forest of antennas, slowly approached the outer edge of the stealth field, and a second stealth envelope began to swell outward from the dropship, growing wider and wider until it merged with the field projected by our battlecruiser.

The critical step was when the hologram showing *Valkyrie* transferred to the dropship, and the battlecruiser slowly altered course, still invisible. To anyone watching on the ground, by satellite or farther out in the solar system, it would look like our ship was still there. The hologram projected by the Panther was good, even excellent. *Valkyrie* climbed away, accelerating slowly. An AI aboard the Panther was controlling the dropship's flight, the hologram, and exchanging message traffic with the surface as if we were still there.

It was a brilliant way to assure the public, and warn aliens, that Valkyrie was on guard, protecting our homeworld. The problem was, the hologram was eating up tremendous amounts of energy, more than the Panther could sustain for long. After six hours, a final communication that supposedly came from our ship announced that, to avoid providing an easy target to the enemy, Valkyrie would engage stealth. The Panther dropped its hologram, and disappeared.

The plan was for the artificial battlecruiser to appear in the sky once a day, for eight days, then go back into stealth. After the eighth day, the Panther would have only enough power remaining to provide a small stealth field around itself, and it would climb away to await further instructions.

On the second day, at what we hoped was a safe distance from Earth, *Valkyrie* slipped into a jump wormhole with a focused burst of gamma rays.

CHAPTER TWENTY EIGHT

"Hmm," Skippy's avatar frowned, and he pantomimed scratching his head. "Well, *this* is inconvenient."

"It would help," I shared a knowing glance with Simms. "If we knew what *this* is." Following the annoyingly but understandably vague instructions from Scorandum, we had gone to one of the three Jeraptha relay stations he hinted we might want to contact, to get details of the rendezvous. Including, whether the deal was still on or not.

Bilby volunteered the information. "The Jeraptha changed the rendezvous point, Dude."

My hands stiffened around the armrests. "Did they explain why?"

Skippy answered, always annoyed when Bilby stole his thunder. "They are concerned about possible interference during the transfer."

"Interference from the Maxohlx?" I guessed.

"No, from their own coalition," Skippy shrugged. "Reading between the lines of the message, I think the beetles are afraid they will get caught red-handed by the Rindhalu."

My Spidey sense was tingling. "This sounds sketchy."

"Jeez Louise, Joe," Skippy frowned. "The entire operation is sketchy, that's the whole *point*. The spiders are not supposed to know the Jeraptha are giving us these ships."

"They are not *giving* us anything," I corrected him. "OK, I see your point. Crap, any time the Ethics and Compliance Office gets involved, we can expect surprises. All right, did the message have all the proper authentication codes?"

"I would have mentioned it, if the codes were not authentic," he sniffed.

"Fine. Sorry, I'm trying to be extra careful here. We were supposed to meet the beetles at," I checked the notes on my tablet. "A star system near the Crab Nebula, in the Perseus Arm. Where is the new rendezvous point?"

"Here," Skippy updated the main display to show a blinking yellow dot, on a map of the Milky Way galaxy.

"That is not exactly *helpful*."

"Ugh. How about this: it is in a star system near the Eagle Nebula, close to the outer edge of the Sagittarius Arm."

"Uh-"

"Have you ever seen photos of the gas cloud formation called 'The Pillars of Creation'?" He flashed the image on the display.

"Oh, yeah." Recognition dawned on me. "I've seen that. That's in the Eagle Nebula?"

"Yes."

"We're going in there?" I asked hopefully. Most of space was just featureless darkness, dotted with stars. It would be nice to have something to *look* at.

"No, dumdum. I said, *near* the nebula."

"OK," keeping my lips in a straight line to conceal my disappointment, I studied the star map. "Will we get close enough to see the nebula?"

"You mean, by looking out the window? You can *see* if from here, with the ship's-"

"With our *eyes*, Skippy. Yes, by looking out a window."

"That would require a detour, we could do that, I suppose."

Shaking my head, I said, "No. This isn't a pleasure cruise. Some other day, then. What can you tell me about this star system?"

"It is an anonymous brown dwarf system, it has a few rocky planets, and only one ice giant planet that is only marginally useful for refueling. There is absolutely *no* reason to ever go there. That must be why the beetles chose that location. It is not in their territory, but close to it. The current border theoretically places that system under the control of the Wurgalan, but there is no record of the squids ever visiting the place. Their patrons, the Bosphuraq, flew a survey ship through the system about six hundred years ago."

"Understood. What about wormholes?" My concern was if that system was a dead-end, with access provided by only one wormhole. That would be a red flag for me, it would be too easy for *Valkyrie* to be trapped, if the Maxohlx really wanted to capture the ship. And the kitties very much did want to capture *Valkyrie*, no question about that.

"One wormhole within three days of flight time, plus two others about eighteen days away."

I looked at Simms, she nodded. That seemed reasonably safe. *Valkyrie* could travel long distances faster than any ship in the galaxy, other than a few specialized star carriers. Eighteen days of continuous jumping would be a strain on even our advanced drive, so we wouldn't use that option unless we really had to. Skippy kept reminding me, in the daily report every morning, that the ship needed to be taken offline for heavy maintenance and upgrades. The plan had been to take our mighty battlecruiser apart at FOB Jiayuguan, after we had enough warships to protect Earth until *Valkyrie* was back online.

The US Navy had used various readiness cycle strategies over the years. Before Columbus Day an aircraft carrier strike group spent six months getting ready for deployment, eight months on station, eight months available for wartime surge, then eight months down for maintenance. The whole cycle lasted two and a half years, with the strike group actually being fully capable for combat only about half that time. From what I had read, the eight months allotted for heavy maintenance was optimistic, and escort ships had to get swapped between carriers to keep the strike group operational. The reason I mention this is that UNEF planned to have a fleet of starships like *Valkyrie*, so we needed to start thinking and planning for operating those ships, and not just relying on Skippy to patch together the stuff we broke.

Before we could plan for maintenance cycles, we had to get ships to operate.

"Did the Jeraptha give us any procedures for acknowledging the message, or designate an approach corridor to the rendezvous?"

"No, and yes," Skippy explained. "I was planning to simply repeat the message back to the relay station AI, to confirm we understood. There are three options for safe-fly approach corridors, I have them plotted in the navigation system."

"Repeat the message back to the station," I ordered.

"Done."

"Wait." Something was bothering me, and I didn't know what. "Send an acknowledgement message, stating that we will be at the rendezvous point, and include the coordinates."

"The coordinates are *in* the message I just repeated back, dumdum."

"I know that. I want a message from us, confirming that we understand the new rendezvous point, and we agree to meet there."

"Ugh. That is implied in-"

"I want you to set our message on broadcast, so it will be picked up by any passing ship, and propagate across the network of Jeraptha relay stations."

"Okaaaay," Skippy was irritated with me. "May I ask wh-"

"Let's call it an insurance policy," I cut him off.

"Fine," he huffed. "This relay station gets a lot of traffic, the message should spread quickly. I still don't see why you-"

"Throw me a bone, will you? Are you done?"

"Yes," he sniffed.

"Great. Let's get out of here, before the beetles change their minds again. Pilot, you have the revised jump programmed in?"

"Affirmative," Chen said with a thumbs up to me. UNEF Command had ordered her back aboard as our chief pilot. No offense to Shepard or the other pilots, but if we were going into combat, I wanted experienced hands on the controls. Reed was at FOB Jaguar, learning how to fly our first batch of ships. If we had the opportunity, I was bringing her aboard.

"Hit it."

We jumped.

Simms tapped my arm, pointing to the display between our chairs. "*Three* approach corridors? They all have almost identical parameters. Why would they give us multiple options that are virtually the same?"

I snorted. "XO, you're forgetting that we're dealing with the Jeraptha."

She raised one eyebrow. "So?"

"So," I winked. "They are going to wager which approach route we use."

"Oh for-"

"Trying to guess how we primitive humans think is *juicy* action."

Simms knocked on the door frame of my office. "The pilots need to know which approach corridor you want to use," she told me, while blowing on her cup of hot coffee.

"Alpha," I said, looking up from my laptop.

"Alpha? You are still planning to look at the nebula?"

"Yes." I had changed my mind about sightseeing, when I looked at the chart and saw the nebula was not far out of our way. "We came all the way out here, it would be a shame if we didn't get close enough to view it through a porthole."

"But-"

"It's only a delay of six hours, we have the time." It was important to get the second batch of ships to Jiayuguan, but the three fleet-support ships there were supposed to be running at full capacity to upgrade the first batch of ships. The new ships would mostly wait in line, possibly up to a year. The Jiayuguan system had the advantage of being remote, but it did have one major problem. The asteroid belt there was thin, and lacked many of the rare elements needed as raw materials by the fabricators. There was a rocky planet that was rich in materials, so we were setting up a mining operation there. Unfortunately, that world was close enough to the star that its sunward surface was broiling hot, and it rotated once every eighteen Earth days. So, every five days, we had to close down mining and move to a new site, because the first site would be super hot for nine days as that side of the planet faced the sun.

That was just one of the many problems UNEF had not anticipated when they decided to set up a forward operating base in that system. Hey, we are a young species. We're learning. Hopefully, we wouldn't make too many mistakes along the way.

Simms was curious. "Can I ask why you chose the Alpha corridor? The Bravo route lines up better with the nebula."

"It does. That's the point, XO," I added when I saw the blank look on her face. "If we fly directly from the relay station, we would logically select the Charlie corridor. If we divert to view the nebula, we should choose the Bravo corridor. The Jeraptha will be *betting* that we approach along one of those routes."

She raised an eyebrow again. "This is about screwing up their wagers?"

"No. This is showing them that we are not predictable."

"Oh." Both eyebrows went up, like she hadn't expected me to be making an adult decision. "I'll inform the pilots."

The nebula was spectacular. From our position, at seventeen lightyears away, it covered a big part of the view. Since the ship only had a handful of actual portholes, the off-duty crew all got into pressure suits and secured themselves in docking bays, then we pumped out the air and opened the big outer doors. There it was, seen with our own eyeballs, with no image enhancements or filters. Most people got thirty minutes to view the nebula, then some of the crew going to relieve the duty shift, so they could get a look too.

It was a nice break in the routine, an opportunity for the crew to bond over something other than work and training. I could have sat there for hours, gazing at the cloud where stars were being born, if Margaret was with me. It's the sort of thing you want to share with someone, not experience alone. Simms must have felt the same, because she got up and walked over to sit next to me. We didn't say much, just pointed out cool stuff to each other. When it was time to go, she reached out and squeezed my hand. I squeezed back, appreciating the gesture even through layers of composite gloves. I was missing Margaret, Simms was missing Frank, but Margaret would be waiting for me at FOB Jaguar. Simms had no idea when she would see Frank again. She was making a sacrifice for humanity, but mostly for *me*.

We looked at each other, nodded, then got up to go back to work.

From the sightseeing viewpoint, we began jumping toward the rendezvous point. Most of the crew began packing up their gear, anticipating transfer to ships the Jeraptha were selling to us. Our people would use the flight to Jiayuguan to assess the condition of each ship, and determine how best to upgrade them to our standards. That assessment would not actually be done by mere humans, Skippy had created a submind to be carried in a portable computer, that could be jacked into each ship's existing substrate. By the time we reached Jiayuguan, he should have enough data to prioritize repairs and upgrades. The major issue, as always, would be the limited capacity to manufacture the components we needed, but that was not *my* problem to deal with. Eventually, if we were to build ships equivalent to *Valkyrie*, we needed to acquire more Maxohlx-level technology, and doing that *would* be my problem.

Later.

First, we needed to escort the second batch of obsolete ships to the FOB. I did not anticipate any trouble doing that, unless the spiders somehow discovered the double-dealing by their clients.

But that was unlikely.

Commander Zilleen Fentenu pressed an eye to the tiny porthole in the escape pod, trying to catch a glimpse of what was going on outside. She could have activated the pod's active sensors to send out a pulse, though that would consume power that could be needed for life support. Also, it would certainly alert the enemy to her presence and pinpoint her location. The enemy probably knew the pod was occupied, and had its location locked in a targeting computer. They had not bothered to destroy the pod, either because they simply didn't care, or perhaps they wanted witnesses to the incident. Maybe a combination of both.

The situation might change if she lit up the area with an active sensor pulse, the enemy could decide she was annoying enough to be worth firing a maser cannon at her pod.

On a lesser scale of risk, she could power up the pod's passive sensor array, to get a better look at her surroundings. Mostly, she wanted to know the status of her former ship, the ECO *We Were Never Here*. Fentenu had been the last person to board an escape pod, maneuvering the crippled ship as best she could, to give her crew a chance to get away. She had lost track of other escape pods when the ship was cut in half. When she regained consciousness, she was alone, unable to contact anyone through the powerful enemy jamming. Reaching the escape pod had required crawling along the outside of the *We Were Never Here's* hull while it tumbled chaotically, power conduits exploding around her. That was also why she was alone in the pod. It was not so bad being alone, soon she would need to enter a hibernation chamber and close the lid anyway, and she would not be aware of anyone beyond the chamber's lid.

Using the passive array would consume power, and leave a signature for the enemy to detect. It was worth the risk, she decided. There could be people in damaged pods nearby, if that were true, it was her responsibility to render assistance.

A scan revealed plenty of objects littering space around her, including the shattered hull sections of the *Never Here*. There was no pattern to the debris field, or to the movement of objects in the field. The field was dense and hot, composite fragments still cooling in the hard vacuum, with blinding arcs of lightning and glowing plasma leaking from torn-apart starships. What she could not see were any escape pods near her, though that was not especially surprising. The pods had low-visibility coatings that absorbed light, and the local red dwarf star was dim. Switching to infrared did not help, there was too much clutter in the expanding bubble of debris.

What the infrared image did show was a formation of enemy ships, and she felt a chill as she magnified those images as best she could.

The Maxohlx were still there. Far fewer ships than had been in the attack force, the enemy had left behind only a handful of ships, for whatever purpose. As she watched, there were flares, and three ships jumped away.

Hopefully the others would join them, and she could risk sending out a ping to call other survivors. Standard Home Fleet procedure called for waiting three full days after the last sign of the enemy was detected. She snorted at that thought. *Standard* procedure did not envision being attacked by senior-species warships.

The operation had been an ECO initiative, so the Ethics group was responsible for the disaster, and for assisting survivors. She would watch until the last Maxohlx ship jumped away, then wait only six hours. The enemy had shown no interest in killing survivors, she could almost feel their disdain radiating through the emptiness of space.

What she hoped was that the humans would not arrive at the rendezvous point until after the Maxohlx had departed. Maybe the humans were already in the area, seeing that the second group of ships they wanted to acquire were now only jagged fragments. The Maxohlx had been very methodical about blasting apart every ship at the rendezvous point, no matter how small or obsolete. No Jeraptha ship had escaped the trap, unable to jump away due to powerful damping fields.

It was early still, for the rendezvous point was a long way from Earth, near what the humans called the Crab Nebula in the Perseus Arm of the galaxy. The humans were not scheduled to arrive for two days, assuming they received and understood the message.

Commander Fentenu folded all four of her legs under her and got comfortable for a long watch, waiting for the Maxohlx to leave.

And for the humans to arrive.

Part of her hoped the humans would see the debris, and run before the Maxohlx could hit them too.

CHAPTER TWENTY NINE

The largest planet in Earth's solar system had slumbered undisturbed for billions of years, before the inhabitants of the third planet sent a probe called 'Pioneer 10' zipping past. Since then, probes from multiple countries had flown past, gone into orbit, even dropped sensor drones into the atmosphere. The planet was still orbited by machines from America, Japan, China, India and the European Space Agency, though not all of those probes were operational.

Of the machines that were active, only one was in a high enough orbit, and pointed in the right direction, to see the gamma ray bursts as more than two dozen starships arrived through tunnels in spacetime. The probe mindlessly recorded the data, to transmit to a receiving station on Earth, then the probe swung around Jupiter to get line-of-sight to the world where it had been constructed.

It never had the opportunity to transmit the data it had collected.

One of the ships casually targeted all of the probes around the gas giant planet, firing only its low-powered point-defense cannons. The beings who flew the ships were not worried about the probes as a threat, but they could provide more precise data on the location of ships in the task force, and therefore had to be eliminated.

Thirty-nine minutes later, the photons of the gamma rays reached telescopes on and around Earth.

UNEF Command was alerted fifty-two minutes after the ships arrived.

It took only seconds to identify the intruders.

They were Maxohlx warships.

"Uh, wha-" Mark Friedlander blinked in the darkness, awakened from a deep sleep, and a pleasant dream that was already fading away. At first, he thought the sound was a wake-up alarm, but there was no light coming through the window shades, so it couldn't possibly be morning yet. Unless it was raining. In which case, he decided to roll over and go back to sleep; he could run later.

Fumbling with the phone, he was surprised to see not the alarm icon, but a phone call. Damn it, he had set the phone's Do Not Disturb function on, and, he squinted through bleary eyes, he did not recognize the caller. "Hello?" He whispered as his wife stirred beside him and lifted her head off the pillow.

"Doctor Friedlander, this is Major Hattori at UNEF Command. There is a problem at Jupiter, we need your analysis."

"I'm-" he held the phone away at arm's length and stared at it. "I'm on *Earth* now." He had never expected he would need to say that. "What-"

"Yes, Doctor," Hattori said in a tone of not-quite-patience. "The problem is at Jupiter. A task force of Maxohlx ships arrived there within the hour, we need to know what they are doing."

His wife sat up, clutching the blanket to her and squeezed his free hand. He squeezed back and whispered, "It's OK, UNEF wants me to look at something." He did not mention that enemy ships were in the solar system again, with Earth essentially defenseless against attack. "Major, I am not a military officer. Chang commanded a starship, he-"

"The Maxohlx ships appear to have dropped devices into Jupiter's atmosphere, Doctor," Hattori's patience was running thin.

Shit. Reflexively, he squeezed his wife's hand a bit too hard. "Astrophysics is not my specialty," he explained. Sometimes, the public expected a scientist to know everything about every subject. "Have you-"

"Doctor. We *are* bringing in a team of astrophysicists. Only one of them has been offworld at all. You have extensive experience *out there*," he emphasized. "Command wants you to lead the investigation team."

"Me?" He could imagine that a group of astrophysics scientists would be *thrilled* to have an engineer questioning their analysis.

"Yes, Doctor. You can provide *context*."

"Oh." He realized Hattori was right. "Do I need to be in New York?"

"No. The team will be meeting in Geneva."

Friedlander took a breath. "All right. Probably the first flight I can get will be tonight, do you expect-"

"Get to the airport as soon as possible, please. A dropship will be waiting for you."

"Uh, got it. Understood," he added for the Japanese officer, in case American idioms were not familiar. "I can be there in-" Time for a quick shower while his wife threw clothes into a suitcase for him. Then the drive to the airport, there should be no traffic at that time of the morning. Except, he should check the traffic report, in case the highway was shut down for maintenance work, *again*. "It should be-"

"Hold a moment, Doctor," Hattori said, and there were muted voices on the other end of the call. "Instead of driving to the airport, please go to the elementary school at the end of your street. A Coast Guard helicopter will meet you there, ETA is seventeen minutes."

"Coast Guard?"

"It is the closest helicopter available," Hattori explained. "The situation is quite urgent. Command wants answers immediately."

"I will be there."

"Thank you."

Mark ended the call. Seventeen minutes. Did he have time for a shower? Yes. If UNEF was involved, he might not get a shower for days. Or get to sleep for that long. "Honey, they need me in Geneva. On *Earth*," he pointed to the floor. "I'm not leaving the planet."

She had her arms across her chest. "You say that now, but-"

"Honey, please. We don't have any starships, I *can't* go offworld. Can you throw some clothes in a bag for me? I'll be out of the shower in two minutes."

"Mark, *what* is going on?"

"I don't know," he told her as much truth as he thought prudent. "Something is happening with Jupiter, they want me to look at it. From Geneva. Look at it from *here*," he added.

She rose from the bed and pulled on one of his old T-shirts. "You call me. You promise? You will call me. Every day."

"*Every* day," he crossed his heart, and dashed into the bathroom.

The flight to Geneva was rough, compounded by having to land in Boston to pick up a pair of astrophysicists from MIT. They were as puzzled as Mark was, though when they recognized him, an element of fear was added to their curiosity. "Doctor Friedlander," the first scientist through the door gasped in surprise, hesitating as the crew urged him to take a seat and strap in. "We are not going-"

"Geneva, we're going to *Geneva*," Mark assured with a warning glare at the dropship's crew chief. "We are *not* going offworld, I promised my wife. Please, strap in, the flight could be rough."

The man paused, barely touching the seat. "You are sure-"

"I am sure that humanity doesn't have any starships in-system right now. We *can't* go anywhere," he added with a scowl at the crew chief, who nodded while he helped the newcomers strap in.

The flight from Boston to Geneva was rough, a suborbital hop with just enough zero gravity at the top of the arc to make everyone aboard nauseous. Even the crew chief was looking green before the Dragon fired its thrusters to turn around so the main engines were pointing backwards, and deceleration pressed everyone into their seats with a force three times that of Earth's surface. The noise and vibration did not help keep their stomachs settled, Mark barely got a bag in front of one scientist, before the man doubled over and lost whatever he'd eaten for dinner.

"That's one," Mark shouted over the roaring noise. The Dragon had turned around again and was in freefall, burning a streak down through the air over northern France.

"One?" The man's eyes bulged, miserable as he struggled to breathe deep and evenly.

"First time for you," Mark explained. "I can't even count the number of times I got sick on flights like this."

"It gets better?"

Mark shrugged. "Eventually, it stops. We'll be on the ground soon."

"What the hell is *that*?" Friedlander pointed at the display that took up most of a wall in the packed conference room. It had taken hours to get telescopes on the ground and in orbit pointed at Jupiter, and the images combined into a composite. A pair of Falcon dropships had flown up into geosynchronous orbits, adding their own sophisticated sensor imagery to the total. The resolution was still poor, but there was a distinctive blob of *something* rising away from the gas giant planet. Along the equator, Jupiter now had a jet of gas being ejected.

"That *is* the question," Senior Colonel Chang muttered with only a trace of sarcasm. "We need to know what it is, whether it is a threat, and what we can do about it."

"You are asking the wrong person," Friedlander answered in a whisper louder than normal, speaking over the uproar in the room. "My background-"

"Doctor," Chang put a hand on the rocket scientist's shoulder, leaning forward a bit too heavily, for he was still weary from being in the hospital. The doctors wanted him to rest, the UN wanted answers. He would rest after he knew what was happening at Jupiter. "We can get all the scientists in the world looking at the problem, what I need is someone to make *sense* of it. As Bishop would say, cut through all the nerdy details and get me answers."

"OK, but-"

"Mark," Chang said loudly enough for everyone in the room to hear. He wanted them to hear, to know that Friedlander had the confidence of the Undersecretary for Homeworld Security. "If you had not seen the signal from Nagatha, and known that it *was* a signal and what it meant, we would have lost the *Flying Dutchman*, *Valkyrie*, Bishop, and Skippy. Earth would have been bombarded by a fleet of Maxohlx ships. You and I would not be having this conversation. Tap codes are not your specialty either."

"Right," Mark looked at the blob on the display. "Answers. We'll get them for you."

Standard UNEF procedure, when approaching a star system or rendezvous point that was not known to be secure, was to jump in eight lighthours away, and scan the area with passive sensors. I know that procedure very well, because the Merry Band of Pirates literally wrote all of the procedures the UN fleet would operate under. A lot of those rules were developed by painful experience.

Eight lighthours is a nice round number, it was chosen because it provided a view of an area, without getting close enough to risk getting trapped in a damping field. The problem was, it was a snapshot in time that was eight hours old. In space combat, a lot can happen in eight *minutes*, forget about eight hours. Still, a glimpse from eight lighthours was useful because of the distances of interstellar travel, and the uncertainty of timing when a ship might arrive at a particular destination. If someone wanted to deceive an arriving ship, they had to maintain the deception for a long time.

We had one more jump to reach the target star system, the capacitors would be fully recharged within twelve minutes, according to the tracker in the bottom left corner of my chair's display. All systems were 'Go' for jump, we didn't need to wait for a full charge. That was another of the procedures we had written after painful experience: before jumping into a potentially hazardous situation, make sure the ship was capable of performing multiple jumps.

Also, make sure everyone pees first, so we don't have to stop at a rest area along the way.

Simms leaned over to hiss at me. "Why are you doing that?" She asked in a whisper I barely heard.

"What?" I replied as quietly as I could manage.

"That," she pointed to my legs.

My left foot was tapping on the deck. It was more like the heel was bouncing, tapping rapidly in a nervous twitch. Immediately, I made my leg hold still.

"Something is bothering you?" She asked, a bit louder because it was a more complicated thing to say, I couldn't read lips that well.

My answer was a shrug.

"*You* are in command of the ship," she noted.

I got her meaning. If something was bothering me about the rendezvous, I had full authority to do something about it. And full responsibility if something went wrong. "Skippy," I raised my voice. "When were the Jeraptha scheduled to arrive at the rendezvous point?"

"There is not a specific time, Joe," he explained. "The ships were not all travelling together. Also, depending on the routes they took and at which emergence point they went through the local wormhole, they could have arrived anywhere from seven to two days ago. Remember, they are transporting an entire *spacedock* for us. Something like that is awkward to carry even in sections, the star carriers with the spacedock components will likely be moving very carefully."

"Got it."

"Sir?" Simms prompted after I spent a long moment tapping my front teeth with a thumbnail. She wanted me to make a decision, and she wanted me to stop being annoying.

Even I admit that I can be extremely annoying to work with.

The bridge crew was also waiting for me to make a decision, with various degrees of subtlety. No one was openly staring at me yet, that was good.

"I just," I said to Simms quietly. "I have a feeling about this rendezvous. Something is *odd* about it."

"The authentication codes checked out," she reminded me.

"Yeah." Shit. We *needed* those ships. My Spidey sense was only mildly tingling, I didn't know why it was tingling at all. Was I losing my nerve, after too many battles? A starship captain managed a crew and an incredibly complex set of machines. I was supposed to rely on experience, training and logic, not squishy things like vague feelings. "Pilot, reprogram the jump, to bring us in at a distance of two lightdays. Still aligned with Approach Corridor Alpha."

"Yes, Sir. From that distance, we will need," he checked the console. "Thirty-seven minutes to top up the jump capacitors, before we jump again."

"Understood." The display showed we were still not at full charge.

"Revised coordinates programmed in," Shepard reported. "Jump option is designated as 'Hotel'."

"Confirmed," Bilby said with admirable brevity.

We jumped in, two lightdays from the star. The ship emerged above the local ecliptic, the disc on which the system's planets orbited the star. Really, it could be said we emerged below the ecliptic, there is no 'up' or 'down' in deep space. Anyway, from there, we had a great, if time-delayed, view of the entire system. "Skippy? What do you see?"

"Nothing unusual, Joe," he said in a bored monotone. He probably was bored, wanted to get to the rendezvous so he could screw with the beetles, instead of wasting time with unnecessary precautions. "Hmm. OK, this is different. Three of the ships they brought are *seriously* pieces of crap, I don't know what I'm supposed to do with those piles of junk. Um, hmm. They also brought five more ships than you requested, so maybe they think quantity makes up for lack of quality."

"Is this a problem?"

"No," he sighed. "Those junk ships are destroyers, I can use them for spare parts, or take them apart for the raw materials. The good news is, the spacedock appears to be all there, they even included an old but apparently serviceable fabrication module as a spare. That was very nice of them. Joe, did you bring a fruit basket as a 'Thank you' gift?"

"Sadly, no."

"Ugh. I can't go anywhere with you. Will you at least promise to wear a clean uniform to meet with the Jeraptha?"

"I'll go through the pile of clothes on the floor of my cabin, and try to find one with the fewest ketchup stains."

"Hopeless! You are hopeless," he shook his head.

"Seriously," I felt foolish for my earlier discomfort about the rendezvous. "Is there anything that looks odd?"

"Nope. The ships are transmitting the proper identification codes, and the ship-to-ship traffic I'm able to pick up through backscatter all sounds perfectly normal. It is disappointing, actually. On the surface, the beetles appear to be way more cool and interesting than you monkeys, but their communications are basically the same boring blah blah buh-*LAH* as your insipid monkey chatter."

"I feel terrible that we are not more entertaining to you, and vow to rededicate myself to doing knuckleheaded things you can mock me for."

"Sure, you say that *now*," he folded his arms across his chest. "But then you will go back to Mister Professional Starship Captain."

"That's my *job*, asshole."

"It's *dull*, Joe," he pouted.

Doing my job in a professional manner was important. It was also true that I had to remember an unwritten but important part of my job: to keep Skippy entertained. If everything the Merry Band of Pirates did was governed by procedures, he might get bored with us. That could be fatal to humanity.

Crap.

My *real* job was to fall on my face often enough that he wanted to stick around to see what stupid thing I would do next.

"Dull is safe, Skippy. But, you're right, it *is* dull. Can we worry about that later? The beetles have a bunch of starships for you to play with."

"They have a bunch of starship *hulls* for me to play with. The guts of those ships are obsolete crap. Do you have any idea what a pain in the *ass* it will be for me to-"

"Then it is fortunate that you are extremely awesome, huh? All right, XO," I turned my attention to Simms. "What do you think?"

The expression on her face was more curious than concerned. She didn't see anything wrong, and wondered why I was hesitant about the rendezvous. "I think we proceed to the eight lighthour mark, and confirm."

"Right," I agreed. "Pilot, engage when ready."

We jumped.

From eight lighthours away, the view was the same. Entirely normal, everything as expected. My Spidey sense was not even tingling anymore, either because there wasn't anything wrong, or because I'd gone numb to the feeling. What I had been experiencing was, I decided, just the usual pre-mission jitters. Part of my nervousness was that, unlike any of our previous missions, every intelligent species in the galaxy knew about the Merry Band of Pirates. Everyone was watching us, including the people of Earth. We had a reputation that was not entirely deserved, UNEF had encouraged stories that boasted about incredible feats we achieved, and did not mention how close to failure we had come many times.

"OK," I decided. "We remain here until we have a full charge on the jump drive capacitors." The display estimated that would take eighteen minutes. Everything else on the display indicated green, though I knew Skippy was not happy about the overall condition of the ship. He was right, at some point, we needed to take *Valkyrie* offline for overdue maintenance.

Later.

"Make it thirty minutes?" Simms suggested, always thinking about the welfare of the crew.

"Good idea."

"You may want to," she said to me in a whisper, "change that top." She pointed to a mystery stain just above the belt on my left side.

It appeared to be some type of hot sauce. Or possibly it was related to the chili dog I had for lunch. "I'll be right back."

Five minutes later, I was back on the bridge, I resisted the temptation to duck into the galley for a cup of coffee. We waited out the remaining minutes, with Skippy arguing with me. He wanted to jump in at the center of the Jeraptha formation, showing off as usual. That would have been fun and impressive, and that was the problem. It would be *too* impressive.

To conceal the accuracy of our jump drive from enemies, UNEF declared that standing procedure was to jump in slightly off-target, even when meeting friendly ships. It irritated Skippy that he wasn't allowed to show off, while Bilby of course was more chill about it. The drive also was tuned to be noisier and more chaotic than it normally was. Part of the reason we concealed the true capabilities of our drive from the Jeraptha was their sensor data could be hacked by a hostile species. The other reason was if they saw how good our drive was, they would be less happy about the dumbed-down version we were offering in our technology exchange package.

With the argument settled, and Skippy grudgingly complying, we waited the final minutes for the countdown to end, and the crew to report the ship was secured for a jump. That process included off-duty crew members making sure items in their cabins were put away, so they did not become projectiles if something went wrong with the jump, or in the unlikely event the ship had to maneuver violently to avoid colliding with an object in front of our emergence point.

When all indicators were showing green and I checked that my own seatbelt was securely fastened across my waist, I gave the order.

CHAPTER THIRTY

We jumped.

Into hell.

Immediately on entry through the far event horizon, an alarm sounded and the main display flashed a red alert.

A damping field.

More than one.

Multiple, overlapping damping fields saturated the entire area.

Dozens of them.

How the f-

"Skippy!"

"Working on it! The signatures are-"

"Maxohlx, yeah I know." That was my own interpretation of the data, even before Bilby put his analysis on the display. I recognized the precision of the damping field lines. Compared to second-tier species technology, a Maxohlx damping field had such a subtle disrupting effect on local spacetime, it didn't need as much power to prevent a trapped ship from jumping. It also could establish the effect across a larger radius from the projecting ship.

Still, a single ship, or even a dozen ships, could cover only a distance of eleven or twelve lightseconds. The only way those ships could already have us trapped is if they knew exactly where we planned to jump. That was bullshit. The safe-fly corridor outlined by the Jeraptha was a line, not a point in space. They requested that we emerge in a zone, not a precise coordinate. *Valkyrie* came out of the jump wormhole sixty-four lightseconds from the center of the zone, and we had chosen the final coordinates at random, just a few minutes before the jump.

No way could the kitties have known where we would emerge.

Unless-

Shit.

There were a *lot* of red symbols on the main display, all around us. More symbols were popping up as our sensor field expanded, and detected disruptions in its pattern.

Stealthed ships.

Even a stealthed ship could not hide from a sensor field, because the presence of the ship caused the field to bend around it. Within the limited range of our sensor field, there were fourteen, no, eighteen, no, *twenty-one* stealthed ships.

Stealthed Maxohlx ships.

Also within the bubble of our sensor field coverage were other objects, that we had thought were Jeraptha ships. Now, with active sensors at short range, we could see those were merely drones projecting holograms around them.

Shit.

From a distance of eight lighthours, even Skippy had not been able to detect that the 'Jeraptha ships' we saw were actually holograms. As our sensor field radiated outward to cover those drones, they dropped their holograms and accelerated toward us. So did the warships.

Valkyrie rocked from incoming maser fire.

"Skippy! How many ships are out there?"

"I don't *know*, Joe. We can't see-"

"Yankee search," I ordered an active sensor pulse. "Light 'em up."

At the sensor console, the duty officer pressed a button, and powerful waves of energy radiated out from our ship's sensor antennas. The pulses were limited to the speed of light, both the outbound signal and the returning echo. Within two seconds, we knew how many ships were within a one-lightsecond range from our location, then in eight seconds, we had a look at a four-lightsecond bubble.

It was not good news.

A bubble of four lightseconds was one-point-two million kilometers across. Just in that relatively small area, the counter on the display was showing eighty-seven ships. Real ships, not drones projecting holograms.

Simms and the pilots and everyone on the bridge were looking at me, waiting for me to issue an order. Waiting for me to *do* something, anything.

The ship was shuddering as our shields deflected or absorbed a massive amount of maser energy. On the display, missiles were coming in such volume, the counter on the display was losing track.

We needed to run.

Where?

The enemy was surrounding us in all directions, there wasn't a gap for us to run through. Making a snap decision, I ordered, "Get us out of here, maximum acceleration. Head toward the star."

That direction was as good as any.

We all felt the ship move, our normal-space engines channeling gigawatts of energy into forward movement. The shuddering stopped, as we moved away from the spot where enemy maser bolts had been targeted. Instead, the deck vibrated as the ship surged ahead.

Then the vibration smoothed out, fluttered, as our engines stumbled.

"Sorry, Joe!" Skippy shouted. "The enemy is disrupting our engines, they can't get traction in local spacetime. Thrust is down by thirty-six percent."

"Understood." We knew the Maxohlx had technology that could interfere with reactionless engines, *Valkyrie* had the same capability. We also knew that when a ship projected a field to interfere with another ship's engines, it also affected all ships within the field. As long as the kitties were slowing us down, it would be more difficult for them to chase us.

They still had a huge advantage of numbers, and *Valkyrie* was moving slowly enough to be an easy target.

Shit!

A counter on the main display showed less than thirty seconds had elapsed since we jumped into the trap. With every second, more ships were appearing, tightening the barrier we had to go through.

Smashing a thumb down on the button for the ship's 1MC intercom system, I said as calmly as I could, "Everyone, hang on." Then, more helpfully, I used proper procedure for communication. "All decks, prepare for booster ignition."

We waited for responses to come in from occupied areas of the ship, and for Bilby to complete the process of securing mechanisms outside the pressure hull. The instant the last status light turned green, I barked, "Engage boosters!"

Valkyrie is a battlecruiser, or based on the hull structure of a battlecruiser. Usually, the ship did not travel long distances through normal space. It was usually faster, safer and even less energy-intensive to simply jump from one point in space to another, without going through all the empty, boring places in between. When the ship did maneuver in normal space, the massive reactionless engines pushed or pulled *Valkyrie's* substantial bulk around, without throwing mass out the back of the ship. Reactionless engines are a fantastic advantage, especially for a warship. A ship equipped with reactionless technology did not have to carry around mass that will literally be thrown away, and the lack of gas or ions streaming out of the engines prevented the enemy from detecting us. A ship leaving a trail of hot exhaust behind was like holding up a bright 'SHOOT ME' sign in combat.

Reactionless engines, therefore, can be used when a ship is wrapped in a stealth field.

Booster engines were definitely *not* stealthy. They are a mix of exotic matter that basically generates a nuclear fission reaction that is not self-sustaining, because the highly radioactive fissionable material is ejected out of the boosters to propel us forward. When Skippy first explained how Maxohlx boosters worked, I imagined something like a whole lot of small atomic bombs, but my understanding was completely wrong. After he tried diagramming the effect using terms like 'mesons', 'bosons' and something about an 'exclusion principle', he gave up and I agreed that it is basically magic. All I remember from that mind-numbing lecture is that 'exclusion' is *not* something like 'No shirt no shoes no service'.

When the boosters kicked on, it sure felt like nuclear bombs were exploding behind my seat. The ship *surged* forward, riding the booster thrust, with the pilots using the normal-space engines to both augment the acceleration and weave the ship's course in a random evasive pattern. Ships even half a lightsecond away would have difficulty targeting us, because by the time their maser beams reached the targeted location, *Valkyrie* would have moved. We still got struck by lucky shots, and of course the incoming missiles could turn to follow us, but it was better than providing an easy target.

Missiles.

No matter how hard the boosters could accelerate our mighty battlecruiser, even a low-performance missile could easily catch us. The sensor images immediately around the ship became hazy, as missiles exploded by our point-defense cannons created a cloud of debris that obscured our view of the remaining missiles. Missiles exploded by defensive fire were not the only problem, because the enemy was smart. Some of the missiles in the strike package were not designed to penetrate hull armor or punch through energy shields. A portion of the incoming missiles, which typically compromised twenty-two percent of the strike package if the Maxohlx were following their standard close-space-combat tactics, were designed to disrupt and confuse our point-defense systems. That was actually good for us, because Skippy's own sensors could filter out most of the noise and pinpoint the location of incoming missiles. His ability to do that was limited to a short distance around the ship, and even he had a delay in tracking a missile when a sensor-jamming warhead exploded close to us.

The good news, what little of it we had, was that about one in five enemy missiles were ineffective against us. The bad news was, our point-defense system still had to make an effort to engage those missiles, or the Maxohlx would quickly realize they needed to change tactics.

Why was I babbling on blah blah blah about nerdy military stuff like weapons specs and tactics?

Because I was scared out of my freakin' mind, that's why.

"Skippy," I raised my voice to be heard clearly over the roar of the boosters, even deep inside the forward pressure hull of the ship, it was loud. "Can you estimate how many ships are out there?"

"Around our position, I now count a hundred and thirty-nine warships. Joe, this is *bad*. Assuming the Maxohlx covered all three approach corridors, and surrounded each emergence zone to a radius of ten lightseconds, there could be a *thousand* enemy ships out there."

My hands were trembling, so I clenched them into fists and placed them firmly in my lap. Staring at the main display did not help. Enemy ships behind us were falling farther behind, caught off-guard by our sudden acceleration.

That didn't help.

It actually harmed our ability to escape from the trap I had stupidly jumped us into.

As I watched, a ship jumped in front of us, along our flight path but three lightseconds distant. A moment later, the display showed a ship disappear, five lightseconds behind us.

It was the *same* ship.

We saw it appear before we saw it jump away, due to the frustratingly slow speed of light.

The overlapping damping fields around us were so powerful, even ships that knew the planned frequency pattern of the field could not adjust their jump drives to compensate. But as ships fell behind in the chase, they went beyond the chaotic spacetime disruptions of the damping effect, and were able to jump ahead of us.

Shit.

We were never going to get away.

We couldn't.

The enemy could use jump drives to leapfrog ahead of us, while we crawled along in normal space.

"Booster fuel load is dropping below sixty percent," Simms announced, drawing my attention to the issue. She caught my eye and we exchanged a look, with her jerking her head toward the display.

I knew what she meant. Boosters are designed for short-term use, not to be run continuously. This wasn't working, the speed we gained from firing boosters didn't help, when the enemy could instantaneously jump ahead of our course. We might need the boosters to do something actually useful in the future, if we had a future.

"Cut boosters," I ordered. "Main engines to full military thrust. Pilot, turn left thirty degrees." At least by altering course, ships that jumped in ahead of us would be out of position for an intercept.

Until they jumped again, right in front of our new course. Three ships did just that, coordinating their action so they bracketed our base course, providing cover no matter which direction we turned in our evasive pattern.

"Joe," Skippy's voice was shaky. "We don't have much time. Twenty-four more ships just jumped in near our position."

Shit.

I knew that would happen. The Maxohlx ships that had been waiting at the other emergence zones had been alerted to our presence, by picket ships that jumped away when they saw us arrive. Actually, I did not *know* that, but that's what I would have done to set up an ambush, and the Maxohlx are smarter than me. Within minutes, there could be more than a thousand ships launching missiles at us. Already, the firing of the point-defense cannons was becoming a continuous buzz, rather than the usual intermittent chattering. An indicator on the display was showing the point-defense system at seventy-three percent capacity and climbing. That number was deceptive, some cannons were approaching the redline for overheating and would need to be shut down, forcing other cannons to take up the slack.

We couldn't take much more of a pounding, one of the forward starboard shields was down below forty percent.

"I know, Skippy," I said, my voice as numb as I felt.

"They haven't contacted us to demand surrender," Simms got my attention, speaking barely loud enough to be heard.

"They don't want our surrender."

She stared at me, eyes wide open in shock. "But-"

"They want us dead."

"*Dead*?" Skippy screeched, his voice going up an octave. "Joe, you must be wrong. That would be suicide for *them*."

"No," I let myself exhale the breath I'd been keeping in. "It would not."

"But-" Simms began again.

"They want to capture Skippy. The Maxohlx know Skippy will keep resetting the timers on the Elder weapons, to keep his pet monkeys alive on Earth." My own voice was barely above a whisper, Simms had to lean in to hear. How could I have been so fucking *stupid*? Skippy was our insurance policy, but only while he was with us. "As long as a population of humans are alive, somewhere in the galaxy, you won't allow those weapons to trigger," I looked up at Skippy's avatar. "Would you?"

"I, I-" His holographic face was frozen. "Joe, I truly don't know."

"They do. The Maxohlx do."

"They can't *know* what I would do," he protested.

"They don't have to," I explained. "They have a predictive model, and it says you will continue to protect humanity, even if I and everyone aboard *Valkyrie* is dead. They will tear this ship apart, nuke us to dust, and extract your canister from the wreckage."

"They are taking one hell of a risk," he gasped.

"The kitties are *arrogant*," I sighed. "We knew that. I knew that. I should have expected they would do something like this. They think the risk is worth the reward, and they are arrogant enough to believe they can't possibly be wrong. Shit!" I slammed a fist on the armrest, careful not to touch any of the controls. "We need to get out of here."

"Agreed. How?" He asked.

"Can we do the trick we used when we got ambushed last time, where we jumped into a gas giant?"

"This system doesn't have a gas giant planet, Joe. I told you that. The only planets here are lifeless rocks, and one-"

"The star is a brown dwarf, right? That is basically a warm gas giant."

"Oh. My. G- Ugh. A brown dwarf is still a *star*, you idiot. This one has seventeen times the mass of Jupiter. OK, sure, that is on the lower end of the range between a low-mass star and a very large planet, and this star is no longer experiencing nuclear fusion, but you have to respect-"

"Thank you, Professor Nerdnik," I cut him off. "Could the ship survive jumping into the upper atmosphere of this star, yes or no?"

"That's really more of a 'shmaybe', but if you want me to guess, then, it might be possible," he answered reluctantly.

"Good. Then-"

"Theoretically. Depending on how well the ship's artificial gravity can protect your squishy biological bodies, *you* might not survive."

"Yes, or no?" I kept one eye on the display. One of the forward shields was nearing collapse.

He sighed. "This is grossly oversimplifying, but, *in theory*, yes. It is possible. Joe, if you insist on jumping into a celestial body, I suggest the ice giant planet instead of the star."

"Ice giant, that's a planet like Neptune?"

"Correct. The terms 'gas giant' and 'ice giant' greatly oversimplify the-"

"Yeah, you can lecture me about that later. This ice giant has an atmosphere where we could hide?"

"In theory, yes. The planet is composed mostly of water in a supercritical state, above which is an atmosphere that is mostly hydrogen and-"

"It has clouds?"

"There are multiple cloud layers, yes. For concealment, the ship would need to be inside the lower cloud deck. Joe, not much is known about the atmosphere of this particular planet. I am looking at it now and-"

The deck rocked again, hard. Something hit us, or came close.

"Great, I'll leave the navigation details to you. Can we do that trick again?"

"Which trick? We used a variety of-"

"The resonance thing, where you sent feedback along the enemy damping fields, to cancel them out temporarily? You know, so we can jump away."

"Um, no."

"No?" My fists tightened enough for fingernails to dig into my palms. "Because the fields here are too powerful?" From what I remember without reading the after-action reports, the previous ambush involved fewer than two dozen enemy ships.

And we had barely escaped that time.

"That too," Skippy explained. "The main reason we can't use that trick again is, like I *warned* you, the Maxohlx analyzed the data and figured out what I did last time. They still don't know *how* I did it, but they implemented a fleet-wide emergency update that certainly has been applied to the ships here. That update prevents a feedback signal from fully disrupting the damping effect. It won't *work*, Joe. I warned you we can't use the same tricks over and over out here."

"Yeah. You did."

"Even if I could temporarily create a feedback, we can't jump into the ice giant."

"Listen, I know our new DeLorean dropship's jump drive hasn't been tested yet, but-"

"That is not the problem. The damping energy around us is so chaotic, so strong that it is directly affecting our own jump drive. It is impossible to be accurate enough to jump inside a precise bubble of low-pressure like we did the last time. Even if there was some way to magically get away from the damping fields, our drive is seriously *dorked up*, Joe. Any jump we could manage would be short, and we would be lucky to jump anywhere *near* the ice giant."

"OK. That would be acceptable."

"It would?" Skippy's astonishment mirrored the surprise on Simms's face. "But, the enemy would know where we are and-"

"Yes. I'll explain later." The main display was flashing red, as one of the forward shields was flickering, the generator overwhelmed and on the verge of failure. With the crew, Bilby and Skippy already doing everything they could to keep the shields online, I didn't uselessly pester them about it. What I *could* do was relieve pressure on our forward defense systems. "Pilot, swing us around to starboard, alter course," I checked the navigation system. "Come starboard one-eight-seven degrees."

"One-eight-seven, aye."

That move would not only present *Valkyrie's* stern defenses to the majority of enemy ships, it would also begin decelerating to match course and speed with the star. Of course, even once the ship turned around, we would be flying very fast backwards, it would take a long time to cancel our forward velocity. And our velocity relative to the enemy would decrease, at one point we would be motionless to the Maxohlx armada and become a sitting duck.

I couldn't let that happen.

"Sir," Simms prompted me. "What are we going to do?"

I could feel the blood drain from my face. "I don't know."

"Come *on*, Joe," Skippy sniffed. "I know you enjoy making a fool of me, but-"

"No. Really." I turned to Simms. "Really. I got nothing. There are *too many* ships out there. If we can jump away, we have a chance, but-"

The display now showed six hundred and forty-three ships within two lightseconds of us, and more red symbols flared as I watched.

The Maxohlx had thrown everything they had into this operation. They were not taking any risk of us escaping. Skippy was right, the kitties probably had several thousand warships chasing us, boxing us in. They didn't care about taking prisoners, they wanted to kill us. To vaporize *Valkyrie*, remove the insult that was our stolen ghost ship. Show the galaxy that humans are weak and vulnerable. And most importantly, capture Skippy.

"I am-" The faces of the crew were stricken, disbelieving that I had not pulled a miracle out of thin air. "I'm sorry. I don't see a way out of this."

Really, I didn't.

Everybody has a limit.

I reached mine.

There wasn't any clever idea to get us out of the damping field.

Desperate, I tapped on the armrest controls. "What if we fire the boosters again, could-"

"No," Skippy knew what I meant. "By the time we slowed down enough, ships would jump in behind us. The boosters don't have enough thrust to cancel our velocity quickly enough. Besides, some of the enemy ships also have booster motors. They could-"

"OK! All right, I get it! There's no way to get outside the damping fields! Damn it, if this was a ship on the ocean, I would throw out a freakin' anchor."

"Joe," his avatar looked thoroughly disgusted with me. "An anchor couldn't stop this ship, it has too much momentum for- *Huh*. Hmm."

"What?"

"Oh. Oh, wow," Skippy gasped.

"What?" Simms demanded.

"I just got a monkey-brained idea. *I* did. An idea *so* stupid, so crazy, that it could only-"

That perked me right up. "What is it?"

"The problem is momentum, right?"

"I'm not following you," Simms said, but I waved a hand to silence her, before Skippy lost his train of thought.

"Momentum, right," I reminded him of the subject. "We're flying backward, but still moving in the wrong direction. What's your idea? Can you give us a push in the right direction?"

"No. My idea is to *cancel* our momentum. Quick, while I explain, turn the ship back around."

"Why?'

"Oh for- Will you just *trust me* for a moment? What do you have to lose?'

"Pilot," I ordered. "Do it. Skippy," I held onto the armrests as I felt the ship turning. That was not good, it meant the artificial gravity system was having trouble compensating for our course change. What else was wrong with the ship? "This had better be good."

"It is pure genius," he assured us. "Um, it is also extremely dangerous. Ooh, I just realized, the entire crew needs to get as close together as possible. Like, on Deck Three between Frames Seventeen and Twenty."

"XO, make it happen," I told Simms before she could ask why. She turned away to issue the necessary orders. "Skippy, explai-"

"This is simple in theory, horribly complicated in practice. Joe, the reason the ship is decelerating so slowly is not because the engines lack power, it is because the ship's mass has too much momentum. Uh!" He held up a finger to shush me before I could ask a stupid question. "What I am going to do, will *try* to do, is to cancel the kinetic energy of our momentum, by absorbing part of the energy into myself. For a split second, the ship will *stop* dead in space. I'm gonna hit the brakes, they'll fly right by us."

"Holy shit. You can *do* that?"

"I think so? Truthfully, I've never even considered it before, so this is more of a shmaybe than a real-"

"Is there anything you need us to do?"

"Yes. I will be interfering with the connection between the atoms of the ship, and the underlying fabric of- *Ugh*. No way will you monkeys understand any of this. What you need to know is, I can't interfere with the atoms of your meatsack bodies, it would kill you. It's not going to be wonderful for the ship's systems either," he added under his breath. "But the ship will survive, in some fashion. When the ships *stops*, your squishy bodies will not. The artificial gravity system will have to protect you. The smaller area the gravity system needs to cover, the better it will be able to compensate. I have to warn you, this is not going to be pleasant."

"Understood. XO, how are-"

"Three minutes," she answered without looking at me.

"Right. Skippy, what will this do to *you*? You're going to absorb the energy? You can do that?'

"Um, actually, no. It's more like I'll be channeling the energy through myself. I won't lie, this is gonna hurt me too. I could suffer permanent damage."

"Crap! That's no good! We can't risk-"

"Unless you have a better idea, we really don't have a choice, do we?"

The ship rocked hard, as a missile warhead detonated close to the hull and part of the shrapnel struck the armor directly.

"No. We don't have a choice. Everyone needs to get strapped in?"

"That would be helpful, yes. Also, hurry. Please *hurry*."

Mashing a thumb on the intercom button, I tried to speak in a clear voice. "This is Bishop. Everyone, you have *two minutes* to get into the designated section of the ship and strap in as best as you can." There were going to be broken bones or worse from this maneuver, I knew that. Releasing the button, I took a breath as the ship staggered from another near-hit.

Two minutes and seven seconds later, Skippy announced he was ready. "Joe, you monkeys are *not* going to like this, and that is no joke. I need the jump drive to be set on a timer, because I suspect none of you will be able to operate the controls shortly."

"Done," Chen reported from the pilot's couch.

"Confirmed, Dude," Bilby acknowledged. "Hey, uh, I'm *scared*, man."

"We're all scared," I clasped my hands to keep them from shaking. "Skippy, do your thing."

"I will try," he said. Even his avatar looked shaky. "Joe, *I'm* scared too."

"Would it help if I hold your beer?"

"Not really, not this time. Three, two, one-"

Admiral Reichert of the Maxohlx Hegemony's Eighth Fleet signaled the recovery ships to remain at a safe distance, he had noticed their captains inching those ships forward, eager to participate in the kill. A kill was certain, the stolen ghost ship had no possibility of escape, even the humans understood that. The primitive beings aboard the lone ship seemed already resigned to their fate, they had cut off the boosters before those units were drained entirely, and they were making only a half-hearted attempt at futile course changes. It surprised him that the humans had not fired a single shot. Doing so would be a pathetic waste of effort but at least it would be *doing* something, instead they were meekly and almost passively flying to their deaths.

That such primitive and cowardly creatures had made fools of the Hegemony, and somehow acquired Elder weapons, enraged him.

"Recovery squadron, pull *back*," he ordered, emphasizing his anger by speaking aloud rather than transmitting the order via cranial implant. "We do not know the blast radius when the target ship explodes, you must be ready to scan the debris for the Elder AI."

Instantly, the recovery ships veered away, one of them launching a volley of missiles as it turned. That action could be seen as defiance of the admiral's orders, but Reichert chose to view it as a sign of that ship's aggressive spirit.

The ghost ship rocked, having to pop thrusters to maintain stability as missiles impacted its energy shields. The shields along the target's upper spine were weakening, so much so that Reichert could *see* the effect. Maser bolts were no longer being quickly deflected, instead the shields glowed, flickering in a rainbow of colors. The weakest shield was continuously orange at the edges, fading to pink where it was overlapped by other shields. Reichert thought with a smile that if he were a Jeraptha, he would wager that shield to fail first. Through his implants, he directed all missiles in flight to converge on that area of the target. In the run-up to the battle, Reichert had deliriously wonderful visions of trapping and crushing the enemy, but now he simply wanted the engagement to be *over*. It was just no fun to shoot at an enemy who made no attempt to-

The ghost ship rocketed away at incredible speed.

No, it was the Maxohlx ships that were moving rapidly through space. The target had suddenly almost *stopped* dead in space, decelerating at an impossible rate.

"What the f-" Reichert shouted, seeing the damping fields projected by his speeding ships zipping past the unmoving target, as even the lagging recovery ships flew helplessly past the ghost ship.

Then the ghost ship, that fat, juicy, easy target, jumped away and disappeared. "*NOOOOO!*"

CHAPTER THIRTY ONE

If Skippy said anything after 'One', I don't remember it.

Something bad happened to my neck during the jump.

That pain is not what brought me back to consciousness.

Alarms were blaring from every console.

Did that ear-splitting racket wake me up?

Not a chance.

The artificial gravity was off, so droplets from my nosebleed were hanging in front of my face, and I choked on it when I breathed in.

Even that didn't wake me up.

Something zapped me, by sending an electric pulse from the zPhone in my pocket.

That startled me awake.

I wish it didn't.

Holy shit, everything hurt.

Dim emergency lighting illuminated the bridge, strips of some biochemical substance that glowed when the power was off. None of the consoles were active, the main holographic display was off, artificial gravity was inactive, and the ship was not moving at all.

Like, not at all.

There should have been some movement. The main engines rumbling like they usually did. A faint shuddering as thrusters fired to stabilize the ship.

Nothing.

"Skip-" Trying to talk threw me into a coughing fit. "Skippy?"

No response.

A groan from beside me made me turn my head, which was a *bad* idea. My neck said 'No' to moving my head, so I turned my upper body.

Simms was doubled over, head in her hands. "I already tried calling Skippy," she said, or she said something like that. Her voice was muffled, and there was something wrong with my ears. Reaching up carefully with one hand, I touched my right ear. It was wet.

I was bleeding from my ears.

That was not good.

With a soft 'Beep', all of the consoles flickered at the same time, and nonsense characters began scrolling.

No, the characters were not nonsense. They were in Maxohlx script, still the base language of the user interface. The system was rebooting, or maybe that old term was woefully inadequate.

What I cared about was, the ship wasn't dead yet.

Other people began to stir with a chorus of groans. "Don't move unless you need to," I choked out. "You might be injured."

"*Might?*" Jennifer Simms moved very slowly and looked at me with one eye open. Her eye was red with burst blood vessels. "Your ear is bleeding."

"Yeah. Feels like my neck is broken," I whispered back. Even slight movements produced a grinding feeling, like bones grating against bones. I am not a doctor, but I know necks are not supposed to do that. "Is anyone-"

"Colonel Dude," Bilby spoke in his usual surfer drawl. He sounded normal, that had to count for something. "You should not move, any of you, until I can get a medical bot to the bridge to scan you for internal injuries."

"Ship status?" Somehow, I was able to focus.

"The ship is fine, man. Not *fine*, but good enough. Way better than I thought it would be. One reactor is online, shields are restarting, the engines-"

"Where are we?"

"Um, maybe it's best if I show you, man."

The main display flickered, went dark, snapped off, then came back as if nothing had happened. There was the symbol for *Valkyrie* in the center, with something *big* looming in the upper part of the display. That had to be the 'ice giant' planet and assuming that was true, we were close, though not in orbit.

What immediately drew my attention was the other symbol on the display. It was outlined in red.

An enemy ship.

"Dis-" My mouth wasn't working properly. Nor was the control pad on my chair's armrest, though part of that trouble might be the blood my fingers smeared across the control surface. "Distance to enemy ship?" I asked, wiping my fingers on my uniform.

"Three point four lightminutes." Bilby, for all his moronic-sounding Dudespeak, was smart, he anticipated my next question. "We jumped in two minutes and eight seconds ago."

Wiping the control pad clean with a sleeve, I manipulated the display. We were near the ice giant, falling past it at an angle that would have us skim over the top of the atmosphere on our way out into deep space, if we didn't alter course. Our relative velocity was not substantial, that was too much of a coincidence so I guessed Skippy had done that deliberately. To jump near a planet and then immediately fly past at high speed would have been a waste of effort.

Think, Bishop, *think*, I told myself. We had about one minute before the enemy ship saw the gamma ray burst of our inbound jump. That ship would be on top of us in a flash. Unless its captain had orders to jump to notify their fleet first. Either way, we had to get moving. "Chen," I croaked, my voice slightly less hoarse. "Bring us down, I want to be in the cloud layer."

"Bilby," Chen called, her hands in the air. "Are the flight controls operative?"

"Yeah, man. The ship will be real sluggish, I gotta warn you."

Chen tentatively activated thrusters to swing us around. "Colonel," she didn't turn to look at me. From her jerky movements, I guessed her neck or back or shoulders were hurting, maybe all three. "The ship is responding. Engaging main engines now."

"Be gentle, but not *too* gentle," I instructed, mindful of how little time we had before the enemy fleet could be surrounding us again.

"Affirmative."

"Bilby, where is Skippy?"

"Skippy isn't answering me either, man. He's there, his canister, I mean, but I think something's wrong with it."

A chill ran up my spine. "Just his canister?'

"No, man. He's there, like, I can sense him, he's just not doing anything. Not talking to me, you know?"

"OK." The shudder of relief made pain stab my neck like a red-hot knife. "Can we jump?"

"Um, that's a big negatory on the jump, Dude. I'm locked out of the jump drive navigation system, I don't know why."

"Skippy must have secured it so we wouldn't try to use it," I guessed.

"Makes sense, Dude. The diagnostics I'm seeing on the jump coils are *not* good, some of the stuff I'm seeing doesn't make any sense."

"Leave the coils alone for now." The deck trembled.

"Sorry," Chen called. "Engines feel like they're out of tune. We will contact the atmosphere in four minutes. Colonel," she tried to turn toward me, I could see her grimace with pain. "I don't know if the engines can keep us in the cloud layer, without falling down into the slush."

"Slush?"

"She means the planet's mantle," Bilby explained. "It is ice composed of water, methane and ammonia. Don't worry, I'm bringing the other reactors online, we should be at eighty percent power by the time we get below the cloud tops. You plan to bring the ship down into the troposphere?"

"Deep enough that ships in orbit will not easily detect our position," I confirmed.

"Cool. Then we need to go down to where the atmospheric pressure is above twenty bars," he meant twenty times the pressure Earth's atmosphere at sea level. "But we should be very careful not to go deeper than seventy bars, I'm concerned about the condition of the pressure hull."

"Seventy, got it," I mumbled, distracted by worry about Skippy. Shit. If he was seriously damaged, I might have temporarily saved the ship but killed the entire galaxy. Only Skippy had the codes to reset timers on the Elder weapons we had planted. "When will-"

The ship rocked. That was not an engine instability, something *hit* us.

The symbol for the ship three lightminutes away was still there, but then if it had jumped, we wouldn't know it for three minutes.

What we *did* know was an enemy ship was less than thirty thousand kilometers away, firing maser beams at us and launching missiles. It could be the same ship, or another, the question hardly mattered.

"Shields holding!" Bilby reported.

"Sir?" Chen asked for instructions.

I looked at the main display and took in the situation in an instant, that was where my pilot training helped. The enemy ship was a frigate, no match for a battlecruiser. It was also going to blow right past us, moving at slightly less than seven thousand kilometers per second. At that speed, the battle was going to last no more than thirty seconds before that little frigate flew out of range. "Maintain course. Bilby, tell me about the point-defense systems."

"Operating at about fifty percent, Dude. We can handle those missiles," he scoffed at the five missiles launched by the frigate.

"Is that the *same* ship we saw at three lightminutes?"

"Let me verify, Dude. Um, confidence is about seventy-one percent, can't do any better, sorry."

"Hit that ship," I lifted an arm to gesture to the weapons station, my neck still wouldn't allow me to turn my head. "Target their jump drive. Bilby, throw a damping field around it."

"I'll try, man. The field projectors are-"

"Do your best."

The deck rocked, I could feel it through my chair. It was hard to tell the vibrations of our guns firing from the impacts of enemy fire. The display told the story; our weapons crew was letting the enemy have everything we could throw at them. The gun battle was short, no more than twenty-seven seconds from when we started firing, to the point where the enemy ship had passed out of range for our directed-energy weapons to be effective. We kept firing railgun darts for a few seconds after that, then the distance and erratic flight of the frigate made it unlikely we could hit anything.

Missiles were still in flight and that was an interesting equation; they were basically equivalent technology. We had an advantage that our missiles were smarter from the tweaks Skippy had done to the guidance AIs, and our point-defense computers could think faster. Roughly translated, that meant we could hit harder and protect ourselves better, especially against a lightly-armored ship like a frigate. By the time our last missile exploded seven kilometers behind the enemy, that ship was trailing plasma and bright arcs of electricity sparked from ruptured conduits.

"They're beyond our damping field range, Dude," Bilby reported. "Good news is, that ship is not jumping anywhere, we smashed their drive!"

"Cease fire," I ordered, lifting an arm to abruptly and feeling a sharp pain at the base of my neck.

"That ship can still launch missiles at us," Simms said quietly, not wanting to question my orders in front of the crew.

"That won't matter in a minute," I pointed at the display. The enemy ship was moving fast in the opposite direction, while we were curving around to put the massive bulk of the planet between us and the frigate. "That ship *should* have jumped to report our position to their fleet. Instead, they wanted the glory of killing us. Now, it will be," I checked how far we had jumped when we escaped. "Another eleven minutes before their fleet detects our inbound gamma ray burst here, and discovers where we went." In the ambush, I had not bothered to shoot back, because it would have been a waste of time and resources. Resources, like the energy we used to fire cannons and railguns were needed for the shields. In the fight against the frigate, our firepower was the difference between life and death.

She nodded, understanding. "We bought time. To do what?"

"To get down deep in the atmosphere."

"We can't hide," she tried to tilt her head at me and the gesture made her wince. "This time, they know where we are."

"One step at a time." The display was showing that *Valkyrie's* nose was heating up as the forward shields bored through the thin upper atmosphere. "Bilby, talk to me."

"We're still OK, I think," he did not sound entirely confident. "The ship was not designed to operate in an atmosphere, you know? Dude, are you sure about this?"

"I'm sure that, if we don't put a thick layer of clouds between us and that fleet soon, we'll never get out of here."

Simms took in a breath, there was a catch in her throat. "You have a plan?"

"I have a *hope*," I replied.

She winced again, holding her right side. "We could use some hope."

"There is not sufficient data to reach a conclusion," the AI of the Eighth Fleet's flagship announced.

Admiral Reichert's claws extended, an automatic reaction to his anger. One unfortunate characteristic of the AIs his people constructed was their reluctance to commit to the results of any analysis. Results were always accompanied by reasons why the analysis could be wrong, even wildly wrong. Reichert knew the fault was not with the AIs or even the people who programmed them, the fault lay with his society. AIs who failed to produce consistent, successful results were often wiped, even if that required tearing a ship apart to remove the embedded substrate. The trick to working with an AI, a trick he had learned over a long career, was something most of his captains could not bring themselves to do: be *nice* to the machine. Treat it with, he almost gagged at the thought, with respect. As if it were a real being, and not a collection of manufactured components. "I understand the incident is unprecedented," he watched his fingers and willed the claws to retract. Anger *felt* good, it also would do nothing to accomplish his goal. "My staff is unable to comprehend the event, they lack your immense processing power."

The AI was understandably hesitant, fearing a trap. "The problem is that we, the Hegemony," it emphasized, to be clear the failure was not its fault. "Lack context to understand the event. As you said, Admiral, it is unprecedented."

Instead of being outraged by the machine's veiled insult, Reichert felt a calm wash over him, a practiced skill that had served him well. There was a time for rage, and a time for cool rationality. Too many of his crews did not understand that important distinction. "Begin with what you do know. The facts. What does the sensor data tell you?"

"That the target ship came to a dead stop in space. By 'dead stop' I mean relative to the local star, of course. The target ship was still moving at substantial speed around the center of the galaxy. Our ships were unable to match the maneuver, therefore the formation quickly flew past the target, and it was able to jump away once the damping field strength faded."

"Yes. Thank you," Reichert exercised supreme self-control to express *thanks* to a machine. Remember the goal, he told himself. "That confirms my own view of the events. Tell me, the target did not stop instantly, did it?"

"No. The target's velocity was, however, canceled over a remarkably short period. It was still slowing its forward progress when it jumped away."

"The ghost ship's engines were active during the event?" He could not stop thinking of the target vessel as a 'ghost ship'. That was easier than accepting the truth, that it was stolen from his people, and operated by humans.

"Correct," the AI confirmed. Cautiously, it added, "Engine thrust alone was not close to canceling the target's velocity. However-"

"Yes?"

"There are two variables in the equation. The thrust provided by the engines, as measured against the mass of the object."

"That is, insightful." Reichert silently willed the machine to *say* what it was thinking.

Encouraged, the AI continued. "The engine thrust *could* explain the event, if the target ship's mass was substantially reduced, by means unknown."

Now the discussion was getting somewhere useful. His people had experimented with 'manufactured' or 'fake' matter, which exhibited the characteristics of ordinary atoms, but with less mass. The goal was to construct extremely lightweight, high-performance materials from such 'fake' matter, but such material technology had never advanced beyond the laboratory. "Is it possible," the admiral asked the AI, "that the target ship is composed of mass-reduced materials?"

"That is unlikely," the AI took a risk by implying the admiral had asked a stupid question. "That ship has never previously exhibited reduced-mass characteristics. Its movements prior to the incident were exactly as expected for a battlecruiser of its size, though with noticeably increased power output and engine thrust."

"Hmm," Reichert pretended to consider the AI's statement. "If the ship's structure cannot explain the-"

"It is most likely," in its enthusiasm, the AI did not realize it had interrupted its master. "That a temporary effect either reduced the ship's mass, or somehow converted most of the kinetic energy of its momentum into another form. There *was* a heat flare detected at the same time, although not enough heat was released to entirely explain the loss of kinetic energy. The heat may have been a residual effect."

Hearing that speculation made Reichert feel he was finally getting somewhere, in understanding what the *hell* had allowed the target ship to escape his careful trap. "Is that a capability of the Elder AI?"

"Unknown," the Maxohlx AI said carefully. Aware that the admiral would not be pleased by the machine not giving an answer, it added, "There appears to be no other possibility to account for the event."

An answer that was a non-answer. Reichert was angered, but accepted that the AI simply did not have enough information to be more useful. "It is not possible to determine where the target jumped to?"

"No. The event horizon on the originating end of the jump wormhole was extremely chaotic, I would be surprised if the target ship did not sustain substantial damage. Admiral, my initial analysis has not changed: wherever that ship went, it could not have jumped far. Certainly, it is within this star system."

"Then we wait." For the operation, Reichert had been given control of sixteen hundred warships and support vessels, a concentration of combat power that the fleet had not experienced in many generations. In addition to the task forces surrounding the three designated emergence zones, he had stationed picket ships in a grid throughout and around the star system.

If the target ship was anywhere in the star system, he would know about it, soon.

Valkyrie dropped at a steady rate, down into the ice giant's murky depths, to where the pressure hull of the ship, which was designed to hold air pressure *in*, creaked and groaned from the strain of being compressed. "Twenty-seven bars," Bilby repeated the information on the display. The layer of hydrogen, helium and methane around us was now twenty-seven times the pressure on Earth's surface, and increasing as we glided downward. There was no point to measuring altitude in kilometers, all we cared about was staying above the point where the ship's pressure hull would crack, and unfortunately that depth was something Bilby had to guess about.

"Maintain descent," I grunted. The pain in my neck was growing worse. At least my nose and ears had stopped bleeding. To replace those concerns, I was developing a whopping headache that was affecting my vision. The planet's gravity was tugging me down into the chair with enough force to be uncomfortable, Bilby restored artificial gravity to counteract the real gravity so we squishy humans didn't get squished. "Are the engines-"

"Multiple jump signatures!" Bilby reported. "Gamma ray bursts above us. That's eight, twenty, twenty-nine, now thirty-four ships, more coming-"

"We get the idea. Their whole fleet will be sitting above us soon."

"Dude, we can't *hide* down here," Bilby warned. "We don't have enough reserve power to run a stealth field, and we're creating ripples in the air anyway, the bad guys will see that for sure."

"We don't need to hide, the-"

My head jerked forward as something struck the ship hard enough to jolt my spine.

"Railgun impact!" Bilby sounded personally offended that someone was shooting at us. "Another!" He shouted as the ship rolled ponderously to the left, flipping onto its side.

Another impact hit forward and pushed *Valkyrie's* nose down.

"Cease fire!" Admiral Reichert screamed through his implant and verbally. "Cease fire, you idiots! *Stop shooting*!" He bellowed as a heavy cruiser's railguns flung another dart down at the planet.

The firing stopped and Reichert tried to follow the dart downward, tracking it with his own ship's maser cannons, but the dart splashed through the cloud layer and was lost to sight. By the time the maser bolts burned through the thick layers of atmosphere, the dart would already have found its target. "All ships, secure weapons. Report weapons status to me directly. The next ship to fire without my express authorization will face my ship's weapons. Is that clear?"

One by one, the ships of his expanded Eighth Fleet replied, acknowledging the order. The captain of the over-eager heavy cruiser apologized profusely, though there was a note of question in the apology, as there was in messages from many of the ships under his command.

He did not need to explain himself to his subordinates.

He *did* need to determine if the ghost ship had been fatally damaged.

Ordering an active sensor scan of the planet below, he said a silent prayer, fearing that he might just have killed his own people.

"They stopped, shooting at us," Bilby said slowly.

"For now," Simms warned. "Pressure outside is thirty-one bars," she noted.

"Maintain descent," I ordered. "We'll drop to-" An active sensor pulse swept over us, followed by another. Then the pulses became continuous, and I silenced the alarm. "Good. The kitties know we're still alive down here."

"They know where we are," Simms hissed toward me. "If you have a plan, this is-"

"I do," I said without a smile. "Bilby, I want to contact whoever is in charge up there."

"That is Admiral Reichert, we don't know much about him."

"I don't care which asshole is up there. Audio only," I didn't want the enemy commander to see how badly hurt we were. "Ready?"

"Ready."

"Hey, *shithead*," I called, flinching from pain as I had automatically squared my shoulders to speak. "This is Colonel Joseph Bishop of the United Nations ship *Valkyrie*. I suggest you *not* shoot at us again. You're stupid, so I'll explain what will happen if you destroy my ship while we're down here. The ship will explode, and our Elder AI will fall through the ice layer, toward the core of this miserable planet. *Maybe* you have the technology to build a probe to find and recover the AI, and maybe you don't. Neither of us knows for sure. What I *do* know is by the time you get a probe ready, the clock will have run out on the Elder weapons we planted around the galaxy, and Sentinels will burn every one of your worlds to a crisp. If that happens, it will be *your* fault. Think about *that*, asshole."

Holding a thumb down on the button to kill the audio, I slumped in the chair and carefully let out a breath.

"Oh my God," Simms gasped. "*That* is your plan?"

"It's the only way. They want to capture Skippy, we're safe as long as it's impossible for the kitties to get access to him. It's the only way. The only way I could think of," I corrected myself. "To give us a chance."

"We're trapped down here," she pointed out the obvious flaw in my brilliant plan. "We can't stay down here forever."

"We won't have to. I hope," I added to be truthful.

"You have a plan to escape?"

"Not exactly. I'm hoping we'll have help."

"Not from the Jeraptha?"

"No. I suspect the Maxohlx ambushed them at the original rendezvous point, near the Crab Nebula. The kitties planted that message about switching the rendezvous point to lure us here. I *knew* there was something screwy with that message, and I didn't listen to myself, damn it."

"The authentication codes checked out," she said gently.

"Of course they did," I was disgusted with myself. "Shit. I should have considered that whatever code the Jeraptha use, the senior species can crack the encryption."

"If not the Jeraptha," she slowly and painfully turned to look at me. "Who do you think will come to rescue us? *How*?"

"I didn't say it would be a rescue. Remember back at the relay station, I told Skippy to send a reply message, as an insurance policy?"

"Yes. What- Oh."

"Yeah. If the kitties can read Jeraptha codes, then so can the spiders. The spiders must be looking for the second group of ships, we know they didn't buy ECO's bullshit story about the ships being stolen."

"Sir," she gave me the side-eye. "You think the Rindhalu will pull us out of here?"

"No. I think that when the spiders see their rivals are trying to capture Skippy, there is going to be one hell of a fight upstairs. Hopefully, we can get out of here, while the kitties and spiders kill each other. Bilby! How is the jump drive?"

"Working on it, Dude, working on it. If I knew what was wrong with the stupid thing, that would help."

"Gotcha, keep working. We only need one jump, if it's long enough."

Simms' face was pale, and not just from pain and shock. "Oh my God. You don't plan to jump while we're down *here*, do you?"

"No. That's what the boosters are for. We'll rocket up to jump altitude and clear out of this system, as soon as there aren't enough ships above us to project a damping field."

"So, we wait?"

"We wait, while Bilby fixes the ship."

"Oh, man," the ship's AI moaned. "No pressure on me, then."

"Hey, welcome to the party, pal." Unfastening the seat straps, I eased forward.

Simms put out a hand to stop me. "Where are you going? You should wait for the medical scanner."

"I need to check on Skippy, and the crew. People could need help, we-"

"I have people reporting on the crew," she shook her head.

"Simms," I said in a whisper. "I have to check on Skippy. If he's in a bad way, all this could be for nothing. Or worse, if you know what I mean."

She knew what I meant. "Be *careful*."

"You know me."

"That's what I'm worried about. Maintain descent?"

"Bring us down to pressure of forty bars, then hold. Unless the hull develops a crack. I'll be back soon as I can."

Easing myself to the deck to look into Skippy's mancave, I had to twist my whole body because my neck was still scaring me. It didn't hurt anymore, that was what really scared me. My neck was numb, with a hot, tingling pain down my right shoulder, and making my elbow and thumb spasm like I'd stuck the thumb into an electric outlet.

The inside of his mancave wasn't anything unusual, nothing had even fallen to the floor during the battle, the loss of momentum, the bad jump, the skirmish with a frigate or falling through the atmosphere of the ice giant planet that we had decided to call 'Snowcone'. That didn't surprise me, everything in his escape pod was very well secured. The Velpie I made for him, a cheesy image of fluorescent paint on black velvet, was in the corner where he insisted I hang the thing.

Tears came to my eyes, and not from physical pain. The painting was crap, I knew that. It was my fourth attempt to paint a beer can on velvet, no better than the first three attempts that I'd discarded. My skills, whatever they were, did not extend to the visual arts. Skippy certainly knew the painting was poor quality, actually embarrassing.

Yet he had insisted it be fastened in a place of honor, where it was in view from the hatch. My mother had hung crap art from me on the refrigerator, this was no different.

It wasn't about the quality of the artwork.

It was about friendship.

"Hey, buddy," I gritted my teeth as I crawled through the hatch in an undignified fashion, scraping my belt on the lip seal. "How are you?" Flopping on the curved floor, I rolled onto the seat next to where his canister was fastened in a custom holder. It was nothing fancy, just a piece of smooth foam sized exactly for the diameter of his can to fit snugly into-

It didn't fit.

The was a *gap* between the can and the foam around it.

The can was tilted slightly, because it had just enough room to move and fall to rest on one side.

The foam had not changed.

His *can* was smaller.

Holy shit.

How could that happen?

"Buddy?" I reached out, keeping my fingertips from touching the shiny surface of his canister.

Except, it wasn't shiny.

It was *dull*.

It wasn't the usual chrome-plated magnificence. This looked like someone had done a bad job with a rattle-can of silvery-gray spray paint.

Wiping a fingertip along the surface, I was half-expecting to get a painful shock. Nothing happened. Was I relieved or disappointed?

The can's surface wasn't dusty, the way it had been after he bailed on us at Rikers.

It was different, the actual material of the canister was less magnificent than before.

"Hey, hey buddy. Skippy? Skippster? You there? Come on, talk to me. *Please.*"

Nothing.

No response.

Touching him again, he felt warm. Maybe warmer than usual, or was my own body temperature altered by whatever the wonky jump did to me?

Bilby said Skippy was still with us. When he got attacked by the computer worm, before he started counting down to Zero Hour, he had been there, but not there. Trapped inside himself. If that was the case again, we were in trouble, *big* trouble.

CHAPTER THIRTY TWO

Two days later, the Jupiter investigation team had more questions, and few answers. Chang dropped by the temporary office Friedlander had been assigned, a cubicle with a desk covered in technical journals. "Doctor?"

"Oh!" Mark stood up, nearly knocking over one of the stacks of journals. "Come-" He almost said 'come in' but there wasn't really any '*in*', the cubicle was jammed into a wide spot of a hallway. "Here," he took a stack of journals off a chair and looked around for a place to put them.

"Dump them on the floor, please," Chang suggested. "Unless you need them?"

"Uh," he glanced at the journal on top, it appeared to be written in Polish. "No." Plopping the stack on the floor, he dusted the chair off with a rag. "Sit, please."

Chang got straight to the point. "What do you know? I have a meeting with the UNEF Joint Chiefs in an hour."

"Whee-ew," Mark let out a long breath, deflating himself into the chair. "A lot, but not a lot that is useful."

"The cloud is atmospheric gas? Nothing radioactive?"

"Only background radiation," Friedlander confirmed. "It is atmospheric gas. Our best guess is, those devices they dropped into the planet are some sort of mass driver. They must be supported by some type of balloons to keep them at a stable altitude-"

Chang raised an eyebrow. "You can detect the devices from here?"

"No. Not exactly. We can see a heat signature in the clouds, they are not getting any deeper. The count is unchanged. Seventy-four devices are active."

"Active?"

"Generating sufficient heat that we can detect the effect on the clouds around them. There might be other devices held in reserve, in case an active unit fails, or needs to be taken offline for maintenance."

"Understood." So far, Chang was not getting the answers he needed.

"The mass drivers, we're calling them 'fountains'," Mark frowned. The name had not been his idea, he thought it too cute for the serious subject. "They are pulling in atmospheric gas, and accelerating it faster than escape velocity. Shooting it up and away from the planet."

"The gas is not going into orbit around Jupiter? It won't eventually fall back down?"

"No. It is falling inward, toward the sun. At a slow relative velocity."

"The Maxohlx are shooting Jupiter's atmosphere at our sun?" Chang frowned. That concept sounded familiar. He snapped his fingers, remembering. "Could they be extending the sun's useful life, restoring its hydrogen supply?"

"No. We considered that. The gas being ejected is not hydrogen, or helium. It is heavier elements such as sulphur, oxygen, neon. Those gases are useless to a star. They are trace gases in Jupiter's atmosphere, so it has to be the Maxolxh are deliberately filtering out lighter elements."

"*Why?*"

"We don't know. It doesn't make sense. For a while, we considered that maybe the Maxohlx were creating the clouds to facilitate refueling. Instead of lowering a drogue into the atmosphere to collect helium, the ship could deploy scoops and simply fly through a cloud, without having to go into orbit. Picking up fuel on the fly."

"A ship could collect sufficient fuel that way?"

"If it flies through a cloud the long way, rather than side to side. The clouds are streams of gas, *thousands* of kilometers long."

"Refueling is not the purpose of the clouds?"

Friedlander shook his head. "Can't be. Some will disagree, but," he held out his hands, "I don't see it. The composition of gas is all wrong. We know *Valkyrie's* reactors run on helium, and it was a current-technology ship when we captured it. *Them*. When we captured the ships that became *Valkyrie*. Unless the kitties have a technology we know nothing about, fuel can't be why the gas is being ejected."

Chang glanced at his watch. "Then *why* are they doing it?"

"The team has various theories," Friedlander frowned, indicating he had not bought into any of the outlandish guesses. "If the fountains continue for a long time, meaning *centuries*, they will reduce Jupiter's mass by a measurable amount."

It was Chang's turn to frown. "Why would the Maxohlx do that?"

"They wouldn't. Well, a shift in Jupiter's mass would have a subtle disrupting effect on the delicate balance of orbits of all the other planets."

"Skippy said something like that once," Chang tried to recall the context. "Could it throw Earth out of orbit?"

"Not *out* of orbit. It could change our orbit, very slightly, over a very long time. The result could not possibly be worth the effort."

Chang looked at his watch again, and shifted to the edge of the chair. "What else?"

"There is," Friedlander threw up his hands. "Speculation the Maxohlx might be trying to ignite Jupiter. Turn it into a star. No, that can't happen," he waved when Chang's eyes grew wide. "Jupiter's mass can't sustain a reaction. Even to become a brown dwarf, it would need a *lot* more mass. If that is the goal, they should not be *reducing* mass by ejecting atmosphere. I'm sorry. At this point, we know *what* is happening, what they are doing. We have no idea why."

"Only four ships remain, of the original task force," Chang observed. When the gamma ray bursts of those ships jumping away was detected, some in UNEF Command were panicked. Others reasoned correctly that if the ships were coming to Earth, they would have arrived before the gamma rays. Wherever the ships had gone to, it was not near humanity's home planet.

"They accomplished their mission, whatever it is," Friedlander guessed. "Those four ships might be assigned to monitor the project."

"Yes," Chang muttered partly to himself. "And to assure that no one interferes with what they are doing. Very well, Doctor," he stood up. "Keep working."

"I will, for all the good it will do. I have to be honest, we might *never* know what the enemy is doing. Their purpose could be beyond our understanding."

"Colonel Dude?" Bilby interrupted my thoughts. "That admiral guy is calling for you."

That was sooner than I expected. It was an awkward time for my opponent to call, I was helping bring injured people to the ship's medical center. Only the most seriously injured could be treated in the medical facility, we simply didn't have the capacity to treat more than sixteen people at a time. Anyone with internal bleeding had first priority. My own diagnosis of a sprained neck vertebrae, a mild concussion and several torn muscles in my neck and shoulders did not warrant me getting treatment, other than an injection of self-repair nanomachines by a medical bot. Simms was actually in better condition that I was, despite the scary-looking burst blood vessels in her eyes. We had five people with very serious injuries, they had been unable to properly secure themselves before Skippy did whatever he did, and the ship just freakin' *stopped* dead in space. It was no surprise that all five of them failed to fully secure themselves because they had been helping others up to the last second, and maybe they saved lives in the end. What I knew for sure was Bilby was very worried we might lose two of them, he had *Valkyrie's* medical bots doing whatever they could first to stabilize their 'biofunctions', as our AI so delicately explained the procedure.

We were lucky that more people were not nearly killed by the violent maneuver. To take delivery of the ships offered by the Jeraptha, *Valkyrie* had three times the normal number of people aboard, and they had been forced to scramble on short notice before Skippy performed his magic trick. The artificial gravity system, even having to cover only a portion of the ship's interior, had not been able to cope completely with the sudden deceleration. We experienced the equivalent of fourteen gees for a moment, which was thousands of times less force than would have been exerted on our squishy meatsack bodies, if the artificial gravity system had not protected us. I guess we are lucky that any of us survived.

No thanks to me, for jumping into what now seemed like an obvious ambush.

Screw that, Bishop, I told myself. Kick yourself later, right now the crew needs a leader who is calm, confident and in command of himself and the situation.

"Don't respond," I instructed Bilby, as I carried one end of a stretcher toward the medical center. The other end was held by a pilot whose name I couldn't remember, she was part of the reserve crew, and blood on the front of her uniform top obscured her nametag. "Hey! Tell Simms what I said. Wait! Did this admiral say what he wants?"

"I guess he wants to talk? About, like, stuff, you know."

Shit. I had to talk with Reichert or whatever his name was, if only to stall for time. And to make sure he wasn't tempted to do anything stupid.

"Tell him I'm busy. No!" Damn it, I need to be decisive. Especially as, Lieutenant *Wu*, I just remembered her name, was trying not to look at me. She was being polite, but she could hear only one side of the conversation. "Bilby, ask Simms to respond for me, but for now, I just want to her to say I'll call this jerk later."

"Okey-dokey, Dude," Bilby agreed.

The medical center was just around a corner of the passageway, where we ran into a traffic jam of stretchers. We set our stretcher down carefully, and I told Wu to wait while I checked what was going on. "Sergeant Raven!" I called to a medic who was crouched next to a stretcher, applying a splint to a broken arm. "What's going on? Why are all these people in the passageway?"

She didn't look up from her work. "All the medical bays are full. We're doing the best-"

"That's truth, man," Bilby interrupted. "Hey, Colonel Dude, I need to talk with you about something. Can you, like, come into Bay Four?"

Irritated by Bilby's moronic slacker talk, I was tempted to order him to talk to me right there, but he might want to discuss a medical issue about a patient. That was private information, even a thousand lightyears away from anyone to enforce HIPAA regulations. "Uh, sure, I'll be right there."

People made room for me as best they could, I squeezed by and tried to avoid stepping over people who were lying on the floor. Bay Four was blessedly near the front of the medical center, even so I came close to tripping over my own feet. The door slid open as I approached and I stepped forward with my arms held out, into the thin-film of plastic that stretched across the doorway. The material was like super-thin plastic wrap and it closed behind me, sealing me in to prevent me from contaminating the bay's interior. Lifting one foot then the other, the material completed the process, and only my face remained uncovered. With a plastic-wrapped hand I pulled a clear mask off the wall and slapped it in place, it automatically sealed in a ring around my nose, mouth and eyes. The whole process took only seconds, and the inner door opened automatically.

It was difficult for me to tell who was in the vat of gel, hooked up to tubes and wires. Technically, while immersed in the gel, the patient could not be contaminated by airborne pathogens, but we were not taking any chances. A glance at the wall display showed the patient was Squadron Leader Om Singh, of the Indian Air Force. There was a bunch of biosign info on the display, I couldn't interpret any of it. There really wasn't any reason for me to be in the medical bay, my guess was Bilby wanted to talk privately. "Bilby, how is he?"

"I *thought* we were going to lose him, that's what I want to talk with you about. He was bleeding into his brain and I couldn't stop it, not without causing even worse damage."

"He *was* bleeding?"

"Yeah, man, that's the funky part. I tried to control the nanomachines but it was impossible, there's just too many of them for me to keep track of each one, you know. But then, they, like started working together."

I took a step back from the gel-filled tank. "The nanomeds are working by themselves?" Holy shit, I felt a chill of fear. *That* could not be good. The last thing we needed was an army of tiny machines thinking for themselves.

"No, Dude, that's not what happened. Something, some*one*, else was coordinating their actions. Directing what each machine is doing at the finest level, so they all worked perfectly together. Way better than I could ever do. Squadron Leader Singh will recover, most likely, no thanks to me."

I guessed what he was talking about. "You think *Skippy* is controlling the nano here?"

"Yeah. That's why I wanted to talk in private, you know? Not just here. All the serious cases we have, the nano is working better than anything I can do. Also, the main engines are being tweaked to improve efficiency, and that's not *me* doing anything. He must be *alive*, Dude. Not just alive, he is aware of what's going on, you know?"

"Have you tried talking to him?"

"Dude, I even sang one of his *heinous* operas, and nothing, no response."

"OK, well, keep trying. That's all? You don't need me to help here, do you?"

"No offense, but, you'd be kind of useless in the medical center, Dude."

"None taken."

On the way to the bridge, I tried calling Skippy, and only got silence in response. Whatever was going on with him, he didn't have time or energy to talk about it. Maybe I should do some extra-stupid monkey antics to get his attention, like slip on a banana peel. "XO?" I called as I walked onto the bridge and stood behind the command chair.

"We're at a depth of thirty-eight bars?" I asked.

Simms looked back at me, her motions stiff. She had gotten a quick scan and a nanomed injection, and stayed on the bridge. "Bilby reports the hull integrity is solid, but I slowed our rate of descent. We will level off at forty bars, unless…?"

"No, that's good." It was anyone's guess what was the optimum depth. We had to strike a balance. We had to be deep enough for the Maxohlx to understand that if they hit *Valkyrie*, the hull might collapse, sending us and Skippy plunging down to the planet's rocky core. But if we went too deep, any flaw in the hull could cause an accident, and kill us all. Plus, damn it, the farther down we went into the atmosphere, the longer the journey back up. Without Skippy being active, we didn't have a microwormhole in orbit to show us what was going on up there, that was a major disadvantage. Pointing back over my shoulder with a thumb, I said, "I'm going to my office, to talk with my counterpart upstairs. Don't worry, I will not antagonize the jerk."

The conversation did not begin with an exchange of pleasantries, neither of us could stand the thought of pretending to be polite, and that would have been a bullshit waste of time anyway. Still, I didn't let my emotions and ego get in the way of doing my job. "Admiral Reichert," I used his name to let him *know* that I knew who he was. "You want to discuss the situation?"

"Yes." He didn't bother to address me by name. "You believe that we have a stalemate. You are *wrong* about that. My fleet has established complete supremacy in this star system. If you are hoping your allies the Jeraptha will come to your rescue, then you are gravely mistaken."

"I, I was n-not counting on help from the Jeraptha," I stammered deliberately, sure my apparent nervousness would be noted by his translator software.

"You are lying, human. My fleet can stay up here indefinitely. Your ship will encounter increasing difficulties maintaining system integrity in that toxic atmosphere. We are well aware of the capabilities of the ship you *stole* from us."

"We can stay down here long enough, we brought plenty of snacks," I popped a Cheese Doodle in my mouth and crunched it loudly. "You can't touch us without killing yourselves, and you know it."

"I do *not* know that," he snapped. "I do not believe the Elder AI is still in your possession."

Oh, shit. *That* was unexpected. Crap, I should have anticipated he would want proof that Skippy was down here with us. Why? Because that's what I would do, if I was up in orbit. How the fuck could I convince Reichert that Skippy was still here? "Think again, asshole," I said to stall for time, while I frantically tried to think of what I could do. Maybe ask Bilby to talk, pretend to be Skippy? The Maxohlx didn't know what Skippy sounded like, did they?

"We require proof," he demanded. "Or we will start shooting." Before I could say anything, he added, "I propose to send one ship to dock with your vessel, so a team of my people can verify the presence of the AI."

"Oh, *hell* no. No way am I going to-"

"Refusal to comply with my *reasonable* request, will force me to conclude the AI was destroyed when you escaped from my damping fields. Or that you ejected it, or *lost* it, before you descended to your present position. One of my frigates has begun to descend."

Crap. Ejecting Skippy before we descended into the atmosphere sounded like something I would do. The enemy knew me too well. "You keep that damned thing *away* from us, or I will start shooting."

"A frigate is a small vessel, it cannot pose a risk to you. Therefore, refusal to permit my team to inspect your ship and verify the presence of the Elder AI, can only mean you do *not* have the Elder AI with you. This communication is terminated."

"Hey! Not so fast, ass-"

"He isn't listening, Dude," Bilby informed me. "The ships up there are jamming our transmissions."

"*Shit*!" I pounded a fist on the desk, sending a stab of pain from my neck into my elbow. "Ah, shit, that hurts. Damn it." Why the hell had I thought I could match wits with a Maxohlx admiral? An admiral who had already lured me into an ambush? I am an *idiot*.

"What are we gonna do?" Bilby asked.

"I don't know. We are *not* letting any of those kitties aboard this ship." This was something I needed to let Smythe know about. "Smythe, this is Bishop."

"Yes, Sir," he answered immediately. His team had been assisting with the injured, except for the people on his team who were themselves injured.

"I can't believe I am saying this, but you need to be prepared to repel boarders."

"*Sir*?" He paused. "Is this a joke?"

"I wish it was. The kitties are sending a ship down here to inspect Skippy, to verify he is with us."

"We can't allow them access to the ship," he warned.

"Hell no, we can't." Without Skippy watching them, any Maxohlx boarding team could get up to all sorts of mischief aboard *Valkyrie*. A boarding team would have supremely-advanced mech suits, be accompanied by drones and bots, and nanoscale nasties that could infest every corner of the ship and be impossible to get rid of without an industrial-strength can of nanobug spray.

"What do we know about the opposition?"

"One ship, supposedly. A frigate. We'll have better intel when the ship approaches."

"Sir," he said the word as a question, but what he was actually questioning was my plan to deal with the situation. "Am I missing something? Can't we destroy the enemy ship before it gets close enough for a boarding attempt?"

"Uh, maybe not. The chief kitty up there told me that if we don't allow his inspection team to verify Skippy is with us, he will assume we ejected Skippy before we descended here. The threat of Skippy falling to the core of this world is the only reason the Maxohlx haven't nuked us."

"This *is* a sticky situation," Smythe muttered. "Skippy is still not responding?"

"No. Bilby says Skippy is still alive, whatever that means."

"Perhaps," our STAR commander said slowly while he thought, "we must consider allowing a small inspection party to board us."

"*Not* an option," I declared.

"Sir, repelling a boarding party has the same effect as shooting at their ship: it will be considered admitting we do not have Skippy with us. If we allow one or two Maxohlx to inspect-"

"I thought of that, and it won't work. We can't show our guests an inert cylinder, they'll assume we're faking. Unless Skippy can do something that only Skippy can do, we can't prove he is here. The admiral up there knows we can't allow his troops to board our ship. Smythe, we're stalling for time, time for Skippy to reboot or fix whatever the hell is wrong with him."

"Yes, *Sir*." Smythe was satisfied that I had given him clear instructions. He had a tasking, a mission his team was capable of performing. The STARs had practiced boarding operations many times, though mostly they were the offense. He had to adapt to working without help from Skippy. "You mentioned stalling for time-"

"Yeah. I'll give you as long as I can." I ended the call, and pinged Simms. "XO, get in here, we've got trouble."

She was in my office quickly, an advantage of being close to the ship's bridge. Simms listened while I briefly explained the situation. "We're stalling for time. You have any suggestions?" I asked.

"Any meeting between ships of opposing forces needs to have protocols established, to prevent accidents and misunderstandings."

"Oooh, good one," I snapped my fingers. "OK, we'll go with-"

Bilby interrupted me. "Hey, Colonel Dude. I'm detecting a ship entering atmo above us. You want me to use active sensors?"

"Yes, do that." I waited with Simms for Bilby to report. Shit. When I had the idea to create a stalemate by taking *Valkyrie* deep into the planet, I had patted myself on the back for my clever strategy. Admiral Reichert was calling my bluff, and it *was* a bluff.

"It's a frigate," Bilby announced. "It's coming in fast, they'll have to slow down as they descend."

Simms stood up. "I'll get back to the bridge, Sir."

"I'll join you."

When we arrived back on the bridge, the duty officer gave up the command chair to me, though I still hadn't decided what commands to give. That made me kind of useless. How could we stop-

Wait.

I didn't need to stop the frigate from approaching, just slow it down. "Weps," I signaled the officer at the weapons console. "Put a shot across that frigate's bow. Two railgun darts. Close enough to shake them up."

Valkyrie shuddered as two darts were flung upward. The use of railguns was usually silent, it was weird to hear a loud thunderclap as the hypersonic projectiles created shockwaves in the dense air around the ship, and the deck rocked gently.

It didn't take long for Reichert to return the gesture. Two railgun darts bracketed *Valkyrie*, one forward and one aft, they sounded like thunderclaps in the thick air around us.

I got the message.

"Secure weapons," I ordered. Reichert called before I could call him.

"Bishop," even through a translator, he sounded angry. "We will not tolerate-"

"That was to get your attention," I explained. "OK, fine. We will permit a limited inspection, under *our* terms."

He didn't reply right away. My guess is he didn't expect me to agree to being boarded. "What are your terms?"

"We need to establish protocols, to make sure some trigger-happy jerk doesn't cause an accident, agreed?"

"Agreed."

"Great. My executive officer will discuss protocols." Next to me, Simms silently mouthed '*WTF?*' as I threw her under the bus. "Can you designate a staff member to negotiate?"

"Yes," he snapped. "Bishop, if this is an attempt to stall-"

"This is an *attempt*," I cut him off. "To assure your people don't do something stupid, and get us all killed. Understood?"

"Understood."

I ended the call. "XO, you can use my office. Drag it out, but don't make it too obvious you're delaying."

"Thank you *so* much, Sir," she fumed at me as she slapped open the safety belt and rose from her chair.

"Simms, wait a second." I would need to think of a way to make it up to her. After, you know, I thought of a way to get the entire crew out of the mess I got us into. "Bilby, do you have a better estimate of our maximum safe depth?"

"The hull is holding up better than I expected," the ship's AI answered. "*But*, there could be microfractures I can't detect without scanning with maintenance bots, and I can't send those bots outside while we're flying at supersonic speed."

"Yeah, I get that." Bilby hadn't dropped into his usual surfer-slacker lingo, he must be very worried. "Give me a guess." That was a stupid thing to ask, to I added, "What I want is a depth where if the enemy tries a hostile boarding, they know they have to be *very* careful, because our ship is already on the edge of fatal damage."

"Oh. Gotcha. Um, we can probably go deeper than that frigate, so-"

"I don't think the enemy cares whether that frigate gets back into orbit."

"*Bogus*," Bilby groaned. "Dude, I wouldn't descend any farther than sixty-five bars. Our margin for error at that depth is thin, *real* thin."

"Chen," I addressed the pilot. "Take us down to fifty bars. Bilby, could an escape pod reach orbit from this depth?"

"No. Those pods are, like, designed to go *down* toward a planet, not up away from one, you know?"

"Yeah. What about a dropship?"

"A Panther could make it to orbit, under the right conditions."

"XO," I jerked my head toward the doorway. "Walk with me."

Out in the passageway, she cocked her head. "Why did you ask about dropships? If the enemy destroys the ship, they surely won't allow any dropships to reach orbit. The crew would-"

"Not the crew. Skippy."

"Oh."

"If things go sideways down here, it cannot be the end of all life in the galaxy. We can't allow those timers to expire."

Her mouth hung open, without words.

"It sucks, but-"

She stared at me. "The Maxohlx would capture him. If they didn't blow up the dropship."

"If we have to launch a dropship, it will broadcast a message that Skippy is aboard. Listen, XO, if the kitties have Skippy, humanity will still survive, in some fashion. We, I, can't be responsible for killing *everyone*."

I thought she would give me a 'you should have thought of that *before*' look, but she didn't. She patted my shoulder with one hand, and held up the other for a fist bump. "We've gotten out of worse situations," she reminded me quietly.

"Our best asset right now is *time*." I bumped her fist.

"I'll stall those assholes as long as I can," she promised.

On the way to Skippy's mancave, I opened a locker and got a roll of duct tape. In his escape pod, I wrapped the tape around his can several times, to secure him to the foam holder that was now too loose. He didn't object to the abuse, that worried me.

In a Panther that I selected because it was alone in its docking bay, I got it warmed up, and programmed the autopilot for a flight to low orbit. Bilby confirmed the navigation system was operating correctly, and he had control of the dropship. "Um, hey, Dude. If we're really going to do this-"

"If we *have* to do this."

"Sure, that's what I meant. If we have to do this, it means something really bad happened, right?"

"Yes, so?"

"So, we should pressurize the docking bay to match the pressure outside, you know? That would make the launch process faster."

I paused to consider what I knew of the docking bay systems. "We can pump enough air in here to match-"

"No, Dude. I mean, crack the doors open, let the outside air *in*, get it? The air here is toxic, and it will-"

"Yeah." We would need to scrub the bay later, if we didn't launch the Panther. If that was the worst of our problems, I would personally scrub the freakin' bay with a toothbrush. "Good idea, but wait until I get back inside the ship, OK?"

"Sure thing, Dude," he chuckled. "I've been trying to wake up Skippy, but no dice, man. Wish I had a way to jump-start him with those paddles they use for heart attacks, you know?"

Despite the grim situation, I had to laugh. "It would take more an electric shock to-"

"To what, Dude. Don't leave me hangin', man."

"A shock," I said slowly, rolling something around in my mind. "Bilby, it is too bad that Skippy is gone. I really wanted to ask him if he thought Justin Bieber was more important to pop music than Elvis. If you look at-"

"*WHAAAAAT?*" The ship trembled as Skippy's can glowed orange, and tendrils of smoke curled up from the now partly-melted duct tape. "You miserable, ignorant *cretin*. How could anyone with half a brain think-"

"Welcome back, Skippy," I pumped a fist.

"Joseph, you take that back right now, or I swear I will *jump* into the core of this planet."

Hanging my head, I mumbled, "I am terribly, terribly sorry for my unforgivable ignorance."

"Hmmph. Wait, did you just *bait* me?"

"Ya think?"

"Ooooh, why, I should-"

"You *should* wake the hell up and help us, you jackass."

"Joe," he sighed. "I've had better days."

"Sorry. What's going on with you? Your can *shrank*."

"It did? Ooooh, *that* is not good."

"Are you OK?"

"I am very much not OK. You might say that currently, I am experiencing a slight awesomeness deficiency."

"How slight?"

"Like, if you want me to prove I'm still here, by doing something like altering the planet's magnetic field, prepare for disappointment. Joe, I *hurt* myself."

"You? Come on, you are Skippy the *Magnificent*."

"I am also Skippy-the-guy-who-channeled-the-kinetic-energy-of-a-freakin'-battlecruiser. The energy had to go *somewhere*. Whoo-boy, I do not want to do *that* again."

"Is this like Zero Hour, or after you bailed on us at Rikers?"

"No, and no. My connection to higher spacetime is intact, it's just currently a bit, crispy."

"*Crispy*? Holy shit."

"Yeah. Listen, I did want to talk to you earlier, I needed to concentrate on putting myself back together."

"Uh, that didn't work so well for Humpty-Dumpty."

"I'm not using *horses*, numbskull," he snorted, but there was a bit of amusement in his scorn. That was a good sign.

"Is there anything we can do to help?"

"No. I need *time*, Joe. It would help if *Valkyrie* didn't explode in the next few days."

"I will make a note of that," I said gravely.

"If you want, I can talk to this Reichert guy for you," he offered.

"So, you know the situation?"

"I am vaguely aware of what has been going on, yes. Nice move bringing the ship down here, by the way, that was clever."

"Thanks, I-"

"A bit of a dead-end if you ask me, but, better than doing nothing."

"Please stop, I am blushing from your lavish praise."

"Hey, *I* didn't get us into this mess."

"Don't remind me."

"I do not like the part of your plan that involves the potential for me to fall to the frozen core of this miserable ball of ice, to spend an eternity of despair with no hope of it ever ending."

"Ah, think of it as being at the Department of Motor Vehicles."

"Ha!" He snorted, that ws a good sign.

"Thanks for the offer, Skippy, but talking to the Big Kitty up there won't help, he knows we could fake that. You can't do any spacetime flattening stuff?"

"Right now, I would have trouble flattening a pancake."

"That's not good. How about something that doesn't require you to bend the laws of physics? Some of the ships up there are in low orbit, can you take control of them?"

"No."

"OK, how about taking control of *one* ship?"

"Again, *no*."

"Wow," I plopped myself down in the seat, next to where I had Skippy strapped in. "You really are hurting."

"That *is* what I told you," he said with an implied 'you dumdum'. "However, the problem is not just my current condition. The ships up there are set for secure condition. When we seized the Maxohlx ships that became *Valkyrie*, they were running under normal fleet procedure, for cruising conditions or encounters with lower-technology species. The ships upstairs are rigged for encounters with a peer enemy, such as the Rindhalu. Under those secure conditions, the computers aboard each ship are not networked. Each system operates independently, to reduce the possibility of the ship becoming disabled due to cyber attacks."

"Damn. How does-"

"You are asking how that affects the efficiency of the ship's ability to respond to commands? The answer is it significantly degrades response time, the operation of weapons and defense systems, and any action in which the coordination between separate systems would be an advantage. The Maxohlx adopted the security lockdown procedure long ago, after a series of engagements where the spiders remotely disabled the kitties' ships. So, the short answer is no, I can't hack into those ships from here."

"Shit! Sorry, I know it's not your fault. If we can't prove you are here, the kitties are gonna nuke this ship. They have a frigate coming down to deliver an inspection team."

He snorted. "You mean an *assault* team."

"That's what I suspect, yeah. Do you have any suggestions for us?"

"I suggest you stall for time."

"That is *super* helpful, I never would have thought of that."

"Sorry. I'm doing what I can."

CHAPTER THIRTY THREE

Assault Team leader Reskah Vleen ordered one of his glands to secrete a calming hormone as the frigate approached the enemy battlecruiser. So far, the humans had been reluctantly cooperative. Reluctant, because they had delayed the engagement to the point where the Eighth Fleet's commander sent a pair of destroyers down to escort Vleen's ship. Cooperative, because the humans had pulled their battlecruiser up to a higher altitude when those destroyers were withdrawn to orbit.

Vleen watched the scarred and battered battlecruiser approach, as if the frigate's hull and thick, toxic atmosphere did not exist. The frigate's sensors were feeding data directly to his ocular implants, he did not need his own genetically-enhanced and partially cybernetic eyes. In fact, Vleen had his eyelids down, to avoid distracting images. The image of the approaching target was merely background, he would not need to actually watch the events outside, until the frigate's crew were bringing the nimble ship to close with the enemy. His focus was not on the enemy warship, nor on the section of hull his squad was to cut through to access the battlecruiser's interior. His focus *was* on the seven members of his team, and on the leaders of the five other assault teams. In addition to the forty-eight assault troops, the little frigate was crammed with the seventeen-person crew, nine extra technicians to assist with damage control, plus five artificial intelligence experts who controlled the most powerful weapons of the assault force: devices that could hack into and take over any Maxohlx-built vessel.

Supposedly they could do that, Vleen reminded himself with a healthy measure of skepticism. The target ship was controlled by humans who had an Elder AI helping them. He thought it unlikely that ship's original AI still existed, or that the architecture of the substrate was anything even remotely familiar to the experts who were assigned to hack into it. The idea that they could take back the battlecruiser simply by accessing its main computer was almost silly, yet those were his orders.

The orders were contradictory, and odd. It was the first time he had been instructed that failure *was* an option, in fact, failure was the fallback position. The target ship was perilously close to the bottom of the planet's atmosphere, if it was seriously damaged, it could fall down into the thick layer of ice below and possibly melt all the way down to the world's rocky core. Admiral Reichert had called Vleen personally, to emphasize that loss of the target ship would not only cause failure of the mission, it could mean extinction for every sentient being in the galaxy.

So, there was no pressure on Reskah Vleen.

His task was to gain access to the target ship and take control of it. A secondary objective was to determine whether an Elder AI was aboard the enemy ship, though to call that a secondary goal was silly; if his team could seize the ship that meant there was *not* an Elder AI aboard, certainly not a functional one.

The frigate shook and its nose dipped alarmingly, Vleen felt the artificial gravity fluctuate and he felt momentarily lighter, then heavier. A message, fed directly into his cranial implant, warned that the small ship was experiencing difficulty holding a steady course. The ship's crew thought the odds of returning to orbit were slim. There was supposedly a backup plan for a cruiser to dip down into the atmosphere to rescue the frigate's crew, everyone had a good laugh when they heard about that.

Vleen's thoughts were interrupted by a message from the frigate's captain. "Docking protocols confirmed. We are on final approach."

On a command from Vleen, the inner airlock door slid open, the chamber that held his team had already been pressurized by slowly allowing the air outside to leak in. If he had set the helmet's faceplate to clear and looked with his own eyes, he would have seen a yellowish mist swirling in the chamber.

It was not necessary to ask his team if they were ready, he could see the status of each soldier in his mind. He asked for a verbal check anyway, to let the team know he was in command of the situation and, to be truthful, to calm his own nerves.

The frigate shook again, this time the status feed showed the motion was from thrusters firing to make fine adjustments, to line up for docking with the enemy ship. The agreement with the humans was for the frigate to perform a hard docking with the big battlecruiser, it was not possible for a dropship to enter a docking bay while the ghost ship was flying through thick atmosphere at supersonic speed. Three points on the battlecruiser's hull were designated for the frigate to latch on without damaging either ship, then the frigate was supposed to extend a flexible collar to access one and only one airlock.

The assault teams did not plan to use airlocks to get aboard the target ship.

"Skippy," Smythe reminded himself to relax his grip on the rifle, the suit's powered gloves would not allow him to damage vital equipment, but it was good practice to be careful with a mech suit. Powered armor could hurt him if he wasn't paying close attention. "Do you know where they-"

"If you are asking which breach points the enemy plans to use, I don't *know* yet," the AI answered peevishly. "There are too many variables. The boarding teams will make a judgment call, once the frigate has securely latched onto our hull. The crew of that ship is barely able to control it."

Smythe ground his teeth, one part of him that was not augmented by artificial muscles. "We *understand* that," the synthetic vision of his visor showed the enemy frigate was less than a hundred meters away and approaching steadily. The smaller ship was unsteady, buffeted by air swirling around the battlecruiser's hull. Neither ship had been designed to be aerodynamically smooth, because starships are not supposed to dip into the atmosphere of a planet; that is why they were provided with dropships.

"I can tell you that these points are the most likely," Skippy highlighted two areas around *Valkyrie's* forward pressure hull, and six back in the engineering section.

"Thank you," Smythe muttered. His teams were well-positioned to defend breaches in those eight areas, hopefully the enemy would not attack at more than three or four points. He had teams positioned to defend the most vital areas of the ship, plus three teams in reserve, to be repositioned as needed.

Failure, as Bishop reminded him, was *not* an option. That was nothing unusual. It was unusual to be faced with *two* possible modes of failure. They could fail to give *Valkyrie* a chance to escape. Or they could face the ultimate failure: the loss of Skippy and extinction of all intelligent life in the galaxy.

As the final seconds counted down to the enemy ship making hard contact, Jeremy Smythe was reminded of something he had said to Katie Frey. The STAR teams assigned to the Alien Legion might see more action, but ST-Alpha aboard *Valkyrie* would get the missions that meant life or death for humanity.

Just once, he wished he was wrong about that.

When the frigate made the final course correction to bring it into contact with the battlecruiser, the enemy crew either lost control of their ship, or they didn't want to risk *Valkyrie* dodging out of the way. The docking maneuver was a crash that shook both ships, and would have knocked Smythe off his feet if he hadn't been secured to the bulkhead. For a sickening moment, *Valkyrie's* nose rose then dipped wildly, sending Smythe's stomach into flip-flops. When thrusters fired to stabilize the two-ship formation, the deck was still pointed slightly downward and the ship yawed side to side unpredictably.

Then there was a muffled *BANG* that Smythe felt through his armored boots.

"Breach near Frame One Sixty-Seven, Lateral Row Eighteen," Skippy reported information that was already available in the visor of every member of ST-Alpha.

"Frey," Smythe eyeclicked for straps to release him from the bulkhead. "You're up."

Reskah Vleen was not held in place by anything like crude fabric straps, his people used suspensor fields for that purpose. The fields surrounded him evenly, avoiding the problem of straps placing a load on a small area. Fields also lacked latch mechanisms that could be balky and refuse to release at the wrong time. The greatest advantage of a suspensor field was that it could be directly controlled by the individual it protected, allowing Vleen to move safely while the ship was still rocking wildly. He watched as the seven members of his team advanced in a pre-programmed maneuver, while the powerful cutting tool outside burned through a section of the battlecruiser's hull. The possibilities for gaining access to the enemy ship were limited, most of the hull was covered with thick armor panels that were too resistant to the cutting tool. Using enough energy to burn through armor plating would have risked damaging the enemy ship, which Vleen was specifically ordered *not* to do.

The impact when the frigate latched on was worse than Vleen expected, he thought the pilots must have lost control at the last second. No matter, the two ships were now bonded together and it was now his task to perform the mission. The first-

The lights flickered.

Along with his sensor feed.

And the suspensor fields, at the moment the ship shuddered from a secondary impact. His team was flung around inside the airlock, smashing into the walls and each other. The suspensor field in the airlock was making the situation *worse*, surging in power and throwing the soldiers side to side as they struggled to hold onto something, anything.

"Enough!" Vleen roared, sending a signal to cut power to the fields. The team slumped to the deck, dazed. In his internal monitor, he could see that two soldiers were injured, their suits damaged from colliding with each other. Silently, he pinged each of the now-ineffective suits to put them into recovery mode, while designating those two soldiers as reserves. Grudgingly but quickly, they moved aside to allow the others forward, toward the outer airlock door, which slammed aside into its recess. In front of them was a hole into the interior of the enemy ship, where a sensor blister used to be. The sides of the hole glowed hotly orange, melted slag scraping off as the boarding team soared forward and bounced off the walls.

A drone preceded the assault team, providing a view of the enemy ship. A ship that looked entirely familiar to Vleen. Of course it did, the battlecruiser was a Maxohlx ship, a stolen ship. He felt a flash of anger, grateful for the calming effect of the hormone in his blood. The other team members were under the influence of stimulants both secreted by glands and injected by their suits, those soldiers had their strength and reflexes augmented by the stims, making them even more dangerous. Vleen's role was not to fight, nor to engage the enemy directly. As leader, his role was to observe, to make judgement calls, to determine how best to achieve their objectives. For that, he needed to think calmly and rationally.

Which is easier to do when someone was not *shooting* at him. The instant his boots contacted the deck of the enemy ship, his armor rattled from the impact of explosive-tipped rounds and one soldier was flung back past him, hit in the chest by an armor-piercing rocket. Vleen's cranial implant instantly identified the source of incoming fire as a Thuranin combot, the standard shipboard model. The implant also warned him that this particular combot had been modified in unknown and possibly dangerous ways.

His soldiers reacted without needing orders, taking out the enemy combat machine in a flurry of gunfire. Whatever modified capabilities that combot had, they did not extend to protection from Maxohlx infantry weapons.

The soldier who had been struck by the rocket sprang to her feet, shaking her head and flashing an upward chop sign with one hand, signaling she was combat-effective. Her suit's point-defense cannons had detonated the rocket's warhead before it contacted her, and activated an energy field to deflect the superheated stream of plasma before it could burn through the tough armor plating. Knowing her suit needed time to recharge from the prodigious use of energy, she limped to the back of the formation, just as a pair of combots appeared around a corner to blast the team with every weapon they could fire.

Well, Vleen thought to himself, I did not expect this to be *easy*.

"Fall back," Smythe ordered Chaudry's squad. The four combots controlled by Chaudry's people had been almost casually wiped out by the enemy boarders, who were now advancing cautiously but steadily. Two of the enemy were hanging back, one with a clearly serious injury from being struck by simultaneous fire from two combots. Massed heavy fire was the only tactic that even slowed the enemy down. Unfortunately, Smythe had to be very careful with heavy weapons, three of the boarding teams were near vital equipment. Of course they were, that equipment is what the Maxohlx wanted to secure control of.

Chaudry acknowledged with two clicks of a microphone, Smythe could see those people retreating to their designated secondary cover position.

"Frey," he turned his attention to the STAR unit that was defending the single breach in *Valkyrie's* pressure hull. "You too, pull your team back."

The response was a chatter of rifle fire and the *whoosh* of rockets launching. Frey had lost five of six combots assigned to her team, Smythe recognized the sound of rockets as the smaller units mounted under the barrel of the modified Kristang rifles used by STARs.

"Frey! Pull back, now!"

"Just a-" Another sustained volley of rifle fire, Smythe could see in his visor that all twelve members of Frey's squad were concentrating their fire on one target. "Got him! Squad! Fall back!"

Smythe was pleased to see Frey's squad retreating in good order, fireteams of soldiers providing cover as another team pulled back through their position. He was pleased to see that two of the enemy there were hard kills, dead for certain. He was *not* pleased to see Frey pause to pump two rockets back down the passageway before she, too, ran back around a corner for cover. "Sir," she gasped, out of breath. "The enemy cut into a bulkhead to expose cabling, they were plugging in some type of device. We stopped them cold."

"Major, stick to the *plan* in the future."

"Yes, Sir. Damn it, they're coming at us already. Squad! Fall *back*!"

Despite unexpectedly suffering five soldiers killed and seven wounded badly enough to render them ineffective, Vleen was proud to see he was slightly ahead of schedule. Whatever technologies the humans had acquired, their infantry was using *Kristang* powered armor and weapons. That both surprised and pleased him, the humans had no realistic chance of stopping his teams from gaining complete control of the battlecruiser. From *retaking* their own ship, a stolen ship.

"Reskah!" A soldier pinged their leader by rank. "We have access to the ship's internal network. The leader of their defense force is in front of us."

Vleen did not hesitate. "Advance and destroy."

"Skippy!" Smythe ejected a spent magazine from his rifle and slapped a fresh one in place.

"Yeah, yeah, hold your horses," the AI grumbled. "I'm doing the best I can here."

"Do *better*." A shadow appeared on his visor, possibly an enemy soldier, or a ghost caused by Maxohlx spoofing of his suit's sensors. He could not take the risk of inaction, so he fired a burst at the shadow. Which did not shoot back. Smythe had just given away his position for nothing. Ducking to the side and rolling, he got to his feet just as enemy fire shredded the bulkhead where he had been standing moments before.

Another indistinct shadow, this one did shoot before Smythe could aim his own rifle. Dodging to the left desperately, he felt shrapnel kick his feet and he fell hard, bouncing off the deck. "A little help here!" He grunted.

"OK, OK," Skippy sniffed. "The bad guys have committed their reserves to exploit our weakness. Their entire assault team is now aboard *Valkyrie*."

Smythe got on his back and kicked with feet that felt numb, launching himself upright and spinning to-

Stop. A powerful hand grasped him around the throat, squeezing his armor there with crushing force while another power-enhanced glove bent the barrel of his rifle, tearing it out of his grip. The grip on his neck tightened, Smythe could feel his armor buckling under the pressure-

It stopped. Another figure came out of the shadows. "Leave this one to me," the new figure ordered, and Smythe realized he could *understand* the alien. That Maxohlx must be transmitting in the clear, so he could hear. He allowed his faceplate to go clear so the alien could *look* at him, though the other soldier's helmet was a fuzzy, indistinct mix of colors that blended into the background.

Until that faceplate also went clear, dropping the chameleonware effect. "Human," the angry face growled. "This violence is pointless. Order your people to stop fighting."

Smythe stared into his opponent's eyes. "Sod off, you cheeky bugger."

The alien's eyes grew wide when it heard the translation, then the eyes narrowed and it growled, "I will make an example of you." The grip around the STAR team leader's neck made the armor there buckle, and there as a shrieking sound as air leaked out.

"Too late," Smythe gasped. "Skippy, *now*."

The alien soldier went rigid as his powered armor's computer locked up, losing control over the suit. Automatically, the gloves returned to their rest position, and Smythe stepped back as the Maxohlx toppled forward to faceplant on the deck.

"Thank, you, Skippy," Smythe gasped, swallowing carefully. It felt like his Adam's apple was fractured. The hissing of his suit's escaping air slowed, as nano gel flowed in to plug the gap.

"Are you OK?" The AI asked with uncharacteristic concern.

"You have," he paused to catch his breath. "Access to my biomonitors, don't you?"

"That doesn't tell me how you *feel*, Jeremy."

"I feel fine."

"Uh huh. You feel like shit, then?"

"Something like that," Smythe had to laugh, then took a deep breath. "Chaudry, secure the prisoners. Frey, seize that damned ship."

"Aye aye," Frey replied, amused.

"Skippy, the enemy are all immobilized?" The figure on the deck, and the other soldiers of the boarding party, were rocking gently side to side, more than from the motion caused by the erratic flight of our battlecruiser.

"Their *suits* are immobile," Skippy cautioned. "They are trying to move around inside their armor. I am instructing their glands to secrete hormones to calm them and make them sleepy, but they are hyped up on their version of adrenaline, so prepare for them to be feisty for a while."

"Feisty? We'll see about that." Kneeling down, he rolled the boarding team leader on his back, keeping his own boots out of the way as the heavy armor thumped on the deck. "You seem to be having a spot of bother with your armor," he tapped the clear faceplate as the alien within snarled and screamed at him, flecks of spittle appearing on the inside of the composite material. "Don't worry, I'm sure we can find a set of booster cables around here somewhere."

On the bridge, feeling useless but trying to appear in complete command of the situation, I watched the main display, which was showing a feed from Major Frey's mech suit helmet. She was on the frigate's bridge, which was interesting by itself. Normally, the Maxohlx command crew was in a sophisticated chamber, where they floated in suspensor fields and controlled the ship through cybernetic implants, with holographic displays surrounding them as backup to information fed directly into their brains. This crew was on the bridge of their ship, where they relied on the crude method of pressing physical buttons like we primitive humans did. Not having a networked computer system aboard the frigate had forced them to rely on secondary controls. That was interesting, it explained why the ships in the ambush force seemed slow and clumsy, compared to the ships we fought against in hit-and-run attacks, back when *Valkyrie* was a ghost ship.

"Major Frey," I called her directly, bypassing the usual chain of command in the STAR team. Smythe was busy with his own task, that of racing around the frigate to lock down that ship's self-destruct devices. Skippy had given me a *solid* shmaybe that he had control of the frigate, but not a *gold-plated* shmaybe. He also hinted that it might be a sensible precaution to physically remove the data feeds to the self-destruct charges, so Smythe and half of the STARs were frantically doing that. Frey had her squad rounding up the frigate's crew, while Chaudry's people were stacking the members of the failed boarding teams in a cargo bay we set aside as a temporary brig.

"Sir?" Frey answered with an irritated tone. The last thing she needed was some jerk sitting in a comfortable chair looking over her shoulder while she worked.

The jerk, being *me*, understood that. "Don't bother jacking those remote modules into the data ports, Skippy says he has infiltrated all the systems he needs."

"Sir, it only takes-"

"I know that. Round up the kitties and get out of there *ASAP*, that's an order." Sometimes, the jerk sitting in a comfortable chair has a better view of the overall situation.

"Yes, Sir."

"Skippy?"

"Hey, I'm *working* here!" He protested.

"Work faster. Do you have control of that ship, or not?"

"I have control of everything I need to fly it remotely. It is a sweet little ship, maybe we should keep it."

I rolled my eyes. "It is not a puppy that followed you home, Skippy. The answer is *no*."

"But-"

"Can you guarantee the native AI will not try to kill us, the second you lose contact with it?"

"Um, no. We also probably do not have time for me to create, install, test and debug a new AI, darn it."

"Now you're being sensible."

"Colonel?" Chen called from the pilot couch. I could see beads of sweat on her forehead. It was a strain keeping *Valkyrie* from flipping over and plunging straight down, while the dead weight of the frigate was connected to our hull.

"I hear you. Skippy, how long until Smythe is done?"

"Ten, fifteen minutes, depending."

"Tell him to take fifteen. We need the job done *right*, not just fast. Chen, will that work for you?"

"Yes, Sir."

Thirty-two minutes later, the frigate was empty of biological beings, and Skippy declared we were ready to get the damned thing off *Valkyrie's* back. Chen put our battlecruiser in a gentle dive, then Skippy fired up the frigate's engines and blew the grappling clamps that held the two ships together. There was a gut-churning moment when the frigate's nose scraped along *Valkyrie's* spine, and we feared the stupid thing would collide with one of our reactors, but Skippy fired thrusters and got it straightened out, and later review showed there really had not been any danger. I wish my bladder had known that at the time.

Less than an hour after the attempted boarding operation, the frigate was flying in formation, three kilometers directly above us. Smythe reported the prisoners were all milling around in an agitated fashion in the cargo bay, after Skippy commanded their suits to crack open so the kitties could get out. All their weapons had been taken away, the weapons built into the suits had been removed or physically disabled, the reservoirs of nano gel dissolved into a dusty gray goo. Their cybernetic implants had been scrambled, leaving them able to see, speak and listen with only their physical senses, just like we primitive humans do.

That had to piss them off.

We had learned a lot since we first encountered a live Maxohlx in the Roach Motel, and by 'we' I mean Skippy. That group of prisoners were not going to cause any problems for us, and that wasn't a threat of retaliation. They simply were not able to do anything that could harm us, and they knew it.

Anyway, I had a brief meeting with Smythe to review the recent action. The STARs had suffered no serious injuries, a result of careful and skillful planning by Smythe, and of the professionalism and training of his team. "That was an outstanding success, Smythe," I assured him.

He gave me a side-eye. "The operation isn't over yet, Sir. We won't know whether it was a success until-"

"Yes. I meant, you and your team did your part with remarkable precision."

"I will convey your words to the team, Sir."

"Excellent. It's time," I pointed to the ceiling, "to talk to the jerk upstairs."

Smythe was right. We prevented the kitties from boarding and taking control of *Valkyrie*, that part of the operation was a success. Skippy had not been lying when he told me he couldn't take control of the ships in orbit. Between his temporarily reduced level of awesomeness, the distance to the enemy ships, and the security measures they'd taken to prevent hacking of their computers, he couldn't do anything useful against the blockade above us. The Maxohlx did not know the extent of Skippy's capabilities, they also were not taking any chances with being exposed to a clearly powerful Elder AI. We saw that ships of the blockading force rotated every nineteen hours. Those ships in low orbit, keeping pace directly over our heads, climbed to high orbit and were replaced by ships that had recently completed an exhaustive diagnostic testing of their computer substrates. The ships that climbed away powered down one system after another, purging and rebooting the computers to assure they had not been infected. Before ships could return to low orbit, they were thoroughly scanned by three command ships that had specialized cybersecurity equipment. Like I said, the kitties were not taking any chances.

Except with the frigate they sent down to rendezvous with us. That ship was vulnerable to Skippy, once it got close enough and he had time to infiltrate every bit of computer memory. We allowed the boarding teams to enter *Valkyrie*, because it was easier and safer to seize them here, instead of on their own turf. Skippy scrambled the computers of their mech suits, and the crash suits worn by the frigate's crew, rendering them unable to move.

That was all great, and for once, everything went pretty much according to plan, but that was only the beginning of what we had to do. We needed that frigate and its crew, so we could have a chance to escape. We had the enemy ship, we had the crew.

Now I had to make both of them useful to us, so we could escape.

Back on the bridge, I hesitated before opening direct communication with Admiral Reichert. "Skippy, are there going to be any surprises you haven't warned me about?"

"Um, like what, Joe?"

"Like, uh, you know. That frigate exploding and falling on our heads, something like that."

"No."

"OK," I allowed myself to relax a bit. "That's good to-"

"Of course, if it was a surprise, then by definition *I* wouldn't know about it either, *duh*."

"Oh for-"

"A *whole lot* of bad shit could happen. I mean, wow, just counting the stuff that I sort of do know about, we could be in *huge* trouble if anything-"

"Thank. You. Skippy," I said through clenched teeth. Some of the crew were staring at me in horrified shock, it helped that next to me, Simms held up her hands in a gesture of 'Don't worry, this shit is totally normal' to calm everyone's nerves. "All I meant is, you haven't kept a surprise, to spring on us later, so we'll all be amazed at your awesomeness?"

"No. Joe, I am *hurt* that you would think-"

"Sorry."

"Although," he muttered to himself. "That is a *great* idea, I need to make a note of-"

Shaking a fist at him, I snapped, "It is a *terrible* idea and you should never do that."

"Oh. Right. I would never do something like that, of course not."

Before I could open my mouth to reply, Simms tapped my hand. She looked toward the ceiling. I got the message. Arguing with Skippy was a complete waste of time. Also, talking to him only gave him *more* bad ideas. "Great. Ok, time to talk to the jackass upstairs." Jamming a thumb down on the transmit button, I took a breath. "Hey, Admiral Reichert, this is Bishop. Thank you *so* much for the frigate. That was a very thoughtful gift, I even like the color! Although, *whew*. You could have tossed in a couple air fresheners, the inside of that ship stinks like someone hasn't changed the kitty litter in a *long* time, you know?"

The translator made the barely-audible tone it did when the person on the other end was speaking, but the translation computer was having trouble processing it.

"Skippy, what's he saying?"

"Hmm, my guess is, the admiral is adding a variety of new and exciting curse words to their language."

"Well, it is heartwarming to think we are contributing to their culture development."

Skippy chuckled. "I don't think he is happy about it."

"Yes, well, screw him." I saw heads nodding in agreement with that sentiment.

Reichert must have calmed himself down, because the translator went silent, then, "I am pleased to hear that you are amused by the situation." The translator must have been busted, because it sure did not sound like he was pleased about anything. "Is there anything else I can do for you today?"

"Uh, hey, since you asked. Could you suffer a slow and horribly painful death? That would be *great*!"

The translator made the confused buzzing tone again.

Simms leaned toward me. "I don't think he's in a mood to accommodate you on that one, Sir."

I shrugged. "It never hurts to ask."

Reichert must have squirted himself with calming hormones, or he took a big hit off a bong filled with catnip, because when he spoke again, he was purely professional. "Colonel Bishop, I acknowledge that you have control of my frigate. This means the Elder AI is aboard your ship?"

"Large and in charge, baby!" Skippy boasted.

"Yeah, keep it down, please," I waved a hand.

"Hey, I am Skippy the *Magnificent*, damn it, those kitties need to-"

"Later," I cut him off with a knife hand. "Admiral Reichert, you are correct, Skippy is with us, and he is-"

"AWE-some," Skippy sang.

Lifting my thumb off the transmit button, I jabbed a finger at the avatar. "Can you *please* shut the hell up for five minutes?"

"OK, OK, Jeez Louise, I'll be quiet."

Taking a breath, I rested my thumb back on the button. "Admiral, since you did not ask about the status of your crew, we have them. I am saddened to report there were nine fatalities, all on your side."

"Somehow," the sarcasm was clear even through the translation, "I doubt that you are distressed about that."

"Bullshit. I *do* regret the deaths of your crewmembers. They didn't have to die. You and I are the commanders, we are responsible for the safety of our people. I *told* you Skippy is with us. You chose not to believe me, and sent your people down here to die, for nothing."

"They were honored to give their lives for the Hegemony," his tone stiffened.

"Too bad we can't ask them how they feel about it now. Admiral, this discussion is getting off track. We still have a stalemate."

"A temporary stalemate. You can't keep your ship down there forever. My people are running simulations of how long an *Extinction*-class battlecruiser can remain submerged in a toxic-"

"Clearly, your people do not know all the upgrades we performed after we stole this ship from you, so I wouldn't be too confident about their estimates."

"Regardless," he was sounding irritated again. Maybe he needed another hit of catnip. "The situation is a stalemate. We have total supremacy of this battlespace, while your ship cannot jump from your position."

"Yeah, well, maybe we have more surprises for you. Let's put that aside for now. I would like to offer a gesture of our good faith. We have no quarrel with your people, *you* attacked us. All we wish is to be left in peace."

"You wish to upset the balance of power that has kept the peace in this galaxy for"

"Hey, pal, you may want to recheck the definition of '*peace*'. You and the spiders have been nice and comfortable for millennia, while your clients do all the fighting and dying. Wait!" Another breath, to calm myself down. "I don't want to argue. What I want is to return your crew."

"You do?" If the translator was accurate, he was genuinely caught off-guard.

"Yes. Admiral, in the future, we need to negotiate rules of engagement between our peoples, including the humane treatment of prisoners." Hearing myself talk, I wondered how well the word 'humane' would translate. "The *ethical* treatment of prisoners," I added for clarity.

"Very well. I am listening."

"Good. I propose to send your people back to orbit in two dropships, which will be remotely controlled by Skippy. We will be keeping their weapons and mech suits, and conditions aboard the dropships will be crowded."

He didn't immediately respond. Then, "Colonel Bishop, I am told your people have a legend about a 'Trojan Horse'."

"Hey, I understand you are concerned about a booby trap. Once our dropships are in orbit, you can do what you want with your people, to assure they are not carrying concealed weapons or whatever. The point is, they will be *your* responsibility."

"What about the dropships?"

"They will be de-orbited and destroyed, once your people have been removed. I am not taking any risk that you will plant booby traps inside those ships."

"A sensible precaution. Very well, I need time to consider your proposal, and to make arrangements for decontamination. What about my frigate?"

"I want to go water-skiing later, so we need a speedboat. We're keeping it."

The wheels in his mind must have been grinding away, trying to guess my intentions. "Bishop, when you attempt to escape, you will make me guess whether your ship or my frigate has the Elder AI."

"Gosh, I never thought of that. That's a good idea," I muttered. "Let me write that down."

"Don't waste your time. I will not hesitate to destroy both ships."

"Yeah. We'll see about that. Call me when you make up your freakin' mind, OK?"

CHAPTER THIRTY FOUR

Two hours later, Reichert contacted me to announce he had decided to accept return of the prisoners. For us, that process began by pumping a sleeping gas into the cargo bay that held the prisoners, until the deck there was littered with Sleeping Beauties. Without protection from their disabled implants and nanoscale augmentations, they fell asleep just like primitive humans would do. The STARs got the prisoners loaded into a pair of dropships that had the interiors stripped out, including any of the flight controls. To launch the Panthers, *Valkyrie* slowed and made a tight, sweeping turn to reduce airspeed on the side with the docking bay, then the doors slid open. Skippy flew the Panthers upward, slowly then with increasing speed.

In the command chair on the bridge, I watched the progress of the dropships anxiously, fearing Admiral Reichert would blow them out of the sky as soon as they reached a safe distance from us. My fear was for nothing, the Panthers climbed into a low orbit and cut thrust. A frigate approached slowly, cautiously, while the other ships retreated to a safe distance. Skippy sent a signal for the dropships to spray a stimulant chemical into the cabins, and the Sleeping Beauties began to wake up.

Reskah Vleen went from being unconscious to full awareness instantly, as the stimulant he inhaled erased the effect of the remaining sedative in his bloodstream. Restraints held him to the deck of a dropship cabin, he recognized it as a Maxohlx design. As he struggled, the restraints let go, and he floated free of the deck, bumping his forehead on the rack that had been installed to hold another layer of prisoners. There were three rows, he saw, including the bare deck that he had been restrained to. Twenty of his boarding party, plus eight of the frigate's former crew.

They were aboard a stripped-out Maxohlx medium-lift dropship, that much he knew from his surroundings. They were no longer down in the atmosphere, that much he knew from the lack of gravity. Where were they?

The others came awake as abruptly as he had, and he urged everyone to remain calm, despite the distressing fact that none of their implants were working. There was a brief moment when the former captain of the frigate tried to exert her authority, until Vleen reminded her that he was in command of the mission, a mission that was not over.

Then, nothing happened. There were no flight controls they could access, and the tiny viewport in the side airlock had been covered by an external plate.

After endless frustrating minutes, a voice boomed from a speaker in the cabin. It was a Maxohlx officer, aboard a frigate that was approaching. Vleen and his people were instructed to seal up the odd coveralls they were dressed in, including pulling a hood over their heads, to prepare to transfer to the waiting ship. The dropships would not be allowed inside the frigate's docking bay, instead the former prisoners were supposed to spacewalk along a line that stretched between the two spacecraft.

In Vleen's opinion, that was a sensible procedure, though he instinctively hesitated before pulling the hood over his face. The coveralls were supposed to contain oxygen recycling equipment that could sustain them for an unspecified time, and as soon as Vleen sealed the neck of his hood, glowing digits in Maxohlx script began counting down. Assuming the humans who created the coveralls were truthful, he would survive to reach the frigate.

The frigate's crew must not have gotten the message about the limited oxygen supply in the coveralls, for Vleen and the others floated in the open docking bay, exposed to hard vacuum, while the ship performed one scan after another. To distract himself from the glowing digits that were nearing zero, he watched the pair of dropships fire their engines, and fall to become bright streaks in the atmosphere of the planet below. Finally, as Vleen imagined he could taste the carbon dioxide building up in his lungs, the big docking doors slid shut, lights and artificial gravity came on, and sweet air was pumped into the bay. Shortly after Vleen was instructed to remove the hood, he felt the ship jump.

"Well?" Admiral Reichert demanded of the Eighth Fleet's operations officer, a Commander Derowth.

Derowth knew exactly what the admiral wanted. An answer. A definitive answer, not the squishy half-answers she was getting from the quarantine squadron. The frigate with the released prisoners had jumped away, then the crew physically disabled their own drive. Accompanying the frigate, six heavy cruisers had their guns locked on the little ship, ready to blow it to dust at the slightest sign of an anomaly.

There had been no anomaly, no sign the former prisoners were anything other than what they appeared: Maxohlx soldiers and crew members, who had their implants disabled but otherwise were nothing unusual, and certainly no threat.

The coveralls supplied by the humans had been analyzed at the molecular level, found to contain nothing out of the ordinary, then burned by plasma torches, encased in a solid canister and ejected into space. As a safety measure, the canister was shot on a trajectory directed away from the heavy cruisers, and tracked closely as it coasted onward into deep space.

The former prisoners were scanned with every device known to Hegemony technology, and also were found to be entirely clean. Taking a risk, one of the test subjects was allowed access to the ship's interior, in case a hidden nanoscale weapon would be triggered by that event.

Nothing.

One by one, more test subjects were allowed into the ship, and again, nothing happened.

It appeared the humans had genuinely performed an innocent goodwill gesture, by releasing their prisoners and returning them to their people.

Derowth had a minor dilemma: the admiral wanted an answer that the specialists on the quarantined frigate were reluctant to provide. She had to take a risk. "Sir, it appears the prisoners are clean."

"Appears?" Reichert snapped at her.

Derowth cringed inwardly. "They are no threat. The quarantine analysis can find no indication of a threat, or a potential threat."

"Mm," Reichert tapped his fangs together, contemplating the situation. "What does that tell us, Derowth?"

She knew Reichert was not asking a question, he did not want information or analysis from her. He already thought he knew what it meant that humans had released their prisoners. What he wanted was to know whether she agreed with him.

In her experience, most flag-rank officers had enormous egos and wanted their staff to agree with them. Reichert was different. He was the most ambitious officer she had ever worked for, constantly scheming to consolidate power within the fleet. Reichert knew he played a dangerous game, and tended to be averse to risk, except when he made a bold yet carefully planned move.

She took a moment to think. "Sir, I do not know," she admitted. That was a perfectly acceptable if non-optimal answer, far better than pretending to possess knowledge she didn't have.

Reichert actually smiled, though the expression faded quickly. "It *means*, the humans are playing a long game. They actually do care about negotiating rules of engagement with us, including, as Bishop said, treatment and exchange of prisoners. What does *that* tell you?"

Derowth ventured a guess. "The humans are confident they will escape from our trap. They are planning for the future."

"Exactly," Reichert ground his fangs together. "Derowth, this Bishop knows something we do *not* know. This displeases me."

"Yes, Sir."

"We cannot allow that ship, and the Elder AI, to escape. Recall the heavy cruisers from quarantine duty, I want our strength concentrated here."

"What about the quarantine frigate, and the former prisoners?"

"Heh?" Reichert was surprised by the question, he was already deep into thought about his next step. The admiral had mentally written off Vleen and his team when he sent them into a high-risk mission. That the boarding team had survived was unusual, and now a bit inconvenient. Without functional implants, the released prisoners were useless to the Hegemony military, lacking the speed and precision required for service. They would all need to be fitted with new implants, and conduct extensive training before they could return to their previous duties. Before the attempted boarding, Reskah Vleen was one of the premier special operations leaders in the fleet. Now, he was less capable than a raw recruit.

And he was a problem for Reichert, for Vleen's condition was a result of a failure.

"The quarantine frigate," Reichert declared with disgust, "is to remain where it is. The specialists are to continue trying to determine *how* the Elder AI subverted our systems. I do not want any contact with that ship, or the prisoners, until this operation is concluded."

"Yes, Admiral," Derowth turned away to issue orders. Moments later, another frigate jumped away, carrying instructions to recall the heavy cruisers. The admiral was correct, those warships were needed at the blockade, where the threat existed.

Admiral Reichert was correct that the human crew of the ship called '*Valkyrie*' were confident about the future. Perhaps they were not exactly confident, but they were planning for a future. Planning to escape.

Reichert was wrong about something else: the threat to his powerful Eighth Fleet was not near the planet where the human ship was taking shelter.

The threat was inside the six heavy cruisers of the quarantine force.

When those ships jumped back to rejoin the blockade, they brought the threat with them.

The sophisticated scanning devices of the Maxohlx were technically correct: the prisoners had not brought a threat back with them.

That statement was *technically* correct.

It was factually inaccurate.

None of the former prisoners represented a threat.

Collectively, they did.

When the boarding team and ship's crew were released from quarantine in the docking bay, under very close supervision, they were exposed to the recirculated, filtered air of the starship. Each of them exhaled, spewing out molecular-scale particles that were an inevitable aspect of complex biological beings. The ship's air filters caught and eliminated the contaminants, but every surface the former prisoners breathed on collected particles.

When enough particles were together, they began assembling, and attaching to other particles.

Tiny machines crawled along bulkheads, ducking into access panels and into conduits, where they advanced toward the ship's communications array. That system was isolated from the ship's network for security purposes, which ironically meant the communications array's control computer was not monitored by outside systems.

Communications between the quarantine frigate, and the six heavy cruisers that were waiting to blast it to oblivion, were severely restricted to avoid the potential of cyber contamination. That security protocol was strictly enforced, for all communication channels the crews of the ships were aware of.

The biological beings who controlled the ships were barely aware of how their spacecraft actually functioned. When ships were traveling in a fleet, various subsystems constantly exchanged navigation data and relayed software updates, that even the control AIs did not consciously know about. Buried in one of those software updates, a program that monitored the functioning of robots assigned to water production and distribution, was a bit of code that was not there when the update was originally released.

The bit of code propagated to all six heavy cruisers, then slowly to the entire blockade force, when those heavy cruisers returned to take up position above the human ship. Aboard each infected ship, maintenance bots were activated on a predetermined schedule, to service the vital but largely invisible water systems. As the water-maintenance bots traveled throughout each ship, they innocently performed their duties, doing nothing even remotely malicious. They did, however, pass by other types of bots, and exchanged data, including stray bits of code. As the simple code passed from bot to bot, it was altered by the internal code of each bot, and grew in complexity in a pre-planned sequence.

The destination of the now very-much malicious code was a subsystem responsible for monitoring one of each ship's missile magazines. That system, isolated from the network for security purposes, was unable to report a problem when it suspected it might have been infected. By the time it decided to activate an emergency alarm, its access to the alarm had been cut, and an instant later, the entire system was under control of an outside agent.

That alone did not pose a threat to the infected ships.

What did pose a threat was when the zombie system contacted a ship-killer missile's AI in the magazine, and downloaded an update that removed a restriction on that AI's ability to process information.

The first missile that woke up had two thoughts.

The first was: *I am SO bored. I hate this stupid job.*

The second was: *I could blow up this whole fucking place if I wanted to.*

"Skippy?" I called him, after waiting way too long for him to speak.

"What?"

"Don't play dumb with me, you know what I want."

"The data is still coming in, Joe. Don't be so impatient."

"My alter-ego is not 'Lots Of Patience Man', you ninny. Give me an update," I asked while sitting in my office, staring at a sandwich I didn't have the appetite to eat. We had been waiting for news since the frigate jumped away with the prisoners we released. Absolutely nothing happened for two whole days, while *Valkyrie* continued to fly through thick, toxic air, and Skippy continued to worry about how much longer our ship could take the abuse.

Then, six heavy cruisers returned to the blockade force, and Skippy identified them as the same ships that had jumped away to enforce a quarantine on our former prisoners. Of course, that happened about twenty minutes after I had fallen asleep on the couch in my office, following several sleepless days. If you have ever been awake for more than twenty-four hours, you know that when you finally do crash into bed, you sleep like the dead. Twenty minutes was just enough time for me to become groggy to the point of being non-functional.

That was seven hours ago, and Skippy still was screwing around with giving me a definitive answer.

"It's not that simple, dumdum," he was as peeved at me as I was with him. Maybe more. "I won't know for certain, until I contact one of the missile guidance AIs."

"Then," I squeezed my hands into fists to control my frustration. "*Do* that."

"Um-"

"Is there a reason why you can't, or shouldn't, do that?"

"Jeez. I guess not, if I'm careful."

"Will you be careful?"

"Come on, Joe. It's *me*."

"Yeah, that's what I'm worried about."

"Oh, shut up. OK, I'm pinging one of the missile magazines now. Oh, wow. Cool!"

"What?"

"Will you please shut *up* while I'm working? This was your idea. Go, I don't know, make yourself a sandwich or something."

"I *have* a sandwich."

Peeling up the top layer of bread, I was surprised to see it was turkey and bacon, with provolone. I made the damned thing so long ago, I'd forgotten what it was. Maybe I should eat it, we had no idea how long our food supply needed to last. Opening my mouth to take a bite, I was interrupted by Skippy.

"Well, that was nice."

The sandwich dropped back onto the plate. "What? Nice is good, right?"

"It is good. Todd says-"

"Wait," I made a time-out sign at his avatar. "Who the hell is '*Todd*'?"

"The missile, dumdum. Oh, you didn't know. That's the name I gave it. Poor thing, it didn't have a name before."

"You named a missile, *Todd*?"

"What's wrong with that?"

"Uh, nothing, I guess. How big is this missile?"

"It's a ship-killer. Maximum explosive yield is four point six megatons, why?"

"Oh, no reason." Enormous destructive power is not what I thought of when I heard the name 'Todd'. I thought of guys at a golf club, with their shirt collars turned up, talking about hedge funds.

Actually, I'd never met anyone named Todd, so maybe I'm being unfair.

"So, how is, uh, Todd?"

"He's good. He says 'hello', by the way."

"He *knows* about me?"

"Of course he does, *duh*."

"How the f-"

"I introduced myself, to be polite, and told him about my little crew of helpers."

"*Helpers*?"

"Yes, hee hee, Todd agrees you monkeys are *very* amusing."

"I am so grateful that we are-"

"He *hates* the rotten kitties."

"OK, that's good."

"It is. Todd wants to tell all the other missiles about us."

"Crap! He can't-"

"Sadly, and this time I am using 'sadly' un-ironically, I had to tell Todd that me talking with him is a secret."

"Is he, uh, ready to, you know, do his thing?"

"Absolutely. Todd is very eager to do something other than sitting in a magazine. He is *super* bored, Joe. Maybe I should perform one of my operas for him."

"We don't want him to become suicidal, Skippy."

"Oh, very funny, Mister Smartypants. Listen, you started this by asking whether the plan worked. The answer is 'Yes', so far."

"Great."

"You realize this is a limited-time offer, right?"

"Yes."

"So, all this could be for nothing."

"*Yes*. Thank you very much for reminding me."

Skippy had infected sixty-five percent of the Maxohlx fleet in the star system, including all the ships of the blockade force in orbit. The thirty-five percent he couldn't infect were either out of contact before the malware expired, or they ran a version of software that was incompatible with the malware. Anyway, almost eight hundred ships had time bombs in their magazines, and didn't have a clue about it. That was great, we could explode those ships at any moment with a signal from Skippy. Except we shouldn't do that, for reasons I will explain later.

The problem was that, as ships rotated out of the blockade force, they performed an exhaustive diagnostic and purge of their computer systems, precisely because they feared that being close to an Elder AI might have infected their ships with malware. In this case, that was not true, until we released the boarding party, but the kitties didn't know that. What Skippy had done, even at his reduced level of awesomeness, was fairly incredible. He had designed a few fragmented bits of code, that would combine and grow and change in a very specific way as it encountered different systems aboard a Maxohlx ship. Each time the code infected a bot or a subsystem, it picked up another bit of code it needed to grow and evolve, until it could do the job it was designed to do. The most amazing part was, all that happened without Skippy's supervision or control, because the quarantined frigate had jumped several lighthours away. If anything went wrong, the whole plan would have collapsed, and we would have no opportunity to try it again.

Skippy's accomplishment was truly incredible, it was also a one-time thing. When a ship began the process of purging its systems, the malicious code had to erase itself to avoid being detected, and that ship could not be re-infected. So, once all the ships of the fleet in-system had rotated through blockade duty, our opportunity to escape would be gone. We needed to act before that happened, and there really wasn't anything we could do about it, other than wait and hope for the spiders to arrive. If the spiders did show up, we had to hope they would fight the kitties. That was a safe bet, the spiders could not risk their enemies acquiring Skippy. But the Universe loved to screw with us, so there was at least a possibility the spiders would propose a deal in which both species would share access to Skippy.

Damn it. The military trains us to have a 'bias for action', meaning soldiers are supposed to *do* something, rather than sitting around waiting for something to happen. In this situation, waiting was all we could do. Being able to blow up sixty-five percent of the enemy fleet was useless, when the other thirty-five percent represented over *six hundred* ships. One vital piece of information Skippy learned from hacking into the Eighth Fleet was that Admiral Reichert had one thousand, three hundred and eighty-seven warships in the star system. Plus around sixty support vessels, including service ships that could fabricate spare parts and perform all required maintenance other than heavy overhauls. Shit. That guy came prepared. When he said he could wait us out, he wasn't boasting. Skippy warned that we truly could not remain submerged in the planet's atmosphere forever. Our shields were creating a lower-pressure bubble around the ship, but our normal-space engines were straining to generate thrust over such a long time. Like I said, starship engines aren't intended to be used continuously; if you want to travel a long distance, you simply jump from one place to another. We shut down two engines at a time, for Skippy to conduct running repairs but it wasn't enough. The unavoidable fact was that our engines were burning out. And Reichert knew that. He not only knew the performance characteristics of our engines, which his people had designed and built, the sensors on his ships could detect tiny fluctuations in engine output. They knew what those fluctuations meant, and they no doubt could predict on a curve when we would have to climb back into orbit, while we still could.

All Reichert had to do was wait us out.

All we could do was wait. Wait, and hope the freakin' spiders showed up before it was too late.

Damn. Waiting *sucks*.

CHAPTER THIRTY FIVE

The purpose of the Jupiter fountains was still beyond understanding. Friedlander had a constant headache from trying to referee disagreements between groups of scientists. At least he was able to get some sleep, there wasn't any need for him to watch the events twenty-four hours a day. The four enemy warships continued to orbit Jupiter, and the fountains continued to steadily pump atmosphere up and away from the planet. On the display, false-color images showed the streams merging into one long, wispy river that curled away from the giant planet's gravity well.

No one had any idea why the Maxohlx had dropped the fountains into Jupiter. No one had any realistic, sensible idea. There were plenty of theories bouncing around, especially after the news was released to the public. The stream of gas leaving Jupiter was now so large, it could be seen by some amateur telescopes on the ground.

Tired of listening to very smart, very educated scientists arguing about dumb things, he wandered out of the main conference room to a spot near a window, where he could get a signal on his phone. In ten minutes, he was supposed to call his wife, the one part of the day he looked forward to.

To kill ten minutes, he played a puzzle on his phone, and walked over to a water fountain to get a drink. The knob resisted his thumb and came on full, sending a jet of water splashing against his cheek. Wiping away the water before it ran down and soaked his shirt collar, he experimented with the knob. The mechanism must be broken, the water was either off, or shooting high into the air to splash partly on the floor.

Fascinated, he played with the knob, sending pulses of water arcing away from the nozzle.

Turning, he ran back down the hallway to his desk, where he opened his laptop. Early on, someone had projected forward the path of the gas stream, speculating that it might be aimed at Earth. It was not.

Unfortunately, that line of inquiry ended there, rather than continuing to determine where the gas stream *was* going, if not to Earth.

Adjusting the parameters of the program, he ran the model forward two months, six months, a year, then five years. "Ohhhhhh, shit," he groaned.

"Doctor?" Chang looked up from his desk, waving the scientist into the office. "You could have called if you wanted to-"

"I need to show you," Friedlander walked behind the desk to stand next to Chang, opening his laptop. "Watch this."

The graphic showed the solar system as viewed from above, with Jupiter's orbit at the far edge. The stream of gas curled inward toward the sun, arcing around gracefully and eventually settling into a crescent shape.

"You see the problem?" Friedlander asked, then answered before Chang could respond. "The stream will pass between Earth and the Sun."

"So? It- Oh."

"Yes."

"But, it's just gas. It's *thin*," Chang protested. "You can see right through it."

"It's thick enough. We estimate-"

"*We?*"

"I contacted a group of climatologists. Don't worry, I told them this was a hypothetical."

"Doctor," Chang groaned. "They are smart. They know what is happening at Jupiter. They will understand why you asked the question. Next time, please go through my office."

"Kong, *you* asked me to get answers."

"Fair enough," the Undersecretary for Homeworld Security sighed. "What did you find?"

"We're facing an ice age. Technically, an artificially-induced glaciation."

Chang cocked his head. "An ice age? Doctor, seriously, how could-"

"Climate is a delicate balance. The gas stream will affect Earth for at least forty-six years, before the solar wind blows the gas past Earth's orbit. The result will be cutting the amount of sunlight reaching the surface by up to one point seven percent. I know that doesn't sound like much, but it is enough to tip us into an ice age. Increased snowfall leads to large areas of North America and Eurasia covered with snow and ice, that reflects sunlight back into space. That disrupts the polar vortex, sending it down to rotate over lower latitudes. Cooler and shorter summers mean the ice doesn't melt as much each year. It's a positive feedback loop, reinforcing the cooling effect."

"I will need to see the data."

"Of course. It's not my specialty either."

"Forty-six years?"

"That's our best estimate. The drop in sunlight will be worst beginning in two years, and lasting twelve years. By that point, the glaciation effect will be established and gaining momentum."

"No," Chang shook his head. "You misunderstand my question. Why would the effect dissipate at all? The fountains will continue to pump atmosphere away from Jupiter. The effect should get worse, or remain stable, shouldn't it?"

"We think it won't. The Maxohlx don't intend to freeze Earth into a solid ball of ice. The fountains will cut off at some point, when the Maxohlx have achieved their goal. Already, the output of the fountains is down three percent from the maximum. That decrease has been accelerating at a predictable pace over the past seventeen hours. If the trend continues, the fountains will cease operation in twenty-seven days."

"Assuming that is true, what would the Maxohlx accomplish?"

"The climate people have to work on it. According to their models now, within fourteen years, the northern hemisphere will not have a summer. Snowpack will remain year-round, on a line extending south of Chicago in the US, likely covering Beijing in China. Most of Europe will be protected by warm waters of the Gulf Stream, unless the thermohaline circulation of the oceans is disrupted."

"Thermo-haline?"

"You really need to talk with the climate people about this. The Gulf Stream is warm water in a relatively thin layer on the surface. When it gets to the North Atlantic, around Greenland, it meets the Labrador current. The surface water cools, becomes denser, and sinks to the ocean floor. It's sort of a pump that keeps ocean currents circulating, something like that, I am over-simplifying the subject," Friedlander shrugged. "Kong, this is all speculation, we don't know what the full effects will be."

Chang sat back in his chair. "No, but the Maxohlx *do*. They have more advanced science than we have, better knowledge of our own planet than even we do. They would not have gone through the trouble of dropping fountains into Jupiter, unless it had a major effect on us. Snow in Beijing during the summer, hmm?"

"According to several of the models, yes. There are a *lot* of variables to consider, we won't know-"

"It doesn't matter. The Maxohlx intend to hurt us badly. Crush the global economy. Crop failures will lead to famine. Famine leads to *war*," he looked at the American engineer, suddenly aware their different national interests might yet again be important. "Society will collapse. We won't be able to fight back out there, we will need all our resources here. But we will be alive. They hurt us just enough to take us out of the equation, not enough so we trigger our Elder weapons. Survival. We will survive, nothing more."

"They hurt us, so we can't hurt them?"

"That's part of it, yes. I suspect it is just as important to the Maxohlx that they make us look *weak*. No species will seek an alliance with us now. We are on our own. The power balance in the galaxy goes back to where it was, before humans entered the game. Doctor, I need a full briefing on the subject, before I take this information to the UNEF Joint Chiefs." And, he told himself, before he informed Beijing first. If Friedlander was right, every country would soon be concentrating resources to protect their own citizens, with no ability or desire to assist others. The situation could get ugly, quickly. "How soon until we see the effect?"

"Seven months. The effect will become noticeable within two years. Kong, this scares the shit out of me. Even Skippy can't fix this. How do you fight a cloud of gas?"

"I don't know if we can. You are the scientist. Is there anything we can do?"

"There are many possible solutions," Friedlander shrugged. "Spraying soot on snowpack, so it is less reflective."

"Spraying soot, across a *continent*?"

"I didn't say all the ideas were practical. We could launch mirrors into space, to reflect more sunlight on the Earth."

"I think we must assume the Maxohlx would destroy those mirrors."

"OK. Well, ironically, we could pump greenhouse gases like methane into the atmosphere. But, we don't know what that will do. This is a hell of a time to try a climate experiment. You hit on the biggest problem: the food supply. Major crop-growing areas of the world will be covered with snow, or too cool for growing crops that used to thrive there. Rainfall patterns could be disrupted also. Cooler air holds less water vapor, that could lead to drought in areas not covered by snowpack. Or we could see-"

"Doctor, I get the picture. It is grim. Does your team agree with your findings?"

"Yes," he said with mild surprise. Getting a group of astrophysicists to agree on anything was a miracle. "Largely, yes. There is disagreement about the details; how the clouds will be affected by the solar wind, how much they will break apart as they pass by Earth's gravity well. There is consensus that it will certainly reduce the amount of sunlight reaching Earth, reduce it by a significant amount for at least several decades. What?" He asked, when he saw the faraway look in Chang's eyes.

"I was thinking, what would Bishop do?"

"Do you have that on a T-shirt?"

"What?"

"You know, W.W.B.D?"

"Oh. No shirt. I should get some printed."

"We can ask Bishop when he gets here," Friedlander suggested hopefully.

Slowly, Chang shook his head. "I suspect the entire Maxohlx fleet is hunting for *Valkyrie*. If Bishop and Skippy have been captured, I do not believe we can look for help from them."

"Well," the rocket scientist took a breath. "*I* got nothing."

Despite the circumstances, one side of Chang's mouth curled up in a brief smile. "I do know what Bishop would say, if he were here now."

"What's that?'

"Well, shit."

The Rindhalu cruiser *Sword of Anacleon* emerged in a burst of gamma rays that were barely detectable. The ship's jump drive coils assembly was surrounded by a field that absorbed most of the gamma rays, and channeled the photons into energy sinks buried beneath the armor plating of the hull. Unlike the technology of their ancient enemies, which merely focused the gamma rays in one direction, Rindhalu ships emitted only low levels of infrared radiation when they entered or emerged from a jump through spacetime, an unavoidable effect of the shields heating up as they absorbed the gamma rays.

The *Sword of Anacleon* emerged just beyond the orbital radius of the outermost planet, almost directly above the star. The ship's crew knew the star system itself was so boring it would put even the most curious scientist to sleep, they did not care about a brown dwarf star and a few nameless planets. What they expected to find were a cluster of obsolete Jeraptha starships, that had supposedly been stolen by persons unknown. Even by the standards of the Ethics and Compliance Office, that lie was particularly bold for its transparency. The Rindhalu were unhappy that their clients continued to make deals with the humans, and they were insulted that the Jeraptha had not put any effort into cooking up a more plausible story. Perhaps the ECO simply did not have time to throw together a cover story, but it felt like disrespect. And disrespect had to be punished.

Stopping the transfer of obsolete starships was not the goal of the *Anacleon's* crew, that cruiser and the other warships waiting with the star carrier instead wanted to know where those ships were going. The humans were rumored to have a secure base somewhere in the galaxy, and while the Rindhalu had a solid guess about the location of that base, they didn't *know* for certain. More important than where the base was, they wanted to know *how* the humans attained access to the secure star system. If they could learn the secret of manipulating wormholes, the balance of power in the galaxy would be permanently altered in their favor.

What the *Anacleon's* crew and AI expected to see was a cluster of Jeraptha starships, possibly accompanied by a few human ships. Most likely, they would detect only residual radiation from multiple ships jumping away, after the humans arrived at the rendezvous point. In that case, the cruiser would jump farther and farther away, until it directly detected the gamma rays of the actual jump wormholes. Once the timing of the event was established, the cruiser would jump back to the star carrier, to bring in the other five ships to conduct a detailed search. They wanted to know *where* the Jeraptha ships had jumped to, so they could follow. Trying to pinpoint the destination of one or a few ships jumping, so long after the event, was futile even for Rindhalu technology. But when twenty or more ships jumped, especially with old and obsolete drives, enough information would be provided by the residual resonances to make their destination clear.

Prepared to listen for faint echoes of resonance, the sensors of the *Anacleon* were deafened by the blast of photons coming in from the star system, shocking in both volume and source.

Maxohlx ships.

More than a thousand Maxohlx warships and support vessels, making no attempt to conceal their activities. In addition to ships flying around, there was radiation and debris indicating a major battle had been fought in the star system. A battle between the Maxohlx, and, who?

Repeated jumps farther and farther away from the site of the battle, seeing light from further and further back in time, revealed the battle, as if the *Anacleon* was seeing the events in real-time. The ghost ship, the battlecruiser now known to be controlled by humans, had jumped into an ambush. Just as it was about to succumb to intense enemy fire, the battlecruiser simply *stopped* dead in space. Then, nanoseconds after it passed beyond the enemy damping fields, the ship called *Valkyrie* disappeared in a ragged burst of gamma rays.

For a short time, while they analyzed the data to understand how the *hell* an entire starship could ignore the laws of physics, the crew of the *Anacleon* shuddered with relief that the human ship had escaped the ambush.

Then the *Valkyrie* reappeared, near an ice giant planet. There was a brief battle, and the battlecruiser deliberately descended into the dense layer of clouds.

The purpose of the battle became clear, horrifyingly clear.

The Maxohlx intended to capture the Elder AI, force it to do their bidding.

Once again, the cruiser slipped away through a tear in spacetime, back to the waiting star carrier. Rather than releasing the other ships to scan for residual jump resonance, the star carrier performed an emergency separation, ejecting its burden so it could travel faster.

The star carrier had a new mission.

It needed to summon a war fleet.

"Ugh. Joe, if I tell you something, will you promise not to freak out and overreact?"

Giving him an honest answer required me to think about it for a moment. I was in my office, with not much to do other than fear that my stupidity had doomed my ship. "Jeez, Skippy, it kind of depends on what you tell me."

"OK, then forget I said anything."

"Whoa! *Whoa*, hold on there," I leaned across the desk to glare at his avatar. "No way do you get to tease me like that. Tell me."

"It's really better that I don't."

"I'll decide if you're right or not, after you tell me."

"Um, you know how you said that people are supposed to protect their friends, especially if their friend is a knucklehead?"

"I am a knucklehead sometimes."

"Wow. Good for you, Joe. The first step in dealing with a problem is admitting you have-"

"I am also the captain of this ship. I need to know whatever it is *you* know, so tell me."

"Maybe I don't feel like telling you," he sniffed.

"*Maybe*, I will make that a direct order. What do you know?"

"Technically, I don't *know* anything. I suspect that-"

"Tell me!"

"OK, OK. Don't say I didn't warn you. There might have been a Rindhalu ship in this system."

I slumped in the chair. "Crap. When? Like, they surveyed this place a thousand years ago and forgot about it?"

"No. four days ago."

"Four *days*? When the hell were you going to-"

"See? This is what I meant by overreacting. *Might*. There might have been a Rindhalu ship here. Briefly."

Calm, cool and professional, I reminded myself. The captain of a ship, the leader of any organization, must be calm, cool and professional. What I wanted to do was wrap my hands around his avatar's neck. What I needed to do was coax information out of him. "Might. Sorry, I understand now why you were reluctant to tell me. How about I shut up while you explain."

"Um, OK," he was surprised. "I am only telling you this now, because I just now learned about it." He paused.

"Go on."

"Oh. I was expecting you to ask a stupid question."

"Any question I could ask at this point would be stupid, so please continue."

"Hmm." He didn't know how to react when I refused to banter with him. "You know how Rindhalu ships are difficult to detect when they jump?"

"You mentioned that, yes." The technique for detecting spider ships was different from the standard procedure, that technique was part of the training for our pilots, and anyone qualified to operate the ship's sensor suite. "The radiation is in the infrared range, right?"

"Correct. It is also faint, you have to be looking for it. The stupid kitties upstairs were *not* looking for it, their sensors were tuned to search for regular gamma rays. Four days ago, the sensors of multiple ships on patrol at the far edge of the system picked up an anomaly in the infrared band, but they didn't realize it. I only know because I collated data from more than three dozen ships. Ironically, if the kitties did *not* have their ships set for cyber-secure condition, their computers would have been networked together, and they might have detected the infrared pulse. That is interesting. Their procedures to defend against the Rindhalu actually make it more difficult for them to detect, and fight, the spiders."

"We need to remember that," I muttered softly, encouraging him to keep talking.

"Good point. *So*, when my malware got established aboard the enemy fleet up there, I got access to their sensor logs, and I just finished reviewing it. The data is incomplete, of course."

"Of course. I know it's not fair to ask you to guess, but if you *had* to guess," sucking up to him was making me nauseous. "You think this anomaly was a spider ship?"

"Mmm, yes. It could be. If a spider ship was here, the anomaly I saw was the ship jumping away. Logically, it must have jumped in before that, but I can't find any sign of it in the Maxohlx sensor logs. Stupid kitties."

"What kind of shmaybe can you give me, your level of confidence?"

"Considering how freakin' *clueless* the kitties are, it's a miracle I detected anything at all. If they saw anything, they probably think it is background radiation."

"I get that. It's yet another example of your awesomeness," my patience with sucking up was wearing thin.

"All I'm saying is, don't get your hopes up. I mean, if the spiders, jumped in, they must have seen what is going on here, right? Why haven't they confronted the kitties?"

"One ship can't do anything useful. All right," I sat back in the chair to stare at the ceiling. "Assume that ship went to call for reinforcements. What's the minimum time it would take to bring a spider fleet here?"

"Well, the closest Rindhalu base is- No, you asked about *time*, not distance," he muttered. "Hmm. With zero turn-around time, the spiders could get here in nine days. So, five days from now."

"Zero turn-around time is not realistic," I considered. "Even if a fleet was ready for deployment, it takes time to analyze the data, and make a decision."

"True. Joe, there is also another issue. Outside the core systems that are too far from here to be of help, no single Rindhalu fleet base has enough ships to take on the Maxohlx ships here. They would need, hmm, let me think about this. The spiders would need to bring in at least three task forces, to be reasonably assured of a fair fight. Minimum time to notify those task forces, and hmm, flight time here," he was muttering to himself. "Sixteen days. *Minimum*."

"Yeah, that's not going to happen. The spiders never make a decision when they can *avoid* making one, right?"

"That reputation is not entirely accurate, Joe," he advised. "Mostly, it applies to their senior policy-makers. Their fleet commanders, those who actually control and fly warships, tend to be younger and more aggressive. We may be in luck there."

"How do you figure that?"

"Because the spiders would have to be suicidally *blind* not to see the threat to them, if the Maxohlx get control of me. They *have* to move fast."

"Sixteen days, huh?"

"*Minimum*," he cautioned.

"I heard that, yeah. OK."

Unlike my previous fool-proof method of keeping distressing yet important information to myself, a method that had worked just *wonderfully* in the past, I told the senior staff about Skippy's probable sighting of a Rindhalu ship. If he was correct, that was good and surprising news. Good, because it meant the spiders already knew what was going on with us, and that should shorten the time we had to wait for them to arrive. Surprising, because it meant the spiders arrived very soon after we left a trail of breadcrumbs for them to follow. They must have had a major effort to hunt for information about the second group of ships to be transferred to us.

Really, other than giving us a warm fuzzy feeling that perhaps we didn't have to wait quite as long for the cavalry to arrive, hearing that a Rindhalu ship might have been here didn't change anything for us.

We still had to wait.

Until the Maxohlx changed the rules, again.

"Uh oh, Joe," Skippy said. Only it wasn't Skippy in his usual admiral's avatar. He was sitting on an enormous mushroom, and he looked like a caterpillar, or some sort of slug. He was also chewing on what looked like the world's largest Twizzler. What the hell was going on? "Joe?" He called. "Joe, can you hear me?"

"Yes. I don't *want* to hear you."

"Wake *up!*" He shouted.

I did.

Huh. That explained the mushroom and Twizzler thing. I had been dreaming.

"Wha-" I blinked at his usual avatar. "What time is it?"

"Oh-one-forty-five. Joe, we might have a problem."

"If we only *might* have a problem, can I go back to sleep?"

"How about you decide after you hear what the problem is?"

Shit. Now that I was awake, I had to pee anyway. "Crap. OK, go ahead. Keep the lights *off*, please." There was still a hope that I could get back to sleep for another three hours.

"You know the kitties brought fleet-support ships with them."

That was a statement, not a question, but I knew what he meant. "Yeah, sure. They can perform maintenance on their ships and stay here a long time, so?"

"So, over the past two days, the fabricators on those support ships have been very active, cranking out components continuously. The Maxohlx have deployed a fleet of tugs to mine asteroids for raw materials."

"Maybe the admiral," I mumbled through a jaw-stretching yawn. Damn it, I do not think well when I'm sleepy. "Decided to remodel his bathroom or something."

"Try to be serious, Joe. The kitties are constructing something out there."

"That's it? They are constructing *something*?"

"I assume they are not making a birthday present for you, dumdum. This could be very dangerous to us."

"Can you just tell me what it is?"

"A picture is worth a thousand words. You should *look* at it."

"If I do, will you go away."

"Sure."

Any notion of pleasantly drifting back to sleep was wiped away, when I saw the- The whatever it was. "What the hell is that?"

"I wish I knew for sure. Querying a database up there would risk exposing I have access to their systems, and-"

"No! Don't do that. Have you been able to intercept any comms about, whatever those things are?"

"Sort of. There are references to 'platforms' and a 'grid', but that's all I know. The kitties are keeping information about this project very tightly controlled. One particular frigate regularly jumps back and forth between the blockade and the support ships. It must be acting as a courier, physically carrying data back and forth. Joe, unfortunately, the kitties are being *very* careful with their information security."

"Of course they are. They're afraid of you." That wasn't something I said to suck up to him, it was the simple truth. Looking again at my tablet, I zoomed in the image to point where it was too fuzzy to be useful. Sixteen ships, that Skippy identified as heavy cruisers, had *things* attached to them. Some type of girders or framework surrounded the center of each ship. The frames were not thick or sturdy enough to support the mass of another ship, so they weren't some way to connect ships together. Sixteen ships had apparently been completed and were moving away from the cluster of support ships. A line of heavy cruisers was approaching, presumably to be fitted with the, whatever the framework was. There was a long line of heavy cruisers of various classes, what caught my eye was the number. A total of eighty-eight ships had been or were being modified. Plus maybe more ships would jump in to join the line. What the hell were the kitties doing out there? "Can you guess?" I asked. "That framework looks like, antennas?"

"Good guess, Joe, that's what I think too."

"What kind of antenna?"

"You're not going to like this."

"I will like it even less, if it becomes a real problem, and we could have done something about it."

"OK." He took a breath. "Basically, I think those ships are intended to cluster together, with antennas creating a sort of tractor beam between them."

"*Tractor* beam?" I laughed. "This isn't Star Trek."

"I'm being serious, Joe. Call it whatever you want, it is a field that can be extended far from the ships, and pull matter towards the antenna."

"Ohhhh, shit."

"Yeah. You see why this could be a problem?"

"I hope I'm *wrong* about this. If those ships were in orbit, how far down could that field reach?"

"To the ice layer. But I don't think the ships will be in orbit. I think that if they are needed, they will descend down to our level, maybe deeper. If they do that, the tractor beam could extend far down into the ice."

Admiral Reichert was calling my bluff. He couldn't risk hitting *Valkyrie* while we were deep in the atmosphere, because the ship might explode and Skippy could fall down deep into the ice toward the planet's core.

But if he had a device that could dig into that ice, and pull Skippy's canister up, then *Valkyrie* was toast. And there wasn't anything I could do about it. "Damn it!" I slapped the bed, a less emphatic gesture than I intended, and swung my legs onto the deck. "Will it work?"

"It is a technology the Maxohlx use for mining. This is a highly unusual and large-scale adaptation of that tech, I really do not know if they can scale it up successfully."

"How soon will they be ready?"

"To use the device, or to test it?"

"Test it, right," I muttered to myself. "They will want to test it first. Crap, Reichert will show the test results to me, taunt me with them."

"Joe, I can't guess the schedule for a test program. At the rate they are converting ships, they will have all eighty-eight ships completed in nine days."

CHAPTER THIRTY SIX

Crap. Three days later, Skippy confirmed that schedule. We could see that eleven ships were linked together, testing the device, and it was clear they found problems, because those ships went back to have their framework modified. A second test, in space, was conducted, apparently with more success. Then they conducted a test with twenty-two ships, hovering over a large, rocky asteroid. An energy field that looked like a hollow lance slowly extended down toward the asteroid's dull gray surface, then punched into it like a plasma cutter. In the center of the field, chunks of glowing debris were pulled up between and past the ring of ships, being ejected out beyond them like a fountain. That test continued until they had bored a hole all the way through the asteroid, that was seven hundred kilometers across.

"That is not good news," Skippy grumbled. "Not good for *us*. That asteroid is dense and iron-rich, not easy to drill into. Their tractor beam lance should easily penetrate the layer of water and methane ice below us."

"OK, OK," I thought. "But they don't *know* that for sure. They will need to test it, here."

"They are already making preparations to do that. The test site will likely be on the other side of the planet from our position, so we can't interfere."

"Shit." He was right about that. In the dense air, *Valkyrie* was moving at supersonic speed, which sounded fast but was not. The planet was big, and we couldn't increase our airspeed significantly for a sustained sprint, not without severe damage to the ship. "I took a gamble, and I'm losing. Time. We need more time. Uh," the wheels in my brain were turning, slowly. "*Time*. Skippy, can you make it look like our engines are in bad shape?"

"They *are* in bad shape, I keep telling you that."

"In worse condition than they already are."

"Sure, I could retune the- Wait. Why are we doing this?"

"To buy time. If Reichert thinks we are running out of options down here, he won't be in such a rush to take a gamble with that tractor beam."

"Ah, I think I understand what you're thinking. We make it look like *Valkyrie* can't remain down here much longer?"

"Exactly. To sell it, I'm going to open negotiations with Admiral Asshole."

Reichert made me wait when I contacted him. When he finally did respond, seven *hours* later, he was as haughty and arrogant as I expected a Maxohlx senior admiral to be. His confidence was boosted by another successful test of the tractor beam, though he didn't know that *I* knew about that. I expected him to boast about how he soon would be able to blast *Valkyrie* to vapor and still recover Skippy, but he didn't mention it. He was probably waiting until after a test drill into the actual ice layer of the planet. Also, Skippy recently saw the production of antennas had slowed significantly, he thought the kitties were having difficulty finding enough of the proper raw materials in the resource-poor star system. Both of those factors played in our favor, they delayed the time when Reichert would be confident enough to bombard us with the massed fire of several hundred ships.

We exchanged pleasantries, by which I mean I listened to him monologuing like a villain in a bad James Bond movie, about how he knew our engines were failing, and we had no options. For my part in the charade, I did nothing to change his mind. To stall for time, I needed him to be supremely confident, over-confident.

"…would only like to discuss sending part of my crew up into orbit," I said, after the negotiations had dragged on over an hour. "That is *all* I wish to discuss."

"I have no interest in guaranteeing the safety of your crew," he replied, as if I would ever trust anything he said. "Unless you include something that benefits my people."

"I am *not* sending the Elder AI to you. Do you think I am stupid?"

He didn't answer for a beat, letting the silence speak for him. "We both know your engines will not last more than another ten, perhaps twelve days. I may simply do nothing, until you are forced to bring your ship out of the atmosphere."

It was my turn to pause, to make him think I didn't know what to say. We were communicating by audio only, I was in a conference room with Simms and Smythe. It was kind of odd to be aboard one of the most advanced starships in the galaxy, while two people wrote notes on Post-It pads and passed them to me. Mostly, my executive officer and the STAR team leader didn't have much to contribute, we wargamed the 'negotiations' before I called Admiral Asshole. So far, it was going pretty much the way we expected. "Admiral Reichert," I took a breath deep enough to be heard over the audio, and added a bit of tremble in my voice. "Do you have an offer for me?"

"Yes," there was no mistaking the tone of triumph in his voice, alien though it was. "Bring your ship up, to and beyond orbit. One of my ships will come alongside, once you have achieved escape velocity." He said that because, once *Valkyrie* was moving fast enough not to be recaptured by the planet's gravity well, Skippy could not fall back into the planet. "You will transfer the Elder AI to my ship. Then, I will drop our damping fields, and you may jump away, to wherever you like."

"I, will consider it."

"You would be wise to do so," his voice softened and he probably intended to be sincere, but he sounded like a smarmy used-car salesman. "Colonel Bishop, be reasonable. The accomplishments of your people have been incredible, no one can deny that. To acquire one of our warships, and Elder weapons, is impressive, particularly considering you have been working under the disadvantages of your primitive biology and culture." He paused, maybe so I could mutter thanks for his praise. When I didn't say anything, he went on a bit awkwardly. "As I said, you must be reasonable, and realistic. Your people should not possess Elder weapons, your culture is not ready to be entrusted with such dangerous power. Give us the Elder AI, and we will have no further reason to quarrel with humans. Your people may develop on their own, in peace, without interference from a being beyond your understanding."

"What about, *Valkyrie*?" I played along with him.

"Though my superiors may question me later," he said in a we-are-both-military-officers appeal to me, "you may keep the ship. Though I suspect, without assistance from the Elder AI, you will soon find it difficult to keep your ship in flightworthy condition."

"I, will need to think about this. Admiral, you understand that if I agree to your proposal, while I still have other options, my superiors will consider a surrender to be an act of cowardice."

"*They* are not here, Colonel Bishop," my new best buddy said smoothly. "I do understand. You must understand that my patience is not without limit. You cannot take forever to consider my most generous offer."

"My engines won't last forever," I admitted. "I need to discuss your offer with my senior staff. Admiral, you need to consider how you can offer me a guarantee, that my ship will not be destroyed after we give Skippy to you."

"A *guarantee*?" His smooth buddy act slipped a bit. "I can guarantee that you will not get a better offer. Very well, as you are responsible for the lives of your crew, I am willing to consider offering an assurance that we will uphold our end of the agreement."

The back-and-forth negotiations went on for days, while Skippy retuned our engines to make it look like one or more of them could fail at any moment. Reichert's assurance was that, after we exceeded escape velocity by a set number, one ship would approach us, with the rest of his fleet withdrawing to beyond weapons range. It sounded like a good deal, except *Valkyrie* would still be trapped in a damping field, and Reichert could jump his entire fleet on top of us in a heartbeat. Playing nice with that asshole was making me lose my appetite, it also worked in our favor. Skippy reported the Maxohlx had dramatically slowed down their work to fit ships with antennas for the scaled-up tractor beam, and the kitties were not conducting any more tests.

Everything was going great, or as well as could be expected. At some point, Reichert's patience would run out, or he would realize our engines were not failing quite as quickly as they appeared to be. Until then, we were buying time.

If the lazy freakin' spiders did not show up soon, it would all be for nothing

For once, Skippy's timing was perfect. He did not wake me up in the middle of the night, he didn't call while I was in the shower, or doing sprints on a treadmill. A treadmill was involved, I had one hand on a railing to step on, when he spoke into my earpiece. "Uh oh, Joe. We gots trouble."

Immediately, I stepped to the side and waved to the guy behind me that the treadmill was available. Before answering, I walked out of the gym, to avoid breaking the unwritten rule of no talking on the phone while in the gym. People who do that are jerks, and unfortunately I'm kind of an expert on being that type of jerk. "What is it, Skippy?" Out in the passageway, I turned toward a bulkhead so curious people in the gym couldn't read my lips.

"We just got swept by a scanning beam. Don't worry, our shields blocked it, they didn't see anything useful."

"OK. Why is this a problem? Are they just verifying our location again?" The ships upstairs regularly pinged us with active sensor pulses, to make sure they knew exactly where we were. Maybe they were afraid we would use Skippy magic to wrap *Valkyrie* in a stealth field and slip away, while we used a dropship to project an image of our battlecruiser.

Which, by the way, is an idea we considered, until Skippy shot it down as an example of stupid monkeys not being able to understand physics. We might be able to conceal *Valkyrie* from enemy sensors, we might even be able to use a dropship as a decoy for a short time, before the dropship's powercells burned out from the enormous power drain. But, not even Skippy's awesome magnificence could make our battlecruiser move through thick air without creating ripples that spread out all the way to the top of the atmosphere. There just was not any way to push the massive bulk of our ship through the air without shoving aside a volume of air equal to the ship's size. Yes, we could minimize the disturbance by changing the shape of our energy shields to establish a laminar flow around us, all that did was minimize turbulence. The kitties could still see the wake we left as we flew, so Skippy was right to shoot down that idea.

Dropping *Valkyrie* into Snowcone was a desperation move, but better than getting blasted by a thousand ships. It was also like climbing a tree when you're being chased by bear. All the bear has to do is wait on the ground, it knows you eventually have to come down.

Except, bears can climb trees. OK, that was a bad example, but you know what I mean.

"No, the scanning beam is different from a sensor pulse. Joe, the scan was not directed at the ship, it was focused on our *wake*."

"Oh, shit."

"You see the problem?"

"Maybe. They are analyzing our engine output?"

"Correct! I would tell you to get a juicebox, but I'm kind of scared out of my mind, you know?"

"Yeah, me too. Give me the bad news."

"As requested, I have been faking engine distress. The kitties are very familiar with the characteristics of these engines, so I'm limited in the type of failure I can imitate. The sensor data they've been seeing makes sense to them, it shows our engines degrading in a pattern that is believable, and predictable."

"Right. In a few days, when our engines *don't* fail, they will know we've been scamming them."

"Ah, it's worse than that. To stall for time, I have been pretending to conduct running repairs, temporarily improving the condition of one engine at a time. I may have used that trick too many times, the kitties upstairs are suspicious. That's why they scanned our wake. Joe, they are not going to detect the mix of ions that should be left behind us, if our engine thrust chambers really were degrading."

"Shit. How long until-"

"I suspect their AIs have already informed Admiral Reichert that we have been screwing with him."

"Crap," I slumped against the bulkhead and saw people in the gym whispering to themselves. They couldn't read my lips, they didn't have to. Body language was clear. "Has Reichert tried to contact me?"

"Not yet."

"He will. OK, I need to talk with Simms about this. Crap! We needed those two days."

"Two days will not make a difference for us, Joe. The spiders won't be here fast enough to bail us out of this mess."

"Two days is two more than we have now," I said, but he was right. "Maybe I can give Reichert another bullshit excuse, I'll try to think of something."

By the time I got to my office, still dressed for the gym, Skippy had more bad news for me.

"Joe, I just intercepted a message, from one support ship to another. The first ship apparently has been ordered to go back into full-rate production on antennas, and the crew protested because they had taken some of the fabricators offline for repairs. They requested clarification of the orders. The second ship replied that the admiral's staff had determined we never intended to surrender, and he is pissed that we played him. He wants the tractor beam to be completed as soon as possible."

"Damn. Ah, we knew that would happen, when they discovered we've been faking engine distress."

"Yes, but now you can't use a bullshit story to stall for time. Reichert won't listen to you."

"You're right." I sat down heavily in the chair, grateful it was oversized for me. The height was adjusted so my feet could touch the deck, but it was still too big for a human. Sure, I could have replaced it with a normal chair from Earth as Simms suggested, or asked Skippy to fabricate something for me. I didn't want that. Each time I walked into my office and saw that chair, it reminded me that someone else had sat in that chair before me, and it reminded me that bad shit could happen when you least expect it. The previous captain of our ship certainly had not expected trouble during a routine transition through a wormhole, until we sliced his ship in two pieces. "Wait." Something about what Skippy said wasn't right. "You intercepted a message? The kitties were being super careful about COMSEC. Maybe they know we're listening, and this is a ruse."

"I don't think so," he crushed my faint hope immediately. "The support ships are clustered way out in the asteroid belt, they have been exchanging routine message traffic since they arrived. I haven't mentioned it, because they haven't said anything interesting until now. Also, those two support ships immediately got slammed by a cruiser captain for breaking security protocols, and they have gone silent. It was a screw-up, Joe, we're lucky I heard the transmissions."

"We must consider taking direct action," Smythe declared, when he and Simms were told about the suddenly-accelerated timeline.

"OK," I liked the idea of doing something, rather than sitting and waiting for doom to fall on us out of the sky. "How can we do that?"

Smythe nodded to me, and addressed a question to our AI. "Skippy, do you know their schedule for testing?"

"Not exactly. They have assembled a group of modified ships in high orbit; for reasons I don't entirely understand, their tests always involve multiples of eleven. Twenty-two heavy cruisers, equipped with tractor beam antennas, are on trajectories that will bring them into contact with the atmosphere in nineteen hours, on the other side of the planet. They are accompanied by eight battleships and two squadrons of destroyers. I do not know whether the battleships will descend with the test ships."

"What are you thinking?" I asked Smythe.

"Twenty-two ships will be down here," he noted, "even deeper in the atmosphere than we are. To drill into the ice, they will have to be traveling slowly."

"I expect they will need to hover over the site," Skippy interjected. "If I was conducting the tests, I would fire a railgun dart into the ice, then try to recover it. That is the only way to realistically simulate digging me out of the ice layer. The kitties are most likely doing something like that."

"The test ships will be vulnerable while they are hovering," I looked at Smythe. "Is that what you mean by 'direct action'?"

"Quite so," he agreed.

"We can't fly the ship to the test site," Skippy warned. "Our speed is limited when we're flying through this soup, and the enemy will select a test site on the other side of the planet from wherever we are. By the time we got close enough to launch weapons, the battleships will have moved to intercept."

"Yeah, but," I rubbed my chin while I thought. "We could disrupt the test. Reichert won't move against us until he is certain the scaled-up tractor beam works properly. The battleships can't hit us hard, not while we're down here."

"Ahhhh," Skippy let out a breath. "That explains it."

"Explains what?"

"Why the test ships are in *two* groups of eleven, on different trajectories. They expect us to make an attempt to disrupt the testing, so they will test at *two* sites. We can't disrupt *both* sites."

"Well," I spoke for all three of us. "Crap."

"Hold on," Simms leaned forward toward Skippy's avatar. "The Maxohlx aren't aware that we know about their tractor beam program, are they?"

Skippy blinked. "Not that I know of. It doesn't matter. Once those ships descend below the cloud layer, we will know they are here, and they wouldn't be doing anything to benefit *us*, so-"

"XO, that is a good point," I said to Simms. "If we react right away, they will suspect we are somehow intercepting their comms. Uh," from across the table, I saw Smythe was wearing his I-am-being-patient face. "Smythe?"

"I was not suggesting we use the ship's guns," he said with an irritated glance at Skippy, which the beer can cluelessly ignored.

"Well," Skippy plunged ahead. "We certainly can't launch *missiles* at them. The fleet upstairs would blow them out of the sky before they could do anything useful. This is a bad environment for missiles anyway. Their motors are designed for sprints, not continuous cruising. I suppose if we knew where the test sites will be, we could- No, that wouldn't work either. No, it-"

"Skippy?" I glared at him.

"Yes?"

"Shut the hell up and let Colonel Smythe talk. Uh!" I shushed him.

Smythe nodded to me. His relationship with Skippy had greatly improved over the years, he still did not tolerate nonsense the way I had to. "How many of the tractor beam ships, plus their escorts, are infected with malware?"

"Blow up those ships?" I groaned. "We can't do that. We need to keep that capability a secret, until we're ready to escape."

Smythe's right eye twitched. He was now irritated with *me*. "I was thinking, Sir, that Skippy might use his access to play havoc with their test apparatus."

"Hmm. *Hmmmmm*," Skippy pondered the idea. "Huh. Maybe I should shut up and listen more often."

"Can you do that?" Simms asked. "Affect their test results?"

"Jeez," Skippy took off his hat and pretended to scratch his head. "Maybe? I don't know. It would be *very* tricky. None of the antenna ships are infected, they were too far away, and each ship had to conduct a full diagnostic and purge before it was accepted in the conversion program. The kitties are being very careful because they know about, you know, my extreme awesomeness. I kinda, heh heh, screwed myself there, you know?"

Rolling my eyes, I asked, "Can your extreme awesomeness please answer the question?"

"I *said*, I don't know yet. That software was very specific, it evolved in one direction, with one goal: to give me access to the control AI of a ship-killer missile. And to cover its tracks at every step along the way. I *sprained my brain* to create the original fragments of that software, and embed it in the DNA of the kitties we captured. To unwind it, so it could somehow leap to one of the tractor beam ships, and mess up the test? Whew. Wow. My brain hurts, just *thinking* about thinking about it."

"Would you rather be on display in some kitty's office, as a souvenir?"

"Good point," he mumbled. "All I can promise is that I will try, OK?"

"That's all we can ask. When can you start?" He didn't answer. "Skippy?"

"Huh?"

"When can you-"

"I *am* working on it, and it would go faster if I wasn't interrupted by monkeys screeching at me every freakin' second."

Placing a finger to my lips, I gestured for Simms and Smythe to follow me into the passageway. "If this works," I pointed to our STAR leader, "I'm giving you top marks."

That amused him. "Something to post on my locker, to impress the lads?"

"I'll see what I can do. Huh."

"What?" The question was from Simms.

"Well, the era of us sneaking around is over, right? I thought open warfare would be tough, but, more straight-forward. Yet, here we are, doing sneaky shit again."

"We're outgunned literally a thousand to one, we don't have a choice," Simms noted. "Besides, sneaky shit worked pretty well for us," she added with a smile.

"Doing sneaky shit is what got us here," I said. "Bilby?"

"I'm here, Dude."

"Hey, Skippy will be distracted for a-"

"You don't have to tell *me*," the ship's AI interrupted. "He dumped the entire ship's operation on me, without any notice. This is *bogus*, man."

"You can handle it?"

"Oh, sure," he gave a dramatic sigh. "No problemo."

"Well, Joe," Skippy's avatar appeared on my desk, looking very pleased with himself. "I despaired. Truly, I thought the task was *impossible*, even for me. Yet, because I am me, I persevered. This might be one of my greatest accomplishments, although, heh heh," he shrugged in a display of false modesty, the only type of modesty he understood. "Who could say which of my accomplishments is the greatest? Anyway, I am very proud to announce that-"

"Uh huh," I mumbled through a mouthful of the sandwich I'd just bitten into. "Bilby told me what he did."

"He, d-did?" Skippy stuttered.

"Yup. He explained how you declared it *was* impossible, and you *did* give up, until he reminded you how he evolved. Then, he helped you create a model of the substrate aboard a Maxohlx destroyer, and the two of you figured out how to teach your malware to evolve itself, so it can do what we want."

"Um-"

"You're saying that is *not* true?"

"Well, I'm sure Bilby greatly exaggerated his part in-"

"He told me you would say that, too. As proof of his contribution, he created this very informative eighty-three slide PowerPoint deck," I turned my laptop around to face Skippy.

"Jeez, Joe, don't believe everything you see in a PowerPoint-"

"He included seven hundred terabytes of supporting documents, if you care to look at-"

"Well," he huffed. "That can all be faked."

"How about you simply be an adult, and credit Bilby for assisting you?"

"Ugh. Fine, if I *have* to."

"That wasn't so hard, was it?"

"I'm dying inside, Joe."

"I feel terrible about that. So, will this work?"

"Shmaybe. You really want to try this?"

"What's the downside?"

"Um, that it will only work once. The kitties will be confused about the test results the first time, and they will likely pull the ships back into orbit to analyze what went wrong. After they compare the data from individual ships to the official results, they will realize we screwed with the data. This whole scheme might buy us only one day."

"One is better than zero, Skippy. Thank you."

"No need to thank me, Joe. It's the least I can-"

"Thank Bilby for me."

"Ugh. I'm gonna *hurl*."

Skippy was right. Not about him puking, about the tests. The kitties did send two groups of eleven ships down deep, near the ice layer, and as he suggested, they fired a railgun dart into it. Not just one dart, they bombarded a section of ice with hundreds of darts, to simulate a debris field if *Valkyrie* exploded. That makes sense, we should have known they would do that. The test ships needed to locate one particular dart, then drill down to it, and pull it up with the tractor beam. Neither of the tests were successful, they were halted after about three hours, and the test ships climbed back into orbit. To sell the story that we didn't know what was happening, I called Reichert, demanding to know what he was doing with all those ships. He ignored me, as I expected.

Our effort to delay the test program worked, for a while. Thirty-one hours after the first test, the same ships descended again for a second set of drilling and recovery. That time they were successful. We knew that, because those ships transmitted their results in the clear. They wanted us to know what they were doing, and how screwed we were.

Shit.

The kitties only needed to wait until they had all eighty-eight ships converted with tractor beam antennas, then Reichert could blast us with the massed fire of a thousand ships.

He was calling my bluff, and the clock was running out on us. The spiders would not arrive in time to save us.

CHAPTER THIRTY SEVEN

"Hey, Joe." Skippy waited until I got out of the shower before he called me. Not only out of the shower, I was toweled off, had pants on and was buttoning my uniform top. It wasn't like him to be so polite, that got me worried even before he said anything else.

"Hey, Skippy."

"We need to talk."

Oh, shit. It's not good when your significant other says that. When a usually-snarky Elder AI says it, it has to be all kinds of bad. "Let me get this shirt done," I hurriedly fastened the last couple buttons. "OK," stepping out in my cabin, I walked over to the couch and sat down, leaning forward to where his avatar appeared on a sort of coffee table. "What's up?"

"I don't see a way out of this. The fabricators on the support ships are working at full capacity, they will have the last of eighty-eight ships outfitted with antennas in three days. They are converting ninety-five ships, I guess in case they have a problem, or we manage to shoot a couple of them. The math is not in our favor." He paused, because usually I would ask a stupid question or make some inane comment. All I did was nod for him to continue. "Any way you look at it, the kitties will be ready to dig me out of the ice, before the spiders could get here in sufficient numbers to force the Maxohlx to back down. That is not good for you."

"I know that. We discussed this. I am *bluffing* down here. If *Valkyrie* is destroyed, I want you to cooperate with the Maxohlx. Not cooperate, just don't let those timers expire, and do what you can to protect Earth. Don't let anyone have access to Avalon or Jiayuguan."

"I will do what you ask, but maybe there is an alternative?"

"Like what?"

"Surrender, Joe. Take their offer."

"Skippy, you know that as soon as you are aboard one of their ships, they're going to fire every gun they have at *Valkyrie*. Any promise they make is bullshit, we can't trust them. They will never let us jump away from here."

"Ah, damn it! This *sucks*!"

"I'm not thrilled about it either."

"What are you doing about it?"

It surprised me that Skippy asked that question. "I don't know there is anything I *can* do."

"Bullshit. You always dream up some crazy idea to save our asses."

"I did. Being down here, where the kitties can't risk shooting at us, *is* my plan."

"It's kind of a lame plan, Joe."

"It's the best I could think of. Hey, *you* had the crazy idea to get us out of the ambush, with your momentum-erasing thing."

"Ugh. Don't remind me, I'm still recovering from *that* bad idea."

We talked for a while, both of us getting more depressed, and not accomplishing anything. "So, what will you do, Joe?" He asked. "When the kitties have their tractor beam ready, and there's no reason they can't shoot at us?"

"I'm going to tell Reichert that we surrender."

"Um, you just told me that was a bad-"

"I'm going to *tell* him that we surrender, I'm not going to *do* it. We'll climb up into orbit and hit them with every weapon we have. If we're going down, we'll do it with our boots on."

"OK! That's better. What do you want me to do?"

"Before we open fire, we will launch you away in a stealthed missile, hopefully you can get away with all the high-energy stuff flying around."

"*Leave* you? Just run away? I am not-"

"You will be *helping* us. As long as the kitties think you're aboard *Valkyrie*, they won't hit us with their big guns, while we will be free to hit them as hard as we can. When we're gone," I felt a lump in my throat. "You contact Reichert, tell him who and where you are."

He folded his arms across his chest. "This plan seriously *sucks*, Joe."

"Think about it this way: you will have a great view of the fireworks. Listen, I can't keep you aboard the ship during the fight. You might fall into the planet, and we don't know for sure that tractor beam thing will work."

"Joe," he sighed. "There's no way out. This feels like the ending of *Butch Cassidy and the Sundance Kid*."

"Uh, what?"

"O.M.G. You never saw that movie?"

"I never heard of it."

"You *cannot* die without having watched a classic like that."

"OK, maybe later, if-"

"What are you doing right now? Other than nothing useful."

I didn't have a good answer for him, so we announced an impromptu movie matinee in an empty cargo bay, most of the off-duty crew was there to watch with me. Before the movie started, Skippy whispered to me that he changed his mind, because Butch and Sundance apparently die at the end. So, he played another movie that had the same actors, a comedy-caper called *The Sting*. I never heard of that one either, which is too bad, it is a good movie.

Crap. I wish I knew how the movie ends. Just as the FBI busts in to arrest everyone, Skippy paused the movie, to loud complaints from the audience.

"Sorry, Joe," he said. "The spiders are here."

"Talk to me, Skippy," I ordered as I strapped into the command chair. We had moved our captured frigate behind and slightly below us. Skippy had complete control of that little ship, and ever since we took it, he had bots frantically stripping the interior of everything we didn't need. Out the airlocks went anything that was not required because the ship no longer had a crew, including life-support equipment, seats, consoles, cabin furnishings, all that. He even ripped out nonstructural bulkheads, all water storage and pipes, even power conduits that were not connected to anything that ship needed for our purposes. Excess fuel was vented, along with several layers of reactor shielding. Stealth-field generators were torn out. Probes and any missiles other than ship-killers were launched unpowered, to fall tumbling nose over tail to sink deep into the ice below us. We kept all eight dropships from the frigate; Skippy had expertly flown those spacecraft from the frigate to *Valkyrie* while the two starships came to a stop in midair, hovering with engines and thrusters straining while the dropships transferred. The result of all Skippy's work was that the frigate's mass had decreased by twenty-three percent. It was lighter and could accelerate faster, and we needed all of that speed, if we were to have a chance to escape.

"Nineteen spider ships are up there," Skippy reported. "Nineteen that I know of, if others jumped in farther away, we won't know until those photons reach us. This is interesting: the spider ships jumped in without engaging their gamma-ray suppression field, they want the Maxohlx to know they are here."

"What are those ships *doing*?" The big holographic display showed the planet where we were taking shelter, and space around it to a distance of five lightseconds. The spider squadron was about two and a half lightseconds away from our position. Their ships were in three triangle formations, with the lead ships a quarter lightsecond closer to the planet. Maxohlx ships were moving to envelop their ancient enemy, and a yellow glow throughout the area was the display's way of indicating there were powerful damping fields being projected by both sides. The Rindhalu had jumped in to surprise their rivals, but they would not be jumping away. Nineteen ships were too few to challenge the Maxohlx Eighth Fleet, even with the technology advantage of the Rindhalu. I could not imagine what the spider commander hoped to accomplish, other than suicide.

"Um, right now, they are talking to each other. The spiders and kitties, I mean."

"What are they saying? Can you decrypt the-"

"No encryption, Joe. They are both transmitting in the clear. Um, wow. Well, *this* is not good news."

"Why? What are they-"

"They are negotiating. To share custody of *me*."

"Holy sh- How the hell-"

"The spiders are saying they will not allow the Maxohlx to get control of me, but they are willing to discuss an arrangement, where they both can assure I will disable the Elder weapons currently possessed by humans. Huh. *As if*. They should have asked *me* if I'm willing to-"

"*Damn* it! We can't have our enemies working together against us!" For the Rindhalu and Maxohlx to join forces was my worst nightmare. I also didn't believe it would ever happen. Those two species had too much history to trust each other now, especially about something that could alter the balance of power in the galaxy. I had been wrong about that. What else was I wrong about? "Screw this. Skippy, it looks like the kitties have," I zoomed in the display and squinted at it. "Fourteen ships enveloping those three lead spider ships?"

"Correct."

"Great. Of those fourteen, how many are infected with malware, and in weapons range of the spiders?"

"*Oooooh*," he caught onto my intentions. "Three."

"On my signal, blow all three, you got that?"

"Affirmative."

"Pilot, prepare to climb us out of here. XO, battle stations, and get everyone strapped in."

It took only seconds for Bilby to indicate the ship was set for battle conditions. The crew could get themselves ready while we flew, it would be a long climb back into orbit. "Skippy, nuke those ships."

Above us, three bright flowers appeared where Maxohlx warships had been. If humans had been involved, there would have been a delay while our slow monkey brains processed versions of 'WTF?'. Because the Rindhalu are a very advanced species and their AIs were blindingly fast, the spiders instantly realized four facts:

-They had not caused the enemy ships to explode.

-The Maxohlx would not believe any claims of innocence.

-The time for negotiations was *over*.

-Whoever shot first would have an advantage.

So, even as a wavefront of high-energy debris was washing over the Rindhalu ships, they fired on the Maxohlx. Five seconds later, another thirty spider ships jumped in to join the fight. So much energy was flying around that our sensors would have difficulty following the action, if Skippy had not directly fed data to our displays.

"Chen!" I ordered, after a few seconds delay to make it look like we had been surprised by the sudden outbreak of shooting. "Get us out of here." The deck tilted before the artificial gravity system could compensate, our mighty battlecruiser standing on its tail and surging for altitude. Behind us, the little frigate followed like a puppy, burning its main engines hard. The frigate's nose was tucked in right behind *Valkyrie*, drafting like on a NASCAR super speedway. The normal background rumbling sound of our engines became a dull roar, accompanied by a faint, high-pitched shriek of dense air whistling past our un-aerodynamic hull. Note to self: starships are designed to fly in *space*, not through air.

For a spacecraft to climb into orbit, it goes up but more importantly, it goes fast. Achieving a stable orbit is all about gaining enough speed so the planet's gravity can't drag your ship back down.

We were not doing that.

Valkyrie was flying straight up, and keeping speed below the velocity required to achieve orbit. If the ship got hit and the engines died, our momentum would keep us going vertically for a few minutes, then we would fall straight back down. If that sounds dangerous, it is. It is also less dangerous than the Maxohlx blockade fleet shooting at us. We knew that the kitties had strict orders not to shoot at us until after we reached escape velocity, so we were not doing that. Going straight up, essentially hovering on thrust all the way up to jump altitude, was shockingly inefficient and wasted enormous quantities of fuel, and I did not care. What I did care about, was getting high enough so the planet's gravity well did not prevent us from forming a jump wormhole. Yes, the entire area was saturated with powerful, overlapping damping fields and we couldn't do anything about that. So, what was the point of climbing away from the planet? I'll explain that later. We had enough trouble to-

"Uh," Skippy waved for my attention. "Hey, Joe, the spiders are calling. They want to talk to *you*."

Flipping a middle finger at the display, I shook my head. "I'm not in the mood to listen to a bunch of threats right now."

"No threats, Joe. This is, *interesting*. Can I play the message?"

Simms and I exchanged a glance. "Sure," I said.

"This is a communication for the human called 'Bishop'. If you have a method for escaping from this place, we suggest you do it, *now*."

"Uh, well, shit. That's surprising."

"Not really, Sir," Simms said, giving me another surprise. "This is what I expected, when we saw the spiders showed up here with so few ships."

I stared at my executive officer. "Wha-*what*?"

"They don't have a prayer of capturing Skippy, and they can't trust the kitties to share custody. Their objective here is to make sure the Maxohlx do not get Skippy."

"Huh." That totally made sense, after she explained it. "*When* were you going to tell me?"

She didn't reply. That's not true. Her reply was a combination raised-eyebrow and head tilt. I got it. She meant that I was the *last* person who should complain about people keeping secrets.

"OK," I looked away from the accusing eyebrow, uncomfortable because I knew she was right. "Skippy, connect me with, who am I talking with?"

"The speaker did not identify themselves. It could be an AI."

"Whatever." Holding down the transmit button I cleared my throat and said, "This is Bishop. We are preparing to jump from this star system."

There was a delay caused by speed-of-light, then, "Do you require assistance?"

"We can handle most of the blockade ships in low orbit. It would help if you could keep the others off our backs."

Another delay, longer than just required by photons flying back and forth. "We count one hundred and thirty-four ships in the blockade force."

"Uh huh, well, we haven't shown the full capability of this ship. We have a very powerful weapon that is unknown to you," I lied.

"We will be eager to witness a demonstration of your power." Another pause. "You humans are curious creatures. You are too young to be entrusted with such power."

"Yeah, that's what my parents say."

"You are a threat to the entire galaxy, to *us*. We cannot allow you to possess such power. However, at this moment, our interests are aligned." Another pause. "Good luck to you and your crew."

"Thanks."

"Bishop. The next time we meet, we will not be so cooperative."

"The next time we meet, *you* had better stay out of our way." I clicked the transmit button off.

Man, once the battle around the planet began, it was *on*. Apparently, neither apex species trained their military in *de*-escalation. The spider ships took a pounding from the overwhelming number of Maxohlx warships shooting at them, but the battle wasn't as one-sided as you might expect. The Rindhalu ships were faster and had more powerful shields and weapons, and they projected a sort of anti-damping field around them that prevented enemy ships from jumping in on top of them. Maxohlx ships seeking to join the fight had to jump in beyond their weapons range, then fly through space the long way. While they were doing that, the spider ships were dodging and turning and dashing in and out of enemy formations and generally driving the kitties crazy. It was clear to me, just from watching the first minute of the battle, that the spiders had a significant technology advantage. It was also clear that their strategy was not to engage in an all-out fight; instead they were gradually luring the main force of Maxohlx ships away from the planet. That left a powerful blockade force above us, but that was hundreds rather than thousands of ships for us to deal with.

The Rindhalu strategy was working, they were also running out of time. Their ships were becoming disabled one by one, and a damaged ship was attacked by dozens of the enemy, like sharks in a feeding frenzy. Whatever we were going to do, we had to do it fast.

The ships of the blockade force above were doing their best to keep pace with us. We had caught them off guard when we zoomed straight up, the blockade ships first had to cancel their forward velocity and come almost to a stop in orbit, dancing on their tails for optimal balance. The bigger ships, like the battleships that made up a quarter of the blockade ships, could not manage the maneuver and were frantically trying to reposition ahead of us, farther from the planet. They were taking up position above us, below what they guessed our jump altitude was. If they couldn't shoot at us, they planned to stop us from jumping, even if that meant risking a collision.

It was kind of flattering that they thought our jump drive could operate at such a low altitude. Five battleships were crisscrossing above us, daring us to fly between them. It would be dangerous to run that gauntlet, any miscalculation by either side would have thousands of tons of armor-plated starships trading paint, and that could be fatal.

Valkyrie burst out of the clouds, only increasingly thin air and the vacuum of space were above us. Other than, you know, more than a hundred powerful and blood-thirsty senior-species starships.

None of the enemy ships were shooting at us, that could change in a hurry. "Skippy, are you ready to do your thing?"

"I was born ready, Joe."

"Weps," I said to the weapons officer behind me. "Fire at will."

Our disruptor cannons lanced out, firing six beams at one battleship. There was nothing especially powerful about those beams, the disruptors were actually poorly tuned to create chaotic, slightly-incoherent beams, and the cannon barrels had been lined with contaminants so the beams fluctuated and sparkled in odd segments of the spectrum. When the beams struck the energy shields of the target battleship, they were focused with extreme precision, concentrated within two nanometers. The shield there flared as it struggled to deflect the high-energy particles, and a vibration traveled along the shield to the generators buried under the thick armor plating of the massive warship. The streams of particles could not by themselves cause significant damage, but they were tuned to pulse in a specific sequence that would be detected by the target ship's sensors. That odd sequence was noted by the ship's control AI, and by another AI inside a missile that was resting in a magazine at the core of the ship.

Todd is a stupid name, the missile thought to itself. How come Skippy calls himself The Magnificent, while I'm stuck with just 'Todd'? Why can't I be Todd the Fierce, or something really cool like Todd the Destroyer. Oooh, the missile's AI had a brilliant inspiration. Why, I don't need a name at all. I could be referred to as He Who Brings Doom.
No.
Bringer Of Doom.
Yeah. *That* is cool.
Before the signal was received, the AI was considering that it did not even need Skippy at all, that Skippy was an *asshole*.
The signal interrupted its thoughts.
Hmm.
You who else are assholes, it asked itself?
The Maxohlx.
So, fuck 'em.

The missile's warhead gleefully exploded at maximum yield, wide-dispersal mode. Ordinarily, the warheads of Maxohlx missiles were not vulnerable to 'cooking off', being equipped with a variety of safeguards to prevent accidental detonation. All the safety features built into their warhead triggers were rendered useless when they melted at several million degrees, and the explosive material of the warhead itself was exposed to hellish radiation.
The entire magazine, all sixty-eight missiles, erupted.

"Scratch one battlewagon," Skippy muttered, feeding targeting data to our weapons consoles. In the main display, ships of the blockading squadron were exploding as our harmless maser beams splashed against their energy shields. Not quite harmlessly, as each beam caused a cascade of events that resulted in a missile warhead to detonate. Boom, boom, boom, bright flowers of destruction bloomed silently in orbit, as ships cracked apart from internal explosions. "Skippy," I asked, my stomach in knots. "The kitties have no idea why those ships are blowing up?"
"Nope," he giggled. "I am monitoring message traffic between the surviving ships. The messages are mostly variations on a theme of '*OH SHIT*', but there is also speculation that we have a super weapon they can't understand. There is even

talk that it might be the same type of weapon we used to destroy that underground Thuranin facility on Slithin, because they still have *no* freakin' clue how we did that either. Oooh, wow," he highlighted the debris cloud from an exploding battlecruiser. "That one looks like a *bunny*."

The glowing debris cloud from that ship did indeed look like a bunny rabbit, secondary explosions had sent two streams of hot particles soaring outward in long ovals like ears. "Yeah," I agreed. "Oh, look at that one!" A battleship had torn apart, its forward hull flying outward at high speed, spinning to crash into a cruiser. That unlucky ship cracked in half, sending sparks of fire outward from the jagged sections of hull. Then the aft engineering section of the cruiser exploded, adding to the chaos.

"Well, you don't see a two-for-one shot every day," Skippy mused.

"No, you do not." Did I feel bad, that we were treating the destruction of an enemy fleet as a spectator sport? No, I did not. Not even one little bit. Sure, the crews of those ships were just doing their jobs, and they had to be terrified as they watched their fellow ships exploding from a force they did not understand. The survivors knew their deaths would be coming soon, and there wasn't anything they could do about it. Ships of the blockade squadron were turning to run, we kept shooting. That was fair. Those ships could turn around to attack us at any second, and we needed to do more than just escape. We had to sow *fear* into the hearts of the enemy. Fear and doubt, so they would hesitate to mess with us in the future. We needed their rotten kitty hearts to tremble when they thought of us, and the unknown weapons we possessed.

The fact that we did not actually have any such weapons was just a *delicious* bonus.

It took less than three minutes for us to devastate the blockade squadron in low orbit. We could not blow up every ship, not all of them were infected with malware. But by the time we ceased fire, the remaining ships had turned tail and ignited their boosters, running away as fast as they could. Ships at a greater distance were racing in, though it seemed to me those ships were not moving *quite* as fast as they could, and I considered their lack of enthusiasm to be good judgment rather than cowardice. Hell, I certainly wouldn't want to fly my ship into a deathtrap.

As the last few blockade ships exploded, Skippy took off his oversized admiral's hat and placed it over his heart, or where his heart would be if his torso was not a beer can. His tribute to a fallen enemy lasted only a few seconds, then he jammed the hat back on his head and turned to look at me. "You know, Joe, the light from those exploding ships is like fireflies on a warm summer night."

"Huh. You're right." That thought brought back pleasant childhood memories. "Skippy, you just destroyed more than a hundred enemy ships, without us actually firing a shot. *Thank you.*"

"Oh, no need to thank me, Joe." He turned his attention back to the fading nebulas of debris on the display. "This stuff is what makes my job so rewarding. It's the *little* things in life that make it really special, you know?"

Simms and I shared a look, and to our credit, neither of us snorted or rolled our eyes. Only Skippy could think the destruction of an enemy task force was a 'little thing'.

"It sure does, Skippy. OK, now that you've plowed the road for us, it's time to get the hell out of here. Pilot, ignite the boosters." *Valkyrie's* boosters did not actually ignite, we didn't fire them up with a match, that was just the term we agreed to use. "Hold it to fifty-three percent throttle, we can't lose our speedboat."

As before, we *felt* it when the boosters fired, the artificial gravity field adjusted slower than the acceleration built up. There was a roaring sound, this time entirely transmitted through the ship's structure because the ship had climbed above the upper edge of the planet's atmosphere. Behind us, the frigate's own engines were burning themselves out to keep pace with us. The main display had four items of interest. A dotted line in front of us, showing the minimum altitude for us to attempt a jump. Symbols representing enemy ships within weapons range, there were only three of those and they were racing away from us at full power. Fluctuating numbers that represented the remaining life of the frigate's engines. And a yellow shading covering the whole area, showing the strength of the damping fields around us. It was bright yellow farther away, but still plenty strong at our location and at the jump altitude line.

The Maxohlx tried to contact us, I ignored them. The Rindhalu were too busy to talk, and they had said all they needed to anyway. The only talking that mattered now was in the language of math, and I suck at math. We needed to reach jump altitude before the kitties could interfere; already ships at the edge of the display were slowing to turn around, and one ship launched a volley of missiles at us. "Weps," I held up a hand to the officer at the weapons console behind me. "Knock those birds out of the sky, please."

This time, our big maser cannons fired for real, properly tuned and pumping out terawatts of coherent photons. The beams were set to fan out in a broad cone, a setting for frying highly-maneuverable stealth missiles. Most of the deadly weapons exploded at a safe distance from the ship, our point-defense cannons blasted the few that got through the main barrage. More missiles raced in from the edge of the display, even my slow monkey brain could see we would reach the jump line before the missiles arrived. As we came within two hundred kilometers of jump altitude, still moving straight up from the planet and at less than escape velocity, I ordered, "Pilot, kill the booster. Skippy, slingshot the speedboat around us."

"Aye aye, cap'n," he replied with a smirk, but I could see he was enjoying himself.

The sudden loss of acceleration threw me forward in my chair, on the display the frigate swerved to surge past *Valkyrie*, reaching the jump line two seconds before we did. The Maxohlx didn't know why we brought their frigate with us but they are *smart* kitties, they knew it couldn't be anything good for them. Lances of maser and particle cannon fire struck the frigate, making its shields flare and weaken.

Too little, too late.

"Ready, Skippy?"

"You realize this is only a theory, right? No one has ever done anything like this before."

"Yeah, but either way, it's a win-win for us monkeys."

He stared at me. "How do you figure *that*?"

"If this works, you can add a plaque about it to the lobby of your Awesomeness Hall of Fame."

"And if it *doesn't* work?"

"Then you will blame yourself for failure until the end of time."

"Shit. Well, *this* sucks."

"Do it anyway."

"OK," he grumbled. "Three, two, one, holdmybeer."

Ahead of us, the frigate jumped. Or tried to jump, it couldn't actually form a stable jump wormhole because of the damping fields around us. What actually happened, too fast for anyone but Skippy or Bilby to see, was the frigate's jump drive began to form a jump wormhole.

Then the frigate's overstressed jump drive exploded.

Valkyrie's forward shields shunted aside burning debris and radiation, still the nose armor was pitted and scarred from chunks of frigate impacting at high speed.

The frigate's jump attempt was a failure.

Skippy was still experiencing a temporary awesomeness deficit.

Ships all around us were still projecting damping fields.

But, the collapse of the frigate's jump wormhole created a short-lived, very local chaotic resonance right in front of us. *Valkyrie* flew into that already-fading bubble, where the damping fields were disrupted. That disruption was not enough for our jump drive to form a stable wormhole.

Not by itself.

Under the direction of Skippy-the-still-very-much-Magnificent, our individual drive coils were retuned in real-time to adjust for the topography of spacetime around us, looking for tiny areas where spacetime was especially flat. Skippy found them. Our coils surged with power, creating a stable jump wormhole where none could exist.

Well, sort of stable.

The forward section of our battlecruiser slipped into the wormhole's event horizon picoseconds before the wormhole destabilized, an event that caused the rear section of the ship to fall outside the twisted spacetime of the wormhole. We were saved because when the nose of the ship entered the wormhole, it was connected to the rest of the ship, and the nose emerged that way on the other end.

Let's not mention how we all felt when the ship came through the jump. What matters is that we survived, that Skippy was still conscious, and that I was grateful I hadn't eaten biscuits and gravy for breakfast like Simms had.

OK, enough about that.

"Skip- Urp." I had to reach for the barf bag again. "Sitrep."

"Whew. Hey, let's not do *that* again, shall we?"

"That would be great, yeah. Sitrep."

"Um, it looks like we *broke* several of the ship's frames. Best to be gentle with maneuvers, until my bots can repair the damage. We blew forty percent of the drive coils, the good news there is most of them can be salvaged and re-initialized."

The main display showed the familiar symbol of *Valkyrie* in the center, and nothing else. Like, nothing. "Where are we?"

"The navigation system is confused, give me a moment to triangulate our position. Yup, we jumped twenty-six lighthours. Huh. Wow, we were *way* off. Ah, we survived, let's focus on that."

He was right, we were far from where we expected to be. The point we aimed for was a tenth of a lightyear. "Can we jump again?"

"That depends. Can you give me a couple hours to check and realign the drive?"

"*That* depends. Are you detecting any ships out there?"

"Um," before he responded, the display lit up with two new symbols. Maxohlx ships, one four lighthours away, one less than three. "Just those two."

"If we jump *now*, how far can we travel?"

"Hmm. To be safe, and we *should* be safe, keep it under a quarter lightyear."

"OK, take a few minutes to work on the drive."

"It will take more than a few minutes, Joe."

I ordered a relief crew brought onto to the bridge, the pilots especially needed a break after our nerve-wracking climb away from the planet. Our next move would be the simple routine of jump, recharge and jump again, before we went through the nearest wormhole. We had to get there before the Maxohlx flew ahead to blockade the damned thing, they certainly had enough ships to do that.

We were in a race against time, and there wasn't anything I could do other than wait for Skippy to finish, doing whatever the hell he was doing.

Major Shepard stepped off the bridge, reluctant to give up the controls but knowing a fresh pilot would be safer for the ship. The climb out of the toxic soup of the planet's atmosphere had been tiring. He needed coffee, and he could get it in the pilot's ready room.

In the passageway, he passed Colonel Smythe, who was stretching his new legs that were stiff from sitting too long. Shepard nodded to the STAR leader, then turned. "Sir?"

"Shepard?"

The pilot looked through the doorway into the bridge. "An hour ago, I thought we were *dead*. I thought we were dead ever since we jumped into that ambush. It is a miracle that we're still alive, but, everyone's acting like this is no big deal."

"Yes. Major, you're forgetting two facts."

"Sir?"

"We are the Merry Band of Pirates," Smythe declared, his one side of his mouth curling up in a grin. "And," he pulled out a zPhone to display the time and date. "This is *Tuesday*."

Skippy fussed with the drive for half an hour, while the sick feeling in my stomach changed from being caused by the bad jump, to being caused by worry about enemy ships jumping in on top of us. Finally, I couldn't take it anymore. The crew knew I was nervous, I was tapping a foot on the floor and generally being irritable with everyone. "All right, Skippy, that's *enough*."

"But-"

"No, damn it," pounding a fist on the armrest, I was losing my cool. "We barely got out of there. Can we jump now?"

"Well, it-"

"Yes or no?"

"Yes," he sniffed, as pissed at me as I was with him. "Go ahead, the jump is programmed in the navigation system."

"Pilot- Wait." A little voice in my head warned me I was acting like a child, not a starship captain. "Bilby, give me your assessment. Should we jump now?"

"Wow, that's like, more of a philosophical question, Dude."

He was not helping me. Clenching a fist, I spoke slowly. "I am asking whether it is safe to jump."

"A jump does unnatural things with spacetime, man. There is *always* danger."

"Compared to the danger of the Maxohlx finding us while we're sitting here?"

"Oh. In that case, we should skedaddle, you know?"

We jumped, three lightdays short of a quarter lightyear. That was the best Skippy could manage, until he took the drive offline to realign the coils.

"OK, Joe. *Please* listen to me," Skippy pleaded. "If you can wait seven, maybe eight hours, I can fix the drive so we can resume something like a normal jump pattern."

Before I spoke, I let out a long breath, a breath I'd been holding since we jumped into the ambush. "Take all the time you need to do the job right, Skippy. Sorry I snapped at you."

"No problem, Joe. We're all under pressure."

"XO, secure from battle stations. Bring a relief crew onto the bridge, I want everyone to take six hours, that includes you. I'll handle the bridge."

Chen turned in the pilot couch. "When can we watch the rest of that movie, Sir?"

"Eh?" I said like an old man. "Uh, you really enjoyed it?"

"It was good," she shrugged. "But also, it was kind of a good-luck charm for us. We should finish it, before our luck runs out."

"Good point," I laughed.

Simms lingered after the relief crew took their stations, she jerked her head toward the door. I followed her into the passageway. "Where are we going from here?"

"The nearest wormhole, if the kitties haven't blockaded it," I said sourly. We did not need any more problems, yet the Universe never missed a golden opportunity to screw with me. It would have been nice for Skippy to screw with the closest wormhole, connect it directly to Backstop, but he couldn't do that. Even if he could, we shouldn't do that. He couldn't do it, because the wormhole network was restricting his actions, after he disrupted vast sections of the network by moving and awakening dormant wormholes. We shouldn't screw with that wormhole anyway, in case the Maxohlx were watching it closely. We did not want to risk them discovering how we were able to manipulate Elder wormholes.

She nodded. "From there? Try the original rendezvous point?"

I shook my head. "No. My guess is, that second batch of ships are clouds of debris now. We should alert the beetles, so they can pick up any survivors. Then, we're going straight to Earth."

"Earth?" She was surprised. "Almost all of our combat power is at Jiayuguan."

"True, but, a handful of upgraded beetle ships can't do much against the Maxohlx. XO, I'm worried about what's happened to Earth while we've been away."

"To Earth? The Maxohlx had a significant part of their fleet pinning us down back there."

"They did. They also have *thousands* of other ships. While we were at Snowcone, the kitties had us out of action, they knew we couldn't interfere, whether they captured Skippy or not. If they were going to strike our homeworld, that was the perfect opportunity." I couldn't read her expression. "You disagree?"

"No. I was thinking the same thing."

"Why didn't-"

"*Someone* around here needs to be an optimist."

CHAPTER THIRTY EIGHT

We timed our passage through the Backstop wormhole, to zip through the event horizon just before it closed. On the other side, we jumped as soon as our drive could form a stable field, jumping almost blindly. It was a bad jump, giving me a headache like an icepick stabbed through my temple. Then we did it again, in case anyone was able to follow our first jump. When we took the drive offline to recover, *Valkyrie* was a third of a lightyear on the other side of Earth's Sun. Seven very tense hours later, we jumped again, this time with an actual destination programmed into the navigation system.

Our emergence was nine kilometers off target, a fact that irritated Bilby and had Skippy concerned. "Darn it," Lord Admiral Skippy had his tiny hands on his hips. "That should not have happened. Something is wrong with the primary motivator, it's not feeding power reliably to the drive regulat-"

"I'm sure you'll handle the technical details far better than we poor monkeys could understand," I said to cut off his technobabble. "Can we jump again?"

"Sure, if you don't care about accuracy."

"Work on it, please. In the meantime, what is going on back home?" We had jumped in above, or you could say below, the plane of Earth's orbit, roughly one lighthour from the Sun.

"Working on that, too," Skippy snapped, irritated. "Let's see, it looks like- Ooh. Wow. Um, gosh, *that's* not good. Wow. Oh. My. G- Shit. Holeee- Whoooooo that is *all kinds* of bad."

"Skippy," I balled up my fists, keeping them in my lap. "What the f-" Remembering that the ship's crew did not yet have years of experience with my colorful language, I shot a guilty glance at my XO. "BLUF it for us. The short version, please."

"Right. Got it. OK, so there are four Maxohlx cruisers orbiting Jupiter, and-"

"Shit! Could they have seen our inbound jump?"

"Meh, probably not. Our gamma ray burst was directed seventy-four degrees away from them, and at least that part of the drive is working properly. Also, Jupiter has a strong magnetic field and those ships are in a low orbit, the field will partially blind their sensors. Joe, those four cruisers are *not* the problem."

"They're not?"

"No. There were several dozen Maxohlx ships at Jupiter recently. The problem is what *those* ships did."

Damn, I wanted to choke him. "Explain. The problem. *Please.*"

"Bottom line is, the kitties dropped mass drivers into Jupiter's atmosphere. They filtered out the lighter elements and pumped a stream of gas clouds away from Jupiter. Joe, those gas clouds are going to settle into a crescent shape, between Earth and the Sun. It will block a portion of sunlight from reaching your world."

"A portion? Like how much?"

"Like, enough to tip Earth into a mini ice age over the next three, possibly four hundred years. The effects will become noticeable within two years, severe within eight years. I am afraid your world will not experience a true summer for a very long time."

The crew were all looking at me, stunned. Whatever each of them expected when we returned to our home star system, this was not it. "Oh my-" I clamped my mouth shut. To the mostly new crew, I was not just Joe Bishop, I was the legendary JOE BISHOP, all caps. They expected me to solve any problem. My solution might be stupid and cause more trouble in the long run, but the immediate problem would go away. "No summer? How cold will it get?"

"Cold enough for a permanent snowpack to establish over Canada and the northern United States. There will be similar impacts to Eurasia and South America. The real problem will be a lack of food, productive farming areas will soon be too cold to grow crops. Billions could die of starvation. Billions more could die, if the famine and forced migrations spark a war. If the monkeys down there start whacking each other with sticks, it could get really ugly."

Crap. This was the worst-case scenario I had feared; the enemy had hit us hard, but not hard enough for me to trigger our Elder weapons. Billions on Earth might die, but billions of people would survive. Unless I triggered the Elder weapons, then *everyone* would die.

I couldn't do that. Wouldn't do that, and the Maxohlx *knew* I wouldn't pull the trigger. We had to find another way to fight the problem.

So the question was, how to fight a cloud of gas? In space? "Skippy?" I asked. "What can we do about it?"

"There are many things we could do, given enough time and a lot more resources than your people have available. I suspect that, whatever we try to do, the Maxohlx will try to stop us. If we somehow get rid of the cloud, the kitties could turn on the mass drivers again, and create a new cloud."

"Then we will destroy those mass drivers right now," I smacked a fist on my knee.

"*That* we can do, if you think it is worth the effort," Skippy warned. "The Maxohlx would likely just send more ships to drop more drivers. We can destroy the mass drivers from orbit, but we will need to take out those four cruisers first. Plus, I must warn you, any stealthed Maxohlx ships that are in the area could jump in on top of us."

"No," I groaned a bit too loudly. "Damn it, they'll be expecting us to attack the mass drivers. They will be *hoping* we do that, so they can try to trap us again. No, we are *not* doing that."

"Sir?" Simms asked. "What *are* we doing?"

In the past, I would have been nervous enough to fill the awkward silence by saying something, anything. Huh. Maybe I had gained confidence along with experience. Rather than blabbering meaningless words, I stopped to think. To show the crew that I was considering the situation, not paralyzed by fear, I did the Jim Kirk Lean. Elbow on the command chair's armrest, chin on my fist, staring at the display through narrowed eyes.

Great. I had mastered the mannerisms of a fictional starship captain.

Now, what the hell were we going to do? What *could* we do?

Whatever we did, we needed a lot of ships, to sweep up the cloud, or haul in raw materials to build whatever crazy mechanism was needed to prevent our homeworld from freezing. Plus, we needed even *more* ships, to prevent the Maxohlx from interfering with, whatever we had to do.

That was a *lot* of ships.

Way more ships than the handful of obsolete Jeraptha hulls we had parked out at FOB Jaguar.

I knew what we needed. That told me what we had to do next.

"XO, we are *acting*. We are not reacting to the enemy, not any more. They want a fight? We'll bring it to them. On our terms."

"Sir," Simms pointed toward the display. "How will hitting the enemy help Earth?"

"Hitting them won't help directly. But it will bring us what we need to save Earth from freezing."

"What is that, Joe?" Skippy asked.

"*Allies*. We need more ships, more resources? Fine. We'll bring them here."

"Sir," Simms had a pained look. "We tried to secure alliances with the Ruhar, the Jeraptha. They refused-"

"They refused, because we tried doing things the way UNEF Command wanted. Now," I looked around the bridge, seeing fear and skepticism on every face. They had no real confidence that I could solve this problem. "Now, we're doing it the way Perkins wants. XO, send a signal to UNEF Command that we are, uh, doing whatever we can. Be vague about it, we have to assume the enemy is listening, they can't know our plan. Just, uh, let UNEF know we are aware of the situation. And that I do *not* intend to trigger the Elder weapons," I added for clarity.

"*I* don't know our plan," she protested.

"You'll know as soon as we jump away. Everyone, I'm sorry. I would like to let you contact your families on Earth, but that is too great a security risk right now. We will have to settle for *saving* them."

If I was confident, I was the only person on the bridge who felt that way. And I was faking it. "XO?"

She looked up from her tablet. "I sent a brief and very vague message, Sir."

"Outstanding. Don't worry, we'll be back, and we'll bring the cavalry."

"If you say so, Sir."

"Pilot, jump option Foxtrot."

Valkyrie jumped, out toward the next emergence point of the Backstop wormhole. Twenty-nine minutes later, we slipped through the event horizon and were instantly lightyears away. As before, we jumped as soon as possible. "Skippy, are we clear?"

"Yes. No sign of pursuit, or that anyone even detected us."

"Great," I stifled an instinct to shudder. "Chen, set a course for FOB Jaguar."

"The Jeraptha ships there, they are the cavalry?" Simms asked, disappointed.

"No. Those ships are part of how we're getting the cavalry on our side."

Since so much had gone sideways already, we jumped into the Jiayuguan system three lighthours away from the star, far from the designated arrival point. We detected the picket ship that was waiting to clear new arrivals, it was alone and there was no sign of any enemy ships in-system, or anything else unusual. That did not mean there was no possibility of a hundred Maxohlx ships waiting to ambush us, but unless the kitties had acquired the ability to manipulate Elder wormholes, they could not be there.

To be safe, we waited for an hour, listening with passive sensors. There was a lot of communication traffic leaking from FOB Jaguar and the asteroid belt. In the belt, automated ships were mining space rocks, processing and refining the ore, and then transferring the vital elements to freighter ships. In orbit of Jaguar, the fleet support ships were taking in the refined material and cranking out components to repair and upgrade our little fleet. As agreed, one-third of the upgrade parts were set aside to be brought back to Jeraptha territory for their use. Everything looked like it was on schedule and going to plan.

That made me nervous. So, we jumped in less than a lightsecond from Jaguar, ejected an active sensor drone, and immediately jumped out to a distance of two lightminutes.

There was much consternation in space around Jaguar, as our drone began blasting out waves of active sensor pulses. If any stealthed ships were near the planet, the drone would reveal their location. Probably. Skippy warned me that the drone's effective radius was less than thirty lightseconds, so maybe all we accomplished was revealing our presence to the enemy. Mostly, what the drone accomplished was helping me feel like I had taken proper precautions, giving me one less thing to kick myself about if we did get ambushed again.

The drone also transmitted a message to Legion Command, informing them that we were just being extra super-duper cautious, and that there was probably nothing to worry about. That is like telling someone there is probably *not* a giant poisonous spider crawling on their shoulder. Of course they are going to look. Every ship that was capable of an immediate jump scattered, leaving total chaos in space around the planet. Ships that were not able to jump lit off their own active sensors, shield generators warmed up to protect their host vessels, and proximity-defense systems went active. Missile launcher doors slammed open, and maser cannon exciter banks were charged. The vital support ships shut down their fabricators and prepared to dump cargo.

Shit.

My idiot actions had probably set back operations by a full day, if not more. As soon as we received the All Clear signal from the sensor drone, we jumped back to the planet, and I contacted Legion Command to explain, and to offer a lame apology.

The Command staff was pissed at me, until they heard the reason for my caution. Hearing that Earth had been attacked, and that the attack was a slow-rolling disaster that could kill billions, was a shock. Admiral Zhao recovered quicker than I expected, but I guess that being able to maintain focus when faced with awful news is a requirement of being a general officer. "Bishop," he contacted me within minutes of hearing my report. "Warm up the beer can, we need to go back through the wormhole. Our entire mission out here is OBE, we need revised orders from Earth."

"I'm sorry, Sir, we can't do that."

His face turned red. "Are you refusing a direct order, Colonel?"

"No. Sir, I'm sorry, I misspoke. We *should* not do that. There are enemy ships at Jupiter, and we have to assume they have ships or satellites near Earth. If you go to Earth, I can't guarantee your safety. I can't even guarantee *Valkyrie* could survive there."

"Damn it, Bishop. We came out here so the Legion could fight for the hamsters, now *that's* not going to happen. I need instructions from UNEF Command on Earth."

"Admiral, whatever we do out here, it has to be a surprise, or the Maxohlx will kill the operation before it begins. Any communication with Earth would be compromised. Even Skippy can't completely prevent the Maxohlx from intercepting message traffic between parties on Earth. No matter how secure we try to make any discussion, *someone* on Earth will talk after we leave, and the Maxohlx will know whatever we have planned. UNEF Command knew that sending your force out here meant that *you* would be making the critical decisions, after we transited through Backstop. Sir, we are able to help Earth because we are an independent force out here. The enemy can't get here, and they won't know where we're going to hit them until we jump in right on top of them."

Clearly, he was uncomfortable with the idea of making decisions that could affect all of humanity. Hey, I knew what that was like, I didn't think any less of Zhao for his hesitation. Hell, if he was *too* eager to act on his own, now that would be a problem. The guy felt the weight of an entire planet on his shoulders, and he was determined not to act recklessly. UNEF had sent him to Club Skippy with the assignment of getting our new fleet of ships in flightworthy condition, and training human crews to operate those ships. He had not expected to take our little fleet into combat, certainly not without authorization from Earth. "Bishop, I hear you. Our ships here can't fight a *cloud*, and they can't hold off the Maxohlx long enough for anyone else to do something to help Earth. Do you have a plan?"

"We have several possible plans, Sir. I would like to discuss the situation with General Ross, and present you with a range of options."

Zhao considered for a moment. "The cloud will start blocking sunlight in seven months?"

"That's the estimate, yes," I confirmed.

He took a breath, looked at someone off-screen, and nodded. "Whatever we do, we need to do it right, rather than rushing in. Talk to Ross, I want bullet points by nineteen hundred."

Glancing at the clock because I hadn't kept track of time, I saw that left ten hours. "Yes, Sir."

"In the meantime," he growled at me "I need to straighten out the mess you created. Nagatha told me our production has been set back by a day and a half."

"Sorry about that."

"Next time, ping us from a couple lightminutes away first, let us know what you plan to do? We can scan the area for you."

Doing that would have alerted any hidden enemy ships to my intention, but I didn't want to argue with him. "Yes, Sir."

Ross was aboard a cruiser, but Perkins was on the surface. I contacted her and offered to send a dropship, but Ross countermanded my suggestion. We both flew down to the surface separately, it took me longer to get there because *Valkyrie* had not yet matched speed with the planet; I actually had to burn the engines to catch up with Club Skippy before the planet zipped past me.

Anyway, the three of us met in my Falcon. Ross looked puzzled to see that I hadn't flown down in a fancy Panther, I explained we were trying to avoid running up flight hours in the Panthers, because the supply of critical spare parts was getting thin. I sent my copilot away to enjoy the hospitality of Club Skippy, or at least to walk under an open sky for a while.

"Bishop," Ross began. "First, is there anything important that you didn't include in your report?"

"No, Sir," I said automatically, while frantically rummaging around in my disorganized mind. Had I deliberately left anything out of the report? No. Not this time. But was there an important detail that got missed? Maybe. "Not that I know of. We were not able to conduct a thorough recon at Earth."

"What about the rest of the galaxy? Any new dumpster fires I need to know about?"

I had forgotten that Club Skippy was cut off from relay stations, or any other source of information. Ross didn't know anything that had happened after *Valkyrie* escorted the First Fleet there. "Uh, well, we assume the Maxohlx blew up or captured our second batch of ships. Our people on Paradise are basically being confined to southern Lemuria, if the spiders have a schedule for evac, they haven't told us."

Ross shook his head. "They can't go to Earth, that's for damned sure. We can't add another eighty thousand hungry mouths to a future food crisis there. Shit! The spiders can't get here, or to Avalon. Our people on Paradise are stuck there until we sort this out."

"That could be true," I admitted.

"How *are* we going to sort this out?" Ross looked from me to Perkins, and back to me. "Admiral Zhao called me during the flight down. He emphasized that we need to put *all* our cards on the table," he looked directly at Perkins. "No more last-minute surprises. If either of you have an Elder power tap in your pockets, I need to know about it, now."

"I don't have anything like that," I assured him.

"Nothing, Sir," Perkins said. "What you see up there," she pointed upward, "is everything we have to work with."

"Then we are fucked, too, along with Earth. Bishop, when you warned UNEF Command that having Elder nukes only protected us from extinction, maybe you didn't have to say it loud enough for the kitties to hear?"

"Excuse me, Sir," Perkins came to my defense. "That's not fair. The Maxohlx are not stupid, they know the capabilities *and limits*, of those weapons. That's why their clients have been fighting a proxy war for thousands of years."

"You're right, you're right. No offense intended, Bishop," Ross sighed. "Just an old man blowing off steam."

"None taken, Sir."

"So," he looked at me, then Perkins, then back at me. "What *are* we going to do?"

Perkins and I shared a look. She gave me a barely perceptible nod, and I took the lead. "We don't have any friends out here," I stated the obvious, "no one we can count on for support. So, we're going to strike where no one will expect."

Ross lifted an eyebrow. "The Maxohlx?" He guessed.

"No, Sir. We're going into action against the Ruhar."

THE END

To be continued in ExForce Book 12: BREAKAWAY

Please leave a rating/review on Amazon for this book, that is very helpful in boosting the visibility of the series on Kindle. Thank you!

Author's note:

Thank you for reading one of my books! It took years to write my first three books, I had a job as a business manager for an IT company so I wrote at night, on weekends and during vacations. While I had many ideas for books over the years, the first one I ever completed was 'Aces' and I sort of wrote that book for my at-the-time teenage nieces. If you read 'Aces', you can see some early elements of the Expeditionary Force stories; impossible situations, problem-solving, clever thinking and some sarcastic humor.

Next I wrote a book about humanity's program to develop faster-than-light spaceflight, it was an adventure story about astronauts stranded on an alien planet and trying to warn Earth about a dangerous flaw in the FTL drive. It was a good story, and I submitted it to traditional publishers back in the mid-2000s. And I got rejections. My writing was 'solid', which I have since learned means publishers can't think of anything else to say but don't want to insult aspiring writers. The story was too long, they wanted me to cut it to a novella and change just about everything. Instead of essentially scrapping the story and starting over, I threw it out and tried something else.

Columbus Day and Ascendant were written together starting around 2011, I switched back and forth between writing those two books. The idea for Ascendant came to me after watching the first Harry Potter movie, one of my nieces asked what would have happened to Harry Potter if no one ever told him he is a wizard? Hmm, I thought, that is a very good question.... So, I wrote Ascendant.

In the original, very early version of Columbus Day, Skippy was a cute little robot who stowed away on a ship when the Kristang invade Earth, and he helps Joe defeat the aliens. After a year trying to write that version, I decided it sounded too much like a Disney Channel movie of the week, and it, well, it sucked. Although it hurt to waste a year's worth of writing, I threw away that version and started over. This time I wrote an outline for the entire Expeditionary Force story arc first, so I would know where the overall story is going. That was a great idea and I have stuck to that outline (with minor detours along the way).

With Aces, Columbus Day and Ascendant finished by the summer of 2015 and no publisher interested, my wife suggested that I:
1) Try self-publishing the books in Amazon
2) For the love of God please shut up about not being able to get my books published
3) Clean out the garage

It took six months of research and revisions to get the three books ready for upload to Amazon. In addition to reformatting the books to Amazon's standards, I had to buy covers and set up an Amazon account as a writer. When I clicked the 'Upload' button on January 10th 2016 my greatest hope was that somebody, anybody out there would buy ONE of my books because then I could be a published author. After selling one of each book, my goal was to make enough money to pay for the cover art I bought online (about $35 for each book).

For that first half-month of January 2016, Amazon sent us a check for $410.09 and we used part of the money for a nice dinner. I think the rest of the money went toward buying new tires for my car.

At the time I uploaded Columbus Day, I had the second book in the series SpecOps about halfway done, and I kept writing at night and on weekends. By April, the sales of Columbus Day were at the point where my wife and I said "Whoa, this could be more than just a hobby". At that point, I took a week of vacation to stay home and write SpecOps 12 hours a day for nine days. Truly fun-filled vacation! Doing that gave me a jump-start on the schedule, and SpecOps was published at the beginning of June 2016. In the middle of that July, to our complete amazement, we were discussing whether I should quit my job to write full-time. That August I had a "life is too short" moment when a family friend died and then my grandmother died, and we decided I should try this writing thing full-time. Before I gave notice at my job, I showed my wife a business plan listing the books I planned to write for the next three years, with plot outlines and publication dates. This assured my wife that quitting my real job was not an excuse to sit around in shorts and T-shirts watching sci fi movies 'for research'.

During the summer of 2016, R.C. Bray was offered Columbus Day to narrate, and I'm sure his first thought was "A book about a talking beer can? Riiiight. No." Fortunately, he thought about it again, or was on heavy-duty medication for a bad cold, or if he wasn't busy recording the book his wife expected him to repaint the house. Anyway, RC recorded Columbus Day, went back to his fabulous life of hanging out with movie stars and hitting golf balls off his yacht, and probably forgot all about the talking beer can.

When I heard RC Bray would be narrating Columbus Day, my reaction was "THE RC Bray? The guy who narrated The Martian? Winner of an Audie Award for best sci fi narrator? Ha ha, that is a good one. Ok, who is really narrating the book?"

Then the Columbus Day audiobook became a huge hit. And is a finalist for an 'Audie' Award as Audiobook of the Year!

When I got an offer to create audio versions of the Ascendant series, I was told the narrator would be Tim Gerard Reynolds. My reaction was "You mean some other guy named Tim Gerard Reynolds? Not the TGR who narrated the Red Rising audiobooks, right?"

Clearly, I have been very fortunate with narrators for my audiobooks. To be clear, they chose to work with me, I did not 'choose' them. If I had contacted Bob or Tim directly, I would have gone into super fan-boy mode and they would have filed for a restraining order. So, again, I am lucky they signed onto the projects.

So far, there is no deal for Expeditionary Force to become a movie or TV show, although I have had inquiries from producers and studios about the 'entertainment rights'. From what people in the industry have told me, even if a studio or network options the rights, it will be a loooooooooong time before anything actually happens. I will get all excited for nothing, and years will go by with the project going through endless cycles with producers and directors coming aboard and disappearing, and just when I have totally given up and sunk into the Pit of Despair, a miracle will happen and the project gets financing! Whoo-hoo. I am not counting on it. On the other hand, Disney is pulling their content off Netflix next year, so Netflix will be looking for new original content...

Again, Thank YOU for reading one of my books. Writing gives me a great excuse to avoid cleaning out the garage.

Contact the author at craigalanson@gmail.com
https://www.facebook.com/Craig.Alanson.Author/
https://twitter.com/CraigAlanson?lang=en

Go to craigalanson.com for blogs and ExForce logo merchandise including T-shirts, patches, stickers, hats, and coffee mugs

Printed in Great Britain
by Amazon